Hand of the Sun

Legacy of the Knight - Book One

Michael D Hill Jr

ISBNs
979-8-9910775-0-7
979-8-9910775-1-4

Mature Content Warning: This work of fiction depicts scenes which may be disturbing to some readers. Discretion is advised.

Mrs. G. Farr - who always told me to "write more".

H. - a dear friend. You inspired more in this series than you'll ever know. requiescat in pace

"The Principles of Truth are Seven; he who knows these, understandingly, possesses the Magic Key before whose touch all the Doors of the Temple fly open."

-The Kybalion

Table of Contents

<u>Chapter 1</u>

On any given night, the roads of Sarat would be free of travel in fear of the wild animals both man and beast which plied their ways in silent darkness, tonight was not one of those nights. Clouds gathered overhead, drowning the moon's full breadth. A suspension of fog consumed a man in silhouette. He wrapped his arms tight upon his shoulders, his breaths blending with the vapors. The faint aroma of cooking meats carried the man to a small home in the distance. Ahead, the road clouded with shadows of doubt. Pain lingered upon his body. Each step more laborious than the last. His gait fumbling within the carved and rutted road from the sounds of a nearby howl.

Clenching his teeth, the robed figure clutched his left arm as the cold cut into his tendons. The shuffle of muddied boots carried his feet to stumble onto his knees. A quiet wane called out to describe his sufferings towards the distant light and met by silent answers. His whiskered mouth struggled to form syllables. Humming vibrations tickled across his chest clung to his neck by a weighted chain. Embraced in a golden alloy, a single jewel glowed within an amulet slung over him. Emitting a green hue, the man sighed. A slight reprieve of the suffering which enslaved him to the jewel.

His mind raced to insufferable torment. The vile stench of mildew dungeons tortured his conscience, the screams of pain called through his ears. Distant untenable thoughts of pleasant memories scarred by stinging flesh on his back. Armored metal claws encompassing a pale hand clasped around the elaborate medallion and placed it against his chest. Snake-like tendrils tore from the core of the pendant. Electric arcs pulsed around his neck to form the tight chains binding him to this trinket. Acridity of burning electricity filled his nostrils reminding him of his curse as the faint cries of children tortured his ears.

Bruised and beaten, his mind fought to hold back the curse whispered to him. A language he begged to erase from memory. He eased to his feet. Aching bones stifled his rise. The fresh odor of roasted foods enticed him towards the welcoming cabin. As he inched his way towards the house his amulet vibrated softly.

His hands gripped familiar wood upon the fence line to aide his lean. Lifting himself with coursing stings of suffering throbbing through his joints, he followed the fence-works towards the gate. Hands glided upon the smooth wood. A dim light cracked the darkness from the windowpanes of the home and seeped through minute seams in the wood walls. Scents enticed his nose towards a trail of flowers lining a path towards the door of the home. Their final blooms performed an encore before closing for the autumn.

He leaned upon his left arm, while his right fiddled with the gate which swung open on quiet hinge. He shifted weight to his right side, relaxing the agony he fought throughout his body. Falling again, he landed upon a patch of violet flowers. Old scents, like those he remembered as a child and ignored the slamming gate. A shadow darkened one of the windows, covering the part with the cup of a hand as to peer outside.

The internal shadow disappeared like a phantom haunting the home. A numbing pulse burning from his trinket deafened his ears from the door opening. Welcoming light encompassed him, hiding the pains in his heart and mind; a light outshining the sun had a savior come to rescue him. He embraced the shine upon his face and creased a smile through whiskered cheeks. Through the faint light searing the foggy darkness, the figure approached him.

"Let me help you inside," the male voice offered. The jewel upon the amulet dazzled into a dark, amber hue.

Lifting the weight of the injured man onto his shoulders, the owner of the house inched his way back inside to the inviting warmth of the hearth. Wood creaked beneath his feet under the weight of two bodies straining the aging planks. The owner eased the man into one of the chairs in front of his fireplace resting him against the comforts of a stitched pelt.

The wood of the armrests groaned as his heft settled in the frame of the seat struggling to hold him with its small width. The warmth of firelight comforted his bones as he settled into the seat. Cracked knuckles drove away slivers of purple and red petals clinging with final vestiges to his soiled robes. Spiced poultry cooked on a skewer over the sounds of a crackling fireplace wafting scents upon his nose. His gurgling stomach distracted him from torturous thoughts yet unable to produce the saliva to savor.

His eyes struggled to see the back room of the two-room abode. He glanced over, catching the silhouette of the host exiting the back bedroom to offer a blanket sewn from thick animal furs. Aging brown eyes focused upon the comforting features of the brown-haired man offering his hospitality.

"What's your name?"

The host's voice mingled with the cracks of the fire as he set stitched fur upon the injured man.

"My name," he coughed. A dribble of spittle leaked onto his facial stubble.

For too long a question he had not entertained before supplying the answer, "Cadeck Wenfier."

"What brings you out to these parts?"

Cadeck studied the young man carefully to find any threat. A small dagger holstered into a sheath on the man's left hip laid upon simple tunics covering his chest stopping below his hips towards a pair of rugged trousers. An ensemble strung together with a tattered leather belt looped into a tarnished buckle the size of a toddler's fist. If the host had the desire, Cadeck's creaking bones ensured his life could be short. The quicker the better, Cadeck thought. The suffering would be over.

"I am in need to return home. Can you help me?"

Cadeck's voice carried from his tongue with the grandeur of a noble linguist swirled in dialect of an aging wheeze.

The boy chuckled, "From your rags, I cannot tell if your home is here with the farmers or in the court of a king. Your amulet you wear, surely more than a day's wage."

The host moved to stand near Cadeck. Covered in the light of the fire's orange tones, shadows crept along the walls behind the host who focused his attention on the medallion. Cadeck could not see the greed of fortune in his burnt hazel irises, nor could he feel the anticipation of riches in his heart.

"You must remove it from me before my body can return home."

Cadeck's heart surged with an ebbing shock from the amulet slung across his chest. A voice called through his mind whispering the name. Cadeck wanted to ignore them. Haunting murmurs filled his mind with the screams of a woman slain before him. His joints struggled to support him upon the armrests as he closed his eyes. A solitary tear emptied.

"Your jewel, did it just glow brighter?"

The amulet pulsated with a bright orange glow. Cadeck disregarded the question, focusing to listen to the voices calling out the man's name. Repeating, beating, incessantly whispering. A hissing, sinister voice rasped like a cowering threat trying one final attack. He tried to focus away, positioning his thoughts and physical mind to another time, another memory. A time in the long past now forgotten; the laughter of a young girl at play in fields of tall wheat and the cries of a newborn boy in the first breaths of life as the eyes and soul of the birthing mother emptied into eternity.

Wrem, Dal – forgive me.

Cadeck strained his voice. Wheezing as he struggled to lift from the chair, "This jewel cries for your attention, Tesh Verdui."

Cadeck raised his body to a standing position with the crackling of aging bone, sloughing the blanket to the floor. Offset, Tesh stepped back towards the bedroom, his right hand grasping the bound leather hilt of his dagger.

"How do you know my name, old man?"

"Whispers from the talisman upon my neck, it calls for your name," Cadeck snarled.

Upon the confirmation the amulet hissed in electrical sparks, the golden jewel blinked into a maroon hue. Startled, Tesh reached a hand to the hilt of his dagger.

"Help me. You are the catalyst to ending this curse."

"I command you out of my home, foul creature. I will not allow the gods I denied, curse me to death by your hands."

The dagger slid from sheathe, yet Cadeck's voice, his natural voice, called from behind his tongue with a purity defying his current manifestations.

"No. I urge you with my life. Take this amulet in your hands and rip it from chest."

Cadeck lunged forward, his eyes glazed to milky white globules consuming his irises. Ignoring any threat, his scarred knuckles seized the collar of Tesh's tunics in forced reprimand.

Tesh winced at the putrid death leaving his visitor's breath, a scent of agony and suffering unfamiliar to the young man. Cadeck's face growled, moans and curses billowed from his voice, the power of the amulet eating at his soul.

"Unleash me or perish," Cadeck sneered, the last word of his speech trailed into a snarl.

In horror, Tesh grabbed the grubby hands from his adversary to threaten the action to push him away. In the struggle, tears of clothing ripped from Tesh as Cadeck's weakened body stammered backward. The last will of his own sentience prevented him from catching his fall onto his back. Cadeck's collapse onto the floor caused the wood to bend. The amulet clutched around Cadeck's neck now engaged into a blinding red.

"You should not have touched me. Destroy this thing."

The last remnants of Cadeck's will stuttered, leaving his body as the words billowed from an ethereal void. Energy erupted from Cadeck's fingertips in sears of sparkling arcs like a violent storm. His body lifted from the floor as though pulled by strings hoisted in the ceiling. Beams of light burst forth from the cursed object encompassing Cadeck in a deadly blaze leaving him unscarred. Cadeck writhed, his head and arms twitched to fight the assault upon his soul. The energies from the amulet strengthened, forcing his body erect into a standing position floating mere centimeters above the floor in cruciform.

4

"Your blood, Tesh; shed your blood onto the amulet. Please. Free me."

Cadeck's soul wrestled to utter his last and final command. Bursts of energy encompassed the small house, extinguishing the fire in the hearth as the ravages of torrential energies crisscrossed around the wooden home. Tesh shielded his eyes from blinding light as each moment passed, bringing him closer to his own death.

"Shed my blood?"

He glanced at his assailant as the pall of violent magick took hold of him, escalating as the amulet outshined the room. As Cadeck drew closer, an image formed within the amulet. A visage of Tesh's own likeness appeared holding a sword of a craftsmanship unknown, gleamed of a metal with the vibrance of sheen unimaginable in Tesh's known limitations.

The hairs on Tesh's neck stood on end. A burning sting of energies filled through him as the impact of a wave coalesced with Cadeck's proximity. Tesh winced in pain as an unseen force tortured his nerves, pricking at his skin and penetrating through to his spine. Cadeck's words rang true; the amulet would destroy him and its host as well. An unfamiliar, androgynous voice screamed from within as a masculine voice in the fore masked by a feminine - *Cut thy hand and grab thine relic. Thy blood will free him.*

Tesh glanced towards his dagger in his right hand. Time wasting. He quickly drew the blade across his left hand and sliced into his skin along the palm. Blood trickled slowly to start, ending in a crimson torrent after carving a fleshy canal along his palm lines. Tesh screamed as the cavity formed upon his flesh. The crimson river escaped towards his wrist and trickled upon the floor. Fighting the stinging pains, Tesh reached upward toward Cadeck's twitching form, breaking through an invisible barrier molding around his hand as it entered. Tesh stumbled, mesmerized to the energy field wrapping around his wrist. Pushing further, the field visible encompassed the rest of his arm until Tesh had reached the jeweled amulet.

Clenching the face of the charm, Tesh's palm stained a crimson smear upon the precious metal carving, creating a surge of energy into Tesh's forearm and sending him back towards a wall. Cadeck's unconscious form stumbled to the floor, cracking panels, as the energies split them apart to cascade them against the wooden structure. Tesh's heart raced as streams of lightning coursed the outline traces of his veins through his skin. Beams of light tore through Tesh's clenched fist as the metallic alloy climbed along his left wrist. Tesh lurched and screamed as golden tendrils tore within his palm.

His fist closed tighter onto the apparatus appearing to crush the metal of his own strength. The golden trinket dissolved into his flesh leaving flakes of metal to seal a scar into his hand. Yellow streams seared into his veins, blocking out the natural blue tint layered into his skin. Tesh released a growling repulsion and as he struggled to remain conscious, a feminine voice released him into slumber whispering through infinity; *All is Was is All.*

<u>Chapter 2</u>

In another life, Tesh would toil for living wage; found a bond pair and raised a family only to keep an iota of prosperity towards the realm. He often wondered, if he were to have joined the military, would today be a different day tasked to some wayward back post village on the border with Silvetzen. Yet, today, he was only a man whose body was torn with pain, sitting slouched on the floor of his home.

Rays of sunshine stretched across the plains as a mother's hand would reach out to her children. Fog-enriched dew-covered green grasses emblazoned across the meadows. Single whiffs of soft white smoke emptied from the lone chimney laden into Tesh's home opening the way for midmorning. Tesh lay motionless against the floor, his left hand cupped against his chest. Crimson stains crusted upon his withered tunics flowing along his left side and pooled onto the floor by his hip.

Scars of carbon searing etched across the wooden framework of the house marred from sinister magick hours earlier. The embers cooled leaving a musky odor of burned bearwood singed from nature's lightning wafting acrid stench across the front room. Tesh's eyes struggled to awaken, blood still rushing into his skull like a night of drunken imbibing lingering upon his thoughts. Numbness scarred his left hand. Fingers bent in burning mortis against his chest.

Cadeck breathed slowly through Tesh's blurred vision. Every joint ached and creaked as Tesh struggled to rise from his slumped position limited to the strength on his right side. Struggling, he collapsed under his own weight onto one knee, the pain ebbing through his left arm only intensified his effort. A clamor of steel vibrated across the floorboards as he fell.

Tesh closed his eyes and through blurred sight, Cadeck shifted where he lay. Peeking his eyes into a lazy flutter, Cadeck squinted to the sunlight creeping across the floor like stretched beams in the early autumn morn. His brain pounding inside his skull as a madman in a blighted cell. Mere feet in front of him Tesh stumbled to stand under the use of one hand, the bloodied left hand cupped to his chest. Tesh clutched to the table rested against a wall to support his body, lifting his weight to his knees. Tesh collapsed once more. The nerves in his body struggling to claim sensation. His blood slowly circulating towards his extremities which fought against him.

One leg at a time, Tesh lifted himself upright to a standing position, pausing momentarily in wavering consciousness. He moved his left arm and gazed at the crusted blood caked in his palm staining his shirt. The pain in his fingers beyond comprehension as he stared at his curled hand. Flakes of golden alloy molded into his skin where his dagger made cut. He used his right hand to aide in the relaxation of his left, pushing each finger one by one letting out an intense moan of agony as his knuckles cracked upon bone.

As Tesh reached his pinky digit, Cadeck's movements distracted him towards the older man. If he could reach for his dagger. The pain in his hand searing across his nerves along his arm. Tesh closed his eyes, hoping for Cadeck to leave. He fluttered once more, catching the man brushing dust from his tattered robes. Creaking floorboards startled Tesh away from his pain.

"Step away from me."

Tesh clutched his left hand, fingers curled at the upper knuckles. Drool spittle clung to his bottom lip.

"Tesh do not be afraid. Show me your hand."

"No. Stay away from me."

Cadeck clutched the ailing hand from Tesh's chest. His fingers coursed over the fresh scar, studying the golden flakes etched into the appendage. Tesh pulled to release from Cadeck's grip, in response Cadeck tightened his stare, forming a stern countenance directed at the youth.

"Your wound shall heal in time; we would do best to wrap it to prevent infection."

In disgust, Cadeck released his grip, allowing the wounded hand to go limp by Tesh's side. Cadeck sauntered toward a window beside the door and peered out as if to wait for a guest. Open sunlight evaporating fog's overnight slumber calmed Cadeck as he embraced the warmth in the window. A sigh left his lips. Calm thoughts entered his mind, old memories bestowed a smile. Seizing his advantage, Tesh leaned toward the floor to grab his dagger with his able hand.

"You would be wise to sheathe your weapon, Tesh. I am not your enemy. *They* will arrive soon searching for both of us."

"How can I trust you?" Tesh readied his weapon.

Cadeck remained in calm pose staring at the light creeping onto his face.

"You cannot. I only tried to kill you. I do not expect you to understand why. Take journey with me for your safety. The gods allow it."

Cadeck turned to face Tesh, "You can set dagger to my heart, but assure yourself those who follow secure better weapons."

"I deny the gods. I cursed those idols months ago. What are you? Who sent you to me?"

Unease spilled from Tesh's voice.

"You can deny the gods all you like, but understand I am a protector of Roth's destiny ordained by those gods. Those who follow do not share my sentiments and only seek the ruination of this world. Gather clothes and supplies, our journey will be arduous."

Cadeck's words commanded a resonance of firm and higher authority. Tesh sheathed his dagger to its rest against his left hip, tying the scabbard cord around the pommel with his free hand. A smirk crossed Tesh's face, a glint of unfamiliar trust clear in his stare as the sun's rays embraced Cadeck in the window. An appearance of a dominating presence spilled from Cadeck's soul lifting Tesh's heart to ponder the man's words. Blood flowed once more through Tesh's legs, allowing him to step slowly. One foot. Left foot. Right foot again. He slumped, catching himself onto the threshold leading into the rear room.

"Your assistance would be grateful."

Cadeck turned to him, "Someone must keep watch. Come along now, we haven't much time."

Tesh leered in the man's direction, pushing with his right arm to propel into the other room. Slowly now. Tesh reached the edge of his bed and slumped onto the corner. Left hand fingers crooked awkward, struggling to overcome the stiffening. Blood still fresh stained his tunic as he slipped it away. His hair caught fabric's cling as he tossed the soiled clothes onto the floor.

"You will need new clothes. I spot uneaten food here upon your table. Toss me a sack to collect if you will, Tesh."

Tesh turned to a satchel lumped on the floor before him and sighed. Blood returning to his limbs. Tesh dropped to his knees and glanced under his bed for a crimson chest tucked below. Inching the box with the one hand, he fell to his side with the container half clearing the bed. Tesh pulled once more, the weighted box tugging to oppose. Another heft, enough clearance to open the latches and lift the lid.

He pulled the sack close to him as it sadly slouched. Fresh, golden flakes seared into his left palm which he used to prop the door to the chest and pushed assortments of clothing away onto the floor. Amassing an assortment of shirts and trousers, he pulled the draw of the bag open with his left hand to hold open then tossed his clothing into the leather bag in a haphazard arrangement ignoring any modicum of respect to his wear.

Tesh yanked one loose shirt slouching over the side of the chest and slipped it over his frame, ignoring the consideration to tuck into his trousers or tie along his sternum. He propped the sack bottom between his feet, then tied the rope cord tight to close. Raising the sack over his right shoulder, he leaned towards a second which he tossed in Cadeck's direction. The empty sack sifted with a thud as it landed.

Impatient, Cadeck approached the doorway and leaned over to grab the stained shirt from the floor, tucking it under his arm. Tesh's meal rested as a scorched husk of blackened roast in the fireplace. Soot and grime painted the stone mantle in pitch. A single loaf of wheat bread and an arrangement of fruits in assorted colors rested on the table as Cadeck examined them for rot or mold. He placed the riper fruits towards the top of the sack and placed a loaf of uncut bread above them, tying the sack with the hemp cord.

Tesh approached him as Cadeck hoisted the sack over his good shoulder. Clothes slouched out of the belt of his pants. Tesh's boot ties unwound and dragged on the floor.

"Wrap this shirt around the wound, we must remain inconspicuous. None can see your injury. The bloodied rag will allow us to deny answers to questions. Do you have horses?"

Tesh shook his head in response to answer *no* as Cadeck handed him the dirty shirt. Tesh obliged and created simple gauze with a piece of the previously stained fabric.

"Then time is terse. We must set leave for Telmen before dusk. They ride on horse, we set to foot. A day ahead of them, we are already behind. Do you have your property deed? We must sell this land to have coin for travels."

Wrapping the shirt around his left arm, Tesh raised his eyes towards Cadeck, "This is my home. I cannot sell it from my name."

"Then it will be taken from you by force if we stay longer."

With an ire in his voice, Cadeck's words swore to truth in his demeanor. The ferocity erupted from his speech sending trembles along Tesh's spine. Cadeck eschewed a fear of dreadful consequence with his threat. Returning into his back room, the leftover glow of a small candle on his nightstand informed Tesh of the hours passed since Cadeck's arrival. Lifting a floorboard beside his bed, Tesh reached for a small box and opened it on backwards hinge. An old smell of wood and wax seal gave Tesh pause.

A crimson seal held the parchment bound. Inscribed upon the seal, rested a pair of eagles; their heads facing away and mounted over a shield – the Royal Crest of Sarat. He traced his fingers over the seal, taking notice of its outlines and the aged drying of the document, a seal never broken in the days Tesh had known to be alive, signed in title by his own father, now turned over to a man who tried to kill him only hours ago. The scars formed on his left hand reminded Tesh of the brevity to Cadeck's demeanor as a branch of three tendrils began to form on the back of his left hand.

Tesh gazed over his shoulder to see Cadeck's filthy tunics turned backside towards him. Cadeck tapped his right foot with hands crossed to tuck at his waist, "They ride quickly, I can only hobble."

Tesh clutched the document, placing it inside his left pocket of his trousers. He wrapped his wound again as he strode to stand beside Cadeck.

"Would you like to grab anything else maybe the tables, perhaps the chairs?"

Cadeck groaned and began limp towards the door, sack resting over his right shoulder, "Let's go."

"You're in no condition to walk far."

"My legs guide me well. Now let us move," Cadeck held his hand firm upon the door handle, cracking it open to sunlight's welcome.

Exiting Tesh's home, past the ruined flower beds, the pair moved beyond the property gate lining the perimeter of his habitation. Cadeck steadied his gait along the corner post of the fence, shrugging off Tesh's noble prompt to grab for him before he regained his hobble along the cart-carved path leading eastward. Cadeck covered his eyes with his open hand, squinting from the light coming off the daytime star. The energies vibrating through the morning air refreshed Cadeck with new breath and warmth, feelings lost for some time. Tesh held pace beside him, clutching the rucksack holding his spare clothes.

The crisp airs of the mid-morning tickled along his senses. Vibrant grasses fresh with dew glistened across the horizon. Fence lines marked other neighbors and farms; their borders etched into the distance towards the rising sun. Hills carried over the horizons wavering and sloping onward into endless infinity dotted by houses and farms. Smoke lifted into the air from their chimneys to signal the beginning of morning ritual. Within the fields, small specks of motion followed with muffled commands to plow mules and assistants signaling the daily chores. Trees dotted the hills flanking their path as stages for the songs of songbirds shouting their choruses.

"Tesh, how did you make profession if I may ask?"

"Odd jobs here and there, helping the local farmers or masters in Telmen with their shops. I am a freeman, you know."

"Can you use steel?"

"I can use a dagger. Mother taught me enough to stab a man or cut down weeds."

Cadeck shrugged, "A dagger will do little good against those who pursue me. Can you use a sword?"

Tesh swallowed, "Not well. I learned what I could from some of my employers."

"We will need to improvise. We must hurry and arrive in Telmen before dusk. We must sell your home for supplies."

"Wait a minute," Tesh stopped, a countenance of surprise washed over his face, "Why should I come with you? Why did you come to me?"

"Look once more at the carving in your hand. We do not have much time, pick up your pace or I promise you what happened to me will be far worse when *they* find you."

"You have not answered my questions. I could turn you into the marshal in Telmen."

"When Marshal Offtil recognizes face, you'll understand the blunder of your act." Cadeck paused, turning around to Tesh.

"Why should I continue to follow? What are you? Who are you?"

Cadeck's stubble scowled into his face, "That amulet, scarred forever into your left hand bares no comparison to what awaits if we do not move. When those following me find your home, they will level it and anyone inside. What am I? A tool for a means to an end. Who am I? Someone who mourns the loss of your father."

Cadeck's words burned a hole into Tesh's heart to the mystery of the man he never knew, "What do you know of my father, Cadeck?"

"If you wish to share his fate, leave me and return. Otherwise, we continue to Telmen." Cadeck started pace.

"Who is after you? I want answers."

Tesh's face furrowed to inquisitive anger.

"Continue with me to get your answers, or you can get them from the bastards riding behind us. Rest assured they do not care to talk. If you want to know who killed your father, go back home. I am confident you would not be able to take them on your own at this time. Help me return to my home, and I will give you any answer you may need."

Cadeck's tone rippled into Tesh's ears as the growl of a wolf approaching prey. Tesh's heart weighed heavy. Cadeck's words carried a sternness of a brick sack slammed into his chest. Cadeck knew information about his father, knowledge his mother never shared. Cadeck resumed pace as best his hobbled leg carried him. Tesh's sauntering kept him behind only to jog to catch up to the aging man.

Half a day's walk passed. Rounding a bend sidelined by a series of knolls, a vista of tiled rooftops dotted into the distance. Wisps of gray smoke left the scattered clay sculpted chimneys. The manor of the regional lord set aside beyond the periphery of the town. Hills hugged the perimeter nearby.

Picturesque, plowed fields of wheat and other grains lined the outskirts along the southern horizon rising towards snow-capped peaks dominating the skyline behind the town to the southwest. Lenticular clouds supplied crowns upon the highest peaks.

The pair continued their trek into Telmen, entering from the northern section of town. Along the fringes dotted the small foundries and weapon smiths for which Tesh had grown accustomed plying his ways among odd jobs. Melted iron stung at Cadeck's nose as the waft of coal-fueled fires billowed from their chimneys marking the iron trade of skilled craftsmen. Red-tinted wood highlighted the plaster and mortar mixed with hints of shellac paste. Brick buildings dominated the industrial shops and trade houses where smelts and blacksmiths plied. Cobble paths lined the streets leading beyond the industry towards the common shops. Orders barked with returned grunts in trade vernacular of the factory district. Traffic of muscled, sweaty laborers hauled carts of ore along with workers carrying completed iron-worked goods along the busy pathways.

"Where does the lord make his office?" Cadeck brushed past several cart carriers.

"Beyond this pathway, into the center of town is the civil office."

Grime and soot layered the brick beneath their feet, aged and caked into the clay from countless years. Cadeck dropped the sack from his shoulder, allowing it to slouch and pulled the hemp rope to expose the contents to the sooty air. Calloused hands with dirt-clogged nails reached inside to remove a purple, bulbous fruit. Biting into the drupe, its juices ran down Cadeck's musty chin which he wiped with the neckline of his soiled rags before returning to his pace.

"Are you going to toss me one?"

Cadeck ceased chewing. Lavender juice dried along his bottom lip. His neck slowly craned towards Tesh, "You have eaten since the past day. My last meal was more than seven ago."

Tiny chunks of purple pulp flicked from his lips as he spoke. Cadeck regained his step, "Come along, we have business to attend. Eat if you must, Tesh, but regain movement."

Tesh glanced to the sack resting at his feet before his sight lost Cadeck into the crowd of heavy labor, the opening of the single sack drooped to the side. For an injured man of middle age, Cadeck's agility moved as a preternatural stalker. Dropping his sack of clothes, Tesh sealed the food bag and lifted them both upon his shoulders. Grunts and moans left his lips to compensate the added weight slowing his walk at Cadeck's behest.

Cadeck spit into his calloused hands to wash away the remnants of pulpy juice, wiping them upon his sullen clothes mired in grime from an unknown origin and caked in sludge and slosh of sulfur's bitter stench. Carrying the extra burden from the aging man, Tesh made his way to Cadeck's side at the edge of the market.

Cadeck stopped to ingest the sounds and sights. Colorful menageries of banners strung along stands. Signs marking goods hung from street shops or various tables. Odors of meats dominated the arcade square. Men and women alike cavorted or toiled and plied their trades in the common fair. He closed his eyes to the sounds of children running and playing with wooden swords or tagging one another in games. He smiled.

"What took you so long?"

"If your skills are as fierce as your sense of humor, we're both dead."

"Your tongue is quick Tesh, but it will not save you for the fight ahead. The civil offices are not far I imagine?"

"No. Just around this bend on the opposite side of the market."

"Pick up your feet, lad," Cadeck led the pace through the crowded square.

"I do not agree with this plan. I have called my father's lands home for years without your interference and have not planned to sell them."

Cadeck turned a surly eye towards Tesh's protest. A couple of passersby clothed in commoner's slops overheard the argument before shuffling to their purpose. Curious eyes wandered towards the pair of men before quickly moving along to their duties.

Tesh continued, "I have taken you to Telmen, I will return home. I protest taking you further. You can find passage to where you live from here, I am certain."

"You can return home, boy, and it will be your grave."

Cadeck's commanding tone reinforcing the demeanor of his convictions, "What awaits you there is death. I am here to keep you from fate."

"What do you know?" Tesh dropped the two sacks upon the cobble brick, "You seem to have all the answers, tell me what you know."

Tesh's voice resonated across the market, an intonation rising for a verbal argument. Commoners stopped their exchanges hearing the sudden burst of voice. Cadeck studied the townsfolk, his eyes wavering across the audience, then back to his aggressor.

"How can I know you don't plan to fraud me?" Tesh unsheathed his dagger, stopping abruptly as Cadeck widened their distance.

Cadeck breathed slowly, exhaling through his nose. The calming motions rested his mind as he closed his eyes. Cadeck's soul reached for

14

strength, inhibited by lingering effects from the amulet once scrawled upon his neck. He looked around as others took attention to their exchange. His thoughts told him to refrain, but Tesh's dagger signaled the man's disposition as he turned around towards the man. Cadeck summoned his breaths to search for serenity through silent whispers kept within his tongue. Inaudible words mustered behind his lips, closing his eyes to focus on his speech pattern.

The moment tore as an instant from Cadeck's perspective. In blinding flash, Cadeck's tongue moved as syllables reflecting the swift shift of position to pause time for his surrounding onlookers. Cadeck's minute prayers of action infused into his words upon his ailing soul achieved to transmute Tesh into slowed time. In prompt motion, Cadeck stood to Tesh's side, removed the dagger from the man's hand and returned to his position mere feet in front of the young lad. With a closing sentence of prayer, the onlookers resumed their harmony as Cadeck returned to his original position.

"You wish to threaten me with this?" Cadeck shook the dagger in a mocking manner.

The townsfolk paused, seeing the older gentleman clutching the dagger that once belonged to his accuser. Shock and murmurs rolled upon the crowd, but none suspected magick, only a man with exceptional martial skills. Cadeck smirked listening to the spoken words of the crowd discussing the quick reflexes of the older gentleman.

"How did you do that?"

Cadeck exposed a purple tinged smile and walked over to Tesh's side, returning his dagger. He clutched his hand upon Tesh's right shoulder.

"Know this, Tesh; people with my skills are being hunted by the same armies hunting you."

Trade speak consumed Cadeck's words to a dull muffle. Cadeck continued his whispers, "What you saw was magick, an ability bestowed upon me to manipulate the natural world. It is people like me whom your father swore to protect."

"My father? How do you…"

Cadeck moved his index finger to his own lips, "I will tell you more, amongst closed company. I hope I proved to you to place trust in me."

Cadeck's words fell upon a stranger's ears in a nearby alley. The slender figure blended within the darkness shadowed by the adjoining shops. With a fleeting grace, the figure rushed away from the market area, jumping over trash and other debris within the passage.

The noises startled Cadeck as he peaked into the alleyway abandoned by the spy.

"Someone eavesdropped on us. Tesh, be on your guard."

Tesh followed Cadeck's gaze into the empty alleyway littered with crates and refuse, indistinguishable from the rest of the alleys in Telmen. Tesh shrugged off Cadeck's thoughts as the rambling of an old man and regained his pace following Cadeck's lead. Cadeck and Tesh continued their intent, approaching the Marshal's building whose unique structure placed it for official business. A lamp hung upon the limestone wall beside the door greeted the men.

Cadeck reached for the doorknob. Above the pair, hung a sign marked by the royal crest of Sarat's twin-headed eagle, the title of "Lord of Telmen" etched beneath signifying the office's purpose. As the pair entered, Tesh covered his left hand tighter with the makeshift gauze. Distinguished gentlemen and landowners mingled within the lobby clothed in finer dyes and wools promoting their increased wealth.

Smoke spice soaked the airs with an aroma of civility and distinction. The pair's tattered attire created a stir amongst the finer crowd gathered as they moved deeper into the lobby towards a clerk's desk a few feet into the building. A staircase pushed against a wall to their left and lined with portraits of various events and individuals noting them special and admired. A couple of the men seated in the lobby puffed on straight pipes, their tantalizing pleasant smokes tickled Cadeck's nostrils with a refreshing taste of lost desires.

The staircase raised into an open balcony lined with papers and books along the railings like a disheveled room kept organized by someone with a proclivity for junk. Polished, bearwood planks answered with creaks as Cadeck and Tesh continued towards the rear desk. Impressed by its structure, a class of building far exceeding Tesh's station, his awestruck pause caused a trio of gentlemen seated at a table to take notice. The men held cards in their hands, Saratian Crowns piled into a central pot beside a single dark bottle of juyo wine. Tesh caught a glance of one hand; face cards drawn in grotesque imagery and various disfigurements and an array of pip values to finish the seven. Gossips of mockery exchanged between the trio before Tesh resumed towards Cadeck.

"May I help you," the clerk asked from behind his desk. A refined voice lingered from his tongue in Sarat's High Accent. Mounds of documents and various books stacked beside and behind him, some on racks with names etched beneath the slots and others loose and disheveled amidst the gathered dust glistening in the sunlight from the forward windows.

"We seek business with the lord of this town," Cadeck answered in calm consternation.

"Do you have an appointment?"

"We intend to seek a buyer for a sale, this man's home, a small one-story hovel about a half day's walk northwest of here. Tesh, your deed."

16

Tesh reached into a side pocket of his trousers and released the parchment sealed with the Crest of Sarat. The man glazed over the rolled document, the seal of Sarat recognizable with its distinctive shield and twin-headed eagle.

"Looks legitimate. I can help you. Do you wish to release it to the lord's possession, or did you have an individual buyer in mind?"

"Whichever fetches a fair price," Tesh replied.

The clerk desecrated the seal of Sarat, peering over the document within his hands. Murmuring to himself the finer details of the property title, he removed a single eyepiece from an inside pocket lining his coat. Sensing the rising intonation of his voice, Cadeck motioned to him to keep the details silent. Clearing his throat in response, the clerk continued his bureaucratic chore.

"Very well, syr. Master Verdui, this document is legitimate. If eyes do not deceive and the residence is in exceptional condition, His Lordship can grant you the total sum of one hundred Crown pieces. You may allow His Lordship to buy the deed at the final offer or allow the property to go upon auction where it may fetch for a much larger price, if the purchaser realizes its significance," the clerk's tone rose in predicted, greedy crescendo on his final phrase.

"The offer from the town is suitable."

"Very well then, Master Verdui, do you concur with your friend?"

"If we put it for auction, I can surely fetch more than the town is…"

"No," Cadeck firmly commanded, "It is adequate for our needs."

Cadeck whispered into Tesh's ear, reminding him of the dangers should they linger longer.

"One-hundred Crowns is fine," Tesh agreed as the fading thoughts of childhood memories stared at him from the blank line requiring his signature.

Scurrying his aging frame into a back room, the clerk returned shortly with a weighty bag, "Sign here."

The clerk pointed to the document unsealed, dipped a quill into an inkwell and handed it to Tesh, "If you are literate, that is."

The clerk grinned. Tesh reached for the quill, producing his signature on the line pointed to. The clerk placed the pouch on the desk in front of Tesh who snatched it into his pocket. Cadeck nodded to acceptance and motioned Tesh to hurry away from the building to continue with the necessary purchases of supplies.

Making their way through the central shops, Cadeck cited a verbal list to Tesh to buy a pair of horses, a sword as well as fresh rations for their broad journey. Cadeck placed his hand into the coin purse, lifted two Crowns from the pouch and summoned Tesh forward to task. Cadeck realized the job before the boy; a menial requirement to fetch rations and methods of travel for a trip leading towards the southern edges of Sarat, through rolling plains and into a mountain pass. Peaks of mountains dominated the skyline to the southwest horizon buttressed by caps of snow. Home. Cadeck's mind lingered on the taste on his tongue of the bliss of enlightenment. But there was a greater goal if Cadeck's intuitions were correct.

Through musky stubble his face did not distinguish him from others in the working crowds. He took care not to expose himself for long for spies were certain within the town and those who hunted behind them could relay information about his whereabouts. It was not just his life to fear for, but millions of others of free men and women.

Cadeck caught smell of a stand in market. The operator behind the counter sat motionless, old, and frail and missing several teeth from his front row. A throw of grungy fabrics clung to the man across his chest exposing a spindly arm and wrinkled skin. The shopkeeper spoke no words, only grunts and whistles as Cadeck approached the tender scents of herbs. It was a familiar call; one he missed for too long.

He pointed to a bin of crushed leaves and stalks and asked the shopkeeper for two pouches of the herb to fit inside his open palm. The owner scooped the leaves into a pair of pouches and tied them. Cadeck motioned towards a row of pipes, perusing each one to consider simplicity and elegance of design before settling upon one of polished erikan wood. The shopkeeper took one of the Crown coins and exchanged his change to twenty pieces of copper.

Cadeck set himself upon the masonry edge of the central fountain. Sunlight formed against his face and spread onto his torn robe as the sounds of the trickling fountain flowed through his senses. Fibers of his robe stung at his back as they clung upon delicate wounds. A knee creaked as he sat upon the cracking stones.

Cadeck took the satchel from over his neck and placed his pipe and herbs inside. He crossed his legs and reached into a pocket in his pants, removing a small chain holding a tarnished amulet on the end of the links. Aging blood stains splattered against the scratches over words scribed in faded etch, rusted, and soured from years of wear. In the early autumn sun, he could see the words cut into the backside of the locket, *To My Love*. With torn heart, he set the dangling chain around his neck and tucked the amulet below the neckline of his robe.

Tesh scrambled through the town, fulfilling the list needed from him and returned to Cadeck's position as he sat upon the stone façade of the fountain. Tesh led two horses, a brown marked gelding, and a gray mare. Upon their dorsal sides rested fitted saddles. Cadeck mounted the fair coated gelding

18

outlined by a blonde mane and brown markings across the hips and back. Tesh set foot into stirrup and slid upon the gray mare and as he set himself upon the animal, h removed the pouch of coin clung around his neck and tossed it towards Cadeck who tied it around his waistline hemp cord.

"I have no doubt we were noticed while in Telmen." Cadeck's voice lowered with rattled nerves.

"Those who follow you?"

"Let us hope the answer to your question is not hard to resolve. I presume you did not find your task too difficult. You picked two fine specimens for riding."

Cadeck discerned the new weapon upon Tesh's backside.

"Your sword, elegant, modest, surely you can manage it well?"

"I imagine I can."

"Remove it. Show me."

Tesh eyed him with inquisition.

"Unsheathe it. Show me how you move."

Tesh obeyed, removing the weapon from sheathe. The sword sheened in the afternoon sunlight. Its formed iron forged to a lightly weighted hilt suitable for his skill.

"Humph," Cadeck muttered, "Not quick, but it will have to do. We do not have much time."

With his statement, he heeled the horse into a quick gallop as he directed his steed southwards into the direction of distant mountains. With a hesitant bewilderment, Tesh sheathed his weapon, and signaled his horse with a heel to follow.

Chapter 3

As a fleeting wind like rushing nightfall, a pack of riders tore along serene valleys in a pace of a wildfire. They numbered four, each of the stallions' black as pitch carrying riders in obsidian armor. Sunlight glimmered upon their metal plate lighting them like the appearance of a raging, black flame. Galloping clangs of the onyx armor echoed across the path to signal dreaded omen. The men burned their pace upon farmers' fields, jumping over fences in a gallop to reach the destination in their midst. Autumn breaths of the horses erupted from the nostrils as their heads cocked with the pull of reins in mad sprints through the valley.

The leader of the pack rode with a grace unbecoming of his companions, free of any armor covered in flowing cloak. As a silk river of obsidian glaze, his mane fell over his shoulders, blending against his garments as it spilled downward along his back. His eyes burned an icy blue as a glacial lake lit by bioluminescent fires. The foursome approached the rear of a small home as the lead rider motioned with a bare, closed fist to come to a full stop. He sat atop his steed, his cape flowing across the crupper plate to consume the hind quarters of the beast in a blackened shroud.

He led his horse into a high-knee trot, bringing the horse to prance perpendicular to the building leading his horse to the front of the home. Arriving to the old gate, the man slipped his right foot from the stirrup, slung his leg over the saddle horn and with the grace of an acrobat, dismounted in single motion to land firm upon leather soles, the flow of his leather cape following to rest. Steadying themselves upon their steeds, the other three men remained in along the western edge of the fence line. Armor links squeaked in their movements as they watched their leader.

Without a word, the slender man strode upon the entry gate, sliding brittle digits of graying rot upon the wood as to glean a vision, studying the loose latch to force his entry into the perimeter. Taking pause to a flower bed in disarray, the man leaned to a crouch, gracing his fingers into the soil patch with a contemptuous sneer. A sheathe of blackened wood carried behind him upon his left hip where the edge tickled the soil path leading to the door. Rising to height, the figure fondled soils within his fingers, lifting them to his nose with a rotted smile.

Blackened leather constricted against the willowy frame of the commanding officer, crunching like a macabre symphony as he approached the door of Tesh's home. Passing along the marked path, his leather vestments glistened with the hints of the sun. Crackling, leather-flesh digits curled the radius of the doorknob marred with scars and fissures across his skin. Flakes and crackles crept along his hand as he twisted the knob and flung the door open with the force of defying momentum. Musty odor trickled in stasis within the building as he consumed the stale air with flared nostrils. Flickers of dirt and dust wasted away in the sunlight.

Clenching his tattered teeth in a state of distorted meditation, the slender man ducked as he entered the room. A blue glaze covered maleficent eyes wandering across the scarred walls to seek information his senses could find. His hide-skinned boots creaked across the aging planks, thundering like a rolling storm, his presence as a towering beast. The silhouette of his figure pronounced by the light spilling from behind him. Pulling apart a series of buckles down his chest, he reached with his right hand towards a pocket lined within. Striking his fist in front of him, he turned his wrist to spread his fingers holding an amethyst crystal resting upon a scarred palm.

"Scrying crystal, reveal to me what I cannot see."

A lexicon of harsh tones, random staccato consonants and light vowel exited his tongue with inhuman speech as the crystal lifted from his hand and shone with internal energies activating to his words. The stone motioned around the room in a silent, unwavering movement drawing no attention to its nature. Flashes of energy highlighted the elongated mineral as it crossed the scarred planks along the wall and carried to hover over the rotting blood stains splattered to the slender man's right side. Flying into the back room with a steady purr, the geode flashed as it stayed stationary over Tesh's bedside and nightstand and lingered over the opened floorboard.

Returning to its master, the crystal rested upon his scarred hand marred with a sigil of an open circle radiating eight pointed spokes etched as a ritualistic tattoo. Closing his eyes, feeling the images fed to him from the vessel, the man hissed a familiar name in the speech of his people, *Cadeck*.

"The Aztmi was here, and he found his target." His words bore into the air like a razor in his native tongue, as he slid the crystal into its home within his clothing.

The man turned to exit the house into an open sky where the sun began to turn to dusk and highlight faint stars dancing against the early evening backdrop. Outside, the soldiers remained mounted to their horses where they carried into a formation behind the taller man's beast. Their armor covered their vital torsos, emblazoned with a red sigil of eight spokes emanating from a central wheel, mirroring the design tattooed upon their leader's hand. Their faces covered by black helmets; eyes set deep within rounded corners.

"We stay here. Make your encampment behind the house but do not enter. This ground is sacred."

The trio of soldiers bowed their heads to acknowledge the order, dismounted their steeds, and scouted for hitching room along the edges of the fence line. A soft breeze lifted through the leader's sable hair as to whisper a call. A faint band of darkness appeared in the early evening sky, splitting the apex to the horizons at a slight degree from overhead. Twinkling stars danced around the plane of void as avoiding a dangerous fall. The tall man whispered a chant in a language dialectically different from his native speech, unheard by the soldiers; he called prayers in reverence to the darkened phenomenon in the heavens.

Through whispers of obscene gods hearing his pleas reluctantly, a rustling hustle in the distance disturbed his prayer. Pale blue eyes gleamed across the southern horizon in front of him, watching a faint figure scurrying in a speedy haste across distant fields. A slow, growling moan leaked from his creased pale lips creaking with putridity. Pointing a long, brittle nail towards the target, he ordered to his soldiers to pursue the runner.

"Vorsk, Storn, bring them to me," the tall man hissed in a curdling growl.

A pair of blonde men heard his call, sliding their helmets to their heads once more and swiftly mounting their steeds. Commanding their horses to pace, the pair of armored men heeled their animals into a gallop beside the fence line, kicking dust and patches of grasses to the hefty strides of their silver and blonde hide animals. Spying its pursuers in the distance the victim increased the pace to a heart-pounding sprint as the taller man smiled.

In pursuit the subject was no equal to the galloping horses as they quickly caught up to the target. Vorsk grabbed the small frame, the figure yelped a squeal in a soprano tone, tumbling and swaying a gray cloak along the ground as the subject came to a stop. Returning with their prize, the captured figure struggled, whimpering in a soft feminine tone as the horses approached their leader. Vorsk dismounted, dragging his victim to his side as the prey resisted fate. The other soldier, named Storn followed, pulling back the gray cowl of the victim, revealing a slender face accented with brunette hair down to her shoulders.

Storn held the girl by her left hand. Golden blonde locks draped over his head and cropped at his chin. His voice was harsh with the slurred accent of poor education, "Well, well. What have we here? Looks like we caught us a fine piece, wouldn't you say Vorsk?"

"Yes, we have. So, what is your name missy? I want to know what to call you tonight."

In response the girl spit upon Vorsk's face.

"Bitch."

Vorsk yanked the girl by a tuff of her hair close to her neck. He sneered at the offending woman who looked upon him with silent eyes and cracked lips. Her slender face surmised her age was young, fifteen they imagined, as he forced her to the ground in front of his horse, planting an iron poleyn firmly in her ribcage. Her face winced as Vorsk pulled her arm behind her back to keep her from moving.

"Lord A'zum," Vorsk called as he produced a small blade from his left boot planted firm to curve against her rounded ass, "Let me cut this Saratian whore."

"No. Bring her," A'zum motioned with a scarred fingernail.

Forcing her to her feet, Vorsk and Storn lifted her arms outstretched between them. Dirt clung to her feet as she danced to free herself, kicking up musty brown residue in vain retaliation to the brute strength bending her limbs against her will. The troops brought the girl in front of their leader whose stare cut into her like an ice shard.

"Morgus," Lord A'zum hissed in his native dialect.

To command, a third man approached from behind the home; heavier, taller, and more robust than the lighter-skinned counterparts, his armor stretched to fill his breadth.

"Take her inside."

Returning to the speech understood by the blonde men, A'zum continued uninterrupted, "Vorsk, Storn, take watch but do not enter."

Lord A'zum turned his back as the brusque man carried the girl behind his master. Sneering in spite, the two blonde men mocked their leader with thumb flicks upon their incisors. Stomping into the wooden floor, Lord A'zum moved before Morgus who tossed the young girl onto the planks with a weighted thud. Releasing a slight yelp, the girl crawled her fingers across the ground reaching for any object to retaliate to her handlers only for Morgus to stomp her fingers carefully so as not to crush them.

"Leave us," Lord A'zum commanded, sliding his digits across the solitary chair in front of the dead, ashen hearth.

His boots halted with successive thuds as he stopped in front of the window. Morgus turned and without a flinch sealed the door behind him leaving the girl alone with the dreaded statue consumed into the shadow. Silent breaths filled the room sensing the foreboding presence of her captor across the chamber where any attempt any of the three men outside would keep her from fleeing. Two of which hinting at a less than fortunate outcome for her existence. Lord A'zum shifted around to the seat, sliding it to position to face her in the darkness of dusk's embrace.

"You carry information, or you were running from something. Tell me child, which is it?"

"I tell you nothing."

She stared upon the tall shadow. Lord A'zum's ethereal eyes offering a fixated point of his position within the room. Her mouth dried from struggle, sweat fell down her brow as her knuckles rattled onto the floor. Lord A'zum lifted his fingers over the wood back chair, placating his digits over the leather-bound tapering crudely stitched across an open gap of wood frame. Copper taste of her own blood tickling her lips with every word she answered him.

"Have a seat, child. If I were to have you harmed, Vorsk and Storn would have their way upon your flesh. As you are, I still see purpose for you."

His hand rested upon the back of the chair, embracing it to ease her fear.

"I beckoned you to have a seat."

Her body hesitated to stand. Her feet scuttled upon the old floor; the young girl shivered before the foreboding shadow looming ahead of her. His clothing carried a foreign stench of an unknown hide tickling her nostrils of sour rot. She scanned the surroundings of the dimly lit room for anything of use to which she could take him out, ignoring the elongated weapon housed upon his hip which she never would see approach her flesh before cleaving her body. She placed her hands outstretched to feel for a familiar scent of leather-backed chair in the shadow, and with the comfort of the acquainted shape, coiled into the heartening confines of the chair as Lord A'zum crossed in front of her.

"We can either do this with your cooperation, or without. It makes no difference to me. Tell me your purpose, and I will let you go home. Resist and I will have to remove it from you."

"Let me go," her voice quivered, "I have nothing for you."

Lord A'zum stood as an immutable force paused to her resistance where he presented his back to her. The discomfort in her tone tickled along his spine. The young girl could readily reach for him, choking him from behind should she dare and overcome the appearance of a weakened and frail, lanky man.

"I have spent considerable time in your lands, far away from my home. I am tired," A'zum tented his fingers in front of his chest, "I only ask your cooperation to my questions, girl. Answer my questions and I shall let you go.

Force my hand, and I shall allow the northern men to have their ways upon you."

He turned back to face her.

"I don't know what you ask of me, but I'm just a girl trying to return to her farm."

A'zum raised a brittle hand and graced soft, gentle face, caressing the contrasting texture with his own. Yellow nails pulled her hair away from her wincing eyes as she whimpered in disgust. He leaned into her face admiring the texture of her flesh. His eyes glowed to the unnatural light within as he reached his other hand around, clenching her temples between infested palms. The girl stared upon rotting teeth; his breath stunk of corpse.

"I allow you ultimatum," he growled into her face, "Tell me your purpose or suffer."

"You will have nothing from me. I obey the Crown of Sarat."

Chants spilled from his tongue in a low growl. Consonants forced into staccato in a spoken pattern. A'zum gathered his thoughts, focusing the pool of his power to which his people referred as "aztunai." His hands glowed between the young girl's face, her eyes closing under the penetrating heat as she begged in silent whispers to be free. She screamed in pain, her mind open to thought suggestion as her voice quickly silenced in ethereal vacuum consumed within a glow of lavender hue coiling within her eyes and mouth. Ethereal pulses vibrated her temples from between A'zum's hands, she grappled the armrests of the chair with vehement, convulsing tugs, crackling the posts connected to the seat.

His voice calmed her in her Common Tongue, "I feel your thoughts, child. You can hide nothing from me. Where you go," his hissing voice whispered, "where you come from; your thoughts are mine."

Through the clouded view, A'zum witnessed the past few moments in his victim's mind. His mind inhabiting hers, A'zum witnessed another messenger. Dressed like his victim stood another woman beside her while a third approached, a sliver of blonde hair falling in front of hooded face. The voice of the approaching woman began, her voice spoke in Saratian High Accent with a quiet, naïve tone:

There is a Magi in Telmen. Another party follows him. Relay this to Her Highness, tell none other.

A'zum's view turned and left the cold alley, scurrying around the pathways of Telmen to exit town before sundown. A'zum stopped his collection of her memories, relinquishing control of her head as she slumped to the side of the chair, destroying the right armrest with dead weight as she fell to the floor. His mouth gaped open in delight, returning his hands towards his sides.

"As I suspected, Cadeck has passed through Telmen."

Lord A'zum stepped over her convulsing form towards the door and exited.

"This one has outlived her purpose for me. Vorsk, Storn, she is yours as you want."

The two blonde men smiled and pushed behind their leader, entering Tesh's home and exited with the limp body slung over Vorsk's shoulder. The woman's face drained of life. Her eyes rolled into her head as her mental state prevented her from resisting the forceful actions of Vorsk and his comrade. Vorsk carried the limp girl as he laughed to his peer, moving their way towards the rear of the home. A'zum paused as the men moved past him while Morgus remained to his master's side.

Lord A'zum turned to Morgus, addressing in their shared tongue, "Assure her death is swift and expedient upon their reward. The draw of her blood shall renew my purpose."

A native of Silvetzen to the north, Vorsk took delight to the inhibitions A'zum rewarded. Vorsk's rugged frame bore resemblance to features of his native land; husky men who preferred steel over books. He carried towards the rear of the house and dropped the girl onto the ground. Storn, his counterpart, stood opposite to deny any feeble escape. She lay still, dirt staining her fingers, blood trickled from her nostrils and her hair in disarray as the pair mocked her with spits and insults. Morgus set the horses to the fence rails for the evening and began a fire from dry firewood stacked nearby.

A'zum entered Tesh's home and seated himself upon the wooden floor in the living room chambers and set the long-sheathed sword to his side. He closed his eyes in silent meditation as the native star fell into the horizon darkening the small home in still silence of evening. Outside, he heard the men taunting and teasing the girl in between her screams and cries. Ripped clothes or skin slaps snarled A'zum's face into a smirk as he pondered upon prayers.

A'zum reached to a pouch upon his hip to remove a tiny black vial with a cork seated tightly upon the mouth. With a swift tug, the cork came loose as he splashed the liquid down his throat with a quick swig. Streaks of green juices spilled from the edges of his cracking lips as he produced a soured grin, scarce of teeth. A'zum closed his eyes, chanting words in the ancient tongue he commanded his crystal only moments before. He tightened his grip around the fragile vial and with the pressure of force, spilled the several shards upon the floor to the sound of the girl's loud screams. Her screams were as prayers as he isolated his own thoughts into focused intuition.

He focused on her pain, absorbing the tortures his men inflicted upon her innocence as the two blonde men cheered one another on. He listened to their profanities, cursing the girl and the subtle taunts of spitting, and slapping. For hours, the unrelenting tortures continued, permitting A'zum a silent vigil in meditative prayer, listening closely to the silent darkness above to which he posed his worship. The girl's voice cried in terror, heard into the black void of the Abyss above as the calls of old demons and demigods took pleasure in her pains. They answered A'zum with encouraging promises, devoid of substance and offered momentary relaxation upon his soul as he uttered Cadeck's name in the ancient tongue.

Upon which he saw a vision of a burning city, the embroidered eagle flags torn asunder in the calamity of ruin, the lamentations of those below him begged for mercy. Cadeck's name cried to him through the voices in the darkness, a calming reassurance to the defeat of lost prey. Yet A'zum discovered another presence in his meditations, a screaming voice through the darkness of suffering to bring with it pain. Pain of a searing light tore into his brain as his mind raced to tangents of infinitesimal magnitudes reaching across his soul to the many who lived in the world. Within the sacred darkness, he found himself amongst the whole to see a light empowered through the ether. A light surrounded by love, bringing with it sacred gifts wrapped in the grip of a pair of children, each one splitting the flank of this ethereal glimmer.

The screams stopped. A'zum's suffering remained quiet, insulated against those outside of the home and contained within his own indulgences of hallucinogenic toxins. Soulless life triggered reverberations like a slithering coil entering from the rear of the home as the smell of the spill of death echoed the cries of the dying, consuming the lost voice of the girl. A'zum focused on the spilled life emptying from the soul, gathering her aztunai, her life essence, to meld his own, mending his catatonic brain from the suffering meditative defeat. The death of innocence consumed him. A vision seen as selfless purity consumed the entirety of his void. A voice of authority whispered to him over the Abyss.

Lord A'zum, I summon for you.

The contrabass voice dominated his mind.

Cadeck was here and he is free from his bind. His quarry is with him, Supernus Magister.

Are you certain of your findings, Magister A'zum?

Yes, Master.

Continue your pursuit. In time, the All will be mine.

***

As a quasar pulses in dead sky, the psychic conference ebbed throughout the lands stunning Cadeck from his thoughts. Amber campfire bristled along the quiet plains and shimmered upon Cadeck's sullen eyes. He picked at a tuft of grass growing through the dirt patch he sat upon, sifting the blades to sprinkle through his murky fingers relishing a quiet moment of freedom. Tesh slept undisturbed upon a nearby tree trunk. Cadeck closed his eyes and listened to the psychic reverberations he sensed within a day's ride. Cadeck reached into his satchel, removed a pouch, and the pipe of erikan wood.

He liberated a pinch of crinkled leaves from the soft-skin pouch and placed them inside the pipe's receptacle. Grabbing a small twig from the ground, he reached into the nearby fire to ignite a starter flame and set the burning end into the leaves. In a burst of sweet-smelling smoke, Cadeck puffed upon the open end, inhaling the mild toxicity to pleasantry. The erikan wood turned the bitter taste of the herbs sweet as the smoke rolled along his throat.

He let out a quiet sigh, savoring the euphoria indulged in the fresh ruban smoke allowing him to forget the experience of his pain. The sweet taste gave way to bitter aftertaste as rolling smoke filled his lungs emptying his mind of the cracked whips once pelt against his ears in deafening halls. As he exhaled, the billows of mist lifted into the darkened sky to excise his tortures. Across the darkness, he followed the starry landscape and paused on the visible bands of emptiness a few degrees from the center sky; the light of the moon off-center to the horizon above.

Cadeck kept his quiet stance, slowly inhaling puffs from his pipe. His thoughts lingered to his mission to return to the ancient temple in the distant mountain valley and to the young man sleeping across from him. Only he and his Ascended knew of its location and to lead Tesh through dangerous plains would test his strength and the boy's own resolve. Sounds of nocturnal animals foraging in the distance alerted his ears as the howls of hunting wolves drowned out the lesser noises. Cadeck returned his focus to the smoke engulfing his brain.

It helped him to concentrate, his mind raced back towards the psychic conversation he overheard in the distance as the faint, female whisper of a voice long silent for his imprisoned eternity tickled his ears.

The servant of the Apophadi draws close.

"Jess," he called as he darted his eyes to the voice lingering in the faint darkness of the starry night.

In haste, Cadeck rose to his feet, clutching his pipe to his side. His ratty cloak flowed to form as he made his way to Tesh's rest. With a shake of his shoulder, Tesh clamored to a steady wake.

"How long was I asleep?"

"A few hours. We must move. Our pursuers linger."

"Pursuers?"

Tesh rubbed his eyes.

Cadeck prepared the horses hitched nearby, "Answers later. Mount your horse so we can take to the mountains."

"Are you sure? It is still dark. It will be difficult to navigate the Koran Mountains with just the light of the moon."

"Trust me, Tesh, I know the way."

"How do you know they're nearby?"

"I sensed magick. Perhaps no more than a few days ride."

"Are they dangerous?"

Cadeck turned his eyes to the question, "The amulet which has fused to your skin is a reminder of their powerful magick. You're always welcome to return home if you question judgment."

Tesh gazed at the wrapped bandage around his left hand where flakes of blood dried around his palm. The etch of mortis crusted tight in his veins as he struggled to move his fingers within the swaddling shirt. His fingers relaxed and tightened in dull pain inflicted two days before. Cadeck continued in his task, positioning his supply satchel behind his saddle mount. He carefully extinguished the fire upon the ground and removed a single lit log from the flame embrace as light for their nighttime journey. He saddled up and raised the torch upon his right arm. Tesh remained next to his silvery gray mare.

"You're welcome to leave, return to Telmen and what may remain of your life. You will not find solace in your decision, only enslavement and death. If your bloodline and your name be true, then you must come with me. It would be your father's wish."

"What do you know of me?"

Tesh readied his hand upon the hilt. A scowl soured his face. Strange words from an even yet stranger man who Tesh surmised was nothing more than a beggar. Cadeck knew magick, Tesh discovered, but at what cost? Magick; a discipline his mother scolded him repeatedly to never pursue.

"I never knew of my father, how is it you do? Do you make bond with demons?"

"And your mother was a wise woman to refrain knowledge from you, rest her soul. Should it be known who you are and what your legacy holds, the armies trailing me would have found you sooner, likely before you were old enough to handle them. You would be dead by now, and Roth would have already fallen into the control of darkness. Death and enslavement follow where they roam. You can come with me, and I guide you on the true path, or you can

30

go home and sacrifice all you once knew, all you loved, and all your father stood for."

"You have raised more questions, I demand answers."

"Questions my Ascended will enlighten your mind upon should we make it to him in time. He will tell you all we know in the sanctuary of the Temple of Light."

Cadeck settled on his saddle.

"So, you are a Magi?"

Tesh released his weapon from the sheath, childhood fears erupted in his gut. The worry of his mother's face flashed across his eyes at the sound of the words leaving his mouth.

"Put away your weapon, Tesh. You have no reason to strike me. I have kept you safe thus far."

"I do not trust Magi. I do not trust magick. How am I to know you will not sell me for some potion or spell?"

Cadeck smiled to Tesh's naiveté, "I would have already done so. I understand your concern, Tesh. Lies do not leave my tongue concerning you. But in the open, it would be unwise to reveal more."

"Why me? I am a lone peasant man of no value to the King or his armies. I work a wage for meager sustenance and tended my father's land for two harvest seasons. Should I sire, they will carry my lands in turn. I pray to no god, nor owe allegiance to any Magi. I do not tithe as the king does. I do not humble myself to the gods nor to any of their agents on this world."

Cadeck turned to Tesh with a sour grimace, "Then this amulet is a false sign. You hold no purpose; you hold no power. The visions I have seen of you since before your conception were hoaxes and dreams brought on by misguided interpretations.

"Fall in your misinformation. What do I care of this poor man before me? Roth dies from my misjudgment. You can follow me and claim destiny or meet your fate and return home. My faith will not waiver with either decision."

"Faith, Cadeck? I only knew faith in sorrow. My mother died while holding onto faith."

"All the more reason to put trust in my words, let us hope her death was not without purpose."

Cadeck heeled his horse to pick up trot. For Tesh, the man leading him meant certain death days before, yet the tone in his voice lent credence to his words. Tesh held the leather grip of the reins as he hoisted himself upon the dorsal ridge of the beast. Cadeck rode ahead, fading into the void with a solitary beacon of ghostly flame to his side. Orange glow danced in the still night over the ground as a silent call to Tesh's future.

Cadeck's lamp faded towards the rising skyline of a distant mountain range. Snow cap shadows hovered over the precipices alit by the glow of the moon above. Tesh peered around his back to reach for normalcy with Telmen's light only to find expansive darkness of fields and farms laying in silence. Cadeck's light shifted in the darkness ahead at a quick pace, leaving the boy behind. Tesh heeled his horse to catch speed, breathing a quick gulp and released a sigh. He gazed down upon the wrapped hand, the words of his mother scolding him on magick rung within his mind replaced by a more ancient voice motioning him to follow. He ignored his mother's kind and mellow words, her hand caressing his face on her death bed.

Chapter 4

Wolves howled in the distance harkening the demarcation to the expansive mountain range splitting the Southern Saratian Plains as a tear through the ground. Cadeck's solitary flame lit the path. Cadeck puffed slowly on his simple pipe as the pleasant smells of smoke flew across Tesh's nostrils stirring thoughts of sophistication. The slow pace of the ride nudged Tesh into a lull daze as he struggled to remain awake from lack of sleep.

The jagged skyline of the Koran Mountains cut into the sky as icy stars danced around them. Mountains towered upon the surrounding plains as protective statues overlooking the expansive valley below. Dots of fire twinkled in the southern distance outlining the many mines and other establishments of settlement etched along the base of the edges of the mountain line. The travelled road spilled into an endpoint while Cadeck motioned his horse forward into the grasslands beyond the dead end.

"Cadeck, there's no road," Tesh reminded.

Cadeck inhaled his pipe coaxing his horse into a steady gallop and ignored the young man. Tesh followed in haste, weary of the journey thus far. For several hours, the pair rode across the infinite wilderness leading towards the foothills of the mountains. Dark azure sky opened into a light pink in the eastern horizon as the monstrous mountains loomed above them. Hues of orange and pink drowned out the stars fading away to the daylight.

"We'll be safe within the mountains."

With his words, Cadeck led the pair south, longer still, as he approached the side of a sheer cliff face. Cadeck called the animal to stop before dismounting the steed. As Tesh approached, Cadeck's neck strained the side view of the cliff arcing to the full height of the massive formation towards the blue skies. Cadeck stood for a moment and embraced light's warmth upon his exposed skin and the squint of his eyes. Frantic in his actions, Cadeck scurried along the cliff face, ignoring Tesh's approach on foot as he led his animal towards Cadeck's position.

"The Temple is just on the other side of this cliff."

Tesh followed toward the man, tracing his eyeline up the side of the sheer cliff wall surrounded in part with a vast mountain range stretching for miles around.

"Cadeck, there are roads into the range from the south, can't we follow them towards your Temple?"

"They lead nowhere, close to the forests north of Kora and other hazardous terrain. No, we must scale this cliff."

Cadeck grinned, his back turned to Tesh.

Tesh sighed and glanced skyward once more, then towards the satchels laid across the pair of horses.

"You spoke nothing of climbing gear, Cadeck."

"No, I had not. Beyond this cliff, is the Temple of Light. What is light, but a mere manifestation of your own perception."

Puzzled, Tesh looked at him with query before Cadeck continued, "The cliff is your reality, but in opposition," Cadeck pushed his left hand towards the wall of the face only for his arm to disappear into the rocks with nary a pain or scratch to his flesh.

"It is the suppression of truth from your limited view."

Cadeck withdrew his hand from the wall, twisting his wrist and stretching his fingers to show Tesh his skin and clothing had not changed. Tesh's eyes widened to Cadeck's ability in the few moments of display. Gasped to the illusion, Tesh approached the hand with inquisitive wonder, studying for any scrapes or scars, blood, or tears.

"How is that possible?"

"As you saw in Telmen, the world of the Magi is not the world in which you live. The Temple of Light awaits you behind this wall and within its chambers, the lesson of my reality and those like me, shall first be manifest upon you."

Cadeck turned towards the cliff, grappling the reins of his horse and as a calming motion, led the animal towards the same illusion and left Tesh outside of the wall. Tesh followed towards the face of the cliff and met the firmness of eons of granite pushed from the ground.

"Your eyes perceive a cliff," Cadeck whispered, "do not use them."

"My eyes? Cliff?"

Tesh whispered under his tongue as he stroked the golden wound in his left palm.

"What does your mind see?"

Cadeck's voice echoed from behind the cliff rock in front of him.

"My mind?"

Tesh murmured as he closed his eyes, listening to the pulsations within his head echoing along his spine and down towards the palm of his hand. In the vacuum of thought, his hand lifted, guiding him towards the wall only for the shadows of void to silhouette the familiar stance of the older man upon the other side. He glanced towards his hand within his thoughts. Hand outstretched, he followed the guide through the wall.

Cadeck placed a hand upon Tesh's shoulder as he breached the illusion and pulled him from his trance. Power surged through Tesh's mind upon Cadeck's touch and culminated into a tickle upon his wounded palm. Before them lay a cavernous expanse of finely cut rock with steep walls reaching high into the open air penetrated by a distant hint of sunlight through the angled path. Tesh drew aghast at the size of the cave towering several stories above him. The cliff walls sheened as carved by a larger hand as layers of rocks marked eons of formation.

"Are we here?"

"No. This is merely the entry path."

"How much farther?"

"Once we clear the cave, but I must warn you to be silenced when we approach the exit, sunwolves cannot see in the bright sun, but their hearing is beyond renown."

"Sunwolves? They exist?"

Cadeck smiled, "I thought you didn't believe in the gods?"

Light shone from the opposite side of the cave as the day progressed into morning marking their long march through the cavern walls. Cadeck made the clearing first, pausing at the exit of the canyon, with his horse in rein behind him. Tesh quickly followed, the light of the sun momentarily blinding him as he settled the reins of his animal lowered to his hip. As his eyes adjusted to the sudden infiltration of the daylight, the bulk of the range came into focus.

As a city unto itself the snowcapped skyline of various heights startled Tesh into a low sigh. A simple road hugged the cliff face from the cave to the cragged valley below. Within the valley taunting Tesh, a pack of brightly colored animals roamed in hunt. Their golden manes glistened from the light of the day star running in pack to appear as one. From his height, they appeared as small dogs roving and raving as little puppies in the valley.

"The horses must remain here. Their noises will alert the sunwolves," Cadeck whispered, "once I make prayer, I can bring us back to these steeds."

"Can you take us to the temple now?"

Tesh whispered.

"I cannot. I shall pray in my Temple before using magick again. The binding amulet drained me. I only hope Ascended Godwen will welcome me back."

"A falling out?"

"More or less. We must be silent now; the wolves do not take kind to noise."

"Can they be killed?"

"I would recommend against fighting them, they are Aeus' hunters, guardians of His Temple, a being more ancient than man. They can smell fear. Show them courage and humility and they will let you pass. Show aggression and you will be torn like rags. I would eat now; your stomach growls may alert them to your presence."

Tesh reached into the food supplies he carried on his steed and removed a small biscuit of bread and a yellow bulb of fruit. Tesh hurried his meal as Cadeck puffed along his smoke, the sweet smokes lingered to mix with the taste of Tesh's morning morsel in a cavalcade of flavors. Cadeck whispered between released circles of smoke and cursed the foul rags clung to his skin. He swiftly extinguished his pleasure before returning his pipe to satchel. He motioned Tesh to follow and continued along the edge of the cliff towards the valley.

The pair hugged the cliff face inching their way down the mountainside. Tesh's feet scraped along the rocky path crunching into a decayed skull. Other corpses strewn about the path in varying states of decay. Rocks slid and collapsed under the weight of the humans bouncing down the cliff side in a violent cacophony of crunchy noise.

One of the beasts below stopped in its motions and pricked at the air with its nostril before returning to its kin. Cadeck ceased and waved to Tesh to do the same. Beneath the bottom of the path, the open valley invited Tesh to encounter the mystical creatures. No longer tiny dogs from the topside, the decreased distance within the luminous valley revealed the sunwolves to be the height of two men. Guttural howls rippled across the valley range.

A mammoth ridge loomed ahead as a foreboding goal blocking the sunlight from the encompassing valley. The sunwolves roamed nearby, shimmering as their own brilliance in the absence of the star's grace. Tesh and Cadeck worked their journey along the trodden path lined with skeletal remains of other adventurers who met untimely fates. Using precognition, Cadeck moved his hand over Tesh's mouth as they stopped in mid track. An angry look in his eye, Cadeck motioned a single finger to his mouth for silence.

A distant ridge clouded the valley in darkness. Hints of sunlight poked around the corner from the path of the walkway. Tesh crunched onto a decayed hip bone and a loud snarl erupted in the distance.

A sunwolf stood motionless and revolved its neck into the direction of the noise. Its ears perked up to listen, while the body morphed from bright yellow to a reddened orange. The beast moved with slow prance. Ears twitched and pulled against the head as it pushed into a full gallop towards the pair. Cadeck caught the beast out of his peripheral vision and slowed his heartbeat to remind the beast he meant no harm. Snarled teeth exposed the beast's intentions.

In reverence, Cadeck stood and bowed in prayer. He showed the beast the intent of his heart and motioned for Tesh to perform the same. Iridescent fangs bore from the mouth of the bearing beast. Rays of light trailed behind as it sprinted into a full blur towards Tesh's noise. Irises of the beast burned like a luminous blaze.

Show them courage and humility and they will let you pass.

Cadeck's warning pierced strong in Tesh's heart as heard from within his head. Tesh's trust of Cadeck remained difficult as the beast bore into gallop towards him. Tesh seated himself along the gravelly path embracing what would be his final breath with a stance of nervous humility. The sunwolf snapped its jaw forcing a gust of wind ruffling Tesh's auburn hair. The beasts gaping maw waved a gush of foul breath like the rot of ancient carcasses, its teeth marked the gnashing entrance to a darkened belly. The sunwolf smelled a kill.

The mythical beast stopped in front of Tesh, its head leaned forward and sniffed him as the mortal dogs the beast shared likeness. It listened to Tesh's heartbeat stilling to calmness with the hint of fear. Its sneer relaxed as the animal kneeled in front of its adversary. Cadeck stood beside it, sharing a glance with the gargantuan beast moving his hand to rub its ear at his face level.

This one is not of your concern, beast. Return to your pack and let us progress.

Tesh unclenched his eyes from inside his face as the golden beast raised upon its legs. Cadeck rubbed its fleece with his hands coaxing the beast into a solemn whimper.

"Did I conquer the beast with my courage?"

Cadeck removed himself from the beast's range and reached down to clutch his satchel and hefted it across his right shoulder.

"Your fear led to his attack. Another moment and the beast would have had his meal."

***

Like a dark tower imposing along a skyline to eclipse the sun, Lord A'zum stood above his soldiers as they struggled to wake. His steely blue eyes ravaged as a storm making landfall into the soul of the lead soldier, Vorsk. Shadowed leathers encompassed Vorsk's view as his eyes adjusted to the pains of daylight's embrace. The menacing sword imposed upon the silhouette's hip like a beacon of death awaiting his arrival.

"Your men have ten minutes to ready the horses for ride."

"Should we bury the girl?"

A'zum turned his head in the direction to the deceased girl and set his hands behind his back. The pale corpse lay in the morning sunlight as flies encompassed their new home. Her last thoughts shone on her silent face with closed eyes and gaping lips. Her naked body lay prone along the ground, blood dried around her slit neck like a pool of lava muddying the black dirt below her. Blood pooled in a bucket beside her, silent and still like settled water.

"Place her in the front of the home and let the vultures show this kingdom what my Master holds for them."

"As you command," Vorsk hesitated. His voice staggered nervously to the order.

Vorsk ordered Storn to hustle into line. The pair from Silvetzen lifted the girl's naked corpse to splay between their shoulders. Clotted blood dripped onto the ground from the festering neck wound amidst the flurry of flies.

"Morgus," Lord A'zum turned to the taller man of red complexion, speaking to him in their native tongue.

"Allow me a moment to commit this girl's aztunai to the Abyss."

A'zum hefted the bucket to the front of the home. Vorsk and Storn lowered the girl as their pale leader walked in and slammed the door shut behind him. A stare of contemplative unease shared between them as A'zum's speech devolved into arcane tongue. Delayed in their removal from the door, Morgus stepped towards the pair and placed a roughened hand upon their shoulders coercing them to their steeds without question.

Moments passed. A'zum exited and mounted his dignified steed. Blood drenched upon his hands, smearing the saddle horn. He straddled the raven saddle of his horse. Onyx barding reflected as an antithesis to the morning sun. A crimson sigil of his command, matching the tattoo scarred into his hand, encased the horse's eyes upon its chaffron.

A'zum commanded his horse into stationary prance. Thunderous legs of immense proportion pummeled into the ground kicking up clots of dust into the air. The horse emitted a whinnying, growling war cry - a trait of generations of selective breeding. The announcement startled the other horses into submission upon the declaration of dominance.

As A'zum and his men moved into the pathway leading towards Telmen, a lone figure made its way towards them in the distance. The distant stranger stopped in its tracks pondering the four-man obstacle ahead. A'zum remained motionless on his horse as a brisk wind flowed his raven hair. The stranger regained his journey after his pause, moving towards A'zum and his soldiers.

Vorsk chortled in response. A'zum silenced him with a motion of his hand as he steadied the reins of his muscular beast. The features of the stranger came into view, a spindly man of cowardly stature. He struggled to reconcile amongst his papers much to the stifled snorts of the two white-skinned soldiers in A'zum's command. A'zum surmised his role was not a threat but allowed the man to continue towards them; waiting patiently as the man approached the horse riders.

"Are you here to inquire about this farm?"

A slight stutter left the man's dry lips. He struggled to press his effects against his soft lavender tunic eyeing the imposing man upon the horse in front of him. Hints of fresh dust clung to his elegant trousers and shoes, of which Vorsk surmised his position had not allowed him to leave a desk in his profession.

A'zum remained silent as the man fumbled in his foibles. The man's eyes turned towards the decaying girl's body beside the door. Shocked in revulsion, he swallowed in fear. His heartbeat drowned out the stomp of A'zum's boots slamming into the ground as he dismounted his horse.

Towering over the craven man, A'zum leaned to meet his eyes. An ominous growl emitted from A'zum's abdomen. The stranger stumbled once more; a piece of document slipped within shaking hand. A smell and smear of blood taste left Tivius' lips.

"Who sold this land?"

The clerk jittered his papers, reaching for the document outlining the sale.

"A young man, Tesh Verdui. Sold just a couple of days ago. I am here to evaluate this property, but the dead girl was certainly not part of the deal."

A'zum turned to the display of the rotting corpse.

"And where is this Tesh now?"

A'zum's question pierced into the man not unlike the blade the clerk saw resting at his opponent's hip.

"I do not know. He and his friend left in a hurry."

A'zum released a hint of a grin, leering towards the man.

"A friend? Tell me more or you meet her fate."

The man swallowed a lump.

"I don't know," he stuttered, "Early fifties. He smelled of wretched vermin. The other, a boy named Verdui had a wound around his left hand. The older man had an air of uncertainty and haste. Look, I am only a clerk. I did not make the transaction. I only saw them while the guild master processed them. Now do you want to buy this land?"

"I care not for this property," A'zum's spade lips hissed, "Once again, tell me where they went, or you end up like her."

"From their whispers, I overheard them discuss the Koran Mountains. I would presume this would be their intent."

In hesitant shake, he pointed a spindly finger in the southeasterly direction. His papers fumbled to the ground. Vorsk chuckled at the folly.

"You have done well, friend."

A'zum comforted words in hissing voice. Crackled hands set along the man's head as to embrace him in a hug. The man cowered in fear as he met the towering man's chest with his eyes. A'zum showered him with adoration as he moved him close to his leather-clad torso in manner to hug the man only to twist his neck with a crackle of bone, forcing the head of the man to face the trail he once walked. The body slumped to the ground as A'zum regained his position upon his charge.

***

A towering ridge separated the valley as a sharp knife. The warmth of sunlight bloomed upon Tesh and Cadeck as they turned the path. A second valley's expanse opened in front of them revealing a cavernous maw bathed from the sunlight above. Across the vale, a large structure embedded within the rock for which Tesh saw columns and spires cut into the face of the mountain. The entrance faced towards the east to embrace the day's first signs of sunlight.

"Is that the Temple?"

"Your thoughts are keen, boy."

Cadeck picked up the pace as his home neared. He limped into an awkward sprint on hobbled leg, and in his hastened stride, managed to speed ahead of Tesh. The sword strapped to Tesh's back echoed its clanks within the valley as he followed behind. His feet pounding into the soft dirt below tracking within the path set forth by the elder.

As the temple drew closer, so did its visible features. Spires towered the height of several meters surrounding an ancient doorway cut out of the cliff. As the pair's sprint ceased in front of the primordial structure, Cadeck paused in reflection, dropping his satchel to the ground. He knelt to the ground; his face strained to the pain of one knee bending and began to peck at the stone staircase to kiss it. His breathing ceased to a welcome ease.

"What is the matter?"

Cadeck regained his posture to a kneeling position craning his neck to look at Tesh towering above him. He did not reply, only stepping up to stand and continued upon the small staircase into the wounded mountain. Ancient glyphs of an arcane language decorated the threshold archway. The most prominent of the symbols presided over the entry; an upright triangle resting upon a small cross mark.

"Whatever happens here; do not speak unless addressed. Do you understand?"

Tesh nodded to confirm.

Cadeck entered first. The musty air of ancient dust swatted across Tesh's nose further permeated by the blinding darkness. The unmistakable scent of stale air rushed from the interior of the structure as the pair approached the threshold. The light of the valley ceased upon the staircase leading into the temple marking a foreboding destiny upon Tesh's unnerved heart.

The echo from Tesh's shuffles filtered into the entry spilling into a vast foyer. Smooth transitions of rock sheered along the walls and ceiling appearing carved of inhuman device by an ancient people long since legend. Sunshine spewed from the open ceiling culminating into a focused shine on the apex of the floor, radiating down towards an elderly man seated in the center in meditative prayer.

Sparks of light emanated from the man's hands outstretched to his sides facing the sunlight as he neither wavered nor focused on the behaviors of the manifestations flowing across his palms and fingers. A flowing beard pooled into his lap like a blanket of white waterfalls as he seated cross-legged upon the polished floor. Wrinkles of an aging wear crossed his brow and cheeks etching their own story carved from a long life.

"Cadeck, I did not invite you back," a faint whisper burst from the man's withered lips beneath his smoke white beard.

In respect, Cadeck bowed to his knees in front of Tesh's stance.

"Ascended, you know why I return."

The old man's eyelids opened, creasing his filled brows of wispy white hairs. Without struggle the man lifted himself to his feet. Lavender robes glistened to the shine of the sunlight above to accentuate the meticulous care of his own patience.

"I had you excommunicated for a reason. Be grateful your tongue remains, though I will not permit you to pray," the man's voice croaked with anger.

Cadeck rose to his feet.

"Ascended, as we speak, *his* armies pursue us."

Ignoring his plea, the older man turned towards a table at the far end of the chamber behind the sun pool. Vestiges of worship littered the table in sacramental ornamentation. Tesh could not discern the actions of the man as the clink and clang of fiddling artifacts brushed across his ears. The older man ceased fondling the antiquities and turned to his student. Withered eyes faded to gooey gray pools studying the words with flittering curiosity in his eyelids.

"Your presence brings them here," his voice waned, "You must leave before they arrive, lest we all be killed."

"Ascended Godwen, this boy saved me from my imprisonment to a binding amulet, and I cannot help him in my condition. I must pray."

Godwen steadily inched towards the pair passing through the basking warmth of the sunlight pool.

"Your soul was bound and this man sacrificed himself to save you?"

"Yes, Ascended. They forced me to seek out this man to kill us both."

Cadeck's statement raised a concern with Godwen, "Boy, tell me your name."

"Tesh. Tesh Verdui." Tesh's voice boomed across the chambers.

Smoky pale eyebrows raised in trepidation upon Godwen, "Very well, Tesh. Cadeck brings you here, to what accord?"

"He bears the mark foretold."

"Cadeck, you raise a strong conviction. Are you certain this man bears the mark of the Azthar Kherdmon?"

"The sacrifice of his blood caused the medallion to fuse with the wound."

Godwen hobbled towards Tesh, his veiny hand grasped Tesh's wounded arm. Godwen traced his purple tinted hands across the course ravine created by the golden amulet. The smear of dried blood painted trails of crimson embedded within his hand and had solidified with the alloy coursed inside him transforming once blue veins into faint golden trails leading along his forearm.

"This wound, your blood has fused with a binding amulet. Astonishing. None have succeeded to destroy a binding amulet. Blood magick."

Godwen turned to Cadeck, "Rituals and alchemy bound in sin, a violation of all that is natural."

Godwen stared into Tesh's eyes, "If you truly carry the ancient blood through your veins; a bloodline tracing back to times before written language, to the time of our ancient progenitors, the Aztmi - the first humans to use magick, then such a rarity beholds my sight. Only magick created of your blood could have crafted such object to seek you out."

"How would have someone acquired my blood?"

"It would have to have been fresh," Godwen smiled, "perhaps, from someone you know."

"Who?"

"A relative. A father, a brother, anyone of male lineage."

"Mother raised me alone. She told me my father was a levied conscript, sent to a war far away."

"Then, whomever killed your father, knew magick. Vile, sinister, blood-drawn magick. Their magick, however, is a legend. A myth. Lost for thousands of years."

Godwen drew a scorn on his face turning to sorrow as he turned his back to the pair.

"Elder, I am afraid their magick is very real. I have seen it firsthand."

Godwen craned his neck towards the mosaic of his god carved into the wall ahead of him, "Just as I feared," his cracking bones turned him around towards his student.

"If, whomever created this amulet is as powerful as Cadeck believes, then there may be more prisoners sent to destroy you both; powerful prisoners such as Cadeck's own children."

Cadeck shot a stern look towards Godwen at the mention of the lost voices of his offspring.

"My children suffer in the hands of the Si'rai. Without me, they weaken."

Godwen heaved deeply and spoke as a death rattle consumed his breath.

"Your children will bring the demise of the Magi," Godwen condemned.

"Let me find them, Ascended, for I must pray to be of any use to this boy. I must liberate my children."

"They will destroy the Council, an order lasting for the entirety of man. You expect me to allow sinister prophecy?"

Godwen's voice echoed a berating tone through the Temple.

"They will not destroy the Council, Ascended, but restore it. I promise you this, Ascended. Permit me to pray and find them. With Tesh, we can restore the Council and the Knights."

"How certain are you of your interpretation of an ageless prophecy? You do not sit on the Council since your removal; thus, your remarks of timeless tradition mean nothing. Your interpretation of codices is moot."

Godwen's words burned into Cadeck's heart.

"Permit me to pray, Ascended and I will see Tesh fulfill the bloodline this mark suggests."

Godwen turned an eye towards his pupil then back to Tesh, "If you are right, Cadeck, then you may pray. But if you are wrong, may Almighty Aeus damn your soul."

Chapter 5

As an ominous obelisk, Lord A'zum rose from a kneel clutching a glob of ashen residue filtered through his bony fingers. Amidst the small squad, Lord A'zum charged a looming presence, their lives at the whim of his own thoughts. He sifted the ashy mud within his scaly skin, the carbon stench of burnt fires pricked at his nostrils. He kept the dirt to his side, watching the specks collapse to the ground below him.

"A campsite. Cadeck's aztunai is still here," A'zum muttered to himself in his native tongue. His eyes aglow with the ire of an icy frost.

A'zum motioned his step towards the southwest following the roadway a few meters. His eyes focused onto a pair of horse tracks imprinted in the dirt, squinting to the direction of the animals. His head followed the direction of the road leading to the mountain range along the horizon.

"There. That is our destination."

"The Koran Mountains?"

Vorsk looked up from his position, standing guard next to A'zum. Storn tended to the pair of horses while Morgus remained on his steed.

"It is there we shall find our prey."

"We should burn Telmen, instead. That will send the message to Sarat that we do not approve of their actions to our people."

With a grasp defying his spindly frame, A'zum clutched Vorsk's exposed neck suspending his trachea from breathing. Like tree roots dredging to secure soil, A'zum's gnarled fingers stretched around Vorsk's bulbous neck and lifted him. Vorsk reached to the black vambrace clenching his contorted neck as A'zum squeezed tighter.

"I did not enlist you to think, Vorsk. Without my leadership, you and Storn would be dead. I loathe your kind. Your kind are no more worthy to lick my boots than the worms I trample beneath them. You serve a purpose for me, do not test my patience any further, lest I summon my Master to burn your lands."

The force of A'zum's release leveled Vorsk's armored body to the ground with a clunking thud onto his back.

"My king will live longer than yours, zealot. Your pending treaty means nothing. Your weapons, your gold, your people will all be Rathmana's."

In swift motion, a slender blade lifted from the sheath at A'zum's side and arced over his towering body finishing with the edge a few centimeters from Vorsk's left eye. The foreign-forged blade dazzled in the sunlight like a beacon, an iconoclast to A'zum's raven looks. Whispers of a howling shriek tore through the arc path of the blade, signifying the cries of wailing torture emanating from the steel. A purple ethereal flame trailed along the tip of the blade before subsiding through the edges and fuller at its stop. Scribbles of an ancient glyph seared into the fuller of the arcane weapon, etched by tools and techniques more advanced than Vorsk's knowledge.

Vorsk's eyes widened to full display, a slivering fraction of space from the point of the silvery, glowing blade. Loud horrors pierced Vorsk's mind as the blade beckoned sinister screams calling for his blood in the whispering haunt speaking only his name. Vorsk heard the blade's shrieks focusing on his conscious thoughts to bleed fear into his soul. Storn readied his hand against the hilt of his sword. A'zum's countenance grew into an intense focus, shimmering with an ethereal brilliance of anger-fueled passion. Wisps of lavender essence spilled from the misshapen, grotesque quillion of the blade, rising through the steel and snaking along its fuller with each horrific pronunciation of Vorsk's name.

"Your choice of words will be your demise, sadakem. I will see that your soul burns for your heresy." Lord A'zum referred to Vorsk by a racial epithet from his language towards Vorsk's light-skin.

In repose, A'zum sheathed his weapon to his side leaving Vorsk to stand on his own strength.

"We move into the mountains. Fill your stomachs now. We leave in an hour."

***

Naked in the bathing pool of sunlight, Cadeck sat cross-legged, his back facing against the entryway to the sacred temple. Streaks of scars etched across his backside in tapered canals of pink flesh exposing the story of his pain. Swirls of energy moved in arcs and streams around the human form as goose bumps reacted to the touch of the stone beneath him. His hands outstretched, palms facing towards the open ceiling of the carved-out mountain.

His thoughts lingered on his meditations and his children; a daughter just reaching puberty and a young son. Cadeck forced the depressing thoughts out of his mind allowing his soul to replenish his need to embrace his magick.

Tesh leaned upon a smooth wall and observed the Magi forming motions with his arms in an enchanting trance while seated upon the carved floor.

"How long will he meditate, Godwen? It has been two days."

"As long as he may need."

"He stressed an enemy follows. Will our pursuers not find us?"

"The Si'rai know not of this place nor the other Temples. For eons they have searched for these nexuses of energy, and yet have they to find them."

"Other temples?"

"Yes, Tesh. Six others. Fire, Wind, Water, Terranroth, the Warrior and the Spirit. Legends speak the Knights have their own Temple, far off to the east which no Magi knows of its existence as to keep the two bodies apart and prevent corruption."

A confused look lined Tesh's hazel eyes, "If no Magi knows of this Temple, how am I to find it?"

"That will be up to you. Come, you have work to do if you are to help Cadeck."

"What type of work?"

"If Cadeck believes you are to become a Knight, each Elder Magi must grant the Initiate their blessing. For you must pass a series of trials, one at each temple. Here will be the Trial of Light."

With a wrinkled, withered hand Godwen grasped Tesh's injured appendage leading him into an antechamber set aside behind the primary altar. A wall of sheered sparkling rock separated the main chambers from the small chamber Godwen escorted Tesh to.

Godwen traced his hands across the golden wound. His eyes fogged into a cataract gray turning his soul inside-out to peer into Tesh.

"This amulet, what did you see?"

"See?"

"Yes, boy, you had a vision. I can feel it. The wound speaks to me."

"I saw a sword, magnificent beyond any I'd seen."

"I can see it too," Godwen walked into Tesh's soul, reaching into subconscious thoughts like a series of tentacles wrapping around his brain.

"Do not fear me, Tesh. I see this sword, and it speaks to me. If you truly carry the bloodline, then you will find it. If, you pass the Trials."

"What is this sword I saw myself holding?"

"This sword; legends say the gods forged it of their own aztmudin. Made of a material unnatural to man and fallen from the Great Sky above. None have carried this weapon in written times. If there is truth to Cadeck's claim, only one with your aztmudin can wield this weapon."

"Aztmudin?"

"The sacred connection which gifts all the Magi. It is what sets us apart from the profane, and a horrible burden among those who bear it."

"I could not wield magick, how is it possible? Mother always shunned it, feared it even."

Godwen cracked a smile through his white beard, "You lot were always superstitious. One should not fear a Magi. We protect Roth, and in turn, the Temple Knights protected us. They protected us from the profane, as well, protected the profane, from us. Twenty years ago, the Temple Knights went to a war they did not win. The last of them fell upon a foreign battlefield. Sarat and other kingdoms sent levies to aide, thinking the numbers would overwhelm the enemy forces of the Si'rai Imperium. None returned. Knights, nor conscripts. An underestimation not foreseen. If your wound bears truth, then their magick has returned upon the world. Only one cursed with their blood rites could have defeated the army of Knights we sent."

Godwen stared into Tesh's eyes, his veiny hands coursing over the wound, "By bearing this mark, a burden now befalls you to become a Knight."

"You said I must go through a trial?"

"Yes, the Trial of Light," Godwen's eyes returned to their atypical shade of hazel, "The first of your trials. Only through this trial, the beginning of your journey, will your Mind be receptive to your Soul. Should you pass, Aeus found you worthy. If you do not pass, I leave you to the sunwolves."

Godwen's threat sunk into Tesh's heart as he returned his hand from the old man's grasp.

"Is this what you expect of all your Knights? Threats?"

Godwen smirked, "No threats, Tesh, only promises. You have entered holy ground to achieve a holy purpose. If you leave now, the wolves will tear you apart. They are the guardians of this temple. Those who fail must face the wolves again, but without myself or Cadeck to protect you. Many fail."

Godwen's voice turned low, "It is why so few become Knights. Only those who share the bloodline of the gods can become Knights. The gods decide if you are worthy to pass."

"And if I pass the trials, Magi?"

"Then I grant you my blessing and your journey to the next Temple."

"Should I find this sword, and pass the Trials; will I find my father's killer?"

"You may find more than you ask, Tesh. You ask too many questions; I will never tell you the answers."

Godwen leaned into a hump, his senile voice slowed into a creaking groan as he walked away.

"You must find them on your own if you wish to succeed, for we are not here to hold your hand. Once Cadeck has meditated, then you will begin the Trials."

***

Reaching the end of the road, A'zum and his men drew their sable stallions to a stop. A'zum removed himself from his mount, pawing on the grassy terminus with his dark leathery boots. His eyes focused on the patchy ground allowing his thoughts to transcend current time. Beams of dusk light blanketed the ground as he made his way along a small ridge ahead of the dead end.

A'zum motioned his hand with open palm facing the ground as he deciphered the energies pulsing from the surface beneath his feet. Cracked teeth exposed from the pale crevice curled open, producing a soft wheeze from his sneering maw in a grotesque display of meditation. Bristling eyes glowed with an intense blue heat while A'zum concentrated his emotions.

"Cadeck continued this way. Vorsk, lead my horse."

On command, Vorsk grabbed the reins of A'zum's powerful steed to lead the dominating beast. Unlike Vorsk's horse, A'zum's horse bred from superior stock, raised for the cruelty of combat and the rigorous musculature needed for its purposes. The fitted onyx armor matched the beast's toned structure portraying a weapon reared for war. Carved sigils marked along the side of the beast's hide, symbolizing ownership in A'zum's native tongue. The broader horse neighed in disgust as the lesser animals stood beside him.

Ignoring the protest, A'zum continued onward. Vorsk took the reins of A'zum's mount, Storn marched abreast mounted upon his steed. The larger beast fought the smaller man, taunting him with each pull of his reins to test Vorsk's abilities. Vorsk pulled, the horse responded in kind nearly sending him to the ground. Morgus laughed at the futility of the paler man's defeats to the beast.

A'zum paced with patient stance. Careful not to slight any vibrations his senses felt. His heart pulsed in unison with the ebbing energies trailing behind his victim, attuned to the energies his caste detected permeating through the world.

Shimmers of vibrant stars welcomed the dusk azure sky as A'zum proceeded towards his impetus. Vorsk released an impatient sigh, blood leaking from scraped skin along his elbows and arms. Mud masked his face between the helmet slits. A'zum ignored the facetious distraction to focus upon the faint band of star-void darkness creeping its way into visibility along the southeastern sky as the sun faded below the horizon. A'zum's eyes glowed brighter.

In mid-stride, A'zum seated himself upon crisp blades of grass. The snow-capped skyline of the Koran Mountains remained in the close distance having traversed half the journey from the end of the road into the open wilderness for several hours on foot. He faced towards the southeastern sky as he focused his prayers into the dark void above. Vorsk and Storn stood at a skeptical distance, setting up camp while A'zum committed to his rites. Morgus remained steadfast, crossing his armored arms against his chest plate as his master entered meditative trance.

Vorsk ordered Morgus to aide with camp and barked to Storn to pursue the evening hunt. Storn snagged a small crossbow from his equipment mount attached to the side of his horse. Morgus hoisted the heavy camping materials onto his broad shoulders shrugging past Vorsk and dropped the supplies onto the ground.

Morgus remained quiet in his chore as Vorsk built the fire. The light of flame highlighted Morgus' bald-skin dome as he removed his heavy plating at his side, taking care to position his armor to leave it in pristine condition. A red dyed tunic covered his chest as two trunks for arms tore through open sleeves cut off at his shoulders. With a precision procedure allowed by the standardized design of the tents, Morgus and Vorsk built their shelters in brief time.

Vorsk seated himself to the crackling flame, stoking the fire with a nearby twig. Sweet smells of cooked bark filtered into the stars as Morgus finished the final tent, lining them in a semi-circle around the fire pit. Vorsk removed his constricting armor, marred in mud, and placed it at his side as he sat underneath his tent.

He leaned his gaze towards A'zum whose isolated prayers continued a few hundred yards away.

"These pieces of shit, Si'rai. For what am I paid? Taking orders from a damn foreigner," Vorsk spat upon the ground, "Blasphemers and murderers."

He turned to face Morgus who sat himself in front of his shelter as a distant cheer echoed in distance.

"Storn must have caught food," Vorsk poked at the fire.

His eyes turned towards the darker-skinned man, a dry inflection of contempt in his voice followed, "You need not had killed that girl. She was quite useful. We could have brought her along. Continued with her as we see fit. To what purpose did you draw her blood? For what manner of god allows such sin?"

Morgus remained silent, removing a small dagger from his right boot placing the edge of the blade into the soft flame. His focus remained on the blade. He mouthed a small prayer in the tongue he shared with A'zum.

"I am talking to you. I asked you a question. Do you speak? You slit her throat and drew her blood. That man took the bucket of blood into the home which you filled and did something I dare not speak. What were we not to see?"

"Acta'unas vohm Volen," Morgus replied in his tongue.

"What does that mean?"

Vorsk's ire burst through his blonde beard as he laid his sword against his knees.

"You see this sword? This sword," he continued in tone of reverence towards his weapon, "blessed by Heseph's Holy Flame, carried by my father and his father before him to serve a line of kings."

Vorsk unsheathed his weapon, "I vowed to this sword to destroy the enemies of my king who may lay barren my lands so as to one day present it to my son blessed to do the same. Your god is foreign to these lands, and I did not vow my sword to blaspheme against my people.

"Your actions are blasphemy, and my sword shall end them."

Unnerved by Vorsk's flagrant boasting, Morgus continued his ritual, then turned to Vorsk with a lingering sneer. Hues of flame reflected on his shaven head adorned in scars. He spoke to Vorsk in Common Tongue, addressing him in condescending tone.

"You would be wise to return your weapon to its scabbard. If my master desires me to speak with you in cordial manner, then he would have allowed as such. As he had not, then I ask you reserve your informalities to your peer."

His words carried with them a heavy timbre.

"Master? A'zum? What are you, a slave? What type of man gives himself to be a slave of another? Do you suck his cock too?"

Morgus lifted his burlap tunic from his stocky frame and revealed a ripped torso. He placed the glowing knife against his left pectoral and sliced a small line cauterizing dripping blood. Verbal prayers calmed his adrenaline. Vorsk shuddered to the grotesque performance.

"What was that for? Is that how A'zum likes his men?"

Vorsk laughed.

The smoldering blade catapulted into the ground a few centimeters from Vorsk's groin.

"Sadakem," Morgus sneered, "Keep your comments to yourself if you wish to spread your seed again. You already know my master is not a forgiving man, do not test him further."

"You make threats to me? I will best you in combat. Right here. Now. By Heseph's Flame I challenge you."

Unwavering in his desire, Vorsk stood to his feet and committing to fighting an unarmed man, dropped his sword in kind. A pair of muscled, freckled arms readied fighting stance.

"You will lose, heathen."

Morgus remained steady in his position, keeping his focus on the lit flame ahead of him and disallowing Vorsk's reaction to flinch him. Vorsk let his anger best him and punched the servant with a closed fist against the framed jaw knocking the servant to lean slightly to his left. In reaction, Morgus kept his stance exposing no emotion to the attack. Unfazed by Vorsk's reaction, he regained his posture and slowly stood erect mounted on large masts of thighs.

A bulk of muscle mass encompassed in leathery red tan skin looked down on Vorsk. Vorsk released another punch aimed for the man's chest. Morgus grabbed Vorsk's right fist to defend, flexing Vorsk's arm into a grapple behind Vorsk's back. With martial superiority, the man leaned Vorsk towards the arcing flame. Hints of burning hairs filtered Vorsk's nose.

"For the Sacred Abyss, home to my god Hadithem, my name is Morgus Kura son of Dakus Kura and honored servant to Lord Tivius A'zum. Feel the flames of your god for my god pisses on him as I and my Master do to you. If you deny this order, then take it up with your sacred fire."

Vorsk struggled against Morgus' hold then relented to a kneel. Morgus released Vorsk from his grapple. Visible singes of burnt blonde marked Vorsk's face angering him further. Storn returned, carrying a pair of furry rodents flung across his back.

"Did I miss something?"

Storn's scruffy voice asked.

"This foreigner nearly killed me."

Vorsk pointed to Morgus in anger. Storn released the dead animals to the patchy ground and raised his armed crossbow towards Morgus' chest.

"If you desire again to feel the warmth of a woman's loins, you had best stand down."

"Your threats mean nothing, Si'rai."

Storn's finger hovered over the trigger.

"You disrespect your king by attacking me in front of my Magister? Your very lives depend on your honor to your kingdom and your god. Harming an ally would bring you disgrace to your homeland."

Vorsk grunted with a scoff towards Morgus as he motioned for Storn to lower his crossbow, "Prepare the meat."

Storn cut into the pelts of the medium sized rabbits and prepared the shanks of meat for consumption in flame. Storn muttered a silent prayer to

Heseph as he offered the meat to the hearth. Vorsk steadied himself to his tent flexing his right shoulder to ease the pain Morgus inflicted.

He moved back to his horse hitched to a tree with the others. From a saddle bag, he removed a flask shaped as a horn and made from tanned and stitched hides. With a large gulp, the purplish wine spilled out of his cheeks to mingle with his beard and consumed several massive swallows. Vorsk let out a solid belch and wiped his chin in ease knowing the ferment would dull his brain shortly to remove the blood curdling screams of the girl from his thoughts.

Morgus bit into a leg of charred rabbit. Succulent juices filtered from his lips as perfect teeth gnawed into the roast. His square-jawed face ravished the morsel as a predator consuming prey. Vorsk returned to camp and in good gesture, Vorsk stood over Morgus' right side extending the flask towards the Si'rai.

"I smell ferment. I cannot accept your drink."

"As allies, you would be wise to partake," Vorsk mocked Morgus' conjectures.

"Your gesture is kind, but my beliefs prevent me from your offering. My priest prays behind us. It would be disrespectful to my god to imbibe."

Puzzled, Vorsk took his seat underneath his lean-to, handing the flask instead to his partner. The blonde men prayed again, reminding themselves of their people's covenant to their god before they consumed the meat and drink.

"Tell me then," Vorsk started in mid-chew, white meat exited from his rotten teeth as he spoke, "you serve Lord A'zum without question, and you murdered that little girl without even so much as taking pleasure from her. Why?"

"You would not understand our traditions. I serve Lord A'zum out of respect and honor as he is a Magister of my people and thus holds title above the common man and warriors. As he is capable to commune with my god, I am his servant as he is my master. He issued an order, I obeyed.

"My god lives in the dark band in the sky vacant of stars for fear of His powers while your paltry gods live here on Roth. Such is the way it should be, beneath Him, as their worshippers are beneath us."

Storn sat silent, continuing his feast. Vorsk closed his ocean blue eyes into a squint consuming Morgus' hurled insults.

"My god gives me fire, a bond mate, and a son. He gives me a king to honor and a farm to protect. Your god sits in the sky. You cannot see him. I can see my god in this fire before us. He has blessed the food you eat and the land at your feet. What about you? Do you have a bond mate?"

"I am denied union to another by profession of my caste; my life for my people, the Supernus Magister and His priests, my blood for His Will."

Vorsk and Storn laughed at this notion.

"Have you not felt a woman's loins?" Vorsk chuckled, spitting out more food.

"I have five sons back home. They are to be warriors like me."

"If you cannot bond pair with a woman," Storn turned to Vorsk before returning to Morgus, "did you rape their mothers?"

Turning to the question in visible disgust, Morgus answered, "I do not defile as you and your friend do to humiliate your enemy and to make her feel as an object and bring her burden, for my station denies me possessions. In my home, all know their worth to the Imperium - men, women, even the children. Their minds or their bodies to serve the Imperium. Any man or woman which denies submission would bring disgrace to their families and either face exile or death.

"Men give their bond mates, as you say, or daughters for the greater cause. These women gave me children and in return must give me compensation so I can train them to fight for our people. This is our way and has been for thousands of years. The warriors fight for the priests and kings, the common man toils for his protection.

"And soon, all of this land," Morgus waved his hand across the lands, smiling as he spoke; "including yours will become our slaves to which we spit on and break them for our emperor."

Without pause and spoken with a new confidence, Morgus continued, "I hope to meet your abrit someday."

He referred to Vorsk's spouse in the word of his tongue momentarily, to break his speech from Vorsk's common speech.

Then returned, "If she is as strong to tolerate you, then she will give me good sons."

Infuriated, Vorsk slammed his meat to the ground grabbing his sword rested by his right hand. He raised his sword to fight, his raging anger steamed through his unkempt teeth.

"You insult my god, my king, and my bonded mate. I will send you back to *your* god."

Vorsk swung overhead at Morgus' body. Responding, Morgus grabbed his sword from the ground and rolled to his left. Vorsk slammed into one of the wooden rods supporting Morgus' tent collapsing the shelter upon the left side. Morgus erected himself, his sword readied in his right hand. Vorsk lunged at him, Morgus returned a block forcing Vorsk's sword to angle toward the ground. Morgus attacked Vorsk with his pommel, punching him in his mouth.

A pair of rotten teeth emptied Vorsk's wounded mouth with a slow burst of crimson copper blood. Startled, Vorsk stumbled backward nearly stepping into the fire. He spat blood into the fire and thought a quick prayer for its blessings.

"Come on Morgus. I will kill you here then kill your priest. I care not for this alliance. I will defend the honor of my home, hearth, king, and god while I piss on your grave."

"It is you who will be in the grave; my master has foreseen it."

Vorsk studied his opponent as he prepared a lunge towards him. Morgus' sword had appeared as a standard issue like other soldiers he had seen from his lands - unlike his own, forged uniquely by his ancestor's hand, custom-made and wielded for generations. Vorsk parried the attack, blocking in a stationary stance, the men close enough for Morgus to ignore the putrid rank of Vorsk's breath. The pair continued their skirmish while Storn remained silent seeing this fight as an extension of Vorsk's temper.

A'zum's meditations ceased to the commotion disturbing his prayers from the distance. His eyes lulled into a steady glow returning to its natural state of icy azure. Tivius stood upon the grassy patches and turned towards the masculine aggression on display many yards away from him.

Tivius' return was swift in the night, enhanced by the otherworldly manifestations serving his meditations to the outward observer guiding him to camp of an ethereal will. Storn looked up in awe at the towering lanky frame approaching behind Vorsk. Tivius wrapped his right hand around the front of Vorsk's neck bringing him to submission with a choking constraint. Tivius' brittle nails cut sharp points into his neck, releasing pricks of blood from the punctured skin.

Morgus fell to his knees, bowing in reverence to the priest as Tivius threw Vorsk to the ground. Puffs of soft soot billowed as his mass pounded once again to familiar turf. Flickers of orange flame shadowed Tivius in ghostly images enhancing his foreboding ethereal presence to the blonde men.

"If I did not require all three of you, I would have allowed my servant to kill you," Tivius hissed.

"Magister," Morgus began, addressing Tivius with their native tongue.

Tivius motioned an open-faced palm towards his direction. In response, Morgus stopped in mid-sentence at the grimy pale palm cracked from brittle age.

"Silence, I will deal with your disobedience."

Tivius gestured, returning speech.

"Of course, Magister."

Vorsk remained on his back, erecting to lean against his elbows. Blood spittle polluted his blonde beard interacting with the slivers of gray. Torrents of anger seethed in his face as currents of a violent flood.

Tivius' next words swayed the Silvetzenian men into a lull as to whisper hypnosis, "You two, begin your slumber. The dawn will be here shortly. We have work to do."

Tivius returned to his native speech populated by harsh staccato consonants, rolling vowels and a visual sneer of the tone of his voice, "Morgus, release your sword from your hand. Come with me."

Obediently, Morgus performed as commanded. Gifted with brawn, his muscular mass bulged in larger circumference to his master as Tivius commanded the gift of speech and insight. Tivius was his commander, and Morgus was destined to obey.

The pair left camp, away from the prying eyes of the Silvetzenian men. The Si'rai foreign tongue marked with staccato punctuations across the consonants. Insipid cries of apology echoed from Morgus' speech in the tongue shared between him and Tivius. In return, Tivius spoke commanding syllables in a hissing dialect recognized as shouts, lectures, and commands. Storn and Vorsk listened on, mulling themselves to uneasy sleep as the grunts of pain and pleasure weaved through the darkness.

Chapter 6

Purple hues of dawn cast upon the carved surfaces of the Light Temple in broad strokes, painting the canvas of the walls like a tapestry. Cadeck wavered his hands in fluid motions calculated to precise meditations, chanting prayers of ancient language as he stood within the sacred pool of energy basked in the light of the sun pouring from above. His feet moved gracefully within the sigil carved into the pool beneath him, a simple triangle pointing upright towards the altar with a small cross attached to the bottom line. Trails of streaming energy flowed between his fingers encircling his outstretched appendages with every pronouncement of his precise incantations, molding the energy form into a dense spherical state as his hands closed tighter.

As he twisted the chaotic configuration, Cadeck released it into the atmosphere rushing it towards the altar wall with a push of energy rippling across the sound barrier, shattering through the air with tremendous force. The sphere extinguished in midflight, leaving a trail of tentacles in the air. Arcs sparked in a radius taller than Cadeck's height.

Forcing the energy from his body, Cadeck unclenched his breath and released a slow exhale. He stood naked within the vacant pool aglow with the warmth of sunlight. He lowered his hands to his sides at an angle, palms outstretched facing towards the front of his body. Muscles rippled across his scarred arms and backside, a testimony of dedication to his covenant. Mingled upon his toned form lay the scars of a tormentor's whip. Godwen studied the actions of his Adept from the antechamber beside the central pool hidden from sunlight's glow.

"I see Aeus has answered your prayers, Adept," Godwen approached the sacred pool, hands cupped against his torso.

Cadeck removed himself from meditations, "Yes, Ascended. Where is Tesh?"

"In the sleeping room, I will wake him shortly to begin the Trials."

"With full respect Ascended, I request to perform them. If he is to be my charge and I am to be your successor, I am ready to administer them to a Knight."

"You know it must be done by an Elder."

"But I am ready to administer the Trial of Light. Aeus has granted such calling."

Godwen shrugged into a quick harrumph, raising his milky eyebrows, "Has He now. Strange, He has not spoken to me of this manner."

"In my prayers, I have seen the boy's future. If the event at his home bears Truth, then he is to become the Azthar Kherdmon."

Godwen scowled, "I have seen his wound, but it does not guarantee the sacred blood flows in his veins. You speak of a legend lost to millennia. Generations of the profane taint his bloodline, and ergo, his legacy, Cadeck. To me, he seems nothing more than the common initiate. I sense a terrible challenge before him; wrought with pain, doubt, and deceit. He must clear his Mind, prepare to receive his Soul if he is to wield Graa'vael."

"The Sword of the Moon. A sword told of in nursery rhymes and other tales," Cadeck whispered.

Cadeck studied his Ascended as Godwen paced in front of the ornate altar adorned with artifacts and other relics devoted to the god of the Light, Aeus. An exquisitely crafted inlay of perfected humanoid form garnished the Temple's altar sporting a headdress of sun rays atop the facsimile. Flanked by a pair of heraldic wolves colored like the sun, the icon of Aeus glistened to the beams of light creeping through the eastern opening, casting a reflection of light directly into the open basin where Cadeck stood.

"A sword lost for two Aeons, Cadeck. Twenty-thousand years of human time. Only one born of the sacred bloodline can ever wield that weapon, as the old scrolls say. Of the sun, his armor shone. Of the moon, his sword struck true. Justice. Vengeance. Virtue. Wisdom. All as One. That which shall brighten the darkness, vanquish the shadows that slay the lands. He That Bears the Seven Signs.

"And you believe he can find this weapon?"

"It is why I ask again to administer the Trials."

Godwen smiled as Cadeck's firebrand demeanor shone forth as brash and honest since his founding. Godwen moved away from the pool of light where Cadeck meditated. Each slow step of movement against the hard floor shuffled towards a small chair resting beside the altar of relics, seated left of the mosaic's position outside from its grace. He set himself slow into the seat, each bone cracking with age at his motions.

"I remember the day when I found you, Cadeck. Tongue spoke of a boy playing in his father's fields who commanded lightning with his words. Without meaning and control, you set fire to your father's prize crops by the whisper of light you spit from your tongue. Word spread in Yumphen of your gesture, and I followed the rumors. As a boy, you were none too pleased when Knights brought you here to serve the Magi."

Godwen's aging lips creased into a smile, "Your persistence harkens back to your candor of that day. I grant permission for you to administer his Trial, but should he fail, then you were wrong. I caution; administering the Trials is dangerous to both the Magi and the initiate. If your words are not precise, your actions performed correctly, either one of you may go mad. The sunwolves would not hesitate to slaughter a follower of their god, especially a disobedient one."

Cadeck paced away from the wide pool on the floor as the small traces of morning sun began to flicker within the cavernous room.

"If I fail, I fail my children."

Godwen creased his wrinkled lips into a small smirk covered by his powder white moustache, "You are incredibly wise, Cadeck. Either wise or a fool. If Aeus has granted the blessing as you say, your proof will be in the Trials. Elsewise, I kill you both."

Tesh stumbled into the primary chambers of the Temple, awakening to the soft argument of the pair of Magi. He paused, scratching himself with a yawn. As his eyes strained to wake, he glimpsed to Cadeck standing upright naked as the day before.

"Cadeck, please, I do not wish to observe you like this," Tesh shielded his eyes with his good hand.

"I apologize, Tesh, but this is how Magi must commune with our god, as the day we came from our mothers' wombs."

Tesh shook his head to widen his eyes awaken.

"Very well, gentlemen. I have led you to this home, Cadeck. If you will excuse me, I would like to return to Telmen since I no longer have a home. I have slept on your thoughts Godwen, and I do not wish to partake of your ways. You have convinced me of nothing short of threats and empty promises. I will gather my belongings and leave."

"You won't be able to leave with your life, Tesh," Godwen's voice lowered into a threatening tone, "You have set foot upon Aeus' Temple and you either complete Aeus' Trials and become a blessed Initiate, or you leave without the Trials and Aeus' beasts would feast upon your soul. What I have told you is true, and once you go through the Trials you shall see this."

"And if I fail the Trials?"

"Then no one knows you ever existed," Godwen assured callously.

"Again, I have no choice. What is it you want from me?"

Tesh's ire echoed against the walls.

Cadeck advanced towards Tesh's position and placed a calm palm upon the stubborn man's right shoulder.

"To accept an idea which you have denied," Cadeck uttered.

He turned towards the pool. The mosaic of Aeus reflecting into the carved symmetrical indentation.

"You turn your back now and deny all I have shown you thus far, who shall trust you should you leave this valley? The man who follows me will not cease his efforts until I shall perish by his hands, and then, he will kill Godwen. Should you survive the attack, no one can begin the Trials without either of us to administer them. You cannot become a Knight, and the last of your line dies with you."

"A Trial I am not even guaranteed to survive."

"If your blood is true, Tesh," Godwen began, "if you carry the sacred line, then you will survive the Trials."

Tesh turned to the older Magi, then back towards Cadeck and finally towards the pool of radiant light reflected from the mosaic before him.

"A bloodline lost to myth and fable. My father was a peasant, a conscript who died for his king. My mother, a widow, who survived on meager wages to put food in my belly. We are not sacred, nor divine. The gods pissed on us."

Godwen sighed. His face turned to distant thoughts reflected in the pool of sunlight in the center of the room.

"If that is what you believe, then the Mind will reject the Trials and you will perish. Yet, if Cadeck's words speak Truth, then your Mind will reveal your Soul.

"Cadeck has decided he will conduct the Trials. If he is to be my successor this is a worthy deed. If he can take to task, then I will grant my blessing. Cadeck, your talk has proven your ambition. I will allow you to continue if Tesh is ready."

Cadeck bowed towards his Ascended in reverence. He paced himself into the pool upon the floor as the early creases of sunlight continued into the circumference.

"I am a simple man, Godwen. Fate does not guide me to this path but to live and die as a peasant, to raise a family and toil the lands. I am not destined for greatness, nor do I adhere to the gods. If I fail, then who will fight this army for you?"

"Our faith has told us different, Tesh. The madman following us cares not for our dreams or hopes; he cares not for the preservation of your lands but the destruction of all you hold dear. If you fail, Tesh," Cadeck tightened his lips, "then we were all wrong."

"My home might lay in ruin because you led me away. There is nothing I can cherish."

"If you make no attempt at the Trials, then there will be nothing left for anyone to cherish."

"And if I'm not this 'savior'?"

"You will die here," Godwen glowered, "Aeus will see to your fate."

"You leave me no choice, then. I join you, take to these trials, or die alone to a god, his servants and to his beasts of which I know no prayers. I am bound to fate either way."

"Do not look at it as fate. Look to it as promise," Cadeck shed a grin and continued, "Tesh, as I have entered the sacred pool, so must you. Your garments, they will hamper your Trials. Father Aeus wishes you as you exited your mother."

Hesitating, Tesh obeyed. He kicked his trousers away as he set them around his ankles, then furiously threw his shirt behind him. Arms bulged with scant muscle matching a torso tanned by the sun. Pale, trim legs supported his weight blinding in the morning sun forced through the open-air archway into the temple chambers. He moved to sit across Cadeck in cross-legged position while Godwen observed the activities from the nearby chair steadying his aging build.

"Within the Sacred Light, your thoughts of Mind will manifest. It is the Mind that creates reality, and it is through the Mind, Aeus will guide you on your path to understanding. I will feel your memories and through Aeus, you shall see. There is nothing hidden here, for within Aeus' radiance, All is known. The Light shows us All. Father Aeus shall show us the way. Through the Mind, is the All. And through the Mind, can you see your new reality. Here is where a Knight begins their journey and the beginning of mastery of oneself."

Cadeck entered a state of meditation, his eyes flickered in rapid succession. Observing the actions of his companion, Tesh followed in suit. At first, he remained hesitant, leering towards Cadeck in a snide grimace. As he closed his eyes, a faint voice shot into his soul with an awakening demeanor. His face winced in inquiry.

Follow my voice, Tesh

Cadeck's familiar dialect commanded.

Focus on my voice.

An expanse of blinding white blanketed Tesh's thoughts as a single silhouette formed in the distance.

I will guide you in the Trials, focus on my voice. Your thoughts will flow within the circle, within the Mind.

Within his thought form, Tesh attempted to speak. Sensing his desire, Cadeck stopped him with a calm assurance.

Do not speak, feel your thoughts. Focus on them. Let the Light of Father Aeus show me what you fear, what you wish - your dreams, your memories. These concepts are Ego. These you must bring forward and conquer to fulfill Knighthood.

Within the thought form memories swirled in front of Tesh representative of wispy stretches of disfigured faces. The forms coalesced into recognizable beings beginning with a quiet woman of brunette hair and a slender frame. A patchwork dress covered the toothpick features of the feminine form appearing in various stages of emotions.

She held a child in her hands amidst a warm hearth of flame in the two-room home; her face sorrowed in loneliness with another man standing behind her. The man's features remained hidden from the earliest memories as a swaddling baby. As other memories processed, the woman took to form of a mid-term bump forming on her belly crying in sadness as the child form hugged her in comfort. Further memories of the mother provided to Tesh the vacant bump emptied of her belly, a bulging purple bulb swelled above her left eye.

The mother spoke of how she suffers to raise her boy, how father died before the boy was born. She called his name each time he hugged her, *Tesh.*

Mother, Tesh's thoughts answered.

Her form faded, emptying into the blank void and replaced with a ravishing woman of blonde hair. Tesh's memories matured towards sixteen. The pair frolicked in fields of flaxseed and wheat. Her smile graced her face with the beauty of the seas as she leaned into Tesh's face to lock lips of crimson.

His mother reappeared lying before him, covered in pus-filled boils. Red bulbs scarred her jaundice-tinged skin destroying her youthful beauty as a wildfire in a forest. He stood before a closed grave beneath a tree, a simple marker etched with her name: *Senas Verdui.*

The thought faded to another life taken. Word spread in his memories of a young woman missing for days. The ravishing blonde morphed into a disfigured, bruised, and bloodied corpse carted through Telmen on the gravedigger's wagon.

Tesh's physical body shed tears streaming down his face, but his thoughts focused further within his mind form; a firebrand woman with locks of scarlet and emerald emblazoned eyes puffing her lips in disgust faded into a mild-mannered girl of dark hair. This other girl stood beside a young boy of blonde head, prodding at the young woman beside him.

She appeared in her mid-teens; water swirling around her in waves of propelling force reaching above her head in manner of spiral towards the moon high above. The boy of middle height appeared beside her, clutching the older girl's tunics in a sign of respective security. His face glowed with the light of the sun, while his spirit remained pure and clean. As Tesh continued to focus on the vision, the young girl morphed into a spiraling column of water rising skyward and likewise, the boy did the same as a glowing ribbon twisting around the other form in a helix pattern.

The thought forms swirled, merging into the haze of pure white focusing upon Tesh's soul. An eruption of force erased the faded thoughts and clear white emptiness, pushing the shadow form of Cadeck's voice into a new memory. Mammoth siege weapons towered upon an ancient battlefield. Hordes of armored soldiers crowded in formations harkening to a battle of which likeness Cadeck did not recall.

Clashes of weapons and pounding artillery from siege rocked the ancient valley. Rivers of blood flowed from the slain soldiers, armored in livery of different peoples as a cacophony of color. The stench of mud and blood, shit-stained bodies, and decaying corpses filled the battlefield. Living counterparts clashed with black-clad armies. Leading the charges with sweeping motions, two forms towered over their respective soldiers.

Encased in a sheen brightness of pure white, one thought form spoke an ancient language in a thunderous boom. Hearing his voice, enemy soldiers armored in sable glimmer ripped apart limb from limb by the multitudes. Unharnessing a sword of equal purity, the form swept the mighty weapon across the frontlines opposing his enemies. Scores more met their deaths in sprays of bloody shower.

Opposite the battlefield, the white thought form blinded Cadeck. Calming its intensity, the thought form billowed forth its voice towards Cadeck's shadow construct. It spoke to Cadeck in ancient dialect, the words in pleasant syllables accented by a flowing pace. Hearing the voice from beyond, the whiteness collapsed with a massive rush forcing the physical bodies of Tesh and Cadeck backward opposing one another.

Cadeck's body slid across the sunlight pool, his hips crossed the edge of the holy vestibule where he lay prone for several moments. He awoke, shaking his head in shock. His eyes struggled to open to absorb the physical sunlight shimmering into the cavernous temple. He spied his Ascended, collapsed onto the floor lying upon his back garbed in his lavender robes.

Cadeck struggled to raise himself, his muscles stung with atrophy. He moved his glance towards Tesh's naked body, lying in a position like a dying bug on the ground. His arms craned at the elbows; his knees bent with one hip lying on the floor the other perpendicular. No sooner than Cadeck spied the boy, Tesh exhaled a whining yell heard faintly across the chambers as his upper torso convulsed in a rhythmic, rocking motion.

Within moments, the numbness snaking across Cadeck's body faded, allowing blood to flow through his extremities. He steadied himself to strength, lifting his body from the floor. His legs buckled, dropping him to his knees feeling the tingling tickling of blood slowly making its way across his arteries. He erected once again to his knees as a position to start a sprint. Steadying himself again, he raised himself to stand.

Cadeck hobbled over to Godwen's body lying next to his chair and knelt at his Ascended's side. He stroked his calloused hands across Godwen's pale forehead. Godwen blinked. His eyes fixated on a blurred vision of his Adept.

"Cadeck," Godwen's vocal cords strained to form words, "help me to the chair."

Obediently, Cadeck carefully lifted his fragile teacher upon the stone chair. Godwen's arms slung to his sides in limp reaction as Cadeck placed him. Godwen wrapped his bony hands upon the sanctuary table. Purple veins brushed against the surface of his skin as his hands labored to prop his weight. Through the blurred whiteness clouding his eyes, the elder man strained under exhaustion towards Tesh's position laying on the floor in nakedness.

Through his leaden sight, Godwen observed Tesh in repose as he rolled onto his back. The young man breathed with slight motion. Brightened sear marks lingered upon his flesh numbering ten in total; one upon his crown, another upon his neck, another between his eyes, another burned upon his chest and followed further towards his groin. Other sear marks touched upon the dorsal elbow and knee joints and finally a single point split upon the arches of his feet.

Godwen dropped his jaw exhausting a frightened yelp through withered beard. He grappled Cadeck's shoulder in horrid fervor. Pain coursed through his body prompting the man to clutch at his chest. Wrinkled eyes shrunk in madness of insanity.

"I have seen the demise of the Council."

Godwen pointed a scraggly finger toward Tesh, his eyes fading into an oozing darkness absent any reflection, "Remove this boy from my sights. I cannot bless him. Cadeck, remove him from sacred ground. As your Elder, I command it."

Godwen's voice strained and wheezed with each syllable. His body rattled independent of Cadeck's grasp as Cadeck set his left hand upon Godwen's forehead.

"Ascended," Cadeck's voice rose, "This boy is our only hope. We cannot save the Council without him. His vision was true. I have felt it."

Cadeck turned first to Tesh, then to Godwen's face tugged between his palms. Fingers snaked through the graying mane and beard. Cadeck's eyes widened. There was a difference in his master's demeanor.

Godwen crept his frail fingers upon Cadeck's neckline. Tesh lingered to raise himself of his own ability, ignoring the raised voices behind him. The ancient man's voice behind him battled to regain composure.

"You disavow my vision? Do you blaspheme my command? Your vision is faulty. The Archons perverted your visions in this time of the Passing as were your feelings for that whore. You too, Cadeck, are a threat to the Council. As my duty to Father Aeus, I shall destroy you both."

"Ascended, no. I saw the mark, the *Dra Nar Azt*, the sign of the Azthar Kherdmon."

"You saw the Abyss as I did," his voice crackled in deathly growls, "A vision of blackness which he created. He will destroy us all, and I must not allow it."

"I will not let you."

Cadeck grasped Godwen by his fragile shoulders and threw him onto the sacramental table. He surrounded Godwen's thin skull with calloused hands as streaks of light formed within the webbing of his fingers outstretched across the elder man's face. Godwen screamed with raspy voice, convulsing in syncopated reaction. The screams ceased into a steady, eased breathing as Godwen closed his eyes and fell into slumber upon the table's surface. Cadeck's light diffused between his fingers as he released a steady sigh.

Godwen succumbed to the superior magick, unable to bring his own powers to fruition and released a closing sigh, "I witnessed *Dra Nar Azt...*"

Tesh writhed to position himself into a fighting stance, yet his muscles collapsed him upon the ground. Cadeck sighed as he removed his hands from his elder. Electric pulses ebbed across his fingers as he closed his fists to ease his nerves. Searing pain arced across the cavernous scars etched into his back as he clenched his dorsal muscles. Cadeck seated himself upon the stone chair, his muscles tensing with forced pulsations of spasm along his spine.

Godwen was like a father to him since his removal from his family farm forty years ago. In all his training, never had the inclination to attack his teacher arose. However, Cadeck sensed a greater threat boiling from within Godwen, a darkness flowing through his eyes and tainting his soul. Godwen did not act of his own devices, this much Cadeck sensed. He had to focus; gather his nerves and move his aching body to permit Tesh and himself time to leave.

Tesh's muscles challenged his decision to stand. Screams of unwelcome angst left his mouth as blood flowed into his appendages. Cadeck stood from the chair, moving towards the back room behind the altar. Beside the bedding chambers, he spotted a chest where he found clean robes of brilliant purple dyes trimmed with golden lined neck and sleeves. Hands sifted over the cotton and silk as he found a robe matching his size.

Old colors brought memories of a young, blonde woman in like robes of emerald hue. Her eyes crisp blue like an ocean wave. He leaned to open another chest nearby and collected a pair of white linens; short pants and a shirt intended to cover him before his robes.

Cadeck returned to the front chamber. He gathered his tattered rags, the tarnished necklace rested above them in careful array. He slipped the charm around his neck. Arms and back burned in rigid pains as he clothed himself. He reached for the shimmering lavender robes and carefully placed them onto the sooty floor. Cautiously folding the vestments in ritualistic practice, tucking the gold-lined sleeves neatly into the creases revealed the traced neckline into a perfect, symmetrical square. With great care, Cadeck cited a simple prayer in reverence and slipped the robes within his satchel. Tesh's muscles tightened as he stood. Spasms waved over his legs and arms.

"What did you do?"

"He will be fine, Tesh. I erased his memories for the last day. He will not even recall his vision."

"What type of vision? What did you see? You said you saw this 'Azthar Kherdmon'? What is special about this name? Why choose me?"

Cadeck sighed, "Azthar Kherdmon was the name given to the First One, the Primordial Man, the First of the Sacred to bear the Seven. Legends say his first incarnation took form nearly forty-thousand years ago during a time known as the Aeon of Creation. He was the first of the ancient Aztmi joined with the powers of our gods. Admired and held to high reverence, a being of renown, when giants walked amongst us. In this incarnation, the legends believe, he was the first material form of a primordial spirit.

"A second form occurred upon the onset of the next Aeon, ten-thousand years later. Around said time, the Si'rai first became made, a sub-race created by their gods, the Archons. It was at this time; the gods went to war and magick faded. As the next Aeon approached, magick began to grow once more. It was then, the Temple Knights came to be, men and women endowed with the gifts, but limited in their displays of magick. The Aztmi knew the bloodline continued, but its purity faded. The Aztmi ordained the Temple Knights as protectors of their newly built temples like this one. Those before us designed these temples to seek the original soul form through prayers and ritual, and always failing. Never understood why he came originally.

"As the millennia progressed, the gift of magick faded within the Temple Knights, some offered promise, acolytes of the gifts, but none of the mastery to fulfill the prophecy of the Azthar Kherdmon's return. I cannot know if you bear the bloodline, Tesh. The Trials shall show us more."

"This Azthar Kherdmon, was that the white Being I saw?"

"I would take a guess so. Gather your things, we must leave and find the Temple of Fire."

"Do you know where we can find it?"

"Never been there."

Cadeck slipped the satchel over his shoulder covered by the ragged robes, "I hear legend it is north of here, in Silvetzenian lands. There is a volcanic ridge on the border of the two nations. We should start there. But lakes of fire and ash surround it."

"Silvetzen? I hear stories they are mounting armies against Sarat."

"As have I. The Council cares not for man's pity wars. The will of the Council and the will of the Knights supersede any bloodshed that may result from failed diplomacy. Our goal must be to travel to the other temples and ordain you as a Knight. We may meet soldiers, highwaymen, wildlife, what have you, but our motive is to press on."

"Godwen said I would need to be blessed before I can leave."

Cadeck looked down at his sleeping master, "Seeing that he is incapable of such a feat, as the Magi who gave you your Trials, I am obliged to bless you. Come here."

Tesh carried to Cadeck's position standing in front of the sleeping elder. Cadeck placed his rough hands atop Tesh's temples. Speaking in the language of his incantations in rough consonants and punctuated syllables, Cadeck's hands glistened with a brilliant fervor twinkling across his fingertips.

"By the Mind, you have opened yourself to Soul. This vessel must prepare to accept its Gift if you are to be Oneness with All."

Cadeck's hazel eyes reverted into a sunlight hue consuming his irises. Tesh's eyes rolled into the back of his head with Cadeck's chants. Standing before him in vision, Tesh encountered the ancient, emblazoned entity once more, looking upon its successor.

***

"I have felt Cadeck's aztunai," Tivius hissed, wincing icy eyes in noticeable pain.

His pace stopped as Morgus, Storn and Vorsk ceased behind him. Morgus approached the Magister Priest with a wavering motion relishing the pain he felt behind his legs and subsidizing in his head with angry prayers to his gods. *Pain makes me stronger* he implored to himself.

"Master, are you well?"

Morgus' tongue recited the harsh dialect of Si'rai speech.

"Yes Morgus," Tivius responded in kind, "I have felt strength; magick grows here. Stronger than I have ever felt. I must find clarity."

A horse's whinny rolled through like an echo ahead of the men's position alerting Tivius to the sound and purpose, "Clarity needs focus."

Tivius grappled the hilt of his blade, beginning its release from its ornate scabbard.

"Focus demands sacrifice."

Ahead of the position, Storn battled to hold his horse steady. His animal kicked and whined, rising, and dragging on his hold to break from its handler. He held to the reins, digging his heels tight to the stirrups in desperation to keep himself from landing to the grasses. Storn called to the animal in harsh commands only for the experienced beast to buck wilder as the animal flung him to land upon his backside. In his heavy armor, Storn buckled, twisting, and rolling to the weight of his raven plate. Prone to his back, the shimmer of the sunlight masked the silhouette of the horse to rear upon its hind legs, the iron shoes aimed upon his unprotected head.

Gauntlets covered his face to the shirked shrills of a wounded animal spraying his exposed flesh with warm blood. Spotted upon his armor, congealed crimson turned black in a macabre mutation. Storn lifted his hands away from his face to see the horse's carcass collapse in split halves devoid of life betwixt the fuller of an ethereal blade. Lavender mists rolled upon the edges of the weapon where the horse's cadaver once stood whole. Storn traced the edge of the blade to a man standing taller than he, aglow in shade darker than a moonless night, like a void within the backdrop of the day.

"There," the shape pointed ahead of Storn's head towards the cliff wall.

"What... what just happened?" Storn stuttered.

"Stand," the void spoke to him, "or you will be next."

The foreboding shadow lingering over Storn turned to the others and commanded in a speech perceived by Storn to be a frightening regurgitation of growls and hisses. As to obedience, the others who accompanied Storn took to the spirit's commands as the specter motioned to sheathe the magick sword and turned to the others before mounting the mighty horse draped in the armor of his rank.

Vorsk carried to Storn, knelt beside him, and offered his hand to lift. Storn's eyes glazed empty as Vorsk pulled him away by his shoulders. Storn stood before his old horse, now a split carcass severed clean. The shadow shape returned to visible spectrum to reveal the raven-mane commander Storn had known as Tivius A'zum, now riding pompously upon his steed. His weapon returned to scabbard as Morgus led the beast forward by the reins on foot leaving Vorsk and Storn. Storn leered towards Vorsk, then back to Tivius' backside as Vorsk set a calm hand upon his shoulder and shook his head.

Tivius heeled his mighty horse into the direction of a cliff wall. The surface shimmered as Tivius entered upon his steed before Morgus, who stood beside. Awed by the spectacle, Vorsk and Storn regained their composure following behind. As the two northerners entered, the lofty ceilings and walls awed them. Carved from preternatural methods to be as sheen as glacial ice.

Tivius' animal strode in parade style towards the opening of the tunnel at the edge of the expansive cliff where the midday sun shone to the height of its power. The pair of horses which accompanied Cadeck and Tesh stood at ease, tied to the rock outcroppings. Tails wafted and swung in the calm breezes. The three soldiers approached the edge of the walkway, turning towards the horses left behind and surveyed the surrounding landscape. A herd of creatures radiating flickers of reflection stalked the valley below.

Sunlight crept onto Tivius' scarred face as he dropped from his animal. Radiant rays pricked upon his skin like pinned knives. To Vorsk and Storn, his pale image shown him to be a man where sunlight was luxury. His war steed commanded authority as Morgus took its reins and commanded the beast to another outcropping to make a hitch. Tivius turned his attention towards the shimmering specks wavering in and out of the sunlight through a display of unnatural illusion masked to the light above. The movements of the beasts like grazing patterns of herd animals.

"We are close," he whispered in Si'rai tongue, "Cadeck's aztunai reveals himself like prey. I thrive on the smell of his blood. Come Cadeck, come meet your fate."

Tivius smiled upon Morgus, "One thousand auduin and a manor with a full complement of uristri await you should you bring me the boy. Double the reward for both."

***

Clearing the opening of the Temple of Light, Cadeck and Tesh returned to the outside world. Energized, Cadeck felt his new purpose awash and reinvigorated by his prayers much to Godwen's behest. The weight of the supply satchel dragged along Tesh's shoulders adding with it the weight of his weapon. Their walk to return to the horses would take several hours, a fact not lost on Tesh's struggle with the equipment.

"Why did you sedate your master, Cadeck?"

"First let us address him proper. A master implies ownership," Cadeck turned towards Tesh, peering down his nose towards him, "His powers are beyond mine, thus we call them Ascended. Powers which could have redecorated the walls with our innards. There was something odd about him, Tesh."

Cadeck's voice trailed to the thought, pondering the eccentricities of his master's demeanor.

"Rather than find out at the cost of my life, I thought it best to subdue him at the first chance. If we can make it to Ascended Philos at the Fire Temple, he may know something as to Ascended Godwen's behavior."

"If it resides in the northern fires, how do you propose we get there?"

"We may be able to find aid in Silvetzen. It is a long ride to the border, more than a lunar cycle on foot. We should secure carriage in Telmen and shorten the trip. The trade routes would be our fastest bet which takes us through Sarat. We must be careful though; it is full of liars, cheats, spies, and criminals. And that is from what I have met within the Court. I would trust myself amongst the beggars before allowing myself within its castle walls."

"You don't seem to hold high esteem for the King?"

"Never cared for politics, my faith lives in Aeus. All men are temporary compared to the gods."

"May I ask you something else?"

"That is all you have done since I met you. I can answer."

"I saw your scars on your back…"

Cadeck ignored the statement, turning his back towards Tesh to venture further away from the Temple. Tesh sneered in Cadeck's direction in a mocking manner that his statement met with such disdain. Approaching the Magi, Tesh attempted to train his attention. Cadeck shrugged his hand away from his shoulder beaming his hazel eyes amidst his scruffy countenance towards Tesh as a dart on target.

Cadeck clenched his right hand igniting a glow of beam from within his palm.

"I never use my magick in anger. Do not tempt me."

I thrive on the smell of his blood. Come Cadeck, come meet your fate.

Cadeck paused from his disgust, scanning the skyline for a voice from the void amidst the cavernous cliffs outlining their path. Tesh watched the older man, asking him about his concern.

70

"I have heard the voice of my tormentor. He is close. Too close."

"The man who follows you?"

"A voice I care not to ever hear again; a recollection of a time I choose to forget and would be better off doing so."

Cadeck covered his eyes as he craned to the sky, "We must hurry to the horses and return to Telmen to secure better passage."

Hours passed as the pair rounded the bend to the sunwolf valley. Cadeck observed a flurry of motion amongst the native sunwolves actively scouring the grounds and howling towards the air. Pawing the ground and bearing their steely-sharp teeth in fight response, a herd of the fierce creatures displayed their ferocity towards the elevated distance like beasts surrounding prey. Tivius stood from a seated position, his eyes focused on the beasts below. An eerie calm settled over the sinister man as he awaited this scenario, repeatedly replaying this very moment in his mind, rehearsing his words to his prey. Storn and Vorsk rose from their leaning positions, their raven armor scraped against the cliff wall.

"There you are, Cadeck. At last, I have found you. I see you have failed to destroy your prey. In your failure, my Master will be most displeased. Give me your life, and he may yet spare your children."

Tivius' voice raised as to call battle.

Cadeck shared no words with his adversary as his eyes grew into a fire of bursting light in response to the threat against his offspring. His demeanor escalated into a fighting countenance. He outstretched his arms to webbed hands circulating in arcane motion. Bursts of lightning curled between his fingertips fermenting the air with the sour smell of burn. Cadeck forced his hands towards Tivius' position sending a burst of electricity towards the opposing platoon.

Storn and Vorsk ducked away as the blast shattered into the nearby cliff face collapsing mounds of rock coursing into the valley below. In reaction to the blast of energy, a nearby pack of sunwolves burst into a torrential level of speed towards the magick effect.

"You missed, Aztmi."

Tivius prepared his own magick. Wisped webs of energy swirled along his right hand as he gripped the hilt of the blade resting against his left hip. With the escalation of his own magick, the tendrils of purple beams wrapped around his hilt, sending a sheen of ethereal ting into the air when he released the weapon. Horrid shrieks of suffering torture filled the cavern to echo with the pull of his blade from its rest.

In response, a leading sunwolf began his ascent upon the cliff side clawing his razor-sharp talons upon the surface and sending shards of rock below. Vorsk and Storn prepared their swords in response to Cadeck's attack. Morgus stood patiently, waiting for his master's next move. A sunwolf hurried across the cliff face upon the right side of the opposing troops led by the beacon Cadeck summoned, hugging the mountainside as if it were ground, unbound by the gravitational pull.

Tivius steadied his sword as the beast advanced the height of the wall. The beast leapt from the precipice baring his teeth in full gap. Tivius reacted to the stench of ozone breathing through the beast's nostrils and with clean cut, swiped his blade against the creature's face. The swift strike of the blade tore through it like a blackened streak of disturbed energy stretching violet tentacles upon the body of the wolf slowly dissolving it into oblivion.

Storn prepared to advance towards the bottom of the valley, sprinting in full stride down the cliff ramp. In blinding speed, another sunwolf hugging the wall leapt into Storn, tearing his torso apart from his legs in a swift motion landing upright on all fours onto the valley floor below. Consuming his enemy in one chomp, the crunch of flesh and iron armor satiated the beast to a full bloodlust boil.

Vorsk screamed in horrid response and tried to flee from battle. Morgus grabbed the traitor by his lengthy blonde hair, forcing him back into defense.

"A true warrior would never betray his children by fleeing in fear. You are no warrior as you have boasted."

As another sunwolf advanced upon Morgus and Vorsk, Morgus swung his broadsword held tightly with his hands into the skull structure of the beast, cleaving the jawline causing the beast to evaporate with the injury in a bursting shower of light. In response, Vorsk geared his sword to battle as a sunwolf burst towards him. He leapt upon the beast's back, crushing his sword behind the neckline, riding the dissolving frame towards the valley below and landing crouched upon his feet.

Vorsk charged towards Tesh displaying his discipline as a warrior to meet the weaker man. Vorsk lunged with his iron, scraping against Tesh's blade as he threw up a block in lazy discipline. Vorsk smiled at the weak attempt before bringing his sword over his head to bear upon the younger man. Vorsk's sword slammed onto Tesh who raised his own over his head. Striking blades reverberated through Tesh's hand muscles stinging his nerves in pain. Collapsing onto the ground, Tesh's knees weakened from the weight of the strike, his blade fell away from his hand onto the ground.

Vorsk grinned with opportunity. Behind him, Cadeck continued to command his sunwolves towards the adversary watching from the precipice above. Tesh craned his neck at the blonde man. Vorsk's grimy beard covered his scarred gums as he whimpered hesitantly in the stance.

"Help me, fellow Rykanian. I am not of my own free will."

Tesh met Vorsk's furrowed eyes bleating for his own life. Puzzled, Tesh gazed into his adversary's eyes at a hint of an icy blue glow within his irises as pulsing stings raced through Tesh's left arm in reaction to the sight. Tesh clamored to prop himself towards his left side as he suffered the agony of nerves firing through his appendage numbing him from physical presence. Vorsk struggled, fighting to keep his sword from raising again.

"I can't, please," Vorsk murmured quietly.

The sounds of Tivius' whispers echoed upon the valley from above, searing over Vorsk's eyes to fade into an eerie blue radiance. He charged towards Tesh to strike a fatal blow aiming for his chest only for Tesh's golden scarred hand to grip the sharp edge of the blade before contact above his heart. Frightened at the bright glow pulsating from Tesh's left hand, he hurried to release his blade from ethereal grip only to fall backwards from his reverse momentum crashing onto his buttocks holding nothing but the iron hilt. Before Vorsk could react to the turn of events, he screamed in agony as his mind clouded with final fade at the sight of his bloody legs shivering on the floor of the canyon, his torso in the death grip of a sunwolf jaw.

Having felled a dozen sunwolves into blinding oblivion, Morgus paused to relish in the death of the infidel. He spoke in his tongue with a confident swagger, the staccato tongue brandishing off the canyon walls like a death poem.

"I shall retrieve the Aztmi for you master. They shall know your Xiatutni bring death."

Tivius grinned as Morgus self-addressed his elite rank. Morgus' mammoth hulk of raven armor sprinted along the cliff trail with the weight like a massive tank. Another sunwolf lunged from a standing pause in the valley below aiming his attack towards Morgus. Anticipating the magical beast's movement, he moved to avoid the crushing jaw to attack the broadside of the ribcage with full blade thrust. Sweeping across the mystical hide in one motion he regained his momentum towards the bottom of the valley, the sheer luminescence of the animal's entrails flowed behind his gait.

Taking pause of commanding the herd of wolves, Cadeck's bristly eyes motioned to the oncoming attacker. Cadeck raised his hands into a formation cocking a bow and arrow. As he performed the motion of the draw, the weapon formed into his hands from the air. The searing missile of light screamed across the cavern. The impact of the projectile forced the assailant against the ground on bended knee, exploding into a blinding beam tearing into his onyx coverings.

Clutching his eyes, Morgus screamed in agony to recover from the flash blindness. Hands and torso flesh boiled from the blast like the light of the sun.

Materializing to form, a sunwolf appeared in front of Morgus' sturdy frame seated upon the rocky surface. Suffering in pain, Morgus did not notice as the beast clenched its jaw into his armor, severing his spine. Too large for the beast's maw, Morgus' body split in two as the sunwolf clenched its prey.

Aghast, Tivius reacted in shock as his superior warrior fell to the beast.

"You fought on my terms, Tivius, and you failed."

Swirls of lightning streamed from Cadeck's hands to await Tivius' response. Sunwolves stood their ground, snarling from all directions to the swordsman. Tivius stood firm to his battle, aiming the blade into the valley, pointed at Cadeck's body. Swirls of mystical energies spilled around the fuller, snaking along the etched carvings of the hieroglyphs in random patterns. With each motion of the lavender waves, the sword whispered to Tivius.

"I shall claim you with this sword one day, Cadeck."

Turning towards his majestic beast, Tivius tore through the air with a swipe of his blade. An eruption of blackened energy spilled down the dorsal trim of his horse, ripping the massive spine and flesh to a form of vacuum void pulling the beast apart. Within the scar, screams and moans of death pulled from the vacancy left into the air, a void of indescribable torment opened where the beast had split at the side. Tivius shorn a rotten sneer aimed towards his adversary as he exited into the darkened vortex, stepping into the open sore of the beast.

The rip of the void pulled Tivius within, closing with the muted sounds of suffering. The bulbous void collapsed in the vacancy left of the air, sheering the horse's body into the shape of the opening, and consuming the beast to scream in death throes. Its remnants pulled towards the center to the minutia of atoms. The spilled guts and flesh plopped onto the ground from the center location where the sword once cut, leaving the only evidence of the animal's existence. Shielding his eyes from the display, Cadeck cowered and turned his back to the grotesquery.

Tesh lifted himself from the ground, ignoring the dust and rocks clinging to his clothes and hefted the sword to his side. His mind wandered to the act, the imagery of a horse split in two by a weapon unseen where its wielder vanished into a vacancy of existence.

"How in… how did he… Did he just…. Where could he have gone?"

Cadeck turned to see Tesh clamoring for answers to the gory evisceration of the massive beast.

"I could not say."

Cadeck turned to see Tesh advancing towards him. Dust covered the young man's tattered rags and grimy skin.

"His magick works differently than mine. We must be on our guard; the blonde men were Silvetzenian. The other two were Si'rai. We must head to Sarat soon and warn His Majesty of their danger."

"I thought you didn't trust the King?"

"King Trebut must know Silvetzen has allied with the Si'rai. I suspect they are the catalyst to the feud. It is wise for us to hurry, Tesh, gather the supplies and clutch onto my shirt."

"Why? What are you doing?"

"Just do this, I will show you."

Tesh sheathed his weapon and gathered his satchel. Gripping Cadeck's clothing as the Magi chanted an incantation. Within moments, the pair vanished from the basin to reappear on the top of the open cliff side startling the remaining horses. Tesh gasped in shock as his body collapsed from the sudden displacement. His knees buckled to the ground as his legs went numb. A rush of vomit spewed from his mouth as he leaned over to exhale it onto the soot below.

"Why are my legs numb?"

Tesh wiped the bile from his chin, his teeth chattered.

"Your body felt a sudden rush of distorted space. Your blood will recirculate, usually takes a few minutes. I will gather any supplies from the Silvetzenian horses which we can use. Feel free to help when you can."

"Why don't we teleport to Silvetzen, then to any other Temples?"

Cadeck approached the horse he rode, "Magick requires our connection to aztmudin; and it is innate within us to those gifted with it. Exertion and the loss of our powers could severely incapacitate a Magi or worse, kill them. I could travel to Silvetzen by thought alone, but I would be useless for days or weeks. Time too valuable to waste."

"You saw what he did with his sword? A weapon like that, a power like his…"

Cadeck lifted his index finger to the notion, scowling through whiskery face at the attempt of temptation, "Do not ever speak of that sword as to wish it to your possession. What I did required nothing; not beast nor man, to die."

"You've seen this sword before?"

"We will not speak of this sword ever again. Am I clear?"

Tesh nodded.

"Good," Cadeck continued, "But I am more impressed by what you did back there with your hand. That is true magick."

"The man felt pain, like he was resisting something, and my arm, I felt it react to his eyes, they turned an unnatural shade of blue."

Cadeck's eyes piqued towards Tesh, "Reacted you say?"

"Yes."

"Then we must hurry to advance your training. In time, the answers may come to you. Now hurry, mount up, we must reach Telmen if we wish to avoid any further danger."

As his senses returned, Tesh stumbled as a newborn deer towards his horse and placed the satchels across the back of the animal. Cadeck steadied beside him and eased him onto his animal, gripping Tesh's collar. Exhausted, Tesh leaned towards the neck of the beast, patted the animal a few times before handling the reins and steadying the gait of his steed. Cadeck reared first, entering the cavern leading to the grounds. Tesh turned, catching sight of a sunwolf over one of the bodies in the valley below gnawing upon the remaining chunks of flesh melded armor.

"I hear Kora is just on the other side of the mountain range. Isn't Kora closer?"

"It is, but no roads lead from this valley or the mountain range out to Kora," Cadeck's voice echoed, "The Koran River begins on the opposite side of that ridge but is impassable from here. Our best trek is the route we came from; through Telmen past your home and onto the main road to Sarat."

He heeled the horse into an obedient trot behind Cadeck. As the pair approached the base of the cliff tunnel, Cadeck motioned his horse to heel, surveyed the other animals and supplies resting upon them. Tesh followed close behind, stopping to the sight of the remains of the once, sturdy horse. Flies had begun to buzz around the carcass to feast and mate upon the buffet.

"Cadeck," Tesh called.

Cadeck ignored the younger man, easing his horse to turn face towards the opening of the chasm leading to the temple valley. His eyes lowered, followed by a quivering jut of his jawline into a curled lip of anger.

Instead of the sheen face of a cliff visible to his physical eyes, a cavern of rotted darkness opened into the grassy plains before him, shadow-like tentacles swirling over the periphery of the cavern entry to mar the portal with a darkened husk of death.

"Gather supplies from these horses swiftly, Tesh, for our time is short."

Chapter 7

After two more days of ride, Cadeck and Tesh crossed the bridge leading into the outskirts of Telmen. The brook sprinkled across shaped rocks and jagged, minute fissures cut into the landscape running towards the south into the fields cooled by winds of the mountain range. A watermill creaked with the tension of bearwood wear as the wheel turned in the direction of the stream repeating the doldrums of time. The pace of the outskirts a reflection of the slow churn. A farmer toiled to pigs, minding the pink-bellied pork to their pens before the fall of sunlight. Thatched roofs dotted the landscape marked with smoking chimneys in the brisk dusk setting upon town. Cart-bearers moved goods and other supplies to their shops and markets to hurry their business before the sun set into dusk.

Tesh led Cadeck through town into the central market square. A wooden crossbow of Silvetzenian markings, a single eagle head decorated the stock, had strewn over his saddle accompanied by an assortment of water pouches and other supplies taken from the Silvetzenian animals outside of the temple valley entrance. Within the commons, the pair came to a three-floor, wood-framed building on the eastern edge. Its structure matured with homely passions having seen days of countless ribaldry and forlorn brawls. The blowing sign of the *Wolves Den* whined with iron hooks above the door. Tesh and Cadeck hitched their horses upon posts nearby.

Tesh entered the tavern first amidst the bustle of raucous laughter and drunken squalor. Cadeck eyed the room of patrons whose attire and demeanor marked them as peasant workers with loose morals. Burly men and surly women imbibed at the bar leaving the stench of gaseous mead and ales floating about the room like a vapor of sin. Two large men scuffled together; a clay stein shattered against the wall next to Tesh's head as he ducked to avoid the projectile while the men pursued their scrap.

A woman graced her crinkled hand across Cadeck's shoulder. A buxom bosom marked by a hairy wart pushed against his ribs as she spoke in drunken slurs breathing a foul taste into his nostrils.

"Wudjou like to taste this?"

The woman signaled her blackened tongue against her putrid teeth.

Cadeck pushed aside the harlot in rank disgust. Her stammer collapsed into a chair causing it to break with her bulbous bulk.

"Thatsno way t' treet a'lady."

"I never assumed you for a lady," Cadeck interrupted her.

Her eyes gazed at Cadeck through mangy hair with an unkempt, pus-laden wart leaking from her nose.

"I will offer you drink, and you will leave us alone."

Cadeck reached for his hips to clutch the hefty coin purse tied around his waist and produced a gold piece emblazoned with a crown on the head side, the double-crested eagle on the tail. He tossed the currency at the woman, hitting her in the forehead. Cadeck and Tesh pushed their way towards the barkeep as Cadeck produced a purse of coin upon the wooden bar. The obese man behind the bar spit into a cup, wiping it with a towel before pushing his hefty frame towards the strangers.

"I ain' seen yer parts in he'r."

His stained mustache whistled with each syllable.

"We will take a room. The simplest you have. Two beds, no questions asked."

Grinning wide, "Whatcho do in yer room is nun my biznes. One room 'tis. Five 'neves, plez."

Cadeck rummaged through the coin purse, removing five pieces of minted copper. Each coin stamped with the pictogram silhouette of a small crown. The barkeep counted them in an impeded pace twice before reaching into his pocket to retrieve a small key. His slow wit tested Cadeck's patience to an unnerving sigh. Cadeck clutched the key in quick response, grinning at the barkeep for his humility.

"Secon' floor, thir door on yer left."

Cadeck nodded. Tesh turned his eyes towards Cadeck as he hurried Tesh away from the bar. A man had passed out beside Tesh with a loud thud against the bar as a river of spittle vacated his open lips. Moaning in dizzying agony, he began to snore.

"We're staying here?"

Smelly flatulence and soured ales tickled at Tesh's nose at the sight of drunken carousing and vomiting unconsciousness.

"It's a warm bed, and you're complaining?"

"I'd rather sleep in the jaw of a sunwolf."

Cadeck smirked at Tesh's attempt at humor. He placed a calloused hand upon Tesh's shoulder as they continued upon the staircase to the next floor. A candle lamp clouded the hood of a thin-framed, cloaked figure seated into a table in the back corner. The table was bare of drink, only a small dagger resting in front of the shadowy figure as the newcomers moved to step onto the staircase leading to the upper floor.

A silk-white hand snaked its way onto the dagger gripping its leather hilt. The weapon moved into the sleeve of the flowing gray cloak. The stranger filtered away into the crowd, sneaking past various drunks and women of ill-repute. With the grace befitting of a dancer, the light steps of the figure followed the staircase towards the second floor.

The stranger took careful stride so not to alert its prey with the creaks of the steps as it followed the pair and crouched to a cover shadowed from the ill-lit hall to mask within the darkness. Cadeck and Tesh entered their assigned bedroom in the antechamber. Small hands swept across the banister. Angelic antipathy escaped the shadowy confines of the cubby hole and followed towards the assigned door.

Paused upon the wall opposite the door swing, the stranger waited amongst the lamp lights. Tesh's faint words echoed into the ear of the spy as its head rested upon the wall hidden by a gray cloak. A sliver of blonde hair fell from the woolen headpiece.

Inside, Tesh placed his belongings upon the foot of the bed he chose on the left of the room. Littered with the least number of stains and filth, he sat himself upon the soft mattress.

"Now that we are in relative safety," Tesh began as he observed Cadeck eyeing the single window opened to the south.

Cadeck swung the single, threadbare curtain closed to block the sunlight and visibility of their occupancy.

"Safety?" Cadeck interrupted.

"Well, we don't seem to be in danger of being followed at the moment."

"There is only safety when their emperor's heart no longer beats."

"Who are they? And what do they want with you and I?"

Cadeck hesitated for a moment and turned to the protégé, "Did your mother not regale you with abominations and warnings of their kind? Histories of legends and stories of old tales speak of the Si'rai in ominous words, none too flattering. What they want is absolute power, and you and my kind are the obstacles to their goals."

"You saw they are also men."

"You also saw what that sword did to the horse. You give them too much credit. They are vile creatures, whose magick is based in death. Their warriors are menacing beasts culled from the darkness of men's fears. Without the sunwolves, the Si'rai warrior would have killed us both. The amulet carved into your left hand is proof of their danger."

Tesh clenched his left fist. His connection to the dark arts of the Si'rai reminded him of the ordeal at his home.

"If the Knights lost to them as Godwen says, do you believe they can be defeated?"

"It would be difficult. Doubtful Sarat will levy more conscripts to fight a war they lost once before. The other lands would surely feel the same. There is something amiss and this proof of alliance with Silvetzen is disturbing. We must find the other temples if we are to succeed in your journey. If legends hold true, two Temples exist within their lands. The Fire Temple is one, and the Wind Temple is the other. This alliance may hamper our progress to them."

"But you said you didn't know where they are."

"True. I have never visited them. Someone surely knows. Loosening a man's tongue with good ales seems like a plan."

"We're just going to march into Silvetzen looking for two temples no one knows where they are?"

"We should first inform King Trebut what we know. The Magi do not wage war on their own, our numbers are too small, but we will need the armies of the kings who pay tribute to be successful. With this information, Trebut could aide in our journey, whatever we might need to move into Silvetzen. From there, we can investigate where the Temples exist."

A faint shuffle brushed against the wooden panels. Cadeck silenced himself, motioning for Tesh to remain still. He took a wide stride towards the door swiftly opening it, catching the lithe spy off balance. Before the dagger could leave the sleeve, Cadeck grasped the weapon, then clutched the edge of the stranger's cloak pulling the assailant into their room.

Falling to the wooden floor with a muffled *oomph* and a soft *thud*, the figure's cowl slipped open revealing a flowing river of silky blonde hair ruffled from fabric's static release. Tesh readied his sword against the stranger as Cadeck shut the rickety door behind them.

"What did you hear, woman?"

Sleek blue eyes crisp like a pure dawn turned towards Cadeck towering over her. Lips pursed in disgust; she reached once more for her small dagger attached in Cadeck's clutch. Tesh burst up, reaching around the woman's neck to defend the older man, holding her in a restraint and pulled her away from Cadeck's range.

"Answer me, and I shall see you spared. If you are my enemy, I will not hesitate to shove this dagger into your chest."

"You must be the Magi," her High Accent strained in a gasp.

Cadeck pricked the dagger against the menial bulbs sprouting from her chest; pointing against the soft woolen cloak reminding the woman her outburst was not welcome.

"State your purpose, woman."

The lady hesitated. Cadeck poked the dagger into her cloak pricking against the skin by the point of the blade. She winced momentarily in the pinch of pain as Tesh tightened his grip around her shoulders and neck.

"I have found no reason not to run you through, admit your purpose."

Cadeck's breaths rolled into her nostrils like aging ale.

"My purpose is for the Crown," her voice confident; defying the strain of Tesh's grapple.

Daylight fainted through the closed curtain hiding the wear of a cobbled face in shadow. Cadeck ordered Tesh to relax his grip, switching instead to holding her arms with his hands at the elbow. The woman gasped, regaining breath before continuing.

"There is a bounty out for two men matching your description. The town clerk testified account and your faces match those who came into the clerk's office a few days ago. There was a sale of a home tied to this record. The other day, the Marshal's men found a murdered girl along with a man at this home. The man was a clerk of Marshal Offtil."

"And the girl?"

"I do not know, but Marshal Offtil has two charges of murder pending."

Cadeck tensed his consternations. He dug the dagger deeper under the woman's left breast.

"What else do you know?"

"I know this; the Marshal is looking for the last owner of that house."

Cadeck sensed a change in her inflection of voice, "Your skills with the hunt need work. What reason does the Crown need with a Magi?"

The blonde girl convulsed her tiny lips to interrogated repose. Her doe-eyed stare blanked in front of Cadeck's stern expression in a vain attempt to hide her fear and deny his question. His grizzled face pocketed with crevices of age wise to her mendacious tendencies as he lowered the dagger to his side.

"What is your name and why have you been following us?"

Cadeck moved away from the young woman. Her tension relaxed as she breathed slowly.

"My name and my purpose are of the intent for Her Majesty's Service only. Let me go and I will not press Contempt of the Crown."

Tesh tightened his grip on the woman, "Contempt? How do we know you will not kill us or turn us over to Marshal Offtil?"

"Her Majesty, Queen Selen, honors the Magi. I serve Her Majesty and Her Highness, Princess Cassica."

"Princess Cassica? You are a Maiden of the Order of the Rose."

The girl's hair fell in embarrassment at Cadeck's statement to slouch her head in shame.

"Fizzlesnits."

Cadeck laughed at innocent cuss directing his inquiry towards her original intent.

"What can you tell us about the persons found at this home?"

"Magi, she was a simple woman, a peasant girl, found with slit throat and ravaged loins. The man had a broken neck."

"And the outcome of the bodies?"

"The girl's body returned to her family in Sarat. The body of the man returned here to Telmen."

"And the house is it safe?"

"No syr. Saratian troops burned down the residence."

Cadeck sighed, crossing his arms amidst his hefty chest, his brow forming to a curious glance at her news.

"Can you take us to Sarat and Princess Cassica? We have information relevant to the interests of the Crown."

"You said something about Si'rai and Silvetzen."

"Clever girl," Cadeck chimed, "What else did you hear?"

"I serve the Order of the Rose. It is my duty to be the extension of the Will of the Crown and if that Will brings me upon information for the safety of the Crown, it is my duty to hold information from those not associated with the Crown."

Cadeck laughed, crossing his arms holding her dagger still in hand, "You stick to your convictions, woman. You remind me of my daughter, feisty and headstrong. We will need safe passage to Sarat, and if you serve the Crown, then you should be able to trust a Magi and help guide him to Sarat. If the information I have is correct, then your service to your Crown should not go unrewarded by this simple task."

"You drive a hard bargain, Magi. The Marshal and his men will find you and have you arrested. How can I trust you? I could turn you over to the Marshal."

"If you want me to trust you, you will do as I ask. The information I have will no doubt clear our names. Our destiny is not to stay in Sarat for we have a long journey ahead which is not of your concern. King Trebut will undoubtedly find our information useful. You are young still and by taking us directly to the Court, you will have served the Crown to highest degree."

The doe-eyed woman smiled. Cadeck's soft words tugged into her heart through an unseen force she could not interpret.

"My name is Venna. Venna Rutin. We could hire a cart to take us to Sarat. You can hide in the bin."

"And who would drive this cart, you? We can hire a driver. Listen, and honor Your Crown with my command, and I am certain favorable rewards shall bestow upon you. Woman, you will make a fine deceiver, but your skills need work.

"We will need disguises. You and Tesh could pose as a couple. I would take the role of the low clergy as we travel to destination to bond pair. She is not much younger than you Tesh, we could pull this off."

"What about our horses?"

"We will return them to the livery. We will have to ditch your sword. Your cloaks, Venna, will surely fail your disguise. Tesh, some of your clothes in the satchel could help her."

Tesh gripped the satchel resting at the foot of his bed and set it upon the hay mattress. A leather strap wound around the bag, bound by tarnished brass buckles. The tongue began to wear its age upon the tattered hide as it cut into the worn leather. He untied the hemp rope bound to the latch with a brass loop on the face of the bag and began to rummage for suitable clothing. He removed a gray tunic with a button collar beginning from mid chest and a pair of brown pants to lay them out for Venna to change into.

Venna removed her cloak followed by a linen shirt and kept her back turned towards the men revealing the bare skin of her lithe frame. Strands of silky, ribbon hair flowed over her shoulders. Cadeck motioned towards Tesh, placing his hand upon his shoulder as he positioned his gaze away.

"Tesh, she is still a maiden. No man should see her in undress except on her union night."

"Oh right," Tesh sneaked a glance over his shoulder before he respected Cadeck's commandment.

Venna giggled with a shy voice as she clothed into Tesh's tunics which enveloped her lithe frame with space to spare. She closed the collar with the buttons, hiding her perky chest and followed to lift the pants around her waist. She reached for the small hemp cord binding her cloak and twisted it to keep the shirt and pants as tight as her body frame allowed within the larger clothes.

"I appreciate your modesty Magi," Venna grinned, keeping her back towards the pair.

She fluffed her hair to remove its grasp from underneath the neckline of her new shirt fitting over her like a rustic dress stretching to her mid-thigh.

"You may look now," Venna cooed.

"Stunning," Tesh commented, "You remind me of someone I once knew."

"Your flattery is commendable, Tesh. But I assure you that I cannot commit to any man."

"The Order does not permit it?"

"You do catch on, don't you?"

Cadeck interrupted their flirts, "We paid for the night. We should bed down. Venna, use my bed, I will take comfort from the chair. We will discuss more in the morning."

Soft light from Roth's solitary moon crept through the window covered by the sheet, a thin glaze of white glow arced towards Venna. Tesh lay in the opposing bed, covered in the shoddy fabric blanket as the blade of light caressed Venna's blonde hair in a wash of silvery sheen. Cadeck set with squirming discomfort in the wooden chair pushed against the front wall of the quaint room. He sighed as he propped his aching feet upon Tesh's mattress watching each breath Venna made in her sleep. Cadeck's torn trousers revealed slits cut near his knees. Worn soles on his boots opened from ripped seams, a size too small for his feet which he crammed in the confines of the shoes.

Cadeck observed the young woman which despite her blonde hair, she matched the spryness of his young daughter. The light of the nighttime orb sprinkled her pale skin. His oldest child he had longed for no longer within his grasp. He reached a calloused hand upon the gold chain hidden beneath his robes while his mind lingered onto memories fading in and out with the environment of drunken brawls. A rowdy raucous echoed from below the floor as drunkards continued their reveilles.

A voice from the square below the window called out the curfew hour as the stumble of drunken collapse forced a thud outside the door. A woman's voice coaxed the drunkard into a room across the hallway, jerking Cadeck to shift in his chair. Venna startled in her precious, soft sleep. Her still breaths lifting and lowering her chest, hairs falling along her cheeks in shambled disarray upon her demure features as she proclaimed an effeminate snore.

Slumber escaped his desires. Cadeck caught slight glimpses of a small girl resembling his daughter standing in the moon light. Ceased in mid-breath, Venna's chest heaved high, a lock of hair paused in place in motion to tumble down her cheek. Cadeck glanced over, likewise, Tesh hung in suspension to twist to his side. Left arm shifted to position only to remain motionless in the shadow of the moonlight's glimmer.

Embraced by the silvery sheen through the window glass, images of swirling water flush flowed into the room. An ethereal mist spilled into the room from the creases of the windowsill, coalescing and sloshing along the floor in slow trickles. Water dripped to wet the bedposts, the cracks of wood plank like riverbeds nourished by a fresh rain. In another flash of shuttering eyelids, Cadeck caught glimpse of the brunette girl in his vision garbed in a silk dress dyed in fashionable emerald. Hair perfected into a golden tiara split over her forehead in a manner apt for royalty.

The figure moved from the window along the floor, feet adorned in open sandals of golden trim which sparkled to the piercing moonlight behind her. The apparition paused to turn towards the blonde girl.

Father, his magick grows.

The young voice spoke in a dialect Cadeck understood as the speech of invocation.

Wrem?

Astunox Graa shall soon appear.

I shall save you before such time.

No. The key is within the Aztun.

Her voice faded into the vacancy of the air around her as a sickly echo. Cadeck pulled at the armrests, stronger than his own frame could muster with unwieldy force.

"Wrem."

Cadeck's voice cried loudly, reverberating the walls like the rattle of a quake. Tesh and Venna continued their actions from the brief pause in time affected by magick's fade outward through the closed window. Sparks ignited from Cadeck's mouth as his words turned into archaic vernacular. Startled by the magick glow billowing over Cadeck's body, Tesh darted to his feet reacting to Cadeck's outburst. With a sprint and a leap, Tesh shook Cadeck's shoulders to calm the man. Cadeck resigned to Tesh's efforts before he cried out the names of his children again.

"Cadeck, please. You will wake the neighbors."

Fierce irises swelled in Cadeck's face; his teeth gripped tight in competition to the man contesting him.

"I saw her, my daughter. Remove your hands lest you suffer the fate that awaits her captors," Cadeck's voice growled with contempt.

"Cadeck, no. It is Tesh, remember? You wish to help me become a Temple Knight."

Tesh knelt in front of Cadeck, easing the older man into submission.

"Temple Knight? You are a fool boy if you think you can lead them. They do not exist. The last of them died twenty years ago."

"I know this, you told me. Calm down, it was a dream."

"No, it was real. You do not know, boy. You do not have children. You know not of what pain I live daily."

"Cadeck, I will help you rescue them."

Cadeck's eyes raced furiously across the ill-lit room recovering from his trauma. His breathing gradually returned to normal syncopation.

"I saw her, clearly as I see you."

"Cadeck, calm down."

"That girl, who is she?"

"The girl is Venna Rutin. We met her earlier this evening."

"Wrem. Wrem stood to her, drawn to her."

"Your imagination, Cadeck. A dream, nothing more."

"No. No dreams, my dear boy," Cadeck dropped his forehead into his left hand, "A vision. She spoke of the Death Moon."

"Death moon?" Tesh turned an inquisitive stare as he stood to his height.

"The darkest night of the Aeon," Cadeck turned his eyes towards Tesh, his hands tightened around the armrests, "Magick swells strong on such night."

Tesh stepped away. The faint glimmer of moonlight hid Cadeck's sorrow in shadow, "Do we have much time?"

"No. I fear it is a ritual necessary for completion. A ritual that will mark your journey to becoming a Knight."

Cadeck dropped his eyes to his hands quivering over the armrests. Thoughts raced to rumors of a ritual so sinister to fear his own children were to be involved brought him to bear. He cleared his mind of such outcome as he slowed his breaths. Tesh sat upon the mattress where he slept.

"Return to sleep," Cadeck whispered.

Venna's covers shifted as she startled to wake. Blonde hair strewn over her face in a gesture of haphazard alertness and half-sleep inquiry.

Cadeck continued, "Both of you."

Cadeck rose from the chair and shuffled along the floor. The threadbare hinges creaked open as he exited the door and quietly closed it behind him.

"What happened?" Venna's soft voice wondered.

"Nothing," Tesh turned to her from across the room, "Just a bad dream."

Chapter 8

An open tear erupted in the middle of the room as the fabric of the air ripped in a single line. The wound spilled open as the color of night, a frail figure fell through the gap and collapsed to the sooty ground. Like a newborn, prone and vulnerable, the figure convulsed in half-risen fetal position upon his spindly frame. Tivius stained muddy wood with the cough of blood. The chambers mirrored the horrid spectacle; rotten entrails and decayed flesh painted the small room with the odor of carcasses and shit. Moonlight pierced through cracks in the walls, casting tiny beams on fetid decay as the magick spectacle faded.

Tivius' body convulsed in full hemorrhage as his mouth evacuated bile. Blood and bile mixed created a caustic whiff of bodily fluids. Muffled whimpers paused the silence between his vomiting and gagging where cold breaths followed from blackened lips stained by his fluids. Tivius propped his knee to lean, his muscles rigid, the pain burned from within. Red and green ooze dripped down his chin, staining his leather garments. His sword clung tight against his hip, sheathed within the sturdy scabbard scribbled with arcane glyphs of a language beyond his comprehension of etymology. Wood creaked with his shift of weight in the direction towards the whispered whimpers.

A threshold sigil marked upon the floor, painted in the viscera of unknown source, the herald of the eight spoke sunwheel laid into a perfect alignment of circumference and design. At the edge of one of the spokes, Tivius sneered towards the source of the sobbing; a young, naked boy quivered in the cold, covered by a small hood over his head.

Bound by chains on his wrists, the boy tightened and panicked at the sound of footstep approach. Tiny traces of moonlight covered the pale boy's prepubescent features. Pus riddled fingers ran trace along the chain links firmly held into the ceiling, down towards reddened wrists where the boy suspended mere inches from touching with his toes. Tivius' nails slid over the left thumb and wrist as the boy trickled piss with a haunting cry muffled only by a gag held firm in his mouth.

Tivius ran his finger further down the arm. The boy's tremored movements increased as sharp keratin ran along his hairless arm, towards his shoulder and along his torso. Now four nails followed the trace along the hips and across the torso causing the boy to scream futilely inside the cloth between his teeth.

Icy breaths billowed from Tivius' mouth, drying stains of blood and vomit along his chin. Each rank breath filtered through the rag over the boy's head with every moment of anticipatory fear of the stranger's will. Four sharp nails slid further downward. Tivius reached for the pleasurable morsels between the boy's thighs, with sneering disdain upon his face. The boy muffled louder to his further touch.

Tivius pulled his hand away with the warm trickle of a second piss stream flooding his fingers. Tivius washed the boy in his own piss as Tivius smashed his open palm against the sackcloth. More whimpers spilled from the dampened rag as the urine turned cold to the air.

"I despise your kind."

Tivius snarled in a low growl in the speech of the boy's tongue, "I grow madder every day I am here in your lands. Every day I am here, every day that your king does not relinquish, another boy such as yourself fills my chambers with blood."

The muzzled boy cried louder in his restraints to the realization of his fate. Another trickle of urine followed. Tivius cased the boy clockwise and stopped in front of an altar surface mounted against the back of the room where the eight-spoke sigil had adorned a cloth mounted against the wall. Each spoke ending in a glyph of his tongue with a single mark in the middle of the wheel

"Here in Rykana, I want more than just the innocent flesh. I want redemption."

Tivius turned his gaze towards the boy's anus, positioned perfectly to the height of Tivius' hip. Metal clanks of straps and metallic buckles entered the boy's ears in the echoes of the hall. The sound of wood crashed upon the floor set the boy at ease if only briefly. Cold hands set against the young shoulders and with a muffled shriek louder than any spilled from his mouth, the boy felt Tivius' flesh intrusion within his bowels.

The faint calls from the ritual chambers muted outside of the door alit with the luminosity of blood. A pair of figures flanked the chambers doors, their clothes an amalgamation of raven, leather skirting, a carapace covered their torsos and shoulders. A muscled figure approached the pair and paused at the door. The dread of fresh death lingered between the towering, non-descript beings.

Atop his shaved head, sweat steam left his body over bulbous ears disfigured as cauliflower. Woolen garments exposed his rounded biceps and strained to hold his muscular form. A chain mail skirt covered his hips and stopped at his shins.

Along the encampment, more warriors built and framed as he trained, exercised, and sparred. An olive, red-skinned countenance reflected years of abuse and battle upon the man as he stood in front of the odd figures. A single tattoo emblazoned across his right eye; the eight-spoke sun wheel, the Sigil of the Abyss, the Herald of the Imperium. Scars marked his face and chin ending into a thick neck hid amidst his inhumanly trained shoulders.

One of the figures protecting the door tilted its hooked spear to impede entry. A pair of organic gloves covered the figures' hands as they stretched around the grip like extensions of roots around the dark wood. A growling echo spoke from the faceless, crimson mask of calcified bone on the right flank guard.

"Master forbids all entry."

It spoke in the language of the dialect understood by the Si'rai soldier.

"I do not wish to enter, the door shows he has returned," a scruff, older and resonating voice left the lips of the balding warrior.

A similar guard on the left flank turned its attention to the mass of muscle, the frontal features of the armor plating signified a feminine shell. Curved sickle blades were bound to its hips by the hilts.

"Your presence is unwelcome," the feminine voice haunted in whisper, "You must leave."

"Inform Lord A'zum, I wish to speak with him when he is 'sane'."

"Your demand will be heard," the masculine spoke.

"Lord A'zum shall determine the necessity of its merit," the feminine continued.

The soldier turned away from the shack. A dark cloak swiveled behind the hefty man likewise embroidered with the crimson religious symbol seared upon his face. His massive thighs trudged across the boreal soot, built as trees standing in thick forests. He approached an elaborate hut decorated with silks and linens dyed in red stained embroidery. As was his tattoo, the Sigil of the Abyss flanked the sides of the tent's entry. Two armored guards of obsidian steel lifted the ever-present herald on the cloth as the commanding officer entered.

As the Field Marshal entered his command hut, he moved towards a wooden desk centered at the rear. A small fire lamp filtered soft, amber lights across the charts and other documents strewn. A hide lining of his tent held aloft by structure poles raised several feet above the head of the officer.

Ceremonial armor rested on a display shaped as a cross, soft tones of the candlelight reflected upon the silver sheen.

He removed his hefty sword from his left hip and mounted it upon a stand beside the armor. A small boy rushed beside the officer and unbuckled the weighty cloak attached to a chain draped around the back shoulder. Without consideration for the boy's stature, the cloak collapsed from its hold. The weight of the shroud caused the boy to toddle slightly as he gathered the heft of the fabric. The superior man's frame sunk upon a plush chair, decorated in ornate wooden sculpt, and set behind the large table where he could face the entry to his tent. Arms bulged out of open sleeves marred in old scars regaling the tales of brutal battles.

As he seated himself, the small boy rushed to a preparation table on the soldier's right side then placed a small cup upon his master's table. Reddish liquid poured steadily from an urn the boy carried into the cup which he set beside the officer. The officer hoisted the cup to his battle-worn nostrils allowing the delicate fragrances to waft into his orifice. A woody sweetness salivated his lips as he swirled the cup below his nostrils, then swallowed the pour in one gulp.

The boy retreated into the corner, plating a meal for his master. Placing the meal in front of the officer, the boy bowed in respect and filtered backwards while facing the imposing man who could strike him for the smallest incompetence. Steam rose from the meal consisting of a full-breasted and meaty shryk with a green puree to dip, a side plate of nuts and garnish and a small pulp of fruit wedge to compliment the dinner.

Aroma of the food lingered upon the man's nostrils. Nervous anticipations tapped fingers upon the wood table. He reached for the goblet to his left and motioned towards his boy with a shake of the cup when two men of similar age entered his tent through the bifold. Shades of gray whiskers and hair covered the men in dissimilar quantity, their flesh equal in reddish complexion with their superior. Each wore signs of their battles on their faces or exposed flesh.

"Apologies, Marshal," one of the men began, addressed in the heavy speech of their tongue.

"Please, Cisian, take a seat," the Marshal beckoned for the lower ranked officer to sit at a stool the boy servant placed in front of the table, "Would you care to join me, I can offer you some wine from these native lands."

The marshal beckoned the boy to fetch a goblet for Cisian and pour the purple liquid. Splatters dripped out of the basin of the chalice as Cisian reached to the fermented drink.

"Update me, Cisian, on how the men fare in the camp."

90

"Pleasant, Marshal," Cisian sipped the wine and set the goblet to his right, "Their anticipation grows weary."

"Our hosts have been more than generous," the Marshal tore into the bird with thick fists and consumed a chunk of poultry breast.

"Their supply of sample stock has been well-received; our men relax in the taverns and brothels as welcomed by our hosts."

"Then what is their complaint," the Marshal sensed unease in his inferior rank's voice.

Cisian leaned upon the table, the stretch of his decorative leather creasing with his movement. Leather adorned his torso down to a pleated kilt exposing thighs like trunks ending in boots. Armor plating covered his shoulders where bare arms protruded as chain mail covered the binds upon his chest. A golden sunwheel etched into his shoulder plate signifying a general's rank.

"The absence of Lord A'zum for many abrani has raised concerns among the men."

Field Marshal paused in his dietary consumption, dropping a chunk of the meat onto his plate, and leaned into the plush of his ornate chair, "We are below the affairs of a Magister, General Cisian. You can inform the wervostri his arrival will be imminent, and his return will be as our Supernus Magister decrees. Now, dismiss yourself from my sight, unless you wish I remove you from rank and replace you with one more obedient."

The scarred tattoo around the Marshal's eye furrowed with his disdain. On command, Cisian rose from his seat and downed what remained of the wine in his chalice before setting it upon the table. He turned to the other officer behind him and motioned to leave the tent.

"Jorast," the Marshal turned to the young boy who sat quietly in a corner by the small, raised partition of the tent, "you serve me well. Better than even my own generals. If you were not uristri, you would make a fine wervostri. May you continue to serve if Hadithem wills you to live."

The man called him a slave in his tongue but commended him to the worthiness of one of his own soldiers. The ember lights of the hearth flickered in the little boy's black irises as he reflected on his master's kind words.

"Thank you, saruf," Jorast addressed his master in delicate sounds of Si'rai tongue.

*

Amidst the silent still of darkness reflected a serenity of a brilliant display of stars. Small fires burned throughout the Si'rai camp as soldiers laughed and entertained themselves into slumber. The darkened band of quiet Abyss streaked across the eastern sky burning desires into A'zum's perverted mind.

Still absent his sanity, he ravished inside his prison. His mind raced in ferocious thoughts swirling with maddening vibrancy. His sins and penance reflected upon the chained boy dripping blood from his anal orifice and soft whimpers crying through the sack over his face. Tivius stood in front of the altar, his back to the boy suspended from the ceiling. Pain tore through the shoulder blades of the young child, stretched to his limits of fibrous muscle like a rope frayed.

Tivius contemplated the sigil hung from the wall, each glyph upon the eight-spoke wheel hid a meaning foreign to most of his people yet learned by those of his rank and caste. He turned to each of the small candles beside the altar dais and with a flicker of his fingers and a slight wave, the wicks bore to life a small burn. Soft light bounced off the pale scars crisscrossing his chest and arms, his long sword rested upon the altar in front of him. Slender nails followed the contours of the hilt, braided with an unnatural build like a semblance of human hair and the sturdiness of fresh bone. The binding resins remained perfect as the day crafted to which Tivius knew not, yet in his whispers, he muttered the respect of his weapon upon the altar before him. The scabbard extended beyond the short table on either side as the sword lay bound and without the hesitation of breath, he gripped the hilt with his right hand and removed his weapon from its bind.

With his weapon to his side, Tivius circled the boy to come to his forward position. The small child continued to struggle, bruising his wrists to purple with his time spent in bind. The tormentor's icy breaths rolled over the mask, the hints of sour tastes, foreign smells of copper and other liquids haunted the boy's nose. With his free hand, Tivius grappled the frock of the sack without concern for any hair underneath and yanked the coverings from his victim.

Icy stare like a pair of frozen lakes filled the boy's eyes with terror and salty tears. Tivius' fingers dug into the lips of the boy and tugged on the rag, ripping several teeth from the child's mouth. Blood sprays fell to the ground as the teeth dropped onto wood beneath.

Now in full view with his torturer, the child screamed louder than any fear he had known come to his fruition at the sight of the long weapon glistening of its own source. Blood gargled out of his lips with liquid screams. Slivers of the moonlight graced the blade through the cracks of the walls. An eerie glow cast upon the pale, naked man. The boy wanted only to flee, hampered in his struggle by the chains cracking his wrists with every movement.

92

"By this blade, I forge my destiny," Tivius began in the words of his convocation. He smiled at the boy in a horrid satiation, drawing the weapon behind him.

"By this blade, I honor Hadithem," Tivius continued as the weapon shined of its own brilliance, lighting the glyphs as he spoke to them.

"By this blade, I sacrifice my enemy."

The boy screamed to the bust of his gut, wrenching, and writhing in the chains to the release of piss and bloody shit.

"By this blade, all are beneath Him."

Tivius concluded his poetic speech as he ran the lengthy sword through the boy's abdomen. Torrents of blood followed, spilling onto Tivius' body. Blood raced from the boy's mouth; the body writhed and convulsed. Tivius smiled with an orgiastic grin. He followed the victim's symmetry, the cleave continued downward through the abdominal cavity. The weapon exited his body above his genitalia and separated them from his thigh to plop onto the ground. Emulsified with the soot and liquids spilt below, organs collapsed onto the floor exiting the clean cut Tivius made with his weapon. A trail of purple, ethereal mist swirled around the entry of the wound and followed the blade as Tivius tugged the steel along the abdomen.

A lone scream pierced the silent night as Tivius thrust him into cold sacrifice. Tivius swiped his sword into dead air, splattering loose blood onto the blackened soil as his gut roared a shattering scream of delight. Tivius dropped his blade and collapsed his knees upon the floor. He reached into the gap his weapon created and removed the still beating heart from nervous reflex. Praying his soul to the Abyss with arcane permutations spoken in an older, consonant-heavy dialect, Tivius consumed the vital organ. A small dagger rested upon his naked hip. He stood and sliced the neck from ear to ear. A fresh spray of coagulation dripped into the ground below.

The boy's skin opened apart as a tear of fabric. Tremors of blood released from the postmortem wound in slow trickle with the escape of the lavender mist spilling from the body and collected by the long blade along its edges. Tivius' mind eased into serenity releasing him from the embrace of pain since his arrival. As with the other corpses strewn across the room, this boy served the purpose of his wishes. In painful sacrifice, the child became a vessel to return him to sanity. Tivius eased his tensions as he finished the ritualistic offering. His hands covered in fresh blood, he slid one around the boy's bloody neck nearly severed at the sinew and dug his tongue between the blood shorn lips.

Tivius drenched his face with entrails. His heart calmed and his nerves untangled across his extremities relaxing the satiated beast into a lulled sleep. As he slept, shadows slithered from a corner, across the moonlit dirt as to snake away from the piercing light and filtered outside into the cold stillness of the Silvetzen nighttime. Several shadows slinked across the landscape, past the barracks, and out into the distance leaving the camp northward into open oceans.

Chapter 9

The rickety cart lumbered upon the deep-rutted road, the small town of Telmen a distant memory behind them. Smoke left the thatched roofs as the early dawn's light covered the town while fresh smells of dew layered the air. A pair of horses led the cart driven by a small fellow in simple clothes and a short hat to cover his head and ears. The box wagon rocked and carried with impoverished swagger as the worn bearwood wheels buried into the shallow ruts cut into the road.

Inside the crotchety coach Cadeck peered outside a cutout window eyeing the town trailing in the distance. One hand covered his eyes from the brightness above filtered by an occasional cloud. Tesh sat beside him, the dagger straddled over his lap. Venna held her own in the small space, her knees crept close to Cadeck's as she seated on the bench across from him. The comforts of the cart were scarce with torn sheets of rough burlap covering the wooden seats and each jolt of the cart knocked her head nearly missing the rough sideboards of the walls.

"You never told me your full name," Venna turned to Tesh.

Alerted to her need to converse, Tesh turned to her, then back to Cadeck to see his head slumped against the sideboard.

"Tesh. Tesh Verdui."

"Verdui? You do not look like a Verdui."

"Pardon," Tesh smiled, amused at her attempt to stereotype him.

"Yes. I have heard of a man with your surname. He was rugged, handsome and a charming man. Could make a woman toss her knickers to him with only a wink of his eye."

"What sort of books do you read, Venna?"

"Not in books, Tesh. My sister wrote of a man she met of your surname. Said he enamored her from the moment they met. They courted, she said."

"Well, he doesn't sound like any man related to me," Tesh pinched at the scant muscle of his left bicep.

"What is his story? I never imagined a Magi to drink," Venna whispered.

Cadeck ignored her comment. He sloped further into his seat to close his eyes at the sounds of the occupants.

"We drink," Cadeck mumbled, "it's that you never see us, you never know."

His eyes fluttered open.

"A drunken Magi?" Tesh turned to Cadeck sitting to his right, "Your vision, right?"

Cadeck ignored him with a grunt.

"A vision?" Venna pried, "Real magick?"

Cadeck sauntered to sit upright, aging muscles resisted his attempt to counter his imbibing the night before. His breath remained sober, yet his ligaments defied his mental rationale either from his age or his troubled night without sleep.

"Yes, girl, a vision."

"A dream, you mean?" Venna's voice approached Cadeck as scolding from her perspective of wisdom opposing faith.

Cadeck smirked, "I don't suppose you understand magick, then?"

"I cannot say. I mean, I have heard stories of Magi, but I have not seen one in all my days."

"You came looking for one did you not? I am sorry I betray your own fantasies by not conjuring some magnificent spectacle to prove my value to your bedtime stories. Magick is not a gift taken lightly for it requires the firmest commitment to one's own reality."

"I suppose."

Venna turned to him then out the small slit window lined with dusty, drab curtains. The twigs of her peasant tiara braided into makeshift arrangement of flowers tangled into the unkempt fabric of the linen drapes.

"I have only arrived to Telmen to look for one, I would not know whom to look for other than I imagine they have long, old beards and carry a staff or something. How do I know you are not trying to trick me?"

She smirked towards Cadeck, folded her arms against her chest and shrugged her shoulders at the men.

"You didn't come alone, did you?"

Her eyes widened.

"The girl," Cadeck continued, "the girl you claim discovered deceased? What of her?"

"Cadeck," Tesh turned to him.

"No," Cadeck set his hand in gesture to halt Tesh's further words, "she knows who this girl is."

Cadeck leaned away, towards the window to his right, "Driver, there's a bend in the road about another marker or two, take the right until you come upon a house."

"Syr," the muffled voice confirmed through the wood frame.

"Cadeck," Tesh drew aghast.

"I wish to learn what this girl knows."

"We should head to Sarat without further delay," Venna whined.

Moments later, the cart took a noticeable turn as the driver directed his lead animals towards the direction Cadeck indicated.

"The capitol can wait," Cadeck urged, "the castle will still be there upon our arrival."

"You don't trust me, do you," Venna pouted.

"I've learned in my day to only trust what I can see with my own eyes, not the words of those I just met."

Tesh remained motionless in his stare out the window as the shadows of familiar trees admitted the turn of afternoon sunlight. Venna ignored Cadeck's verbal victory and returned her gaze out the small window towards the vistas.

"Cadeck," Tesh began, "I agree with her. I do not find this idea comforting. If my home is truly gone…"

"Then you understand the stakes of which I have laid upon you and why you must bring yourself to trust all I have said to you."

The sudden lurch of the cart slid Cadeck and Tesh to jolt into the backside of their bench as Venna steadied herself from dropping forward into Cadeck's lap. The fearful whinny of a pair of horses jolted the cart to a sharp turn to the driver's left as he fought the animals from breaking their wooden attachments to the carriage box.

"Driver," Cadeck yelled. The driver did not respond, only yelling to his animals as he commanded them to a halt.

"Driver," Cadeck commanded once again, ignoring the rapping of the side wall of the carriage.

"Syr," the driver moaned, "the horses do not wish to advance. I apologize."

Cadeck motioned to Tesh to open the door as he squeezed himself by the younger man.

"Driver," Cadeck burst.

Before he could continue, the driver aimed his finger towards a darkened husk of a home, charred and decayed in a stillness of suspended breath absent the calling of birds or other animals. Remains of the wood lay dormant and barren, a beacon of sickness and disease. The air loomed silent, absent. Vacant as in vacuum. The surrounding landscape contrasted to the home with vibrant reds and oranges. Sunlight poked through overhang clouds which shadowed the rugged forests in the distance. The horizon filled with rolling hills, covered in patterned crops from farms and border fences.

"We should turn away, syr."

"No," Cadeck motioned towards him, "Remain here."

He turned back towards the carriage to see Tesh and Venna stepping down the small footstep beneath the door.

"Cadeck," Tesh looked on, his mind focused upon the vacancy in the distance. A moment out of time from the surrounding features of recollection and happiness.

"Do you understand now?"

Cadeck turned to him as the young man approached his side. A whisper of wind floated the hair along his brow. Tesh could only gaze in awe at the silhouette frame of his old home where his childhood once flourished. Yet it was not the darkened char of wood, nor the broken glass or the patches of old burn brush around the front of his home and broken fence which caused him pause, for those were mere effects of the curse placed upon his lands, yet it was the statues of figures suspended in motion. Their backs to the home, chased by something at the center of his hovel and frozen where they stood.

"Stay here with the girl and driver," Cadeck moved forward towards the horrific scene.

"Cadeck, wait," Tesh proclaimed.

Cadeck ignored him.

"Young syr," the driver began, "there is something afoul here. I want to have no part of it."

"We paid you to drive us to Sarat."

"You did. But this was not part of my bargain."

"Wait. I am sure all will be fine once he returns to us," Tesh looked towards Cadeck slowly approaching the fence line of his home.

The ashen statue stood in motion to run. Features of a feminine outline sketched upon the husk in a position of mid-sprint, looking over its shoulder, a scream opened from its mouth in perpetual eternal silence. Eyes fixated upon an unimaginable horror, half organic and bloody while other portions of the skin crackled and streaked with decaying rot and flaked with the flash-burn. Cadeck surmised she was the farthest figure from whatever had befallen her demise, barely escaping. Other figures were mere fragments of armor, suspended in their own positions minus the flesh or bones to support the steel where other organic features remained like half-broken toy soldiers, disassembled, and the organic matter sucked dry.

Cadeck paused in front of the frame of the door as a third figure, more violently destroyed than the others had paused in its demise; a splattering of fragments of flesh and armor into thousands of tiny pieces separating from clutched fingers gripping its sword forward as to attack whatever killed it. The Magi paused in the open room, bereft of ceiling and walls, now visible to the distant onlookers. He closed his eyes and motioned his hands into a triangle formation; his index fingers resting a few inches in front of his forehead. His eyes shuttered behind his eyelids with every syllable and nuance leaving his tongue.

Beleth

Venna stood a few feet behind Tesh and the driver, darting her eyes around to the name she heard across the meadows. She paused, turning towards Tesh's backside again and once more heard the name in sinister whisper as trace arcs wrapped and began to burn upon Tesh's left wrist.

Tesh screamed, gripping his left hand now culminated into a fiery sear, the marks of golden tendrils brightened into a discernible glow through the clasp of his right hand.

"Your hand," the driver screamed in a panic and readying his cart to flee.

"No, wait," Tesh dropped to his knees, the last words of his sentence hefting to leave his tongue with every surge of pain coursing through his arm.

"You are of a foul magick. A curse befalls you, young syr," the driver's superstition worsened his experiences, "I must report you to the Blue Guard post haste."

A young, dark-haired woman stood to Cadeck's left as a trio of armored men studied the home around her, each of them in non-descript cloaks and blue chest plates. Variants of the heralded accoutrements marked them as Blue Guards. The sun shone brightly upon the home as the first of the men leaned towards the corpse of an older man, his neck twisted in a manner to separate fragments of the flesh and muscle from his shoulders.

"Who could have done this," the armored man questioned.

"Add it to the report and we'll worry about that answer later," the woman moved past Cadeck's position at the frame of the door, "we have a job to do. Regulars will be here shortly to collect the bodies."

"Justiciar," another man beckoned, "come quick."

The woman hustled into the back room where Tesh's bed had overturned and the sigil of a blood sunwheel painted onto the floor. Eight spokes carried from the center circle, each one formed of unknown viscera and an array of vials and other vestiges of ritual lay in the center. One bloodied instrument lay in center of the sunwheel, a white rose patch, caused the young woman to freeze.

"This is the flag of the Imperium," the man spoke.

"What could this mean," the woman pondered, "Surely they are not behind these two murders."

She leaned towards the sigil and swiped the outer ring with her fingers. Familiar copper tingled her nose, "Blood. Female. Estrus."

Her eyes dropped to the realization the young girl, a maiden of her order, had become a sacrifice.

"Mistress Saun, look out."

The man beside her screamed as shadows coalesced from the center of the sunwheel in a violent rage of blue fires. Through a gape of orange eyes to the shape of triangles, the shadow form appeared to speak in threatening tone the sound of a single word, "Beleth."

The appearance of the shadow figure violently tore Cadeck away from the scene as he buckled to his knees within the periphery of Tesh's old bedroom. He turned his gaze upward from his kneel at the blackened iron blade aimed towards the center of the burned sunwheel painted upon the wooden floor. In the center of the sigil painted upon the floor laid a solitary cloth. The white rose embroidery, blood-stained, yet undamaged and unaltered by the fate of the home crinkled in Cadeck's clinched fist as he lifted it from the ground.

Tesh winced in pain clutching his temples. Scarred veins in his left hand ebbed with golden light. He did not hear Venna calling to him in her innocent voice of High Accent, instead his mind focused on an unwelcomed and intrusive shared vision. With the discarded embroidery held firmly against his chest, Cadeck reached into the soul once in possession of the signet. A tear crept along his cheek at thought of the pain of her violations.

"The suffering she must have endured at the hands of brutes. Spare my daughter the pains."

Cadeck turned his focus towards the tree in the distance as he reached deeper into his soul, listening to the sounds of the suffering, the screams of the young maiden echoed into his head as his magick returned to see the vision once more only that of the girl's neck slashed over a bucket. Her essence poured into the receptacle in a torrential fountain from a cut administered by a wide blade. In the ghastly hue of greying blue surrounding his form, he turned to see Tesh writhing upon the ground. He held his hand to the pain from beyond his existence through the void.

Tivius' familiar voice whispered through time and space, smearing the bucket of blood onto the floor of Tesh's darkened room, "With her sacrifice will begin the end of this realm."

"Tesh, are you alright?"

Venna administered her concern. She shook his tapered shoulders to wake him from his trance. Stutters spilled from lips as Tesh awoke, breaking his bond to Cadeck. He lay on his back; the sunlight beat upon his face masked by the shadow of the girl crouched over him.

"What?"

"Tesh, you passed out."

"I did? Where am I?"

Venna gazed around, first to the void of darkness in the center of the fields, then to the surrounding vistas of farmlands and outward to the horizon where the sun began to set into dusk.

"I do not know. You said this place is your home."

"My home? I…"

Tesh leaned to sit upright as Venna rose from her knees to stand, "Cadeck? Where is he?"

"I'm right here," Cadeck's scruff voice responded.

Neither Tesh nor Venna heard him approach as his voice carried a weighted heft of concern.

"What happened to you? What happened to Tesh?" Venna's voice raised with fearful inflection, "What's going on here?"

"Soldiers didn't burn down this home," Cadeck leered towards Venna, "you had to cover for something didn't you?"

"What?" Venna gasped.

"A Mistress and three Blue Guards arrived at this home; their fates are too horrific to divulge to you. How would you have known this place burned if the Mistress did not return?"

"I…um…"

"Answer."

"Contingency response, Magi," Venna stifled a tear, lowering her eyes to the ground, "After three days, a second team came, reported the fate of the first back to the station."

Cadeck grunted, "Probable. But the bigger question now, where is our driver?"

Venna pointed to the cart, "Inside."

Cadeck released the latch to the door, the flash of sunlight's wane shed shadows upon the man, bound and gagged in the forward seat with leather reins. An open container skirted slightly from beneath a bench alluded to the origin of the ropes. Brown eyes darted through matted hair draped along his cheeks, dread fell upon him like a weighted sack to Cadeck's intrusion as inaudible and futile screams billowed through the rope tightened in his jaw.

"I do not intend to harm you," Cadeck assured.

A pair of kicks towards Cadeck knocked the man off balance with bound ankles to slide onto the floor of the carriage.

"What happened here?" Cadeck turned to Tesh and Venna.

"He threatened to report us to the Blue Guards," Venna responded.

"Tesh?"

Cadeck turned to the younger man who returned a shrug.

"I mean you no harm," Cadeck spoke again, calmer, "We mean you no harm."

The driver responded, this time, leering his widened eyes towards Venna as beads of sweat filled his brow.

Cadeck followed, glancing back to his left shoulder, "You did this?"

Cadeck clasped his hands in front of his torso.

"It's in my training," she spoke bluntly, her demeanor never wavering from calm. The orange sunlight glows lit her hair to an aura of benign beauty accentuating the waif-thin appearance of her frame.

"He made notion to report us. On behalf of the Crown and those who serve, my goal stays priority."

Cadeck turned back to the driver, "Nod your head if you understood her words?"

The driver affirmed.

"Good," Cadeck continued, "Now, I will release your gag and I need you to answer very honestly, do you understand?"

The driver nodded once more. Cadeck leaned into the carriage and with minimal effort, loosened the rope bound around his jaw. The driver craned and stretched his mouth, chattering his teeth and silently recalled the ones he knew to be missing. Heavy, panted breathing left his lips as Cadeck hefted his body upon the opposite bench. Venna and Tesh enclosed his escape route.

"Tell me your name."

"Jovin," the driver replied, spoken in the Low Accent.

"Jovin, is there anyone to which you are close? A mother, a bond mate, a father, son, daughter, anyone?" Cadeck seated opposing him.

"Yes," Jovin nodded, "three sons, and a daughter."

"You would do anything to protect them, wouldn't you?"

Jovin nodded again; his senses calmed by Cadeck's tone.

"I am going to remove the bind around your ankles, and I want you to step outside. Do not make any sudden moves, for I will not hesitate to harm you should your aggressions call for such response. Do you understand?"

Jovin nodded.

"Good," Cadeck welcomed with a smile, fulfilling his promise to release the cords. Tesh responded by gently gripping Jovin's legs to help him outside of the carriage as his sodden shoes planted upon the mired and rutted road. Cadeck lifted himself behind Jovin and stepped to his right.

"Look over there," Cadeck pointed to the gruesome remains of Tesh's home as Jovin obeyed, "What do you see?"

Jovin hesitated, his mouth stuttered, lips did not form words. Only one thought fell upon his mind that could encompass the unfathomable visage in the distance, "Death."

"What happened there awaits the rest of this realm, your home, your family, and unless you take us to Sarat with your skills of the horse and cart, me and the boy will have no chance to stop this fate. Do you now understand?"

"There's a curse here," Jovin sobbed.

"A curse that will only grow. A curse that I know too well and a curse that has given this boy the injury on his hand. I promise you this day should we defeat this evil, you can revel in whatever fanfare you claim with myself, the girl, and the boy to profess your deeds without denial, but we must make haste to Sarat. Am I understood?"

"Yes syr." Jovin nodded to approval.

"Very well. We are short on sunlight, and I suppose camping near here is not agreeable to anyone. We should move swiftly and get as far away as possible to ease our nerves," Cadeck motioned everyone to return to the cart, "Jovin, how far of a ride till we reach Sarat?"

"A good three to four days."

"We should be quicker if possible."

###

"I saw her last breaths," Tesh's voice cracked to pitch, a crackling fire warmed their camp, "she needn't had died by my actions."

"Her fate was not of your doing," Cadeck assured, "now you see the suffering that awaits if we do not fulfill your training and obligations."

Tesh lifted his face from his bent knees held in place by his arms, "She would still be alive had you not made presence to my house. She would still be alive had I not left."

"You cannot be certain of her fate. She could have died by any other means at that exact moment on the exact day. Tesh, we do not live on a reality predetermined on a set course. Everything we perceive, we act upon, are predetermined manifestations within our own thoughts, here," Cadeck pointed to his temple, "in the mind."

"Someone thought of her death, and she died?"

"No," Cadeck looked along the horizon to see the fields of stars awash upon the blackened sky. The darkened band at the center, the Abyss in his folklore, suspended like an omnipresent bulge pressing the symmetry and forcing the nearby stars to dance around in fear.

"The actions which led me to your home were a commandment of another. I knew where to go, where to find you and had your presence not existed in your home, I would have found you even had you moved into the city. This journey which I have brought you upon is unravelling towards a larger scale. To master the mind is to master reality and a greater power is well ahead of you. Only through this training can you expect to defeat him."

Tesh stared towards his injured hand, the flakes of golden veins reflected the sparkles of the campfire as he turned to see Jovin sleeping over his driver seat. Venna tucked away upon one of the benches, the carriage door swung open to gather the heat from the flame.

"Yet they came to my home, drawn to me, drawn to you."

"And had you lived in Sarat or another city, they would have followed. What then? What death would have escalated with their rituals? You saw the shadow."

"I blacked out. I saw… the men, the woman like their very lives erased."

"You saw what I did when I reached into the history of the wood, the frame, the fence, the yard."

"You gave me the vision?"

"No."

"The amulet in my hand," Tesh rubbed his injured wrist.

"No. The vision was entirely of your doing. I projected nothing to you. You bonded to the magick in your presence, and you channeled your latent gift."

"My hand."

"It awakened your bloodline, Tesh. A bloodline myself and others who have taken similar oaths swore to protect."

Tesh looked over to him. Light from the fire twinkled in his eye, "What of my bloodline? And why do you mourn my father if he was a mere conscript?"

Cadeck sighed, jostling his crusted boot into the dirt, "Because I feel guilt for why he died and why this curse upon your hand is vital to the future of man."

Tesh lowered his head, setting his chin upon his knee. He turned towards Venna as she slept soundly within the cart, "This girl, here, Venna, once we arrive in Sarat, where does she fit into your plans?"

"She does not. But if we are to gain an audience with His Majesty, she would most assuredly be able to allow us. Yet, there is more to her connections to the dead girl than she has let on."

"The dead girl was a member of the Rose."

Cadeck's words warned in impenetrable elocution of a stern lecture. The warm morning sun sliced into the windows of the cart.

"How do you know?" Venna's hands trembled in her lap.

Cadeck revealed the frayed cloth from the satchel at his hip, "You've been lying to me," his deep voice forced towards her ears in the raspy voice of his low-born status, "Why were you looking for Magi?"

Venna bit her lip and spoke sheepishly, "The Crown sent us to find the Magi. That is all I knew. We knew a Temple rested in the Koran Mountains but did not know where. We were lucky that you came into Telmen, and I spent a day trying to find you," she swallowed her spittle.

Cadeck's body swayed in the motion of the ride, "And this girl?"

"One of my couriers. She along with another girl left Telmen in haste as commanded."

"How did you know about her murder?"

"I overheard rumors. I went to wait for you should you return," her voice lowered to a whisper, "There really is a bounty for you."

"Well, Tesh, seems we are wanted men. The evidence we have though, points to other men, men we met before we came back to Telmen."

"You can't just acquire an audience with His Majesty," Venna muttered.

"Which is why I need your cooperation. The Order of the Rose is far too secretive and clandestine to aid the Magi outright. We would need a more specific impetus to garner favor yet keep a modicum of caution to make the involvement of the Magi officially unofficial."

"It's the Imperium, isn't it?"

Venna's voice wavered.

Cadeck leaned closer to pry her observations, "Tell us what Sarat, specifically King Trebut, knows."

"Nothing. There have been rumors. Secret alliances mostly. I wished I could assuage my fears of such dreaded thoughts, but when I saw you and Tesh in the town, I had to make sure Her Highness knew the Magi still existed. I sent a courier back to Sarat, and another to Doningsen. When I returned you had left town square. I picked up your trail later in the day and followed you until you left town."

"Why didn't you follow?"

"I got a way up the road, past the mill and creek when I noticed four men ride across the plains, not along the main road. Their clothes like pitch tar. There was a large man with reddish skin and shorn head. I followed them till they made camp, the darkness helping to conceal me. A tall man seemed to pray away from the others. I noticed on the second night they fought, and I knew they were serious. I ran as fast as I could back to Telmen. That was a few days before you had returned."

Cadeck leaned back to his seat, "Those men you describe, they were following us. You can be at ease; three of them are dead. Had they found you, you would have ended up as your friend. The man you describe as tall, he is a most dangerous man indeed."

Venna's eyes sank into solemnity as her mind calculated the gravity of her actions, "I sent my best friend to die. We met in Academy and…"

"You did well, Venna," Cadeck interrupted her from releasing sobs, "Do not believe your friend died in vain, but she died for service to your King. I am sorry for your loss."

Cadeck's words simplified her grief but lent little to comfort her. She sank her chin into her chest as she peered out the cutaway window. The fading sun edged upon dusk washing the fields and sky into ethereal auburn. The rickety cart jostled and tossed shifting its inhabitants in uneasy discomfort. Tears formed in her eyes as her memories faded to those she shared with the lost girl.

"You remind me of my young girl, Venna," Cadeck sighed, his thoughts followed his eyes towards the vistas of rolling plains and fence lines as the slow wavers of the cart lulled Tesh to snore beside him.

"I wasn't aware a Magi could have children."

"Can, yes. Should we? No. It is a burden made all the heavier now."

Venna glanced into Cadeck's withered face. His whiskers created a pock-marked battlefield of age and disarray clamoring for an answer.

"Where is she?"

Cadeck ignored her for a moment then turned to her, "Where the tall man came from, and where his master holds her prisoner."

Chapter 10

If there ever were a city as powerful as Sarat, it did not lie on this side of Roth. Sarat soared on the horizon with chiseled mason peaks. Chimneys billowed hazy gray residue over the rooftops. The city rose from the countryside as a mass of amalgamated stone and iron. The risen sunlight of morning dawn sprinkled hues of the rainbow across the windows of grand spires watching over its keep. City walls stood several stories high, the extent of the city border stretched for miles. The skyline dotted with many buildings and towers risen higher than the walls, yet securely wrapped within its ramparts and embellished its domineering presence.

Rutted and abused, the trade road path graduated into smooth grade as the cart approached the declared outskirts of town. Miles of fields encompassed the city as centralized blocks of houses distinguished communal pockets of hamlets and villages along the landscape. Watchtowers made of bearwood rose over the communities in effort to protect them from outside invasion or criminal activity. Tributary roads branched into the fields, through the communal lands and connected them to the larger network of the kingdom's capitol.

Haystacks stretched across the fields. The straw shimmered in afternoon's sunlight. Multitudes of carts and production traffic congested the advance of Cadeck's rental cart with smells and sounds of mewling animals.

The driver pushed the horse pair to the extent of their patience. His beasts trudged through the industrial carts and workers through the path leading into the city walls. Large gates, several meters high, welcomed Jovin's cart. The two-headed spread-winged eagle crest decorated the doors and split at the seam. Passing through the gatehouse, the cart pushed aside from the flow of traffic into a side street lined by small apartments and various shops jutted against the walls. Jovin stopped his advance and tapped his left hand against the edge of the wagon.

"We're here," he ordered.

Cadeck exited the cart with a foul face. The smells of urban living permeated across his senses. Body odors mixed with the stench of fresh meats and waste products created a profane pool of putrefaction. Animals and people coexisted in this egregious concoction of civilization where soot painted buildings. The smog of cooking, smelting and musky scents blotted the pristine skies enjoyed by those who lived far away.

Tesh followed behind, reveling in the massive clamor of city life, a foreign distinction from the simple existence he knew as a youth. His eyes absorbed the marvelous sights of various people mixing about, plying their trades and wares. Crests of rooftops lined the skyline before him, some arching over avenues and streets where whole sections of roads or alleys lived in shadow day and night. Protective walls sheltered the urban center welcoming Tesh with an enamored presence. Venna released herself from the wagon, her face openly excited with a smile at the familiarities of home.

Cadeck reached into the coin purse, counted out five pieces of gold marked with the Crown of Sarat upon the head side, the two-headed eagle on the tail.

"Remember our bargain? Return home, cherish your family."

Cadeck dropped the gold coins into the driver's grubby hands. Torn gloves snatched the currency as he smiled a scarce-toothed smile and nodded his head in agreement to the payment. Tesh climbed to the roof of the wagon and dropped the satchels to the muddy ground. Soils and muck stained the leather fabric. Venna fought to untwine the lily wreath from her golden hair. Tangles of fray remained in its wake. She frizzled her hair in a vain attempt to straighten. Jovin turned his cart, the wheels ground a rumbling roar against the brick streets. The horses sprinted to his whip as the distant sound of the portcullis gates whined ajar.

"Venna," Cadeck turned to her, "can you get us an audience with Her Highness? We have no time to waste."

"I can try. But there are procedures."

"Procedures?"

"We can't just walk into the castle," Venna gazed to the taller man. Her voice inflection reminded Cadeck of her stern adherence to law, "we must go to the processing building so we can make an appointment and present my findings."

"Processing?"

"I must provide my information and purpose as to your visit since your matter involves the security of the Crown."

Cadeck's whiskered face nodded a respective smile towards the young girl. Bureaucratic actions left a sour taste in his quiet grunt.

"Very well, Venna. Lead the way," Cadeck turned to Tesh, still enamored by the bustling sights of city activity, "Tesh, come along."

Cadeck reached for a sack upon the ground and handed the second towards Tesh. He paused a moment and adjusted his balance upon the limp in his leg. The slosh of the road hampered his gait. Tesh tied his dagger to his waist and heaved the other sack along his back. Venna led the party through the dissonance of population, through avenues and small streets where shops and business lined the brick streets. The paths snaked through town like symmetrical lines cutting between blocks of buildings.

Mired amidst the mazes of streets and alleys, the bustle of activity continued to amaze Tesh. Buildings rose several stories in height, made of brick and wood while others formed of daub and stone. His mother told him of the large city and warned him of its dangers, fearing what may occur to her only son should he become lost or snatched by ne'er do wells. The activity of the city appeared foreign although no different than activity in Telmen which he accustomed to, albeit in a much grander scale. Meat butchers cut their inventory for consumption, millers and bakers molded wheat into delicious breads and pastries whose sugary scents tickled at Tesh's nose with the air of delicacy and a sweetness of honey or other unknown spices and sugars. Masons, blacksmiths, potters, and other artisans numbered along the shops and activity as the harried lifestyle of the larger city yearned Tesh to return to his simpler life.

Venna stayed a few yards in front of the men, absorbed into the patterns of the foot traffic. Cadeck studied her moves and every back alley they ventured. His mind cautioned if her words were trustworthy as she guided through streets with ease. Occasionally Cadeck or Tesh would rub shoulders with another citizen, causing a stir in the man or woman only to return an apology. Cadeck's intuitions served his thoughts with probabilities; she could have killed another Rose, took her signet, and falsified her past then led the men to untimely deaths in an unknown crevice amidst the grand city's inner workings. Her innocence denied his thoughts, for anomalies in her demeanor admitted subtle truth to her words. Venna turned down another alley and stopped her advance at a three-story non-descript building hidden within a dark alley of similar constructions where the afternoon sun strained to warm.

Cadeck motioned for Tesh to stop before moving to catch up with Venna.

"This may be a trap."

"You don't trust her?"

"Not this far from the castle. We must be cautious."

"What you said on the way here. Her story sounded true."

"That is when I thought we were getting a direct audience. There are no guards at this building."

Cadeck proceeded assiduously, absorbing the surroundings as he perceived. Venna's looks coerced Tesh although Cadeck did not share the sympathy. Venna's innocent stare met Cadeck as he arrived at the building where no sigil or sign denoted its purpose, its solitary door closed off the outside world from external influence as the pair of men came under the awning where the second story crept overhead.

Venna reached with all her height to the iron knocker and stiffly produced a singular knock. A small slit in the door opened leading to further speculation in Cadeck's eyes. Venna produced the orange signet from a pocket on her hip and placed it within the slit. She stood quietly, her eyes darting behind her towards Tesh and Cadeck, back to the door. Her mangled hair belied her virtue as she produced a steady, patient whistle.

A creak of iron opened the door to the whines lacking lubrication. Venna's svelte frame writhed into the crease consumed in dark obscurity before the door shut behind her leaving Cadeck and Tesh outside. Tesh's face turned to surprise as he heard Venna's muffled conversation with another female voice through the thick door. A few moments later, the door opened as Venna beckoned them to enter.

Two men flanked the inside doorway outfitted in lengthy cloaks covering cerulean armor breastplates fitted upon their frames like extensions of their flesh. Twin-headed eagles emblazoned in golden tint upon the pairs' breastplates noting them on official business, protectors of the contents inside. Their arms spilled from the cloaks covered in blue-armored vambraces and hoisting a pike upon their stocky shoulders. Their helmets protected their noses and jaw line and seamed to the neckplates. Tesh jittered his eyes nervously at the pair filtered by the scant light.

Simple lamps hung from the distant wall, their amber lights flickering onto a wooden desk lined with parchment documents some stacked a few feet high. A lone, frail woman sat at the desk where the lighting tinted her gray hair purple. An expanded pictograph of the elaborate Rose emblem engraved upon the wall behind the desk where a motto etched beneath, reminding the girls of their code of ethics – Diligence, Mercy, Justice – written in a manner of half-circle. Hints of candle oil burn mocked the perfumes leaving the older woman. Stale aromatics suspended within the shadows of the dim light. Venna sat herself upon the right flank of the room beside a brunette woman whose voice Tesh recognized was the other girl she spoke to before they entered.

Cadeck's face formed a smile as did the older woman behind the desk. Venna removed herself from the conversation and approached the woman at the desk in hesitant manner. A purple signet of the Rose sewn above the left

112

breast of her fitted dress with the bloom of five petals, sleeves stretched to her wrists in unwavering modesty.

"My name is Venna Rutin, Aspirant of the Rose. I have brought to Sarat a Magi whose name is Cadeck and an Initiate of the Temple Knights, Tesh Verdui."

The purple-rose woman filtered through her papers reaching for a document she read to herself.

"Did you make it to the Temple of Light?"

The woman's High Accent spoke in scripted manner.

"No madam."

"Your orders say you were to go to the Temple of Light and bring back the Magi who lived there. Records show this Magi's name is Godwen, no surname provided," disgusted by Venna's disobedience she grilled the young woman further, "How can the Crown verify this Cadeck is a Magi since you did not visit the site by physical means clearly disobeying your orders and the Crown?"

"Madam, there is more information I have to provide."

"As you did not obey your primary objective, how can I verify the rest of your report is accurate?"

The woman's voice pierced at Venna's heart as a stern schoolteacher scolding her students. Tesh reached to speak but before his lips could form words, Cadeck shut Tesh's mouth with his hand and shook his head to consider silence.

"Madam," Venna replied, "the rest of my report is pertinent to the safety of the Crown and His Subjects."

"Can you verify the next piece of this report?"

Venna reached into her pouch strewn underneath Tesh's used tunics and removed the blood-stained sigil of her fallen friend's white rose. Placing the remnants on the desk, the purple rose woman drew her face into a silent disgust and pity.

"Silvetzenian soldiers murdered one of us."

"She could have died by anyone's hands. The Crown has received notice from Daryn Offtil, Duke of Telmen where a recent murder took place outside of the village, and did we not send a detachment to the scene, only to never return? Murder of a member of the Rose in Saratian land is tantamount to regicide. Two, if these reports are true, is punishable by hanging, drawing, and quartering," she swallowed briefly, "the murderer's entire family.

"Your implications it was Silvetzen could hamper strained diplomacy between the two lands. You must have undeniable proof of this atrocity."

"What if the Magi could prove it? He has requested an audience with His Majesty. He and the other man need passage north to Silvetzen. His concern is not with our affairs, but with broader affairs with the Si'rai."

Venna's words challenged her superior.

"The Si'rai? They keep to themselves on the other side of the oceans, they have no business here outside of trade. There will be no further discussion of your rumors and conspiracies. The Crown alleges Tesh Verdui as the culprit in the murders and should henceforth undergo detainment."

The elder woman turned towards the soldiers and shrilled an order toward them, "Guards, arrest these men."

The men lowered their pikes to ease their hands into brutish action.

"No madam," Venna protested, "I saw them in Telmen while Bri was very much alive. The two argued in front of the market. I ran to my couriers and informed them to return to Sarat with the news that a Magi was in Telmen."

With her honesty, Cadeck opened a stubborn smile.

"Are you certain this Cadeck is a Magi?" The older woman called off the guards.

Venna nodded. The woman sifted through the pages laid before her peering over the documents with deep study.

"I don't see a Magi bearing name in this list of known Magi."

Cadeck's face dropped into trepidation, "With all due respect, madam, why does Sarat have a list of Magi?"

"I do not believe such is your concern, syr. If you are a Magi, why is your name not listed? Are you falsely claiming to be a Magi? Have you seduced this girl with your proselytizing?"

Cadeck approached the desk and slammed his palms upon the deck disturbing documents to a flitter. Venna stepped away as the guards readied their pikes for defense of the room. Strong smells tickled Cadeck's nose to stifle a sneeze.

"Woman, you are as stubborn as a dying mule and your bureaucracy can take a flying leap off a cliff. Look under my tongue and see the Blessing of the Council for your proof."

Cadeck opened his mouth, lifting the underside of his tongue to touch his tip against his top incisors and revealed a tattooed rune scarred under his organ; the shape of a triangle sitting atop a small cross.

"This is the mark of the Council, it is the mark of my Calling, the Aztin of Aeus. Only a proven Magi, gifted with his or her powers can achieve this responsibility and assigned his or her mark. What Venna has told you is true, and I must relay it to Trebut."

"I can file a report and filter it to the Court. The Crown will act on it accordingly and in a prompt fashion. If you require passage to Silvetzen, due to heightened restrictions north of the Saratian Forest, you must file a claim of waiver with the magistrate granting you official passage along the Saratian Route."

"We do not have time to waste with this inane bureaucracy."

"Please madam," Venna interjected.

"I'm sorry Venna, but you know the procedure."

The woman directed her eyes towards Cadeck. His face tightened, his bottom lip curled thin against his teeth, his eyes lowered to disdain.

"To obtain audience with the Court, one must file the proper requests. These are the laws we must follow through the proper venues. The Order of the Rose is not the place to do this. I can take your testimony and Venna's report and file them for research amongst others of my rank. We will issue the statements and respond appropriately."

Infuriated, Cadeck excused himself from the office and encouraged Tesh to follow. Venna's face dropped into a frustrated demeanor as she began to follow the men outside only for the elder woman to call her away from the closing door. A rolling thunder boiled across the sky; clouds thickened overhead.

"She was right behind you," Cadeck huffed.

"I know, but I heard the elder woman call to her."

"We do not have time for this procedure. I once had direct access to the Court, to Trebut."

"But you don't now?"

Cadeck shook his head to the clamor of thunder, "They don't know what they risk."

Cadeck drifted his eyes left and right towards the brick houses and structures. Covered by an overhang street, the taller buildings hid from Cadeck's view in this back street. Pedestrians milled along sodden brick roads where the pair's presence in the alley hid them.

"All of this, gone."

A delay in rescuing my children weighed down by the banal procedures of bureaucrats.

"What if you're wrong?"

Tesh's doubts puzzled Cadeck to turn his attention to the young man.

"Wrong? Look at your hand and tell me I am wrong again."

The door to the small hideout crept open as Venna removed herself from the shadowy crevice, "I'm sorry that Madam Rygard was so stubborn, but she is right."

"There must be a better way to get to Silvetzen," Tesh responded to the door closing behind her.

"There's only one secure route into their lands," Venna reminded.

"You observed Tesh's home, Venna. What will happen to your home here in Sarat with your bureaucracy?"

Venna reached for a coin purse against her hip and hoisted it towards Cadeck's hand, "I just told her. She provides you with this."

Cadeck hefted the purse into his palm and heard a pair of coin clanks. He unwound the tie and dropped the contents into his opposing palm. A pair of heavy coins collapsed onto his hand bearing an older herald of a single eagle crest and minted in a shining, silvery ore. Quickly, he shoved his hands into the purse and closed the string tight. He shuffled Venna and Tesh to turn away from the street behind him.

"Rykanian eagles? The Crown has not minted these in five centuries."

"Exactly," Venna whispered, "they are currency still recognized at The Brounden. Where Madame Rygard requests you to stay the night."

Another clap of thunder. Pedestrians hastened their activities in the distance behind them. Cadeck raised his withered face towards the sky.

"Brounden?" Tesh muttered.

"You enjoy this city, don't you?"

Tesh nodded to Cadeck's question.

"The Brounden will show you its true face."

Venna hurried the men towards a nearby bazaar and rounded a corner past a fountain. Splatters of raindrops splashed into the water. Ripples radiated across the surface of the pool. A nude, feminine crouched into position, holding a stone bucket giving the appearance of pouring water into the base of the decoration. Venna escorted the men through several streets and avenues away from the small hideout, past rows of artisan shops and buildings Tesh recognized as homes stacked two, sometimes four stories high. As the trio traveled along the city, many men and women gathered to head towards shelter. Tesh observed the different layouts of activity; small squares of shops and fountains, homes and other services cloistered along class diversity and as the young girl led them towards the northern edge of the walled city, the Brounden's dominating brick and cobble plaza introduced itself.

More width than height, the Brounden spanned several blocks of landscape within the walled city. Surrounded by gardens along the building's periphery, the red stone structure contrasted to the less well-to-do confines Tesh encountered in Sarat. A gabled roof topped the building as decorative windows offered the patrons with unrestricted views of the plaza below where fashionably dressed citizens milled and cavorted as they paced towards stately townhomes before the storm intensified. The inn advertised its name across the symmetrical wooden door where Venna, Cadeck and Tesh paused underneath a balcony overhang.

"I must bid you farewell from here."

"You won't be joining?" Tesh inquired, his eyes wandering over her angelic face.

"No, I have quarters in the castle. Please find yourself some rest."

"It has been too long since I've slept on a quality bed," Cadeck sighed, "Come Tesh."

Venna nodded to the pair before scampering away in a swift sprint to race the sprinkles from becoming a downpour. Ornate linens decorated the windows of the lobby parlor, closing the room to sunlight. The glimmer of a wide chandelier bloomed overhead, where Cadeck's and Tesh's attire lured the eyes of the well-kept concierge behind a carved table of dark colored wood. He stood reverent in his attention to the polish of his desk.

A slight murmur of inaudible consternation escaped his lips as a waft of stench exuded from the pair. As the table formed a wide curve, braided wrapped posts accented the corners with rounded tops, molded to the bottom surface of the desk. Exquisitely carved tables matched the concierge desk within the lobby bearing mahogany accent and polished smells. Large candelabrums suspended by wrought iron chains from the rafter beams highlighted the red brick walls

"Excuse me," the concierge proclaimed in the refined dialect of High Accent, "but I do believe you are lost."

"This is the Brounden, is it not?" Cadeck inquired. The man stepped back from his approach. Cadeck's grime infested hand touched down upon his domain.

"It is," came the reply.

Disgruntled at Cadeck's uninhibited approach and unmistakable presence of poverty, he stood regal to the stranger. He fidgeted his vest tight and taut as he cleared this throat. His next words to border the periphery of couth or absolute disdain.

"Yet, your kind belong in the southern districts, where you will find shelter more to your," he took another whiff of Cadeck before furrowing his nose, "income."

Cadeck smiled, set the small pouch upon the desk, and tipped it over to reveal a pair of the silver, shimmering currency of an older time.

"I do believe these two coins will suffice for the evening. Two rooms."

"You either stole those, or…" the man stuttered.

"We're guests of the Crown," Cadeck grinned.

117

The concierge lifted an eyebrow, followed Tesh and Cadeck's attire, then back to the shiny coins of the rare silvery metal.

"Of course, for only a respected benefactor of His Majesty's kingdom could dare produce such coins, of which have not been minted in a time long forever."

"They are still legal tender, if my history is still in modest recollection," Cadeck's voice spoke sternly, his eyes surveyed the concierge for any deceit.

The man turned to a drawer and removed a single key from a shelf, "Although such coins are so rare only the Crown would dare legally own them, I cannot give you the rooms such coins would fetch today. However, I cannot allow your friend with his bandaged arm into my establishment. I will not expose my guests to Rust Skin."

Cadeck turned to Tesh, "I can assure he does not have the Rust. He burned his arm a few days ago in a smelt, the wrapping is to protect his flesh."

Tesh unwrapped a few of his fingers to show the concierge the golden flecks adhered to his flesh. He nodded to the affirmation and produced a second key, "Here, second floor, rooms twenty-two and twenty-three and please for the courtesy of any other guests, allow yourself to the washroom. I will waive the charge."

Cadeck nodded to the agreement, "Of course. And another matter, tonight's meal?"

The concierge laughed, "The Eagles will only get you far enough for a room in your condition, you will have to arrange to pay for the meal of your own coin. Five crowns each, but unless you have worked for any of the High Houses such as the Rutins or the Denwiches for a good sum of your lives, and they were quite generous to you, I am afraid the price is still too far out of your pockets."

Cadeck reached into the coin purse, shifted his fingers within the heavy coins and counted ten gold coins stamped with the image of the Saratian Crown on the head, and the eagle sigil on the tail. With closed fist baring worn knuckles and grimy nails, he placed his muddled hand in front of the man. Fingers lifted to produce the required coinage.

The concierge grinned at the shiny objects laid before him before turning his eyes to look at Cadeck, "Dinner is promptly at sundown. You shall see tonight's course presented in menu when you return. But please, for the sake of our other guests arriving tonight, do present yourselves to the washroom."

Cadeck nodded and beckoned Tesh to follow him towards the stairs. Cadeck gripped the polished dark wood with rough clutch of their travels while Tesh graced his hands into a steady balance of the elaborate design. He glazed his rough hands upon the surface of the railing, studying the intricacies of smoothness in its design. The current patrons of the inn were scant, limited to a few travelers who discussed finer events of society. Their accents varied from the Saratian High to the romantic Proper Cadeck recognized from Koran nobility. Cadeck approached the pair of rooms and motioned Tesh to take room twenty-two.

Cadeck beamed towards Tesh as he unlocked his room, "I will see you at dinner," and shut the door behind him.

Tesh's door pushed open with delicate and lubricated hinges that jostled Tesh at the cleanliness of the swing, unlike the creak of old wood and iron. His eyes drew to the painted red door, carefully colored in to keep paint from splattering upon the iron hinges, or such a wayward spackle decorated the handle. Tesh moved his satchel against the foot of the cleanly fitted bed. A soft sheet of luxury covered a simple hay mattress neatly tucked in a woolen sack. The quiet roll of thunder clapped against the glass window shaking the bubbled pane, while the soft shower tickled the air wafting the fresh wash of evaporation across the room.

He watched the rain spatter across the window, The showers blurred the view of the decorative buildings and courtyards of the nearby neighborhood. He wiped the condensation away to see a carriage approach the circular driveway of the inn's entry. He had not recognized the livery of the house which owned the carriage, only noticed the distinct appearance of a red dragon on the door of the vessel. Tesh turned to see an armoire across from the bedside and with the tug of his arms, the doors swung wide. A set of clean wash linens of assorted sizes folded on the bottom of the wardrobe. Finding a pair to fit his frame, he draped them upon his left hand, covered the golden wound, and carried himself towards the door.

As scant and scarce as the afternoon crowd had appeared, the evening crowd did not fill in gaps. For an establishment boasting a history over six-hundred years, the livelihood of the dining hall gave the appearance of a failing business. Tesh sauntered down the staircase in a pair of pressed and clean trousers, with a long-sleeved jerkin covering his arms and chest. He managed to wrap his left hand in straps of wash linens provided to him in the washroom.

Women dressed in fineries dashed about the hall and tended to the several guests that had arrived for the evening meal. Dressed in a uniform manner, Tesh surmised they were employed by the Brounden. Tables filled with several guests dressed to their class of the upper establishments of Saratian society while not adhering to any specific liveries of the various houses Tesh had known from rumors to run Court.

He turned his head to glance over the room to find Cadeck already seated in a small lounge, wearing his battered clothes he wore when they met. Tesh carried himself towards the table and slid into the bench across from Cadeck, "You didn't bother to change clothes?"

"My only other pair of clothes are my Magi robes," Cadeck whispered, "It would be unbecoming of a Magi to be seen outside of official Crown business."

"I see," Tesh replied. He studied the room once more, "Do you recognize any of these people?"

Cadeck grunted softly, leaned back into his seat, and produced his pipe from his satchel next to him. Cautiously, he removed the pouch of the spiced narcotic, pinched a sliver, and placed the leaves into the receptacle. A sconce bolted into the wall beside their table held a candle lit to a low flame. Cadeck lifted the pipe to the candle, set it between his lips, and drew a long breath.

"Every single man seated at these tables are worth less than pig's shit. They could not work an honest day's wage if Aeus forced them, instead they rely on peasants like yourself to bring them coin. Peasants slave for them while they revel in their wealth. However, they are not the nobility. These men come here to flaunt what wealth they believe they have, only to answer to higher authorities. You know what men like this do?"

Tesh shook his head.

"They would slit each other's throats or sell their own children if it meant an audience at Court. These men are just another ring of the tree. The true power exists in the nobility. These men are merely the gentry; landowners and coin pushers, not to mention, tax collectors and judges. But what I am interested in right now, is what is going on behind that closed door over there."

Cadeck motioned his pipe to a sealed, split door bearing the signage of the Brounden. Above the door marked the words, "Private Hall." Tesh turned to follow Cadeck's motion.

"For the last hour, several of the staff had been seen leaving the room carrying pitchers and food."

"You don't think it means anything, do you?"

"Perhaps not, perhaps a family event paid for by another of the gentry."

A young waitress interrupted Cadeck as she approached the table. She wore her sable hair in a bun behind her head. A blue dress covered her thin frame to her toes, pale shoulders exposed to the dingy air of the room. Aromas of ales and pipe smoke hung close to the ceiling.

"Juyo wine," she asked, holding a clay pitcher with both hands.

"Two please," Cadeck pushed a pair of wooden cups towards her as she began to pour into each.

"Have you had the chance to peruse tonight's menu?"

"There is only the choice of verdasnik steak, or roasted chicken breasts in a cream butter sauce. I will have the steak," Cadeck smiled.

"Chicken, please," Tesh replied.

"Thank you," the woman turned and moved towards the concierge desk to set their orders to the inn's manager.

"You see that woman over there?"

Cadeck pointed towards the concierge's long bar where Cadeck's target made casual chatter with the man. She hefted a sigh and brushed golden hair away from her mouth.

"The blonde-haired woman, tall and fit to frame, wearing the blue dress like the others."

Cadeck turned his eyes to see the woman, Tesh followed his gaze.

"She has been the only one to enter and exit the private hall consistently. I must speak to her."

Upon Cadeck's words, as to hear his whisper from across the dining hall, she turned to him with an attentive glint in her brown eyes. As a cat to prowl, she slipped away from the bar and ruffled blonde locks marred with the sweat and oils of the toils of her labor. Quiet murmurs of her dress fabric whispered into Tesh's ears upon her approach like a cresting wave of sea waters slammed to the shore. Quietly, she reached into the apron clung to her curvy chest and produced a small envelope to lay next to Cadeck's gnarled knuckles upon the polished table. Before Cadeck could reach to her delicate fingers, she pulled her hand away from the note and tucked them clamped behind her back.

"Do not read this here, the men in the private hall are not aware of my role," she muttered, "For the Crown."

Cadeck nodded his confirmation as his fingers slipped the envelope close to his chest.

"She's another one?" Tesh queried.

"The Rose sprouts everywhere I see."

As he slipped the envelope into his parcel bag, the young, dark-haired waitress approached Cadeck's table with a pair of plates steaming with food.

"Chicken, for the man with the bandaged hand, and the steak, for the older man, am I right?"

"Aye," Cadeck nodded as the thickened brown meat smoked before him paired with a side of green vegetables arrayed as a salad. A large knife stuck from the center of the protein which Cadeck permitted to remain solemnly risen from the fleshy steak. Tesh ripped the chicken breast with his good hand, aided by a two-prong fork to his side. He drowned a piece of the meat into a gooey, buttery sauce and consumed the savory dish like a ravaging beast.

"It is customary for a Magi to produce words of offering to my god before I consume meal."

Tesh halted his chew, speaking rudely with his mouth full, "I don't believe, remember?"

"Your hand should remind you otherwise," Cadeck affirmed in low murmur.

Tesh eyed the wrappings around his left arm then followed his eyes towards the older man seated across from him. Without a flinch, he bit another morsel of his meat dripping with the oozing sauce.

"Very well," Cadeck clenched his hands and bowed his head quietly.

After a few moments, he cut the steak open to a soft, pink center and with his first bite, closed his eyes to a satisfactory smile. His eyes closed, the taste of his first bite lingered in his mouth with each chew. He took a swig of the juyo wine next to him and waved his fork at Tesh as he chewed through a thought.

"You spend time in a grimy, cold prison for two harvests and you appreciate these tastes more."

"The place you were taken, when you were captured?"

"The place, yes. I only remember it was in the north, from the way the winds howled through the halls and the unforgiving cold of the dank cell. Periodically, I sensed a warmth beneath my feet preceded by a shuddering of the walls. Likely it were the fire horses of Heseph plodding and sprinting along their sacred rivers of flame as the occasional stench of sulfur would crowd the halls, a welcome relief from the piss and vomit that otherwise went with the cold. But…"

Cadeck's voice trailed to hide a tear resting against his eye, "I do not care to talk about it any longer. This meal will not consume itself, my friend."

After several minutes of drink and food, Cadeck and Tesh wrapped up their meal. A pair of dirty plates remained beside a pair of copper Knaves for the servant girl. Cadeck waved to the concierge in polite manner as they left their seats and went ahead up the stairs. Tesh followed and as the pair approached their rooms, Cadeck followed behind Tesh and hastily slammed the door behind him.

"Now, let us see what is so important with this letter."

He removed the sealed parchment from his satchel. The wax seal of Sarat's eagle mark bound the folds of the notice. Cadeck slid his fingers along an edge of the fold and carefully broke the bond. The note folded away to a square with the writing crafted with an elaborate quill. Tailed letters trailed and lifted into an intricate pattern with a darkened ink which Cadeck recognized to be from the royal family.

Magi Cadeck Wenfier and Initiate Tesh Verdui,

I hope your stay at the Brounden is to your most pleasurable, I assure you the Crown spared no expense for this arrangement, yet my father was not aware. I am delighted that you were the Magi to heed my call, as father has graciously accepted your company for many years in his Court. In the morning, a carriage shall arrive, bearing a seal of a Rose. I ask of you a simple protocol and do not address the occupants of the carriage upon entering while within earshot of others. The occupants will remind you when to speak freely as circumstances become acceptable. You and I share a mutual desire to enter the lands to the North. I will do what is within my power to meet your needs if you are able to meet mine. Upon reading this letter, you must discard in flame.

Her Royal Highness
Commandant of the Order of the Rose
Cassica Diaysus of House Bovariàr

Watermarked behind the signature appeared a pink form of the Rose symbol. Cadeck sighed. The note fell to his side clutched in hand, "This letter is from Her Highness, the Princess Cassica."

He turned to the lamp resting on the small table beside Tesh's bed and followed the command to incinerate the parchment.

"Why burn it?" Tesh looked at Cadeck inquisitively, seating onto his mattress.

"The letter commanded so."

"Can you be certain it wasn't a forgery?"

"The mark in the signature is the same on the patch left behind at your farm, and the same that Venna bore."

"You mean," before Tesh could finish his sentence to reveal the name of the Order of the Rose, Cadeck silenced him with a soft shush against his own lips.

"I did not expect them to be as involved in Magi affairs as they have become. Either this is an elaborate ruse to subdue my order, or they too are aware of our engagement at the Temple of Light," Cadeck turned from Tesh to exit the room.

"What do you think?"

"The latter," as Cadeck sealed the door shut.

Chapter 11

Several shadow forms slinked their way across vast expanses of ocean approaching a darkened shoreline. They slithered like sinister snakes beyond a harbor where ships of many sizes had anchored, beyond a fortified embankment and various rows of barracks. No moon shed light upon the sentient shadows, giving their appearance a sinister and eerie presence, like tendrils of an ink-colored void consuming their surroundings, only to leave the scant light of fire torches and braziers unscathed.

Various soldiers on their watches or leisure paid no attention to the invisible shadows that lurked around them, as they moved to climb upon a massive mountain blanketed in the contrast of snow and volcanic pumice. Rising beyond the beachhead deep within the landmass, the shadows writhed towards a large raven stronghold mounted upon an overlooking precipice.

The shadow forms slunk through a grand foyer composed of obsidian stone lit by fires shadowing the shadows. Shadows slid through hallways and chambers, moving swiftly past more anonymous soldiers garbed in raven armor. Some marched, others manned posts throughout the dimly lit corridors. The sentient mass moved with a sinister grace, twisting along walls and walkways as soldiers remained oblivious to their presence.

Arcing and flowing along the antechambers, slithering through staircases and ramparts, gliding through doors, the snake shadows flowed as guided by an unseen force. A double door graced with the sunwheel Sigil of the Imperium carved from the iron and painted in blood-red hampered the slithering forms. Without a pause, they navigated below and above and between the colossal doors like flowing ink seeping into crevices. Inside the massive portal, the shadows slithered into a large room made of an obsidian stone and lined with tables of various relics and instruments. A single pedestal erected in the center of the chamber amidst the Sigil painted in grand, vermillion scale upon the floor, like a splattering of bloodletting intended for the decor.

A raven form towered within the prominent circle of the sigil clothed in black robes covering the entirety of the frame. Free from entrapment, locks of blackened hair flowed along the spine. The figure fingered the pages of a leather-bound tome resting on the pedestal to find the one reference or subject matter vital to its research. Behind the reader, the shadows rose and coalesced above the floor into a humanoid shape.

Crimson eyes seared from the rounded outline of a malformed head in the shape of inverted triangles touching at the corners. Shadowy arms grew from the mass ending in pointed razor fingers visible within the faint light burning from lamps and torches whose lights strained to reach every point of the circular room.

"Report, Choronzon."

The reader spoke in a deep bass voice, the timbre within the elocution of his words thundered echoes against the stone. The syllables and pronouncement of Imperium dialect flowed from his tongue with the natural pace of a rapier fight.

"Master," Choronzon hissed, "Tivius A'zum has returned to Silvetzen. Alone."

The shadow's hissing verbiage caused the reader to gradually cock his head into an upright position away from his study.

"Alone?"

"Yes, Master."

"Displeasing yet expected. His propensity to engage with his hunt is most admirable, but disconcerting and if he lost, then the prey and its quarry have invoked destiny."

"The Azthar Kherdmon is still untrained, unmolded, Master. He is still vulnerable."

The raven figure gleamed his pale hands over the texts, covered by lengthy claws of raven armor. He filtered his fingers like dancing talons across the pages of glyphs and ancient words. On this page, scrawled with crude markings covered in an ancient ink, scribbles and symbols surrounded the drawing of a cube within a cube, transitioning in the artwork from multi-faceted and colored to absolute blackened void.

"Cadeck was strong and resilient. Tivius revealed his hand too soon. The flesh of the Azthar Kherdmon is that of a boy, a young man still crude and worldly. Through him, *she* shall reveal herself and return to me."

"*She* has hidden for Aeons, Master."

"The Aztmi protect *her*. The darkness of the Imperium shall fall upon them. In their lands, I shall lay my seed. The abin (daughter) of Cadeck shall reveal *her* to me."

"What of the treaty, Supernus Magister?"

The voice of an aging man beckoned behind him, standing with the support of a gnarled cane, and hunched over in deep, crimson robes. Face wrapped beneath a cowl, the shadows of his fabric absorbed the glare of a monocle clung to his left eye.

"Trebut and Rathmana will not accept domination."

"Magister Philatané, you shall be my emissary to Silvetzen. I do not expect the formalization of treaty if Cadeck informs the sovereigns of the threat Tivius presented. Fifty legions shall be with you. Upon your arrival, inform Lord A'zum he will be of better use in Sarat. Forceful compliance shall show the realms of Roth we have laid dormant for too long. Go now, bring our enemies to conquest."

"As you Will it," Philatané bowed, supporting himself with his cane.

Choronzon flittered away, spilling his blackened form through the crevices of stone and grout beneath his apparition, dissolving into the surface like ink. As the aging Magister in the crimson robes approached the wide doors to the chamber, a pair of crimson armored men standing like statuary reached to whine the doors open for his exit and followed with an obedient closure. The tall reader whom his inferior addressed him as Supernus Magister remained paused over the page in his tome, the scribbled texts and ancient glyphs promoted the importance of the imprint of a mysterious cubic relic before him.

"You do not yet realize your importance to me, Azthar Kherdmon."

***

Rain-slicked stone moistened the soles of Tesh's shoes as the songs of birds harkened to call the sun to rise. Lush hues of pinks and blue covered the eastern sky behind the palatial inn as Tesh had a moment to contemplate the bustle and clamor of the city around him. Even as sunrise encroached, several vendors and shopkeepers in the surrounding square took to their stores, performing chores to clean or otherwise prepare their wares for the day's services. In this benign corner of the city, more prestigious and elegant fineries lined the shop windows and merchandise stands denoting the noble and gentry class of wealth dominating the presence around him. A short sniff sent unfamiliar smells into Tesh's nose; aromas of spices and foods prepared for demanding clientele. Fabrics and dyes freshly tailored and woven permeated their scents embellished by the fresh, dew-soaked air.

Yet, despite the strangeness of the climate, the randomly placed movement of carts and personnel, a slight sense of familiarity reminded Tesh of the days he would spend in Telmen, toiling for the various merchants and craftsmen he found employment. A smaller town in scale, Telmen excelled in the craftwork of the metal armorers, having access to the nearby mines rich with various ores smelted under the bureaucracy housed within the capitol city.

While Tesh was versed in the manufacture of smaller weapons intended for the home or the random farmer needing to fend off wild animals, the more robust weapons and armor remained reserved for the regular army and Capitol Guard which patrolled the streets around him.

Cadeck seated himself on a marble bench beside Tesh, resting his aging knees to the comforts of a brief respite. His satchel slung over his shoulder as he allowed his tarnished locket to hang openly around his neck, draped over the fresh set of tunics provided from the hospitality of the inn. He leaned against the backrest, one leg crossed over his knee and with a sigh, turned to his companion.

"I've never known the Court to be late on schedule for any affair."

"Do you think Her Highness was lying to us?"

"She has no reason to. We travelled here with one of her maidens, and the information we have is beyond the scope of Venna's knowledge."

"Would our ride have become lost?"

Cadeck chuckled, "Tesh, look around you, if a carriage driver in service to the Crown is unable to navigate this city in their sleep, then how would they keep gainful employment? Anyone in service to the Crown, knows this city and the many streets and avenues within."

"There is so much here to learn, so much here that still amazes me."

"I admire the virginal impressions the scale of this city consumes you, I was once the same way too, but do not allow yourself to become entrapped to the physical goings-on of this eyesore. This," Cadeck motioned his hand along the plane of the street before him, "All of this is arbitrary. What you see now is but one side of the scale of the wealth spectrum pervasive in this city. If I took you over there," Cadeck pointed in the southerly direction, "you would see a side of Sarat which would make you sick with disgust.

"The disease, the blight, and the neglect contrast to this exquisite luxury, for that is the nature of cities. The poor stay poor, while the rich continue to grow more wealth. For a Magi, and especially a Temple Knight, our purpose is not the greedy accumulation of gold and silver, but to the institution of service."

"But you were on the Court," Tesh turned to him.

"Was on the Court. Tense of your sentence is important, Tesh," Cadeck leaned forward, positioning his hands to form into a tent, "The Magi do not regale in the niceties of our charges. We are still humbled, acting in service and advisory positions when needed. Our influence only carries to words of encouragement or education to the crowns we serve. In such positions, you can say the Magi learn more than what we teach."

"Do you miss it?" Tesh seated next to him.

"Sometimes. It was always nice to know you have a roof over your head, a soft bed to your back and three warm meals. But we only stay in service until the sovereign, or the Council dismiss us."

"Then why did you leave it?"

"That is a question for another time."

Upon Cadeck's words, a single, azure carriage carried by a pair of sturdy horses approached the courtyard of The Brounden. The hooves of the animals clamored upon the cobblestone, leading the soft echoes of the carriage wheels to follow. A pair of men rode at the front of the carriage on the driver bucket as another pair of men stood on either side of the carriage, standing on running boards as straps wrapped around their waists to anchor them to railings bolted along the edges of the frame. Each of the four men wore a light cloak; drab and brown as cerulean helmets covered their anonymity, allowing Tesh to only gaze into a set of eyes dug deep behind steel plating. Quietly, the man on the right side reached to a lever opening a door which bore the eagle crest of Sarat pinching a blue rose within its talons.

Cadeck stood to his feet, "This must be our ride."

The soldier who opened the door ushered the pair inside. Tesh gathered his satchel and lifted the bag from the ground as the two men entered the carriage to the command of the man. With the door shut, the driver signaled the horses to move. Tesh and Cadeck found empty seating at the front of the carriage, across from a trio of figures garbed in raven cloaks. Beneath the cowls, strands of hair colors draped down, slightly shadowed by the scant sunlight piercing the window slits on either side. Each remained still, motionless, and quiet and as instructed, Cadeck motioned for Tesh to emulate the same.

The darkened shadows inside the carriage offered little comfort to Tesh as the horses led the vehicle along city streets, consumed in the traffic of other carts and carriages. The city closed to him, only offered by the slight glimpses through the window slits fabricated upon the iron plates lining the exterior of the carriage. With a slight clearing in the congestion, the horses clomped louder, faster before leaving through a pair of iron gates to the outside of town.

Pulling back their hoods, sat a trio of three women with only Venna recognizable. A brunette flanked the other side of the middle woman which struck Tesh's attention with an awe-inspiring beauty. Locks of ginger hair fell down her shoulders like a river of delicate saffron as a pair of emerald jewels for eyes stared at him from across the carriage.

"Your Highness, Lady Cassica, it sure has been a long time since I last saw you," Cadeck greeted.

"Likewise," her voice spoke like a chorus of angels, "I hope my furious writing delivered to you late yesterday was legible?"

Cadeck nodded, "Aye. Yet I don't suppose we are in this carriage for a quaint jaunt through the Northern countryside?"

"No, but I must say, you were not the Magi I was expecting."

"You refer to my Ascended, Godwen?"

"That is the name I was informed, yes."

"I am afraid he could not join us. But if I may ask, why the haste to get our services?"

"The encounters that Venna has informed me has piqued my interest."

"You assume we encountered something?"

Cadeck raised the pitch in his voice as to misdirect the conversation.

Cassica smiled sardonically, "I am concerned of the influence of a foreign power upon my father's lands. One that is not Rykanian. A foreign peoples Venna encountered while on your trail."

"In my defense, she discovered what is about to leave your tongue of her own doing."

"The soldiers she saw outside of Telmen you mean? But what of the events at the home of your charge? Tesh Verdui, I presume?"

Tesh nodded to confirm.

"Magi business. She happened to see the encounter."

"I don't suppose this cloth is any less Magi business than it is mine," Cassica opened her fist to reveal the soiled patch cloth of the white rose emblem once belonging to the body Cadeck found at Tesh's home.

"I suppose this is where our paths meet. Where is our destination?"

"Silvetzen. To which I understand, your itinerary directs you there also?"

"Clever. I must say you have grown into a studious and intelligent young woman, far advanced than the young girl that showed me her dolls and toys when she was a child."

"Fifteen harvests ago, before you left my father's service. I barely knew how to effectively use the latrine."

"You understand matters arose then that required my full attention?"

"I do not fault you."

"Your father, is he not aware of this meeting?"

"He is, and he has fully engaged the protocols when summoning for a Magi."

"With all due respect, Cassica, as you are not the acting sovereign of this kingdom, I cannot fulfill my representation on behalf of the Council to speak to you."

"Then, you should know the information Venna has shared matches information my proxies have gathered in the field. Sarat is fully aware of the situation to the North involving our ancient brothers and sisters of Silvetzen. However, my agent in Silvetzen has added information which I must obtain in person, the purpose for our paths to cross."

Cadeck turned to each of the flanking girls, seated in shadow, "Then you're aware of the Silvetzenian alliance with the Si'rai?"

Words growled from his tongue.

"Yes Cadeck. Unfortunately, Father preoccupies himself with matters about Founder's Day. I am to function as envoy in his absence concerning the tensions both here and abroad. Firstly, to meet with my contact in Silvetzen and secondly once I have obtained my contact in the Council, to hasten a peace treaty with all parties."

Cadeck's eyes grew stern towards Cassica, "The only peace the Imperium knows is enslavement."

"Which is why it is imperative upon Father's insistence, that a Magi accompanies my entourage."

Cadeck raised his index finger to emphasize his disgust, "I will only take this boy to the Temple of Fire found somewhere in Silvetzen to help him fulfill his training as a Temple Knight. I have no desire to act on the affairs of mankind's kingdoms to ally with the Si'rai. This treaty you speak of is a sham.

"What is the information your agent has which requires me to join?" Cadeck folded his arms.

"She did not say, for fear of her own life should it be read by the wrong hands."

"I suppose her statement is reasonable. But I will not mediate for any allegiance involving the Si'rai. You must act on that for yourself, Your Highness. My obligation is to the Magi, and the Temple Knights."

"I understand, Cadeck, but your words sorrow me."

"Then it means I am speaking truth. Any alliance with the Si'rai will only lead to dangerous futures for you, or your lands. I will not allow myself within their company."

Cassica folded her hands within her lap, picking at the nails upon her fingers, "You served my father for many years before I was born, why turn your back on him now?"

Cadeck leaned against the plush velvet seat. The narrow slit covering the window frame offered views of the meandering landscape of fields and farms as the carriage entered the primary road leading northward from Sarat.

"I served your father because he asked. This time, I do not serve in the role of a secular kingdom. There is a far greater danger the Si'rai pose than that of being foreign mediators in a dispute of Rykanian lands."

"Would this danger involve the rumored use of their magick?"

Cadeck turned back to face her, grimacing at her words, "What do you know of their magick?"

"I have read the histories and how their form of magick faded away to legends and myths. Long forgotten by scribes and scholars, relegated to mockeries and superstitions."

"A common belief amongst those who cannot wield magick."

"As a woman of education, I will need proof, not conjecture."

Cadeck leaned his chin upon bent index knuckle, refusing to answer her question. An air of uncertainty filled the cramped carriage quarters as he pondered her words, "Then you will not understand the importance to take Tesh to the Temples."

"Excuse me," Tesh muttered, attempting to lighten the conversation, "Your Highness, if I may ask, how long is the ride to Silvetzen?"

She turned to him bewildered of his brazen attempt to address her. Her eyes delicately dancing around the question asked of her of one of her subjects as not to berate him for crossing his caste, "Several days by carriage at best speeds, with this war carriage likely double."

"When do they expect you, Your Highness," Cadeck followed.

"A few weeks, before the next full moon."

"Amuse me, Cassica," Cadeck addressed her informally, "What information has Venna shared with you?"

Cadeck's face closed into an inquisitive stare. Venna's face sank into a rosy blush, feeling the ire of Cadeck's inquiry. Cassica turned her attention back to Cadeck, her mouth slightly agape at the position his question placed her.

"That information, I'm afraid, is proprietary to the Order of the Rose."

"Her information riddles with half-truths. Words that if spoken improperly, or even uttered under breath, could lead to ruination of her own mind and thoughts. These matters should not concern you, nor your Order, but left to the Magi to investigate. I am afraid your Order is out of its bounds."

"And what will the Magi do? Sit? Wait? Fiddle their thumbs? Perform incantations? Read leaves or runes? The Temple Knights are gone, Cadeck. The Magi cannot rely on them, and it is now up to the secular governments to act of their own interests and sovereignty. I cannot sit idly by while an inept body of aging men ponder the futures of my people or this world. If the histories I have read have shown anything, it is that their conclusions have not always been correct."

"The Council has always and will continue to act for the security of man. The Council has ordained wars and skirmishes and settled just as many; all their decisions guided by Natural Will. The Si'rai are the enemies of the Council and as such it should be our duty to respond to them accordingly," Cadeck leaned towards Cassica with disconcerting stare, "Your Roses can not defend against their magick, of this I can assure you."

"I have heard rumors of their magick in my father's lands," her face furrowed to sorrow, "whispers mostly, hushed voices. Nothing more than conspiracies relegated to town gossip and mocked accordingly."

"It is not wise to trifle with magick. A misspoken word, an ill-timed gesture or even the mere mention of magick leaving the tongue could invoke horrid atrocities upon those who commit the acts, and that is the magick that is favorable to Natural Will, never mind mentioning the chaotic results of using magick to one's selfish Will."

"I have always doubted magick, and the gods, ever since I was a little girl. I never believed it, yet Father tithed to the Magi as needed every year. He was and still is a firm believer in your ways to the point of unwavering, zealous trust. But do the gods favor him? Does Aeus give him wisdom to see? Does Heseph burn a fire into his heart? Does Tiasu give him a just tongue? Does Sokut heal his pains? Does Gedesh give him fertile seed? Does Vebest give him the will of a warrior? Or does Desed give his spirit comfort in his days? No. None of these things. All those thoughts and feelings are up to him. Me. Us."

"To question the gods is to bring great tribulations upon your lands. You teeter upon beliefs that you may one day wish to regret. To underestimate what Venna has told you will be perilous to your people and the blood-stained cloth in your hand should be proof enough to dissuade your incorrect opinions. If I am to help you, you must realize the danger of this treaty and the danger presented to you and your entourage. In turn, you must help me bring Tesh to the Temple of Fire, and we cannot pass into Silvetzen without official decree from your Crown. So, it would appear we have an impasse. I must have your confidence in my words and my warnings if you want my aide, but I ask you to not sign the treaty.

"You may wish to act on your own, even despite my trepidations. You may believe that the strength of your quill is enough to subdue the Imperium. But for how long? Months? Years? Decades? Time only allows them to grow stronger and with time, they also grow their magick. For thousands of years, the Magi have never underestimated their abilities. You do so at your own risk. With all due respect, Your Highness, you are walking into a trap."

#

Several days passed since leaving the capitol. Cassica's carriage continued along the Saratian Road leading across hills and dips as the dense forest separating the two lands loomed ahead in the distance. The road continued to wind past small huts and farms and the occasional village or hamlet, passing across small creeks active and dried out where aging bridges supplied a secure passage over the obstacle. As the forest boundary drew closer, a pair of stout guard towers draped by the Saratian herald flanked the entrance to the darkened wood as the day lowered to sunset. A guard posted on the left guard tower waved toward the approaching wagon and the driver motioned in return. Towering bearwood trees presided over the forest canopy protecting the fauna grazing below. The road winded into a narrow path allowing for single file traffic consuming the carriage amidst the dense woodlands.

Shadows of forest consumed the interior of the carriage, settling hard upon Cadeck's nerves. He darted his eyes to focus outside the window slits watching as passive animals pawed at the flora below their feet consuming the grasses and other plants. The sounds of the forest filled Cadeck's ears like the purring reverberations from a kitten. Insects and larger rodents scurried along, mingling with the tense echoes of birds ready for nocturnal hunt. Tesh stroked his hand upon the hilt of his dagger as the darkened forest slowly consumed their light.

"Calm, Tesh," Cadeck placed his right hand along Tesh's left knee.

"No need to be nervous," Cassica assured.

"I've never traveled this far before," Tesh choked on his words.

"There is nothing to fear here. I assure you the Blue Guard is more than trained to manage anything which may cause us harm."

Cassica's words carried into Tesh's ears with the serenity of a songstress, but a hint of derision trailed from her tongue at the notion her loyal guards could ever lose a battle.

"I'm not worried about the bandits and thieves," Cadeck motioned, "I sense uneasiness in the forest."

"Magick? Legends say a witch lives here," Venna burst forth.

"No. Old wives' tales my child, I sense something else."

Wind rustled across the forest canopy startling small limbs to fall to the floor below. Dusk painted the sky with eerie reds and orange clouds as the dim light darkened the canopy with the haunting aura of deep blue glow. The driver flicked a match and lit the lantern to his left. The soldier on the right repeated the action for the headlight to his right. The pair of lights beamed in front supplying a dim shadow of luminescence to guide them. The clamor of the horse hooves and iron rut wheels rolled through the forest echoing against the trees alerting the forest to the arrival of the carriage.

The heavy carriage rickety rocked along the winding road with the sway of the lamplights shifting with the ruts cutting deep into the path. Nocturnal beasts began their evening chorus to the signal of the slicing beams of the waning moon above cutting through the forest canopy like a series of silvery knives. Leaves rustled, jerking the driver's head to his left. The lantern shook in the wind. The soldier next to him calmed him with a shoulder pat and leaned into the back of his seat.

"I feel something. In the woods. The trees, they call to me." Cadeck whispered.

Tesh turned to Cadeck with concern, "I hear nothing, Cadeck."

"Request your drivers to stop here, Cassica."

Cassica nodded before marking her command through the open window slit. With her order, the driver pulled the reins carrying the beasts as the side panel burst open. Released from the confines of the carriage, Cadeck stepped aside, shifting his weight, and limped onto the detritus below with the sound of a sloshed thump against the decaying leaves. Whispers carried his name through the leaves as the winds fluffed a tuft of his hair. Cadeck turned to the driver board and encouraged the man to begin camp.

"You're not serious, Cadeck?" Cassica's sanguine locks cascaded through the open door and into the fresh airs.

Cadeck did not answer, only motioning from the road and around the rear of the carriage to the western embankment of wagon ruts. Cassica landed her suede boots onto the soft dirt, as the drab color of her musty cloaks absorbed the creeping moonlight spilling through the dense woods. Tesh came from behind her, leaning his hand against the cargo bin on the rear of the carriage.

"Tesh, remain with them. Do not follow."

Cadeck's words trailed through the air muted as he continued westward through thick shrubbery into the awaiting darkness.

Cassica turned around to see Tesh within distance of her personage, "Move."

Her voice scorned to the peasant, demanding he allow her to pass.

Tesh lifted his arm allowing her to return to the door side. The pair of soldiers on the right side of the carriage dropped from the running board onto the ground.

"Find a clearing not far from the main road," Cassica barked, "We'll hitch there."

The soldiers beside her bowed.

"Driver, move the carriage off the road, stay with the horses. You two," she called to the other pair on the left side, "hunt for game. Venna, Eris, help with removing the supplies."

The remaining soldiers bowed acknowledging orders and performed as commanded. The driver signaled the horse to motion as Cassica and Tesh followed the hefty carriage into a nearby clearing. Fallen twigs cracked upon hoof step as the heavy wheels coiled along the brush with a rolling crunch of weight. As the driver halted the vessel, the horses released a heavy whinny. He stepped down to his left, moving along the climbing steps carved into the iron side. He moved with his comrades, lifting into the cargo bin to remove the supplies for camp and tossing them onto the forest floor for preparations.

Venna and Eris emptied from the carriage, their plain cloaks covered their bodies, matching the attire of their superior. Venna wore her hair with dangling bangs covering her eyes as the brunette girl wrapped hers into a tight twist upon the back of her skull. The men hastened to setup camp, lifting a deep blue awning over the edge of the carriage emblazoned with the golden herald eagle upon its roof. One man lifted inside, sliding mechanisms from beneath the benches converting them into a folding mattress. He continued and pulled another latch, enclosing the windows to fit seamlessly flush with the rest of the iron plating. The other men setup simple tents: two soldiers apiece with an open tent reserved for Cadeck and Tesh as the driver began the process to start the campfire.

One of the guardsmen, light-skinned and skinny, climbed onto the roof of the carriage, like the others, he wore his armor hidden beneath gray cloaks, a small sword hung at his side. He reached to his feet and grabbed a blue, crested helmet to rest over his blonde locks and strapped it to the chin. He reached towards a case and eased the latches from the constraints revealing an assortment of weapons for the men. He loaded a crossbow with an array of bolts, slung the strap across his shoulder and readied his finger over the trigger stop to begin the watch for the evening.

Another stirring of wind rustled through the leaves, sending a cold chill along Cassica's spine as she readied herself on a cushion next to the campfire. Her emerald eyes reflected the flickering firelight emblazoned against the brush like a ravishing doom of orange glow. Tesh sat on the edge of one of the running boards, coaxing his left hand glazed by the wound of golden trace. His leg propped up next to him. The blue in his veins formed to yellow gold, with the cut gash in his hand molded over. Metal mingled with cauterized skin and blood.

He flexed his wrist and fingers, sensing the muscles tingling with movement. Nerves appeared as veiny, gold spiders along his hand, numbness rolled with the sensation of prickles. He flexed his fingers feeling no pain. The approach of the soldiers startled him from his thoughts as the pair dropped to sit, flinging a pair of small rabbits by the fire.

Eris worked to help, skinning the animal furs with diligence provided by her skill. Venna readied the meats, disemboweling the skinned animal and setting the skewer in place. Tesh observed the pair as they followed procedure as a master hunter, approaching the flame and sat next to Cassica. He rested his right foot upon a rock beside him. One by one, like clockwork, the pair prepared the animals for cook, placing the animals on a spit for the tongues of the crackling fire to braise the carcasses.

"They work well, Your Highness."

Cassica turned to her right to Tesh's attention, "They learn in Academy. It is a requirement to become a Rose."

Tesh continued to watch the pair, each of the young girls' delicate appearances defied their roughened skills, "They look like nobles to me, not fit for working the outdoors."

Cassica sighed, turned back to look at the pair and her soldiers, "You would do well to mind your place, Tesh. What the Roses do is not the business of the commoners."

Her High Accent tore through his supposition like a ravishing wolf.

"I meant no disrespect, Cassica," Tesh turned towards her jade eyes reflecting the dancing campfire upon soft, pale face.

One of the soldiers seated beside her rose to height. His bulked frame topped off with a brown beard covering his face. Spit melted into his whiskers as he scolded Tesh, "You will address her with respect, citizen."

Tesh dropped his foot to the ground. Taken aback by the sudden bolster of the man in front of him, "I meant no harm. Mingling with royalty is foreign to me."

Tesh's words revealed his fealty.

"Stand down, soldier. He travels with a Magi and carries his role. He may address me as the Magi does."

The soldier obeyed, grunting discouragement towards the wishes of the royal in silent thoughts.

"Thank you, Your Highness." Tesh nodded. Cassica rose to her feet, her face reflective in the fire like a smooth-skin statue.

"Tell me, Tesh," she began, "did I know your father?"

"No. He died before either of us was born," Tesh craned his neck towards her.

"A man's portrait hangs in the Hall of Champions with your surname."

"Well," Tesh shrugged, "probably another man with the commonality of my name."

Cassica grinned to Tesh's sarcasm. Her mood lightened slightly from the regal rigidness of her station, "He was one of father's best in the Blue Guard. Are you certain you do not belong to the nobility?"

"Mother and I were simple villagers, Your Highness. We never ventured to Sarat, keeping between Telmen and Stonebear."

"Venna says you had a farm outside of Telmen."

"Aye. I lived there my life, mother passed in recent years," Tesh turned his stare into the fire.

"I may be above your station, but I humbly share sympathy when those words spill onto my heart. Come, walk with me."

Tesh hesitated, looking upward towards her.

"Come along," she motioned with her neck.

He rose to stand, brushing the dirt and grass off the back of his pants as she strode towards the parked carriage. Cassica strode slightly ahead of him; waning, pale moonlight splintered the tree line above them, cascading gentle white streaks upon her skin like tiny slivers of brilliant radiance in the darkness.

As she passed through the moonbeams of waning cycle, Tesh caught sight of another figure. A shadow of a woman silhouetted against the frame of the princess, matching her height like a ghost imprinted upon her as she passed beneath each attempt of the moon to strike the forest floor. He scratched his eye only to see the reflection again through another shadow of moonlight. She paused in her stride taking Tesh by surprise as he steadied himself beside her.

She reached her right hand to touch upon his left. His eyes widened in shock. A stinging pain filled his nerves, etching into the golden veins hardened into his left hand. Whispers called to him like a haunting ghost calling his name in sultry indulgences. Tesh reacted to her touch, removing his hand from hers to cower it close to his chest and massage his fingers. Ethereal clamors splintered through his nerves unraveling them like a hewn cord.

"Did I hurt you? You never said how it happened."

"No, I felt no pain. I felt something strange."

Cassica scorned, "I assure you; Father betrothed me to another noble once I have completed my service to Father's causes. You had best refrain from such animalistic thoughts."

"No, it was something else. I do not know."

"How did you get it?"

"Cadeck caused it."

"Cadeck? Why?"

"He came to me, cursed with an amulet. I cut myself and the amulet bound to my skin freeing his curse."

"Can you feel it?"

Tesh clenched and opened his fist completely in response, "Sometimes."

"Does it hurt?"

"Not until you graced your hand. Why are you interested in my wound if I am just a common villager?"

"Legends, Tesh," she whispered out of earshot of her guards, "All my life I have heard old legends; legends of ancient warriors and the founding of Sarat and ingrained into me since birth."

"What type of legends?"

"Saratian legends speak of an ancient warrior, a savior to our people. In his left hand he is bound in gold and in his right, he carries a mighty sword gifted to him by the gods. The superstitious believed his words spoke death to enemies and brought life to those considered worthy.

"He transcended from the gods, blessed by the heavens above. They say in his last death, mankind fell into disarray. Tongues scrambled and brothers warred with brothers. They believe should he return one day; we will know him when he pairs with the sun and moon to his sides. In victory, he would unite man, end wars, and give man his gift back."

"My mother never taught me any prophecies. Mother forbade speaking of magick. She called it a secret, that it was fragile and of the darkness. There was a hint of untrustworthiness in her tones towards those who would manifest such deeds. She treated magick as though it were a curse upon man."

Tesh's eyes became solemn as his mind wandered to memories of his mother, "She always spoke with a resounding fear about magick, and as she spoke of the subject, it truly scared her. Sometime after her death, I renounced the gods entirely."

"Your mother seemed very superstitious, Tesh." Cassica kept her tongue couth, hinting depreciation of his stature in class, yet keeping it to herself.

"It is not important. You mentioned some gift. What gift?"

"Stories say man could always wield magick. It was the gods who gave man this gift. But man abused their powers, and the gods stripped it from us; destroyed those who flaunted the gift and selectively chose those of purity to continue the traditions."

"Is this what you were told?"

"I have read of many stories, Tesh, in old dusty books when I was younger. Like you, I have always doubted them. Since I was a girl, I saw them as superstition and fable. I read them again sometimes to humor myself. I never believed them. Madame Rygard only told them to me when I was a young girl, told me it was to better my learning, to be well-versed to the ways of our world, but I was more interested in the explanation of things; the sky, the plants, the birds, surely magick did not bring all of this to life. There must be something else, something more complicated than saying it was 'begotten' into existence by some mystical force."

"I noticed you don't hold the Council to high esteem."

"They take when they can. They laud power to keep their hold over man. They would subjugate man into submission using their magick and never allowing man free will, holding back man's true self. My father trusts them, but I cannot. If I were in line of succession, I would change our stance towards the Council. I would give back to my people. Let them choose free will."

"What about governments? Wouldn't you say the same about them?"

"Father respects his commoners; he is working to make Sarat better. We hold the interests of our subjects high. He wants to change things, Tesh. We understand man's purpose and work to keep man free, remove some traditions if we can. But we are still beholden to the Magi and the Council, in service to them in duty and tithe and reminded of the divine plan the gods have laid forth. Some courtiers believe a foreign outsider coaxes him and the Court to question and doubt the Magi, but that is only hearsay. Cadeck was the only one I could trust, and he speaks highly of your name."

"It is only a surname, princess. I have no ability to wield magick and can barely wield a sword. My father carried it, and I am sure others do too. I am so common even Venna says her sister wrote of a man with my name."

"Venna told you of her sister?"

Cassica refrained her voice from rising in suspect.

"Shall I guess, she's your contact?"

Tesh turned a raised eye in her direction. Cassica did not answer; instead, she removed herself from the running board before joining the others. She turned to the younger brunette girl, Eris, and whispered to her ear. As to obey, Eris removed herself from her seat and carried off into the woods in the direction Cadeck ventured. Venna approached Tesh, crossing beside Cassica, and provided Tesh with a leg of rabbit meat.

"What did you say to her?" Venna inquired.

"Nothing really. I may have touched a nerve."

"She doesn't look so happy."

Tesh gnawed on the cooked flesh before him, "Talking with nobility is new to me."

Venna giggled, "You just need to learn how to address them. Never disagree and always flatter."

Her tone came across to Tesh as lecturing.

"That's how my father expected it."

"If you're nobility, why are you involved with the Order of the Rose?"

"My father saw it as an honor of myself to join. The highest of service a lady in my stature could adhere to within the kingdom. Otherwise, I would have several children by now."

"Your friend left I see."

Venna turned to see Eris removed from her position once next to hers, "Her Highness assigned her a task. It is not in our interest to question assignments she delivers. But it is in interest to Sarat as she speaks for her father in her position."

"You obey without question?"

"I should return. She will call for rest soon and as before, we must be ready to help with her wishes."

Venna turned around and walked towards the campfire to sit next to Cassica as the other soldiers prepared for sleep. Tesh studied the princess with intuitive gaze, watching her movements as she commanded Venna and the other soldiers with a polite demeanor. Fiery hair slung over her pale shoulders exposed by her linen dress peeking from her loosened cloak, fitting to every curve of her features. Like a dancer, she moved with grace accentuated by the bright fire behind her as though to follow the rhythm of a chant with drums. He watched with a careful eye to not pry into her business only for Cassica to catch his gaze and return with a subtle smile.

Chapter 12

L antern light burst into the small shack like an eruption of pearly white flame. Tivius flinched away shielding his icy gaze from the sudden rush of light assaulting his translucent eyes aglow. Dark hairs draped across his broad, exposed shoulders concealing ageless scars and pale wounds. Fresh cuts formed upon his faint, naked body searing like small canyons of dried blood. Tivius positioned in meditation, the rotten cadaver of his victim still clung to the ceiling by his chains.

"Magister A'zum," a feminine voice called from the fading brightness, addressing the pale man with the coarse words of the Si'rai language.

Tivius slowly craned his neck to face the open door. Strands of raven hair fell into place onto his left pectoral muscle.

"You may speak."

"Field Marshal Jabar requires your presence at his command tent."

"Did he state his purpose?"

"There is information he must disclose, and he wishes to only converse with you."

Tivius' hairless skin appeared as pastel paint in the shimmer of the faint lamplight as he erected himself from the ground soil in his ramshackle holdings. He began his towering stride towards the blazing light disregarding decency to dress. The feminine figure stepped aside, bowing in reverence, her body clothed in full cloak. To her flank, the other masculine figure bowed in unison, standing slightly taller than the feminine.

Each of the mysterious guards held a lantern burning blue flame and panned to follow Tivius away from his shack. As the pair turned, their light shifted upon the rotting cadaver chained to the ceiling, its chest torn open, and a lengthwise slit skewered the boy to his loins. The shadowy figures followed Tivius' lengthy gait as he callously strode naked through the encampment towards the command tent draped with black-dyed skins, ignoring any protocols of decency to his appearance. A pair of armored soldiers lifted the heavy flaps separated by the Sigil of the Abyss. Passing between the two, red-skinned guards, Tivius' shadowy followers carried an energy of dread to the men. Their resolve faltered, assessing their ability to remain in attention. Their weapons trembled within their hands.

Jabar's deep eyes surveyed documents and maps, his rust-colored, shaven scalp reflected the oil light on the desk. As Jabar raised his head to meet the magister with his eyes, his chiseled face squinted in disgust at the appearance of his superior. Tivius' guard floated in their cloaks to either side of him standing a synchronized distance behind their master.

Jabar stood to attention, saluting Tivius with a closed fist at his chest and following with a bow of his head.

"Lord A'zum," Jabar's calm, deep voice addressed returning to ease, "If my repulsion to your appearance may be excused?"

"You will address me as standard. Why do you interrupt my meditations?"

"We have received notice from Sarat an envoy is en route to sign the treaty. It is rumored Her Highness, Princess Cassica and an Aztmi is part of this party."

"An Aztmi?" Tivius' shaved brows raised upon the revelation.

Jabar nodded.

Cadeck, he whispered to himself, inaudible to Jabar, "Cassica will sign her nation's downfall, and Supernus Magister will be pleased."

Jabar paused, and continued his briefing, "King Rathmana has accepted full occupation, relinquishing his title under the intention of becoming our vassal upon signature of treaty. When the envoy from Sarat arrives, the formality of the signing will include them."

"Rathmana's death will be a display in front of his people. I shall have the pleasure of savoring his demise for Supernus Magister. I presume the details of the treaty are not fully known to King Trebut?"

"No, Lord A'zum. He only believes the treaty is a formality with Silvetzen. To our knowledge, Sarat is unaware of our direct involvement."

"Not if the Aztmi is with them."

"This Aztmi, Godwen, would certainly be following our guide while joining the Saratian envoy. Afterall, he did accept our 'offerings'." Jabar's naked eye lowered in concern, questioning his superior's knowledge.

"No, this Aztmi is not Godwen. His Adept rides with this envoy, and he is fully aware of our presence."

Tivius erupted in fury, raising his voice against the calm demeanor of his inferior, "Those Silvetzenian fools you assigned to me fell easily to the Magi and his Knight, allowing him to continue to live. I have no doubt Cadeck has informed Sarat of our involvement."

"A most disagreeable turn of events," Jabar's tattoo squeezed tight around his eye socket.

"When is the envoy from Sarat expected to arrive?"

"Many days my Lord, but before the next abranus."

Flames flickered against Tivius' icy eyes shining an ethereal aura within the tent.

"Assure those within the envoy receive treatment as ambassadors. Our involvement must continue to remain secret, despite any allegations to the contrary. When the time comes to sign the treaty, detain the entourage swiftly. They must not leave this heretical kingdom."

Tivius removed himself from the tent as Jabar bowed in reverence to the command. The ghostly cloaks followed behind as Jabar grappled his shaking right hand to cease the aura of dread trailing behind them.

**

Flickers of moonlight knifed through the forest canopy as slivers of blades to a torture barrel. Cadeck seated himself in motionless meditation, his knees bent to ground, his hands formed to a tent with his index fingers touching his nose through reverberating chants in a primordial tongue. Whiskers formed along aging crevices in his weathered skin, and his jaw made subtle movements in his prayers. Breaths rolled through his fingertips like cold smoke. A crude circle drew around him in the patchwork grasses beside a subtle growth of mushrooms whose caps appeared to grow with each moonbeam tracing upon them. The faint voices of the Saratian camp permeated across the landscape, dulled out by his concentrated efforts.

Removed were the tattered robes worn since leaving Tesh's home, replaced by a sleeveless white cotton shirt draped upon his fit body revealing the cavernous scars reaching over his exposed shoulders. A hemp belt tied around his waist joining a pair of white trousers to his torso ending just below his knees.

"I called to you, Cadeck," an aging feminine voice waned speech.

"I heard your name in the trees."

"Which one?"

"The several. I do not pray to you, but why did you summon me?"

Cadeck felt a lifeless hand reaching onto his shoulders. Moans of death rattle echoed into his ears. He saw whiteness void in his thoughts etching into his soul. He heard screams of a young woman straddled on her back on a cold slab amidst a darkened tower. A massive figure covered over her; his long hair melted into hers. A muscular man forced upon the crying woman sending

145

shrieks of torture through the hall surrounded by crimson robed figures. Cadeck could not move in his thoughts as the brunette hair straggled across the girl's face in whimpering cries of pain. Soon, a deluge of water covered him within the vision.

Cadeck collapsed, his hands catching his fall as his mouth and eyes widened to gaping horror. He shook in hesitation to move; his mouth stuttering syllables in vain attempts for detectable speech. The once lifeless hand removed from his shoulder, only for him to hear the crackling female voice once again.

"I have shown you a future, Cadeck. Your children will suffer so truth may reveal."

"No. Please. I must rescue them. Remove them from this fate. Cry to your goddess so she may save them."

Tears streamed across his cheeks as the realization settled in.

"You know I cannot, Cadeck. Natural Will flows immutable."

"Then I will abandon Tesh and find sail to the Imperium. I will rescue them myself."

"And you will meet fate along the way for abandoning purpose, Sokut would have it so. They must endure, Cadeck. Your children are strong, bring the Azthar Kherdmon to his trials and those who harm your children will see their demise. Your children are the future of Roth; do not deny your world their pain. The gods have spoken."

A low, young voice called to Cadeck through the woods. He wrestled with the words spoken through his soul, tormenting him as to the condition of his children. The vision was undeniable, a sense of torture and dread at the hands of his former captors. Nails turned soiled as he clawed into the moist mud begging in futile screams to the voice calling to him to vision. Only silence heard his screams, as the patter of a guest ran towards his hunched body lit by the scant moonbeams piercing through thick forestry.

"Wrem."

His voice burned with pain as he clutched Eris' cloth cloaks along her neckline. Echoes of his suffering tore through the forest. Faint yells called his name from the distant campsite as he stood to his feet. Eris' hazel eyes caught with fear as Cadeck lifted her by the collar of her tunic, her feet dangling from his lifting strength.

"You are not my daughter, where is she?"

"Elder Magi, Her Highness requested your presence at camp," Eris muttered with fright.

Cadeck forced her back against a tree, his eyes turned to muted whiteness.

"Where are my children?"

146

Feet sprinted towards him in the faint darkness of the forest. Cadeck heard his name called aloud in the forest in Tesh's voice, only not spoken in the common speech but echoed through his soul in the soothing vernacular of the gods. His eyes returned to dull hazel as he lowered Eris to stand upon the moist soils. The young woman sobbed frightened tears as a pair of Blue Guard accompanied Tesh to meet with the Magi.

"Cadeck," Tesh began, "is everything alright?"

Cadeck shook his head, lifting his palm to his face. A pair of fingers flanked his right eye, "I saw a vision, Tesh, placing priority upon our journey. We have no time to waste."

Cadeck paused and reached to grab his satchel upon the detritus before pushing beyond Tesh towards the hint of amber light from the distant camp. The soldiers crouched next to Eris as they readied to coax her to stand. A smaller soldier rose to his height, reaching to Tesh's nose and lifted his sword from its sheath at his hip before aiming the tip towards Cadeck's backside. His ginger hair slipped below his helmet line separated by freckled cheeks rosy like a newborn. Thick lips covered a gap between his teeth as his tongue rolled words in High Accent.

"This Magi placed vile hand upon Her Highness's maiden. Such act is a crime against the Court."

Cadeck paused before turning his head over his shoulder, sensing the point of the sword several yards behind him. Tesh did not move only paying attention to the situation prepared to unfold.

"I once served your Court, young man. Your king and his family place high appraise upon my services. How would you answer to Her Highness if you were to run me through within this silent forest? Would you be safe? Would your family be safe from your crime?"

The other soldier rose with his arm around Eris and coaxed his peer to sheathe his weapon. As to obey, the younger soldier slid his sword into the wooden sheath as he followed his peer towards the camp light. Tesh approached Cadeck as the Magi stepped off towards the campsite.

"What did you do to Eris?"

"I will apologize to Cassica when we return to camp."

Tesh sensed the undertones of sarcasm, "You felt a vision, Cadeck? Like the one in Telmen?"

Cadeck ignored his statement as he led the young man along the dense forest skirting beyond trees and shrubbery, "Let us return to camp. It will be several more days ride into Silvetzen."

#

Sunlight cleared the shielded woods as the azure war weapon carried itself past the towering trees. The path broadened into a wide road scarred with wagon ruts and horse prints. Simple guard towers flanked the roadway composed with logs carved into sharp spikes. Two archers stood at the ready within the confines of the adjoining structures. A similar soldier, carrying a sword to his hip, stood upon the ground at the border entry. His body bulged through the custom chain fashioned for his frame and overlaid by a leather pelt covering his chest. A crude tattoo etched upon his bald scalp. Worn nails scored with mud scratched at his face.

The Saratian carriage arrived at the single man who walked with the gait of sore legs and the odor of unkempt hygiene. The driver of the wagon heaved his reins to bring the large horses to stop as the Silvetzenian guard approached the vehicle.

"You must be the envoy from Sarat?" The bald soldier required of the carriage.

The cold smell of fresh dew filtered through his nose as he sniffed a load of mucus before coaxing it upon the ground by way of his tongue.

"Here are the orders," the driver reached into a small satchel on his board, produced a small paper and handed it to the guard.

The man perused the paper following his eyes across the carriage marked with the Saratian herald and studied them in the best of his illiteracy.

"Eh, this appears in good order. Carry on."

His rotten gums reeked from morning meal. He returned the slip of paper to the driver and beckoned the carriage onward while the snipers eased their bowstrings.

"How far is the ride?"

"You will reach Silvetzen in another week. His Majesty awaits your friendship."

"Very well," the driver carried his horses into a full gallop as the guards on the sideboards clutched the handrails in response. The carriage rolled past the border patrol along the widened road lined by remnants of wood and open meadows.

Cadeck leaned away from the window slit, forming his wide frame into the plush cushions. His shoulders touched next to Tesh's as the three ladies seated before them opposite the cabin.

"Your Highness, what is your plan once we reach Silvetzen?"

"We must find our contact. Once we find her, we can then act on the next part of the plan."

"My purpose is not to involve with any affairs which may jeopardize Roth, which includes signing a treaty with the Si'rai. If this agent has information of vital importance, I will aide you to meeting her. However, my vision two nights ago impedes me on acting as your accomplice and hastens my goal to lead Tesh to his training."

Cassica shuddered upon his insistence before clearing her throat to continue, "Cadeck, I assure you Sarat's goals are in line with yours. My agent will go with me as my escort into the meeting. If a Si'rai official is present, she has assigned orders to assassinate him and prove the alliance is a lie."

Tesh raised his hands in a defensive posture as if to push aside the notion, "Wait. Political assassination was never part of *my* plan."

"These politics affect Cadeck and yourself."

Tesh produced a queried look, "I don't follow."

"My contact informs me she has information vital to the Council."

"This information is why you needed my assistance?"

"Precisely Cadeck. She has not told us in correspondence for fear she may expose her cover. There have been changes in the Council, changes which strengthen my feelings of doubt towards them, and which may hold dire relations for our world."

"Changes to the Council?"

Cadeck leaned back against his bench, "I have lain in a dungeon for two harvest seasons, and I am afraid I must know of these changes. Are you certain your contact is still unknown?"

"Aye, she's made cover as a courtesan."

"How do you plan on contacting her?"

"Venna will take care of those details. She will bring my contact to our quarters, and we discuss our plans then. She may know the location of your Temple."

"You plan to bring me into diplomatic relations with the Si'rai only to have your spy assassinate them? Are you aware the ramifications endangering Sarat should the Imperium learn of this?"

Cassica sighed, contemplating her words carefully, "Your assistance is required to maintain protocol as Silvetzen has decreed."

"Do not underestimate the Imperium. You recall your attempt, and once you have contacted your agent, you are to leave from Silvetzen with her. Leave Tesh and myself to our own accords."

"I'm afraid, Cadeck, the writ is official."

"You drive a dangerous bargain, Your Grace," Cadeck gritted his teeth.

Cassica remained composed at Cadeck's incessant anger, "Cadeck, if her words are to be true, I'm afraid what she has uncovered will change your misconceptions."

The Saratian carriage straddled through the countryside as a cerulean beast lumbering across the widened highway beyond farms and fields. Disheveled farmers clutched their children as the carriage of their aggressor strained past them. A few farmers readied their pitchforks as if to predict an ancillary attack from the mounted soldiers, their faces clearly masked in anger.

Tesh peaked through the armor slits admiring the soft countryside filled with gourds and livestock plowing fields. His journey continued into a territory both physically and politically of which his experience as a tradesman never prepared him for. He wondered if his father had made this journey more effortlessly as required by all Knights and how many failed in their quests.

Sighing, he returned to thought. His mind recollected the past few days. He paused and closed his eyes to the outside world. A bright light flashed within his memories forming into humanoid form. He grasped a handle on the side panel in sudden jerk as a fresh pulse of surging pain gripped across his left hand. In response, he contracted the appendage, wincing in visible agony.

Death awaits you in Silvetzen. A voice boomed from within his mind. He released his hand as tentacles of golden energy flowed across the crevices fused within his veins.

"What's the matter?" Cassica asked, witnessing Tesh's pain.

"I get the feeling we're in danger," Tesh gasped.

Chapter 13

A saddened face glistened with fresh sweat draped with silvery, blonde locks clung like barnacles to the soft cheeks of the woman. Her mouth gripped tightly upon a tree bark. A newborn's wailing cry sparked to life. Tears streamed down the woman's face as the child erupted with cold exposure to the open air. Relief at the sound of the breathing cries allowed her mouth to release its grip, the rod of wood collapsed to her side.

She struggled as she welcomed the blood-drenched child in fresh swaddling amongst her calm embraces. Lips collapsed into purple tinge as her vessels in her skin shorn through sickly paleness. A young man released the birth grip of her hands to allow the woman to welcome the bald child. Her warm eyes sunk into a void as she held the boy amongst her bosoms. Her head tilted back straining her neck to look at the man at her side.

"Cadeck, I love you."

Her voice waned into emptiness as her soul faded into lifelessness.

"Jess, no. Do not leave me now. No, please."

Cadeck immersed himself in the white sheets of his deceased lover. Blood stains spilled around her thighs. His thoughts trailed into despair as he wailed over the loss. He burst into haunting screams, recalling the past as he rose from his nighttime slumber to a screaming fit.

Disrupted by his clamor, Venna rose from her rest inside the armored carriage as Eris startled beside her. She heard cries coming from outside as she stumbled to her footing within the wagon. Barefoot, she set to the cold ground as she wandered aimlessly towards the crying moans and palmed her still sleepy eyes.

She approached the single tent, her silhouette masked by the orange light of the fire with the scented smokes rising into the air with the sting of burning wood. She lifted the hide flap to see Cadeck shirtless, his whiskered face sobbing into his palms. He gazed towards the young girl; his eyes swollen with reddened tears. Pain washed over him like a memory of ancient time. He could not make out her features, only the height of the woman standing at the right stature he remembered of his daughter.

"Wrem, you come to me?"

"No Cadeck you're having another dream, 'tis I, Venna."

"Venna? Where am I?"

"We are in the heart of Silvetzen. We have made small camp off the Saratian Route."

"Silvetzen? What am I doing here?"

Cadeck looked around his small confines. Fur rugs strewn across the topsoil; small wooden boxes rested at his feet holding simple rations for his short night stay. Bending a knee to his chest, he leaned back upon one arm to gather his thoughts.

"Cadeck, what troubles you?"

Venna seated herself upon the ground at his feet.

"The vision in the forest, I'm haunted by it."

"Did you see her?"

Cadeck shook his head at the young woman's simplicity, "See who?"

"You know who. The Forest Witch."

Cadeck smiled at her naiveté as he pressed his left palm against his forehead to soothe a tapering headache.

"I can assure you Venna, there is no such thing. Magi scorn witches as perversions of magick, they are as outcasts, or persons who do not wish to conform to the ways of the Council. The Temple Knights used to hunt them down when even the slightest rumors spread in a village. If there were such a person, she would certainly remain hidden to not allow a Magi to find her."

"But I've been told since I was a little girl…"

"I am aware of the stories, Venna. Girls across Rykana have heard them, my daughter being no different. But we have more pressing matters before us. We should wake and prepare camp to move soon."

Their journey continued several more days as the Saratian envoy reached the military outskirts of the Silvetzen capitol city. The Saratian Route shrunk into a narrow road lined with military barracks and training grounds occupied by a multitude of fit warriors garbed in chain mail, loose-fitting tunics and kilts exposing fit, toned appendages. Various soldiers of pale complexion toiled in training or preparations with a variety of builds and hair colors. Their camp stung of sweat and labor wrought among communal fires fueled by whale oils. A gray malaise of clouds overhead blotted out the sun in random patterns lending an eerie, drab cold to the breaths of the soldiers.

Mud soaked the grounds of the simple boreal clime as sooty smoke rolled over the valley from the campfires lit in the military foothold. The road spit forth towards a large city walled with thick mortar embattlements and guarded by a battalion of archers and heavy battery along the towers. The massive portals yawned in reprieve allowing the Saratian envoy entry into the structured city.

The gates swallowed the wagon as if it were a small insect in proportion. The main roads filled with pedestrians stopping their tracks to eye their newcomers with a harsh disdain. The inhabitants of the town composed all castes of life from the dregs of poverty to the splendor of luxury as the envoy carried past various shops and warehouses. Square buildings shaped like wooden, cubed fungus mired the lower-class districts. Their roots and walls growing from the tundra lined the roadways of innumerable heights and proportions with thatch roofs overextending beyond the entrances in various states of neglect or disrepair. As the wagon moved further, the city gave way to rows of smaller mortar apartments, shops, and various accoutrements to desired living before coming upon the inner-city gates marking the more opulent centers of nobility.

As the wagon cleared the inner-city portcullis, a contingent of men approached the wagon on horse carrying a white banner with a blood red eagle silhouette. The larger man led the pack stopping his advance in front of the carriage. Quiet winds blew through his ragged red hair poking through his iron helmet fashioned as a small face ending below his nose. Atop his helmet rested a raven plume signifying his rank over the men behind him. A red flowing cape fell along his back and draped across his steed's backside.

"Greetings," the officer announced, "You must be the envoy from Sarat? Our King, Sorithen Rathmana is pleased his cousin sends regards."

The officer's accent was thick with guttural speech spoken in broken High Accent. The driver of the wagon accepted the offer and displayed his orders towards the Silvetzenian officer who glanced over the official parchment as his breaths rustled against his ginger moustache flowing from his nose.

"We welcome you as a member of Court; King Rathmana demands it. We will escort your carriage to the castle."

"Very well," the driver followed.

"I don't like this," Cadeck protested from within the cabin.

The wagon rocked forward as the driver commanded his workhorses to trudge.

"We must be patient, Cadeck," Cassica comforted in her hypnotic voice, a single bang of scarlet curls slung down her left cheek, "It is vital the treaty commences, and we can locate our contact."

"Venna's going to sneak out and find your contact? If we are in Court, I find this plan highly dubious."

"Do not underestimate my ladies, Cadeck."

"If I remember right, I think I stumbled upon her vain attempt at espionage," Cadeck grinned.

Tesh peered through the iron plated eyelets in the side boards gazing across the ramparts and scaffolding across the city. Onyx-armored soldiers interspersed along positions bulked in massive frames and red skin blazing against the cool northern sunlight randomly peeking through the overcast.

"Cadeck, look," Tesh pointed towards a couple of Si'rai men laughing and conversing along a rooftop balcony.

"They mingle within the city and the citizens pay no concern. Our meeting at the Light Temple was not just a chance encounter of a band of sanctioned help. The Si'rai are active within this city."

"What do you mean?"

"It's not a treaty, Cassica, it means assimilation."

"But if the treaty has not been signed, how are the armies of the Si'rai presiding in the city?"

Cadeck pondered Cassica's question with concern showering his face, "The Si'rai must be preparing a formal appearance. What is involved I do not know. I do not feel you should execute your plan. The treaty will only allow the Si'rai to march into Sarat unopposed, your attempt to assassinate may end up doing more harm to Sarat than you imagine. I do not think they will hold mercy to the ruling class and subjugate your people in turn. You must not sign this treaty."

Cassica pondered the Magi's words. She respected him and his position, but never the Council body in her lifetime. She muttered to herself an inaudible statement; her index finger slid across her lush lips in concentration cupping her delicate hand against her chin. She slumped her shoulders, her regal dress sunk against the plush cushions on her bench. Her hand cupped against her chin while her eyes wandered along the floor of the wagon.

The armored cart drove further into the town reaching into the drawn portcullis of the imposing castle. Flags bearing the red eagle herald rested in the calm air atop the guard towers flanking the gate. The armored horses rested to a stop deep within the courtyard edged by armored Silvetzenian soldiers and officers protecting their liege. The rattles of the armor carriage grinded like unoiled metal gears ceasing action as one of the Saratian soldiers on the running board prepared the exit of the riders.

He lifted the latch to open the carriage as Cassica released herself left hand first in elegant royal demeanor to welcome her distant relative. Venna and

Eris followed, clothed in simple attendant dresses flowing of cerulean seas capped off with silver tiaras. Cassica greeted her host with the elegance of a foreign dignitary, curtsying in respect as her ladies repeated the same.

The attending soldier announced her formal name to the host, "Her Royal Highness of Sarat, Princess Cassica Diaysus of House Bovariàr."

King Rathmana welcomed his guest adorned with golden jewelry and gaudy attire accentuated with a bright red cloak draped along his obese sides down to his hips. He stroked his balding dome marred by sickly string hair in a desperate attempt at grooming along his surly head in contrast to his regal status. His appearance belonging amongst perversion of brothels and alcohol than the elaborate luxuries of the wealth he notably exploited.

"Surely your beauty graces our kingdom as the fires of Heseph warm our hearts," he spoke as though food spilled from his mouth. His neckline ample as to have multiple chins like a goiter.

"Your flattery is amusing, cousin, but understand my respect when I decline your indulgences and urge haste in our matter."

Rathmana formed a garish sneer dotted with the stench of mead, "Of course, our common allies would be willing to hasten our business should you wish. I have welcomed them in my home the past several months and they have been most gracious visitors."

Cassica followed her eyes across the castle ramparts lined with a mix of Silvetzenian and Si'rai men with a pleasant nervousness as she inhaled swiftly through her nostrils before speaking.

"I can see, cousin. I hope we can avert any further conflict with our affairs."

Rathmana chuckled, nearly choking on his own saliva, and muttering to himself under his breath, "Affairs?"

Cassica shrugged off the shrewd, unnoticeable comment as she continued to walk into the castle confines by her cousin's hand. She could feel the sleaze pouring through his glands epitomizing his debauchery of endless nights amongst whores and drunks. Rathmana escorted his cousin with a flank of his armored men. Venna and Eris followed a few meters behind the royal relations as custom to their stature.

Rathmana's eyes leapt from Cassica's down to the visible cleavage from her exquisite dress, eyeing her beauty with perverse desire. With gallant courtesy, he allowed the entry of the three ladies into the walls of his castle first, and followed behind them with slathering abhorrence, staring without impedance to the shapely backsides of the trio. Rathmana's gait waddled, following the ladies through the doors.

Cadeck and Tesh appeared from the wagon as the pompous fanfare of formality subsided. The driver handed Cadeck the single sack holding the supplies Tesh carried from his home. A pair of Silvetzenian officers distinguished by full breast plates, crested helmets and flowing capes stood in front of the pair awaiting their move. The burly officers met the pair of men with chain mail hands before they could follow the women.

"You will not be going with the fair ladies. We request you to other quarters for their discretion," the officer spoke with a rough accent pitched low.

"Understandable," Cadeck encouraged.

"What about...?"

Cadeck hushed Tesh's words expecting the conclusion of his sentence. Two of the Saratian detail stayed with the wagon to move it for parking. A pair of guards escorted Tesh and Cadeck into the awaiting gates of the stronghold, keeping their distance behind the Silvetzenian officers.

Tesh and Cadeck sifted through rugged hallways lined with flaming torches ensconced in black iron chandeliers. Ashen soot scarred the ceiling and the walls smelled of a mildew flavor trickling onto the tongues like rotting beer as the soldiers moved them like cattle through ill lit halls, down flights of stairs to a wing used as a cellar. The first officer stopped at a small door of wooden plank and opened it to reveal a small windowless room lit with a single lamp. The drab air rushed into the hallway unchanged from the sooty aroma stinging their nostrils.

A rat scuttled across one of the beds dropping onto the floor before disappearing in the darkness below one of the frames leaving a pile of globular feces in its wake. The room seemed more fitting for a political prisoner than an official envoy of dignitaries.

"This is your quarters. You are to remain here and allowed only to see Her Highness during the daylight."

Cadeck nodded his head as Tesh's face befell a curious glance. The officers exited the doorway closing the door behind as if to seal the pair's fate.

"What's this all about, Cadeck?"

Cadeck settled his satchel upon one of the beds, scooted the rat droppings away and set his aging frame upon the soft hay. He scratched his stubbly beard in thought allowing the oily light to sting his nose.

"Standard procedures, my boy. As the acting Magi, I must not allow myself access to interact with the parties taking part in official discussion should a sovereign ask for the Council to preside upon diplomatic purposes until requested by a formal audience."

"I do not know if I can acclimate to these 'official procedures.' It is all confusing."

Tesh moved to seat himself upon the opposite bed. Shards of hay stalks poked through bitten holes in the molded mattress cover.

"Do not worry. As a Knight, it was never the duty for them to interact. Only act on the Council's blessings to invoke peace through force."

"War?"

"No. Far from it," Cadeck ignored the odor of mildew rot covering his bed, "The Council of Magi saw the Knights as a practical mediator. A brigade of Knights could take out whole armies and for this reason kings feared them. As a precaution, the Magi used the Knights sparingly and only as a last resort among the affairs of man."

"What about Cassica, and Venna and Eris?"

"I am certain they will be fine. We would do best to bed soon, to not lend more of our words to Silvetzenian ears posted outside."

But Cadeck was wrong. A pair of gargantuan tanks of men flanked the doorway covered in sheen raven armor lit from the grimy fires. Shaved stubble covered rounded heads marked with scars of battle wear across their chiseled, red-tinged faces. They carried war pikes topped with serrated blades anchored against their outside arms. A crimson symbol, an open circle with eight, fine-lined spokes emanating in symmetry scarred along their breastplates.

As a nervous performer, Cassica paced within her lavish chambers. Her crimson dress flowed behind her as a fresh flow like lava gracing the finely cut stone floor beside her canopy bed as Venna and Eris prepared the sleeping arrangements. A sturdy armoire stood across from the bed close to a beauty stand, plush couches upholstered with exotic furs supplied creature comforts to the diplomatic party. Rathmana's kitschy portrait displayed prominently above the fireplace as it burned warm embers into the room.

Cassica brushed her brow, moving a single strand of scarlet bangs behind her ear shifting her dazzling emerald hairpieces fastened against the back of her head. She walked an index finger across a daintily laced sleeve absorbing the fine textures of her outfit. She turned back away from the bubble-paned window to face the blonde maiden who remained silent awaiting her mistress's word.

The maidens replaced their formalities with simple, loose-fitting tunics and leggings befitting their agile frames.

"Venna, Eris," Cassica spoke in command. On request, the girls ceased their activity as the pair paused to listen.

"You must go quickly and find our contact. I do not know where Cadeck and Tesh stay, and this uncertainty makes this situation unbearable. If her information is vital to the Magi, Cadeck must be aware. Eris, bring a message to Sorithen, inform him I wish to be privy to the location of my entourage. Since I brought the Magi in my envoy, I should be welcome to his council at any time. Girls, go."

Obediently, Venna and Eris bowed their heads, exiting the chambers as commanded. Cassica pulled at her fingertips, reaching up to bite at her delicate nails. She paused again after the first two nips before devolving her emerald eyes into worrisome, blank stare at the cold stone floor.

Chapter 14

Elegant and fruity perfumes mixed with the aroma of blooming flowers flowed through the room with a sense of freshness and luxury. Quaint chairs of elegant upholster lined against a wall with a large mirror in landscape display sprawled above them. Pastel paints covered the walls sprinkled by the light of a chandelier hung from the arcing atrium of the foyer. A nearby quartet played music on harps and stringed instruments in the lavish parlor room clothed in fine linen attire. In this room of sophisticated inhibitions, Venna's innocence stuck out like a delicate flower mired by thorns.

Men cavorted in the chamber with ladies of several sizes and attraction in a display of undress. Silvetzenian aristocratic dandies conversed amongst each other, laughing, and cavorting with an ensemble of courtesans who returned their amusements over wine and ales. While Si'rai dark-skinned men rudely fondled a naked woman standing between them. Some of the more unsavory types, brusque perverts who managed to gather some coin to partake of the establishment, licked their lips towards Venna's direction.

"Meh I hep ya?"

An aging voice called from behind beaded curtains.

The Madam came forward, dressed in a lavish gown flowing pink across her frame, a corset pushing her sagging, rotund bosom in a grotesque elegance of wrinkled beauty. Strings of golden tendrils weaved within her salty hair lining them like a spectacle of opulent pageantry.

Venna's body tensed up. Her spry frame paused as her eyes fleeted around the parlor room. She fidgeted in her position, unaware of how to answer.

"A' ya he'r to find work missy?"

"No, I'm here to find a friend."

"A friend? Yule fin' manee friends he'r." The madam's accent spoke as a drunken mule, "Ladies."

On command, a bevy of women clad in various disarray of dress entered the parlor entrance from behind the beaded curtain. The ladies came in diverse sizes; spry and lissome like Venna while a couple of others were large as the concierge. Venna spied blondes, brunettes and ginger headed women, but none of them looked familiar. Each of the women displayed low taste; missing teeth, displeasing odors, scrummy hair in all places and one whose face scarred with an old burn.

"I mus' apahlagyze, girl. But my bes' girls are with the King on th's evenen. He has speshul gests t'night."

The madam's breath blew the foul stench of liquor as she spoke to Venna's virgin nose. Venna studied the dregs again, each of them enticing the young maiden to make her special.

"Or p'haps, you may want to join us to help the men?"

"No. I must apologize for taking your time, madam. I imagine your ladies find no complaints amongst their clientele, but I must decline your offers and return to my stay."

Venna revolved towards the elegant double doors and exited the parlor chambers into the frosty night. Disdain scarred her innocent face upon the sight she had just beheld as she made her way past dim lit buildings and inclined-roof homes. The stench of unbridled inhibitions and perverted sophistication lingered around her longer than she liked. Her training as a Rose required her to be accustomed to the sophistications and at times the underbelly of the world to form her to become an excellent assassin should she obtain such role. She thought that using any means at her disposal to get to her potential targets was not her calling. *I am staying chaste. I am never giving myself to a man after seeing chaotic spectacle.*

Sorithen Rathmana's private chambers prevailed as vulgar as he existed. Portraits of the perversely vain king adorned his lavish antechambers as he surrounded himself with a diversity of courtesans in stages of undress. Lamplights flickered on torches and sconces around the room, bathing the garish hallway in a splash of orange flame flickering amidst the soft faces of the ladies. He gorged himself on fruits and meats while a brunette woman with a flaunty bosom pampered him by massaging his fingertips. Sorithen sprawled lengthwise against the plush cushion sinking under his corpulent opulence as he shifted his weight.

His mouth salivated with the juices of his indulgences dripping onto the spidery weaves of hair crawling across his naked, rotund chest. Girls giggled and cavorted with his actions only to laugh at him in his obese display of sickly engagements. One of his guards entered the chambers. Sorithen groaned in the guard's direction as a dominant male would meet his rival.

"What do you want?"

Sorithen yelled to his guard visibly shaken by internal fears. Splattered fruit juices dribbled out of his rotund lips, the unmistakable stench of filth and sweat coalesced around the folds of his torso.

"Your Majesty, Her Grace, the Princess from Sarat, sends a messenger."

Eris stepped forward. Her frail frame caught Sorithen's eye in rotund glee. Eris was an elegant creature; naïve, clean, fresh, unlike these harlots occupying his room. Her simple tunics flowed below her hips advancing with a pair of loose leggings fit against her ankles. A brunette courtesan seated at Sorithen's feet shot her attention towards the young lady as she followed inside.

Eris swallowed her pride trying to hide her discomfort of the scene. She advanced towards the perversion as the soldier closed the massive iron doors behind her, sealing her with the king as the only man in the room amidst the congregate of whores.

"What does my cousin want, little girl? Or did she send you to pleasure me in her absence?"

Eris stopped on his question to engage the scents of fruits and ales mixed with the sweat of corpulent flesh. Her eyes shrunk in displeasure of his advance. She carried herself not as a regal official but as a disgusted woman taken offense by his gesture. She collected her thoughts and regained her composure trying to conceal her feelings towards him.

"Her Highness requests unrestricted audience with the Magi and kindly inquires why this access is being denied as she brought him here."

"Inform Her Highness she knows the procedure when Magi join in diplomacy. He and his Adept are not to remain alone in secret chambers with any singular party of this treaty unless all parties are involved. Tell Her Highness our mutual partner needs a week of preparedness. They plan some sort of surprise for us. Now, you can either dismiss yourself, or come over here to pleasure me."

Sorithen slid his trunk-like fingers within the loose trousers falling from his rotund waist and approached his loins. His hand bulged inside his pants, moving like a spider against his genitalia causing Eris to voluntarily excuse at his debauched display. In defeat, Eris retreated through the doors shaking her head to remove the memories of the encounter.

Sorithen consumed his pleasantries throughout the evening ending in the sleeping stench of sweat and the sour aroma of semen filtering in the air. Girls cooed and slept along his dais, a single blonde courtesan rested her head next to his naked loins, his hand lazily entwined within her hair. An auburn-haired girl resting at his feet sat up, gazing across the bevy of sleeping women she entertained with.

Her locks remained unhampered while she wore a sheer top piece fitted over her ample chest accentuating with a frame of athletic measurements. She moved in grace, careful not to allow the trinkets hanging from her translucent leggings to stir her compatriots to wake. She slid her left hip across a sleeping girl, the slit in her legging moved in action to uncover the soft ink tattoo of a thorny red rose marked upon her hips. Her feet touched softly in response to the cold stone floor as she glided with ease towards the front of the chambers.

Carefully, she opened the giant iron door while the guard studied the action with curiosity. She slithered herself through the slim opening of the door and slid the door to its closed state. The guard paused, blocking her advancement down the hallway holding his lance across his chest to ready it for action.

"Where are you going?" His scruffy voice whispered to command, "You were paid to remain the night."

She slid her elegant hands behind his unarmored neck in soft embrace as if to pleasure his ear with her tongue. Eyes glistened like storm-washed seas flirting with his emotions in the soft light. A tongue graced his ear sensually as she glided a small metal pick from beneath her flowing hair and swiftly poked the guard in the soft flesh below his jawline. He started to groan before she covered his mouth with her caressing hand. The guard collapsed to the floor in mild convulsions.

She carried herself through the darkened hallways dimly lit with torches and wrought iron sconces. Two Saratian guards stood outside the doorway covered in simple, gray tunics marked with the Saratian double-headed eagle. A pair of armored boots rose to their knees, trousers tucked neatly within the shin guards, and a belt tied around the waist slightly above the tail of their tunic shirts. The woman sprinted in their direction approaching the guards with the grace of her profession. Likewise, the Silvetzenian, the two men crossed the doorway with their standing pikes. She split her leggings along the slit to reveal the mark on her hip.

Ignoring their obvious, manly desires, the guards recalled the calling card, nodded their heads, and eased their stance allowing the lady entry into Cassica's chambers. The double doors popped open unnerving the still-awake guests inside. Firelight crept along the walls of the room, creating dancing shadows of flicker. The high windows reflecting the orange glimmer, as the smells of candle soot and native plants arranged for their elegance filled the room. Cassica sat on her bed still dressed in her regal crimson dress as Venna turned from her duties tending to Cassica's hair towards the intruder as the guards returned the doors to their closed position.

Venna stared at the intruder, their eyes met to familiar gaze. Cassica followed the woman's pasty skin mottled by the flickering lamps towards the tattoo barely visible from the sheer leggings. She bore the mark of the Red Rose, the secretive line of the Order of the Rose who acted upon the actions of the Order in covert handlings. Cassica's contact.

"Your Highness," the brunette woman bowed to the princess.

Cassica rose, permitting Venna to slide to the side of the mattress and in polite response, curtsied to the gesture.

"Your name, Justiciar."

"Rensel. Rensel Fiasti," her voice spoke in High Accent of the Saratian noble class.

"Ladies, retire to your chambers for the evening."

Cassica turned to Venna then to Eris as the pair bowed in obedience, gracing their socked feet upon the marble floor, and exited towards a door painted in pastels with gold trim. The handle obscured to the structure walls of the chambers in the shape of an eagle's head. Twisting the knob, the pair opened the door outward towards their antechambers and sealed the room shut to leave Cassica and Rensel to their own audience.

"You may speak freely, Rensel."

"I hear rumor you arrived with a Magi?"

"You have heard truth. There is a Knight Initiate traveling with him to the Temples to become a Temple Knight."

"Then, our situation is more dire than I have surmised."

Cassica's eyes widened amidst the candlelight awash with a new sorrow, "Continue."

"I do not have much time, Your Highness. Through my contacts and endeavors, I have surmised the Si'rai do not plan peace, they plan to assimilate the two nations in exclusive agreement. The signatories would turn over their respective sovereignty to the Si'rai."

"Then the Magi was right."

Cassica stooped to the bed, her dress painting the white linens in a crimson flow pouring towards the drab, cold floor. She returned to prodding upon her fingers, her eyes awash in sadness as the emerald darkness before a storm.

Cassica returned her gaze towards Rensel, "Do you know where he is being kept, Rensel?"

"The east wing of the castle, there is a lower chamber below the grand atrium. He is there with another man whom I assume is this Initiate. What is this Magi's name?"

"Cadeck Wenfier. The other man, his name is Tesh Verdui."

"Verdui?"

Rensel sunk her head as if to hear her heart strung like a lute unravelling its strings. *No, certainly he is no relation to the rugged man you fell in love with. Verdui is just a common name.*

"Yes, is something wrong?"

"No, Highness. But I have not heard this Magi's name before. Are you sure he is part of their ranks?"

"I have seen him use magick and he has been a friend to my family for years. I am fully confident in his abilities."

"His name did not appear on the records."

"But why would he not be listed?"

Rensel's mind raced towards thoughts only she knew, "Unless the census removed him? He may know the reason. It is starting to make sense."

"What is?"

"I need to speak to him. Find out the truth of the information I carry."

"Rensel, find him, please. Inform him of the situation."

"Yes, Your Highness."

Rensel curtsied in respect to her liege and excused from the room as the door sealed shut with a soft crash. Cassica turned back to somber tone, standing to move towards the expansive window beside her canopy bed, the dress flowing as a waterfall ending in a frilly, scarlet pool around her feet. Her silhouette drowned out the candlelight behind her, allowing her to see the darkness of the city dotted with random blazes of warming fires.

Cassica pressed her hand against the cool window glass peering across the landscape strewn with armored soldiers encased in Si'rai livery along the rooftops below. They worked like beasts along the ramparts and balconies installing rigging and ropes calling to one another, barking orders as men constructing buildings. Their curses were inaudible and in unintelligible tongue through the glass but could clearly decipher commands being issued and followed and superiors yelling mad obscenities to humiliate their greenhorns. *What they were doing and why*, she had wondered. The future of her kingdom lied at stake with the information Rensel presented and what Cadeck could prove.

Chapter 15

The image seared deep upon Tesh's visions. A sharp blade penetrated through a frilly scarlet dress evacuating below the woman's breastbone, blood dripped in sheen drops down the sharp length of the weapon. Each drop rained upon the stone rampart like a ticking clock. Streams of gargled blood crept from the creases of the woman's soft lips mingling with strands of crimson bangs like mangled strings of thread. She struggled in vain to remove the blade from the front of her chest as it thrust deeper, impaling her behind her back. Her neck jerked in reaction to the deeper thrust.

Tesh save us.

The sharp weapon withdrew from the front of her body as she dropped to her knees, slumping into a limp position in front of her assailant. A dark figure towered the woman like a menacing shadow draped in black robes along the height of the body.

Show yourself, Azthar Kherdmon, so all may suffer.

The voice rang deep as a choir filled with bass voices echoed from the eons past. A voice heard through cyclic iterations into ancient time. It was a voice he had heard before, but not within his current expanse of life.

Cassica, I am sorry.

Tesh screamed as he awoke from his sinister vision part from pain and part from fright. He clutched his left hand as it throbbed incessantly, glowing in tendrils of magical light arcing across his forearm and knuckles tracing his gold-laced veins through his skin. His groans continued in long tones as the pain intensified shifting Cadeck in his slumber next to him.

"What's wrong, boy?"

Cadeck grunted as his body tried to wake.

"Cadeck, my arm, it surges with pain."

"What do you mean?"

Cadeck shifted his body and rose into a seated position scratching the sleep from his eyes in the dim lamplight. The whisper of a rat scurry squeaked beneath the beds. Streaks of lightning sparked through Tesh's fist, ceased in mid-clutch, as the feelings of rigor mortis settled upon only the left arm. He stood to his feet, stepping next to Tesh as he sat upright in his bed. Cadeck's eyes awakened to the sight.

"You possess True Spirit, not seen in Aeons."

"I know Cadeck," Tesh grimaced with disdain, "We have discussed this already. How does this stop?"

"I do not know, Tesh. It is a legend not seen in thousands of years. Tell me, what happened."

"I saw," Tesh scowled, his pain shooting through his arm in muscle spasm.

"I saw pain, suffering. I saw Cassica murdered by a robed figure. He called to me and told me all will suffer if I show myself."

"Your vision, it is a possible outcome."

"Outcome? I do not want to see this outcome."

"Then we should leave soon. The longer we stay, the longer it delays your training."

"What's going on in there?"

A booming voice commanded from the other side of the door.

"Bad dream," Tesh yelled in return.

The sturdy door crept, squeezing sausage-sized fingers covered in thick onyx armor through the break as they clutched the edge of the wooden portal. Tesh's wounded arm sprung to full spread arcing in purple tendrils swimming through his veins and knuckles. The brute squeezed through the opening; snug armor fitted to his body. Cadeck eased his right elbow behind him, crossing his left arm across his chest; tendrils of yellow energy hesitated across his finger movements as he tickled the air spaces between his hands like wisps of limp, golden feathers. A sphere ignited within his palms. He steadied his position, conjuring the orb to hesitate before striking, thinking of his target's threat assessment.

But Tesh beat him to the punch. In a reflexive motion, Tesh spurred towards the guard, leaping from his bed in one swift motion, and squeezed his left hand around the guard's high neck sending surges of violent magical pulses coursing through the soldier's body. He lay helpless, convulsing as a blinding light absorbed his muscular mass. His body dissolved in the light flare; atoms of his individual flesh disintegrated as energy pattern into destruction leaving only a hulk of armor behind like a black shell.

The other soldier fell silent, collapsing to the ground as if attacked by an unknown assailant. Tesh straddled his dissolved enemy, his knees bent across the abandoned armor. He could not move. Tesh's body froze in rigor as he processed the stream of magical energies flooding his senses.

"Can you do that again?"

A sultry voice of High Accent appeared from behind the door covered by the fragrant taste of exotic perfumes indulging the stale air of the room.

Tesh turned to the direction of the voice moving his eyes, following his nose across the athletic female in thinly clothed attire standing before him. His hormones took the best of him, but his speech stopped short of making an advance. He hesitated to speak only to collapse backward from the unfolded events.

Cadeck regained composure, releasing his hands from his magical energies. He dropped to Tesh's side and clutched Tesh below his shoulder blades. Cadeck struggled to move Tesh's legs over the hefty breastplate once worn by the massive guard. Rensel snaked her way into the small room, swiftly closing the door behind her. In the frail light, her fit frame silhouetted her features as if she were an entrancing entertainer.

Her washed-emerald eyes percolated in the fire light set amidst her brunette locks. Cadeck ignored her sensual figure, asking her to help him get Tesh onto the small cot. Rensel stared at Tesh's tapered frame, his face struck familiarity. She studied him deeper in her thoughts as they raced towards a past life she would soon rather forget. *No, he is not your love.*

"Who are you and what do you want with us?"

"My name is not important to you, but yours is to me."

"If you are here to kill us, I warn you it will not be easy," Cadeck swanked.

In Rensel's eyes, his pitted face had etched with years of abuse and confidence. She had no reason not to doubt his boast. He looked like a fighter; one she would have no trouble bringing down with her training. She sensed an air of worry in his inflections, as if the older man before her had nothing to lose. The receding smell of electrical energy wafted from Cadeck's rough frame as seared by lightning yet unharmed.

"Which one of you is the Magi arrived with Her Highness?"

Cadeck's ears perked into observation. This virile woman knew of his existence, what is more, she knew of his profession. Cadeck leaked a whisper as he spoke his next words.

"You are an assassin of the Order of the Rose, are you not?"

Rensel stepped back. Nerve endings in her scalp reminded her she had one poison barb in her hair. It would be enough to knock out the aged man who inquired of her profession, but she would have to be inventive with the young man. She had no reason to harm either as the man on the cot had taken out the larger adversary with a manifestation of magick.

"What do you know about me?"

"I know I travel with three others of your Order. Judging how you handled the guard outside; you must be a Red Rose."

Rensel lifted the lining of the thin strand around her waist to reveal the small thorny tattoo of the elaborate pedals of her Order.

"My name is Rensel Fiasti," she whispered, "Again, I ask who you are."

Unthreatened by her tone, Cadeck obliged, "Cadeck Wenfier, Magi of the Temple of Light, this man over there is Tesh Verdui. I believe you may have information to help us get to the Fire Temple."

Rensel nodded her head. *Verdui. Oh, he does look like your love, but you cannot get your revenge today.*

"I can discuss the details about getting you to the Fire Temple, but Cassica requires your presence."

"I cannot leave him here. Eventually the Si'rai will discover one of their guards is missing and the other is dead. We cannot leave him here alone. We must complete his journey to the Temples. He is to be a Knight. If the Si'rai discover him here, he is dead."

"How long will he be out?"

Cadeck monitored Tesh's hibernation and rubbed Tesh's forehead. He traced his fingers along the golden canals carved into his palm as the etched scab dissolved marginally into his skin.

"I have no idea. But your handiwork outside may lend suspicion."

"This room is nearly cut off from the rest of the castle, it may be several days before they change duties."

"Bring him in here then tell me what you know about this treaty."

Rensel glided outside the door, peering down the hallway in observation for other soldiers. Cadeck followed behind, picking up the soldier by his feet as they dragged him inside, struggling to lift him mere centimeters above the ground straining from his bulk. The door squeaked close as minuscule as a mouse as Rensel kicked the soldier with her feet moving him slowly out of the walkway.

The soft hay cushioned Cadeck as he sat next to Tesh studying the injury in his left hand.

"What happened to him, Magi?"

Her eyes followed Cadeck's hands across Tesh's injury.

"Magick," his tone was abrupt, ending any continuation of exposing secret knowledge before shifting focus to his questions.

"But your information is more important. Tell me, woman, what do you know about the treaty with the Si'rai?"

"They have assimilated their forces within Silvetzen as you may have seen. A few miles outside the city, the Si'rai have built a camp blockading traffic to the harbor. The treaty would bring Si'rai troops unabated into their lands, and eventually a pathway through all Rykana."

"Conquest by consent. What of the sovereigns?"

"I did not discover, Magi."

"What you did not discover remains a secret and for suspicious reasons. Her life and Sorithen's are in grave danger. Before Tesh awoke, I heard him yell out Cassica's name then commented about great pain."

"His?"

"No, everyone. When is the treaty scheduled for signatory?"

"The Si'rai Command has held off. The officers have requested a full seven sunrises before signing the treaty. They wish to plan it when the moon is fully dark for this cycle."

"They plan something," Cadeck's thoughts pondered upon Tesh's vision, "they would not intend the timing to coincide with the moon unless," Cadeck's thoughts paused with his whispering words before he turned to another subject.

"When can we meet with Cassica?"

"Sorithen has denied you access until the signing of the treaty."

"Inform His Bloatness, the Magi will have no accord with the Si'rai, and I wish to leave this abomination of protocol."

Rensel swallowed her saliva blinking her eyes at his remark, "I am afraid, Magi, all parties involved believe otherwise. I did not hear you would be the Magi in presence, but a Magi named Godwen."

"Godwen? What about him?"

Cadeck's face decreased into stewing dismay.

"He had agreed to act for the Council as a representative."

"The Council would never work in an agreement with the Si'rai. Godwen is aware of history."

"But the Council themselves signed a treaty with the Si'rai did they not?"

Cadeck sunk, feeling his heart plummet deep within his torso. Eons of training, legends and tradition disappeared as if the fires of history torched ancient libraries. Cadeck choked, his breathing simmered to shallow as his palms welted with sweat and strained to hold his tightening fist. Tears welled within his eyes as a lonely trickle streamed down his left cheek.

"You retreat your statement or be accused of blasphemy against the Council."

"I make no remorse for my statement, Magi. What I say is true."

"When?" Cadeck's tone grew darker, his face scowling with discontent.

"I hear about two harvest seasons ago as the harvest gave way to the low-sun."

No. "Decided by Quorum. If the Council has betrayed mankind, then we must leave with Cassica swiftly. If we can save one kingdom, the people of Roth may have a chance. Cassica said you may know how to make it to the Fire Temple?"

"I followed a Magi to a volcanic ridge southwest of here, but he detected my presence and left me behind a wall of flame preventing my advance. I pursued him to try and confirm the information I have obtained."

"Philos. Either he is complacent or did not wish one of the profane to follow him. Right now, I suspect the former. How far of a ride?"

"Not long, two weeks by horse and cart, longer by walk."

"I would rather not stay for what the Si'rai have planned, but we must remain to prevent suspicions from arousal. Can you prepare an evacuation procedure?"

"I have made contingencies for all possibilities to leave Silvetzen and have routed accordingly."

Cadeck grinned, allowing a burly smile along his pitted face, "Rensel, as I suspect which to not be your real name, perhaps one day your sister will be on par with your skills."

Rensel ignored his assumption, darting her eyes to his statement. In her mind she fidgeted to scurry from his words betraying her outward poise. Cadeck continued, "What about our friend on the floor, he is surely dead?"

"No Magi, the poison I administered is a mild intoxicant administered directly into his blood. He will feel like he just woke up from a long night of heavy drinking and whoring with the stain in his pants to show the latter. We should take measures to secure him before he wakes."

"How long and will he remember anything?"

"The most he'll remember is hitting the floor in about several hours."

"We do not have much time. You need to return to your position before they notice your absence. Help me get him back outside, and when he wakes, he can answer his own questions. I will deal with the other armor."

Cadeck strained as he lifted the large man once again. His muscles bulked as the soldier's arms spread wide at the shoulders under Cadeck's grip. Rensel fared little better as she struggled with the man's feet.

"What are they feeding their soldiers?" Rensel gasped.

"The flesh of virgins and the blood of young boys. Vile men occupy the Si'rai lands."

Somehow, I believe the Magi.

They dropped the man into the hallway producing a clumsy thud. Cadeck tipped his head to the young woman. Rensel curtsied in response before evacuating like howling winds through the cramped hallway. Cadeck returned to his room seating himself to Tesh's side. The flesh tears marred by the golden veins trickled with an electrical arc pulsating over his arm.

Tesh remained sleeping, his breathing slow and steady as he lay in peace. No dreams, no visions, no horrors. Cadeck sensed his mind through his aztmudin. Peaceful dreams permeated as the wounded hand streaked in soft streams of preternatural energy. Tesh's wound reacted to the tracing of Cadeck's fingers against the golden scab, following the yellow tint lining his ventral veins. As the energies pulsed within his hand, Tesh startled slightly with each jolt.

Cadeck muttered a prayer in a rolling speech exquisitely pronouncing his vowels as the consonants emphasized in return. He prayed to his god, Aeus, turning remorseful as he muttered Godwen's name in curse. Tesh's wound reacted in kind reflecting the strong powers emanating from the Magi.

He continued to pray focusing on thoughts of his sadness wrought by his excommunication. His children, Wrem and Dal and his bond mate, Jess the last Water Magi. He recalled the last moment he saw his children; the trio separated by cramped cages leading to different ships. He knew nothing of their fate after the Si'rai magisters obeyed their commands and sailed the family across the ocean.

Cadeck felt a tug at his loose-fitting pants to see an illusion of his blonde-haired boy clutching at his leg. Glazed tears fogged Dal's brown eyes as he called his father's name.

Dal, are you safe? Where's Wrem?

Cadeck spoke to his vision not expecting an intelligible answer from his subconscious dreams. The ghostly boy did not speak, only trailing off as to walk towards the corner of his room.

Wait? Dal?

"Dal."

But his boy did not answer as Cadeck pawed at his knee expecting his son to be there.

Chapter 16

Lumbering alone amidst a modified dock, a massive warship loomed as a towering city against the boreal landscape nearby. An armada of thin landing boats stretched the shorelines, unleashing thousands of raven clad men decked with full war readiness. Tivius A'zum stood along the harbor line of the docks, listening to the clamor of the distant platoons and the smattering of waves crashing the beachhead. As specks in the distance, a fleet of ships weighed anchor in the vicinity of the harbor, forming a crescent blockade leading towards the mainland. Beside him stood Field Marshal Jabar, his silver armor glistened in the cool autumn sunlight. A slight breeze ruffled the crimson plume in his helmet. Tivius stood beside him, encased in his leathers, and swaddled by a cape. Where his pale skin broke through, ritual scars marred his flesh.

Tents and temporary barracks littered the close encampment to the sequestered docks filled with soldiers armored in the sable protection of Si'rai gear as they toiled and marched in disciplined motions. Commanders barked orders to the incoming waves of new soldiers. Si'rai soldiers occupied buildings and blocks of confiscated warehouses along the pier. Armored men committed to their orders while workshop trade continued to the retrofitting of the Si'rai accompaniment and their needs.

A wide, solitary ramp angled upon the mooring leading from the immense vessel like a large, blackened tongue ready to devour its meal. Upon the wharf, the gargantuan ship succumbed the periphery of view like the silhouette of a dark sky. Sails did not form on this ship of satin or silk, but of a cloth inorganic and mystical in the way they directly absorbed sunlight and constructed of sinister magick. The ship itself an amalgamation of horror and elegance. Organic design meets function.

A contingency of eight beings, dressed to appear as men and clothed with entirety, flowed from the gangway. Raven armor enclosed their frames as sanguine capes slung around their backs like scarlet waterfalls as they floated down the ramp of the vessel docked in front of Tivius. Long skirts covered what may have been feet, they hovered like floating wraiths over the ground. Their heads covered in organic looking helmets to appear like faces whose eyes glowed a dull blue and indistinguishable from the masks. The bodies covered beneath the armor with obsidian fabric where like the ship, appeared to absorb all light.

No heralds marked their armor plating which morphed and transmogrified over the formation of the bodies to their movements. The guards stopped short of the commanding officers, turning to face in file along the foot of the ramp path. On the precipice of the ramp, a menial stature of crimson robes stood in presence like a bloodied ghost as the piked men at the base of the ramp readied for his arrival.

A pair of grotesque statues flanked the ramp to the height of the hull from the keel. Incongruous statuary formed to the shape of tortured souls. Their forms made to appear of eternal pain with the shape of the mouths emanating the glow of orange lantern light. Rhythmic tapping of a gnarled cane along the wooden plank pronounced the arrival of the man standing at the height of the ramp. The robed ghost's presence commanded all nearby to pause to attention. Tivius and Jabar fell to one knee and bowed their heads until the man shadowed their humble respects at his feet.

"Rise," his voice commanded his rank to those around him in the tongue of the Imperium.

The gentlemen obeyed. Tivius pierced his eyes towards the noble man hidden within a deep crimson hood.

"Your presence is unexpected, Iostana Magistrata." Tivius addressed the man as Most Revered Magister.

"I am not here to purvey your accomplishments, Lord A'zum."

The robed man's jowls sneered in scowl hidden beneath a deep cowl. Moving as a phantom in the early morning sun, the figure floated ahead of his inferiors. Jabar and Tivius followed a pace behind, the flowing sea of decorated armor behind them. The boots of the living men crushed a trail of footprints within the early morning snowfall, a precursor reflective of their intents.

"I presume my accommodations have been prepared in advance of our engagement?"

A frail finger excavated from the figure's right-side billowing from the robed sleeves in advance of Tivius' processions.

"Your Reverence, your presence is," Tivius swallowed, "surprising."

As a force slammed against a thick wall, the figure stopped his stride, "You had adequate time to prepare. The Guardian tells me you were informed of my arrival."

Tivius felt the impact of the superior's question as if he were the unstoppable force slamming into his wall, "My Lord, my men work with fervor. Your residence is in construction."

174

"If it pleases Iostana Magistrata, you may stay in my command bunker," Jabar offered, bowing his head.

"Of course, Jabar."

The trio of men continued into the encampment, rising upon a hill separating the outskirts of city from the docks along the beachfront below. Si'rai soldiers ceased their activity, falling to one knee in reverence of their God-King's avatar and murmuring prayers in their native speech. Many of the seasoned soldiers had only heard of their own God-King as an immortal being, Supernus Magister, as they knew him. Many faces existed in as many voices, but most never saw his visage. Even to his own legions, their ruler's face and true appearance remained mystery.

The avatar's commanding appearance sent waves of emotions searing across his men flooding them with an emotive response befitting the established personality cult. Hulks of soldiers erupted in sobbing drenches of glee as his presence blazed upon the camp as sacred fire. Campfires pilfered the air; roasting pots of scant meats and flatbread ovens hinted the simple breakfasts of the soldiers. Many who stopped in their activities appeared in various states of dress; armored, underclothing, or naked. Their solemn breaths rolled in patterned unison in the wintry air.

Armored men standing guard at Jabar's tent slid the double sheets open, splitting the herald to envelope its High Priest within its protection. He moved with grace and cane, seating himself into Jabar's desk embellishing his perfection amidst the Marshal's effects. Jabar emotively sunk in his fear as his liege's emissary took command at his own seat. The envoy raised his sleeves gripping his wide hood with his frail fingers and unsealed his balding head from the imposing confines.

Wavering eyes lingered thin within his face marking his age along a low-bridged nose. He reached into the collar of his elaborate robes and removed a monocle to place into his left eye. The ornate chair consumed him along with his enveloping vestments. As were the ship he arrived in, the robes likewise shared a form of fit to design embracing his frail body in a ghastly visage of crimson dye. Elaborate, regal, and befitting a man of his stature, his attire hefted heavily onto his body as his appearance deceived his ability to wear his manner of clothing.

As he began his speech, his mouth moved the aging jowls hanging below his necklines, "I have ordered a new legion to supplement your numbers. They will sweep the lands of this infernal kingdom, cooling the flames of any resistance. Field Marshal Jabar, your garrison will remain in city. I want the sovereigns executed upon the signatory of treaty."

Tivius scorned at the man's orders, clutched at his sword, and imagined in a single swipe, the figure before him would be gone, "Lord, Sorithen has informed me Cadeck and this, Tesh Verdui, are present in Silvetzen. Princess Cassica takes her father's place as envoy from Sarat. If he is to become this Azthar Kherdmon, I presume the executions of Cadeck, and this boy, are our top priority?"

The elder man opened with a sneer, "No, Tivius. I am only here to oversee the assimilation of Rykana," the older man turned to Jabar, ignoring the seething hiss from Tivius' lips.

"Has the envoy of Sarat been made aware of my arrival?"

"No, Lord. Sorithen has informed them our plans were to delay the signing of the treaty for a grand preparation," Jabar replied.

"Excellent. Jabar, send a messenger into town informing the parties the treaty will occur in two rakini." He commanded Jabar for his new timeframe of two days.

"Yes, my Lord," Jabar bowed, excusing himself from the quarters.

The emissary erected from the desk. Shorter in stature than Tivius, he gleamed over the maps and documents laying before him. Tivius cleared his throat, gripping at the braided hair hilt resting to his side.

"You would be wise to remove thoughts from your mind, Tivius."

Tivius released his hold upon his weapon, crossing his arms, "I trust your travels were safe, Magister?"

"More so than I can say for those who willed themselves in the service of our emperor to expedite our speed, but I am not here to discuss matters of our rites, Lord A'zum."

"Why did he send you, Magister Philatané? I am more than capable of overseeing this treaty in Silvetzen."

The older man peered up from his study. Aged, blue eyes peered along wrinkled nose to the towering man across the tent, "Your Raka'ir does not see it this way. Your encounter with Cadeck supplied the evidence Supernus Magister required of your failure and your unworthiness in his eyes. He commanded explicit orders to follow."

Philatané reminded Tivius of his failure in his father's eyes.

"The Azthar Kherdmon will grow in power if I allow him to live. He will bring the end of the Imperium."

"An Imperium you will never rule, Tivius."

Tivius gripped the hilt of his weapon once more, wrapping his spindly fingers around the hair braids sewn in jagged formations where portions of white bone were visible beneath the patterns.

"Cadeck and Cassica will not oblige to his treaty."

"He has counted on it. With or without her signature, his wrath will blanket her lands. Your Raka'ir has higher aspirations than the suffering of one Aztmi. Your raka'ir's plans are fulfilling flawlessly. Trebut sent his daughter in his stead. The treaty shall place her into our custody and sent to Abaddon. The seeds we have sown in his lands are bearing fruit."

A messenger burst into the command tent interrupting the exchange. He at once dropped to one knee in reverence to the men. His breaths bowled in visible moisture as his panting gave notice to his expended energy. Pores on his welterweight arms opened from the descending cold exposed by his slight tunic. He addressed the pair with proper title.

"Magisters, I bring message from the garrison in Silvetzen."

"Rise and speak," the older man proclaimed.

The messenger obeyed, "A soldier has turned up missing and his partner has been detained."

"Where were they stationed?"

Tivius turned to the man, folding his arms upon his chest.

"They were protecting the Aztmi and his Neophyte."

Tivius cracked a grin, "Inform their sergeant to remove the wervostri from post permanently and he is to assign a new guard as needed if the order has not yet fulfilled. Dismissed."

The messenger bowed in reverence, clicked his heels, and exited the tent.

"Tivius, I have no doubt Cadeck and his ward are connected to these wervostri's disappearance."

"Then allow me to deal with them."

"Do not arouse suspicion amongst our guests as the envoy from Sarat must continue to believe the parties in treaty are to continue protocol. This turn of events will feed into the fears of our host. He will trust us even more."

Tivius bowed with a slight smirk and turned to exit the command tent. Thoughts of contempt boiled in his mind as he marched towards his ramshackle confines. His confines suited Tivius, rather than lavish in extravagance but to mingle amongst the impoverished and filthy. They fit his style of ritual; dirty, grotesque, and obscene. The letting of blood eased his mind after spending his aztmudin. Tivius relished in the sacrifice of life to replenish his own.

Tivius' mystery guards stood to either side of the entrance to his shack, the female to his left and the male to his right. Neither said a word as he entered past them. Wood scarred with the chiseling of his sigils and hieroglyphs formed from the ancient tongue of his people meant nothing to the victims whose corpses littered the floor. Whereas no trace of his recent offering, the small blonde boy, lingered in his sanctum save for the various array of rotted meat taken from the corpse and set upon a workbench to the right of the room. Stench of decay stung at his nose like the pleasant odors of a fresh bath. He stripped bare, then pierced the hooks of the chains suspended from the ceiling into his shoulder blades.

Blood lamented from his wounds as he lay in suspension, curling his knees close to his chest. The chains creaked from the unsupported weight, wailing, and straining from the ceiling. Adrenaline pumped through his body as the pain continued unabated, blood seeping from his wounds to drip down his back in slow torrents.

Rivers snaked down his backside before collapsing into the circular sigil beneath him. His lips spoke slow chants as the drops soiled the muck where his sigil had drawn in the blood of old victims. Blood pooled in the center of the Sigil before easing, coalescing of its own sentience towards the inner circle. Flowing in form, his liquid stretched at the apex of the eight lines, easing towards the outer edges of the markings before encircling the drawn glyph upon the dirt. His mantras increased in vibration as more blood spilled down his backside.

With further chants, the markings on the ground erupted a small flame of purple hue, blazing around the inner circle to start before lighting in trails upon the spokes. Within moments, the full sigil had burned, the stench of copper flame filled Tivius' nose as the flames grew hotter and brighter to his magick. As the flames dissipated to a lull, the form of a silhouette took shape in the center beneath his feet, covered in the shadow hue of light lavender. A robed figure stood vigil over the circle as called into summons.

"You summoned for me, Lord A'zum?"

The figure hissed in disdain.

"Supernus Magister has denied me to take the lives of Cadeck and the Azthar Kherdmon."

"Then he has been found?"

The figure spoke with a feminine hint, speaking as to create a self-manifested echo of two separate auditory frequencies mashed together out of harmony.

"Yes," Tivius replied.

"He is still too weak for his power to be worthy. Claim him when the time is right."

"I will find the Temples and wait for him."

"With their deaths, we may proceed with our rebellion against Raka'ir, and our raki shall become the true Supernus Magister."

Upon the final words, the image within the center of the circle faded.

Tivius sword lay on the ground, the memory of the cave where he found it and the stench of corroding acidity still fresh in his mind. The image of the weapon embedded into a mummified corpse imprinted into his mind as to trace through hundreds of years of blood memories. Old death surrounded the weapon from a time where legends shadowed into myth. With each touch of its hilt, he heard suffering in whispers. Tivius craved the power the sword brought him with each use as thoughts of destroying his adversary perverted his mind.

Their rituals lay in blood and the sacrament with the Abyss above, his weapon blessed in covenant to his god. Tivius prayed to his god, where his people believed whose throne rested within the visible band of darkness in the nighttime sky. To his people, Tivius' father was the embodiment of their religion, their savior who would unite man under Si'rai rule ushering in a generation of peace. Apophadi. The prophecy emboldened those of pure Si'rai blood and whose merits were accountable with their faith in the Abyss. To appeal to his graces meant everlasting life in the Abyss, but to falter meant enslavement in the afterlife.

Tivius permitted his dogma to accentuate as he hung upon his cords. His icy stare shed no tears, only continual glare towards his weapon laying upon the murky saturation of mud and blood shaped to the eight-spoked sunwheel of his Imperium. He embraced the pain accentuating his nerves, the tendons through which the steel cut and the muscles which bled down his backside, snaked over the healed scars and wounds upon his pale flesh.

"You shall fall to my sword, Cadeck, then your peers. Then, my father."

Chapter 17

"I do not approve of this plan," Cadeck panted.

"It is our only chance. Besides, you seem to know about the danger Cassica faces."

"Yes, but leaving the castle now and violate protocols? So much for our cover," Cadeck shook his head towards Rensel.

"Cassica trusts your word, Magi. She has devised this escape based on what I have relayed to her."

Rensel pranced over the comatose soldier slumped in the hallway. This man was different, his facial features while Si'rai red skin, distinguished him as another individual. Her hair flitted side to side as she peered down each end of the passage. Her gentle fingers traced the pitted creases on Cadeck's palm reminding him of Jess' soft grace. He withdrew his hand from the careful aid Rensel granted him recoiling into his own emotions.

"What's wrong, I'm trying to get you out of here."

"I am sorry, but your hands. They reminded me of someone."

"We should discuss it later."

She threw a winking glance towards the older man.

"Of course, for now we need to move. Tesh, make haste."

"Right behind you."

Tesh reached for the dagger tying the scabbard to his hips. He hoisted the single satchel across his shoulder as he exited the musty, moldy room. With an assassin's grace, Rensel escorted Cadeck along the antechamber careful not to disturb loose mortar. Tesh followed a few meters behind, eyeing in amazement at Rensel's handiwork with the new guards.

Rensel craned her neck in either direction of the intersecting walkway. Her hair flittered in motion as her head jerked to face opposing ends to her left and right. A pair of Silvetzenian soldiers marched along the hallway in lockstep motion. Their chain mail clanked in syncopation; their sandals paced as feathers upon the stone. Red and white covered their surcoats, split down the center in two-tone. Thin helmets covered the tops of their heads like hats, leaving faces and neck exposed.

"How many?" Cadeck whispered, his back against the wall, embraced by the shadows.

Rensel crossed her right hand over her chest to hold up two fingers.

"Did you hear that?" One of the guards pointed out. His voice spoke like crushing rocks in broken Low Accent.

"Have you taken juyo before your shift? I heard nuttin'"

"I haven' drank since last night. I heard a voice," the first guard scolded in gravelly tone.

"Maybe one of those redbacks. Aren' they supposed to guard that wizard?"

"I have heard 'em speak. They do not speak Rykanian. They speak a foreign tongue I have not heard before. I heard Saratian accent."

Rensel steadied herself. She glided her left hand into the fitted tunics hugging her shapely hips removing a concealed stiletto between her index and middle fingers. The guards continued to listen for any anomalies. The sooty embers blowing from the torchlight flickered as dust in sunlight onto the floor.

"You're hearin' things. Come on. Our shift ends in a few hours, this hallway will not patrol itself."

"Aye, you're probably right."

The armor returned to lockstep clank as the soldiers continued patrol. Rensel guided Cadeck into the opposing direction. Her hips swayed in motion, gracefully propelling her in lithe sprint across the stone surface. Cadeck's age struggled to keep pace, his tunics ruffled against his skin. Tesh's satchel brushed against his tunics announcing their presence to the guardsmen.

"I told you I heard something," the first guard turned around to watch as Tesh stopped with frozen fear in mid-stride.

"Prisoners escaping," the second shouted.

Cadeck and Rensel readied for battle stance as Tesh removed his dagger. A piercing stiletto caught the advancing guard into his unprotected neck. Blood rushed along his braided armor, staining the metal with crimson rust as he grappled his wound in dying vain. The other soldier unleashed his sword to lunge towards Tesh. He blocked the advance as the sword swung overhead.

Like a predatory feline, Rensel pranced in motion towards the battle. She removed the fallen man's sword from the ground and in a broad sweep across her right hip cut the edge against the attacker's mail shattering cords of his protection onto the floor. His weapon reacted to his pain, sliding towards Tesh running parallel to the wall as the guard fell to his knees.

Tesh took the opportunity to lunge his dagger into the wounded man's clavicle erupting geysers of crimson upon his body. His dagger stood upon the man's shoulder as a testament to his action. The soldier's knees buckled sideways collapsing the man onto his left hip. Sprays of gore drowned the stone floor professing the horrible act.

"Nice teamwork. You manage yourself well for one untrained in martial combat."

"Thanks. I guess."

"Here, take this sword. You will need a new weapon."

Rensel handed Tesh the sword from her steal. He wrapped the sheath over his shoulder as Rensel rushed to catch up to Cadeck leading the way out of the antechamber. The rest of Rensel's planned escape involved avoiding further entanglements before leading into a lower hallway occupied by smelly game animals in preparation for slaughter as they approached a sewage grate along her planned route. Blood and refuse from the kitchen slaughters spilled down the grate and into the stench of wastewater below. Rensel pulled on the bar to release the mesh lid to the gate and slipped her shapely frame into the opening, dropping to her feet with a sloppy splash.

Cadeck followed as Tesh protected the rear. Realizing they were alone, Tesh followed into the sewage canal landing in the water with a slippery *thud*.

Rensel giggled, "Are you hurt?"

Her High Accent taunting Tesh's misfortune.

Tesh lifted himself from the murky smut, ringing his tunics from the dirty water staining his clothes. Tesh gagged as the reek drained from his clothing. His satchel remained dry, caught in Cadeck's hands as Tesh continued to drain the filth.

"I'd rather be hurt than wringing this filth."

Tesh threw her a terse glance of displeasure. He reached for the satchel from Cadeck's hands. He forced his hands into the satchel to remove a fresh change, tossing his dirty rags into the sewage canal. Rensel studied his movements as he removed his clothing revealing a slender frame culminated into loosely toned hips. She moved her eyes towards his manhood.

No, he is not your lover.

"Excuse me, Rensel. Do you mind?"

Rensel's cheeks disintegrated into a rosy blush. Her face decreased into a mixture of a mocking smile and displeasure. Not for her, but more for any lover Tesh may meet. Her hand moved to her lips to hide her insulting giggle at Tesh.

"My apologies, Tesh."

Cadeck moved past the juvenile conversation, "How much further till we get to your safe house?"

"A few blocks through the sewers. Cassica, Venna and Eris should have already made it."

"When you two are done flirting, we should hurry."

Tesh fit his shirt over his chest and picked up the sword over his shoulder.

"Trust me, Cadeck, I wasn't flirting," Rensel smiled.

Rensel floated past Cadeck in a swift gait. Following the torches burning the walls of the slimy passages, Rensel moved through her memories as she darted left, right, and other directions towards perceived west. Her sprints guided her as if she were a native inhabitant of these sewers, which Tesh did not know if she was playing the delicate courtesan as a ruse. Cadeck and Tesh struggled to keep up with the agile woman's nimble pace. After several minutes in the rotting wastes, Rensel came upon an exit highlighted by an escape ladder leading to the surface.

Climbing the ladder and skipping every other rung to hasten her lead, she reached the iron manhole above. She lifted the obstacle without a strain as she scanned the stillness of the street chilled by winter's touch. Rensel signaled an all clear to Cadeck below her as she lifted herself from the darkened waste pit. Cadeck's leg hampered his climb, as Rensel assisted his escape, grappling his hand as he drew closer. Tesh followed, passing his satchel and sword to Cadeck as he removed himself using the strength of both shoulders. Rensel replaced the manhole cover before the trio advanced along the soulless alley consumed in darkness save for a few burning lamps from windows overhead.

Amber lights flickered in frosted windows dimming activities of the various buildings nearby as they snuck through the peasant's district of Silvetzen. Two-story buildings lined the streets, various apartments and low-class shops surrounded the streets and alleys of their advances. Unlike the hovels met before, these buildings housed the majority of the bustling city's tenants and shopkeepers. Rensel reached the doorway of a small apartment and rapped on the door in a three-knock code. She repeated the short signal three times. Tesh recognized the pleasant, azure eyes peering into the cracked door into the outside alley. The door flung open quietly as Venna greeted them.

Soft glows from the oil lamps dimmed the scarlet features of Cassica's athletic frame accentuated in the loose fittings of a raven ensemble. Fitted trousers and a sleeveless shirt squirt her arms out of the fabric. Functional attire intended for rigorous athleticism. Eris laid out the hay mattresses upon the floor while Rensel greeted her superior with a soft nod. Venna closed the door from the chilled air creeping behind them.

A stitched-back chair made of cobbled craftsmanship beckoned to Cadeck's withered body as his mind continued to race. A pot of stew warmed over a fire pit next to him, wafting smells of warm meat and broth through the small room. Lamplight danced upon Cadeck's unwavering eyes as though every breath in the room waited on his words. Snowflakes of a new fall pecked upon the lone window beside Tesh in soft harmony.

"My apologies, Rensel, Cassica's plan worked."

Cadeck reached into his satchel rested upon his hip, removed a small pouch and his pipe. He pinched a small bit of seed and leaf into the chamber. Before taking a seat, he carefully removed a small piece of firewood from the hearth nearby and used it to light the narcotic. Sweet burn broiled through the room as he huffed on the smoke. Cadeck coughed from old lungs and chilled air brushing against his throat as he took a seat in the cobbled chair.

"Well, Cadeck, we have one plan. What about yours?"

"Of course, Your Highness. We need to leave soon, is your carriage ready?"

Cadeck consumed another puff.

"My guards have been aware of our intuitions, but we cannot leave tonight. Rensel tells me Si'rai guards patrol the streets with Silvetzenian men. There is an active curfew, and the city seals the gates overnight. I have also seen Si'rai soldiers working at night. They look like they are preparing for something."

"Preparing? A celebration of the treaty I imagine."

Tesh announced his observation as he moved away from the window. An unease washed over him at the sight of the small lamps burning on visible rooftops where Si'rai soldiers stood around on watch.

"Tesh, I imagine they plan their own form of celebration of which I do not wish to stick around to revel. Rensel, you recall the way to the Fire Temple?"

"Yes. Southwest of here."

"Good. The soldiers will ride in the empty carriage leading to Sarat. We on the other hand will evacuate in the hay cart Rensel can obtain."

"What?" Cassica protested, "I did not agree to this. I must return to Sarat in the carriage with word of the malicious intent of this treaty. We must have time to prepare troops, send order to the Houses to levy men to prepare for battle."

"Cassica, the vision I had, Cadeck feels you'll be safer with us."

Cadeck's eyes flickered with soft reflection from the fire to his side. He inhaled a long puff as the ash from the receptacle kickstarted into orange glow.

"Tesh is right," he exhaled.

Stinging aftertaste rippled down his throat, "You cannot leave with the soldiers. You must come with us. There is far less risk."

Venna followed Cassica's pace with her eyes as the princess carried across the small living space stopping short of Rensel's position. Cassica turned her attention to Tesh as her words came short of supplying tears.

"Vision, what vision? What do you mean?"

"I saw you on a balcony of a castle. A dark figure thrust his sword through your back to murder you. You cried for help, but I could not save you before he threatened me with an ominous warning."

"Are you bringing curse upon my sovereignty?"

She leaned upon the short table, slamming her palms upon the surface.

"No, Cassica. I mean no disrespect to your House. I cannot answer to where this vision came from. Only, my left hand surged with pain afterwards."

"I have attested to his vision, Cassica. He means you no harm. I have suspicion the Si'rai plan on vile intent upon you and Sorithen. You must return with us should his vision be true. We cannot defeat this evil alone. Tesh's destiny is with the Temples.

"The loss of two governments is inconsequential to the loss of mankind. You could return, sign the treaty, and allow the Si'rai to march into Sarat unabated and with little resistance. The people must see their intent firsthand so they might form a movement to fight the oppression. Even if Sarat falls, you must remain safe, so the people have hope of rebuilding.

"They will need a leader to light the lamp of their darkest hour; you must stand for their hopes as a leader. The decimation of the royal family would leave no hope among the people and the Si'rai would be victorious and our deaths as a result."

Cadeck's words etched into her heart as a mason would chisel into stone. The heavy burden drove her to pause as she seated herself on a small stool next to the single desk. Rensel moved a comforting hand onto her exposed shoulder. Cassica reached to embrace her palm in a motion of confidence and security.

Her mind raced to unimaginable thoughts of her kingdom burning in ruin as bright as the noonday sun. Thoughts of the crying and lamentations of her people scored her ears as unseen hordes pillaged the land. Streaks of tears boiled in her eyes upon the arcane thoughts. Her father's realm, destroyed, at the slightest wrong move, wrong thought, wrong plan of her doing burned into her chest.

"All those years ago, when I knew you as a child, your words have always been trustworthy. Tonight, they bear a heavy burden on my heart. With reluctance, I will agree to this plan."

"I promise you, Cassica, when Tesh completes his training, more will be gained than lost."

Cassica slumped in her emotions. Venna and Eris kept away, allowing the senior Rose to console the Princess. Tesh made attempt to move as Rensel shrugged him away with the sway of her head. But what if Cadeck was wrong? Would she be able to return to Sarat in time to save her kingdom and warn her father?

Tesh moved to make bed on the sturdy planks reddening his rear from weight seated upon them. His silhouette flickered amidst the soft light flushing the single room unit on the bottom floor of the building. He turned his attention to Cassica, watching her as her bold scarlet locks tugged at his thoughts, the lamp light highlighted the soft textures of her exposed skin.

Her darkened tunics flushed into form within the angular shadows as Rensel remained to her side. His mind raced to his vision at the Temple of Light, the scarlet woman coming to his aide seeking help of her own. Was she the vision? He looked upon her as though she was the entirety of the universe, his eyes drew concerned and yet, filled with awe as she caught him with brief glimpse, only to turn away towards the attention of her ladies.

"You like her, don't you?"

Cadeck took a puff of smoke. His fatherly whisper startled Tesh from his obsessions.

"What? Cassica? No," Tesh struggled to hide his embarrassment, "I am just a commoner, there is nothing I can offer to her. But she is beautiful as if the stars collapsed to Roth and what remained was her."

Cadeck chuckled at Tesh's naïve comment and placed a warm hand upon Tesh's shoulder.

"Do you think she's going to work along with your plan?"

"I hope so. For the sake of Sarat."

"Does she know? You know, about Godwen?"

"I haven't told them yet and I would hope Rensel has not either."

Cadeck placed his weight upon his withered shoes as he carried towards the small fire pit opposite his chair. He set his pipe upon the table, its sweet smoke rising into the room. The smell like home, a welcoming earthy taste upon the noses of the occupants soothing their minds. He grabbed a small clay bowl from beside the fireplace, seized the ladle and prepared a bowl of meal. He reached for the wooden spoons resting on a shelf and provided each occupant with a bowl of steaming food and a spoon. Venna and Eris indulged the morsels as they sat next to each other on short stools. Rensel remained to comfort her princess as Cassica picked at the meat chunks with her utensil, her head resting against her left palm.

"Food comforts the soul, my dear," Cadeck urged, discomforted by Cassica's denial of base stimuli.

Cadeck seated to the stool across from her. Toughened hands seeped through the tattered robes covering his shoulders as he positioned them to flank the bowl.

"We should thank Venna for preparing from my stock," Rensel reminded.

"We should thank the gods for this comfort. We have a hearth to warm us, a roof to shelter us and food to nourish us this night. It may be some time before such luxuries arise again."

"The gods may damn us all before we're done," Rensel proclaimed as she sat herself beside Cassica, lifting her spoon to the bowl.

"If the gods willed it so, we would all be dead by now. Help us reach the Fire Temple, and we shall see how far their Will leads us."

Chapter 18

"No. No."

Sorithen's anger echoed along the musky hallway as he stood over a pair of deceased guards. His throat tightened as he clutched a hand over his chest. Slow wheezes left his lips as he propped a lean upon a wall with the other hand. A Silvetzenian soldier rushed to the side of his king, aiding him with his lean.

The stench of his nightly liaisons brushed through the air trickling into Tivius' cracked nostrils several yards away. Tivius' sable figure trounced towards the hallway where two of his guards lay dead. Torrents of blood had pooled upon the floor leaving the gashes from their throats.

"I'll be fine," he moaned in disgust, brushing the hand of the guard away as dabbles of spit burst from his tongue.

Tivius returned to Sorithen's side and kneeled beside the dead soldiers. A glimmering glint of a small projectile caught his eye embedded in one of the men's necks. He released the stiletto from the grip of mortis as tears of flesh followed the eviscerated skin. A cold stare pierced against the projectile blade resting between his scarred fingers, his icy eyes focused intently upon the blade to the curvatures and indentations of the manufacture. His eyes widened flushing like a pool of clean water frozen in mid-stream. A grisly moan expelled from his gut splitting his cracked lips in a sneer.

Tivius' vision morphed into a gray visage, the image of the blade left the buxom brunette assassin piercing the stale air, striking the wind with hues of black and gray as it traveled to the guard's neck. Streaks of pushed air encircled the blade as it screamed through the hallway to connect with its target in gory display. Tivius kneeled against the other dead soldier coursing his hand against the handle of the dagger. His vision moved and electrified his hand in charged bolts of magical energies like writhing tentacles across his fingers and wrist. He recoiled at the onslaught of magical energies pounding through his body, streaming away from his fingers like water trickling from a bath as he pulled away. Magick energies pooled upon the handle of the forced blade embedded within the shoulder of its victim.

The eminence of Tesh's spirit form thrust the blade into the Silvetzenian guard encased in magick light searing into Tivius' skull. The purity of white blinded him, drowning out his senses to segregate him from the cold embrace of his magick connection. He clutched his eyes as shrieks of pain pounded against his skull, retreating into the fetal position while two Si'rai warriors readied their hands against their hilts.

"What's wrong?" Sorithen waddled to his side.

Tivius answered in the Common Tongue spoken by his ally, "My eyes, they burn…. the vision… I have seen."

"Vision? Seen? What happened?"

Tivius clawed away from the bodies pursued by an unseen force. His eyes melded into clouded fog twinkling with streaks of bright blue forcing his soul to overcome the enchantment. He erected to all fours, his slight towering frame lingering to regain stamina. His chest weighed heavy, breathing restricted and forced. The hold upon his soul gripped and tugged his fears. He clutched the sidewall of the hallway in a desperate attempt to erect to his full height.

"A woman killed these men, so did this Tesh, the one which travels with the Magi."

"Woman?"

"Are you deaf?" Tivius growled, "Yes, I said a woman. She threw the stiletto, and the boy killed the other one. She must be working with Cassica. An assassin in her party."

"Only two men; one older gentleman and one about twenty and two women about seventeen and fifteen accompanied Cassica's security detail," Sorithen protested.

"Then the assassin was already here, within Silvetzen," Tivius scolded.

Sorithen's bulbous frame blurred within Tivius' vision as he felt his way along the wall.

The pudgy liege responded, "Then she knew her way around the castle. No one knew about the location of the Magi and his Adept except your men and my personal guard."

"Your perverted mouth blurted to your nightly harem. One of those women was an assassin and working with Sarat."

Tivius reached his long arm like a raven tentacle and squeezed his slender, cracked digits around Sorithen's fleshy neck. His guards responded to the attack, while the Si'rai guards reacted in turn, readying more powerful armaments against the weaker foes.

Tivius continued, "High Magister must not become aware of this failure. We will sign the treaty as scheduled, with or without Cassica. I will return to camp with the news from the Saratian bitch. You better hope your soul is pure, High Magister is not as forgiving as I may seem."

Sorithen struggled as Tivius' grip released from his rotund neck. Tivius' anger echoed through his heavy, trodden march upon the hallway filling the shadows with his own raven leathers. Sorithen's coughs reverberated through the antechambers as the rotten stench of the corpses lingered upon his lungs. His commands interspersed with his wheezing as his men hurried to pick up the cadavers. Sorithen waited impatiently to ensure Tivius imposing form vanished from his sight and sound.

"This deal's getting worse all the time."

Streaks of daylight tore through breaking clouds and beat down upon Tivius dehydrated figure sealing its welcome heat within his dark leather. A fresh sheen of snow blanketed the courtyard of Silvetzen's castle where looming towers and keeps spread behind the entry door. Glittering icicles grew from the edges of the overhangs as random flakes of lingering snow made their way to the ground. A dry wind rustled through his sable hair flowing behind his shoulders. He mounted an armored steed as its heavy hooves pranced in the powder creating craters exposing the icy stone below.

A trio of escorts followed mount upon horses awaiting Tivius' arrival. Scars of battle crossed their exposed faces and heads. Leather armor strapped across their torsos and thighs leaving their arms visible to the elements warmed only by fur cloaks bound by loops on the flanks of their necks. Each of the men chose various weapons of obscene design and strewn them upon their backs or hips. The foursome signaled their horses to ride as they exited the drawn portcullis from the castle grounds.

A spectacle of darkness propelled through the prestigious sections of town in a swift motion of elaborate stride, an imposing sight. Nobles dressed in decorative fashion stood mesmerized at the hypnotic display, ceasing activity as the winds of oppression enraptured their audience. The dark riders continued into an outlying district of peasants beyond the walled inner city through the production shops and warehouses where the sweat of labor, smelting iron and fetid rot lingered into the air.

The road spilled into cascading farms rolling across the boreal plains with fences covered in a fresh sheet of snow a few centimeters thick. The horses galloped in exasperated breaths of misty evaporation spilling from their nostrils as the riders rode them steady and hard in a continuous pace. The riders continued along the path as the hills lowered towards the Silvetzenian harbor in the distance where new shipping houses lined the wharfs constructed by the visitors.

Tivius' lead carried them into base camp. A pair of guards saluted him with closed fists as he made entry beyond the arched fencepost marking the territory his armies occupied. Drawn by the count of sixteen muscular beasts, a gargantuan war wagon paused in the center of camp. Slabs of iron plate shielded the framework, protecting the fragile purpose of its occupants. The brusque shoulders of the gertoums carried the weights of chains as reins. Hooks attached to the reins sank into their muscular, fleshy skin in sadomasochistic display spilling streaks of orange blood into the crevices of their hides.

Tivius approached the carriage, removing himself from his steed. His motion carried him into a swift kneel as Magister Philatané removed from the command tent followed by Jabar and his boy slave. Brisk winds filtered through Jabar's pompous plume, billowing the folds in his cape. High Magister stood as a hunched caricature enclosed in a heavy cloak silhouetted in a deep shade of dyed crimson wool protecting him from the harsh elements whipping through camp. In the presence of the elder Magister, the foray of soldiers and arms masters, servants and craftsmen ignored the exchange, leaving the business of the higher ranks to their own. The sole audience in front of the command tent dismounted and bowed in reverence behind Tivius. Philatané's wraith-like guards floated to surround the carriage.

"My Lord, the king prepares for your arrival. Sorithen anticipates the official ceremonies to be underway. Unfortunately, I have a piece of news you may find most displeasing."

"Rise, Tivius. Share your news."

Tivius reached into his leathery ensemble and removed a folded parchment whose seal had previously broken and handed it to his Magister. Philatané struggled with the parchment, pushing his monocle closer to his left eye, his hands trembling in his frailty. He unraveled the folds and eyed the official crest of Sarat in the footer before reading:

> *Most Esteemed Tivius A'zum of the Si'rai,*
>
> *It is with great regret that I inform you I must leave for home to Sarat as this foreign climate renders me ill and unfit to perform to ability. I would request your representation would be welcome within our kingdom at your earliest convenience. I am certain our peoples can achieve the peace wished with Silvetzen, to secure prosperity for further generations.*

"She dispatched another note specific to Sorithen providing the same reason."

Philatané smiled at the note, turning to Jabar then back to Tivius, "This presents us with an opportunity. Has her carriage left?"

"Her carriage departed at sunrise."

"She has," Torkas smiled, "outsmarted you. No surprise. I have decided a new course of action," the Magister consumed the note in his left hand while aiming an arching index finger towards Tivius.

"Gather your Xiatutni. Hunt the carriage down and assassinate all on board. Supernus Magister requests you to leave for Sarat. What better motive than to hunt down their Princess? If she is among them, hold her and have her returned here for her transport to Supernus Magister. Then infiltrate the royal house and get rid of Trebut and the rest of his family. You have the blessing of Hadithem, and the support of forty legions behind you. The legions will arrive before the abra'in draws full once more. Enough time to fulfill your new duties. Upon completion, you are to be the Magister Durustratum of Sarat. Her failure to sign the treaty peacefully will lead to the collapse of her realm and the enslavement of her people."

"What of Cadeck and the Azthar Kherdmon? I have felt their presence here."

"As have I. He would not be present with the Saratian carriage as his priority will be to take the Azthar Kherdmon to the Temples as the training of an Azthar requires. As our armies infiltrate the two kingdoms, it will be impossible for him to remain hidden for long. Fleets sail to Racoren to complete the invasion. If he is still in town on this morning, we can surely find him and should he leave, he will have difficulty leaving by sea. And if he wishes to see his tuistrina again, he knows what he must do. Now, leave from my sight and bring Sarat under our rule."

"Yes, My Lord."

Tivius bowed in reverence before leaving the sight of his superior and the surrounding entourage. Jabar remained steadfast beside the emissary in escort both as physical and military support. His silver ceremonial armor strained to hold his muscular bulk as his bulbous head erupted from a gold-trimmed, crimson-plumed helmet. Jorast remained behind, carrying a gold-sheathed sword across his arms as he followed his master aboard the carriage.

Magister Philatané lifted himself into the grand carriage, aided in his physicality by Jabar and another soldier as his aging frame struggled to enter. He seated within the crimson plush cushions next to an open window where an angled plate prevented an aerial attack upon the windows. The crimson-caped escorts flowed across the running boards tightening their formation like blood clots sealing a wound.

A crackling sonic boom struck the air from a whip ordering the sixteen large beasts into motion. Seated alone upon a solo chair, a muscular, bare-chested man recalled his enormous whip and repeated the process over their heads. Trodden clumps of snowy mud melded into the soil as the thunderous beasts pummeled the roadway below them, straining to pull the heavy war-tank. Wide wheels made of iron and other alloy creased into the trail, their ruts damaging the roadway. Soldiers stood at attention following in worshipful bows as the massive carriage whined past them.

Silvetzen's roads were ill-fitted to handle the weighty vehicle. Brick-paved roads cracked under the intense pressure presented to them by the large beasts towering a story high. Likewise, the wheels ground into the roads like a bread mill leaving disfigured mortar in its trail. The Si'rai war wagon squeezed through the streets as paste through a tube, the sharp angle of turns tested the red-skinned driver's patience as he cursed the skinny roads in his native tongue.

Breath roiled from the beastly nostrils as their cries recalled the collapsing sounds of cascading mountains. Silvetzenian residents paused in awe of the horrid beasts shaking the foundations of their town as they pummeled along the snowy streets, collapsing the bricks and shaking dust and ice from nearby balconies. The walled gates of Simonoma's castle squeezed the Si'rai carriage within its portcullis as it suffered to accommodate the width of the vessel. The towering gertoums encircled the courtyard leading back towards the exit of the portcullis stopping the massive wagon. A timorous sound of a grinding halt like unlubricated gear rocked the stone.

Sorithen gawked at the ominous vehicle and the horned beasts which squeezed the armored carriage into his courtyard. A pair of his men stood in flank, each carrying a banner of his herald. The crimson caped figures removed themselves from the Si'rai carriage in a syncopated unison as each appeared to float in rigid attention upon the fresh powder. Sorithen's heart murmured tighter in his chest at the sight of these ghostly figures. Two stood along the side of the massive transport; the Sigil of the Abyss emblazoned into the iron door as the color of blood. The specters gripped the iron handles of the door, splitting the Sigil in symmetrical width.

Erupting from the omen, the figure of the man Sorithen surmised as the Supernus Magister of the Imperium lingered from his position as if to birth from the womb of his power symbol. Commanded by the flick of a finger, iron stairs clanked into rhythmic position allowing egress. Metal met metal as the crimson robes flowed along his aging frame exiting the carriage with the aid of a pair of his personnel. Sorithen quirked his head in query and cleared his throat from any assumptions he would make towards the weaknesses of the man before him. His heart trembled within his chest; his hands flittered against his stomach at the sight of eight entities whose armor appearance defied reason. The Revered Magister hobbled on his own strength towards the overweight king.

"Greetings, friend," the Magister smelled fear upon his host.

Evaporated breathing settled as rapid immolation devouring the countryside upon Sorithen's ears like death calling for him. Stories of the strengths of the higher ranks of the Imperium pushed Sorithen's nerves to shiver. Despite the weakness shown before him, he surmised the man could kill him without effort. Sorithen's brow sweat in the cold. For months, he had dealt with Tivius and other officers of the Si'rai. He could prepare for them, diplomatically avert them as needed yet who acted on the will of the weakened man before him.

The Si'rai mingled with the people of Silvetzen, relishing in their commerce and boarding. They supplied needed income as a visiting guest, acting on their own as ordered by their commander, Tivius A'zum. Sorithen concluded Tivius acted to an authority who instilled fear into Tivius' cold stone of a heart. A heart satiated by the bloodlust of the innocent during his crazed rituals, the old man before him did not impose such gesticulations. Sorithen proceeded with caution.

"Your men do not announce your presence, you must be Lucivus A'zum?"

"Forgive the informalities, Sorithen Rathmana," the emissary presented his response with a snide smile, continuing the ruse to the overweight king who knew no other name to address him.

"They fear to call my name should it become mispronounced in our speech. Doing so would be analogous to blasphemy. As your people do not follow my creed, your elocution of my name in your tongue was well versed."

Philatané's words mingled through Sorithen's body as the pair turned in eloquent procession into an awaiting archway. Jabar exited the carriage, his slave boy followed, as the pair of men ahead of him carried through a quaint antechamber leading from the courtyard into a wing of the castle.

"It is unfortunate House Bovariàr of Sarat has chosen to decline this offer. You can rest assured the Si'rai Imperium stands behind our words."

"Most welcome words, my friend."

Sorithen's tone echoed vibrato in his timid voice. The intonation raised a cunning smirk upon Philatané's aging face. The raven guard followed behind them.

"Is the Magi prepared to function as mediation in our affairs?"

Philatané detected Sorithen's answer as he struggled to form his response. His thoughts betrayed his existence, as the Revered Magister had well predicted the question and answer before his arrival. He would ensnare Sorithen with his response. Sorithen gulped on his own breath swallowing a lump of spit before he stuttered his answer.

"The Magi... I am afraid the Magi had left Silvetzen when my cousin did."

"Go on," Philatané raised a fluffy eyebrow.

Philatané's crimson robes flowed over his feeble frame advancing in inertial motion as his hunched figure stopped abruptly. Sorithen choked in hidden fear to form his next answer as though his very life depended upon carefully chosen words.

"We found two men each of mine and yours murdered near the Magi's room. The Magi was not present. This is the second instance concerning your men, my friend."

Tivius warned him not to alert his liege choosing to remain their secret. Philatané's presence commanded answers pulled from the air as though the aura of rampant torture prevailed in the room.

"But the Magi does not travel alone," Sorithen continued, "He has accomplices."

"Your allegiance is more valuable than I surmised, Sorithen. A shame my lesser Magister had not informed of this news."

Philatané's eyes burned with a stinging pleasure. He craned to look up to Sorithen's pudgy, rotund jowls as though a mouse watched a hawk in the sky only for this mouse to lay a trap. He lifted his cragged, bony fingers to wrap upon a chain around Sorithen's neck, tracing it to a trinket of an arthropodal representation where a darkened, amethyst crystal suspended in the thorax of the figure.

"You value the trinkets we sold to you, these tokens of our honesty?"

The reverberations of the Magister's words crumbled Sorithen's throat to mutter in response, whimpering his lips together in timid breaths which coiled from his nostrils and chattering teeth.

"All of the Houses do friend."

Philatané turned towards the hallway leaving a trailing sneer at Sorithen's direction. The rotund king lingered as Torkas and his guard advanced deeper into his castle. Sorithen's enchanted stupor vacated his vacant eyes as he understood the speech he invoked to his ally. Jabar edged past the shocked king sneering at the imposition of a future only he would be privy to.

Sorithen dawdled in anxious pace as he cleared his head from words reaching deep into his subconscious thoughts. He clutched the walls in weakened stupor with his left hand over his chest as he struggled to keep pace with the party. He reached into his soul; Tivius' threats reverberated through his mind. He felt bound as though an invisible force extended into his heart and confined it with cold, steel chains cutting with each twist.

Chapter 19

Cadeck's whispers summoned deep emotions billowing through his soul. The burning fire of the hearth warmed his body in quiet solitude. Murmurs and chants of magick prayer echoed through his crackling lips covered in whiskery beard and moustache. With every breath, the roll of chilled vapors swirled in the vacancy, puffing in command to his words from the deepest recesses of his soul. Names of memory, times of happiness and gratitude, chanted through an ethereal manifestation within his mind and turned into scarred, cragged cliffs and doors leading into infinite decay.

Along voids defaced with jagged cliffs and the present void of ashen decay raining down upon him, he tried to call for his children. Darkened shadows of the emptiness consumed his words, holding them to his lips and appeared as stitched mouths closed by surgical clumsiness. He teetered on temptation, the souls of the damned reaching through the Abyss calling his name. Each lead to his children brought him deeper into shadows crawling over the tattered cliffs of darkness, held only to the sky by large chains beneath their surfaces. Upon one of the surfaces, the image of an island inhabited by a dark cave appeared before Cadeck. He called their names into the cave and heard only a growling laughter whose very intonations mocked his torment with each call.

Cold deaths chilled him as only voices of the damned replied to his vain requests. He called out to his god. A gurgling noise cursing the name of his chosen deity answered.

Your god does not exist here. In this domain, I am the Master.

The voice rolled with a drowning warble growling at Cadeck before a pair of angular eyes of darkened red appeared mere inches before Cadeck's perceived space. In the void of pitch, the figure swirled to coalesce before him, winding into the darkness, limiting the exposure to Cadeck with a pair of spindly arms beneath the neckline.

I pray in my own meditations, what is this?

Welcome to the Abyss, Aztmi. Here you will find only torment and pain.

No. I do not allow my soul to be here. Leave me, demon. By the Sacred Aztun, I command you.

Rolling laughter mocked his plea.

You see in the shadow, Roth's future. In the presence of thine enemy, you will find only darkness. Here, in the darkness, you will find me as I have found you. You cannot escape, Cadeck. His Lords will find you, praying only makes it easier.

Send them and I will defeat them.

They are many and you are but one.

The rolling cackle stilled Cadeck's heart into a slow beat as his mind returned to a numbed body. Cold prickles tickled at his fingertips and his toes as a shooting pain punished his spine and lower legs. He stayed in a meditative pose, the light crackle of decayed fire spilling into his ears in a welcome ease on a crisp autumn morning. Wood fuel blackened with each spit of orange ember dancing on whitened timber. In moments, Cadeck felt his eyes blink to waken from his trance and to see the emptiness of the silent room, the tangled mess of strewn pots, and various clutter of disarray around his perimeter.

Behind him, within the small room Rensel used, the sheets and bedding had tossed in frenzied manner and a small nightstand had toppled over with a broken leg. Artifacts and effects stripped from dumped chests broken into pieces. The simple wooden door swung wide waking Cadeck from his meditations to the form of a familiar lad bursting with new confidence.

Tesh reached to Cadeck's hand as he aided him to his feet.

"Is something wrong, Cadeck?"

"No," Cadeck withdrew his feelings from Tesh's presence and focused on the task required, surveying the room.

"If Rensel's consistency with hiding her cover is any sign, I assume you left the ladies with her friend?"

"Yes, but this town has gone into a strangely calm, maniacal fury. The criers are calling for all citizens to bear witness to news."

"News? I presume it is related to the treaty."

Cadeck reached towards the floor to gather his satchel and hoisted upon an aching shoulder.

"Might be. Rensel's friend said the town's gates stay closed. All citizens must hear the news and gather at the castle balcony. I asked the ladies to stay at the stable while I came back for you."

"You were lucky you weren't caught."

Cadeck slid his frame towards the solitary window. Fresh snow crested upon the windowsill as Cadeck's breaths frosted the poor fixture frame. He could hear the bustle of the crowd lingering in the nearby street along the hidden alley. A small cat scuttled across the fresh snow marking paw prints in the virgin ground. It craned towards the human in the window before pelting out a soft cry of affection towards the stranger and scurrying further down the alley. Cadeck arose from the window to catch Tesh gathering belongings for the journey.

"What can I say, I blend in well."

"Yes, but we still need to figure out how to get past the locked gates. I presume Rensel has discovered such a way and secured an exit already so we can leave. We must make haste."

Cadeck reached for the cold iron handle of the door and swung it wide balancing the warm air with the low cold of the outside. Tesh brushed his arms to protect from the sudden change and closed the door behind them. Mortar-walled tenements flanked the snow-laden alley ending into the bustling street ahead.

Heralds made announcements along the streets promoting the crowd to move in the direction of the castle. Groups of armored soldiers harried loiterers to business enforcing the herald's words. Cadeck measured the temperature of the town leading his eyes towards the rooftops and the various pairs of Si'rai soldiers positioned above.

"To blend in, we'll need to follow."

"What about the women?"

"Cassica can take care of herself and if Rensel's prowess is any sign, I presume they shall have no problems. We will catch up to them when we can, but we do not want to stand out."

Cadeck led the pair into the agitated crowd to mingle with the peasants and various peddlers moving eastward towards the large palace. The flow moved towards a gated entrance, marked by a sign noting the area to belong to the nobility with the name of King's Square. Here patrician met peasant as the drab and often ill-educated lower class harried into the area reserved for the intellectually inclined. The main road emptied into a large plaza surrounded with mortar structures of delicate colors framed by wood beams topped with gabled roofs. Mounted soldiers kept order within the square while crossbow snipers in Si'rai armor kept to the balconies.

Pairs of men without armor had stationed in various positions around the ramparts and galleries appearing to show they did not belong. Their clothing signified them of Si'rai employment with the Imperium sigil embroidered on their left chests. Cadeck and Tesh positioned near the edge of the sprawling, circular plaza, away from mingling with the primary crowds and close enough to leave should they need. Overseeing the large arcade, a decorated balcony jutted from the outside wall of the castle which rose upon a small cliff, keeping the peasants and lesser dregs away from the prestige of their nobles.

Iron fencing marked the edge of the cliff topped with pointed bars lining the perimeter to prevent climbers from entering. Marksmen patrolled the fencing along the snow-covered grounds of the cliff rock. Silvetzen's eagle crest flag flew from the bannisters along the veranda, heralding the nationalist pride of the Silvetzenian people. Soldiers of Si'rai and Silvetzenian armor stood in positions above the crowds, upon verandas and ramparts where pairs stood watch of the events.

The crowd swelled in mild anxiety. Their murmurs soon quieted by the appearance of Jabar's crimson plume burning in the brilliance of the daylight. His silver armor glistened against the drab chain mail decorating the Silvetzenian contingency. Amazed revelers of the lower class clapped and hollered as though a god appeared before them before foot soldiers urged calm silence within the crowd with shouts and bursts.

The silence broke when the rotund girth of Sorithen Rathmana revealed through the decorative door onto the portico. He encouraged his celebrity amongst his people, raising his hands in fierce pomp. Peasant men brandished swords and daggers to praise their king. Surly women hoisted their children as if to offer them to his service for a lifetime while those of the upper classes applauded respectfully to their king. Tesh and Cadeck met face eyeing the peculiar devotions.

Sorithen urged his subjects to calm. A hush fell over the crowd as random murmurs and coughs percolated to break the silence. He hobbled to the edge of the balcony to secure pronunciation to all gathered within town. He spoke with an ethereal confidence, contrast to his apprehension with his ally and staff.

Behind a veiled curtain draped to cover the exit to the balcony, the true puppeteer stood silent. Flowing drapery lined the mortar walls in various hues of luxurious dyes. Candelabras stood as guards between the sheets signifying the room as one to heighten the celebrity of the attendees. The imposing darkness of the Revered Magister stationed within like a fervent vacuum consuming the jubilance of the theatrical room. Philatané's fingers weaved in strings of an orchestra, wafting his thoughts towards Sorithen as the burly man stood on stage as the dummy played by the ventriloquist. Philatané stood in pause; his eyes glowed with a purple tint as the vision of Sorithen's commanding pose glimmered like a faint image.

"Citizens of Silvetzen," their king began, "it is with great honor I address you today. For too long we have lived with the threat of Sarat knocking to our south. They rattle their swords and bang their shields to prepare to battle their brothers and sisters. They call to unite Rykana by force; King Trebut following in the shadows of his ancestors to spill the blood of his fellow men.

They have set fire to our farms, pillaged our outlying villages, and made threats against my life. His daughter's harlotry tempts our men and youthful sons with lustful entrapments. Even now, amongst you, Saratian spies could enslave your children, rape your mothers and sisters, and kill your fathers and men of union.

"We gave them the choice to lay down their swords and take up plowshares with their brothers and sisters. Instead, they did not agree to our terms and left our proceedings. In their wake, they have murdered two of your men and two of our prized guests. They show they stay untrustworthy, even with a simple signatory."

The crowd swelled into simple-minded surprise and nervousness. They clamored with anticipation upon the uneducated masses hanging to their king's next speech.

"No fear, my subjects. I have guaranteed their threats will not go unmatched. For months, we have allowed our humble guests to quarter in our town and share in our pleasures; break bread and enjoy the fruits of our labor."

As his voice reached a stubborn crescendo, Sorithen took pause to wince to a mild pain between his temples.

A protest yelled amongst the crowd's silence, "Find our missing children."

Recalcitrant murmurs followed in the crowd before nearby soldiers subdued the noise. Cadeck watched the proceedings, swallowing nervously as Sorithen hissed his lies. Sorithen reclaimed his dignity as the soldiers removed the suspected interrogator.

"Today marks a new day in Silvetzenian history," Sorithen growled, recovering from his mild malady, "By the grace of Heseph's fires, we have secured a beneficial treaty with the Si'rai Imperium. They will work in conjunction with your men as we unite to war against Sarat. Their weapons and culture will improve our ways of life insuring a quick defeat of our enemies. But do not let my praise be alone. Permit your ears to hear their own words."

Sorithen stepped aside, swinging his arm to present the robed nightmare breaking into the balcony from a grand entrance. As though floating like a bloodied ghost into the white virginity of Silvetzenian snow, Philatané humbled himself upon the crowd. Frail and weakened, he filtered to the edge of the rampart as Sorithen proceeded to his right to stand besides Jabar.

The crowds did not see a weakened man. An image of a strong and able brute of strength towered over their own king with the confident charisma spilling in his wake. The crowd drew gasps as the man echoed an aura of energetic hypnotism and quelled the gathering into programmed silence.

He split his robes exposing fitted black armor to the sunlight shimmering above. The crowd awed at his chiseled face mimicking a perfect statue overseeing an overgrown garden, withering, and decaying. His armor sealed to his figure like an extension of his own flesh. Raising his arms in charismatic splendor, the crowed obeyed his call to silence.

Cadeck whispered to his ward, "This is not the Magister we saw at the Temple. His aztmudin is… mesmerizing. I sense a mask; this image is a lie."

Defying the physical stature his counterparts saw, Philatané erupted in firebrand speech washing the populace in silent awe. Scripted promises flowed from his hands as they waved over the audience, enticing the crowd into various responses of cheering. Cadeck parted waves to leave the grounds as Tesh paced to keep up. The crowd ignored the disturbances as Philatané maintained his thrall by the dominating prominence of the bass timbre resonating from the speech.

Surges of glow flowed across Tesh's left arm responding to the orator. He ignored the stinging pain, instead sending his injured hand to grip Cadeck's tunics. Cadeck stood as an automaton set to obey. A calm breeze flowed over him like the winds washed over fields of flax shaking the plants to tickle one another. In the still of silence, he isolated himself from the crowds, from the booming voices and Tesh behind him.

In the fields, he saw life. A wreath of yellow primdil flowers covered flowing blonde hair cascading down the woman's shoulders. Aging wisdom sprinkled along the fair face as the maiden white dress flowed around her body in carriage to the winds. She touched the stalks with her fingertips, sleeves finely curved to her wrists. As the woman spoke, Cadeck numbed.

Cadeck. Leave. Now.

"Jess?" Cadeck paused, his eyes consuming the reality of the crowd around him. Only Tesh heard his question as a single tear rolled down his face.

Cadeck turned to his student.

"No," Tesh responded. His face squinted at Cadeck's question.

"Tesh?"

Tesh nodded in confirmation as Cadeck moved attention towards the pulsating appendage drawing his eyes to full agape. His mind refocused towards Tesh's purpose.

"Hide your arm, let's move."

Tesh removed the cowl covering his face and wrapped his supernatural appendage in tight bond. The Revered Magister's speech reached orgiastic culmination upon the crowd. Silence proliferated, polluted by the sheen slink of metal gracing metal in familiar song to the warrior clan people. The cold stillness released Jabar's weapon as a beacon upon the audience. As seared through meat, the sword cleared Sorithen's head from his bulbous form as the crowd turned to fear. The severed head graced the virgin snow with the spilling of crimson blood as the body dropped in response, crashing onto the rampart of the balcony.

As commanded by signal, the riggers and engineers moved in unison to release the seas of black Abyss in a flurry of fascist fury. From the balconies and ramparts, the unfurling of the heraldic flag of the Si'rai Imperium flooded throughout the town. Cadeck turned towards the commotion to witness Si'rai soldiers cutting their way through the Silvetzenian guard. Snipers on the rooftops engaged with single bolts to remove Silvetzenian men climbing the ramparts to defend their king. Rioters fled a fresh flush of Si'rai black marching into the plaza.

"Tesh, run."

Parting through the rampage, the pair separated amidst the rioting crowd as they clamored to leave the courtyard. Tesh pushed through, charging left and then right trying to recall the path to the rendezvous point. Cadeck attempted to follow, losing Tesh in the crowd. Tesh craned his neck towards the balcony trying to turn against the flow. The escalating riot pushed him away. He snuck into an alley to escape the mob. Alone and cold, he gripped the satchel tight against his chest as he trudged into the snow-covered street. Reaching the end of the alley a pair of Si'rai warriors confronted him in suspicion.

"Where are you going, sadakem?"

One of the soldiers growled in his native tongue, backhanding Tesh's face to knock him to the ground. Standing as towering trees of charred, glints of armor, the pair mocked and sneered to the young man lying on the cobblestone street. Beneath the fabrics covering his hand, the tendrils in his left arm coalesced into a slight glow visible beneath the cloth.

"No, wait," Tesh muttered, involuntarily aiming his hand towards the men sending a beam of energy through the fabric and striking each one in succession, evaporating the pair within their confined armor.

He sheltered his eyes from the blast, shyly removing his hand from his eyes at the clank of steel upon the stone. Crowds surged towards him and realizing the danger, he shuffled clumsily, gathering his satchel, and making haste along the streets.

Tesh jolted through the streets. Dodging around crates and boxes, carriages left by their carriers as the ever-increasing horde of Silvetzenian citizens surged his direction. Sweat steamed from his brow. He reached his destination; a two-story shop built over a stable filled with horses and hands. Soft lamp light spilled onto the ground from an overhang. Hearing the roar of a frightened crowd, Rensel hurried Venna and Eris into the back of a cart resting below the awning and aided them with cover. A towering, lumbering man stood next to Rensel to her aide, reeking of pig slop and laziness.

His motions were slow as he made simple responses of monosyllabic words to Rensel's requests. As the younger girls were situated in their cover, Rensel patted the slow man on the side of his rough cheek. He responded in a rotten tooth smile as though she had given him sweets.

A look of concern washed over Cassica's face as she approached Tesh, "What in the Bogs of Er'tahar is going on?"

Tesh gasped to respond, grasping for his knees to regain breath.

"Sorithen…. Murdered…."

"What? Where's Cadeck?"

"I lost him. Come with me, we need to find him."

"Rensel, stay here."

"As you command."

"Tesh, let's go."

Cassica tapped the man on his shoulder trailing behind him in sprint. At this point of town, the crowd filtered away, returning to homes, and locking doors in frantic panic. Tesh returned through his route, tracing his way to the point where contact faded. Moving through the alleys and streets, they worked in conjunction to avoid Si'rai patrols, passing sparse pairs or pools of Silvetzenian citizens crying in shock to the loss of their king or the separation of others. A blast of energy flashed in the distance over the buildings sending a shock wave rocketing through the ground rumbling against the structures nearby. Specks of spackle and mortar crumbled beside Tesh and Cassica to the vibrations of energy pushing through the air.

Tesh felt a surge through his left hand, wincing in response. Cassica began a swift sprint towards the sound of the commotion. Tesh struggled to pace, grappling his left hand in pain as he trudged slowly through the snow towards her direction. From afar, the echoes of soldiers rolled through the streets shouting words of blasphemous tone in a foreign tongue.

Cassica reached the end of their street to see a man stammering to escape a squadron of pursuers more physically fit than he while several fragments of Si'rai armor shells lay scattered upon the snow or thrown in mangled iron mesh into the stone of buildings. Tesh matched her position and yelled out Cadeck's name. Cassica rushed to meet the Magi down the street, passing him to continue an attack against the pair of men behind him.

In swift strikes, she worked the two men into a dizzying martial frenzy. Tesh approached the Magi, grasping his shoulder as the men watched in awe at Cassica's prowess with the Si'rai guards. She moved as a graceful angel in deadly combat slamming her open palm into the nose of one man, while kicking the other behind her across his jaw. Both men collapsed to their knees in pain, grasping their injuries, as she removed a blade from her hip and sliced both necks to spray upon the snow. Cassica never lost pace as she rushed to catch the two men encouraging them to follow.

Cadeck's discipline kept him in stride with the young adults at the cost of heaving breaths upon reaching the stable. Cassica leapt into the trunk of the cart, grasping for Cadeck's hand to lift him into the bin. He struggled and slipped as he hefted his weight collapsing upon his back into the haystack. Tesh followed suit, guarding the pair as they made cover. The large man gripped Rensel in a bear hug. Her face responded in sarcastic surprise as she hesitantly patted his back in favor.

She mounted the driver's seat commanding the horse to full gallop. Axles squeaked through the town as the horse rushed swiftly at Rensel's command, passing wayward revelers awed by sprint of the carriage while afeared of what they fled. The pace of the cart drew Si'rai guards to notice, yelling above to the balconies to alert the sniper positions.

Bolts rained down upon Rensel's cart as she dodged and flanked the attack. Erupting from the haystack, Venna readied a bulky crossbow and aimed the bolt at a sniper positioned on a passing rooftop ahead of them. Bumps and jolts knocked her around, causing her to lose aim with the speed tightening closer to his position. With the *thwip* of the bowstring, she struck the assailant proactively, catching him off-guard with a single shot to his trigger arm, sending his arrow to shoot wildly away into a nearby roof. She ducked into the hay again to dodge a return volley whipping at the cart which outpaced the leading aim of the projectiles. Without slowing pace, Cassica arose from the cover and in a single step, balanced herself upon the edge of the cart. Sensing her first opportunity, she leapt out of the cart and onto a building ledge nearby.

She climbed her way to the rooftop and glided across the thatched canopy over the buildings. She reached a building abutted against the castle wall, leaping towards the mortar in single action. Cracks in the wall aided her scaling of the towering barricade. The cart outpaced her movements as she soared from rampart to rampart across the wall. Cassica approached rigging line and sliced it with a concealed blade in her sleeves and without hesitation swung around the tower impeding her advance to reach the opposite parapet at angle.

Tesh attempted to watch the proceedings, yet Eris tugged at his shirt, forcing him back into the hay. A turn of the cart around a corner slowed the movement. Cassica's sprint caused confusion in the Si'rai snipers across the street on the buildings as they caught sight of her movements aiming their crossbows in her direction. Anticipating the bolts, she leapt to a roll below their aim as she followed her grace to turn her roll upon her feet, crouching low and continuing her run, outpacing the reload time of their heavy weapons. Her swift actions brought her to a gate house guarded by a pair of Si'rai pike men.

She reached into her knotted hair releasing it into crimson flow like a blood stream, and in a single stroke, she tossed a pair of piercing pins whistling through the air into their necks. She entered the gate house and with one kick released the brake on the pulley causing the counterweight into a free fall slamming within the walled structure. From the open-air control room, Cassica's eyes followed as the cart made headway towards her position. Timing her action, she leapt once again into the back of the cart safely protected by the hay as Rensel steered the escape vessel away from Silvetzen.

Chapter 20

An immaculate lake loomed in the far distance as the single-horse cart raced along the snow road. In the low sunlight arcing towards evening, the sky mirrored within the clear waters. Smokestacks dotted along the far shores of the lake with the onset of late northern autumn. The cart raced through winding lanes and paths, past snow-covered farmlands, passing glacial peaks to the northern horizon. The walled city of Silvetzen drew smaller in the vista as the cart hurried at blinding pace towards a westward direction.

Rensel steered the cart through the trodden path beyond pristine snowcapped fields. Farmer huts sprinkled the landscape in sparse distances like spackled dots. Winds carried the sweet smokes from their chimneys as the carriage rode through the open terrains denying Rensel the comforts of a hearth. Snow drifts pelted her face and sprinkled into Rensel's brunette locks dotting them with flakes of cutting ice. She craned her neck to glance behind the cart, the walled city no longer in her sights. Witnessing no pursuers, she cooled the gallop of the horse into a steady walk as she approached an intersecting road defined by a solitary sign delineating town names in various directions. She called the horse to halt before slapping her hand on the backboard.

"Are we clear?"

"Yes, Your Highness."

Cassica appeared from flittering hay. Strands of straw stuck tight within her scarlet hair quivering in the cold breezes. She turned her head in either direction of the intersection, the baseboard meeting her chest.

"Which direction?"

"This road leads east returning to the Saratian Road. If we head west, we run into the town of Vorstak where Silvetzen trains their soldiers. We should continue to head south. There's little farmland and risk of running into hostiles."

Cassica nodded her approval and signaled the remaining occupants of the carriage to reveal from hiding. Cadeck stood against the backboard, picking strands of hay from his clothes. Tesh sat upon the side boards breathing in open relief. Venna arose to stand next to Cassica, the cold winds flowing through her golden hair. Eris remained seated, clutching her knees to her chest coddling within her warmth.

Cadeck hopped onto the driver board beside Rensel causing Cassica to steady herself as the carriage shifted forward. Cassica pushed hay away from her hair struggling as reluctant strands hesitated to remove from their grip. She dropped to sit as she leaned against the rough backboard; her spine straightened against her will by the right angle.

"Let me help," Tesh scooted besides her placing his hands within the scarlet rivers.

"I don't need your help."

Tesh plucked a strand of hay without discomfort to its host.

"What are you doing?"

"Be still."

Cassica slumped in disdain, almost insulted, "I can do this, you know."

Tesh ignored her plea and continued working within her glossy hair, removing hay straws one at a time. Cassica furrowed, wincing at every tug of her hair, yet reluctantly giving to the deed. He worked his hands in a magical fervor acting as his sole destiny meant to perform this duty. He executed until the last strand of hay left the vermillion sea of flowing silk.

"Now, that wasn't hard, was it?"

"I never gave you permission to touch me."

"I think we can disband with the formalities, Your Highness. We are fugitives now. Besides, you displayed magnificent footwork back there. You are more than just a princess."

Tesh changed position, staring deep within her emerald eyes, "It was always you," he whispered, trying to sneak the words under his breath.

"I know not of which you speak, citizen."

Cassica's stare met his in polite anger.

"Your eyes, I had seen them my whole life. Dreams. Visions."

"Your vain approach at romance is humble, yet unwelcomed. Now, if you do not mind," she ushered him out of her proximity.

"Apologies, Your Highness," Tesh shifted slightly away from her.

"I am not here to romanticize with you, I am only acting now to hold my part of the bargain. You offered to help me see through this treaty with Silvetzen which turned into trickery. Now my girls and I will aide you to get to the Fire Temple and I request to return home upon your completion of task."

"And how do you plan to return to Sarat? We are in hostile territory, remember?"

"We can make it. We can rely on our wits."

"Judging by the cart handler's fondness for Rensel, I'm sure wits are not all you can rely on."

Tesh smirked as he returned to his sideboard. Cassica shrugged her shoulders and crossed her arms. Her lips snarled into a curl. She looked around for anything; loose wood, a brick, anything hard but the best she could muster was a clump of hay flittering away into the wind as she launched it towards Tesh. Tesh joked at her gesture. Amused by her futility, he stretched one leg out and leaned backward against the sideboard and crossed his hands behind his back allowing the cold chill to wash against his face.

Venna scooted closer to Cassica and began to whisper.

"I think he likes you."

"Nonsense. And you would best to remove those thoughts. It is not proper for royalty to romance with the commoners."

Tesh turned his attention to the catty chatter executed by Venna and Cassica. At times feigning interest then removing them to peer into the road passing behind the cart as Rensel commanded the horse into a slow ride. His thoughts turned to ponder the ramifications of their latest adventure. What did they want and why are they there? A veracity immeasurable, godlike in precision and brutality. The enemy was close, and he was in no position to help Cadeck fight them. He felt Cadeck's immeasurable pains in the fleeting moment he touched his shoulder amidst the chaotic revelry.

Tesh moved his left hand to his front. His veins were calm, tinted through his skin with the golden hue of the amulet's alloy as he stroked the searing numbness tickling his limb. He recalled the intense pulses in his arm only moments before in memories that seemed to exist in the entirety of his existence. This time, it was not his vision, but a higher calling to another power, a connection so strong Tesh's focus no longer became his but that of something he could not understand. He could not hear the exchange but felt intense heat when he laid hand upon Cadeck's shoulder in Silvetzen urging the man to leave his temptation alone. Something, someone must have called out to Cadeck the moment he set hand.

Hours passed as the cart stretched into the evening sky. The winds calmed to still as Rensel drove the cart into a small outcropping dotted with craggy cliffs. Cadeck pointed them towards a small cave carved into one of the cliff sides. He and Rensel dismounted the cart and went ahead to scout the shelter for wildlife. Cadeck ascertained its safety and whistled towards the cart a few meters away. Tesh aided Cassica with a heavy chest as Venna and Eris positioned hay in front of the horse.

Venna and Eris returned to shelter, strands of hay interspersed upon their tunics. A low fire welcomed the young women as they snuggled close to

Rensel for warmth. Cadeck stoked the fire to coax the flames to burn brighter, his thoughts shifting to match his eyes as he lingered silently on the safety of his children and his companions. Cassica carefully opened the chest to keep prying eyes away and handed Cadeck an enclosed pot of leftover stew. Cadeck scooped a handful of snow upon his hand and dropped the ice into the pot to mingle fresh water within the stew. Stirring the pot to melt the powder the stew began to emulsify with new liquid aiding the contents to an easier stir.

Cadeck rationed the warmed meal to each of the women in the bowls Rensel managed to salvage. He then provided Tesh and himself with meal and turned his attention towards the next step as the inhabitants consumed. He focused away from his pains so not to allow them to interfere with the task at hand. He would find time in his meditations to center on his children when permissible. The cold ate at his bones within the cave, yet he took no time to ponder the aches. His thoughts lay only on the goal of the mission.

"Once we reach the Tanakian Ring, you girls will need to remain behind. None other than a Magi or a Knight are to approach near a Temple."

He shoveled a spoon of stew into his mouth.

"What if we're caught or ambushed?" Cassica addressed concern after swallowing her taste.

"There is no way a Silvetzenian will come near it. The Silvetzenian hold it as sacred."

"The Si'rai do not, Rensel. Unless there is a Magister amongst the search party, you should be safe," Cadeck reminded.

Cadeck turned his attention towards his own words almost sinking in his speech to reveal his lie. The meditations before leaving Silvetzen worried him as the demon of the Abyss warned him of the odds he met. Cadeck continued to converse about the plan but supplied little relief for Cassica assurance for safe journey home.

"He's lying to us," Cassica turned towards Tesh who was half-entertained by Cadeck's words, "Another reason it's hard to trust the Magi."

"Listen, he knows it is not safe yet. He will not put you in danger by allowing you to return."

"Cadeck's seen the skills of the Order of the Rose before. He knows we can manage ourselves."

Cadeck turned away from his conversation with Rensel to pay attention to Cassica's whispering as he were a teacher interrupted by an unruly pupil.

"But not against one of their Magisters," Cadeck scolded.

"We're being pursued by one, aren't we?"

Cassica crossed her arms upon her chest as Cadeck shifted uneasily in his sitting,

"I wish I could answer your question honestly, Your Highness."

"Like the others of your kind, you're lying to those who do not hold your beliefs."

Cadeck turned into disagreement. His face scowled at her blasphemy, "You underestimate them, Cassica. If one were to follow us or find us, yourself or Rensel would hold no match to them. They would not hesitate to kill or capture your ladies after they disposed us."

"Your Highness, Cadeck's right," Rensel affirmed, "Tivius was acting as shadow governor for Silvetzen, until the formal handing over of territory today. I have seen the dangers their wizards impose. I had observed the camp, seen his personal hut, and watched as a pair of dark-dressed figures forced young children into the shack regularly, only for the children to never leave. Sorithen did not ask, only supplying little children regularly to save his own hide.

"If a beast of his like could hide such atrocity, what makes you think we fare any safer? Their soldiers are just men, but their wizards are vain and powerful."

Cassica drew aghast at Rensel's horrid statements. Thoughts of dead children dare not entertain her mind, yet in Rensel's words, inescapable. Eris withdrew into her knees, frightened at the mention of thought. Venna remained silent, staring into the fire, gripping the bowl tight between her hands as Rensel's words disturbed the far stretches of Venna's mind. A fate she did not dare to think as the descriptions uttering from Rensel's mouth of torture and debauchery, violent cruelties and seductions concocted vivid imagery within her head. The campfire sprinkled soft light onto the ghastly responses on their faces as Rensel further described Tivius' sins she had seen.

Rensel continued, "I do not doubt Tivius would harm any of us, and knowing he has baited Her Highness, would take vile pleasures in her death. We stand a far safer chance allowing Cadeck to fight any Magisters pursuing us, than let us go alone into a trap."

Cadeck studied the exchange amongst the ladies. Cassica withdrew herself into timid calculation as she picked at her fingernails. Glimmers of fire escalated her concern as Tesh looked on mesmerized. The Magi could sense her fears as bubbles of sweat built up around her forehead leaking her stress between her arms. He placed his comforting hand upon her raised knee even with her chest.

"Know this Your Grace; I would not allow harm to come to you by my own doing. Your father would not have it. I make it my vow to protect you."

#

As the morning dawn rose upon their third day of travel, Rensel harried the cart as fast as the horse would allow. Cadeck rode to her side, shrouded by a deep cloak disguising his appearance. The shaky ride bumping and rattling the heavy chest in small distortions within the carriage bin. Tesh propped his feet upon the box as he relaxed amidst the quick pace carried by the horse.

Tesh's thoughts lingered for his mother and how she always made it home from her random jobs as sundown approached to make sure she told him a comforting story before bed or fed him a warm meal. The glow of her face or soft voice in her lips hid true pains she never told him. Even if she came home late with bruises on her face, she would be available for him. She kept her words firm yet pleasant never revealing how hard she had it. But Tesh always knew.

She never revealed who his father was, preferring to never answer when he asked. Her reply always stayed the same; he left before he was born and would never see him again. As Tesh grew older, he pushed the question to reveal a more specific response, but she only revealed the small truth; he was a conscript levied to fight a foreign war and left the topic alone from then. Cassica gave him a glimpse of name, but nothing more than the notice he should have become royalty.

His eyes opened from his slumber and favored glare towards Venna, recounting as a youth the nubile farmer's daughter he courted before closing them again to sleep. As he grew into trades, they met in happenstance while he browsed market one day. He did not have much to wine her, favoring simple purchases of fruits or tanned meats he could save for from daily pay. They had flings into the fields where he would seduce her with simple ballads he heard from the travelling bards.

He told her of a tale of star-crossed lovers, a roaming play travelling into Sarat by a performance troupe. His allowance lacked coin to give her a seat in the theater, but he did his best to tell the tale. His rhythm fell short of intended purpose, the story befuddled by the crossed stanzas. She laughed at his tone-deaf attempts as he concluded the story of tragic deaths correctly. Despite his methods, she would never allow consummation vowing her father would kill them both if she were not chaste on her union night. He respected her wishes. Yet the day would never come. She turned up missing and Marshal Offtil formed a posse to find her. Days later, the men found her near a known highwayman's hideout, the mark of the Wolfsblood gang led to the arrest of three suspects.

His dreams turned to speech amidst the passengers. Startled by his disturbing thoughts, Cassica reached over towards him in attempt to wake him.

Her silky skin caressed his face recalling days within the embrace of his nubile farm girl. Her lingering whispers formed in his ear as spoken from the peaceful winds.

In deep sleep, he raised his left hand to touch the vision only to grace the elegant skin of Cassica. Golden flakes of skin tickled with energies as full lips of an ethereal scarlet goddess planted upon him. The goddess in his mind cackled with seductive voice, a flow of scarlet robes clung to her shapely, nubile, and naked form underneath as it spoke to him, *Blade is not yet ready*.

Cassica attempted to retreat from the sudden clutch as his sleep-induced vision forced his lips to hers. Sensing the indulgent kiss, Tesh burst his eyes open in shock as she clutched at his face to escape in earnest.

"What was that?"

Cassica snarled at the advance. She shunned his stuttered apologies leaping from his mouth like a diseased rat before withdrawing from his proximity.

"I would suggest to never attempt flirtations again."

"But I…"

Venna giggled at the exchange giddy as her youth. Cassica shot her a look of misconduct, prompting Venna to cough at her disorderly remark. Cassica retreated into the corner of the bin moving further away from Tesh. Venna grinned towards Tesh as he threw a clump of hay at her to flitter into the cold winds behind them.

Tesh returned to his thoughts. Cassica's dainty kiss still tingled on his lips. He pawed at the clumps of hay with his left hand embarrassed with himself for his transgression and lingered on the kiss tasted like the warm glaze of honey layered over tart cakes. Plush lips pressed upon his in fleeting moment soothed him in an ethereal enchantment of otherworldly beauty.

Rensel drove the cart through the intertwining valleys and dips as the climate spilled from snow-laden fields of blinding whiteness to sod and tree marking the early borders of the vast Saratian forest stretching between the nation boundaries where the smells of coniferous needles filled into the air. She approached another intersection which she at once steered west. Craggy mountain fingers lined with faint glowing trails stretched across the sky reaching over the horizon distance. Patches of blackened dirt sprinkled along the ground as a powdery soil. Lush grasses and moss covered the grounds where the snows had yet to fall.

She continued along the road coming short of a displaced streak of pitch smoked grass seared as fused, green-tinted glass across the road. Cadeck urged her to stop a few meters in front of the anomaly.

"Is this where you followed the Magi?"

"Yes. For many days I pursued him and when I caught sight of him again, he created this," she pointed at the charred ground, "I couldn't get beyond the wall of flame he scorched upon the ground and when I would try to go around, the wall of flame reacted, impeding my advance. As he was not my pursued purpose in Silvetzen, I returned."

Cadeck turned his inquisitive mind towards the distant mountain range. He rubbed the growing whiskers encroaching upon his chin.

"Where does this road end?"

"The western port town of Blorak."

Cadeck turned his shoulder to scan for any encroaching pursuers.

"We must be quick. The Si'rai will mobilize their forces to spread through Silvetzen. The Tanakian Ring lies ahead. If you followed him this far before he stopped you, I am certain the Fire Temple is there."

"We're heading into a volcano range?"

Venna raised her voice into a questioning pitch as she stood up in the back of the cart. She brushed off fragments of hay from her garments in a vain attempt to appear tidy.

"Fire Temple, my child. Try to keep up with the formalities," Cadeck turned his attention towards Rensel, "Get us close, but do not enter the range. You ladies will need to remain behind while Tesh and I continue into the Temple. Make camp in seclusion. After his trials, we will return and meet up with you. If a Si'rai army arrives with a Magister in our absence, run. Run as fast as you can into the Wood and do not let them find you. Do not return to Sarat. Make your way towards Racoren and lay low. We will find you there."

"Racoren? It is a den of thieves and pirates there," Cassica sighed, her voice rising in disgust.

"You will be safer there than in the hands of the Si'rai. This I promise you."

"I hope you're right about your plan, Cadeck."

"I hope so too, Your Grace."

Rensel commanded the horse to continue as they rushed forward through the wood-flanked path. The wheel ruts sank into the blackened road trailing volcanic sand in its wake. Ample fauna grazed within the lush fields interchanged with pockets of forestry as the cart swept along the dense paths winding along the carved trade route. Hazardous cliffs signified the baseline of the Tanakian Ring intruding upon the serene landscape as though cursed by the anger of the gods.

The trade route skirted north of the range passing through empty fields of pristine grasses wavering in the cool winds. Riding further as the sun lowered to dusk, the outcroppings loomed closer along the road as rises of gray rock faces pierced through the grasses. Cadeck moved his hand onto Rensel's shoulder and motioned for her to cease the cart. Growths of volcanic rocks tore through the moss-covered fields like fingers through mud. Daylight waned to reveal a shimmer of stars above.

"Tesh, come."

Cadeck steadied himself to lower to the ground. Tesh removed himself from the rear of the cart carrying the fallen soldier's sword and his simple belongings. He shook his pants to remove any excess hay as he met Cadeck at the front of the wagon.

"Is this it?"

"I would imagine the Fire Temple is somewhere in this range. Cassica, I see there is a clearing of forest to the south of here, make your camp there."

Cadeck pointed towards a tree line bordering the craggy outcroppings of the baseline of the volcanic rim. Without hesitation, Cadeck turned his attention towards a small path leading within the volcanic mountainscape. His head never turned away from his goal while he spoke advice towards the female party staying behind him.

"If there is an eruption, you will feel the ground shake. I would suggest running."

"More running," Venna sighed.

Cadeck ignored her sarcasm, pressing Tesh to move onward into the rocky distance flanked along their route by massive boulders of pumice rock dotting the countryside. Rensel aided Cassica with the preparations to move the cart off the path as nighttime gave way to the howls of distant predators.

"Well, he's a load of cheer," Venna remarked as she jumped to the driver seat beside Rensel.

Rensel led the horse-drawn cart into the appointed clearing. Cassica watched as Cadeck and Tesh moved into the dangerous range, a flicker of light erupted in front of Cadeck's palm to guide their path. Her heart drawing upon Cadeck's visions and thoughts. She valued her dynasty's alliance with the Magi throughout the ages. Rumors and legends of their corruption formed her opinions as she stared to the path to follow the pair. She knew Cadeck as a trusted friend and advisor and relied on his truth in following his plan.

On the other hand, Tesh introduced himself as a mere commoner whom she had no reason to speak to other than cordialities. Charming, yet naïve to the ways of her station, he humbled himself to her in clumsy manner. Despite his awkward attempts, his doddering speech in her presence, she felt something unique about him. Throughout her life she had known royalty and nobility, guided in the principles of the position her family guided for her. Cassica spent no time learning romance in her youth, occupied by other endeavors. For her role one day was to become the chosen bond to a prince or other royal, adhering to the laws of a kingdom her children would inherit. She rubbed her left-hand paying attention to the veins shadowing through her pale skin and with each dialogue with Tesh, with the touches of his hands upon her figure, she too sensed a destiny unknown. *Tesh's hand is so… different. I will not know if the legends are true, until he proves himself.*

Chapter 21

Blood soaked the rich green foliage of the sparse forest clearing, trickling as a gushing torrent from the gaping neck wound of the verdasnik. A serrated knife blade cut deep within the furry hide of the game animal as Rensel prepared the beast for field dressing. The head splayed apart from its neck facing the ground, its two small horns only a few centimeters from touching surface. Venna raised the creature with its hind legs pulleyed along the branches of the bearwood tree with hemp rope allowing the blood gore to drain from the beast.

Venna winced over the rough stench of the beast's hides as Rensel swiftly separated the edible muscle from the continuous streams of gelatinous fat oozing from every cut. The muscles were stringy and tender as Rensel slung them into the metal bucket at her feet carving her way through to the soft guts of the animal. She reached the verdasnik's heart and added it to the collection of meat. She moved closer to the stomach, dissecting it from the digestive tract and placed the whole organ into the bucket.

Venna did her best to cover her face from the stench as she watched Rensel remove the rations. Venna's nose fought to distract her attention from the smells of the gore to the morning dew sprinkled across the grasses in the scarce dawn light. She surveyed Rensel's methods of fervor to organize their meal, carefully carving away skin and fur from the animal to prepare the hides for use. Specks of blood spray littered across Rensel's unruly brunette hair betrayed by a few days lack of attention.

"Why'd you do it, Ysalir?" Venna assured none were in earshot of her question, addressing Rensel by her given name.

"Do what?" Ysalir continued her meticulous task, unflinching from her deed, "And why did you use my birth name? You know protocol."

"We are alone. None can listen and you are my sister. I should be able to address you informally. Why did you sleep with strange men?"

"I did it for the Crown, Venna. In my profession, you do what you must to obtain information and secure your targets. I do not regret it. It brought us out of Silvetzen and saved your ass, right? Do not address my name in front of Her Highness, understood?"

Ysalir carved the thick blade into the stubborn hides of the carcass, peeling the remnants away with her open hands as the edge fileted the skins. Birds fluttered from the trees calling towards the rising sun while a cool breeze trickled over the landscape from the north.

"But when you first went on assignment, you held a respectable position as a nurse maid. Your letters filled my heart with wonder and admiration," Venna's voice fluttered with her eyes.

"You misled yourself, dear. Being a killer is not respectable, nor commendable."

Pooled blood spilled from the animal as she punctured an organ in the torso cavity, covering Ysalir's hands in fresh gore.

"I had to do what I did to secure my cover. Once I got close to the Court through the ladies of the nobility," she sighed heavy as she struggled onto a new piece of hide, "I could then turn my lure towards the men."

Ysalir never paused in her work. She spied the samples of provisions in the bucket and mentally declared a full ration for a couple of days.

"Do me a favor would you? Stuff the incision with grass and leaves. It will hide the smell so other predators do not sense the kill and approach camp."

Venna performed as requested gathering the thick foliage between her hands in the surrounding brush. She winced to vomit as her hands fell into the open torso with each push and shove of vegetation.

"But your letters," Venna continued her pry, "You boasted of a man, a handsome man. I had my eyes set on becoming a Justiciar so I too may find love like the one your heart poured out."

Ysalir cracked a shot of grimaced stare poking through a furrowed bang stretching down her right cheek. Venna's question volleyed an arrow into her heart. She dropped the bucket of meat onto the dense floor of the opening forest and cut into Venna's face with a stare of spite.

"There is no love in my profession, only pain. The pain is of my target, and I feel no sympathy for their misfortunes at my blade. The task of being a Justiciar is assassination. Getting close, spreading your legs, it is all part of the job."

Ysalir turned away from her sister, grabbing for the bucket.

"But your letters were filled with love, until one day I stopped receiving them."

"My mission came before family. As a servant of the Crown, you would be best to remember."

Ysalir hoisted the bucket upon her shoulder while Venna stuffed the remaining pieces of verdure into the prey. She wiped her hands upon the soiled tunics with fresh mud to cover the stench of rot. Her doe eyes contrived the sense of displacement her sister displayed towards her.

"Then I do not want to become a Justiciar. I will be a Benedicer... or a Scrivener, a spagyrist, or a scholar."

Ysalir started to walk away from her sister as she spoke. With her strength, it wasn't the bucket that hurt her. Each step a torture upon her heart with every word spoken from Venna's bleating. She knew her guilt yet told Venna the truth she wanted her to hear. She returned a response to Venna as the younger girl arrived at her side.

"You'll perform as the Crown commands," Ysalir poked her left index finger into her sister's budding chest, "Queen Selen will mark your rank, and you will obey as Princess Cassica declares. You have proven ability as a killer when we escaped."

Ysalir turned and began the arduous march through the clearing towards the hint of campfire.

"But if Tesh becomes a Knight, the Sun Warrior if the legends are true, there will not be a need for the Order any longer. The Knights shall resume their roles."

Ysalir pierced a stern eye into Venna's soul as the pair walked abreast, "Do not pleasure your mind with thoughts of fools, Venna. The Knights are a legend, a fairy tale. There are no more Knights as the last one is surely dead." *As well he should be for ripping out my heart.*

Ysalir returned to her trek slugging through the dense foliage upon the ground with the reeking bucket slung onto her shoulder. Venna followed, ducking, and weaving through the thicket. Her hands sprung up to protect her face as a twig snapped towards her direction after Ysalir cleared it aside.

"Your lover's actions, it's why you became a courtesan?"

"We will have no further discussion of this matter. You would do best to clear your mind of it."

"Don't hold back truth from me, Ysalir."

Venna's voice rose as though her conclusion was correct. A solitary tear rolled along Ysalir's right cheek. Venna's naïve inquisition rolled over Ysalir's ears as a shiv to her gut as the pair approached camp. The welcome aroma of the fire brushed through the pre-dawn woods carrying its smoke like a low haze. Bubbling sounds billowed from a boiling pot hoisted over the low flame of a campfire. A simple, lean-to tent had covered a side of the carriage where Eris rolled up the sleeping arrangements. Tied upon a tree nearby, the single horse gnawed to the welcome grains of hay beneath its mouth. Ysalir dropped the bucket to the ground with a heavy thud upon the plush grass. She stretched her arms, relieving the muscle tension gripping her biceps.

Cassica seated herself upon the foliage; the soft damp wetness penetrated her loose leggings as she pressed her thighs along the ground. She released a burlap sheet into a lengthwise rollout. Finely cut accoutrements gleamed in the orange firelight. Different knives and blades of assorted sizes and purpose holstered within the leaf. She counted each of them once, twice, then a third time deducing the tally to accommodate all materials were intact.

Each of these weapons served a purpose from long range stilettos used for tossing towards a pursuing target, or handheld knives used to cut attackers in melee. A pouch held caltrops while another held axes for wood chopping. There were also pin-sized needles intended to store in bobbed-hair and dipped in toxins to administer to a mark.

"A fine assortment you have here, Rensel."

"One can never be too certain, Your Highness. Never know what you will need for a job."

"How long do you believe they'll be gone?"

"I wish I could say. A day or two. You are more familiar with the Magi than I am, Your Highness."

Ysalir unrolled a burlap mat upon the ground and prepared the meat for broil. She carefully placed strings of cut meat into the boiling pot to preserve their length for cooking. Eris seated herself next to Venna as the two younger girls helped Ysalir. Venna maintained her inquisitive stare at her sister, her heart saddened by Ysalir's cold responses at the site of the hunt.

"Your thoughts may be true, Rensel. But I am not familiar with their ways. Mornika never discussed it."

Ysalir nodded in agreement.

"Father saw Cadeck as more of an advisor and a friend as did I. I was too young to ask about his ways before I left for Jorin."

"A lot troubles him. And I am afraid I may have compounded them back in Silvetzen."

"He needed to know. He understands now why I cannot trust the Council as a whole. If they turn their backs to secure their fortunes, they are nothing more than greedy charlatans."

"He didn't want me to tell you, Your Highness, but it is my obligation."

Cassica nodded in response with Ysalir's statement as she continued, "However, I've observed you don't see him that way."

"No. Something is different. Do you ever get the feeling someday the world will change? Possibly we are living in those times. I asked Tesh if he believed in prophecy, but he did not seem to care."

"I used to believe too, Your Highness."

"Explain?"

Ysalir ignored her question instead focusing on the preparations at hand, "Your Highness, if I may decline answer?"

"She lost her heart to a man."

Venna shouted in cold agitation. Ysalir shot her a disgruntled stare curling her lip into a sneer. She balled a fist ready to strike her sister but realized her audience and calmed herself with an exaggerated release of breath.

"Is this true? While you were on assignment, you let your emotions guide you toward a man? Did you compromise your name?"

Cassica returned her tone to her formal rank as Ysalir's superior.

"His information was vital, Your Highness. I did what I needed to, for the Crown. Without it we would not have known about the Si'rai involvement with Silvetzen in its earliest stages."

"Who was he? Does he know your name?"

"He is dead now. He betrayed the Si'rai, and he met fate after leaving Silvetzen."

"Are you certain? Did you see his body? Does he know your name?"

Cassica's anger rose as she asked the question a second time.

Ysalir stomached her lie in hopes Cassica would believe it, choking back a response. Her eyes, her face unmoved in her conviction of words to her superior.

"I told him my name before I murdered him. I buried him in secret."

"You do not sound very forthcoming with me. What else did you expose while you were on assignment?"

Cassica reached for a blade amongst the arsenal, prepared to handle the sudden betrayal.

"Your Highness, please, you can trust me. I got you out of the riot, didn't I?"

"For what? Are the Si'rai going to find us out here? As did his heart, did yours likewise betray your Crown? Do others know of your name and your worth?"

Cassica sprang from her position, the dull end of the knife leading against her forearm as she rushed it towards Ysalir's neck dropping the woman to her back. Cassica's emerald eyes turned to a low glimmer. Venna stumbled backwards, crawling as a crab away from the fight.

"You are my most trusted asset in the field. You are as an older sister to me, and you revealed secrets to our enemies? We trained together. I should gut you now and leave your corpse to the predators."

Ysalir struggled to keep the business end of Cassica's blade away from her neck, her hand gripped around Cassica's fist curled tight upon the hilt. Two pairs of bare white knuckles buckled around the blade's pommel.

"No, Your Highness, I revealed nothing to him of the sort. He told me he was Si'rai, an executor for his emperor's will. His most trusted servant. When he told me who he was and how he came to serve the Si'rai, I had to tell him."

Cassica poised over Ysalir's chest, her hips spread apart straddling Ysalir. She split the hold Ysalir had on her knife and hoisted the weapon in a stabbing motion above her head, her palm on the pommel. Cassica fumed with fury allowing one last ultimatum before she would plunge the knife through the traitor's heart.

"What did you tell him? You told him your name because you loved him, didn't you? You revealed my father's secrets for cock between thighs."

"I told him who his father was - Teru Verdui."

"Which means…" Cassica dropped the knife to the ground, her eyes leading her thoughts towards repose as she slipped from Ysalir's body. Ysalir sat up, leaning against her right arm.

"Yes. And why he left Silvetzen. He ran, where he went, I do not know. But I stayed on assignment and repositioned myself into the court but could not return to being a nurse maid. I learned what I needed from him. He divulged plans for the Magi and the Si'rai conquest for Sarat and the rest of Roth. He did not tell me why or how, but it has something to do with the Temples. I never intended to fall in love with him."

"But you did, and you could have jeopardized your mission. You allowed your heart to get close which aided you to obtain information vital to the safety of the Crown and with heavy heart I have entrusted to our decoys."

Cassica's thoughts trailed to her family as she stood to her feet and offered an open hand to her friend. Ysalir accepted the friendship offer, joining her in stand.

"Those men are our last hope, Your Highness."

**

The blue streak of Saratian bulk bolted through the Silvetzenian landscape with thunderous calamity as the wheel ruts swayed the carriage to each side. Cold darkness gripped the air surrounded by the dancing stars. Waxing moonlight cut to the east, splitting its orbit against the backdrop of the dark band hovering close to the apex of the night. The horses whinnied with whipped haste as the driver clutched the reins in white knuckle, commanding grip. The sounds of rocketing steel and heavy wood barreled over the landscape. Behind him, a Blue Guard kneeled against the flat board of the carriage's rooftop, a wrapped cord tightened around his waist tying him onto the roof.

His arms angled to secure the butt of a crossbow against his shoulder made difficult by the rocking of the wagon. He eyed along his sight, as he readied his breath for the trigger pull. He aimed the weapon with precision as a single bolt evacuated from the barrel with a *thwip*. The bolt pierced through empty night into the direction of a wall of darkness pursuing them.

Another guard secured along the running boards, repeated the action of his peer. The bolts cleared the fearsome attackers as their horses parted, allowing the projectiles to harmlessly fall onto the ground. As the void loomed closer, the Saratian men caught sight of eight orbs of eerie azure glow encroaching upon their escape. Like a consuming void, the attackers made pace and soon matched speed with the fleeing cart. One man bounded from his horse, an astounding feat with his size and clutched the trunk board of the war carriage with calloused hands like peeled sausages. His leather armor stretched with a whine as his grip tightened against the alloy plating.

Ignoring the speed of his target, Xanos Coron climbed his way onto the roof of the carriage and removed a pair of axes with serrated blades from his back. Elaborate curvature adorned the blades into half-circle shape against the hilt as he readied them to strike. Unwavering from the swaying carriage ride, he took a ferocious swing from his right-hand axe towards the single man mounted on the roof. In defense, the Saratian guard brought his crossbow to protect his face buying him time as his assailant cleaved his bow along the stock. The impact allowed him to reach for a broadsword resting at his feet.

The young Saratian guard readied his blade to battle his adversary. He caught a glimpse of the shadow riders behind his carriage, the middle one lit with an icy blue glow for eyes like wispy orbs of a haunted graveyard dancing in the darkness of sin. In ferocity, Xanos split his arms in war stance; his axe blades darkened by the night as he let loose a fearsome war cry through his split goatee. His eyes matching the ice blue stare of the middle rider. Dropping his weapon, the Saratian guard cowered from the horror of the foreign beast pronouncing his superiority of strength and steel. Xanos' bald head and fierce cry intimidated the well-disciplined Guardsman, as he swung the barbed blades into either side of his redheaded prey spilling blood and skull fragments across the vehicle. He pulled his axes away from the wound, showering the Saratian man's collapsing body in blood stains.

Another Si'rai soldier made pace with the driver of the carriage, jumping onto the right of the driver board. Cold heat smoke rose from his bald scalp as a tightened braid bound Jagoth Reanar's lengthy ponytail into a barbed tip. A quick plunge of a dagger gutted the Saratian driver's throat. The pony-tailed man grabbed the reins of the horses commanding them to a gradual stop as the driver's body slumped forward, falling into the path of the carriage crushing him with a pulp of blood, flesh, and bone.

The remaining Saratian men fought in vain, their lives ending by the superior blades and conscripted ferocity of their attackers as the new driver jerked the carriage to a full stop. Tivius A'zum dismounted his horse; his icy eyes surveyed the damage his men inflicted as a proud father boasting of his offspring's accomplishment. Blood splatters painted upon the sides of the wagon and soaked the armor of their dead. The door to the carriage flung open exposing the empty ruse, finding only a solitary box and a lit candle secured in a silver sconce beside it.

Tivius sneered upon his discovery. His eyes glistened with anger as he wheezed an unpleasant hiss. None of the Saratian envoy was onboard. He reached for the parchwood box. Finding fortune, the box opened with ease. A wax seal kept the parchment from unauthorized eyes bound with the sigil of the Order of the Rose. He removed a small knife from his hip and defiled the classified document.

Tivius smiled as he read the letter, glossing it over with his brittle hands as his eyes dimmed to a cool sheen in the cold of early winter frost. His assassins removed the armor from the Saratian bodies, assessing their sizes and binding the plates to their bodies as they would fit. He called the soldiers to his attention who obeyed their master without question, lining up in front of the carriage like a ragtag assortment of depravity and violence.

Tivius glanced at each of them along the line, sneering as he surveyed their haphazard accoutrements. The first, Surar Tudok; built stout and muscular as his Si'rai brother-in-arms, Jagoth Reanar and carrying a quiver of arrows slung over his shoulder and a blackened stock crossbow polished raven to a shiny gleam. Quinias Degoros stood taller than he, dwarfing beside him with a dark-skinned complexion and lanky as Tivius carrying a large sword on his back. Two other men approached the wagon late, mounted on horses like black silhouettes of war against the dim twilight.

"Men, the Saratian envoy was not present onboard this carriage," his leather croaked as he walked in front of them with slow pace, "Instead, she sends a letter to her father we have conquered Silvetzen and will return to Sarat in time. No matter, our task is not to find her. Don the armor of our enemy; we ride as though we were them. Clean up the blood, to not arouse suspicion and burn the bodies. You two," Tivius pointed to the mounted men, "return with the horses and inform Iostana Magistrata of our findings to send the legions soon," he turned his attention to the sky, recalling the position of the moon, "Abra'in will be full in fourteen rakini. My armies shall arrive then. We have thirteen rakini to conquer Sarat.

"I have no doubt our ruse will grant us unprecedented access direct into Court. Reward for our endeavor will be five Saratian uristri and one thousand auduin. I grant you this by my commission."

Tivius' speech delivered in his tongue, the language called Sheebal, inspired by the reward of five slaves and currency, the men moved to obey his command. The pair of horsemen wrangled the other five animals and harried off to return northward. The rest made quick time, fervidly moving to take on the armor of their kill. They stripped their own tunics and splashed them with the water from the Saratian supplies to rub out the fresh blood before it could stain the iron plating. Tivius sealed himself within the carriage and placed his long sword along the opposite bench in front of him.

He felt a fading essence. It was a taste he once pursued lingering in the carriage like the smells of a satisfying meal. The magick signature was strong and weighed on his own mind to recall his failures. He ran his spindly fingers cracked with dehydration through the open airs of the vehicle as it lurched forward. The tastes of magick tickled his digits as he consumed the remaining vibrations of his adversaries before retreating them in closed fists.

"Raka'ir's servant will find you Cadeck, and where he fails, I will not."

Chapter 22

Dim sunlight crept into the shallow darkness of the middeck chambers. Beams of amber candlelight swayed to light in futility. Shadows bounced along the curved cabin chambers in grim reflection of the obscene, decorative motif. Torkas Philatané sat behind a rickwood desk decorated by the talents of a commissioned madman with distinguished taste of art. Before him stood several men with various disfigurements, each one studied contemptibly.

He sensed their dread. An air of distrust circulated about the room with each man before him unwavering in their motives. They too, studied his frail senility, the meek and hunched man in the crimson cloaks who stood as the one fragment to gaining the full trust of their emperor and taking place to be his administer.

Before him stood Magister Ragres Shabririn the Blind; eyes covered by a thick, soiled cloth. A tattoo of the Abyss burned upon his scarred forehead devoid of hair. Beside him and slightly taller, stood the burning, crimson corneas focused from Magister Malphas Corant. His red flesh mired by chiseled flakes of an obsidian infection across his face and exposed hands which ended in keratin talons. Each servant wore the distinguished leathery bindings of their caste fitted tight upon their flesh appeared as stitched upon them at birth.

Malphas' voice rolled as a shallow growl speaking in their native tongue, "Lord, I accept with great humility your honor bestowed upon me. But if I may approach with question as to your purpose?"

"I assign you as Commandant Magister of Silvetzen. A position of which should require no inquiry. Would you rather I find," Torkas paused, his voice squeaking as a coughing wheeze were to overtake him, "someone else?"

"No, my Lord."

Torkas ignored his response, directing his voice towards the blind man.

"I have received word this morning from Lord A'zum concerning the fate of the Saratian princess. We expected her ruse, thus conquering Sarat by force is now a necessity. Magister Shabririn, you have your orders. This Aztmi orchestrated her escape, thus, to conclude he, the Azthar Kherdmon and

Cassica still live. It is to my understanding the Guardian of the Abyss discovered him in prayer before he left this city?"

"Yes, Lord." Shabririn spoke through rotten gums and a slight hiss to his speech of their native tongue.

"Good. Follow him. Do not engage. When he meets the temples, leave evidence so we can find them. He is already several days ahead of you. It is imperative you do not arouse suspicion. Find the Temples, but do not desecrate them. Supernus Magister would rather deal with the Aztmi at each temple himself, so says his word."

Shabririn made no comment but released a hiss of acceptance as he bowed towards his master. His figure shambled away from the room leaving Torkas with Malphas and another Magister covered in crimson robes. A crimson veil adorned his scalp and hung by a mesh of wired entanglements gripped across his skull.

"Malphas," Torkas reached for a stack of papers bound in a rope, "These documents came from the endeavors of Lord A'zum's predecessor. They are the names of the Silvetzenian royalty who have assured their loyalty. Go now, assume your place upon Silvetzen's throne. Magister A'zum will secure Sarat. Magister Nybas," Torkas pointed to another stack of documents, sliding them towards the crimson-robed man with the gnarled skull, "These are the same for Sarat. Fifty legions are ready to support his conquest."

"Magister, if I may ask; what of Tarlakana? The land certainly holds Temples," Malphas pushed one last question as Nybas ruffled through the papers in his possession.

"Our spies among the Tarlaki have assured Aztmi exist there. Once Admiral Focalore secures the port of Racoren, he will take Magister Shabririn by sea. Should Shabririn fail, Supernus Magister has assured of contingency. Now leave me, for your next question may be your last."

Malphas shuttered his vermillion eyes as he bowed in respect towards his High Magister and removed himself from the cabin.

"Magister," Nybas growled through hidden lips, "this one here, we can be assured of his loyalty?"

He pointed to a document near the top of his stack bearing the House surname; Denwich.

"He fits our criteria."

"From the dossier, he will be entertaining to me," Nybas bowed in reverence, turning his back, exiting the cabin.

Another man remained with the emissary. Dyed, vermillion fabrics formed slender as a flagpole topped with broad-shouldered pauldrons. His crinkled face etched with years of wear sinking his blackened eyes amidst the dark abyss of the room. Long sleeves entombed his hands to nigh invisibility as they crossed upon his chest. His stocky frame bore years of wisdom in service to the Imperium. Torkas turned his attention towards the older man, announcing his civilian title in their tongue.

"Durustrata, you may return to Abaddon to report progress to the Durustratum. The Imperium will obtain victory during this Passing of the Abyss."

"The Durustratum will be delighted of this news, Iostana Magistrata, but they question Supernus Magister's insistence on placing Magisters in positions of rule."

Torkas leaned against the back of his chair, folding his arms within his sleeves, "This is a war front. Once we secure the realms, Supernus Magister shall appoint a Durustrate to represent this colony."

The lawman nodded in appreciation of the words, "The clans will be delighted, and what shall I provide to the Durustratum to rumors as to the purpose of the Aztmi's tuistrina?"

Torkas lifted his eyes through the crimson cowl concealing his face in shadows. The legislator pushed the belief of the populi to state the Imperium holds children of a Magi prisoner. Meek and intimidated, his jowls shook to form a response at the request. His thoughts processed the words, yet the illusion of frailty belied his position to the legislator.

"How many in the Durustratum believe in rumors, Abigar?"

"A handful, my Lord. Others not holding position have been spreading accusatory tongue. The Durustratum requests confirmation of them."

"There are no prisoners of the Aztmi in the custody of the Imperium, nor have there ever been. Durustratus Abigar, return to Abaddon and quell these rumors permanently. Any citizen of the Imperium, even the nobility would not be immune to punishment for sponsoring gossip. Should insidious words leave the tongues of the people, remove them, and not just their tongues."

"Yes, My Lord. Another agenda I should bring to your attention, my Lord, if I may?"

Torkas nodded his approval of the question, his chin lowering with little observation, "Proceed."

"Drahak Abra'in is upon us soon, celebrations are underway in the Triopolis for Babalon's consummation, but the priests have not seen the Visraair Abra. They have begun their fasting in Shemhaiza in preparation for her arrival. Shall the people expect the possibility of their Sacred Queen?"

Torkas postulated the concern, "It too has been a concern of mine. Supernus Magister continues to lead from the war front and has placed his convictions upon the womb of the Aztmi's abin as holding the gateway to the future Aeon. I must leave in time to prepare for the ritual, yet the populace must believe their Supernus Magister is infallible.

"Isolate a uristru; she must be slender with supple, yet firm breasts. She must be Si'rai, no other race and virginal. Induce her, drug her, and primp her for the ceremony. Reveal her to the gatherers and worshippers and parade her as called for. A Magister from Shemhaiza will serve in our master's stead to the ceremony. Let the public continue to celebrate as they may; orgies, sacrifices and bloodletting to appease Hadithem. It will please Supernus Magister to know his people continue to hold pride. Victory should not falter from the minds of the populace, victory for us in this Procession. This Aeon belongs to the Si'rai.

"Inebriated and seduced into splendor, the populace will be unawares of her fate. After the three-rakinis time, I shall command the Magister to take her into isolation and splay her insides in Antexum Cruci, and he shall also take his own life."

Abigar swallowed a lump, his eyes opened with fear. Hesitation rolled from his voice like a lumbering, broken wagon.

"My Lord, are you so certain punishment is necessary?"

Torkas did not hesitate to deliver his response, "Would you prefer I perform thus to you on the bow of this ship?"

"No, my Lord," Abigar regained composure.

"Then leave. As Volen Absikar, my words are absolute. Follow them or see your fate manifest in the Abyss." Torkas proclaimed his title to the lawman as the Will of the Abyss.

"May the blessings of Hadithem grant your endeavors good tidings my Lord."

Abigar bowed and dismissed himself from Torkas' cabin. As the creak of the wooden door sealed him from prying tongues, Torkas contemplated upon the orders issued. He swiveled in the chair to gaze upon the waves splashing against Silvetzen's docks. A dusting of light snow blanketed the base of the sea wall between the piers. Ghostly lanterns posted in several intervals casting dancing shadows in the light wind swaying them. Untouched virgin frost covered the harbor posts like white capped sticks hoisting the refined planks of wood. Harbor men tended to the massive Si'rai warships docked like floating, obscene castles painted against the high cliff sides.

Like little insects building their mounds, Torkas observed the dock men loading cargo into the Si'rai ships. Biting winds tore upon their exposed, light skin as Si'rai officers barked profane orders of indentured servitude. Each of them, like innocent little minds ripe for corruption bent to the will of their conquerors. A futile uprising occurred as a Silvetzenian dock worker hefted a cargo crate in the direction of a Si'rai soldier, followed by the man's unfortunate decapitation. Torkas smiled at the sight as the creaking of gears and machinery signaled the masts to open sail.

The listing of the ship with the direction of the light angle put the skyline of the Silvetzenian harbor within Torkas' view. The rest of the smaller, embarkation boats released their organic cargo onto the outlying shores, spilling seas of Si'rai raven armor towards the inland city in a wave of enforcement. The Will of the Abyss completed as commanded by Torkas' master.

Torkas counted the days. Nearing three centuries to Tivius, Torkas sensed the younger Magister would strike at the chance to remove the liaison between himself and their master. Though Tivius was a natural offspring, the hierarchy of their command structure did not offer Tivius line of succession. Torkas had proven himself decades before. Though physically frail in appearance, none without skill dare raise their aggressions towards him; those who did found themselves at the mercy of a man who spared none. He recalled the times when several lesser magisters tried methods of usurpation. Torkas punished them with catatonic psychosis from forced sensory deprivation while they slept as unknowing victims of his distant magicks.

Torkas carried the Will of the Supernus Magister of the Imperium. Orders dictated came to fruition under his guidance. His presence was symbolic as laying eyes upon the Supernus Magister himself. Where he carried, so did the breath of their God-King. He earned his place over a century ago when he bore witness to the striking blade in the hands of a young man. The boy, no older than thirteen shone with the glee of death in his eyes. The skull pommel of the serrated blade cast in ivory rested atop his thumb as the striking instrument clung to fresh blood and tissue. The victim strewn on the cold slab in a manner of sacrifice, the heart removed still beating as the young boy ingested the fresh muscle.

It is done. The dying man's final breath whispered. Torkas moved his fingers to close the man's eyes. Ceremonial robes covered him, sheen in white fabric, exposing the thick olive-skinned tone beneath them. Golden jewels laced his neckline with a flat headdress capping his attire. He counted his age then, nearing a century. Jewels adorned his ear lobes and nose, his fingers fitted through ornate claws extending beyond his nails. As he reached for the blade in the young boy's hands, he dropped to one knee in the grace of obedience. He bowed his head lifting the ritual tool with both hands and proclaimed the young man with title, Supernus Magister. Chants and bows followed among the priests and priestesses presiding over the ritual.

Torkas' thoughts lingered to distant dreams interrupted by whispering hisses billowing within his cabin. The daylight now absent. The shores of

Silvetzen long given way to the ocean. He turned to see a pair of floating crimson eyes before him casting themselves in shadow unimpeded by the small candles upon the desk.

"Master is pleased with your progress, Torkas."

"You can inform him I will be returning shortly for Drahak Abra'in."

"He is aware," the shadows slithered to form a spindly figure ahead of the ornately carved desk.

"And the Aztmi, Ragres informs me he cannot pray."

"It is true. The Abyss covers the lands of Silvetzen and soon it will cover Sarat. When he prays, he will see it."

"And when Ragres marks the locations of the Temples, he will have no safe place to commune with his gods."

"You place too much assurance in his mortality, Torkas."

"I have commissioned his replacement should he fail."

"She is reckless, Torkas," the slithering spirit moved in the shadows, only his eyes visible, "Like her brother. Leaving her with Goborah was not a wise choice."

"Supernus Magister has trusted my judgment for nearly two centuries, demon. Since the day I crowned him."

"But a speck of time to me, Torkas."

Choronzon pushed his shadowy figure over the desk. Torkas heard the demon seething his name, berating his mortality.

"'Tis true, demon. Yet, you are still obedient to him."

Torkas looked up to see the pair of eyes floating in shadow to remind the ethereal beast of his place.

"Only in as much as his devotion. Should he fail, the Archons would surely claim him as they will with you," Choronzon slithered away, towards the cabin door.

"The Imperium shall not fail, demon."

"Another outcome may yet come to realization. The Aztmi's tuistrina will bring ruination."

"Subdued they are mere tools, pawns to be used against Cadeck to bring him and the Azthar Kherdmon to death at the hands of Supernus Magister."

"You would be wise not to underestimate them, Torkas. The Aztmi's devotion is incorruptible, his tenacity is venerable."

And as the haunting specter appeared, the shadows withered away with the faint dimmer of Choronzon's fiery eyes into the darkened void masked by the lamplight. The demon spoke through his own kind, the representative of their gods of death to their religion as a gateway across the Abyss. Magisters

232

channeled their own desires for the shadow demon to ferry them back to their ancient gods. He functioned as a guardian to their ethereal host, and as a foul specter commanded by the Supernus Magister as his own personal ferryman of information. Torkas watched the stars above, dancing out of the way of the ghostly void appearing in the nighttime sky above the fleet. Chanting occurred on the decks above, his loyal zealotors and lower priests working magicks to their fabled heaven.

"We will command the gods, doubter, and they will obey."

A hissing laugh not of his source followed his whisper.

Chapter 23

Sharp-scented ember smoke rose from the dying campfire flaring its specks to cling to the fading simmer. Stinging sulfur scents blew across the valley covering the taste of the varkin meat Tesh consumed with a bitter aftertaste. His stomach struggled to overcome the stench of the caldera around him as he swallowed the meal. He studied Cadeck standing several meters away, surveying the bleak surroundings. Amidst the bubbling springs of clear water and caustic acidity, there existed a sliver of arcane beauty like a bathhouse of certain death.

Tesh readied his feet to work another day. He stretched his legs and glanced down towards his left hand. Steam and sulfur wafted along the air clouding the skies above, blocking the visible sunlight through the valley. What he would give to return to Telmen to work any of the laborious jobs he had taken. Today, he was in the harsh and unforgiving wasteland of a caldera.

Cadeck scouted side to side in anxious manners. Tesh sensed unfamiliarity in his mannerisms. No clear road marked a path, only juts and crannies of ashen rocks and gravel allowing stretches of barren landscapes where the slightest slip would end in fatality. Small animals scurried across the rocky terrain penetrated by steaming cracks scarring the landscape like pressurized wounds. They exhibited a doggedness withstanding the odd heat pressing upon Tesh's body. An occasional rumble rocked the deadly terrain followed by the release of noxious vapor pockets like a vicious geyser burst.

Cadeck turned back towards Tesh, scratching his graying whiskers now forming long upon his cheek. The short beard hid the cracks of age in his face mirroring the landscape around him. He kicked up a fleck of volcanic dust from his stride, the land around them a dangerous vista of random geysers and pockets of steaming, basaltic lava. Cadeck's breaths strained short as he covered his mouth with the neckline of his dusty tunics.

"We should leave, Tesh."

Tesh's meat chunks mixed with the pink hues of marrow as he nibbled his way to the bare bites. He filled his mouth with his meal and chunked the leg bone to the ground.

"Do you know where we are going? We have wandered aimlessly this past day."

"I have my hunches. The hot flows tend to drift towards the center of the valley. I imagine the Fire Temple is not far. We need to be careful."

Cadeck wiped his brow with the sleeve of his robes. He paused, pondering the new stain on his clothing evaporating as he watched. His short hair clung against his neck with the refuse of sweat and grime. Every smell reminding him of his torture. Every breath like the dungeon he left where every thought and every dream centered upon reuniting with his children. He could never hear their nighttime cries, but he was certain they could hear his screams under torture.

"Then how can we find this place? How did other Knights find this place?"

Tesh kicked ashen dust beneath his feet as he stood in angry impatience.

"Back when the Knights still existed, the Magi of Fire could always guide them. I never knew. I never administered a trial until you came along. Godwen reminded me the journey is not about the one we take with our feet, but the one within our soul."

Cadeck's cryptic words rolled through Tesh's ears as riddles and anecdotes, much too sophisticated for his upbringing. Cadeck picked up his belongings to rest over his shoulder, worsening the deep journey into the volcanic hell. Tesh followed, lagging as he cursed the hotness of the air and the pools of sweat upon his skin staining his clothes. Teams of cauterizing water bubbled in sparse pockets, every pop and fizzle watered Tesh's desire for fresh liquid. He touched his water flask and tried to drink only to discover the water inside was warm to his lips. It quenched his thirst but supplied little to stave the increasing discomfort of the aether around him.

Tesh struggled in his journey as the hours progressed, occasionally stopping to have a seat on the heated ground. He winced in pain as he removed the leather shoes tugging against the blisters forming upon his feet. The exposure of saturated air allowed them to breathe momentarily. Cadeck turned to him, scowling at the delay of their progress. Thick steams blotted out the sun lending a hot darkness to their plight turning otherwise pleasant hues to a sickly orange.

Tesh massaged his burning feet in visible discomfort, "Where is this damn Magi?"

"I wish I knew. With the Temple Knights gone, it is likely the existing Magi would ne'er believe anyone would come and would allow any invaders as hostile, allowing the burning air to kill them. I sense a pull upon my aztmudin, a heightened effect, if you will. It is as though it is what keeps us alive."

The ground trembled with a fresh onset of tectonic activity. Rocks and dust collided along the faces of cliffs as they tumbled towards the ground, collapsing, and shattering upon impact with each other. Fissures of steam erupted in the distance causing Tesh to jump from his position from the rumbling beneath his feet. The chaotic spectacle shifted and moaned beneath them like an upset stomach before settling to an uneasy lull once more.

"We should hurry. The Fire Temple will offer safety from the violent grounds."

Tesh replaced his shoes onto his feet, hissing in his pain as the sweaty fabric touched the spotty blisters on his heels. Tesh limped in a gait to avoid placing weight upon them.

"If you understood the trials we take as Magi, Tesh, the burns on your feet would be the least of your worries."

The ground shook again. Cadeck stumbled in his movement, collapsing hard into the soft dust. He puffed the soot away clinging deep into his whiskers. The shaking rippled into his muscles preventing him from rising to his knees. He buckled to the ground, imbalanced from the sudden disturbance.

Cadeck struggled to feel his limbs in the constant quaking, his muscles stiffening to the jerking shifts beneath his feet. He hastened to stand; the tremors of the caldera collapsed him back to his knees. A quick glance stolen over his left shoulder, Tesh collapsed to the dirt with a successive quake, slipping to impact upon his stomach. Tesh groaned with the slow reach of his arm to lift himself before his eyes widened.

A small crack formed in front of Tesh's face splitting the ground along a seam. Fear moved him as he rolled to one side of the fissure. The flaw increased in width as it split through the soft dust crumbling and rising with the tectonic movements. Cadeck extended his left arm towards Tesh whose face shone fear of the violent and raucous earth movements around them. The crevice widened between them. Cadeck felt his body rise as the ground continued to split below him extending into a large gap hungering to consume him. Cadeck slipped into the growing fissure as his hands clutched the edge of the fresh cliff face upon Tesh's side with a burning red glow lit below him.

Cadeck's fingers dug into the soft soils. A death glow billowed from below. Tesh crawled towards the Magi. Another quake stymied his approach as he struggled to close the distance. Boulders collapsed from the shifting cliff below Cadeck's position, rocking his left hand away now making his perch single-handed. His fingers worn from past callouses as he strained to clutch to the shaking and shifting rocks supporting his weight. Many meters below

Cadeck's dangling body, the pit spewed with the bile of mantle inching towards the expanding maw of the rock. Sweat rushed from Cadeck's pores, his teeth gritting through whiskered face only to feel the muscles tightening within his body with each passing moment, the lava creeping towards him.

The burning emissions reached closer, pushing towards the surface by an unseen force. Bubbles popped in ferocity consuming the rocks along the new fracture like the spit from a devouring beast hungry for new flesh. Tesh grabbed Cadeck's hand, yanking in vain to lift the weight of his friend. He would not die here. Not now. Not with the Imperium close to their backs. He pulled to lift Cadeck with the might of his will, veins in his face stretching into his skin. Sweat covered his woolen tunics as his muscles tightened and strained by Cadeck's weight.

"I'm not dying here, boy."

Cadeck reached with his free hand to grasp the cliff edge aiding as best he could to raise himself to the surface. Impending incineration flowed faster than he. Flashes of pleasant memories began to filter through Cadeck's mind. He recalled the days of his own youth when he first learned about his powers. So much simpler.

Tesh pulled harder. Feet gripped into the ground to brace with knees bent and ass positioned deep into the soil. Using the fulcrum of his thighs to lift Cadeck's weight, his hands slipped from a full grip clutching the ends of Cadeck's fingers.

Cadeck's hand slid through Tesh's fingers as he succeeded to give himself another chance with the quick clutch of his free hand onto the soil. The lava rushed faster, erupting from the fresh split. The liquid rock consuming its meal as it yearned for the consumption of the Magi and would soon devour Tesh. The gravity of the situation prompted Cadeck to fight harder. He reached with his free hand once held by Tesh, the sweat slipping along the dust. Gravity kept its hold upon Cadeck's figure as his stronger hand lost the fight allowing free fall towards incineration. Tesh called in anger at his own futility to keep the man from his fate.

"No."

Orange death glowed upon Cadeck's free-falling figure as he plummeted several stories to his doom. His body reacted, tensing in shock, and denying him the calmness to initiate his magick to teleport to safety. Cadeck closed his eyes and accepted his destiny, the vision of the young girl and boy forever held within his arms. As he plummeted to his death, a wave of burning energy swept across the magma's surface and wiped the orange gleam into a sheer face of hardened rock glass. Cadeck impacted the fresh surface with his left hip within a few seconds after his acceptance of fate pronouncing a loud scream as he collided with the obsidian glaze in a freefall that lasted a few moments of time. Every nerve in his body registered the collision simultaneously as his thoughts processed the change of fortune.

Steam erupted from the fissure in front of Tesh emptying across the length of the split, He contemplated the quick death of his companion accompanied by the screams of agony he briefly heard from below.

"Cadeck, I'm sorry."

"He's not dead," a sarcastic voice replied behind him in Koran Proper Accent. Tesh recalled the elegant, refined dialect in the brief conversations overheard in the lobby of the Brounden Inn.

Tesh cocked his head behind him to see a man close to his age standing in the gloomy dusk. His hands alight in fiery flame as a pair of pearl-white irises lit aglow in full brilliance. He chanted words in the language of magick speech, commanding the silence of the grounds around them. Vermillion robes covered his frame etched with orange highlights along his neckline tapering in strong right angles in the center of his chest. As his fires in his hands subsided, he scratched rustic hair salted by streaks of silver white lines and pushed his lips as if to ponder the scene.

"I could have done better. Philos will need to see this."

"Who are you?"

Tesh stood to his feet, his eyes questioned the stranger.

"Kenat. You can thank me for saving my fellow Adept, Cadeck. You must be Tesh?"

"How do you know who we are?"

Tesh reached for the sword sheathed against his back.

"You should steady your sword to sheathe. I have been watching you since you entered the valley. Why would you leave those pretty girls by themselves?"

"Cadeck said only a Magi and a Knight could enter the Tanakian Ring."

Kenat rolled his beady, pearl-colored eyes, "Oh yes, the sanctity of the gods, or something rather. We should get Cadeck out of the pit. Ascended Philos is expecting your audience."

Tesh leaned over the cliff side to see Cadeck writhing in slow pain. His body cemented upon the hardened magma surface crackling around his frame. He rotated himself upon his stomach in a rough struggle to erect to his fours. Cadeck moaned as he positioned his knees to support his weight. Cooled basaltic rock beneath his aging body continued to stream steam vapors from random pockets along the frozen lava flow.

"Cadeck, can you hear my voice?"

Cadeck steadied his nerves, calming his body and mind to release the pain. Tesh's question eased his suffering knowing the initiate was safe. Full light encompassed his body illuminating him in ethereal glow as he chanted murmured prayers to ease his mind. He felt his aztmudin through the molecular fabric of his being as his cells dissolved in exponential quantities fizzling through his core. His fingers disappeared first reaching towards his arms and across his torso across his legs and culminated with his head. In the moment he began his meditations, his body instantaneously disappeared in a flash-burst to reappear crouched in front of Tesh and Kenat.

"Well, that was certainly interesting," Kenat proclaimed as the shining silhouette of his peer manifested to solid form.

Cadeck collapsed to the sooty ground from his magical shock. Low breaths of pain followed as Cadeck coughed through aching lungs.

"Aren't you a Magi? Wouldn't you have seen such magick?"

"Did Cadeck explain to you we don't get out much?"

Kenat's voice was dry in his demeanor and brash in his responses sounding like a spoiled child of nobility.

"I believe those words came from his tongue once."

Tesh positioned himself behind Cadeck's shoulders and prepared himself to lift the ailing Magi. He reached underneath Cadeck's limp shoulders causing the older man to tense up into alertness. He waved his hand to shrug Tesh away.

"I can get up. I will be fine."

"Are you alright?"

"I said I'm fine."

Bones cracked in audible tones as Cadeck stretched his extremities into release. He moaned with a mix of pain and pleasure. Nerve fibers in his body sent sharp electrical charges racing along his flesh, accentuating the endorphins flowing through him. The feeling was euphoric as Cadeck's body went numb into relaxation. He paced his breathing into a steady rhythm preparing to erect into standing position. Pain shot through his nerves; the entirety of his microcosmic energy spent to teleport his being. It stung deep, penetrating to the very core of his spine. He winced with each motion; an action spending short bursts of magick jolting his soul into near torture.

He brushed off the sickly green dust from the bland tunics and motioned for Tesh's water flask. He poured a quick handful into his hand and coursed his rough whiskers with the warm and relaxing liquid. Cadeck turned his attention towards the young man standing next to Tesh dressed in the robes of an adept Magi. Water mingled within his graying stubble, clinging briefly before steaming into small droplets.

"You must be Philos' Adept. What is your name?" Cadeck's voice strained.

"Kenat. Kenat Denwich."

Cadeck shrugged at the Adept's abilities pointing to the cooled magma in the crevice below, "I suppose your magick cooled the lava?"

"What can I say? You caught me."

"Impressive," Cadeck quickly regained his attention towards the overlying task, "We should get to the Fire Temple lest our breaths suffocate in this environment."

He heaved a deep breath. Singeing sulfur stung into his lungs.

Kenat extended his arms towards his sides, "We're just getting to know one another, what's the rush?"

Cadeck moved into Kenat's space towering over the man who stood to his shoulders. Kenat's sarcastic tone did little to comfort Cadeck.

"Perhaps your Ascended never informed you about the Si'rai?"

Kenat's tone retreated in the presence of the commandeering Magi, "Oh, them. Then, Philos *will* want to talk to you."

Kenat led Tesh and Cadeck through harrowing rifts of steam vents and beyond curdling pools of sulfuric water. Tesh's stature became woozy amidst the horrid stench of toxic emissions which supplied little comfort to his already aching body. He questioned how Kenat, and his Ascended could survive amidst the vapors and fumes tearing into his lungs and in the same reply, Kenat informed Tesh how their commune with the gods allows such sanctity. The trio trekked beyond the skeletal remains of those who tempted fate littered across the sacred valley before arriving at a vast lake of molten magma.

Boils popped and spewed across the creeping surface welcoming instant death to those trying to cross. Kenat stopped at the shoreline of a volcanic flow, his figure blurred by the hot gasses rising through the air. Kenat moved his hands with the grace of birds in flight, swinging them around each other as cracks of flame began to encircle his fingers. He started chants in the ancient vernacular whose vowels flowed as thick as the volcanic resin before him.

Cadeck's eyes receded into an attentive, studious stare towards the young magician. As Kenat was still an Adept, a fouled word or incorrectly conjugated verb could provoke an undesired result and end their lives unexpectedly. Kenat performed his magick with ease as though his short years of study made him Ascended. As he continued his conjurations, the ground trembled with the ferocity of stampeding horses causing Tesh to buckle to his knees with the sudden tremors.

Cadeck stood firm. The vibrations of the ground rippled through his bones and the light fabric of his peasant clothing wafted in the pulses. The caustic flows of lava ceased movement, reacting to the ripples below the surface. A bulbous form poked through the magma surface, climbing from below the liquid as it were water.

An orange manifestation appeared from the viscid flows forming a tapered head resembling a horse. The robust front legs took shape, stomping onto the dusty surface to free itself from the pool. The heavy torso followed, lava dripping from its figure leaving the creature unscathed. The beast lifted its hind quarters to the shoreline rising to full height, towering as two men standing on each other's shoulder.

Pumice oozed from the creature's skin pooling in steaming, pyroclastic puddles. The beast glowed with the intensity of flame brighter than a thousand candles. Tesh stood to his feet staring agape at the animal before him.

"What is this?"

Tesh's voice raised in intimidation.

"Firehorse," Kenat replied, "This is how we will make it to the Temple."

"Is it safe to ride upon?"

Kenat gripped the firehorse's glowing, orange mane. It's wispy hairs like keratin Tesh had known of its normal counterpart and hoisted himself upon the mythical beast's backside. His robes straddled against his legs, forming him as one with the animal. He stretched his youthful hand towards Cadeck.

"Hop on. Though, I would not step in the puddles below," he turned to Tesh, "I heard you complaining about your feet. Step in the puddle and you will have a worse pain to worry about."

Cadeck accepted Kenat's hand and gripped it with the tightness of toned muscles, carefully sidestepping the small puddles below. Tesh took a running leap, clutching onto Cadeck's arm and struggled to mount the high beast. This was no ordinary horse, he thought to himself. He oriented his way for all three to face forward as Kenat motioned the beast to stride.

"How much farther, Adept?"

"Not far. The Temple exists in this fire lake."

The fire horse galloped with flame trails as it traversed the magma flow with an intense velocity. Heat rose from its wake splashing deadly lava along the sides. The riders jostled in sturdy rhythm and clutched one another tight to prevent fall. Tesh glanced down towards the fatal ooze, gripping Cadeck's tunic taut.

"Is this the only way across?" Blistering winds galloped across Tesh's face deafening his words.

Kenat smiled at Tesh's question, "You could always walk across, though I would not recommend it. I have heard others have tried many centuries ago."

"How did other Knights make it?"

"You will have to ask Ascended Philos. I never knew any Knights."

Kenat's answer supplied little ease to Tesh, though seeing the young man of age slightly younger than his own, would consider his answer plain. The journey evolved into ever more danger and even more questions. One slip here and there would be no return as shown by the emaciated ruins decorating the valley. Tesh assumed countless individuals tried to continue their quest to become a Knight, few succeeding. What was the reward? Was it wealth? Was it serving mankind?

Neither Cadeck nor Godwen hinted at those resolutions but vague responses to say the Knights were the protectors of the Magi, serving at their command. When the Magi ordered the Knights to crisis, they obeyed without question. With the Knights extinct, Tesh thought, there was room to change the status quo.

The mystical horse galloped across the lava; the canyons of the Tanakian Ring rose along the skyline marred by crags lined with pyroclastic flow like archaic ruins left to history. A series of volcanos cut into the sky forming around the valley where two landforms met. The trio came upon an island floating within the fiery secretion separating the primordial formation.

This island formed alone, cut into creation by the violent magma melting around it. Crackling bursts of lava shot through the glassy surface of the island as Kenat eased the fire horse upon the shoreline of the obscurely formed glass. Defying its form, the beast's weight prodded like a feather upon the fragile surface.

The men disembarked. Kenat extended his hand towards the creature and uttered ancient words in flowing dialect. Upon command, the beast bowed its flaming head, knelt upon one knee and merged with the glossy surface below it. Rivers of mystical pumice formed like tentacles into the ground as sentient extractions leading into the lava surrounding the island.

"Your skills are impressive, lad," Cadeck bolstered.

Kenat turned towards the wizened man and thanked him for the words. He resumed his attention towards his charges and motioned them to follow. His march advanced towards a formation upon the cliff side carved into the hardened magma. Artificial carvings molded into the pumice stone resembling old glyphs like those Tesh recalled at the Temple of Light.

Crimson glows burned from the gaping maw leading into the temple structure. Flustering heat exited the building like feverish breath of old beasts.

Built in the same design as the first, its ancient builders carved their language upon the borders of the entry in the hieroglyphs. The dialect unknown to Tesh's mind and the same broken script Cadeck had little knowledge of despite his experience. Kenat kneeled into humility before he entered the holy site as Cadeck followed his honor and rose to his feet. Cadeck urged Tesh to repeat the process of which he performed in fumbling complacency.

The simple act was an arcane gesture for Tesh's upbringing. His awkwardness showed in his reluctant response to Cadeck's request which Cadeck shot him a glaring disdain in return. His mother never raised him on religion only cursing the gods for her vile fortune. She had reason, for it was the will of the gods that sent his father to his fate, leaving Tesh without a father and his mother a widow.

As he confronted the Temple, pulses of pain surged through Tesh's left hand tickling through his nerves. Tendrils of magical energy fluxed through the limb lining its movements across the golden veins carved into his hand. Cadeck paused to study the anomaly, interrupting Kenat's advance.

"What's wrong with your hand?" Kenat's pearly eyes focused intensely.

"A reaction, I guess."

"Quickly, Tesh," Cadeck turned to the man watching as the glowing tentacles formed along Tesh's hand, "Your trials must begin soon. Your blood is sensing your destiny."

Cadeck reached his arm around Tesh's perspiring shoulders edging him into the welcoming Temple past their host. Like a young child, Kenat's pearly orbs turned his fascination towards Tesh's obscene ligament.

"Make yourselves at home."

Kenat opened a welcoming smile.

Chapter 24

S earing air glazed over Tesh's skin like the sizzle of a hot iron as he entered the confines of the Fire Temple. Air cooled as he passed the threshold of the entry to a moderate temperature. A bubbling cauldron of hot magma simmered in the center of the singular chamber shaped as a dipped basin in similar design he recalled with the structure of the Temple of Light. Glimmers of seeping lava inched within cracks of the walls, stretching like fingers reaching for the floor, benign, like decorations placed upon the structure by an insane architect. Cadeck strode abreast as the pair moved into the ancient building.

Moving magma shifted the ground below Tesh in a steady flow, lighting a carved sigil within the pool of an equilateral triangle pointing towards the altar on the back wall. He could sense the petite ripples moving underneath him which did not faze Kenat who hurried ahead of him to meet his Ascended. An older Magi stood beside a table studying the relics of his service. He lifted a glowing rock between his fingers. Veins of burning magma trickled through the artifact rested upon his fingers as he bent them in a manner to resemble a pedestal to display the piece.

The glow of flame erupted from the relic lighting a soft luminescence against the short beard formed upon his chin. He allowed the fire stone to extinguish itself within his hand. Like flowing water, the viscous lava trickled down his wrist and merged into his forearm to which he felt no pain. Cadeck stood in attentive pose and observed the Ascended at his craft.

"Magi Cadeck, I presume," Philos' voice spoke as fire, gravelly and hoarse.

"Philos. Your Adept is a gracious servant. You have taught him well," Cadeck bowed his head in reverence to the elder Magi.

Philos poured over Cadeck and Tesh as a scrutinizing study, watching every detail of Tesh's timorous repose. Cadeck's verbal recognition of Philos' ability as a teacher came with an appreciative tone rolling gently as a spring wind over a fresh field.

"Your kind words are humbly welcome, Magi. I sense you have a greater purpose than bringing this Initiate here," he spoke in a calming, appreciative voice absent the youthful garishness of his Adept.

"Tesh has succeeded in the Trial of Light. I present him to the Trial of Fire."

"You know well Initiates must pursue the Trials on their own accord, not by the coercion of other Magi. The remains littering my valley are a testament to fact."

"Ascended Philos, with all due respect to the House of Heseph, you know there are no further Knights pursuing the cause. You may also be aware of the threat Roth faces."

Philos studied Cadeck's rough demeanor. His voice returned to the pains of torture and uncertainty at the hands of an enemy Philos knew too well. Kenat had told of stories of Dark Armies moving through Silvetzen emblazoned with a foreign sigil of legend. Philos motioned Kenat away, allowing him to retreat into deep recesses of the Temple. Philos set the flaming stone upon a pedestal whose twisting knobs of sparkwood flickered with the placement of the artifact.

"The Trial of Fire will assess the Initiate in what he sees as truth. The Fires of Heseph will consume those who fail."

He turned towards Tesh whose face sunk into defeated stature, "Should Tesh fail, he was not worthy to burden this mantle and the fate of Roth has been written."

"I won't fail the trials."

Tesh boasted, the look of concern on his face. Stinging pulses coursed through his left hand circulating through every fiber of his body and ended with tingling in his hair. Philos felt the coursing of magick through Tesh's systems, reflecting the culminations of eons of souls standing before him.

"Father Heseph will tell me for sure."

"Then I am ready."

A soft rumble chuckled from Philos' belly at Tesh's assertiveness. He waved his arms to full width in front of his body as he motioned across the flowing pool of liquid fire separating him from Cadeck and Tesh. The crimson river glistened against his coarse flesh in hinted hues of reddish flame darkening his tiny eyes into an ethereal tint.

"Heseph's voice has not told me as much. My feelings suggest you should ponder your decision to become a Temple Knight. Sure, you have passed the Trial of Light, but the Fires of Heseph will scar you forever if you let them. If you let your guard down during the Trials, you will melt away as the rocks flowing below this temple. It is not too late to return, if you can master the Fire Horse."

Cadeck's knowledge of protocol took a back seat to an erupted aggression. His aging frame paced around the holy pool of lava towards the stubborn Magi and assumed position close to the man's space. Breaths roiled down towards the shorter man as his gaze followed the bridge of his scarred nose towards Philos. He commanded physical presence towards the Ascended. Breaths heaved in a steady rhythm as his impatience escalated with each stuttered moment.

"We should make haste for his Trials, Philos. There is no time. The Abyss is in Passing, and there are no Knights to challenge the Si'rai threat."

Cadeck's rough, experienced knobs of fingers clenched the neckline of the vermillion vestments of his opposition. Anger flowed through him, denying him calm serenity. Tesh watched the temper of his friend flare up sensing their lives depended upon Philos' next word. The concern Cadeck shared for his fellow Magi was in question since the discovery he learned in Silvetzen from Rensel. He would as soon as launch Philos into the smoldering pool rather than spit upon him. His own children in danger and Philos prevented advancement towards their rescue.

Philos concern towards the Magi's disrespect caused him to blink in response, "You dare assault me in the House of Heseph?"

Balls of flame engulfed Philos' fists laid out towards his sides.

"No, Philos, you have two objectives to do; administer the Trial of Fire and answer my questions. We do not have much time for both."

Cadeck released his enraged grip. Sweat spilled from his brow. His emotions overcame his anger in fear of his own children's fate and the fate of the Magi.

"Kenat," Philos demanded. He brushed his robes into proper appearance. His Adept returned from the living recesses.

"Ascended."

"See Tesh to his sleeping quarters. Cadeck and I have much to discuss. I shall administer the Trials in the morning."

Philos stared into his colleague's dark eyes. Cadeck's concern for his family and Tesh's fate bled through his face like an open wound. Kenat joined Tesh and escorted him into the rear recesses like a child would show his new friend his favorite toys. The sheen rock muffled the footsteps of the pair as they exited the sanctuary.

"What do you want to know, Cadeck?"

Cadeck located an edge of the sacramental table and propped himself onto the surface, "I heard tongue the Council of Magi made an alliance with the Si'rai."

Philos stared at the flowing magma within the sacred pool. A small flame burst upon Cadeck's question.

"The loose tongue speaks truth. The alliance forged over two harvest seasons ago."

Cadeck followed, "Shortly after the time of my capture."

"Correct. The Quorum voted on the proposal to avert all-out war. With our lack of Knights, preventing their threat was impossible."

Cadeck dropped his head and returned an icy gaze into the older man's eyes, "Without a full Quorum, those decisions could not be made."

"With the absence of a Water Magi, Godwen affirmed the proxy vote via his position as Supreme Elder."

"How did you vote?"

Philos considered his words carefully. Betrayal soaked through Cadeck's face like a wet dog.

"I opposed. Godwen assured us our position was secure with this alliance. The Si'rai would leave us alone so long as we allowed them access to standard diplomacy. Godwen wished to oversee this alliance. For reasons known only to him. Was he not present?"

Cadeck burned with fury as he dropped to his feet. Pacing away, his back turned, a small glow from the magma pool intensified the tears building within Cadeck's eyes.

"I interfered. I went with the Saratian envoy, unaware of Godwen's position with the alliance. The Si'rai beheaded Sorithen and I fled with Princess Cassica and her entourage with Tesh," he turned to face Philos, "The Si'rai do not seek peace, Philos. They tortured me, bound me to their magick for two cycles. Godwen betrayed the Council and Roth. My family suffers for his works."

Philos swallowed his saliva, "You know why you were excommunicated."

"My own Ascended betrayed me," Cadeck's tone irked the lava pit to a caustic boil, "Sold my family for imprisonment so he could have his vote? All those years ago, he ordered the Knights to their death field. And for what?"

Now standing close to Philos, Cadeck's breaths of old, sour ruban smoke rolled along his face.

"Godwen believed the Knights were a threat, you were still an Adept, a non-voting member of the Quorum. Based on what you had told him of the threat in Tarn, he, like us, underestimated them. The Knights lost, eliminated, along with any bannered conscripts. He contrived falsehoods to spread to the populace how the Knights challenged their sovereign nations; amassing wealth and forming armies to threaten kingdoms and the rulers believed him. Something changed him, Cadeck, but you were just his Adept. You would not have known, nor would you have seen his manner. He assured us the Knights were becoming selfish. We doubted him. He was convinced the future of Roth was with the Imperium."

"You could have stopped him. Free him from whatever curse lay upon him."

"We tried. Two of the elders had died. Yourself, with the other Adepts, were on your own journeys."

Cadeck clutched the locket around his neck, "My mission to Tarn. When I met Jess. When we returned, she summoned for me to tell me her Ascended was no longer alive. She retreated from her temple, sought me out."

"You comforted her, and you grew closer," Philos shrugged away the rest of the story before continuing, "While you were away, serving Natural Will, we confronted Godwen. He could have killed us all had we not submitted. Nerthu died protecting her Adept from Godwen's betrayal, knowing she was not yet ready. We could not subject her to this role, to this plan, as we all saw the visions of your children. With the Knights eliminated, the visions of your children only grew stronger."

Cadeck shot an inquisitive stare. His voice lowered to a protective tone, "What of my children?"

"Godwen feared them, their power, their potential, and I fear this is what changed him. Were a vision we all shared. On a night of a full moon. Yet, he did not know of whom the children belonged. He was unaware his visions came true until the boy was born."

"Jess and I gave over to our flesh on such a night against the teachings of the Council. We took vows in secret in a glade close to Kora."

"The Circle," Cadeck gazed towards the lava pit beneath his feet, "kept our secrets."

Cadeck's eyes lowered to his realizations, shifting his feet to the edge of the lava pool to stare into the bubbling caldera.

"I see sorrow and guilt within your eyes. Do not be. Without a Water Magi in Temple none can complete the trials without Sokut's vicar. Godwen insisted to reserve the gift among those showing our rare blood. But your children were raw and pure. Born of two Magi, powerful magick flows in their veins. Something within them posed a threat; they would bring the demise of the Council which Godwen could not allow. As you may have surmised, without the Knights, Godwen could not order your family's capture using our resources."

"Even after informing him of the threat the Imperium posed, he still arranged for my excommunication and my capture?"

Philos sunk his head. The flames in the sacred cauldron burned hotter. The shame washed his face.

"As Supreme Elder his word is absolute. I do not believe a curse befell him, Cadeck. His old age led him astray. His mind wrought with fading memories, I fear, but none dare betray him again. I am sorry, friend."

"Then my children, Jess, all of this?"

"You won't find your answers here, I'm afraid, yet I am rapt by another topic," Philos shifted his voice, "If Tesh is truly to be a Knight, what is his purpose?"

"He bears the mark of Azthar Kherdmon."

Philos turned his eyebrows upward, a low chuckle vibrated from his gut, "What makes you believe legend?"

"The Si'rai sent me to kill him with a binding amulet, an artifact of their magick infused with life-draining powers attuned to what I believe is with a sample of similar blood to the target. When I found him, I nearly killed him. Had he not sacrificed a cut upon his palm, neither of us would be here now. The amulet fused with his left hand. I have seen him use magick and with further training, he could return as the Azthar Kherdmon. Godwen examined him, his mark on his hand. Then, after he allowed me to perform the Trial, he cursed us before I subdued him."

"How is he now?"

"I didn't stay to find out."

Philos' slight amusement echoed through his sanctuary, Cadeck soon followed before Philos returned to studious conversation, "Does Tesh know of his parentage?"

"No," Cadeck shook his head, "his mother never told him, and all he knows is his father was levied and sent to die in a foreign war."

Philos stared into the glowing pool. A memory flickered in the reflection of his irises.

"Do you believe it was Teru's blood used to bind this amulet?"

Cadeck raised his eyebrow in inquisition, "Who else could it be?"

"If you recall, Teru had two sons."

Philos turned his attention towards the sacred pool as the flow pulsed with intensity.

"The older boy died along with his father. A tragedy of collateral damage serving as a page," Cadeck reaffirmed his knowledge of history.

"True, as the story says. Evidence may point to the contrary."

Cadeck grew inquisitive, "What else has been hidden from me?"

Philos grinned as a jovial friend, "Do you really want me to answer?"

Cadeck shook his head, "I think you have answered enough. We should rest. Tesh has a long day in the morning."

"He does. Yes, he does."

#

Tesh stood before the Fire Magi with blank inquisition. Philos studied his hand, tracing the golden remnants through his veins. Each motion ignited sparks of magick within the fused skin. The crevice carved into his palm had shown signs of advanced healing, merging the golden flakes with fresh epidermis.

"Simply remarkable, Tesh. I have not seen such a wound infused by melted gold and the victim still alive. If the stories and legends are true, then we may be bearing witness to Azthar Kherdmon."

Tesh shot Philos a puzzled glare with intense ferocity of a blazing wildfire, "But these marks were the cause of Cadeck's binding amulet merging with my blood."

Tesh retreated his hand from Philos' grip, "They are nothing more than an effect of sinister magick, Magi."

Philos raised his fiery stare into Tesh's bold eyes. His flush lips ravished as a crimson river burrowing through canyons of gray, "The Azthar Kherdmon was a legend. He was the first of the race of men to become our Knights. He was as proficient with magick as he was a sword; a true merge of our people of which our gods had not intended. Cadeck believes in you and as his friend, so should I. I will administer the Trials of Fire, and if you are truly the progenitor of legend, you will be able to wield the Gifts of Heseph.

"Please, come forward."

Philos gripped Tesh's wounded hand escorting him towards the sacred pool. Kenat stood by the sacramental table preparing oils and incense burning through Tesh's lungs as a sour flame. The viscous flow within the sacred pool cooled into solid surface allowing the pair to stride towards the center.

"As with any of the Rites, you must appear to the gods as you left their world and entered ours so they may recognize you."

Philos removed his vestments of his profession revealing flows of wrinkled skin covering his body from shoulders to thighs. Aging gray clumps pocketed across his arms and chest as a bear in the woods were to take to nature. Kenat took care to retrieve the garments and folded them ritually in programmed fashion, careful to avoid wrinkles and creases before placing them upon the ritual table.

Tesh followed in suit, slipping his ratty tunics from his chest and unbuckled his trousers to drop to the glassed lava. Tesh's youthful figure tapered into form at his hips clashing with the degradation of the aging man before him. Philos motioned Tesh to seat himself in the pool as he joined in cross-legged arrangement.

The basin of the sacred pool felt as long-cooled glass. Movement of lava flowed beneath them. The glow of the liquid rock brightened the room in a dull orange and pulsed with each reverberation of Philos' tongue as he spoke. Magma jerked and jolted with every syllable he spoke in the magick speech. His consonants burst into staccato pulses; the lava responded as quickly. With each vowel, the lava returned to a mellow pace.

Returning to common speech, Philos instructed Tesh to his prayers, "By the Light you saw your memories, by the Fire they will burn. Through the Mind, you opened to see Soul. Here, your Heart will attune to Soul. Guided by Heseph as your Heart so is the Will you project onto the world. As within, so without."

Philos abruptly returned to his ritual speech causing the viscous liquid to flow once again between the bodies. Tesh experienced no pain as the glass morphed to liquid form steaming around him as their bodies came into contact of the lava flow. The magma flowed in a clockwise pattern as a whirlpool, increasing in ferocity as it rose from the confines of the stone border. The tornadic magma churned violently hiding the pair from Kenat's view. He shielded his pearl-white eyes from the brilliant display of crimson glow.

Tesh's memories flowed with the flame as his attention turned towards his saddened mother. Her fair skin graced against his youthful face with a soft touch. Tears washed upon her bruised cheeks as flecks of flame opened upon her countenance. Pockets of lava burst from her pores before consuming her memory construction.

More memories appeared; the blonde maiden in Telmen whom he frolicked within the fields. They ran in pair clutching their hands together. They stood within the open fields whose grasses swayed with the gentle winds. A broiling fire erupted in the distance consuming the wheat fields with the hunger of an invading army. Tesh tried to yell. The roaring blaze of a flash bang silenced his screams as the fires smashed into the blonde woman ripping her skin from her bone with the burn of a thousand suns.

Tesh dropped to his knees within the burning fields as the flames jumped over his body. Plumes of smoke smoldered around him signifying the remnants of a great battle. Corpse littered meadows stretched for miles as maggots and buzzards feasted upon carrion. Armor older than time adorned the dead marked with the livery of many nations mixing upon the graveyard as a broiled stew. Rotting flesh wafted across the battlefield stretching through the vision like sop. Tesh stood to his feet, naked before the carnage. He looked upon the smoldering sky above him, to his left rose the flaming sun and to his right stood the moon amidst a darkened sky.

Remnants of large siege weapons and other ballistics rotted in decay, smoldering from the chaos of fire consuming them. Tesh carried himself over the decaying men and swatted flies in his wake. The skies burned orange with haze searing into his flesh which added to the misery of his vision. He felt pain as the suffering of his loved ones hung heavy into his heart. The ground below shook from rapid movement forcing Tesh back to his knees to stabilize his body. Cracks split the soft ground into a distinct rift in front of the young man. A flaming humanoid figure ascended from the opening as lifted from an unseen platform.

Intense flame engulfed the form as the scorching heat quickened from its body kissing Tesh with the magical aura. Beside him, stood two figures in silhouette, masked by the radiating fires sourced from the center figure. Tesh squinted to recognize them, only to see the one to the right of the figure taller than the one on his left and clearly of a female shape while the silhouette on the figure's left was like a young boy. He reveled in the mighty shadow of the figures bowing in reverence. Boiling winds blew in intensity with each syllable spoken in the ancient tongue from the primary figure. Tesh collapsed face first into the scorched earth, his body throbbing with intensity of pain as searing fires of holy touch coursed over his naked flesh. Breaths and words cascaded over his body in searing heat.

His vision dissipated, solidifying the volcanic tornado into shattering glass violently sprinkled across the cavernous temple. Kenat dropped to his stomach to shield his eyes from the projectiles leaving Tesh and Philos in the center of the sacred pool sheened with glass rock. Pockets of wispy smoke erupted from Tesh's extremities centered towards his left fingers glowing crimson with the magick of flame.

Tesh lay motionless as Philos yelled for Cadeck's aid to remove Tesh from the pool. Cadeck's meditations outside interrupted, his body crept slowly to stand as he heard his peer call from within the sanctuary. Cadeck sauntered into the Temple, his fragile knee carrying him with all his muster. Weakened, Tesh muttered inaudible speech as the older men escorted his limp body clear from the pool beginning to boil from viscous magma. The pair dropped Tesh's dead weight onto the ashen surface as he moaned.

Ten smolder points formed upon Tesh's naked form; his crown, neck and forehead, the inside joints of his elbows and knees, upon his sternum and upon his loins and the last one at his feet as his arms lay angled out from his mid-torso. Philos studied the markings etched into the smolder sources.

"Cadeck, those markings. Do you know what they are?"

Philos raised his eyelids in astonished gaze.

"Godwen confirmed my suspicions at Temple. As I released him into slumber, he proclaimed it too - *Dra Nar Azt.*"

"Exactly, but it is only legend. Ascended Elders long dead discussed this in their aging, rotted tomes."

"I too have read the legends."

Philos continued to study Tesh's smoldering points, his eyes darted between Tesh's relaxed form, Cadeck's studious visage and the flowing pool behind them.

"My Ascended feared this form, and why I had to subdue him."

"What did he say?"

"The fear in his eyes was like none I'd seen. His eyes blackened, rambling how he observed the Abyss."

Philos sighed, the vote of the Quorum provided evidence to his actions, "Then the Si'rai had truly cursed him. I do not know how, or when, but his actions are clear to this fact."

Cadeck dropped his head into his right hand, bracing it with his fingers. Decades of training compromised by the only man he knew as loving as his own family.

"Godwen sent me on a fact-finding journey, leading to the events to send the Knights to their doom. He made an alliance with our eternal enemy and damned myself and my fruit to suffer at their hands. What will happen to Godwen?"

Cadeck's concern for his Ascended and children exuded from a single tear boiling in his eye.

"I do not know what will happen to him, but you should not feel guilt upon your heart. The death of their emperor might lift his curse. I do not believe he did it for power, Cadeck."

Cadeck shook his head in agreement, "No, his motives were worse, or controlled. Would the other Magi know?"

"You could ask them, but your reputation amongst the rest of the Magi is in doubt."

Cadeck returned to his steadfast demeanor, an air of confidence surged with a deep breath, "When have I ever shied from risk, friend?"

Cadeck gripped Philos shoulder in confident camaraderie as concern returned within his gaze.

"Something troubles you?"

Cadeck dropped his pitted face, dropping his hand back to his side. His wrinkles withered by stress crept deeper into his flaky flesh, "Of my children, I have not felt them in days, nor have I felt Aeus' grace. I grow weaker, friend."

"It is darkness, Cadeck. Only here are you safe."

Cadeck raised his head from his chest, "Before we left Silvetzen a few days ago, I meditated. In my meditations, one of their gods visited me. He speaks to me when I meditate as to have his aztmudin remain with me."

Philos comforted Cadeck with a gentle hand upon his shoulder. He craned his neck to meet his peer eye to eye, "Then as we have feared. Their darkness will overshadow us if we are not careful. Only in a Temple can you pray safely. Do not fear, brother. If the prophecies are true, our order shall return to its former glory and your children will prevail, the darkness will fall. You will discover the truth and aide Tesh in his plight."

Cadeck did not share his optimism, "I pray you are right," he turned his attention towards the ailing lad, "Tesh, can you move?"

Tesh moaned to startle. His left hand glowed with crimson burn coursing along the golden lines molded into his veins. He strained to raise upright, cursing his pain. He gripped forehead to dull his senses and he replied to the question with a carping yes. Kenat rushed to the men with Tesh's clothes pressed against his vermillion vestments onto his chest. He kneeled towards Tesh's side and aided Cadeck to dress him.

"Cadeck, I ask you to take Kenat with you on your journey."

Cadeck shot a stare towards the elder as Kenat likewise matched his surprise, "Are you certain?"

"Kenat has proven himself as worthy. He needs to find his own Adept to someday continue his craft."

"With all due respect, Philos, he has shown his ability to wield magick, but has he received his Aztin?"

Kenat opened his mouth and flicked his tongue to tap the roof exposing the scorched tattoo burned into the muscle. Precision branding of Heseph's Blessing scarred into his organ drawn of an upright triangle.

"I accept him Philos," Cadeck gazed towards his peer, "I can always use the help."

"Guide him, Cadeck, but he is not your Adept."

The pair of elder men nodded in agreement as the three Magi turned to each other, sharing smiles, and shaking hands.

Chapter 25

Cold, coarse fingers curved in brittle joints like gnarled roots clawing through the ground and waved over the ashen soot of an extinguished campfire. Bitter winds pierced cold through the musky cave, disturbing the blackened dust across the charred wood left in the pit. Fingers bowed into aged amber nails, each one caked with decay and extended into the sharpened edges of keratin. Canyons of cracked skin stretched across the hands, the wrists and forearms covered by leathery bindings attached to charcoal sleeves.

The hands clicked into position upon leathery poleyns squatted in form next to the powder. The leathery trappings screamed as they stretched, shifting the figure into standing height. He split his blackened lips crusted with maltreatment. A gaping maw filled with rot and cracked teeth. His bitter breath circled the icy winds in front of his face of which he could not see.

A blindfold covered his eyes, soiled with abuse, and spotted blood. It formed to his flaked, white skin below a carved tattoo of the Sigil of his Imperium upon his forehead. Ragres Shabririn encircled his hands against the ancient walls around the campfire keeping in silent meditation as he surveyed the room using his magick. His brittle mouth gawked in curled lip as a sharp growl burst from his gut like a death rattle echoing in necropsy within the abandoned cavern.

Through scarred eyes, cauterized in ritualistic fashion beneath the fabric, his sight blurred into a conical focus pulsating with hues outside the visible spectrum. As he followed his ethereal sight, the visions of figures shaded into his view. Near his feet sat the glowing silhouette of a man close to middle age burning with a violet hue tainted by hints of darkness. Ragres ignored the shadows of feminine stature flamed in shades of blues and greens with one singular being red, concentrating upon the mixed souls before him. Black hands penetrated his conical vision as he waved them in ritual dance.

He turned his attention towards the slight taste of a shadow, isolating it from Cadeck. He wrapped his hands into the thickness of the glowing form as if to feel his sacred Abyss. The magick scent lingered near the spiritual imprint, but he could not focus on its source. He continued his meditative focus as a predator upon his prey taking ecstasy in the vibrations coursing through his body from the taint enveloping Cadeck's soul. Like a dog picking up scent, Ragres' crusted lips peeled open as convulsive moans erupted from his gut in orgiastic joy.

He prayed in the ancient speech of magick, "Thank you, Father Hadithem that I may serve you in locating your vicar's goals, I will honor the gift you have given me so I may find the Temples of our enemies."

He fanned his focus across the room; a shimmering glimmer caught the peripheral of his blurred cone. Ragres beamed his beacon like a spotlight to focus upon the hint of magick signature spilling with radiance. Burning white singed his vision, his mouth widened in pain as though the flare of a thousand suns erupted into his face. His crackled fingers clutched the putrid cloth covering his eyes as he stumbled in agony. His legs moved as a cripple as he twitched in haste to leave the confines of the enclosure.

Ragres dropped to his knees, writhing in slobbery slosh percolating from the corners of his mouth. His face collapsed into the snow embankment at the opening of the cave. His convulsions escalated into a frightening seizure before coalescing in calm vibrations while a young aide ran and kneeled to his side. The aide draped a fur pelt upon his master easing him to warmth as he arose from the pain. Ragres rose to one leathery knee, the hides creaking in the cold winds brushing across the bindings. Ice particles crept into scarred pits buried deep into his skin across his hands and face like drought-stricken riverbeds clinging to nourishment.

His soiled skin blushed red with freeze burn which Ragres ignored. The pain seared into his heart embellishing the strength surging through his tall, broad, and spindly frame. Icy, rotten breaths pushed into the open air as he stood to full height. A coat made of rawhide, dyed with the blackness of winter hearts draped the man towards his ankles enhanced by a high collar resting against his hairless neck.

His ethereal vision blurred into focus as he gazed towards the young man standing at his side. He gripped the fur hide draped upon the servant's shoulders with a crackled hand and shoved his appendage into the young man's chest, dropping the fur into the snow. A guttural moan erupted through his decaying gums before straining his head westward. Like the wound of an injured animal, the whispering taint of enveloping darkness trailed ahead of the hunter towards the faint mountains peeking into the distance.

"We move west," Ragres croaked in his speech.

Unnerved by the plight of his aide, Ragres trudged through the snowbank as high as his knees. The single page hurried towards the pair's single Si'rai war-horse. The horse neighed in adamant struggle against the weaker slave tugging at its reins. His small frame skidded amidst the trodden road as the animal protested his commands, its muscular frame outlasting the small human. The cold snow bit at his knees as he collided to the ground, the beast showing no resistance to dragging the boy.

Tears formed into the younger man's trousers as the beast drew him a few yards in slow trot. He took the advantage to rise to his feet and regained command over the animal bucking and rearing into obedience. The horse followed his lead as the lad paced many yards behind his master; a silent stalker covered in oily blackness capped with a scarred baldness draped in rotten blindfold. The boy's servitude was absolute, commissioned to Ragres the better part of the past star cycle.

Chains of servitude bound him to the Magister as he recalled his purchase in Erabu, the land of the seven deserts. Pain and humility encompassed the life of the Si'rai slaves as the boy learned early on being born to another master's employment. There was no record of his pedigree as he only knew the nature of being a slave. Magister Shabririn made his purchase, including him with several others on the market for scheduled day's sale. Shabririn branded him with a new name, Asvidar, and through brutal treatment still scarred on the boy's face, forced him to learn it swiftly.

Ragres advanced in the blistering snow along the road cut deep by the ruts of trade. Asvidar continued his pace, struggling to advance towards his master's expedited march. Ragres chose to keep his hunt simple, no soldiers or armaments, relying only upon the abundance of the wilds. The march progressed into the evening lending the bitter cold into an escalating ferocity absent the heat of the sun.

Ragres pushed further, fighting back against the biting winds pricking at his scars. Glowing starlight glistened upon the sky like dancing ghosts flying through the heavens. His call to prayer was soon as twilight grew into darkness. He summoned Asvidar to a clearing in the scant fields and ordered him to make shelter. In hastened ferocity, the boy, a uristri all his life, obeyed.

He fastened fitted poles into their connections made of the sidgen woods native to the lands of the Si'rai. Asvidar aligned the notches in the barks to fasten them into position. His assignment had taught him timing in this assembly as within minutes he pulled the thick hides of the canopy taut into the wooden supports. Ragres observed the quickness of his movements, smelling the air to find the boy's actions. The undeniable scent of the Erabian juvenile's pheromones permitted Ragres to time the activity with scrutinizing accuracy. Ragres would beat his properties for lesser offenses.

Ragres wanted his life to the letter, no mistakes, and no makeovers. He expected the same of his servants. As the boy finished his chore, Ragres ordered him away into the open for the nightly hunt, denying him a moment to rest. The magister skirted the flap for entry and sat upon the woolen mat protecting his body from the cold ground below. As commanded, the boy placed a satchel inside for Ragres's sacraments and prayers. Ragres shed his leathery confines piece by piece, unbuckling the binds strapped around his ribs. His clothing dropped upon the mat, unleashing a canvas of scarification across his body.

Scars overlaid upon scars. Deep wounds crisscrossed his cracked skin, like plowed fields torn asunder in a whirlwind. He placed his naked body onto the warm animal pelt and removed a small glass vial from his bag ending in a bulbous base. He followed this ritual by removing a sheen blade a foot in length; its curved hilt carved from bone, etched with hieroglyphs of his arcane rituals. He placed his blindfold upon the woolen carpet, carefully unraveling it into a perfect line. Vacant pits of cauterization replaced his eye sockets. Putrid flecks of green residue caked around them, meeting the scarred flesh of his face. He followed his ritual with the removal of a small cloth and removed the cork from the shiny blue vial.

With each step of his sacraments, he prayed through his breath using his vernacular. Sprinkles of absalin oil rained upon the small cloth and dotted his decaying flesh. Sweet aromas filled the tent, like the flower blooms the oils derived from on warm, full-moon nights. The welcoming smells filled the tent contrasting with the rotten stench of Ragres's skin. The blade cut along his left pectoral muscle sending blood to drench into a straight fall down his chest. He widened his jaw and followed with a clench to suffer through the pain. He dabbed the wound with the cloth of his oils sending a stinging pain coursing through his nervous system. The fresh wound festered in bubbling ooze as he hurried to place his blindfold to absorb the fluids.

"By the blood of my flesh, I enter the darkness of the Abyss. I sacrifice my sight so that you might give me yours," the words of his native tongue hissed from his lips with unpleasant growls.

Soiled with the mixture of sweet copper blood and the smells of the absalin oils flickering through his nose with a pleasant taste, Ragres bound the soaked blindfold upon his eyes, taking care to wrap the coverings in ritual fashion. He allowed none to see his sacrifice so the disbeliefs of heathens could not taint his sacrament.

Ragres remained in solitary prayer within his small tent, feeling the vibrations within the air outside. His mind raced with the vibrations of hallucinogens filtering through his open sores into his bloodstream percolating his brain into a euphoric orgy. Ragres closed his thoughts to outside stimuli and embraced the beating blood coursing through his head as visions of his gods painted his thoughts like a fresh canvas. The snow drifts spoke soft whispers as they stirred upon the winds, each of them singing their own tunes as he continued his ethereal trance. The loud crunch of footsteps entered his senses with each step like a pounding drum. He focused on the intensity and tuned in on the pacing of the crunch with the guidance of his meditations and calculated them to belong to a bipedal creature. Asvidar must be close with food.

He heard the boy start a fire outside as the crackling whips of flame announced the presence of their camp, each prick of flame poked into his eardrums. His ears tuned into the cutting of a knife against tendon as the muscular bindings tore one by one from the carcass. Each cut produced a twanging sound as though the boy were plucking a lute. A strange scent of raw meat made entry into his tent of hog hides dipped in beer. The acoustic vibrations of the boy echoed through his ears as he placed each tender cut upon plates carved of bone. The sounds mingled with the ethereal vibrations of his beacon causing his head to jerk to which an outsider would believe him to be paranoid.

A rush of air followed the boy as he released the flap of the tent to bring his master his supper. He gripped the fur coat wrapped tight around the boy's arm with a force enough if he were to crush it and violently removed the plate of meat from his servant as he sneered with jagged gums to instill his brand of fear. Releasing his grip, he flanked the plate with his rotted hands and ran the food close to his face. A curved, fungal tip of his nose skirted over the slices like a dancer on stage.

Ragres' gurgled moans curdled Asvidar's stomach with fear. Yellow nails of worn keratin squeezed the tender cuts between the blackened fingers of decay as the seer shoveled the first morsel of food between his begrimed gums. What teeth did grow, swiftly ground the first bite into a palpable mush seeping through his lips more than down his belly.

"You did good, raka. The meat is raw to my taste," Ragres croaked with mouth full.

With the congratulatory speech, Ragres motioned Asvidar to leave his tent. Asvidar's night would be cold and lonely amidst the biting winds of the northern roads of Silvetzen. He and his master had left the capitol city days ago by foot and Ragres was no closer to catching his prey. Where they journeyed, Asvidar wondered, was only known to his master. They had no troops to escort them, which gave Asvidar concern over their safety. If they fell to the elements none would know, and they would die in a cold, foreign land lined around with enemies of the Imperium.

Asvidar prepared his lean-to shelter to face against the winds plowing from the west and lit his campfire in front of him within the shroud of the hides. He wrapped himself within the fur linings supplying little comfort upon the snowy ground and consumed himself like an insect inside a cocoon. Here he escaped to pleasant times within the servitude of a more forgiving master of the nobility.

He recalled he had a name provided to him at birth, but through the cruel indoctrination in servitude to the Imperium his last master weaned it from him. Ragres was neither nobility nor a warrior and in Asvidar's brief time serving him, Asvidar could not understand Ragres' profession. For being born in the uristri, illiteracy was normal. He bore the symbols of the Imperium; the eight-spoke wheel with the open center, but knowing the man was blind was clueless as to his method of survival.

Asvidar had heard rumors and legends growing up of ancient leaders of the Si'rai who could commune amongst their god and Ragres took great care and protection with the vestments of his practice. Asvidar's previous owner had kept many secrets of their worship hidden from his slaves and through curiosity Asvidar had inquired what he could about them. Legends told to him in his youth by the woman he presumed his mother were their people, the Erabu, worshipped seven gods, corresponding to the deserts, but the Si'rai were different.

In times past, a Si'rai clan conquered and assimilated the Erabu and relegated their legends to conspiracies leaving the Erabu to worship their one god, Hadithem. Punishment met those who disobeyed. But by Asvidar's time those stories had also fallen into myth. Everyone he had known of his people were always a slave to their overlords.

Crackling embers of firelight soothed his aching mind and body. Huddled within the scant pelts afforded towards his caste, Asvidar did the best with the warmth as he could. Should he die in the frozen fields of a foreign land, Ragres would move on for his mission was priority and would quickly find another servant. Nocturnal choirs of roving wolves groveling for prey soothed the young man towards a nippy slumber.

*

Ragres rose before the sunrise, forcing his servant to pack camp with only the light of the stars. From a short distance, he waved his face in motion with Asvidar's movements following his scent and sneered at each wasted time of momentum his servant lingered. Asvidar continued this ritual and had begun to roll the pelts when Ragres turned his back and continued his vector towards the Tanakian Ring.

Through icy sheets of matted, black hair, Asvidar's glazed emerald eyes watched as the obsidian silhouette floated in the distance away from him as a wight willowing in the pre-dawn snow. Asvidar rushed his actions, placing the camp supplies upon the single beast of burden. His small frame fought with the horse once again to lead it towards Ragres's advance. The massive animal slowed Asvidar's speed to catch up with his owner who had outpaced him into a distant dot.

Ragres ignored the major roads leading across Silvetzen's lands. Their path made a straight line as the raven flies towards the Tanakian Ring trudging through snow-laden fields. They crossed fences of farms and strayed from crossing towards any villages. Their march lasted days passing through the snowy north into the boreal plains. Upon the twelfth day, they met the peat and bogs leading towards a day's journey of the volcanic ring. The hunt continued ignoring the blisters forming upon Asvidar's feet.

After the thirteenth day, Ragres trekked into the crackling underbrush of the sparse forestry bordering the warring kingdoms. His sight motioned him towards his victim, cautioning his gait into a silent stride as he approached a sparse campsite within the forestry. He turned towards Asvidar, signaling him to stop as he continued into the woods.

Ragres moved branches from his sight, taking care not to disturb the leaves and detritus at his feet into a crackling cataclysm. Through his gift, the ethereal spectrum focused into view as the faint signals of four female figures tended to an encampment glowed in hues of greens and blues though the fourth silhouette burned in angry red. Yet one of the figures shaded curiously with shadow. He tuned his ears towards the ground, cautiously approaching the campsite and leaning into the floor to crouch. Feminine pheromones and perspiration flittered through the air scraping through his nostrils to his perverted smile of putrefied gums.

Within his ethereal vision, the wafting essences lingered of lasting darkness snaked through the women, beyond their carriage and towards the valley leading into the volcanic ridge. Ragres followed the stream through his own connection to the Abyss leading him towards Cadeck's soiled soul. He observed Cadeck exit the valley towards the campsite, followed by a foreign spirit, glowing in bright crimson intermingled with orange flame. Ragres remained vigilant and turned his face away as a faint brightness began to shimmer towards his vision.

Though he turned his supernatural gift away from the searing blindness haunting him at the cave, the curse of his gift allowed his other senses to blare with the glow of an effervescent spirit, a blinding and haunting vision his absent eyes saw within the Abyss. Whispers of his curse filled within his ears rolling through the forest with the ferocity of a burning blaze. Sour sulfur overcame his nasal cavity while he experienced an invisible immolation upon his rotting skin like his very bones cremated from within. A being of pure light overcame his senses.

Ragres suffered through the pain consumed upon his flesh like flakes of bloody tears ripping from muscle and sinew in maws of sinister beasts. The stinging burn flooding his nose consumed his senses encasing him in a prison of disembodied torture. He remained unwavering, holding his position amongst the wood. He muttered chants and curses to dull the agony while creating soft whispers of forbidden tongue, trailing like haunting echoes upon the forest canopy.

"I heard something, what could it be," Eris turned towards the disturbance.

She paused in her motions, turning the fire pit into a mound of soggy soot with cool water. Simple tunics covered her body tucked into a pair of trousers torn on one knee.

Ysalir paused in her conversation with her sister to perk her ears upon the sinister speech, "Fersyn, the Forest Witch. We should be cautious."

"Forest Witch? So, the legends are true."

Venna's fascinated eyes appeared as azure saucers fitted into her face shining through her golden mane draped across her cheeks. A laced, white dress covered her body as her blonde locks frayed into split ends.

"Aye, she boils the flesh of virgins within their own blood," Ysalir's tone moved into a sinister chide hinted with sarcasm, "The brew keeps her young. She is an abomination of Sokut, one of her Forsaken Children."

Venna picked up Ysalir's embellishment, "You're lying."

"Am I?"

Ysalir raised an eyebrow to continue her legend, "Mother used to tell you tales when you were still swaddling. She warned you to never leave into the woods."

"I'm not buying it either, Venna," Eris proclaimed, taking her friend's side, "The voice was like a man's."

"See, I told you she didn't exist," Venna huffed to the realization the stories of her youth might be false.

Cassica ignored the banter of her lower ranks and remained vigil towards the volcanic ridge. She observed as three figures returned from the mountainside. Cadeck led the way followed by a strange individual in front of Tesh. She watched as the men followed the wide valley path, marking their way through the crevices and crannies avoiding the steep grades and continued towards the base. She huddled within a slim coat protecting her from the cool clime. Unease lifted from her heart at the sight of the familiar men after more than four days of their absence.

264

She shifted from the approaching men to observe Ysalir taunting the younger women with tales of phantom crones. Venna's playful mischief turned into taunted anger as she raised her voice at her older sister. Ysalir continued into the strange legends of the Forest Witch. Venna's behavior unwelcomed for further training in her Order. A trait necessary to wean. Venna's admiration and carefree attitude were unbecoming of the disciplinary practices required to obtain the rank of Justiciar. Cassica slid her form from the seat board of the carriage, planting her feet firm upon the underbrush.

The princess approached the inferior ranks, clearing her throat to grab their attention, "Ladies, hurry, we need to pack up camp. Tesh and Cadeck return, and I see we are to have new company."

Ysalir followed the horizon towards the trio of men, "Shit, we barely fit into the carriage on our own."

"Figure it out, Rensel. Ready the carriage for departure. Wherever Cadeck wants to go, we will not have much choice. Then, we should return to Sarat post haste."

On her command, Ysalir rounded the lower ranking women to her side and rushed to prepare the tear-down of camp. Cassica stood in poise at the edge of the brush line. Slight rustling jerked her attention towards the distance. A cold chill rolled through the brush bringing with it the putrid stain of pus. Cassica crinkled her nose from the repugnant odor assuming it an animal as she returned her attention towards her command.

Ragres returned his vigil, catching glimpse through the Abyss as he gazed upon Cassica's trailing form. Redness burned into his eyes filling her silhouette within his view. An ancient blood flowed through her veins dribbling her presence into the Abyss like cascading waters. Years of sacred ritual, cutting and tearing of his own flesh had wrought Ragres of his own will led only by the beacon of Hadithem. Within the Abyss, Cassica's lineage churned with sacred form inhabiting her body.

Silken robes trailed through Cassica's soul adorned in sacred garnish. A golden necklace cut across her pale shoulders highlighted by an elaborate tiara made gold carved into deep scarlet strands of hair as a river would border a nation. Transparent robes flittered upon the delicate framework of the hallowed woman accentuating her shapely seduction.

"Visraair Abra, Babalon," through scarred gums, Ragres praised his goddess he called "Sacred Mother."

Chapter 26

Tesh and the Magi continued across the scarred valley towards the awaiting encampment at the edge of the wood, descending past torn fragments of rocks and grasses lining the rough trails along the ridges of the mountain range. Rocks and boulders dotted the dangerous valley welcoming them into the woods and the familiarity of calm serenity. Cadeck led the trio, guiding them through the lush fields clashing against the hellish landscape behind them. Cassica disbanded from the encampment and sprinted towards the men's stride.

Tesh caught the hints of an unkempt aroma masked by the musky stench of the woods. Vermilion locks graced her worn face dropping like thin ropes upon her covered shoulders encased within the slim coat embracing her athletic build. Drained by restless unease, she studied the men carefully taking note of Tesh's new confidence disguised with a ferocity of pain fallen upon his trusting eyes. Streaks of purple and red tore through the golden veins encrusted into his left arm as he carried his swagger with a calm serenity. But her focus cornered Kenat upon her spotlight.

Wisps of white streaks cut through his blonde hair like flames kissing a forest watched over by the pearly orbs of his eyes. They appeared as two moons counterbalancing the destruction of unkempt grooming. He carried his gait with an uncaring brashness befitting of his sheltered youth. His face carved as the statuesque features of noble blood pale with the absence of sustainable light. Cerise vestments laced by golden threaded frock covered his short stature emboldening his demeanor.

As Cassica approached the men midway, the stern cut of her eyes unleashed a fiery tongue towards Cadeck's attention.

"And might I ask who we have added to our company?"

Unnerved by Cassica's repose, Kenat took a bow of sarcasm towards the princess embracing her hand towards his lips, "Kenat Denwich at your service, madam."

He addressed her in torrential tone mocking her status as she jerked her hand away from the youth.

"Denwich," Cassica raised her inflection in acknowledgement, "of the Koran House which bears the name?"

Kenat drew aghast at her salutation as she reminded him of a past he chose not to remember, "I may carry the surname, but do not choose its titles."

Cassica acknowledged his decision with a firm bow of her head, "I apologize, Magi. Allow me to introduce myself, I am Princess…"

Kenat interrupted her introduction bursting through his scrawny face with an air of boasted confidence.

"I know who you are, Your Grace," he smiled once more, mocking her station with his politeness, "My Ascended has told me about you and the Bovariàrs."

Cassica scowled in admonishment to Kenat's disgrace of the formalities entitled towards her. Kenat reminded Cassica of his status as a Magi; irreverent to secular titles and discouraging her use of his surname in relation of a stature foreign to him.

Cadeck interrupted the exchange of disconcerting opposition, "Are your ladies ready to move onward?"

Cassica cocked her head towards the older Magi, "We should be ready. Where does our journey take us now?"

"We take Tesh north, towards the Temple of Wind. Kenat says he knows the way."

Cassica's eyes turned as a violent sniper shot piercing from a kilometer away, she twisted her nose in angry consternation, "Northward, deeper into Silvetzen? You made promise we could return to Sarat when you completed your task here."

Cadeck looked downward upon her as a father scolding his child, "I did. But priorities guide my intuitions; I feel you should continue to come with us."

"My people need me, Cadeck."

"They need a leader, not a corpse."

Cassica turned away from him, crossing her arms in protest to his warning. Her backside shielded her thoughts expressed upon her face from his lecture as she led the men towards the closing camp. Tesh trailed behind Cadeck while the trio joined the women loading up the single horse buggy. Venna and Eris paired up in their duties to pack the heavy vibark chest with the supplies of their profession, being careful in the intricate concealment of their wares. Kenat admired with careful observation as a glint of mottled blonde hair caught his eye when Venna wiped sweat from her brow. He moved in closer to the cart, leaning against a tall tree nearby.

Ysalir lifted a cloth satchel towards Venna who struggled as she tugged it close to her budding chest. She found difficulty heaving the heavy satchel into the open container and in her clumsiness, several small knives emptied from the wrappings and clinked in a metallic melancholy upon the planks of the cart and settled into the mossy ground below. Kenat gained advantage of the opportunity as he moved closer towards the blonde girl. He crouched upon the ground and gripped a stiletto hidden between blades of grass.

Ysalir gleaned her eyes towards her sister to silently scold the younger woman. Kenat held the blade between his index finger and thumb, allowing him to study the intricate craft work of the tool.

"I believe you dropped this," he returned the blade towards Venna's pale digits gazing into her doe-blue eyes encased by tangled blonde locks.

Kenat's calloused hands met her silky fingers as he placed the blade within them. Ysalir pushed him aside, hurrying to gather their tools of their trade and verbally unleashed a torrent of cursing towards her younger sister. Ysalir turned towards the young wizard erupting in a fiery flare admonishing him of his interference.

An aged hand graced the young man's shoulders as he turned towards the older Magi. Pitted cheeks adorned an early onset of graying beard upon Cadeck's face.

"She meant nothing by her tirade. We travel with Saratian royalty."

"You didn't tell me we travelled with Roses," Kenat whispered in sly demeanor, belittling his elder's casual tone.

Cadeck turned a sharp eye towards his colleague, "Philos let you know of them?"

"No. These blades are not native to Silvetzen's armies. I have seen them upon dead bodies. They are the blades of specialty killers and the weapons of state terror. A hallmark of Sarat's resources and proliferations within this realm.

"At times, Philos would assign me into Silvetzen for weeks, watching as the developments of Silvetzen and the Si'rai continued. One night, I saw this one leaving a target's home. She found me and I fled. She was persistent, I must say. After many days, I saw her in pursuit of my retreat to the Temple. You may have noticed the charred remnants of my barrier a way to the east. I could not allow one of the profane to take notice of our secrets, Cadeck."

"Then be careful, lad," Cadeck tapped his shoulder twice with a firm tone in his voice and a fatherly smile gracing his face, "Rensel is sweet, but would not hesitate to cut you ear to ear."

Kenat swallowed at his words in scared surprise. Despite extensive training of his craft, if Ysalir gained the upper hand, his lifeless carcass would be unable to counter her blade's handiwork. Cadeck worked to comfort Ysalir's anger as he aided her to finish her tasks. Cassica held a clump of hay towards the horse's mouth while petting its mane in readiness for the new day's ride. Tesh and Kenat followed Cadeck's warm advice and aided the ladies prepping the cart.

#

Ysalir casually drove the rickety cart through soft-rutted roads winding through thin tree lines edging the border of the two realms. The occupants of the vehicle strained the single horse in its efforts to move as the dark-colored wooden bed overflowed in compact seating. Cassica leaned her back against a sideboard of the carriage, Eris sitting beside her. Tesh flanked her on her right as Venna and Kenat sat opposite. The latter propped his foot upon the heavy chest constraining the other occupants in tense seating of bent knee upon thick hay. Kenat removed his thin sandals from his feet, allowing them to plop upon the vibark chest with a soft thud muffled by the thick wood.

Tesh stroked his left arm, the ebbing pulses of crimson followed his rhythmic heartbeats in subtle sensations. He strained to flex his fingers; each motion caused them to ruffle with the sound of crackling skin baked in weeklong sun. Cassica studied his movements and took interest in the sudden change of his handicapped arm.

"Tesh, your hand. It glows… differently."

Tesh turned his attention away from her topic, watching the landscape passing behind them. She saw him as he looked to the path behind them; trees and grass flowing into the distant horizon with the towering mountains of the disjointed volcanoes covered by the mists of water vapor and poisonous gas.

"Are you worried, Tesh?" She followed in a casual tone. Her demeanor half-condescending towards his station.

"Yes. I feel… different. I saw things. For another conversation."

Tesh did not address her eyes, but focused on the path behind him, reflecting in kind to the thoughts racing within his mind of his experiences at the Temples. His somber tone alarmed Kenat who addressed Tesh in brash rudeness.

"Wait. You do not feel stronger? Like all of Roth would fall at your command?"

"No, I don't," Tesh mumbled, glaring towards the young Magi.

"What about the prophecies? Philos mentioned something special about you the other day."

Kenat's tone reverberated like an enthused juvenile. Cassica turned to him abruptly, silent, crystalline eyes stared at his outburst.

"Kenat, enough," Cadeck reprimanded from the driver board of the carriage.

"What about those prophecies, Kenat? Is this world worth saving? You do not know what I saw."

Tesh turned a focused eye like a beam of lightning towards his challenger. Cassica darted her eyes towards Tesh, quickly following the terse exchange between the men.

"What do you mean, 'worth saving'?"

Her question sounded more of fear than condescending, "You've witnessed the abilities of the Si'rai."

"And you damn near formed an alliance with them if I'm not mistaken, Your Grace." Tesh confronted his ruler in argument, raising his inflection to make his point, "Even after we informed you they had violated one of your own Roses."

"Wait a minute," Kenat raised his right hand to gain attention to speak, curling his fingers to make his index finger prominent. His slender face made his nose protuberant like a beak as he made his thoughts known. His voice echoed of noble lineage in the inflection of his concern, "Are you saying Sarat signed a treaty with the Si'rai?"

"Almost, Kenat," Cadeck replied, "Had I not intervened."

Cadeck sensed Kenat's concern. Knowing the scholarly studies imposed upon Magi Adepts, Philos would surely lecture Kenat on their past histories.

"But you still would have, right, Your Grace? Philos was right about your secular ways. Whatever benefits through coin or power, despite the consequences, will serve man to defy the ways of the gods."

"Excuse me, Kenat; you neither know the ways of Sarat, nor our laws. What business do you have to vocalize your disfavor?"

"I once…"

"He doesn't," Cadeck interrupted him, placing hand on Ysalir to motion her to stop the cart and turned his body into the conversation. His voice commanded amidst the travelers.

"Kenat, you will learn your place in the absence of your Ascended. Philos entrusted me with your well-being and while I am not your Ascended, I am an Elder and you will listen to me as I were your Ascended."

Cadeck's tone struck child-like fear into the inhabitants as a father would admonish unruly children. Tesh perked up, turning his mind away from the pain throbbing through his nerves. Venna's innocent stare snapped to military attention as she craned her neck towards Kenat with a facial expression to mock his reception of Cadeck's scorn.

Cadeck's voice returned to natural calm, "We still represent the Council in this trip though we travel with secular authority. But our aim is to administer the trials to Tesh. As a representative from the Council, you will respect Cassica and her entourage and address them in kind. Keep your opinions to yourself, lest you misrepresent the Magi."

Cadeck leaned downward to capture Cassica's attention, "I trust you were not offended, Your Highness?"

She shook her head to acknowledge no offense.

"Now, Kenat," Cadeck returned, "Where did Philos say we could find Ascended Tijoa?"

Like a defeated child, Kenat sat back against the sideboard and answered the question, "North, towards the town of Vorstak." Kenat slumped against the wooden side panel, picking at a clump of hay strewn on his robe.

"Vorstak?" Ysalir protested.

Sea-teal eyes seared within her statuesque face making Kenat the full brunt of her fiery tone, "The center of Silvetzen's training? There is also a large Si'rai camp there from what I have heard. It will be like the rat climbing straight into the eagle's nest."

Kenat choked on his next statement in a sarcastic manner, "Well, he lives outside of town if concerns are eased."

"Look, Kenat, you have already twisted my loincloth once today. I am not putting Her Highness, nor her entourage in any further danger. I think the Si'rai may be following us," she turned to Cadeck, "We heard a voice in the woods not long before you returned."

Venna piped in to correct her sister; her innocent inflection proposed thoughts of child-like fantasy mocking her sister's scary story, "It's the Forest Witch."

Cadeck lowered his speech, speaking in a low, whispered tongue through his burly face. Crusty words billowed from his mouth as he focused Ysalir's concern towards him, "What do you mean, voice?"

"Eris heard it," Ysalir nodded her head towards the young girl.

"It was whispers, mostly," Eris asserted in soft High Accent, "like a chant. But I did not hear anything more and it was clearly deep, like a man's voice."

"They are following us. They must be seeking a path to the Temples," Cadeck's voice reflected a tone as to the realization of clarity, "We clearly have the advantage and must make use of it. Kenat, how far is Tijoa?"

"He is about three to four sunrises from the Tanakian Ring. His hovel is about a day's ride from Vorstak due west, with a healthy horse at full pace."

"We're being hunted?"

272

Ysalir's voice flowed like a folly of daggers.

"Not by an assassin, like you. He will not target us. He is following a trail to find the temples and I suspect myself and Kenat are like the crumbs. He is still dangerous; like a snake, he will attack when cornered. He will find Kenat's temple. We need to make sure he does not find the others. How fast do you figure we can drive in these conditions?"

Ysalir surveyed the ground; noticing the soft moss of the boreal soil, the prevailing winds snapped through her hair from the northwest. A looming cloudscape in the horizon stretched into grounds demarcated by snow. Cadeck turned and dropped his legs into the open-air cart as Eris scooted aside.

"Your Highness," Ysalir began, "we will need to destroy the chest. It is adding weight to the cart, and we cannot outpace this hunter if we do not."

Cassica reacted to Ysalir's suggestion in empathetic approval as she ordered Venna and Eris to sort the supplies. Ysalir signaled the horse to stop, hopped into the bed and removed handfuls of clothing from the container. She sorted those intended to conveniently hide stilettos and daggers and tossed two sets to Cassica. The princess removed a burlap satchel housing various knives and daggers, removing the weapons and placing them in the carefully sewn places within the fabrics for easy access.

Tesh and Kenat helped the ladies in their endeavors. Kenat's pearly eyes glowed in fascination as the simple tools of the Roses emptied from the cart like a furious maid removing old things to prepare for new cleaning. Ysalir removed the only crossbow from the chest, but Cadeck assured her to leave it within.

"Too unwieldy for the disguises we will need. A travelling band of nomads would look foolish with Saratian weaponry. Especially that which bears the herald."

Ysalir begrudgingly disassembled the weapon in methodical procedure and placed the weapon within the chest as Cassica began a survey of clothing and weapons necessary for their status while listening to the suggestions Cadeck relayed.

"We'll become as a nomadic family," Cadeck followed, "If the Si'rai or Silvetzenian armies spot us, we are a travelling family of entertainers. Which means, Kenat, you will need to discard your vestments."

"But as a Fire Magi, I cannot…"

Cadeck's calloused hand silenced further speech from the young man, "Do I wear my vestments? We can place them in my satchel with those of my worship. Rensel, is there an outfit he might wear?"

"Venna's about his size."

"Good," Cadeck joked in grinning approval.

"But…" Kenat protested.

"Go change. Venna, hand him some of your clothing."

Venna reached into the chest to remove a velvet tunic with a frilled collar line which when fitted to her build would expose her shoulders. She followed with a pair of leggings of teal color and motioned him away from her sight. Kenat eyed the ensemble with curious disgrace causing his eyes to squint and curled his nose before forcing his pursed lips to blossom in accented crimson disapproval.

"You expect me to wear girls' clothes?"

"No," Venna replied, "I expect you to look cute in them."

Venna's High Accent softened the sarcastic response as Kenat hopped from the edge of the cart into a dense wood a few yards beside them. He turned his scrawny frame backside towards the party as he removed his religious habits. The vermilion robes slid from his head and neck and carefully placed on an overhanging branch nearby. Unspoiled, white undergarments covered his pale skin exposing his arms and shins bare. His frame was frail and lanky like a pale rail sprouting limbs with the voice of a young man.

Kenat studied the violet tunic, grunting and sighing at the mismatch of designs. He slipped the tunic first, stretching it to fit his slightly larger frame. Discomfort showed as the bottom of the tunic rose slightly above his spine when he placed one leg at a time into the teal trousers, sliding them up his legs causing his looser undergarments to shift around his crotch. Kenat moaned as he bunched his jewels in an uncomfortable assault of fabric. Kenat adjusted the unfavorable conditions as he heard Venna's soft laughter in the background.

She had been watching him the whole time. *Curious little nymph,* he thought. She was an admirable thing, barely the age of seventeen and innocent of her days. He removed his robes from the tree branch and carefully folded them within his arms in ritualistic fashion leaving the neckline forward and the sleeves tucked neatly within sacred form. As he turned towards the party, he caught Venna playfully dropping behind the side wall of the carriage. Drapes of blonde hair slowly fell from her escape like trapped liquid dripping into a puddle below. He was onto her.

Kenat heard soft giggling before Ysalir warned her to be silent. Cadeck greeted his return, seeing his near perfect fold of the sacred garments.

"You will learn in time. You have creases in front of your sleeve folds and your tail, scrunched and loose where it tucks underneath. It should be a perfect square, no creases, no loose fabric where your folds are. The square is the completeness of your vows, the acceptance of your gift. When you unfurl your robes, it is to symbolize the ways of magick as it flows into your soul, and which have prepared your body for its eternal use."

Cadeck's voice did not scold, nor did it condescend, but the older sage provided Kenat with reassurance as he escorted the young man back to the others. Kenat circled towards the rear of the cart as Cassica, Tesh and Ysalir struggled with the vibark chest into an outcropping a few yards away. Venna and Eris tended to the remaining tools, though the blonde woman's giggling incessantly increased, darting her eyes towards the other maiden and Kenat's attention.

"What's so funny?" Kenat spoke in Proper Accent.

"You look like a harlequin dancing in front of a bastard's court."

Eris joined Venna to laugh at her playful joke.

"You're the one who dressed me like this."

"I know. I did not figure you would accept it."

"Ladies," Cadeck interrupted the juvenile banter, "It'll do for now, Kenat."

Sour burning stench wafted into the air as Ysalir set the vibark chest alight. The stink burned into Cadeck's nose reminding him of the fetid swamps near Sarat's shorelines, and the aroma of the native trees as they decayed. Cadeck aided Kenat into the cart, while Eris and Venna continued to tease him silently as they exchanged childish glances in his disfavor.

The fire crackled behind them as Cassica, Ysalir and Tesh returned from the immolation. Tesh clutched his left hand as it surged with pulsating red traces across his veins merged with the golden amulet melted into his skin. A jolting pain, unlike any he had felt in his lifetime, surged across his hand, up his arm and through his spine. He stumbled through the clearing before collapsing at Cadeck's feet behind the small cart. Ysalir turned towards his direction, glancing through her raven locks with a piercing acuity.

"Is he alright?"

Cadeck dropped to his knees at Tesh's aide. Dirt and foliage clung upon his ragged tunics as Cassica aided Cadeck to lift the young man. His left hand ebbed in tighter contractions before coursing with a raw, orange flame coursing across his appendage.

"Tesh, your hand."

"When the flames ignited, I felt it in my body, as it were part of my own blood."

Cadeck pondered the boy's words, craning in meditative thought towards the ground.

"What did he mean?" Cassica asked, struggling to lift Tesh to his feet.

Cadeck paused within his thoughts. Cadeck hoisted Tesh's opposing side back upon his shoulder relieving Cassica of the strain upon her body.

"Can you make it into the cart?"

The flames upon Tesh's hands subsided into relaxed hue settling into his fingers, "I think I should be fine."

"Kenat," Cadeck beckoned.

The young man rose to his feet, gripping Tesh's right hand as Cadeck hoisted him into the wagon. Tesh's legs gave way as he arced his rear foot onto the flat bed. Tesh collapsed onto his back while Kenat held firm to his hand, twisting the man into an awkward position with his right hand lifted across his chest. Kenat released the limb permitting Tesh to stroke his forehead in subsiding agony.

Cassica lifted into the cart, "If he is going to be like this on the journey, he will not be of much use. We will need an army to defeat the Si'rai."

"I'm sure he'll be fine Your Highness," Cadeck glanced into the sky tracing the sun's trail into noon, "We need to get far to keep distance from this hunter."

Cadeck carried himself towards the front of the cart and hoisted himself onto the driver board next to Ysalir. She signaled the horse into gallop as the cart jolted with wooden creak from the forward momentum.

"What happened to him?"

Ysalir's words rolled from her tongue like a soft melody. Cadeck ignored her words as he held to the riding bar to his side, keeping his composure as the horse carried lighter weight in faster stride.

"When I figure it out, I'll tell you."

Cadeck's thoughts drifted into quiet meditation as the northern winds picked up to rustle through the scant trees like a river changing course. His mind focused on thoughts of raising his children, the waning stench of the vibark wood reminded him of more pleasant days. Ysalir ignored his brash comment, thinking it the babbling thoughts of a middle-aged man beyond his prime.

She raced the horse deeper north along the sparsely travelled path through the thin forestry leading into boreal peat. Bitter chills whipped along the air. Venna, Kenat and Eris covered themselves with the hay stocks and fur blankets Cassica scavenged from the chest. In prideful boast, Kenat freed a hand from beneath the blankets, and twisted his fingers into a dance with syncopated speech whispered from his tongue. With the quickness of spoken word of ancient vernacular, flames burned from his palm as he split apart his curled fingers mesmerizing the younger ladies in awe. The added warmth allowed them to snuggle closer to the Magi to bask in the warmth of his flame.

Venna rested her blonde mane against his right shoulder, gracing his arm with both of her hands. Eris clutched upon his left as the pair rested their heads comfortably upon him. He cherished the attention as he leaned his head against the side wall of the cart creasing his face into a callous smirk.

Cassica placed a fur blanket over Tesh who faded into sleep upon the rough boards covered with scarce hay. His left hand simmered into golden spackled flesh as he clenched it tightly with his right. His sheathed sword slid quietly down his back towards the pull of gravity on his left side. She curled her knees to her chest, burying her face into the cover. Her crimson locks blended into the black and white blanket like a flowing carpet upon a grand foyer.

Ysalir carried the cart into dusk as the fading light of the sun drifted into the western horizon. Scant boreal permafrost flanked the road as the cart rolled beyond scattered farms dotted with small homes in the distance puffing welcoming smoke through their chimneys. Cadeck motioned Ysalir away from the farmers' road into a clearing between a series of rocks and cliffs judging a spot of ground to be suitable for a campsite.

By the finalization of the setting sun, Cassica had made camp aided by Eris and Venna. Kenat seated himself next to a small stack of kindling and outstretched his palm as a burst of flame coughed between his fingers into the wood. Venna's eyes widened, and a grin split her lips at his supernatural skills. Cadeck stood over the spectacle, arms folded, shaking his head in dismay.

"This is the last time I want to see your magick for prideful purpose, Kenat. Our powers are not meant to impress, but to protect."

"As Magi, we possess abilities they do not."

Cadeck groaned at Kenat's snide reply, "Philos entrusted me as your superior, and I will continue to remind you of his teachings. Now, go, check on Tesh. He should be waking soon."

Kenat grumbled as he lifted himself from his seated position. Peevish at his assigned task, he made his way towards the cart a few meters away from the campfire surrounded by the sleeping furs laid upon the ground. With Kenat's back turned away, Cadeck snapped his fingers and waved an open palm towards the rising flame causing the flame to disappear, reversing the kindling back in time to fresh, dry fuel in front of Venna's and Eris' naïve facades.

"Ladies, start the fire as you should, please."

Cadeck grinned at his command, turning his back towards Venna to peer behind him. Venna gazed upward towards the older man as he did not see her disgruntled face and mocking tone as a child whose father took away her favorite toy. She let out a low sigh followed by a grunt as she grabbed a strike of flint from the supply pouch next to her. She tussled upon a free piece of wood and struck the flint against it to spark in flame. Placing the wood gently upon the formation, the lit source ignited the rest of the wood.

Cassica ignored Venna's misfortune, her demeanor a serious tone as she stood and moved to meet Cadeck at his side. Across the eastern edge of the horizon, a series of orange lights and gray smoke painted the sky with the backdrop of fading daylight, reflected like drops of ink onto the pristine canvas of the calm lake. Short reflections of dotted flames glistened across the vast Lake Vorstak bristling on the edge of their sight. Their breaths rolled into vapors as Cassica crossed her arms to tighten the coat around her shoulders.

Cadeck's chiseled face craned silently in a short panoramic scan across the view. To the south, faded brown towers erected as small triangles with guard flames burning from them. From his position, he discerned a faint black flag with a red center erected from a fort equidistant on the horizon rose upon the stone walls.

"The Si'rai have made their presence known within Vorstak and its training center. We will need to hurry to find Tijoa and move Tesh into his next phase of trials. From there, we must find voyage into the Oradan Sea to find the Water Temple."

Cadeck's statement exuded his strict regimen to discipline and order and as sharp as the low winds cooling Cassica's soft skin. Cadeck spoke of the Water Temple in manner to ignore a painful memory, reflected in the timbre of his voice staggering upon his sentence. Cassica's concern returned to thoughts of her kingdom. Several weeks passed since leaving Sarat, her father and her realm. A time lost to warn her father to prepare an army.

"You should be able to find friendly passage in Racoren. Once there, I wish to return with Rensel and my maidens back to home and leave you, Tesh and Kenat towards furthering your journey."

Cadeck ignored her statement, focusing instead on the faint calls of barked orders rippling across the lake's waters. He stood as a stoic statue listening to the words of a devoted follower of his icon. She turned her neck towards Cadeck's potted face. A whiskery beard denoted both wisdom and suffering in one person.

"You will be safer with us Your Highness. The Si'rai have conquered Silvetzen as we saw. I have no doubt their handiwork repeats in Sarat."

"It would take a massive army," her eyes followed his towards the camp in the distance, calculating the response her father's army could muster.

"The Imperium has those resources. Their leaders are well regulated, conquering and conscripting to increase their numbers. There would be large movements of men; many from lands across the oceans conquering in foreign soil thousands of miles from their farms and families. They either obey or lose not just their own lives but those of their loved ones, if the Si'rai leadership has not performed deed already behind their backs. You commit folly if you underestimate them."

Cadeck broke his gaze to lean his head towards Cassica's angle on his right shoulder, "I guaranteed your safety, Cassica. I sent your men with your carriage to lure the Si'rai away from you. If you were aboard your carriage, they would surely capture you or worse."

Cassica drew inquisitive, "Then what happened to those men?"

Cadeck returned to his view upon the distant lake, "Murdered. If the Si'rai acted for the bait, upon discovering the ruse, the men would have fell victim to their pursuers. If you were with them; I dare not fathom the outcome at their hands before they handed you over to their emperor. Then it only gets worse.

"I have followed your family since I earned my tongue. Godwen discouraged my further involvement with the Saratian Court, but upon my first introduction when you were still swaddling, I sensed something about you he did not."

"What is it?" Cassica turned to him inquisitively.

"Something powerful the likes of which I have not felt before or since."

"A spirit?"

Cadeck patted the young princess on her shoulder ignoring her question, "I will meditate away from camp. Troubling thoughts consume my meditations since Silvetzen. I should not disrupt the camp with my struggle."

Cadeck marched towards a mossy embankment of rocks yards away from the campgrounds. Cassica did not pursue him, only shrugging her shoulders and letting out a short sigh as she revolved towards the fur blankets laid upon the ground. Venna cozied up next to Eris close to the fire. Ysalir returned from hunt, dropping a couple of rabbits upon the ground, large enough to sustain the campers till the next morning.

Tesh rested upon Kenat's shoulder as the pair walked towards camp. The warmth of Venna's fire comforted the aching man as Kenat rested him into ease upon the soft peat grass covered by the warm fur. Tesh settled into the soft skins, wrapping another blanket around his shoulder for warmth. Cassica seated herself to his left as Kenat joined next to Venna and Eris leaving Ysalir at Cassica's left, her back turned towards the quiet winds.

Gray clouds painted into the horizon dimming the last remnants of sunlight across the skies. Rabbit hides crackled within the flames as Ysalir lifted one of the skewers away. She peeled apart legs and muscle tissue splitting it between herself, Cassica and the girls. Venna devoured her meal politely with

Eris and Kenat beside her. Ysalir prepared more meat for Kenat and Tesh, handing them each a morsel of cooked flesh which they devoured without courtesy.

"Is he not joining us tonight?"

Ysalir's attention focused to Cadeck seated several yards away.

Orange flame reflected upon Cassica's emerald eyes as she turned towards the Magi, "No. Something troubles him."

She turned back towards Ysalir, "We should remain with him and Tesh until we learn more about the stability of Rykana. He does not feel it is safe to return to Sarat anytime soon."

"What about your father and mother? Your brothers? You have been adamant to rejoin them since we left Silvetzen's capitol."

"Rensel," she returned to watch Cadeck, "he's right."

Cassica's heart sunk. She fought her instincts and her upbringing in her simple words to her friend. Diplomacy failed many days ago in Silvetzen's capitol. She sent her soldiers on a decoy mission whom she hoped had returned safely to Sarat with her letter to warn her father. Cadeck's instincts suspected otherwise. Had she been on the transport with Si'rai soldiers ransacking it, she could have suffered a far more sinister fate than theirs.

She watched in the distance as Cadeck seated himself in the faded darkness released from the campfire's embrace. His back turned to his companions; he stretched his hands against his knees in meditative posture. Cassica watched him as a concerned friend. Unguarded, he was cold and alone but preferred none go with him during this time. Cassica made her watch orders and commissioned them amongst the party permitting Tesh and Kenat minimal watch duties. Kenat protested, but Tesh reassured him of his role in the endeavors.

Cassica admitted her role in the journey; not only were there a need for her protection, but she also had to make her command aware of their own duties and she needed complete participation. She understood she traveled amongst commoners; but held no authority over their citizenry in her neutered facility. A burden placed upon her in recent weeks, now succumb to the whims of an aging Magi and a boy pupil. Her youngest charges required direction, a capacity she could offer. The weight of Cadeck's sorrow relied upon her acceptance of his truth. A truth she dared not contemplate, but a likelihood she understood to come to fruition.

Chapter 27

The banter of camp dwindled into a low hum as voices faded into drifted sleep. Cadeck remained silent amongst the cold stone rock jutting above soft peat grass. Chilled air whispered across the landscape vibrating the faint hairs growing along his ear. His eyelids remained closed, focusing on sounds coming through the mortal plane before drifting into meditation.

He first admitted his soul to his god, Aeus, in hopes for favorable blessings. He called the god's name both in common and the speech of invocation but heard no answer. Instead, he only heard muffled whispers through the darkness of the Abyss with Wrem's voice. He called her name. She returned maniacal laughter. He resumed searching, calling names of his fallen ancestors along with Jess. He called out ancient names of deceased Magi long since turned to ash from burial. More laughter.

Then, he called for the haunting demon, "By the Aztun I command you demon to reveal yourself."

Shadowy whispers tore down the walls of vacuum surrounding Cadeck's meditation as the demon slowly revealed itself within his mind. Choronzon's sinewy wisps whipped around Cadeck's spirit form like a whirlwind of noodles snaking through the Magi's mind before molding into his familiar dark embodiment. Crimson globes glowed like baleful flame beset into a shape of a head. The demon assumed his spectral form upon Cadeck's command.

"I linger, Cadeck. The hunter is close."

"I won't let him find another Temple."

"If you kill him, then Master will send another. As many as he needs."

"Your darkness only prevails in Silvetzen. You cannot haunt me out of this realm."

Choronzon laughed with the voices of a thousand souls, "Soon, Sarat will succumb to the Abyss, and I will prevail there. You delay the inevitable, Aztmi. Once Ragres informs Master you ride with Mother Babalon, he will not delay in the demise of your children for they would no longer serve his purpose. Unless" Choronzon paused with a long hiss, "you make a bargain."

"I do not bargain with demons."

"Then you may as well have killed your children yourself," Choronzon's spirit hissed a tiny laugh and continued, "But I am willing to make an offer. You turn Cassica over to Ragres and we release your children. I leave your soul alone to allow you to pray and you may then continue with the Azthar Kherdmon, if you believe you will be successful."

A tempting bargain. One sovereign sacrificed so he might unite again with his own blood. A selfish notion. One that a man composed of a lesser soul would entertain. Until he realized the supposition in tone.

"Such pleasures will not derive from me."

Choronzon laughed, "You fail to comprehend Master's power; the link to the Abyss is strong where his presence looms. Spirits roam, and voids open and close where he conquers. He is the embodiment of our god and his vicar on Roth. Connected eternally to the Abyss, all who possess the gifts, though your dogma has denied truth for Aeons. It is the Oneness of the All which creates and completes Life. You know this, your Magi know this. And with the presence of Babalon within a virile vessel, the ushering of a new Aeon is upon us.

"Your Ascended foresaw this. The Azthar Kherdmon, Babalon and the Apophadi; all three now exist in one Procession, but there lies the conundrum. This Aeon will be like none other. Two will exist, but one shall fall. To the victor goes the Aeon. Give my Master what he requires, and you shall live well in his Aeon. The offer is simple."

Cadeck's soul form raised his voice towards his adversary, "I have already told you what I think of your offer. You can take it and send it back to the Abyss where you belong."

Cadeck mustered his strength in his subconscious, gripping the thin neck of the demon's form with fists surrounded with an intense light from his source. The demon struggled as to appear gasping for non-existent air, flailing his spindly arms, whipping his ethereal abdomen ending into a pointed tail absent legs.

"I'm not done with you, Cadeck."

Choronzon commanded a harsh dictation as his form disappeared from the overpowering magick ending the spiritual conversation with a fading laughter in the void. Mystically weakened, his soul form crouched to his knees before collapsing onto an ethereal ground. The stone felt cold like the emptiness in his heart as icy winds washed upon his uncovered face and hands. Ice pellets clamped upon his open digits and sprinkled onto his eyebrows as though the frost would become his grave.

Cadeck.

A familiar voice called to him. Thrice it rang his name. He writhed to respond, unable to discern the tone calling for him. Cold hands graced upon his withered face, tracing along the pitted furrows and rough stubble covering him. Cadeck groaned in pain, crying the name of his lover.

You must hurry to the Temple of Water, love. There is urgency in my message.

"Jess, I hear you. Where are you?"

Do not concern yourself love. Morning approaches, Tesh must go to Tijoa. Then you will be closer to me.

"Cadeck," a soft feminine voice called out to him within his conscious hearing. The soft melodies rang through his ear drums as the pitter patter of children at play. His eyelids cracked open with the pain of cold frost's clench. He felt the tingling numbness of the night-chilled air drenching his hands in icy sweat.

Eris called his name again, this time enhancing her cries with the slight shaking of his rough shoulder.

"Where am I?"

"Wake up, Cadeck. Torches approach us from the north."

"Torches?"

Cadeck split his eyelids open to reflect what simple lights bounced in the cold darkness of the northern tundra. Whispering flames of orange vibrations danced in march-step from the northern horizon of the road. The orange dots blurred in focus as his mind attuned to the callings of the physical realm. A faint cadence followed the ghostly lights flickering with the occasional wind blowing from the northwest.

Cadeck groaned as he lifted himself to all fours. He stabilized himself onto one foot, left knee firmly planted on the bedrock where he rested through the night. With all his might, he gripped his right knee with both hands and raised himself to his feet with the arthritic cracking of his bones. Movement caused his legs to shift on the embedded rock he stood upon as he abruptly adjusted to his center of gravity.

He gazed around towards camp as Ysalir and Cassica worked quickly to conceal blades within their fitted tunics to cover themselves with the warm fur hides by the faint light of the moon turning to sliver. Kenat did his best to shelter his lavish, girly attire as Tesh moved in clumsy grace to obscure his weapon in furs upon the ground, the hilt of his sword within reach should he need it. Venna stood next to her sister who forced a small dagger between Venna's fingers, coaxing her to use it for defense. Cadeck could distinguish a distinct argument in soft whispers as Venna reminded her sister she did not feel she was a fighter. Cassica's command reprimanded her of her protest, insisting she conceal the weapon.

Cadeck ignored the exchange and focused his ears upon the speech coming from the dancing flames in the distance. He motioned Eris to return to the camp and ask what preparations she may need from her commandant. The speeches from the flames spoke in a foreign dialect uncommon to the Saratian-Silvetzenian blood. Cadeck reached upon his soul to muster what ethereal strength he could and chanted in speech of invocation. Cadeck's body froze as a statue. Motionless, his hands joined into the shape of a triangle in front of his forehead.

Vision came into focus as the men were still many yards away from approach. Cadeck released his soul, focusing it to march side-by-side with the encroaching flames. Their voices harsh of tongue and their flame-kissed faces bore the signature olive-skin roughness of his enemy. Their bulky armor chimed as a sinister dirge on lockstep rhythm towards the distant camp, each step crushing into the peat moss stones with clamor of syncopated death. A crimson-crested plume capped the helmet of their leader, marching in forward formation ahead of his six soldiers. They bore no flag relying instead on the haunting, vermillion symbol of the Abyss crested into their breastplates.

A gust of spiritual energy swept onto Cadeck's body marking the culmination of his enchantment. Mustering his might, he hobbled towards the encampment in swift pace. The soft peat grass provided little comfort to his aching bones in his harried steps. The burning campfire stung at his nostrils like prickling needles forced inside them. He chose to ignore the horrendous stench of the dying wood and focused on his friends.

"There are seven in total, they're all Si'rai," his whispers caused Venna to clench at Kenat's left arm.

"Nod your head if you remember our cover."

Cadeck received unanimous nods from the men and women and continued, "Good, follow my lead. If these men get out of hand, on my word, Kenat, you may defend yourself. Rensel, Cassica, you know how to deal with them. Venna, Eris, I want you to run for the cart. Tesh, stick to my side."

The air calmed to a still sending the echoing clanks of metallic plate into the cold silence of camp. Breaths rolled in coordinated unison from the mouths of Cadeck and company in anticipation. All motion ceased in momentum as all of existence relied on their next breaths. The sounds of stamping soil, metal plates mashing and scraping and uneasy voices speaking in a foreign dialect approached the travelers. Cadeck felt the ale-fresh breath of the men boiling through the air as the enemy soldiers hastened pace.

Cadeck eased his emotions as the cacophonic concerto approached closer. There was little doubt in his mind the soldiers had spotted the camp from afar and had changed their patrol towards their direction. He watched the faces of his travelers, paying close attention to the younger girls while their thoughts gave way to intimidated faces. Ysalir steadied herself, paying attention to the presumed leader of the troops. Kenat turned his attention towards the flame, the light glistening against his pearly orbs drenched with mental focus.

The lead soldier halted his company with movement of his hand. He motioned another soldier to follow. Their metal boots clinked against the rolling hill while climbing the jutted rocks and crags of the small embankment. Each step pounded into Cadeck's ears with the jarring memories of the dire fortress of tortures once endured. The leading man's pitch helmet was unique from the others; curved eyelets formed at the brow with a singular mold covering the bridge of his nose. The bottom of the helmet exposed his open jaw and adorned with a single red plume, erected from a notch on the forehead and remained as a steadfast monument to his lowly rank.

He commanded this simple company trudging through the barren sod fields of foreign lands. They would just as soon spit on the ground and burn it than spill blood upon alien soil. The pair approached Cadeck with disgruntled fervor. Cadeck calculated the chances; the enemy outnumbered them by two, which he and Kenat could take out all of them by themselves. Cadeck figured they would pose no opposition but chose to remain calm despite the odds being favorable.

Cadeck watched nervously as the sergeant surveyed the camp. The burning flame of the hearth bristling upon his blackened steel promoted the shadowy magick of the masters he reported to. Cadeck waited for his words although the commanding man chose to pay special attention to the young women in the party, studying them with a sneer. Cold breaths rolled from his mouth as he began to speak in his foreign tongue. His breath reeked of sour, Silvetzenian ales conflicting with his finely kept teeth as his tongue rasped his coarse language at Cadeck's direction.

Ysalir bit her lips and translated the sergeant's words in her mind but did not aide Cadeck with them. She was a professional and continued the ruse lest she blurt out the translation and expose their disguises. Finishing his sentence, the sergeant permitted the younger soldier to speak to Cadeck in Common Tongue. His structure was premature, and his conjugation broken. His voice cracked with uncertainty to translations.

"You intrude on Imperium land. Demand your citizen papers, please."

Cadeck eyed the sergeant with calm concern, "We are a poor family of travelling entertainers. We do not own these papers you ask, for we are citizens of Sarat, to the south."

The young warrior spoke to his commanding officer in the words of his native speech. He broke the phrases that rolled from Cadeck's mouth into a variety of words, some longer than others resembling nothing of Cadeck's tongue. Ysalir nodded towards Cassica in obvious concern, for the soldier translated Cadeck's speech into a Si'rai protest chant. The sergeant barked an order towards his company, hands covered by thin, raven vambraces, he pointed with shouted commands at each of the individuals with emphasis on the young ladies.

He gripped the lapels of Cadeck's tunics with his gloved hands, pushing the Magi into the rough terrain. With a metallic ting, he revealed his sword from the scabbard upon his hip pointing the tip towards Cadeck's wrinkled neck. Venna called towards Cadeck, addressing him as father. The five remaining soldiers trudged in unison step upon the rolling knoll towards the campgrounds.

Tesh reached into the sash for the hilt of his blade. Kenat chanted under his tongue, working his thoughts into perfection so his spell would be untainted. Venna and Eris obeyed as preached, darting their nubile bodies towards the horse-drawn cart. The translating soldier unsheathed his weapon giving chase to the young girls.

Calculating his timing, Kenat opted to protect Eris and Venna. He turned his slinky frame towards the direction of the soldier and extended his hands. The tips of his thumbs and smallest fingers touched, with the other fingers spread outward as a web. Between his palms coalesced a burning orb of flame; fire-hot tentacles wrapped around the center before discharging into a powerful stream aimed at the pursuing soldier. The focused energy kissed upon the man's exposed neck, torching his skin upon contact before crawling within his metal shell cooking him from inside. His screams were loud yet short as he dropped to flaming knees disintegrating into ash with the rest of his organic coverings. A burning hulk of steaming steel remained, melted in orange goo at the tips of the fittings where his skin once extruded from the armor. Exhausted from the efforts spending his magick, Kenat bent over and dropped to his knees. His breathing turned laborious.

Tesh leapt over the camp flame, his legs straddled over in sequential motion, sword in hand as he took a swing at a soldier attacking Cassica. The soldier blocked the attack, before planting his metal boot into Tesh's torso. Tesh struggled as the kick of his adversary knocked him over. His imbalance landed his back next to the flame, his left hand falling into the fire. Ysalir flew into action, her fur coverings slinked away from her athletic build as she lifted a small dagger from the loose tunics fitted against her hips.

She mounted Tesh's attacker upon his shoulders. Her thighs gripped her knees tight upon them as she thrust the dagger into his neck. A shower of blood sprayed against her clothing; his sword dropping to the ground. Ysalir remained perched upon her opponent as he fell backward, clutching his wound till his life drained.

Flames burned against Tesh's crippled hand. He felt no pain as his hand consumed the chemical reactions, sending burning surges through his gold-laced veins. Voices spoke to him from another time mingled with the present sounds of metallic conflict and screaming. Tesh sprang from his encumbered position to rise onto all fours, surveying the battle. The sergeant kept Cadeck hostage against the ground only to quickly look over his shoulder to see Tesh charge towards him.

A clear advantage over the lad, he raised himself into a defensive position to counter any move Tesh may employ. Tesh's left hand burned with flame trickling along vein lines carved into his skin. Kenat regained his composure and surged another blast of magick behind Tesh, propelling his flame jet towards a soldier running towards Cassica's unprotected backside as she struggled with another Si'rai warrior. Kenat's target fell as the last one, screaming in whimpering pain, gurgling into melting sounds of organs and blood, then fading into lifelessness. As his flame dissipated, Kenat's body jolted to a sudden pain in his chest, collapsing him onto the ground once more.

Cassica handled herself in a two on one situation. Her graceful kicks and limber form held her attackers at bay before gaining the upper hand upon one. What they carried into battle with sheer weight and strength, she danced around them with nimbleness. Taking advantage of her situation, one of her men fell with a dagger thrust through the bottom of his jaw.

The gambit changed. The older women were fighting back and at least one of the men knew magick. The sergeant surmised the younger man was a serious threat. Watching the spectacle of two of his soldiers incinerated like victims cooked in torture ovens reorganized his thoughts to order his men to focus on Kenat. His curiosity jerked his head at Tesh's left hand undamaged from the flames beneath his skin.

Utilizing the distraction, Cadeck's aging bones cracked his body into a crippled stature lifting him to stand upon his feet. Ysalir and Cassica followed the men disengaging from their combat and followed their sergeant's orders towards Kenat. His spellwork required timing and articulate phrasing which panic and unbridled discipline prevented him from accomplishing. Realizing his predicament, he turned to retreat towards the cart.

Ysalir gained momentum against her target, leaping upon his backside planting him face-first into the ground. She thrust a stiletto dagger into the right side of his neck, severing his carotid artery. Cassica's target paced quicker with his pursuit of Kenat. Cadeck studied the attacker. Tesh's sword took aim to confront the sergeant.

Cadeck extended his arms to full length in front of him. Chanting sacred words, a bow sizzled into form in an erratic display of static electricity. He pulled back the drawstring, as a projectile lengthened with the pull of his right hand. His magick fizzled and reenergized with his ailing strength. He chanted his words faster. His weapon glowed into form as the missile of energy launched from the bow with the simulated release of his right fingers.

Frigid air squeezed tight into Kenat's lungs as he sprinted to reach the cart. He turned to see the lone pursuer whose sword rose above his head in a fanatical run of obeyed commands. The man towered twice Kenat's height and bulged with muscle even more so. For his frame, his muscular thighs outran Cassica and Ysalir gaining considerable ground against his target, Kenat. Venna and Eris would be no match for the soldier and Kenat's frantic thoughts forced his ethereal talents into submission.

Kenat watched as the soldier closed distance upon him. His eyes darted towards the incoming projectile pulsing with the powers of Cadeck's speech. Perched upon the higher ground, Cadeck observed his weapon fired towards his target only to have the arrow disappoint him and fizzle out yards before reaching its goal. Kenat regained focus as the mighty blade of his attacker came crashing towards him. He ducked away, snaking his skinny figure underneath the wheels of the ragged cart. Shards of splintered wood showered in the air as the beast lowered his massive sword shattering the edge of the sideboard. Venna and Eris squealed from the impact, clawing their way towards the opposite side of the cart.

Cadeck turned his attention towards Tesh who held his own against the trained sergeant. He focused again upon the cart as Ysalir and Cassica carelessly lunged for the brutish soldier before he threw the trained ladies away from his back with a swing of his right fist, knocking them to the ground. Cadeck heaved a sigh, grasping for his chest in weakened state to see Kenat struggling against the mightier man attacking the younger girls. Cassica frantically struggled to gain footing, turning her eye towards Cadeck in disdain. She strained to stand, breaths panting, and hair frayed in front of her face, but a shimmer of disappointment carried into her eyes before she refocused upon her goal.

The sergeant's relentless lunges and arcing swings started to weaken Tesh. Against the Silvetzenian soldiers, Tesh could hold his own and take advantage of their styles which were close to his rudimentary training. Si'rai were more disciplined in their focus, regimenting years of fighting from the time of childhood bred specifically for their cause. The sergeant did not tire in his combat, focusing on removing the man with the odd hand threatening him. Sweat drained down Tesh's brow, soaking his face and burning his eyes. Chilled air tickled his eyebrows forming minute icicles with the perspiration.

288

Ysalir regained a jump upon her target, causing him to collapse from the imbalance. Kenat motioned himself to the opposite side of the cart, rolling from underneath. Ysalir distracted the trooper from Kenat, forcing him onto the soft permafrost. They struggled in melee. His closed fist punched Ysalir into the nostril. Her nose burst with blood. He pushed her from him, gripping for his sword and cursing at her in his tongue which she mentally translated he wished her to become his brood slave.

Insulted by his taunt, she reached for her fallen dagger and lunged towards the thick neck outcropping from his armor. He swiped her futile effort with a swing of the hilt of his sword, and then sliced into her clothing. She clenched her right arm with her empty hand as blood spilled through her fingertips with the open gash. Venna called her sister's birth name in fright as a string of tears kissed her pale cheeks. The brute readied his killing blow.

Cassica reached into a pocket within the fabric against her breast and removed a throwing knife. Propelling the weapon towards its mark, the blade stabbed into the thick neck of Ysalir's attacker. Blood sprayed across his armor as he exclaimed pain into the early morning air. Unphased by his wound pulsing crimson life onto his armor, he turned and sprinted towards the princess.

His armor clanked into rhythm, a chorus of metallic bulk heaving with his weight. Each strain of his massive muscle placed a burden within his anatomy as his heart struggled to pump blood. Weakened, he raised his sword to ready his swipe into Cassica's skull. A war cry erupted from his throat yards away from her prone, tired body. As his vector closed in to within a few feet, he collapsed to his knees. Like a programmed machine, he swiped his massive blade with his right hand, the weight collapsing his torso with forward momentum upon the ground. The sword clamored upon the rock surface inches from Cassica's body. The man clutched his wound as he hemorrhaged into death.

Back on the campsite, Tesh's adversary wore him into submission. The sergeant tasted victory with each attack which left Tesh weak. He heard no commands, no cries, or no battle calls as the last of his soldiers fell to the family of entertainers. He realized he was the last of his squad, the strongest tactician, only for his hardened soldiers felled by women and one proficient in magick. His inferiors were weak and unworthy to be wervostri, their matriarchal bloodline a curse upon the Imperium, he thought to himself. His attacks continued to deteriorate Tesh's resolve. The silhouette of Cassica rushed towards them, followed by Kenat clutched in Eris' welcoming arms as the pair struggled to return.

Tesh succumbed onto his back with a blow from the sergeant's fist into his face. Cadeck had watched the fight, unable to help in weakened state strained to a prone position on one knee. He felt helpless as his charge fought to survive. The sergeant raised his sword above his head to lunge into Tesh's torso. As Tesh lay in sacrifice to the blade, tired and frail, unable to lift his own sword to defend, voices called once more to him.

In slowed time, the blade lowered down the height of the sergeant. Tesh listened with interest; the voices dulled the call of the sergeant, the scream from Cassica and the pounding of his own heart. Burning surges coursed through his left arm tingling through to his hand. His hand glowed with intense flame snaking along his gold-laced veins. As the sword inched closer towards his unarmored heart, his hand instinctually lifted from the ground. Ignoring his fragility and pain, his palm faced towards his attacker sending a pulse of fiery flame towards the face of the sergeant.

The impact of the energy propelled the body a few feet above the ground, throwing him many yards behind Cadeck. As his body graced the air, it glowed as a bonfire. What landed into the ground was a calamity of armor pieces devoid of organic life, instantly incinerated of flesh and bone. Cadeck stood vigilant as the battle concluded, the thoughts of his helplessness at the forefront of his mind. Cassica, Kenat and Eris returned their way to camp. Tesh breathed in agony, his hand cooling to simmer as perspiration covered his shirt and face.

Tesh lay on his side propped by his right elbow in a moment of reflection. The darkness of sky began to brighten into a dark blue in the eastern horizon as the nighttime clouds started to fade. The voices dissipated into faint whispers before leaving altogether. He had heard them before with each passing of the Trials. He would ask Cadeck if he could.

However, Cassica's arrival would impede his attempt as she had more earnest questions to ask of the Magi. Her matted hair and sweat stains defied her inherited beauty. She clutched at her left ribs sensing a bruise bulging under her clothes. A stern look graced her lips, eyes furrowed to anger beneath entangled locks straying over her face.

"What happened to you back there?" She opened a berating query towards Cadeck as he rose to stand.

He declined her ears the luxury of an answer. The tear of fabric overshadowed a muffled scream from the cart. Cadeck turned his attention towards Tesh gripping the young man's arm to aide him to stand. Cassica pursed her lips at Cadeck's refusal.

"I asked you a question."

Cadeck bluntly answered, "I do not have to answer. You, of all your Roses, know the ways of the Magi best. You're wounded, Cassica."

Tesh lifted himself under Cadeck's aid. Ysalir's distinct voice blurted obscenities at her sister in the distance.

"I am fine, just a bruise. Nothing broken. But my pressing concern is that your magick failed, Cadeck. Which may cause us to lose Rensel."

"Where's she wounded?"

"Her left arm sliced open, a bloodied nose," Eris answered, Kenat stumbled next to her as he seated onto the ground.

Cadeck turned towards Kenat whose heavy breaths from his battle hampered his walk. The glimmer of a cresting sun filtered into his pearly eyes.

"Can you heal her?" Eris followed.

Cadeck looked back towards her, "I am afraid magick does not work as you would like, child. Sokut blesses the gift of healing, not Aeus nor Heseph. Kenat are you weakened?"

"Aye," the younger Magi nodded in wheezing breaths.

"Can you cauterize her wound?"

Rolling sweat rolled along his face, staining his hands and armpits, "I have never tried. Cadeck, my magick, I feel unnecessarily weakened by simple procedures."

"Eris, grab a flame from the fire to seal her wound. Tesh do what you can to gather camp."

Tesh nodded in agreement moving swiftly to gather the furs and supplies. Eris ran to the campfire and removed a small glint of kindling and with caution, made her way to return to the cart.

"Cassica, we'll need to gather the armor pieces, take them with us and burn the bodies lying here."

"No Cadeck, I demand you answer my question."

He turned to her, grunting in malice upon his pitted face, lips mashed upon themselves with clenched jaw as he approached her position. His anger sprayed her face with random spots of spittle.

"You would never understand, Cassica. If we train Tesh, I can rescue my children and save your kingdom, maybe then you will understand. Until then, I kindly ask for you to never request of my logic again."

Cadeck felt responsible for her charge since their introduction to each other while she was a baby. His loyalty to the Court of Sarat had been undying to the disdain of his Ascended. As he informed her the previous evening, he felt something within her from birth. He knew little of the spirit living within her, looking to ancient texts from the Magi and written lore of the Si'rai. Godwen instructed him to consume such words could lead to a tainted heart, ending with insanity or death. His heart sunk as he turned away from her. Tesh stopped his chore as Cadeck's rage billowed towards Cassica.

He strode towards the hulk of armor near the campfire that once had organic material. Kenat incinerated its owner as his second attack and Cadeck, using the force of his leg, propelled the helmet a distance with a swift kick. Cadeck slumped to seat himself upon the rocky surface carpeted by mossy grass.

He lingered on thoughts now vanished memories. For fleeting moments, Jess' plush kisses tickled upon his lips. The raucous laughter of his boy marched through his ears while the loving hugs of his daughter encompassed his arms. A streaming tear jerked from his eyes, cascading along his pitted face washing over his dried whiskers. He could not answer the question because he did not yet understand. Each time he prayed, each time he reached to his soul, he felt the taint of the darkness of the Abyss stretching over the lands like a dense fog enshrouding all in its wake. He saw too, it affected Kenat.

Cadeck realized urgency to leave Silvetzen and move to lands untainted. Could he return to Sarat and to his Temple? Risky, yet he knew the Temples were untouched and communing to his god would be welcome. What dangers awaited him along the way, he thought to himself. He was in no shape to face the hunter who lingered after him alone. He remembered his meditations and how his lover required him to join at the Water Temple. This gave him hope.

As he lifted himself from his seat, he straightened his tunics and trousers from wrinkles and verified his satchel remained closed as he hoisted it over his shoulder. Creaking sounds of unkempt wheels whined to a stop upon approach.

"Are you coming, Cadeck?"

Venna's high voice called to him. Memories of his daughter sprung to life with each moment he shared with the blonde girl. Each moment he gazed upon her innocence. His mind harkened to a simpler time. Yet each time, a haunting familiarity intruded his thoughts. Cadeck glanced around, fumbling his thoughts to recall the task at hand. Kenat and Tesh began to settle the remnants of camp into the cart as it parked upon the road near Cadeck.

"Right," he made approach to the cart, "Kenat, how much farther do we ride?"

"Tijoa's hut is about another day's ride."

Chapter 28

Tivius A'zum stood as an obsidian statue crested by an onyx mane as he overlooked the carnage he had wrought upon his conquest. Clouded by thick smoke wafting over the horizon mingling with the gray sky above, Sarat lay in siege. From his view atop the forward ramparts, scattered fires burned within the city across the river scarring the sky with lucid tears and the acrid stench of copper-tinged blood running through the streets. Screams and moans of women and children, the death rattles of men and soldiers rang through his ears as fifty-thousand seasoned warriors laid waste to the capitol city.

Flanked to his right stood Quinias Degoros wearing skin-tight leather upon his dark-complexion frame and standing near to Tivius' height. His muscular arms poked through fitted holes in his sleeveless shirt, a heavy sword defying his stature slung across his back, like a trained and fitted beast bulging from his discipline. He wore his hair short, cropped upon the top and shaved on either side with a single nose ring piercing through his septum.

"Iostana Magister's timing was impeccable," Tivius spoke in his native Sheebal. His eyes focused through an elongated viewing scope encrusted with jewels. The twin-headed eagle crest of Sarat minted against the shiny works, cut from a single piece of a crimson jewel. He lowered the scope to his side, being careful not to damage his loot. Blood caked his hands, dried, and etched into the cracks of his pale fingers

"Lord A'zum," Quinias addressed in the same tongue, "fifty legions command their way through Sarat. This kingdom is yours."

Tivius' eyes stared across the horizon in stoic pose. Winds carried the smoke in an easterly direction, whipping his hair across the shoulders onward upon his chest.

"Go and find the general in command. I require his report in the court of this fetid kingdom."

"Lord," Quinias saluted bowing his head and clenched his right fist against his heart. He turned and removed himself from the edge of the rampart. His boots rocked the wooden staircase leading towards the outer courtyard of the castle as he sprinted downward into the open enclosure. Tivius continued his gaze to admire the handiwork of the soldiers ravaging the city across the river from his position. Rampart towers smoldered with decay leaving charred remains of mighty ballistae. Walled by towering brick and mortar, the city of Sarat crumbled under the iron heel of his command.

The sun's light turned to fade on his second day of charge, a slight reminder of the former brilliance hidden in the musky soot consuming the grand city. He lifted his left hand forward, skin flaked and crunched as he constricted his digits into a fist. He released them to relax. Caked blood embedded in the pitted ravines stretching across his hand recalled the lives he took in recent days. The guards were viable, yet easily fallen. As his entourage assembled their way through the castle, the occupants drew into disarray amongst their vanity. A'zum slid his blade through the heart of the silver-bearded king and his older sons, his Xiatutni took out any soldiers who interfered. Sarat's crown fell in a few recalcitrant hours.

Selen was missing, not seen in Sarat and the last of the royal court. Tivius' thoughts pondered on his failure to wipe out the full royal family. Another failure should his father ever learn of it. He erased thoughts of punishment from his mind as he lowered himself along the rickety staircases into the outer courtyard. Saratian heraldic banners remained, hanging from the sides of the square towers facing the entry yard. Tivius drew breath, ushering in remaining strength his stamina could muster. Two days of solid fighting withered upon his body, his magicks provided him the abilities to withstand the burdens but the strains on his muscles escalated the more he drew prone to relaxation as though his body collided with a wall.

Crisp winds of the harvest season blew through the courtyard whipping up mini cyclones in fury along the corner walls and below thatched awnings flinging his hair to whip in frenzy to harmonize with the breezes. He paused a moment and stretched his bones cracking them with each successive release of pain. As each bone released tension, a long sigh escaped his breath.

He stood poised, confident with the accomplishment before him. He turned quick step towards the walls separating the outer courtyard from the towering ramparts marking the exit of the inner walls. Tivius remained silent as he passed through the opened doors towering like giant trees exposing the castle's inner grounds to the outer chaos. The piercing whiff of decay caught his nose.

Tivius' remaining assassins stood in attention as their commandant exited the inner fortifications of the palace and into the outer courtyard. Jagoth Reanar and Surar Tudok stood abreast next to Xanos Coron, a shorter man with lighter complexion. Xanos' distinguishing mark was the split goatee braided below his chin as Jagoth held his long ponytail over his shoulder, a metallic barb tip capping off his hair, swayed close to his left hip. Blood stains painted across their armor, the metallic scent of the smeared viscera festering into the crevices of the inlays. Wounds and scars fresh from battle cut into their skin. He did not smile at the accomplishment of his orders, only admiring with a rigid contempt towards the lingering Saratian servants within the courtyard.

Murmuring flies buzzed around the yard behind the men standing at rigid attention. Stench of rotting flesh loitered in the air as Tivius turned his attention towards bodies resting on slabs behind his men. Planked awnings covered the death trolleys where mounds of firewood lined delicately in pyramid shapes against the cut stone walls. Hay mounds covered the dusty ground. He crossed path beside the Si'rai man on his left. Five carcasses rested on individual cadaver carts prepared ritualistically in sacred fashion.

Elaborate trinkets and royal display dressed the oldest man, his grayed beard matted in bloody discoloration and his eyes closed tight. Bound to his eyelids with grotesque cruelty were crests of sewn fabric bearing the Sigil of the Abyss. His hands tied at his hips as were his legs with his throat cut post-mortem. Each of the bodies decorated lavishly to mock their vanity in death with the ritual bindings and scarred surgery committed likewise as their father.

Tivius reflected on the last moments of the older boys before him, the careless ambition in their eyes as they faced their father's attacker. Red hair marked the pair as twins. A gash cut along each of the twins' torsos traced in matching symmetry. The other bodies were children no younger than the age of six.

Tivius moved to the middle boy. He graced his right hand, etching his gnarled fingernails along the budding fuzz. Hair paused growth upon his fair face. Tivius tousled his hand within the boy's blackened hair in admiring fashion. He venerated the young boy's tender face flush of empty blood. He leaned over. Flowing raven tresses graced the gentle skin of the prepubescent boy as he split the boy's purple lips with his crusted, spade tongue.

Tivius leaned up from his necrophiliac embrace, licking his lips of the decay festering within the young child's mouth.

"This one," he crooned, tracing an index finger across the incision along the boy's neck, "send him to Racoren and impale him upon a stake. Burn one twin in Yumphen, impale the other in Telmen's town square. Send the last boy to Kora and hang him with a noose. Finally, hoist King Trebut upside down and mount him upon a pole in the primary market square. His body is the most contemptible; old and weak. He put up no fight in his death. Pathetic and feeble attempt for a man and for that he is to suffer the travesty of Antexum Cruci. Here, his soul will wander Roth searching forever for atonement only to find none.

"The message will be clear to the Saratian people; resistance to the Imperium shall result in death, the fate of their leaders is clear. The male lineage is extinct here."

Tivius clutched his spyglass tight into his left hand and placed it carefully into the hands of the stockier of the Si'rai men, "Surar, ready this tool of vanity, smelt it into coin. By itself, this abomination once coined, will be more than enough for your rewards."

Surar opened with a pearly grin of kept dental features, "My master it would put shame on the Saratian people for it to be smelted here."

Tivius returned his favor with a smile of his own. His darkened teeth an antithesis to the hygiene of his own soldier, "You have the spirit of a true pillager, the breed of your astu. Your raka'ir, who was he?"

Tivius' words fell from his lips in a lurid tone. Surar swallowed his saliva surprised by the Commandant's question as Tivius praised his bloodline and requested who fathered Surar. Ingrained to be instantaneous and the slightest hesitation in his response would turn anger upon his superiors. With each split second of time of his delay, the anger boiled within Tivius as he waited for the indoctrinate answer.

"Magister, raka'ir was Riger Tudok, Lord of Megid."

Icy blue eyes burned crisp into Surar's native hazel irises as Tivius approached the warrior's face. Tivius stared at Surar, his mind focused on the pedigree before him.

"You are of quality astini. I expect you within my bedchambers this evening. Leave me and perform your duties and have this abhorrent decoration smelted."

Surar wavered in his obeisance as he excused himself from the courtyard. Tivius' reputation preceded him among the wervostri; he regularly lusted the finest of men serving him, built of primal stock, and fit for battle. Like others of his caste forbidden from life-long unions, Surar had no bonded mate, yet had fathered multiple sons from multiple women back home. Surar favored women and Tivius' unsated carnal tastes against nature were disagreeable among many of those who served under him. But a denial of his requests would mean denial to return home alive.

The outer yard entry of Sarat's Royal Residence stood silent as lingering death enveloped the air. Bodies and corpses of peasants and servants littered the courtyard with few men and women standing in silent confusion, waiting for the aggression of the oppressors. Tivius barked an order in Common Tongue towards a group of stable hands standing idle on the opposite end of the courtyard. Intimidated by the occupation forces, the Saratian workers obeyed his request with hesitation.

One of the men buckled to his knees as he came upon the carcass of his king, streams of sobbing erupted from his face like a violent storm. An armored fist struck the mourner across his jaw led by the other Si'rai assassin. The assassin hoisted the man by his arm. The cracks of separation ripped inside his shoulders as Tivius repeated the order in condescending tone. The mourner screamed and clutched his right shoulder as he fell into the dirt. The group of mourners carted the bodies away from Tivius who commanded his men in Imperium tongue to escort the civilians as they began the journey to cross the bridge over the primary river.

Tivius paused, staring at the man whose cries melded to the mud. With a swift stomp of Tivius' heavy boot, the man's neck severed from his spine and silenced him. Tivius moved his eyes across the courtyard glancing across the remnants of life. Fearing retaliation, laborers hesitated to return to their various chores to the upkeep of the grounds. Turning, Tivius retreated deeper through the outer courtyard before entering the heavier portcullis leading towards the opulence of the inner plaza.

Amidst the bricked pathway cut around a central fountain, Tivius followed the extravagant, azure carpet following through to the doors of the structure. Two bodies flooded the clean waters of the fountain with their blood. The statuary casted waters within the centerpiece. Clever carving etched the statuesque shape of a curvy, naked female, her hands lifted above her head in a praising stance to the sky. The waters flowed from her palms, downward her arched fingers and into the basin below her feet.

A golden plaque mounted below her feet gave prayer to the goddess: *Sokut - She who gives life, her waters make us calm. Her breath is our strength, and her heart is her love.*

An ethereal ting echoed through the pristine stone walls like a ghostly yell from a corpse as Tivius' sword glistened against the mired sunlight. Scribbles lined the side of the blade in a language predating his own modern tongue. As tall as his height, the blade shimmered as he steadied it to his right side perpendicular to his body. In one swipe of his blade the marble statuary slashed in two below the left ribcage at an upward angle, severing the right breast. Cracking rocks and tumbling rubble preceded the top half of the relic as it slid at the angle crashing into the water below.

*

Dense fog settled upon the pristine valleys below as Ragres Shabririn climbed along the steep cliffs leading into the Tanakian Ring. Walkways and jutted paths lined most of the trail, while other stretches required climbing with one's own hands and feet to make progress. For a man with full sensory perception and the proper gear, this journey would take a half day, or longer. For Ragres, a full day had passed since he began his ascent, never stopping to rest or eat.

He denied Asvidar the burden to make the climb ahead and lowering any ropes or other equipment they may need for he explicitly carried none, so to spare his life for a grander purpose. As ordered, Asvidar lingered behind, making camp at the base of the mountains. Daylight broke above the eastern horizon splitting the soupy mixture of fog and sulfur.

Ragres's hands turned to blistery pulps carving into the limestone cliff sides. Like a black, tattered shadow, he scaled the paths to reach the summit into the opening of the volcanic caldera. Torn, battered and exhausted, he lifted himself upon the flat surface covered in patchy grass and weeds; he shifted his weight onto the rock and collapsed onto his ribs.

A sharp moan of anguish billowed from his gut as he rolled to his stomach and lifted to the tension of his burning thighs. He cried to his god with a shrieking roar, cursing the pain searing through his muscles. He sealed his crusted lips to silence as he stood like a shambling corpse freshly risen from its grave.

Through the Abyss, his vision caught the trails of his bait. Touched by the Abyss, Cadeck's track shimmered like a blackened goo reflecting spackles of light kissing sinister bile along the valley leading onward into the Tanakian Ring. Signatures of heat mottled into the magician's ethereal vision erupting in violent fissures and flows throughout the hazardous region. The jagged mountain range crumbled and buckled with cataclysmic fate stretching as far as an able eye could see. He curled his fingers to rest upon his sides in anticipation of the arduous journey ahead.

The Tanakian Ring symbolized the ancient blood feud between its neighboring kingdoms. Like historic conjunctions between the two rivals, the volcanic ridge would also turn ferocious. The Silvetzenians believed this was where Heseph honored their warriors in the afterlife. Neither Saratian nor Silvetzenian would venture into the western borders for fear of the encounters rumored to exist and only a Knight or a Magi could calm the ghosts of the battlefields here. The Saratians believed Sokut returned life to Her honored warriors whose blood spilled from the fires of battle upon the river. It was this primary channel where the souls of the slain returned to be honored in their capitol before heading into Her seas for eternity.

Ragres stood in crumbled disarray, unsealed the binding trousers wrapped to his legs like a second layer of flesh. He took a piss and smiled as it streamed towards the valley before him. Magick pulsated around him as his connection returned signatures of Cadeck, another Magi and the being which haunted his thoughts, the brightened essence of purity lingered upon them.

"You shall take no further steps, dark one," a commanding voice billowed from behind the scarred man. Ragres paused his stream, lifting his pus-addled head, turning over his shoulder to sneer at the voice's direction.

He sealed his trousers with knobby hands fleshed with calloused fingers, body reeking of sweat and pain sealed within leathery bindings. Through his vision, the pulsating aura of a figure shrouded in gray ash with a red hue manifested within the silhouette. A staff hoisted to his right masked in black with an ebbing stone hovering within a trident spiral glowing with an orange burn. The stone erupted in flame as the figure aimed the staff towards Ragres, launching a billowing broil of rolling shapes in blackened shadow of Ragres' vision.

Chanting through hissing whispers, Ragres proceeded to step forward towards the flame launched from Philos' staff and with the flash of shadow wisps engulfing his form, Ragres pushed into the silent ether of void. He sauntered casually past the fire streaks spilling from the staff, and strode to minimal effort, past the ejections towards the silhouette of the Magi. Before the gushing flame emptied from Philos' chants, he paused to the vacant air where his target once stood. Before his thoughts processed the void, wisps of sinewy shadow spilled into shape, wrapping from the sulphury ash beneath his feet to culminate into the figure once standing meters in front of him.

Calloused fingers wrapped around Philos' wrinkled neck, bound to leather gloves stretching into long sleeves encasing Ragres' arm as he tightened his grip to the older man. Philos' staff dropped to a puff of sulphury disarray as he clutched the single hand wrapped around him. In swift pull, Ragres hoisted Philos' by the single reach as the older Magi kicked and carried his legs in vain attempts to remove himself from the pain crushing his larynx.

"I would not prevent my Master from taking pleasure in your death, Aztmi," Ragres hissed, cocking his blindfold to one side.

Philos glanced to his assailant's scarred and bloodied flesh. A tincture of gray-colored, sad skin muddled by years of flagellations and lamentations covered Ragres' face. A visage of sin adorned the bloodied rag where the eight-spoke sunwheel scar glowed upon Ragres' forehead.

"Your Master will never find this Temple," Philos' wheezed as the grip tightened around his throat, "You will not tell him."

Philos' hands erupted to flame burning into Ragres' leathery bindings.

Ragres released his hold on the Magi, dropping him to his back. Ragres clutched the vambrace on his left hand to remove the armor in haste. Philos shifted in crab crawl backward and reached his hand forward towards his

299

assailant. In a blast of expulsive spray, fire shot from Philos' palms shrieking through the air towards Ragres' body.

In repetitive expedience, Ragres uttered a chant, dissolving him into the air, appearing behind Philos' shoulders and with a quick strike of his decorative dagger, plunged the weapon into Philos' skull, piercing the bottom of the old man's jaw. In the realization of death, Philos' jetting fire billowed into emptiness, retreating to source as a torrent of blood spray followed Ragres' steady drop of his body to its back. Ragres set Philos to the ground, pulling his blade with irreverent tug through a collection of brain tissue and skull fragments spilling upon the ground.

"All who die returns to the All, Aztmi. Yours is no different today."

Ragres licked his blade of the blood and gray ooze before sheathing it into his leathers. Stepping to the side, his boot graced the edge of the wooden staff relic whose stone ebbed in vibrant display. A kick of his boot propelled the staff into the air, his scarred fingers grappled the object. Smiling with a wheezing whistle through his decaying gums, Ragres reached towards the stone hovering within the coiling trident and pulled it from its magick bind. In silent glow, the stone whimpered to a lull cool as he tossed the staff aside, shattering it upon the ground with hefted force.

*

Nighttime sky welcomed Ragres as he set foot into the grassy embankments along the edge of the vast mountain range. Asvidar's small camp rested in the lingering fog highlighted with shimmering fire glow. Ragres caught whiff of roasted meat and the rhythmic clamoring of utensil upon plate. His face snarled in cringed anger, rotting teeth punctuated his jawline. His feet clamored upon the soft meadow cold from autumn breeze. Like unwilling prey, the young boy did not hear the animal approach.

Ragres's knobbed hands of bulbous pus gripped the edge of Asvidar's make-shift lean to, ripping the fabric from its rudimentary pole support causing it to collapse around the young lad. Asvidar stumbled in response, his cheeks puffed and saliva dripping through the corners of his mouth. Dirt lined his lips and fingernails, unkempt from several days of constant walking.

Afraid of the Magister, Asvidar dropped his plate onto the ground. Greased contents spilled onto the grass and leaves. Fury burned through Ragres's visage, ravaged from a flame which singed his flesh as teeth shown through fetid lips. With clenched fist, he lunged at the boy's face, knocking him towards the ground.

"I ordered you not to eat till I returned raka. Your disobedience angers me."

"Saruf, it was three rakini. I felt weak."

The words trickled from Asvidar's bruising cheek as he trembled from fear, reminding Ragres of the length of days Asvidar hungered.

"Weakness makes you stronger, uristri. For your weakness, I will make you stronger. Now, go, find me a fresh kill."

Without hesitation, Asvidar scrambled to his feet and gathered his hunting equipment to trek into the wilderness for his master. Ragres moved with corpse-like awkwardness towards the elaborate tent Asvidar built for him. The air burned cold against his crackling skin as flecks of flesh slivered away from his face. He picked at a fold of skin to notice the cauterized remains of the dead epidermis, tossing it aside into the tent. His breath rolled from his rotting lips in wind-swept spirals.

Ragres entered the shelter amidst the dark cocoon enshrouding his being and seated himself upon the plush rug made from the furs of predatory animals native to his land. He began meditations, chanting in the ancient tongue he used to cast his magick.

Supernus Magister, I have found the Fire Temple.

The Aztmi's death is an inconvenience, Ragres, but one I shall exploit. His Adept is young and weak. Malleable.

I shall destroy him.

No, Ragres, he plays into my plans. Finish your task and fulfill the Volen of Hadithem.

Acta'unas vohm Volen.

Morning came with the violent boot lunged deep into Asvidar's ribs. The stars danced their pre-dawn ensemble in the nighttime sky as the streak of the Sacred Abyss drew upon its nightly curtain call. Wiping his eyes from the brief sleep speckles, he could make out his master standing before him with seething madness.

"Break down camp," Ragres commanded.

Asvidar obeyed. While he moved like a wild stallion to dismantle the two tents, Ragres unstrapped the large leather bags from their horse's mount and tossed them onto the ground beside the animal. The blind man returned to his slave as the boy finished his task and gathered the supplies for storage.

"I have spared the horse from the burden of carrying our supplies; instead, you will serve his place. The animal has earned his reprieve, a burden which you will now bear. If you do not keep pace, I shall dine on your sinew."

Ragres's words blew with a cold, decaying flavor upon Asvidar's face. Ragres's cruelty lived to his reputation once more as he followed the order. Strapping the bags bulging with supplies, he tied them around the six tent poles he used to build camp. His knees buckled under the intense weight and sweat followed down his cheeks while he hoisted the supplies upon his back, straddling the poles in a full nelson maneuver within his arms. Ragres lifted himself onto the horse and stirred it into stride leaving Asvidar in painful march behind him.

Chapter 29

Frosted winds whirled among the sleeping bodies covered in cocoon-like furs numbering six. A frail figure stood above the resting individuals encased in heavy furs to protect his frame from biting cold. With Cadeck asleep, Kenat lit himself a small flame within his hand to aide with warmth sending his shadow to prowl behind him upon the small cart. His pearl, ghost-like eyes glistened with his magical power whose tendrils flowed in a whirling fashion within his palm. As he meditated on his flame, his frocked locks curled with the chilled breezes as a slight surge pulsed through his body. He tucked his magical energy within his furs to keep the light from exposing position.

Kenat gazed across the landscape of rolling cliffs and meadows covered with fresh blankets of snow from the days' earlier fury. Kenat counted hints of fences to demarcate properties to occupy his mind. Glinted lights flickered in the distance giving position to homes as the waning moon spilled soft reflection onto the whitened snow. The night was pure and quiet with the ebbing pulse of billions of stars calling to him like tempting maidens of nocturnal delight. The dark band of the Abyss stretched above him in line with the rotations of Roth. He heard its demons calling for him, crying to him as if to drown out the meditations in his mind. Focusing on his flame became difficult as he prayed in silent whispers to keep the little fire in his hand alight.

Was he delusional? The strains of his magick use exhausted him to a point which pained him to walk. The cries of the Abyss above churned in his soul, coaxing him with temptations each time he used magick. He turned to the camp; Cassica, Ysalir, Venna and Eris huddled among another while Tesh and Cadeck flanked them. He watched as the two younger ladies respired leisurely in slumbering bliss, bundled tight in their fur blankets torn from the skin of a verdasnik. He thought of the denials of his luxury during his tenure with Philos. He had heard of the libertine carelessness of the aristocracy of Kora, how many a youth of his prestige showed raw passion amongst the finer ladies of the city. If Sarat was the conservative capitol of its namesake kingdom, Kora was its debauched opposite.

History reminded Kenat of the several times Kora sought independence throughout the ages with each instance quelled into submission. He knew an ancestor, Finnel Denwich, 1st Baron of Kora, had led the first uprising several hundred years ago, long before the current dynastic reign of Cassica's family, only to be systemically imprisoned and hung for his crimes. Nevertheless, Kora stayed a strong and reluctant vassal state to her rulers and supplied countless scholars and artists for the kingdom.

Kenat thought of the possibility to serve his family in the aristocracy. He could have sired several children by now of several willing and flirtatious debutantes. Philos only told him he found Kenat as an orphan in Racoren. He had only learned of his heritage in recent years, taking up the scholarly history of Sarat to discover the truth of his name, Denwich, a name of nobility and status among the Koran populace. He learned his mother and father abandoned him when he was nearing ten and continued their recklessness, producing several more offspring none of which matched him. The paintings of his family held the Denwich trademark of blonde hair, blue eyes, and pristine face devoid of defects. Kenat knew he was different.

To Kenat, magick came as a natural extension of his Will. As he closed his eyes, he could hear the hearts beating of his companions, each of them beat a different tone and with each heartbeat, another sinister whisper. Kenat ignored the haunting murmurs, listening to each one of his companions focusing on them one at a time; Tesh's fiery reluctance and passionate chivalry, Cassica's uninhibited proclivity for justice and preservation of the status quo, Venna's naiveté and Eris' stubbornness. Rensel, as he knew her, produced a raw, unsatisfied thirst for something eluding Kenat's thoughts. Cadeck's heart burned the hardest; mixed with anger and torment, love, passion, and revenge. Of all of them, Kenat heard Cadeck's heart cry the loudest.

In fright, cries echoed from above. He opened his eyes and removed his flame from his coat but could see nothing with his physical senses. A haunting whisper filled upon the landscape like a fresh wind of splintering ice striking upon his face and penetrating his ethereal senses. Panic set into him resulting in the erratic movement of his right hand holding his flame, searching like a lost child for the tears of torment pounding into his ears but the night remained still. He listened to the ancient whispers as the flame coiled to the form of a shadowy and sinewy snake-like figure which evaporated the tiny fire and laughed with sinister hisses.

Kenat dropped to his knees; extinguished flame with a prayer of thought and clutched his forehead as the cries of mourning pummeled his mind. He burst into screams of his own; loud, guttural piercing moans that brought the attention of his companions. Cadeck was the first to awake, shaking his head with startled realization. Tesh stumbled to an upright position, clutching the icy hilt of his blade to defend. Ysalir darted to stand as swiftly as Cadeck beside her. Cadeck rose to foot, guided by legs limping with open circulation.

"What's wrong, boy?"

Cadeck rushed to Kenat's side as fast as his bones would allow. Venna and Eris were slow to rise, Cassica followed suit, clutching her furs around her shoulders.

"Something happened, Cadeck. Something happened to Philos."

Moonlight overhead began its wane, amplifying Kenat's teary pearls as he met Cadeck's withered eyes.

"What is a Philos?" Ysalir's tone implied uncertainty.

"Philos is the name of his Ascended, and my peer."

Cadeck leaned into the younger man's vision, coddling Kenat's face with his brusque hands as the younger Magi continued to weep. Venna rushed to help while Eris stood next to Ysalir bundled in her furs.

"Now what do we do, Cadeck?" Cassica piped in.

Cadeck rose to stand, "The hunter is several days behind us still."

"If he's following you, Cadeck, I'll stay behind and take him out."

"He took out a Magi, Rensel, what chance would you have? He will rip out your soul before you ever see him, even if you were in full condition. Then, what would you do? Kenat, will you be alright?"

Kenat ignored Cadeck's question, turning a teary-eyed stare towards the horizon. Venna moved to wrap her arms around him, draping a set of furs to his shoulders. Kenat nodded to accept the comfort, taking the blonde maiden's offer as she coddled him with her arm around his shoulder. Cadeck observed the party as they lowered their guard, the waning moonlight glistened against the soft slush of the grounds. The crackling campfire lit the inhabitants to the welcoming warmth as they assisted Kenat through his pain.

"Dawn will be soon," Cadeck continued, "Everyone, return to sleep. I will finish his watch."

#

The morning sun hinted pink hues from the east casting across snowy fields. Cadeck seated upon the edge of the cart's backboard, pricking at the soft wood with his disheveled hands to occupy his time. He closed his worn eyes to embrace the stars' approaching grace. He felt a brief surge of his magick as the light hit his skin, coursing through his veins with the ancient energies of his god. It did little to comfort him as each brush with magick writhed like a fleeing parasite within the Magi. Little by little, he focused beyond the darkness covering his prayers to touch deeper to his god, yet the cold darkness kissed at his soul with each attempt.

The cold churned within his bones when the winds howled from the frosty north. He heard a stir coming from camp as Ysalir rose with the faint morning pink. She bundled her furs tight upon her structured frame, clutching her right arm as best she could and approached the older man. She stood as a statuesque idol whose curved, toned features accentuated against the warm hides wrapped tight against them. Cadeck watched her approach; her shapely figure reminded him of Jess' gait as she once welcomed him in the mornings.

"Did you have a good rest?" Cadeck opened.

"I'll be fine."

"How's your arm?"

Ysalir reached below the fur shawl and gripped at the taut fabric fitted as gauze around her upper bicep, "The fire stopped the bleeding."

"You're resolute, Rensel, a quality amongst your profession."

"The wound did not break muscle."

"A blessing, nonetheless. The gods were with us yesterday."

Ysalir's eyes shimmered in the early morning sunrise. She sighed at Cadeck's statement, "I wish I could honestly agree with you."

"You hold no value upon the gods?"

She ignored his question, "The gods created the chaos present in Silvetzen and if your fears are correct, will soon come to Sarat. What value is there in holding to such beliefs?"

"The gods did not cause this, Rensel."

"No, but your own Ascended did."

Cadeck turned towards the rising sun, "He is not the only reason for this demise."

"Then who," Ysalir turned towards Cadeck's weathered eyes, "You?"

Cadeck nodded. Ysalir gripped the knobbed hilt of a blade tucked at her hip.

"You would not be wise to strike at me. Cassica trusts my judgment."

"But your ways, the ways of magick caused this destruction. Cassica is right in not trusting the Magi. I should not trust you."

"It is not as you think," Cadeck rose to stand, being careful in his tone to not wake the others.

"Did you betray Sarat? Did you betray the Magi?"

"I admit to betraying the Magi. But for the same purposes you leaned away from your Crown."

Ysalir pursed her lips. Cadeck knew her secret. A feeling of betrayal covered her thoughts, her eyes lowered below her bangs, "How did you…?"

"It is best not to hide secrets from Magi, Ysalir," Cadeck grinned upon speaking her true name. Ysalir attempted to stutter upon hearing her name from Cadeck's tongue, "We should discuss this later. We should leave soon for the moon will be dark in six days' time, and I would recommend being off the road by then."

#

Flush powdery snow shone bright in the mid-morning sun canvassing the horizon across all angles. The single horse drawn cart lumbered in pace. Ice crystals lined the edges of the animal's nostrils as shivering breath roared between them. Cadeck stifled the reins as the horse jittered along the route. Smoke trails lingered into the crisp daytime sky inviting the cart from a distance.

Silence fell into the sky with a heavy presence as the cart continued towards the simple structure where the smoke originated. Sharp cliffs and jagged walls carved a serrated trail into the western horizon. Cadeck studied the air and heard still silence, an eerie calling chilling his bones with each burst of wind. Furs draped across Cadeck's stocky frame; the titillating whispers of fleece strands tickled through his ears.

"We're here," Kenat's words rolled through frosted breaths.

"That's Tijoa's hovel?"

Kenat nodded his head to acknowledge, "He'll be none too happy to see you, Cadeck."

"I'll keep such thought to mind."

Cadeck struck the reins to liven the pace of the single animal as it started a slow trot towards the home. As the cart approached the wooden and thatch structure, Cadeck observed minimal activity coming from within. An axe rested in the wood chop while a pyramid of firewood stacked against the home, covered with fresh slush. Fresh kill of small game hung from a rack beside the logs.

Cadeck stopped the cart a few meters from the entrance. He climbed towards the ground and returned to the rear of the cart. He motioned for Tesh to remove himself from the bundled women huddling together for warmth.

"Kenat, stay here with the women. If you are right, I do not assume our visit will go well."

Tesh jumped from the cart to Cadeck's side and adjusted the fur coverings draping his shoulders. He steadied the sword against his back and crossed his arms to warm from the searing cold. Ice pocketed in his hair, gathering along his eyebrows. He wiped the ice with a crunching slush from his face while his cheeks blushed to warmth.

He followed behind the older Magi as the pair continued towards the framed door of the thatched hut. A smell of sweetwood filtered from the framework delighting Tesh's nostrils to flare with a welcoming smile. Cadeck hobbled along the snow-clumped path leading to the abode and struck the door with a soft knock of his knuckles. No answer called to him. He knocked once more with the same result.

"We came all this way and no one's home?"

"Disappointing. He will be the only one to get us to the Temple. I would hope the Si'rai have not discovered him."

Cadeck turned towards Tesh, exposing his back to the door. A creak exited the door frame and exposed a small crease into the hovel. Cadeck returned his attention behind him, the winds bristling against his burgeoning beard.

A whimpering voice called from within, "Who dares to disturb me?"

Cadeck stuttered towards the door, opening his arms to width offering no danger to the voice should it shed its eyes upon him. He lowered his hand and glanced over his right shoulder to motion Tesh to stand down.

"It is I, Cadeck Wenfier, Magi of the Temple of Light. I come to meet Tijoa Örfdag, Magi of the Temple of Wind, and Keeper of the Dragon."

The voice did not return his address. A slow wheeze followed with a cough before answering.

"You are no longer a member of the Council, Cadeck. I shall not address your presence."

The man's voice rocked harshly, speaking in the Rykanian Common Tongue with a northern accent as his confidence opened. The speech broke through the air like rocks grinding on glass. Cadeck rushed towards the door. The man inside resisted his barging momentum as Cadeck slammed his shoulder against the wood.

"Tijoa, I come with an Initiate. He has passed the Trials of Light and Fire. You must give him the Trials of Wind." Cadeck's desperation yelled into the door crease.

"You know the rules, Magi."

The man's face hid behind the crease in the door. A solitary eye peaked through, caked over by withered eyelids shadowed by a flurry of gray brows across his forehead like a wispy whirlwind of dust.

"I have no time to explain outside. Permit us entry, and I shall discuss these matters with you."

"I see others with you on your travel. You lie to me. You are no Magi, as you claim. If you are Si'rai, then I shall send you back to your god."

"No Tijoa."

The violent, inward fling of the door to the hut interrupted Cadeck's burst. Inside the door, Tijoa lifted his pale hands skyward towards his ceiling. His tongue muttered ancient words spoken through a short white beard stopping at his neck. Pale blue robes covered his body from head to toe in the sacred vestments of his keep. Gusts of wind flowed between his wavering hands sending sonic shrieks across the land. Cadeck leapt for Tesh sending them both towards the ground while Kenat stood ready, forming his own words in defense. Ysalir covered Cassica and clutched her sister and Eris to draw them in closer.

Tijoa extended his hands towards Cadeck as rushing gales spun the game rack hurtling through the air. The food rack cleared Cadeck's back a few feet above him. Strings of food ripped from the harness flying in many directions from intense power sweeping in gale gusts over the travelers. Kenat ducked to avoid the wooden framework flung towards him as the gale caught him off guard catapulting him across the driver board and into the snows beside the cart. The powerful winds caught the horse as it trudged its hooves into the snow in vain. He whinnied in reaction to the winds freeing him from his harness in a violent symphony of wood and iron snapping and splintering. The horse fell to his left, crashing into the snowbanks beside him.

The right wheels lifted from the ground. The ladies reacted in fright as the gusts forced the wagon in vector before slamming back towards all four wheels, splintering several spokes of the passenger front wheel, collapsing the cart in direction. Impact slammed the cart back to grind into the ground, jolting the four ladies forward to press into the headboard.

Cadeck lifted himself from the snowy embankment of Tijoa's front yard. Specks of ice gripped in his fur lining and clung to his beard. His eyes shortened gaze in anger as Tijoa readied himself for another spell. Overcoming the bitter pains creaking within, Cadeck rushed his peer with a full tackle. He burst through the door frame into the simple hut. The impact of his tackle spun the two men to shatter a chair from their weight. Phased and in disarray, Tijoa attempted to free himself from Cadeck's clutch as Cadeck propelled a fist into Tijoa's jaw.

"If you feared the Si'rai, why make alliance with them?"

Cadeck's irritation erupted from his tongue.

Tijoa fumbled in his words trying to find the speech to react to his punisher. He broke tongue, splitting his sentence between the ancient speech and common tongue.

"We had no choice."

"No choice?"

Cadeck removed himself from Tijoa's body, lifting the older man by the collar of his sacred garments. Cadeck shoved Tijoa into a cushioned chair crunching with the sound of hay. Cadeck's face steamed through his ice-flaked beard.

"Why do you come here, Cadeck? You are no Magi. You are a fugitive deserving exile to the dogs," Tijoa's harsh accent tore into Cadeck's heart with the violent words of his motivation.

"I come here with a Knight. He must receive the Trial of Wind."

"The Trial of Wind? Don't you remember? The Knights are dead. They are nothing more than a legend and the Council of Magi holds sway now. Your Ascended should punish you for your insolence."

"My Ascended is a mad man, just as you are. The Initiate travelling with me bears the mark of Azthar Kherdmon, the Dra Nar Azt, the sacred blood. You must aid him on his destiny."

Tijoa coughed at his suggestion, "Kherdmon? Dra Nar Azt? Do you believe those tales? Those legends proved nothing. Who gave him the Trial of Light? You? No wonder you believe those stories. You have fabricated them then came to me to find those who conspired against you. You will get no such pleasure from me. I should shatter your breath within your chest."

Interrupting his words, Tesh entered the small hovel. Cadeck crossed in front of him, passing by the cast-iron stove.

"Who is this you bring before me, Cadeck?"

"Tesh Verdui of Telmen."

Tesh extended his left hand to greet the elder Magi. Flecks of golden shimmer cut within the man's veins of his left hand ending with the golden seal in his palm. Tijoa wheezed at Tesh's sight, his eyes widened amidst his furrowed brow. Tijoa's pale grip curled around Tesh's injured hand, tracing his fingers along the infused veins. Tesh's veins reacted, sparkling with tendrils of purple and red energy reaching across his hand and wrist, stopping below his elbow.

"You were telling the truth, Cadeck."

Cadeck turned to meet Tijoa's words, creasing his beard with a grin.

A clamoring interruption burst through the doorway bringing a rush of cold inside. Ysalir clutched Kenat's body across her shoulder, twisting to turn parallel to enter the doorframe. Kenat's limp body straddled Ysalir and Venna as his arms draped around their necks. Kenat's face dripped with blood along deep cuts in his face and arms dyeing the white and brown fur coverings upon the women's shoulders.

"What happened?" Cadeck demanded.

Ysalir set the unconscious man upon the sodden floor, "The old man's magick knocked him off the cart. He landed a few meters into snow covered rocks."

Venna scrunched her face in anger towards Tijoa as Ysalir held her back. She dropped to Kenat's side, removing her furs to warm him. Frustrated, Venna removed her orange rose patch from within her attire and used it to aid Kenat's wounds. Cassica and Eris followed the pair within.

"Any further injuries?"

Cadeck's tone lowered to a concerning nature. He received unanimous shakes of heads.

Tijoa released the grip held upon Tesh's hand and lifted himself to his feet, "I have poultices to apply, in the cupboard behind your red-headed friend."

Cassica turned to face the cupboard at her head level. An aging creak of iron opened the hinge revealing to her multiple pouches and unmarked bottles covered in layers of frosted dust. Cassica huffed in anger at the discolored and fogged vials stained by age, distorting the familiarity of the contents. Impatient with her ineptitude, Tijoa rose to his feet and shuffled to her side.

His raven eyes scanned the cupboard contents before gripping a medium-sized bottle in tight clasp. Tijoa met Cassica's eyes with a disgruntled glare, moaned at her incompetence and sealed the door beside him sheltering them from the cold. He muttered an insult towards her secular position and popped the cork to the poultice. He shoved the bottle towards the young blonde and instructed her how to apply the medicine. Venna dipped her fingers into the bottle removing a milky, porous gelatin and smeared it across Kenat's cuts. The gel sealed into the wounds, absorbing the thick blood pooling in the scars.

"This is Philos' Adept, is he not?"

Cadeck nodded his head at Tijoa's question.

"He will be fine. Let him rest here on the cot and when he returns to conscious, you should lie to him. He has much practice before his powers will be on par to his Ascended. Now, you have a pressing matter I believe, Cadeck?"

"I have many, but these matters do not concern them," Cadeck motioned towards the ladies, "Can we discuss this on the way to the Wind Temple?"

Tijoa seated himself on a chair beside the crude couch. Tesh and Cassica lifted Kenat into the straw mattress shoved crudely over a wooden chest pinned against the wall. The young man collapsed in fluid motion upon the platform, his breathing slowed from the relaxing sting as Venna continued to apply the healing medicines. Tijoa furrowed his eyes towards Cadeck. He grew impatient with the heathen, moaning at the suggestion for Cadeck to go with him.

"Wind Temple? What makes you think you are coming with me? If you want this boy to take the Trials, you will remain here with these ladies and allow me my rites. I know a hunter follows you. I will not allow the hunter to follow you to my domain."

Ysalir rocked her unease as she shifted her leg to rest upon the bench across from him, "We can handle him."

"Woman, I suggest you let the adults talk. I never invited your kind here," Tijoa returned his attention towards Cadeck; "I can see Philos let you into his Temple? He was always soft, his vote being the only dissention to the alliance with the Si'rai."

"Philos is dead, Tijoa. Kenat felt it a few days ago," Cadeck burst, "This alliance killed him."

"So, the Council did vote; to hand over Roth to the Imperium?"

Tijoa craned his neck towards Cassica's statement and realized his blunder of information leak. She stood next to Ysalir, arms crossed, her scarlet hair splayed across her fur-covered shoulders. They stood close to shoulders while Eris slid beside them, seated herself upon a rugged table, and curled her knees against her chest.

Taking a stance, denying his own gaffe, he continued, "You ladies should really learn to be quiet in my house. You have no business asking about the matters of Quorum as they do not pertain to the profane."

Cadeck raised his voice towards the superior Magi, "You will respect them, Tijoa. The lady you address is Princess…"

Tijoa raised his right hand to silence Cadeck, "I know who she is, heretic. If you want your answers, everyone but you, Tesh and Kenat must leave. You want your answers, you said so yourself, *not in front of the ladies.*"

Tijoa rose from his seat. His gait quivered across the floor with a slow pace. Covered by his furrowed brow, his eyes pierced into the occupants standing before him with inherent displeasure. Cadeck met his peer to the face. His breaths billowing with a ferocious impatience at the older man as he kept his eyes fixated upon the elder. Tijoa motioned Eris to remove herself from his table, murmuring a cursing statement about respecting the host's house before crossing over towards the stove.

Acrid air of crisp meat burned through the cabin as Tijoa tended the overcooked meal left on his stove. Fumes poured from the pot as he removed it from the oven with the piercing creak of iron hinge work. He threw the steaming pot to the table towards Eris' direction sending the girl into a dizzying removal as pieces of stew polluted the wall and table next to her. Ysalir unsheathed a small dagger from her hip as Cadeck motioned her to calmly return it.

"I asked you ladies to leave my home. There are matters to discuss you do not need to hear," Tijoa rose to the height of his lungs.

"I change my mind. I allow them to hear these matters as they concern the state of the Kingdom of Sarat and all others of Roth."

Tijoa meditated words in ancient speech as his back remained facing Cadeck. The harsh syllables carried weight into Cadeck's mind, building into a cacophonic dissonance within his brain as he clutched his throat to grasp for air. Cadeck dropped to his knees, his eyes widened in pain. Ysalir sprang her blade towards the older man before she too succumbed to an invisible throat clasp. The blade collapsed towards the ground and clamored with a steel dance against the soft wood.

"I requested they leave, Cadeck, as you previously implied. Now you change your mind and refuse to obey me in my house? I would have hoped to never teach you a lesson."

Tijoa turned towards the man, his eyes shining into an icy glow. Ysalir dropped to her stomach, clutching her throat with both hands. Her eyes widened as the green seas; her mouth gaped wide as she clamored for breath. As Tijoa's magick swelled, Tesh's left hand stung with streaks of pulsating energy rippling through his veins. Tesh squinted with discomfort searing along his wrist. Tijoa ignored his reaction, concentrating on Cadeck's suffering.

"Let her go," Cadeck cried. His voice strained with short breaths.

"If it's me you want to punish do it but leave them be."

"Then ask them to leave."

"No."

Tesh's left hand caught swift wind clasping against Tijoa's neck. Streams of searing pulses rippled through Tesh's veins and arced through the webbing of his fingers as his grip tightened against the older man. Tesh's instinctual response sent Cadeck and Ysalir into coughs reclaiming their air intake. Tijoa's eyes returned to amber as he turned them in fear towards the young man. Venna squealed at Tesh's response.

"You will not hurt my friends, Magi. Tell us everything."

"You dare strike me?"

Tijoa's words cut off as Tesh squeezed tighter.

"I have seen innocents fall due to the actions of the Council. You will tell Cadeck what he needs to know, even in front of these ladies."

"Or what? Without me, you cannot become a Knight."

"I'd just as soon die a pauper than see harm come to my friends," Tesh released his grip permitting Tijoa to speak normally.

"Friends? What worth are they to you if your bloodline is true? I can arrange your words to become fate, boy. There is nothing you have done convincing me of your lineage. Your wound in your hand? Just a lucky brush with death. If I take you to the Wind Temple and you fail the Trials, then what good are you? What good is your line? You would have become a failure, pissed on by Tiasu as He breathes the winds into being."

"I have not failed the Trials."

Tijoa hobbled to his chair with a smirk and slight giggle, "Many have come before you boy, and many have failed. Some have passed one, sometimes two trials. Others; four or five before succumbing. The legacy of the Knights is not service, it is a prison. You are no different than your father; forced into this destiny."

"What of my father?"

"Your father was a fool, a common thief. Teru Verdui owed a debt to Trebut, and in turn the king sentenced him into service."

"But he was a champion of Sarat," Cassica chimed in.

Cadeck rose to his feet, gasping for air. Ysalir too, attempted to regain her breath as she and Cadeck aided each other to sit upon the bench of the hovel.

"Oh yes, in time. Before then, he was a scoundrel, a beggar, and a pickpocket nothing more than a common street urchin. The Council needed Knights and we took the lowest of the low. The world was changing. Boys no longer wished to serve the Knights; they sought adventure. No longer did boys wish to serve a noble cause. Their numbers were dwindling. Yes, the gods would gift a few Initiates and kept their ancient bloodlines through sheer luck or grace, I could never recount whom or how. So few turned out to pass the Trials and become Knights, that they were all seen as disposable."

"But by blood, by the gods, they were all worthy."

"So, they were, Cadeck. But they were the worse of the bunch. The gods pissed on them with disfavor, and the Council sensed this. They came to servitude, serving their Temples but turned to personal gains in their homelands. Your father was no different, Tesh.

"Her father may have seen him to be his champion on the battlefield, honored after his passing, but he was horse-piss to the gods. The gods care not for your secular kingdoms and your honors. He passed his Trials and became a Knight as did many others. He returned to Sarat with favors from your king. Knighthood was his freedom, and lands were his reward. These vagabonds were vile. Only a few, including your father, honored what had bestowed upon them. We had to remove them."

"But the stories, and the evidence they sought to overthrow the Council, amass wealth beyond many kingdoms of their service?"

"Fabricated evidence, Cadeck. What good would the Knights have become if the truth revealed incompetence weakened them, and the gods no longer blessed the ancient order and had forsaken Roth? The common folk would devolve into mass psychosis. Your secular armies would not be able to fight the rioting. Instead, we created a legend that the citizens could respect and uphold to, some seeing them as heroes to upend our archaic ways. Although the Si'rai Imperium looms around them and threatens them daily, they still have hope."

"And the treaty with the Si'rai?"

"Your Ascended's own greed and self-service. Each passing of the Abyss brings about a change and the dawn of a new Aeon. Godwen wants to hold on just a bit longer and feared the impending change. The prophecies of an upheaval to the Magi were foretold centuries ago. Godwen refused to believe them. The Si'rai brought their curse to him, poisoning him, the same curse lingering upon you, me, and the boy," he pointed to Kenat resting on the soft hay cot beside him, "I was the only Elder who knew of this curse. If the prophecies are true, then Tesh and your children will end our reign, and the reason he had you conveniently removed."

Tijoa turned his eyes towards Tesh, "But it would appear with Godwen's actions which set action into motion. By tempting fate to withhold the prophecies, he inadvertently created them."

Cadeck reached for Tijoa's hand and clutched it tight, "I must know, Tijoa, what of my children? Why did you forsake them at the cost of a prophecy?"

Ysalir perked her attention towards the exchange.

"Godwen lied to us all. He told us you and your children would bring the demise of the Council, the fall of the gods and show the people the truth behind the lies we had set in motion twenty years ago. Excommunication would see you silenced and removed from threat. Your children were always a danger to the Council. They will bring the dawning of a new era. The old ways will fall. A fate, we discovered, we cannot change."

"But you believed him. Philos led to rumor you tried to fight him. Why didn't you?" Distrust shown in his eyes.

"At the risk of death? Two Magi died sensing the curse laid upon him while you were cavorting in Tarn, which actions culminated towards the birth of your children. Your children's power grew over time, the time to excommunicate you was long past. Yet, Godwen called it to vote. Knowing had he not committed to removing you from the Council, you could initiate your children to be bound to their Gifts. Philos' cast the only dissenting vote to banish you in a show of pity. Godwen spared him mercy in his vote, punishing him to forever remain in his Temple, never to leave, never to venture away from the grounds, a lesson to us all. He spared him death as Kenat had not received his Aztin at the time."

"Aztin? What is that?"

Venna piped from her seat at Kenat's head.

Tijoa stared her down, the secular question shot to him like a fast blade. Cadeck tousled the man's hands.

"Tijoa, she means well. Spare them your anger. Venna, I will explain for another time, but know it is how we recognize another Magi."

"Like being branded?" Ysalir inquired. She paced her body across the floor and returned to the bench next to the table.

"No different than your mark you hide for your secretive Order of the Rose."

Ysalir turned a spiteful stare towards Tijoa, "How did you know I was…"

Tijoa smiled to her ire, his passive-aggression soothing her mind to remind her he was in charge in this home. Ysalir calmed, nodding her head as she retreated to turn her back towards him and pace towards a small table edged against the wall. Tijoa continued his scold towards Venna as a foreboding teacher lecturing her with condescending voice.

"Understand, ladies, should a person use magick without the mark, it is heretical, and the Knights could put them to death if they are not an Adept to anyone. Witches, shamans; they are all seen as sacrilegious in the eyes of the gods, may death fall to them for perverting our ways. But with the Knights gone, many priests and witches come forward bearing blessings from a god here or there. Shit on them I say."

"Like the Forest Witch?"

Tijoa laughed at Venna, "Such a naïve little girl. You are too old to be believing in those stories any longer."

Sunlight crept into the western horizon signaling an end towards the day. Amused by his company, Tijoa stood to his feet. His aging bones creaked into position as his stride carried him towards the door. The iron handle whined as he opened the door. Bitter winds gnawed at his skin.

"One of you will need to find our food if you wish to sleep well tonight. I have ruined my stock and I would expect my guests to replenish it."

Cassica shot disapproving stare towards Cadeck who humbly nodded in her direction, "Entertain him."

"I'll go," Ysalir barked, gripping her holstered blade at her side stomping away from the table.

"I'm coming," Venna announced, leaping from her seat by Kenat's head.

Cadeck held his arm out before the girl could pass him, stopping her solid.

"No. Stay here with Kenat. Eris, go instead."

Eris nodded and removed herself from the opposite bench where Ysalir began. She followed behind Ysalir as the older woman shot a discomforting grunt towards Tijoa. Ysalir tucked her furs close to her shoulders and wrapped them tight around her bosom and hips before venturing into the evening chill. Eris followed suit as she shut the door behind her. Cassica followed Tijoa with a discomforting gaze as he seated back into his chair.

"You don't hold us highly, do you, Tijoa?"

Tijoa coughed, ignoring Cassica's question almost laughing at the notion, "What passed upon ear, Cadeck? Did this woman try to address me?"

"Speak to me, Magi. Why do you hold disdain towards the people of Roth?"

Tijoa's wrinkly neck craned into her direction. His furrowed beard disheveled and split from years of unkempt grooming. He grinned towards Cassica, mocking her question, and laughing with a snide titter. His words cracked into her like a poisonous whip fresh with laced arsenic searing into her open wounds.

"Because, Princess, you people are stupid and ignorant fools. You come to us for prayers and offerings, and we in turn share our blessings to keep the masses in line. Without the Council, and our ancient progenitors, the Aztmi, you people would be extinct eons ago. We keep our secrets to keep you tame, to herd you around like cattle. If we unleashed magick upon the populace, if we let just one human be prone to magick without ritual, you people would kill yourselves trying to harness it."

Tijoa lifted a curled finger towards her direction, misshapen and curved by age, "Our secrets are too important to entrust upon the profane. You have learned too much today, woman. I pray you do not take it for granted and dishonor Mornika's teachings."

"You knew?"

Cassica whined, her emerald eyes widened with surprise.

"The whole damn Council knew, and how I know who you are, what you do and the little order of flowers that you command. But Godwen did not. If he found out; he would kill you, your other bitch, and your bitch of a mother. Mornika would be without a tongue and imprisoned in The Spire," Tijoa turned his punishing eyes into Cadeck's direction, "Do not think we did not know, Cadeck. Your treacheries with the Saratian Court came back to our ears. As the Arch Elder of the Quorum, I kept you safe, defended your actions in their Court as to your role as an advisor. I knew what Godwen would have done at the risk of my own life."

"You speak harsh tongue, Tijoa," Tesh began, his left-hand tingling with supernatural energies with his assertiveness, "Are these people not worth saving? Is mankind worthless?"

"Verdui, would there be Knights if the gods did not see? The gods have forsaken mankind. Bloodlines failed and no true Knights have existed in three generations. If this wretched rock were worth saving, the gods would have given their aztmudin to true Knights. Prove me your worth at the Temple, Tesh. I might reconsider."

Tijoa peered towards the door, "Your friends need to hurry with food before the cold claims them. I lock my doors promptly at first howl."

"You can't leave them out there to die," Cassica protested.

"Watch me, woman," Tijoa smiled through his ruffled beard.

"Tomorrow will begin an arduous trek. Tesh, you and I will travel alone to the Eternal Ice. The rest of you may remain here until we return, including you Cadeck."

"The hunter will find me here. Your place is not safe for Cassica and her entourage."

"Deal with him, Cadeck," Tijoa rose towards the door to lock the latches for the evening, "I will not have him finding the Wind Temple. The Si'rai have already found two of the temples, I will not allow them to find more. It is imperative you limit the chaos of darkness filling Silvetzen."

As Tijoa approached the door, Ysalir rushed in. Her arms cradling small animals freshly killed. Eris followed behind, the frosted winds blowing with them. Their faces were flush with the bitter cold, ice crystals encased within the brunette locks of the pair.

"You arrived in time," Tijoa scolded, "I close the doors promptly at sundown with the first wolf howl. Broil your meat; I will eat mine in the morning. I prefer my game with the spices in my cupboard; a sprinkle of garn, a dash of resu to give it heat, and a thick juyo sauce."

Eris looked at the man with scorn, "But we do not cook. We are warriors."

"Learn to cook maiden, if you ever expect to pleasure a man."

Tijoa latched the iron bolts to bind his door to the frame. He turned to hobble towards the rear of his hut into the smaller room. A single bed and the soft warmth of an oil lamp greeted his aging body. Tijoa extinguished the flame, leaving the rear room immersed in dim darkness as his groans and creaks signaled him to rest.

"Can you believe the gall?" Cassica shrugged, her breaths inhaling aghast.

"He was kind enough to let us stay here, Your Highness."

"But he holds those of us who do not know magick in such contempt."

Cadeck sighed, his emotions weighed heavy between the devotion to his friend and his faith, "It is the gods you must blame Your Highness, not the Magi. We can pray for Tesh to complete his trials and a new awakening will fall upon Roth with his success."

Cadeck's words rang true to Cassica's heart. Since the death of the Knights, the Magi have fallen into retreat, their ways kept hidden and their appearances scarce. Prayers and offerings went unheeded and calls for the Magi ignored. Cadeck remained loyal to his friends in the Saratian Court, her father's only contact with the Council. Had it not been for Cadeck's arrival in Sarat so many days ago, Cassica may never have avoided eventual fate at the hands of the Si'rai. Cadeck's trust had come at an opportune time, and she would forever be mindful of it.

Chapter 30

Cadeck's trail lingered in the air like the putrefaction of decayed flesh. Ragres stood motionless on the small precipice off the road like a soaring, obsidian statue. His shorn head blushed with icy pains settled upon the crevices carved into it. Frost formed in the cracked folds of dried skin sloughed fresh. Frostbite stabbed at his face, covering the soiled rag draped across his eyes with the Sigil of the Abyss clouded by rot. Ragres counted three men, larger than he and all met violent deaths. Blackened ash scarred the surface of the ground where Ragres' nostrils sensed the dying embers of a campfire.

Ragres reached his right arm towards the north as the hazy silhouettes of vision came into focus. He released a guttural wheeze through scarce teeth while he pinpointed the ectoplasm trace of his prey.

"We are close," he whispered to his companion in his tongue, "Rest will be secondary. Cadeck is only a few rakini from here."

Ragres calculated the number of days needed to reach his target. He turned in lockstep, his tight leather overcoat swayed into vacuumed form with his action. Ragres glided down the embankment like a writhing ghost as he met the road and joined Asvidar. The boy laid on his side, barefoot and blistered, the frost biting into his bones like a vicious predator dismembering its meal. Ragres gripped Asvidar by the lapel of his tunics, hoisting him onto his feet shading to purple.

"I do not reward weakness, raka. Gain your ground and follow me."

Ragres fit his boot heel into the stirrup of the war horse as he crossed his other leg over the saddle stretching the inner skirt wrapping his legs to his ankles. He draped his overcoat across the backside of the animal as he handled the reins and tightened his thighs into the ribs of the beast. He reined the horse into a steady walk. Asvidar lumbered behind.

Ragres kept stride into the night with Asvidar trailing in a decaying pace of marching death. Darkness lingered with the waning moonlight shard hovering in the evening sky marking the culmination of the current moon cycle. Stars danced around the fading satellite, twinkling in quick time, shrouded by cloud curtains closing around them. Patches of snow drift covered the ground as Ragres guided his horse in the direction of his haunted visions following the rough gouge of wagon wheels carved into the week-old powder.

The night carried into morning with Ragres in full attention upon the horse, guided by his mission in bound torment. Asvidar fell behind. His feet burned into a numbing purple hue. He dropped the supplies with his weight, collapsing into the snow drifts with a soft thud. The puffing sound of animal hides remained in melody with the clatter of wooden poles collapsing into the rocky surface. Ragres called his horse to stop and turned to see his slave fallen into the snow meters behind him, the supplies scattered into the slush.

"This one has failed me," he whispered to himself.

Ragres removed himself from the horse and joined Asvidar's shivering body. Snowflakes covered Asvidar's dirty tunics embedding into his ruffled hair. Ragres turned the boy onto his back. Icy flakes clung to his open eyelids with the life drained from his irises. His lips turned clammy purple flush with new death.

Through the Abyss, Ragres saw a voided silhouette. Asvidar's soul lingered in emptiness near the boy's chest. He dropped to his knees beside the cadaver and reached into his leathery trappings fitted upon his body and removed the ornamental blade against his left hip. He stabbed into his boy's chest, drenching the elaborate etchings written into the side with the taste of fresh blood spilling into the icy drifts beside him.

Ragres cut into the chest carefully and removed the boy's heart. He lifted the bloody organ above his head and began a slow chant in ancient tongue while the heart sustained a slow beat. Rivers of blood flow meandered along his carved hands and embedded into the brittle keratin of his fingernails. The streams flowed down the charred flesh of his left hand, meeting the sleeves of his wrappings, spilling like an overflowing dam before continuing down his arm. What left of Asvidar's withering life now cut short.

Ragres approached the heart to his mouth, grinning with the ecstasy of his commitments. He gnawed a chunk of the organ with his scarce, sharp teeth drenching his lips and chin with the life-force of his victim. With one bite consumed, he held the heart to his right side, imbibing like a drunkard in the flows dripping from his lips, onto his chin and lingering onto his neck.

With the ferocity of a madman, he shoved the organ into the chest of Asvidar and removed the blade from the wound. Ragres pricked his knife into the boy's left neck and slit a cut width wide across the jaw spilling coagulation into the snow. He returned his knife into its sheath and buried the heart deeper into the chest wound to secure it from dripping out of the gap. He hoisted the boy onto his shoulder and draped him stomach down onto the backside of the horse. As the rush of cold blood spilled along the horse's backside, the animal produced a slow whinny and nostril breath to the sudden adjustment of gore contacting flesh. Ragres proceeded to gather what he needed leaving the building materials for Asvidar's tent in the desolate snow.

Ragres rode the horse through snow-covered fields following the rut of the road lined by a single horse cart. The trail of the dark Abyss guided his vision through the daytime and night, unrelenting through hunger and thirst. Bitter chills nipped at his exposed flesh like gnawing ants consuming their prey. Massive cliffs scarred the western horizon along his path separating the pristine fields from towering formations carving through the ground. In his northward vision, the guidance of the Abyss formed a dark void sealing the horizon in veiled ice. This, he found, was the farthest north civilization could exist. Without Asvidar's sight, he could only rely on his own precognitions and guidance in faith.

He followed the outlines of his vision as the white snows traced like darkness and overbearing cold. A solitary signature stood in antithesis. The outline of a small hovel with patchwork thatch roof cuddled amongst the stinging cold embraced by the heat of fire. Lingers of his gods remained motionless there.

Ragres removed himself from his steed and carelessly released Asvidar's body from the horse. Dried, frosted blood pricked away; icicles embedded upon the horse's backside as the cadaver collapsed onto the ground. Ragres moved in quickened pace to keep his actions untraceable at this distance by those of able sight in the cabin. With his limited use, he set up his tent in crude manner. The poles leaned in grotesque fashion and when he applied the hide coverings, the structure collapsed in dissonant disarray.

He sneered at his failure. His tent mocked him. Ice crystals fused with soiled flesh as the process carried into the night before the Magister ceased his own torment. He settled with a rudimentary lean-to blocking the prevalent winds from the northwest. With ease, a campfire lit, blocked by the hides of his shelter from the peering eyes that may peak from the distant cabin. Encasing himself with the trappings of his slave, he removed a limb from Asvidar's torso, preparing it as best he could with his handicap, and placed it to roast on the fire.

He focused on the hut while his meal seared with scalded flesh stinging his nostrils with a grin of his blackened gums. Cadeck's unmistakable signature glistened in the hovel, the connection to Aztunai lingering within Cadeck stayed still. The hint of Babalon caught his attention while the signature of the Azthar Kherdmon remained elusive. His countenance sniveled with resentment as failure would find him.

For three days he watched in secret. Choronzon's signature did not leave the perimeter of the home, neither did the Azthar Kherdmon return. The occupants continued casually as daily routines kept their minds focused. A pair of ladies whose features voided through his vision hustled to keep an outline of a travel cart. For hours, the pair would study the wheels and axles and try to fit a new wheel onto the vehicle. On occasion, Cadeck's signature would exit the home but return briefly if only to remain outside a few moments. Not with time for him to strike, Ragres thought. This bothered him.

The Magi of Wind must have lived there and took the Azthar Kherdmon signature to the Wind Temple. With Cadeck staying behind, he would not find the Temple. Kneeling upon the arctic ground, his leathery knees protecting him from the biting frost, Ragres meditated on his failure. Dried specks of blood flecked upon his lips as he spoke his arcane tongue.

Ragres reached for guidance within the Abyss, searching with his aztunai in a wild journey into hellish torment of the creation void of his beliefs. Voices spoke to him, torturing him and lying to him, sending his thought in a frenzy of direction as he sought his answers.

"Father Hadithem, I come to you in humility. I have offered my natural sight so that you have given me Blessed Eutin. I beg you to answer my prayers," His voice echoed upon the darkness, his words referring to his talent for blessed sight.

"Begging is for cowards," the echoes of a multitude of voices screamed at him; moaning and hissing, "Do you fail the Apophadi, servant?"

"Guide me, so I might fulfill his Volen and find Wied'stritastum (Sacred House of Wind)."

"You have guidance from the Guardian. It is you who has failed. Choronzon has led you as far as he will. This is the Will of the Abyss, so mote it be. This Will is Law."

"To what purpose have I followed a lie?"

Like a billion chortles of sinister laughter the voices responded to him, "In time, you will see your usefulness to its end."

Ragres returned from his focus. His mind faltered with thoughts of failure; his breaths deepened into draining sighs. The Voice of the Abyss had spoken and revealed his fate. Ragres rose to his feet, the leathery bindings creaking into form. Frost clung to the scarred crevices carved into his skin atop his baldness and embedded themselves into his bare hands. Ice crystals flaked into the soiled rag covering his eyes as he curled his gnarled top lip into anger.

"I will destroy Cadeck to repent for my failure. This I promise you Hadithem."

He raised his right fist into the air as to curse his god. He reached for the sacred dagger sheathed against his hip and unfurled his fingers across the polished bone hilt, gracing the weapon with his cracked hands. Ragres focused his anger upon his blade, praying for guidance that his weapon would meet his target with blood and truth. With arcane prayers, Ragres made pace towards Tijoa's hut, dissipating into the air like a haunting shadow.

#

"You like him, don't you?"

Ysalir interrogated her sister with a stern voice and the hint of flirt in her eye. Cold winds bore down upon the pair as Venna steadied a piece of wood for fire upon the cutting stump. Ysalir wielded the axe with toned strength to bear down into the sturdy coniferous wood cleaving the halves clean. Venna gathered the halves and carried them towards the stack laden against Tijoa's hut by his front door. Venna collected a new piece of timber for split, her soft furs clutched tight against her frail frame protecting her from the bitter winds.

"Of whom do you speak?"

Venna's coy reply sprinkled with innocent sparkle in her doe eyes.

"You know to whom I refer."

Venna ignored her statement, placing a piece of wood upon the stump as Ysalir readied the axe to chop.

Ysalir shook her head, "I know the look on your face. Your heart flutters in your chest, your knees turn weak and your loins tingle with joy. Kenat's not attractive, dear. He is spindly and lanky. He should be an artist in Kora, not a Magi."

She cleaved the wood in a single strike.

"I guess I like him."

"You're only impressed by his magick, which Cadeck has warned him not to do."

Ysalir rested the axe blade into the stump at an angle, "Even if you do form a relationship with him, he will only burn your heart into the ground. It is what men do best."

Ysalir sighed with her statement recalling the pain she once felt the morning her bed turned empty. Ysalir gathered her thoughts and continued to aide her sister to stack the wood against the hut. The sun peered into the western horizon leaning into late afternoon. Hints of melting snow dripped along the sides of the hut and slushed along the solitary path leading from the hut into the road.

"But Kenat's not as you say he is," Venna protested as she floated to her sister's side, stacking the tough sweetwood in tight formation against the front wall.

"They all are, dear. Kenat has a cock. It is what men use to think, and his head is just a space to hold air. You will find this out one day, love."

"You judge him like you do others."

Ysalir turned towards Venna, looking down to her younger sister as the top of her blonde hair met close to Ysalir's chin.

"Save yourself the heartache and take my advice. Kenat will fuck you till you cry tears of joy then abandon you with tears of shame and guilt. I just want you to be careful."

Exasperated, Venna dropped her shoulders as she turned away from her sister. Fury glazed across her face. Ice crystals tangled in her matted blond locks freezing the tears drenching into her eyes. Frustrated, she clutched her furs tight. She stomped down the slushed path to the main road. Ysalir dropped the wood by her feet and called her sister's name. Venna ignored her pleas.

"Where are you going?"

Ysalir followed behind her sister who advanced at hastened walk.

"I'm going for a walk."

The blonde girl refused to turn her head towards the question. Venna turned her path southward onto the road leading away from Tijoa's hut.

"It is dangerous out there alone. Look, I am sorry if I hurt you."

Venna continued along the road ignoring Ysalir's compassion. She wiped away salty tears streaming down her cheeks ashamed with the knowledge Ysalir laid upon her. Ysalir sprinted into a steady run to catch up to her sister.

"Come back, Venna."

"No. You have never been there for me, why now?"

Venna's statement boiled hot temper into Ysalir's heart. The packed snows beneath her feet trudged and crunched as her pace escalated. Ysalir caught up to her nubile sister, clutching a tight grip onto the smaller woman's shoulder. Venna shrugged her away twice before Ysalir forced her to face with a clamped grip against her shoulders.

"You were the only person I wrote unofficially, and why I show concern for you. I did not want this for you, but you insisted. I warned you before I left for my assignment. Father should have never let you join the Academy."

Venna's cheeks fumed red with melancholy. Eyes shimmered with fresh glaze tears as Venna released Ysalir's grip and raised her voice.

"You do not know me. I looked up to you till you became a whore. You allowed your heart to soil, and you no longer offer compassion. I care about Kenat. He will not hurt me, and I will not allow him to."

"You are naïve, Venna. The Magi cannot court, and you know this."

326

"Cadeck did. Don't you think he has compassion for a woman? You can see it in his eyes when he is alone. He compared me to his own daughter once."

Ysalir shot a stare to Venna with stern accusations, "Cadeck's fucked up. He violated rules and dipped into a woman's loins and now you, I, Cassica and all of Roth are in a shitstorm because of it. We are lucky he is alive to help us if Tijoa's harsh tongue is any sign. Your heart's falling in the wrong direction. A Magi cannot love you."

"What if he is different? What if…" Venna choked on her bubbling emotions. She looked away from her sister collecting her tears upon her fingers.

She turned to Ysalir on her left, "What if things change like the Magi have been telling us? What if Tesh changes things as their prophecies say?"

Ysalir pursed her lips and followed with blinks of her sea eyes. She inhaled a quick breath through her nostrils.

"That's a lot of 'what if's' Venna, and they could all be wrong."

"You cynical bitch. You truly are a killer. You killed men, you killed hearts, and you have for sure killed mine."

Venna turned towards the southward direction, continuing her dejected walk.

"Venna wait."

"No, I am going back to Sarat. I will find my way. I will whore around like you did if I must."

"You will die alone. If you cared about Kenat, you had come back with me."

"What's the point?" Venna came to a halt a few meters on her resumed walk, "you said it yourself - he cannot love. I will find love with seedy men as you did."

"No. You are wrong about me. I did what I had to."

"You were a whore and a murderer."

Venna reached into her tunics and removed the soft felt patch emblazoned with the sigil of the orange rose. She graced her silky hands across the stitched embroidery and threw it onto the ground.

"I will not do this. Not for you, not for myself, not for Cassica."

"Then do it for the Crown."

"The Crown is dead, at least to me. The Order is nothing but a brothel of murderers serving a vain king."

"Your king is dead."

A slithering voice coalesced from the blank ethers with hissing groans followed by a swamp stench of decaying rot.

"What was that?"

Ysalir steadied into a defensive stance, quickening her glances around her as she clutched the knife sheathed at her hip.

In a shroud of rippling fog, a shadowy figure rose in front of Venna. The frame of the apparition materialized in streaks of crackling sparks bouncing from the billowing cloud two meters in height. A hand gripped around Venna's neck startling her doe eyes into a widened scare as the crackling of the Abyss broke apart with deafening moans of undead shrills. The gangling frame of Ragres finalized from the void gripping his blade in his right hand pointing the business end at Venna's eyes. Scaly hands continued its strenuous clasp at her throat. Venna struggled against her captor gagging with each strain of her muscles as his hold clamped tighter.

"Take me to Cadeck, virgin, lest I gut you from neck to womb."

Ragres's voice hissed command in Common Tongue. Rot breathed from his words as crackling skin covered his hands. Encased in a full overcoat made from a distinct foreign hide, he towered over Venna's frail body like an obsidian monument. An inner skirt surrounded his hips made of the same material stretching towards his ankles as Venna caught notice of the soiled rag emblazoned with the Imperium herald over his eyes.

"Venna," Ysalir screamed from the metered distance.

"Approach me boshani and she dies," Ragres reverted to Sheebal as he addressed Ysalir as a female hound.

"Take me to the Aztmi and I may let her live."

"Let her go, gertoum piss."

Ysalir commanded her insult towards Ragres, returned in his tongue. The magister turned Venna's back against his chest, clutching her puffed lips with flaked fingers preventing her from screaming. He brought the blade to her neck in coercion towards Ysalir's threat.

"If you value your abinisa's life, you will take me to Cadeck. Run ahead of us actatnu, fetch me your Aztmi." Ragres ordered Ysalir to obey his command, addressing Venna's relationship to the older woman and Ysalir's profession in his tongue. He returned his speech to Venna's innocent ear with the putrid stench of rotting gum and slimy tongue seeding her purity with thoughts of salacious deed.

"I sense a shroud within you, girl; haunted by it - the Guardian called to me."

Venna's innocent gaze turned to terror in Ragres's clutches. Her eyes cried desperation to Ysalir for rescue, yet Ysalir offered none should the magister hold true to his promise. Ragres' desiccated lips cracked into an empty-toothed smirk of rancid gums as his threats waivered through the air with billowing breaths. Ysalir sheathed her dagger against her left hip hiding it

328

beneath her fur cloak. She mouthed her affection towards Venna, turned and began a sprint towards Tijoa's hut.

Ragres harried Venna to march, keeping his hand against her lips and blade tight against the skin of her svelte neck. The short walk seemed like a brutal exodus with each passing second as Venna whiffed the years of scars and soiled flesh emanating from her captor. Ysalir sprinted towards the hut. Her grace swung the door wide. Venna's azure eyes teared up unknowing if her final moment to see her sister would be at the hands of this disgusting individual.

Seated at Tijoa's chair, Cadeck rose as the older sister burst through the door sending the cupboards on the wall to a wide swing as Ysalir slammed it shut. Cassica sat at the bench table preparing garnishes for the evening's meal. Eris and Kenat stationed at the stove, working to prepare the main dishes as Ysalir's rant turned to fright.

"Cadeck," Ysalir began, her throat choked with tears, "the hunter is out there, and he has Venna. He is going to kill her."

Cassica rose to attention at Ysalir's plea. Cadeck lifted his hand to calm the ladies.

"No, this fight is not yours."

Cadeck met Ysalir's watered eyes graced with salted tears and touched his calloused hands against her blushed cheeks. A wash of calmness embraced her. He shed a smirk of confidence as he lifted the door handle.

"Cadeck," Cassica protested, running to catch him before he left the hut.

"Do not concern for me."

Cadeck shut the door behind him leaving the ladies to question. Outside, Cadeck embraced the cold enveloping his form. He closed his eyes opening his mouth with a slight grin through salty whiskers. His arms wound the tight furs against his wide shoulders, his leather boots trod into the soft slush lining the path from Tijoa's hut. Cadeck strode the walkway with steps of uncertainty. The axe remained lodged into the cutting stump as Ysalir left the weapon. The foot marks of the sister pair fresh in the muddy snow slop.

Cadeck caught his eye with the shadowy figure clutching the nubile woman against him. He sensed the fear rising in Venna's emotion followed by cadaver rot. Cadeck's aztmudin swirled majestically within, boiling, and bubbling with the intensity of agitated water. Cadeck's salted hair flittered in the bitter winds. Split ends teetered with unkempt hygiene brushed against his forehead.

"Release the girl, hunter. She is of no concern to you."

Ragres ceased his walk, his grip tightened against Venna's mouth, "Killing her would dull my blade for its intended target, Cadeck."

Ragres forced Venna into the ground with a thrust of his wrist. The girl collapsed into the snow onto her stomach and face. She lifted herself with pain and brushed the ice and snow from her face and matted blonde locks.

"Run Venna," Cadeck commanded, and turned his attention towards Ragres.

"You followed me through my prayers, Magister. The darkness of your master lingers over Silvetzen, but I will not allow you to find the Wind Temple."

"I have accepted my failure, Cadeck. Your death shall atone me."

Venna darted towards the Magi.

"And your master, who wishes to kill me and the Azthar Kherdmon, you would deny him pleasures?"

Ragres seethed his tongue against his rotted gums, "Killing the Azthar Kherdmon now would be a waste of my magick. In time, my Master shall reward me for my deeds. I do not wish to kill you now, Aztmi. Take me to him."

"You will not find another Temple, dark one. Your attempt shall stop here today."

Cadeck remained calm as his opponent paced side to side in anger.

"Strong words, Cadeck, from a Magi weakened in the presence of Hadithem's glory. You will do as I ask if your children are to live. Master awaits his prize, and you denied him by refusing to sign the treaty. Now, do not delay, Cadeck. I will return to my Master victorious no matter who dies today."

Teal tendrils encircled Ragres's right hand stretching across the sacred blade. The etched glyphs on the sides glowed with energies empowering the magister with heightened awareness. His vision blurred into focus; the blackness caused his aztunai to coalesce into a tunnel vision of emptiness. He raised his hand over his shoulder into an arced throwing motion to release the projectile in Cadeck's direction.

Ragres outstretched his fingers and wiggled them to guide the weapon. Cadeck shut his eyes and calmed his emotions. In blinding flash, his body flickered from his position to return a few inches to his left, catching the blade's handle with his right hand. The magister winced with rage.

"How," Ragres burned.

Cadeck wheezed as his body collapsed in pain. The blade dropped into the slush empty of blood of the intended target.

"Cadeck."

Venna yelled as she passed the Magi in her sprint. Her fear collapsed her into a slip on the ice, pounding into the muddy mire. Venna crawled to the huddled man a few feet in front of her face. More mud and ice splattered into her cheeks, staining her clothes.

"No."

She continued in sob, clawing her way towards his body. Cadeck remained unresponsive. Venna and her friend's chances to survive this encounter lay in the collapsed body slopped before her, his resolve weakened and bruised. Ragres's pace slowed towards the fallen Magi, meters separated the point from the hut.

The lingering doom called to Venna; her ears perked to its haunting tones. She looked behind her, watching as the shadow approached. Ysalir and Cassica exited the hut from the girl's screams. Kenat followed, hobbling under the pains throbbing through his back. His ruffled hair covered his stark face, pearly eyes emblazoned with the essence of his fight.

Kenat twirled his fingers into a ball in front of his chest as they glowed with energy. Ragres stopped at Cadeck's ailing body, standing over Venna. He smelled the woman's fear as she turned rigid in fright. Ragres hissed towards the culminating fires forming from Kenat's hands. He reached into his leathery hides over his chest and removed the small, crimson stone, discolored in blackened shades stretching in minute veins around the rock.

"Calm your boy-Magi girl if he knows what is good for him. Hadithem's grace weakens him. He will fall by my hand as did his Master."

Ragres's tongue slithered his guttural command, parading the stone within his fingers.

"No, he should hurt you as you did Cadeck."

Venna protested, leaning over Cadeck's body, and faced the sinister man. Ragres coiled the stone in his right hand and swiftly struck Venna's face with the same backhand. The force of impact dropped her to her side as Ragres leaned towards the knife.

"No," Kenat muttered in anger towards the attack upon Venna.

Ragres shifted his hands, sliding the stone into his left hand as he hoisted his knife with the other, taunting Kenat with the rock with a sneering grin. Kenat's hands raised towards the leather-bound man and shot a stream of flame towards him. In skilled martial grace, he ducked the flame, clearing the stream jet of blazing magick, and hurled his dagger in Kenat's direction striking the boy in his thigh. Kenat crumpled in pain, gripping his leg to the rushing blood. Cassica rushed to his aide, holding him to ease his agony.

Ysalir hastened a rush with readied blade towards Ragres in retaliation for Venna. Ragres paused, focusing his vision on his adversary charging him, her auras glowed with furious redness. He commanded the ethereal plane through his sight, manipulating and forming it to his Will. The Abyss answered as he commanded as dark spirits hurtled towards the weaponised threat blitzing towards him.

Ysalir dropped to her knees, gripping her forehead crying with paranoid delusions of hallucinated fear. Ragres commanded the spirits further, calling them to retrieve his weapon from Kenat's leg. Cassica's eyes widened with shock as the blade removed itself from his thigh, guided by invisible forces to her sight. Kenat screamed while the wavy blade tore through sinewy muscle evacuating with a gush of blood. The blade seared through the air, handle-first as it returned to Ragres's right hand.

Cries of terror called around Venna. She heard her sister shrieking from delusions. Kenat moaned with pain behind her pounding ears. She lifted her head from the ground, her right cheek pounded with fresh throbs as a hissing whisper seared within her skull. She jolted her head to attune the odd beacon and caressed the numbing welt forming upon her cheek. She craned her neck towards the attacker as the hisses continued to rattle within her brain of several voices.

Venna's head jerked to clear her thoughts. She watched as Ragres knelt against his adversary. His withered knee settled against Cadeck's ribs, ignoring the humans nearby. His hands gripped the bone hilt, preparing the blade to thrust into Cadeck's neck. The other Magi focused on his pain; two ladies huddled around him to calm his nerves denying them effort to attack. The stronger woman lay writhing in fear, the spirits of the Abyss clutched at her mind, beating her heart into increased rhythm. The madness would drive her into shock, exploding the organ within her chest or so Ragres had hoped.

Ragres turned his head towards Cassica's direction; the spirits of the Abyss lingered in his thoughts, his vision, and his soul. The spirit of Sacred Mother glowed with the embodiment of blood-shorn lace. The physical vessel tended to the wounded Magi as Ragres summoned prayers upon silent breath in his tongue. Absent any other wish or command, seething in his own volitions of carnal intuition, Ragres whispered towards her spirit.

"I call to you, Babalon. I do this for you. Visraair Abra, I will vanquish the weak surrounding you and make you my eternal bride so we may unite and rule Roth."

Ragres ignored the lithe girl beside him as his hands thrust the weapon towards Cadeck. Venna reacted, jumping to her feet, and tackled the magister into the ground, sending the blade and sacred fire stone into the slush. The perpetual motion buckled his knees, cracking one of them for dislocation. His face flopped into the snowy slop with a soft thud. Ragres groaned in agony as Venna's weight straddled his torso.

332

As he turned onto his back, he threw Venna into the ground with a yelp.

"Boshani."

Venna reached for the bone hilt caked into the slush. Ragres struggled to move and as he twisted into position to rise to his feet, he moaned with the crackle of his dislocated knee. Venna revolved to face Ragres who lied on his back; right leg twisted into unnatural position from the knee down.

Through matted hair and disheveled furs, Venna's innocent stare turned to anger. She pursed her lips at the attacker and snarled as she pushed the blade towards the Imperial herald on his flaked forehead. Ragres's hands stopped her, his strength twisting the skin around her spry wrists to crush the bones within. The pain released the blade from her grip; the paused momentum dropped the weapon against Ragres's rag upon his left eye socket as it harmlessly followed the curvature of his face into the ground.

"You have failed, girl," Ragres shed a snarling cackle at the amusement of her fealty,
"Killing you will bring me pleasure, a task which is long overdue."

Ragres's strength collapsed into Venna's wrists as she fell to her side. Tears streamed down her cheeks as he crushed his fingers upon her wrists. Ragres ignored his own pain as he turned to his right side following his victim's reaction. He turned his gravity onto his left knee, his crooked leg drifted in the clotted snow. Crackles of bones given tightened pressure rippled through Venna's forearms. Ragres forced his fingers to crush her wrists, crippling her abilities to fight back.

"You are weak," he taunted, "useless."

He reverted his dialect to the ancient litanies with a snarl, calling to the spindly demon Choronzon as he stared into Venna's eyes through his bloodied coverings.

#

Cadeck, my love, hear me again.

Jess?

You are close to me, my love. Save your friends from their suffering, in time your god will answer you.

Jess?

Cadeck whimpered the final call of his lover's name. His soul warmed inside him. A light glowed within him upon Jess' words. He struggled with his thoughts, hearing Venna's cries beside him. He focused the blur of his vision into the ground. Wet blood lingered in the etching of the wavy blade causing them to release faint glows. Cadeck lifted his hand towards the hilt, and with every bit of remaining strength, hoisted himself onto his feet.

He turned his head around the scene; Ysalir struggled with the ethereal attack a few meters behind him amidst the throes of pain within her head. Turning towards Tijoa's hut, Kenat leaned against the cutting stump. Eris tied a tourniquet around his thigh while Cassica coddled his head against her chest and calmed him with stroked hair. Cadeck breathed slowly, his mind returned focus towards the magister. Pain and suffering dripped from him like matted water from a submerged dog returned to land.

"Release her, hunter."

Cadeck's familiar voice echoed behind Ragres. The magister set his weight upon his left knee as he removed his hands from the little woman. Ragres turned his rotted rag in glance over his shoulder to find his weapon removed from the ground. Without hesitation, Cadeck forced the blade towards Ragres splitting the Imperial herald on his blistered brow crunching into the skull beneath it.

"My gods have not forsaken me, magister. Your gods have failed *you* instead. By Aeus, I release your god's curse upon us."

The wound oozed with blackened blood expelling onto Ragres's face. Through his vision, the void of the Abyss disintegrated into ghostly static before fading to empty darkness without form or lining. Cadeck stood over the man as his crippled body collapsed into the slush. Viscous liquid spewed from his skull polluting the virginal slush beneath his body. Cadeck gazed around to see Venna upon her back, contracting her arms close to her chest with sobs of pain. Ysalir's ravings lulled into whimpers as her lunacy recoiled into somber release.

Cassica rushed towards Cadeck and draped a warm fur blanket over his back as he stumbled in reaction. Her soft whispers in High Accent comforted his mental wounds as they discussed bringing the wounded into the hut. He listened to her words blurred by the humming drones of pain both his own and the girls. She aided his limp towards Tijoa's hut guiding Eris with the task of abetting the others. Cassica steadied him into Tijoa's chair. Cadeck's hair matted, his tunics dirtied from the stains of slush and mud and his mind rattled from a sudden release of energy lifting from his soul. He closed his eyes, embracing the internal warmth of the fires and listened to his own heart as he clutched the locket beneath his shirt.

I love you, Cadeck.

Jess' solemn voice lulled him into relaxing quiet.

Chapter 31

Tesh awoke to cold prickling winds brushing against his face. His eyes fluttered amidst the whipping stings filtering the stark whiteness along the sky. He lay silent, studying the intake of light spilled into his eyes like a rushing flood. Numbness filtered from his feet up his legs and through his torso. He hesitated to move. Pain ripped through his joints as his nerves rekindled feeling with the morning airs.

Tijoa's wrinkled face interrupted his thoughts. Gnarled knobs of clumped beard polluted Tesh's vision as the Magi's heaved breathing warmed his face. Tijoa's eyes huddled within his furrowed salty brows as moles burrowed in their holes peeking out amidst the brightness of early morning sun.

"Wake up, boy."

Tijoa moved out of Tesh's way to allow the man to rise. Chilled hesitation calmed Tesh as he rose, clutching the warm furs tight around his torso. He unfurled the wrappings covering his borrowed blade from becoming brittle in the harsh climate of the northern reaches. His left hand clinched with tight muscles; the golden tendrils scarred into his veins burned bright flickering in the morning reflection. Tesh lifted to his feet standing firm within fluffed boots of bear and wolf furs. Brown and black pelts entombed him in an armor of warmth.

Tijoa harried the boy to march. Furs covered the frail shoulders in matted disarray, along his backside, and covered the bright azure vestments furrowed along the rest of his body to meet a pair of woolen boots. He carried the scant articles of his faith, while Tesh carried the supplies of their camp stocking them and packing them into a tight satchel. He fumbled carelessly to sort the pots and sleeping wraps to bury them in neat packing within the small binds of the sack.

Tesh rushed to catch up to the older man who betrayed his age with his walking speed. For infinite distance, the blinding white glacier covered the horizons below the orange sky opening to the east. Tesh respired heavily as his stride rushed to catch Tijoa.

"How much further," Tesh panted amidst the muffled clanking of pottery in his sack. His knees and calves shot with cold stiffened pain.

"When you feel the coldness of extinction, we will be there."

"I do not follow. It's cold now."

"If you still breathe, if you still walk, you are not there."

"You're testing me, Tijoa."

A rare smile covered Tijoa's puffed lips through his gnarled beard, "You are smart boy, but you have a long way to go. This Trial will break your soul. I have seen many Initiates breathe without heartbeat as their bodies give up. Through the Winds, carries vibration. When you feel cold emptiness, you will find its source. When Vibration ceases, then you will know."

Tesh lowered his head in thought. His left hand vibrated with the stinging contemplation of thought. *No winds and no breaths. It is the cold stillness permeating the valley around us.*

Tijoa turned to Tesh's realization, "That is where the dragons live. Where they exist, no wind exists. Only from their wings do the winds form, does the minutia of life vibrate. If you fail this Trial, the Great Dragon, the Dragon of the Northern Wind, will consume you."

"Why don't the dragons show themselves?"

Tijoa followed his journey unrelenting in his ambition and easing a sigh into the wind, "Only one dragon still lives. In the past, Four Great Dragons held dominion over the winds: North, South, East, and West. Each of them fell as the Abyss passed overhead, leaving only one behind. He has seen eons of time all in the fleeting moments of thought. He is the Guardian of the Wind Temple. We tread cautiously around him."

"But you are the Magi of Wind; Cadeck called you its keeper."

Cold winds buried into Tesh's hair flowing in misdirection. Daylight burned against the whiteness of the infinite glacier stringing the pair's shadows in elongated western growth.

"He is a temperamental beast. He would not hesitate to kill me should I fail. You have faced the blinding veracity of Cadeck's dogs, the fiery fleeting of Philos' horses, but the dragon holds dominion of them all. He is vicious and impatient."

"And if I fail the Trials?"

Tijoa shot him a disturbing stare with a callous pause to his next answer, "He feeds on your soul."

Tesh swallowed an audible gulp as he paused to contemplate Tijoa's warning. The Trials have proven difficult on his mental sturdiness and given his body a reason for pain. He longed for the night of a warm bed, free from the troubles of the world and free from the burdens of man. An encumbrance weighed upon him, the culmination of thousands of years of prophecy rested on his heart as many have told him. If he failed, none would come after him and his friends, Sarat and Roth would suffer.

Tijoa outpaced him along the expansive ice sheet. Tesh sprinted as best as his pain would allow. With each stride, the numbing cold gnawed at his knees and joints breaking into his heels and toes as he pushed his ligaments to hasten. He felt the bunions wrapping around his toes like vines of ivy. For hours they journeyed, Tijoa never faltering from his walk while Tesh would break occasionally to soothe the spasms in his knees.

"We have travelled for days. Our only shelter has been the clothes on our backs, Magi. Is this Temple any farther?"

Tesh wheezed in short breaths to address Tijoa.

"You still feel winds, don't you boy?"

Tesh replied with a short acknowledgement, "Yes."

"Then we are not there. There is a deep rift in the center of the Eternal Ice. We move until we feel no wind."

Tesh's expedition pressed on for another day. As the midmorning sun crested into noon along the southern edge of sky, the glacial sheet sloped towards the crest of ocean in the north. Jagged ice sheets rose from the oceans like a lethal sea maze broken away from the main glacier. The winds were coldest on this edge. Ice fragments pelted into Tesh's hairs, in his eyebrows and furrowed into his fuzzy beard. With each bite of the air, the wound in his left hand tingled not from magic but from his injury.

Tesh discovered a colder cold than any winter wrought upon his home. The winds of the Eternal Ice nipped at any exposed flesh in attempts to rip it away. Tijoa assured the boy covered himself head to toe, masking his face in linens and thick furs. Travelers passed through Telmen telling of lands to the far north which froze the sweat on your body and your tears if you dared to cry from the pain should you linger too long.

Tijoa walked a distance ahead before stopping in the middle of his path as though he met an invisible wall. Tesh gathered his strength, lifted the cargo sack, and harried to make pace to him. When he stopped, his jaw reacted to awe.

Below their feet, an expansive cavern carved into the ice, tempered to appear if a blazed sword had sheen cut through. Ice sheet walls cooled to a light blue appearing as frozen glass down the sheer drop. An eerie stillness fell upon Tesh as he looked over the edge of the canyon. The cold winds ceased at the edge of his feet as he followed his eyes towards a basin on the horizon of the cavern.

Tijoa turned to face him. Ice pellets clung to his discolored and unkempt beard. His puffed lips crept into a cold smile.

"This is where the dragon lives and where you will die."

Tijoa rushed to grip Tesh's pelts with his withered right hand. With the speech of ancient language cursing the boy, Tijoa's free hand reached into his robes to remove a small knife. Tijoa's eyes burned into a malicious offering as he raised the kitchen blade into a striking stance.

"Cadeck was a fool to believe those legends. The Azthar Kherdmon has not lived in over forty-thousand years. You expect me to believe He returned in this pathetic, weaseling brat?"

"What is this?"

Tesh struggled to remove himself from Tijoa's grip. He grasped the frail man's hand with his left hand. Tendrils of crimson energies coiled along his golden veins tightening his hold upon the lithe wrist. Tijoa reacted in pain and struck at Tesh with his blade, cutting against Tesh's elbow joint only to gracefully slip against his sleeves. Tijoa stabbed again, this time breaking the cloth. Tesh moved quickly, skirting the blade to scrape inside only to sear dead skin flakes against the blade.

"Here you will die in the cold of the North, Tesh. You failed the Trials of Wind, and the dragon consumed your soul. That is what I will tell your friends."

"You'll be lying."

"No one will know. Who is going to come here to claim your body? A Magi's word is absolute, Cadeck knows this. You are not a prophecy, or a legend. You are the bastard of a criminal."

Tijoa struggled with Tesh and made further attempts to cut into him. His blade met mark and cut skin into Tesh's shoulder staining his tunic with a flow of blood. Tesh tightened his grip further, causing the pair to waver on the edge of the ice wall. Tesh set his furred boot into the ice floor, slips of crystals pushed into the crevice below. With the advantage, Tijoa calmed himself and released his hold on Tesh permitting the fall of gravity to hold. With the force of momentum, Tesh gaped wide, his eyes embraced the realization of his slip. His boot buckled from underneath, sending his legs into the air as the ice slid him over the edge back-side down.

Tijoa watched as the man raised his arms in futile attempt to grip at a ledge. His feet flew from underneath as his body jerked to fall. Tijoa's scraggly beard clung to his face, whipped to a frenzy in the gale winds. His robes followed suit, crackling in the rush of wind to his back.

"Sorry, boy, but you were not the Azthar Kherdmon."

338

Tijoa tossed his blade into the canyon, turning his back to return south. He meditated in the speech of the ancients, guiding him along his walk away from the demise of his Initiate. His element picked up faster, rocking the old man's gait to waiver towards the east. He regained momentum, holding his hand against his face to block the onslaught of ice pellets rushing towards him like a hurricane.

A freezing burst erupted from behind him, knocking Tijoa to stumble onto his knees and stomach. A rushing echo boom burst with the sound of a flapping wing. A mighty roar echoed along the ice sheet escalating in a high crescendo like the sound of a thousand storms. A long rush of air flowed across the glacier sending a wave of free ice pellets to scatter along the surface as ripples across the waters.

A thrusting shockwave burst into the glacier with the arrival of a gargantuan thud. Tijoa turned onto his backside to look behind him. A fresh glaze of crystalline pellets lodged into his clothes and beard. Before his eyes towered a reptilian quadruped.

Wings crested upon its high shoulders above the forward legs. The translucent, azure scales grafted onto the creature like clean brush strokes. It stood on three of its legs while its forward left had gripped in tight formation. It eased its left hand onto the surface, releasing its steady grasp to flex wide. From the towering claws rolled a human body clothed in icy furs and remained cowered in sublime stasis upon the frozen ground.

Tijoa cowered as the creature craned its massive neck to lower at the Magi. Bony horns covered an elongated snout protruding across the ventral and dorsal sides of the beak. A cartilage shaped ridge covered the baseline of the head joining the neck as slit-pupil green eyes flanked the beak in front of the ridge. The beast moved its left claw away from the human body in a protective stance from the Magi.

The creature bared no teeth, only to open its jaw wide and release a deafening roar at Tijoa. As the echo screamed, shards of ice littered across the glacial surface, the beast's horns shuttered with the rush of air through the sinus canals culminating as visible breath rolls. Its wings flapped a mighty storm rolling along the ice as it reared its front legs in displeasure.

"Æiutherion?"

Tijoa's physical mouth hesitated to structure the name of the beast standing before him.

Æiutherion placed his feet upon the surface of the ice and rested his stance. He moved his elongated neck with an ease of slithering snake to face the Magi. His lips did not move, only commanding a voice calling through the air telepathically. He spoke his words in the ancient speech, a dialect consisting of arcane vowel movements and staccato consonant sounds. A vernacular the Magi called Tereswa, or Speech of the Divine. His voice boomed in Tijoa's head with the echo of ancient eons flowing through his silent tongue. The creature's voice flowing with the slow pace of a meandering creek.

"For eons I have seen ancient ways and known ancient men. Many have come through the walls of the Wind Temple, and likewise many have failed. The Aztmi have mastered the Elements since the ancient of days, respecting the Aztun which created us and created you. On this day, I bear witness to a sinner."

Æiutherion paced in a calamitous boom to his right keeping his snout pointed at the Magi, "The cursed sons of the gods are upon Roth like a stone pressing to flour. The primitive sons the gods created eons ago bloom their fruits for conquest."

The dragon continued to circle the scared man, "I have seen the Magi fail their guardianship with this Passing. The Council is unruly and unworthy. It is the Magi whose souls turned corrupt and in turn followed to the Knights. A plight foreseen. Your frail minds feared this. You made alliance with the ancient curse, defying the creeds set forth by your gods."

Æiutherion's slit eyes closed halfway as to lecture Tijoa, "This boy, Tesh Verdui, bears the mark of the Azthar Kherdmon, he is the prophecy of the Primordial Man made manifest. I see her, with him, in a reality still to manifest. The Mother, and her Children. Your Council has denied your teachings, your fellowship, and your creeds. It is by this denial; you have forsaken your savior. You *will* present to him the Trials of your Calling. Failure to do so will result in *your* consumption."

Tijoa cowered as the ancient dragon's head towered over his frail body. He feared Æiutherion could fill his lungs in one swift moment to inhale the old Magi into his mouth to never see light again. The dragon's imposing legs straddled across the ice sheet as vast expanse separated Tijoa from Tesh. He swung his spiked, crystalline tail in wide arcs disturbing the ice pellets dancing nervously in the throes across the glacier.

Æiutherion was the chief dragon, the primordial beast under Tijoa's ward in his role as the Wind Magi and Tijoa had disappointed the ancient creature. Tijoa found himself consumed by Æiutherion's shadow as his head rose to blot the low hanging sun to the southern hemisphere. Tijoa covered his scraggy face with his weak hands, palms out fearing the worse.

Tesh lay still on the ice sheet, his hands blushed from the frost chilling over his body. Wayward whipping gusts blew above him swaying from left to right, east to west. His eyes strained with the nipping frost clinging to them as he craned his neck towards Tijoa. Æiutherion's rear foot imprinted into the ice beside him, the scaly lattice rose with muscular weight into the sky. A claw extended from the beast's heel to match Tesh's height in length.

Stinging energy cut through Tesh's golden stems carved into his left hand. The surge of magick coursed through his body in the presence of the dragon. His mind slowed to form the imposing spectacle. His physical senses denying the beast while the thoughts coursing through his soul believed otherwise. He rose from his coiled repose, screaming through the fight of the burning cold. His exposed skin prickled with frostbite.

Æiutherion shifted his weight upon the ice, careful not to squish the fleshy humans. His skeletal, crystalline wings fluttered to offset the balance as he craned his elongated neck to catch sight of Tesh in his struggle. He lowered his head to meet Tesh, the bony growths covering his snout lowered into flush with his beak as a sign of welcome gesture. He met his right eye to Tesh's body.

Tesh ceased his scream, panting to near shock as his face met the visual organ as large as his head. Tesh heard the beast's crystalline eyelids crackle like stones rubbing with each blink. His body calmed to fear, too petrified to defend himself. Æiutherion began to speak. His voice lulled Tesh into relaxation as he spoke not with mouth but through mind. As though every fiber in Tesh's body reverberated with the dragon's speech like his very blood translated the beast's language for him.

This feeling lowered Tesh into a steady breath as he felt the course of his bloodline pounding through his body. He recalled this feeling from his Trials, but this was not the true Trial of Wind, yet this beast spoke to him in a manner to the voices from the past. The feelings rippled through his body beginning at his skull and like a crashing wave flowed into his neck, his heart, his hands, his torso, and loins and following through to his feet.

"You are the Azthar Kherdmon, the Primordial Man created by the Aztun to live with their soul, their *Dra Nar Azt*, their sacred bloodline. You hold the history of your kind within your body. You are as the son of the gods as you are of man, the entirety of your world. Prove your worthiness with your Trials and your gifts shall bestow upon you."

"What are you? I do not understand."

Tesh stuttered his words, his mind struggled to understand the enormity of the beast.

"Your physical self cannot grasp the knowledge you have seen and witness to now. When you achieve totality of your being, Oneness, only then will you understand. I cannot answer your questions. You must discover the answers on your own. There is nothing more I can tell you, for time is terse and your achievements are of the utmost."

Æiutherion hefted his weight to motion behind Tesh. His crystalline wings blew overhead canvassing over Tesh dwarfing the human beneath a canopy blocking the sun. The dragon sunk his weight into the glacier, bending his four knees as he thrust himself to flight. His wavering wings sent infinite pellets of ice dust in his trail as he gained altitude into the sky.

Tesh watched with awe as the massive beast flew in low altitude and began to circle the land. Æiutherion started descent yards in front of Tesh and Tijoa's position, lowering himself from his circling altitude into a swift drop. Ice shavings obscured the massive beast under his violent wake as his quick flight grazed the surface of the glacier.

Tesh dropped to duck as the beast rushed closer, fearing the beast ripping him in two. As he coiled into the kneeling position, covering his head, he felt a slight tug as the dragon flew past him. Æiutherion reached with skill, gripping the two humans in his forward claws as he approached them in blinding motion. The icy scape blurred beneath Tesh as he opened his eyes to look below.

Violent rushes of cold winds swept through his auburn hair as their echoes crossed his ears. He wrapped his arm length around the teal crystalline claw, white knuckles bore into his flesh as his hands did not touch another with his frightened grip. He laid his face upon the gentle giant's frosted finger as the beast made a swift descent into the cavern below. Tesh felt surges rippling through his left wrist calming him from the beast's violent flight. Æiutherion hugged the edge of the wall almost for Tesh to touch. As he approached the floor, he lifted himself and swept his wings into aerodynamic grace as he darted tree-height above the surface.

Deceleration alerted Tesh to remove his toughened grip as Æiutherion released his claws dropping the human pair onto the frigid surface. The dragon continued his flight, approaching the carved Temple etched into the ancient ice. He coiled his body around the icy stalagmite centering the building against the wall. His tail flowed in a helix pattern towards the Temple's dark opening. Æiutherion placed his forward claws around the central spire as his slender neck slid upon his right side watching the human pair as they slowed to rise.

Tesh stumbled, slipping his knees on the sheen surface of the cavernous crater carved into the ice. Furs slid from his shoulders under the weight of gravity. Tesh rose to his feet with the cold stillness stinging through his layers. Before him rose a massive crater cut artificially into the glacier. Embedded into the wall, cut from a single layer of ice, the carved structure of the Wind Temple rose before him straddled by the giant dragon's body.

Downbursts tore through the crater forcing the howls of hurricanes to scream through the walls. Tesh shielded his face from the onslaught of air as

342

blistering pellets of ice followed the streams. Tesh paused to gaze at the pristine carving shimmering with dazzling azure cut into the ice wall. His feet wavered as he lowered his arm to his side. Æiutherion released a calm breath, his eyelids blinked as the man below him recognized the structure.

Tijoa blinked his eyes rapidly as he awoke from his shock. He rose to a seating position and steadied to ease his center of gravity. His tattered furs clung tight to his body covering the sacred vestments dangling against his ankles. Pieces of ice clung tight into his frazzled beard as he raised himself to his feet. The silent cold nipped at his exposed flesh with the scent of frozen seas surrounding his senses as the winds cut through the cavern. Tijoa lifted his head towards the mighty beast straddling the ancient structure as the vast expanse separated the humans from the building.

"You spared me, dragon," Tijoa stuttered his words with disbelief.

"Honor your sacrament, Aztmi," Æiutherion began, his lips remained closed as his voice echoed across the crater, "If your premonitions are true, Tesh will not survive the valley and you may return to your home and away from the cold. If you are wrong, Tijoa, your penance will be to remain in the Temple through your dying days."

"Dragon, Tiasu has allowed me to live as I have since I assumed the mantle, to live with my countrymen. Why do you forsake covenant?"

Tijoa shook his extended hands, digits outstretched at the beast.

Tesh peeked over his shoulder watching as the Magi and dragon exchanged words.

"The gods have spoken," Æiutherion's voice roared through the valley, "The Magi will fall. Your fate foreseen. You have broken your atonement with your secular dealings. You have dishonored your vows and you will atone for your sins."

"I bring this Initiate to the Temple. I will grant him the Trials. I request to leave when I finish as I have done before."

Æiutherion's head craned skyward, his neck extended to full length. His eyes highlighted to a cerulean glow as the beast cracked his jaw into wide gape. The dragon's claws gripped into the ice sculpture sending shards of icicles to collapse below as the pressures of the beast intensified. The dragon lowered his head as swirling winds encapsulated within the open beak at the end of his snout. Bony outgrowths extended to full length rippling with anger.

The energy of a thousand storms rippled sonic booms from the beast's mouth cutting a damaging ray of wind into the ice walls behind and above the humans' heads higher than the temple. Energies carved into the walls with the piercing screams of furious winds sending thousands of shattering shards of ice tumbling into the glacial floor below them. Tesh covered his head to shield himself from any fragments sent into his direction as the dragon's anger carved a straight edge into the ice wall many meters behind them, splitting a symmetrical cut against the face of the surface.

Æiutherion relaxed his neck; his bony horns flowed into parallel against his beak as his words spoken in standard calm demeanor, "You will obey as commanded by Tiasu, Magi. Lest I strip you of your aztmudin."

Tijoa collapsed to his knees in obeisance to the beast, "Spare me Tiasu's wrath."

"Enter the Temple and prepare the boy for Trials. Anything other than decreed will certainly call for fate."

Tijoa approached Tesh, gripping his spindly hand against Tesh's tapered shoulders as Tesh gathered his materials for warmth. Tijoa led him along the clear white cavern surface towards the matriculate sculpture carved from a single, uninterrupted line upon the cavernous wall.

Hidden from the glare of the sun, the Wind Temple rose high above the floor. Æiutherion's spiked tail twitched in anticipation as the pair approached the hollowed entry. The beast raised his tail above the frame of the entry. Intricate hieroglyphics carved into its surface. The writing matched the ancient script adorning the other temples, undecipherable to Tesh. Ripples coalesced and surged across his hand as his body crossed the boundary. Tijoa stopped to bow upon one knee, urging Tesh to repeat the vigil. Tijoa recited ancient words in the Divine Speech before rising to his feet.

Light reflected from the icy surface above, the interior of the temple glistened in an ethereal hue of dazzling azure and cerulean crystal. An empty pool marked the center of the structure's interior like the design he had seen before. Carved to inlay within the pool, set the glyph of a triangle facing upright with a horizontal line crossing near the apex aimed inward, towards the icy altar. Frigid stillness of salty ice brushed against Tesh's skin and through his nose, the building appeared virginal to any visitors, unwavering in its sterility.

Tijoa dropped the fur trappings covering his shoulders onto the ice-laden floor then followed with his teal robe. He removed the white cloth covering his torso. Tijoa stripped his leggings to his feet, tossing them away to reveal his frail, aging nakedness. His flesh began to blush from the lingering chills while he focused on his meditations in silent murmur. Tijoa immersed his body into the sacred, empty pool and turned to face Tesh.

"We are starting now. No time to rest?"

Tijoa cocked his head in sarcastic demeanor, "No, Tesh. The dragon demands the Trials begin now. You either pass or fail. Any other result will lead to our demise."

Tijoa motioned his fingers to coerce Tesh to join him. Stripped bare, Tesh touched his naked feet onto the floor jumping and hiking his knees to prevent his heels from freezing to the surface. He reached to his genitals, cupping them in his hands as his body's reaction to the cold curled his testicles into his torso. He steadied himself towards the Magi, stepping carefully into the empty pool filled with emptiness of zero density.

"By the sacred winds of Tiasu, the Trials of the Wind will test your resolve. With His Winds, All is in Motion, All is in Vibration. In the Light, your Mind reached to Soul, to seek the All. In the Fire, you saw Correspondence, your Heart, so your Will. In the Winds, you will see Vibration. Your breaths to speak as Soul."

Tijoa laid his hands upon Tesh's temples, chanting an ancient prayer reverberating into his soul. Tesh's eyes rolled into his head which tilted back in submission to the ancient prayers.

"Listen to my voice, Tesh, feel your soul carry along Tiasu's winds."

Tesh's hand glowed. He focused on Tijoa's prayers as violent swirls twisted and spun around his feet. The words pounding through his very soul like the words spoken by the dragon while the tornadic ice continued to lift around the pool in an erratic display of nature. Tijoa's prayers echoed through the hall, focusing the crystalline ice to spiral towards the ceiling in a helical pattern. Tesh's mind echoed eons of time against his thoughts as the fiery flames of battle came into focus.

Tesh's mother stood over him, her soft voice rolling from her mouth with cold smoke. Her brunette locks draped across her bare shoulders stopping at the frills above her breast line flowing into a ragged peasant dress to her ankles. Winds outside the framework house howled with the rapping at the door. She motioned to answer as violent gusts from the wind shoved her with the door's swing.

A brusque shadow stood at the frame, calling her name mixed with threatening insults. The man reached for his mother, but Tesh arose to stop him. The man flung Tesh with a violent grace. Tesh crashed into the table behind him.

The burly man clenched at his mother's hair, forcing her to her feet and standing her upright. The man dragged her into the back bedroom, punching her across her cheeks crashing her onto her mattress. Frosted cold covered the man's beard and calloused hands. His eyes grew with the chills of frozen lakes.

"Mother."

He called from his physical form convulsing in the sacred pool. But she did not answer. His soul form continued his vision leading to a familiar voice call from outside the house.

"Senas."

A stark call echoed through sacred winds before a stoic man burst through the open door. He bore the vestments of a Magi; a slender robe of lavender hue encompassed him. His face was majestic, glowing with the energies of the yellow sun as his hands prepared the workings of a spell. His raven locks curled back against his head. His face full of youth. The burly man took notice to the intruder and approached the door as a cold giant lumbering to meal. His feet stammered into the wooden planks with the howls of the low-sun winds.

"Who are you," spit trickled from the fat man's lips, "and why are you interrupting my evening?"

His vile words coursed from his mouth with blackened breaths of still coldness.

"My name is Cadeck Wenfier, Magi of the Temple of Light and I'm afraid I cannot let you harm this woman."

"A Magi? I thought they only existed in books. Then if you are a Magi, you can pay off this woman's debt. I lost a good harvest from her lack of focus, and I will reclaim my losses one way or another. My taxes will not pay themselves and taking out her debt on her crotch with a good, solid fuck will ease my anger."

"You will leave her and this boy alone."

"Or what?"

The brusque man stood toe to toe with the Magi.

Cadeck's form lifted his hands against the man's temples, embracing them with the white heat of light. The man screamed in agony and slumped to his knees.

"You will have no memory of this entry, or any memory from the past two days. You will leave this home and return to yours never to bother them again, do I make myself clear?"

"Yes. Yes. As clear as the midday sun burning into my eyes."

The dirty man withered his reply, pain tightened upon his face, the searing intensity of Cadeck's focus forced him to his knees. Cadeck's vision form released his grip as the man collapsed onto his stomach. He hesitated to stand but gazed towards the Magi towering over him. He pleaded with Cadeck to remove himself from the premise with the closing breaths of a swirling wind as to vanish in the dust. Tesh's mother returned to her living room, a welt forming onto her cheek bristling with the ice of winter frost.

"Cadeck, what are you doing here?"

"I am leaving the Temple and returning to Jess. Our daughter is about to be born. Come with me, leave this farm. You can stay with Jess and I back in Yumphen. I have regained our family's farm and I was on my way to Racoren to meet with Jess. Tesh will be safe with us. A new Procession arrives during this time of the low sun. I have felt its cold tremors these past few months. Roth will not be safe for long."

"No, Cadeck. I cannot leave here. The quieter and simpler our lives are, the easier it is to protect him from his fate. I cannot allow him to leave, especially after what happened to his father."

"Which is why I ask you to join me."

"No. He is safer here, Cadeck. I do not want the Magi finding him. I have seen the tremors in dreams. Traces really, a sword which screams and your daughter… and a son."

"You saw it too?"

"Yes. Now go, Cadeck, leave. Give Jess a life away from the Magi. Your daughter, and a son yet to born, spare them your suffering."

"You must not speak a word of this encounter to no one and if little Tesh does not remember this, then the better for all of our fates."

Cadeck's spirit form turned towards the door, winds whispering as his form and Senas' faded into emptiness.

Senas approached Cadeck to hug him, "Thanks for saving us, cousin."

Tesh's house swirled into wisps of frozen precipitation surrounding his spirit form. A blonde maiden close to teenage years embraced him. Her hands cold as she touched them to Tesh's face. Cold shocks graced his cheeks while her face broken as a patch of icy fog, disintegrated as a breath of air extinguishes in the winter.

"Jaena," his voice trailed with the gusts of a storm as the figure dissolved into an ethereal void.

Snowdrifts covered carcasses; swords erected upright stabbed into the ground with blood-drenched hilts iced over from bitter winds. Relics of damaged artillery scattered like a graveyard of salvage as far as Tesh could see. Soldiers in various armors; blues, blacks, reds, and silvers stood around. Some clenched wounds, others hobbled to find a safe, relaxing place to die. Tesh felt a cold swirl embracing his left hand.

As he lifted it, he outstretched his digits in front of his face as ice caplets rotated in a tornado around his gold-laced fingers. To his right, buried into the ice erected a hilt of a sword drenched with the fresh snows of winter. Ice covered the outline of the hilt masking all appearances of the weapon in grafted cold.

Tesh attempted to fit the weapon to his grip and in struggle, collapsed to his knees. As his spirit turned to face the forged obstacle digging into the snow, the outline of the sword flittered with the frosted winds into infinity. Children's screams tore in the distance of the ancient battlefield. Sons, daughters of the slain come to mourn their dead. The arrival of a new Aeon? Tesh saw this vision twice before, each one countered with the element of his Trials. But the screams were new. They carried with the dark winds flowing around him, erasing the scarred field into the emptiness of vacuum.

Hurry Tesh. He seeks the Sacred Mother, Babalon.

Babalon? I do not understand. What is this Babalon?

Return to father. Hurry. He can tell you.

Who are you?

I cannot speak much longer; he can hear me when I call. Go now. Please.

The sounds of the girl trailed into the darkness. Tesh's vision collapsed around him as his physical body succumbed to gravity within the icy darkness of the Wind Temple's pool. Tijoa released his hands from Tesh's face as his body stumbled and drew into the fetal position. A pocket of ice scarred upon Tesh's forehead dancing in the reflections of the glorious structure. Tijoa followed his sight upon Tesh's body as similar spots formed upon his arms and legs, his torso and neck, and his loins. Tijoa clutched his jaw, wheezing with the discovery before him.

"*Dra Nar Azt.* Cadeck was right."

Tijoa's eyes followed the sacred points on Tesh's body. A single tear glistened in his left eye to begin its journey upon his cheek.

Tijoa scrambled to lift Tesh from the sacred pool. His frail body heaved with insufficient strength as he lumbered to heft Tesh's dead weight towards the edge of the chamber. He erected himself away from the meter high embankment. He squatted, his knees crackling with age as he draped his arms under Tesh's shoulders.

During the struggle Tesh awoke. His eyes lingered to open as his mouth mumbled incoherent ramblings. Tijoa released Tesh's feet upon the embankment, dragging him away from the sacred chamber to carefully lay him upon his back. As Tesh's body contacted the frigid surface cutting into his nerve endings, he reacted and lifted himself awake. The pull of his skin from the sheen floor erupted pain as blushes formed on his back and shoulders at the contact points. Tesh clenched his forehead; breathing and moaning to process the stimuli both physical and spiritual.

Tesh shivered as his thoughts raced. His left arm tingled with a stinging frost flowing upon the golden veins in perfect parallel symmetry. His erratic breathing bordered on hyperventilation as his body was slow to grasp the situation. He burst his eyelids open clenching his jaw with the seething of sufferings.

Tijoa dropped to his knees, embracing the boy's tapered frame with his spindly arms.

"I saw pain."

"Tiasu's winds showed you change. The past, the present. All in Vibration, ever-changing. Nothing rests; not time, not space."

"But I did not see the future." Tesh's breathing slowed to normal, his jaw relaxing into a confused stasis of intoxicated calm.

"The future you see comes later, but not this Trial. If your soul is ready, you will welcome it."

Tesh turned his head towards Tijoa, meeting the man's bright blue eyes, the window to his atonement.

"You must hurry and return to Cadeck. The rest of your Trials await you."

The pair rose to their feet. Tesh hurried to gather his clothes and apply them to his body. Tijoa ritualistically clothed himself beginning with the white linens covering his body lifting his trousers in sacred fashion to cover his nakedness. With each action, he recited a prayer before placing the undershirt upon his chest. The ceremony completed with the drop of his azure robes. He moved towards Tesh who concluded his wardrobe to place on the fur-lined boots. Tesh draped the shoulder strap to the sword sheath across his chest as Tijoa placed a calm hand upon his face.

"I was wrong about you. You have proven me wrong to Cadeck and to my god. I permit Æiutherion to return you to Cadeck. When you return, take what you need from my home to aide on the rest of the journey."

"Thank you," Tesh smiled. He hesitated but embraced the Magi with a tight hug.

"Before you leave, I must grant you the Blessing of Wind."

Tijoa embraced his palms against Tesh's cranium, chanting in ancient speech a calming soliloquy of verse to which Tesh heard all too familiar from Cadeck and Philos. As the others before Tijoa, the words silenced his memories, stilled him into a lull to cherish his birthright culminating in a stinging release along his left hand which glowed with a cooling blue color.

Returning to Common Tongue, he patted Tesh on the shoulder, "Rescue the girl, Tesh. Cadeck's children are the future of Roth and of our line."

Chapter 32

Howling winds rolled through the pristine valley, pushing from cliffs and jutting mountains towards the calm occupation of a small hut. Faded black smoke rose from the thick thatch surrounding the chimney outlet reaching into the star-studded heavens above. Tijoa's hut stood like a silent guard upon the snow blankets as winds hammered against the windowpanes shuttering the occupants from the predatory winds outside. Nighttime sky littered with stars like specks of sand upon the beach invaded by a solitary void stretching from north to south splitting the sky in clear demarcation.

Cadeck rested his body in the small chair at the foot of a mattress on the right side of the room. His head leaned backward; snores crept from his forming beard. Kenat rested upon the dense mattress beside him, propping his left leg upon cushions. His legs were bare, a tourniquet strapped around his upper left thigh as white goo hardened into his injury near his knee. Venna sat upright, leaning her head onto his shoulder. Strands of golden, matted hair clung against her bruised and mottled face. Her arms folded against her chest.

Eris straddled the bench upon the other wall, her legs split sideways along the width of the bench seat as she propped herself upon the back wall. Her head rested close to the window banging with the winds. In the backroom, Ysalir stood silent watching guard over the occupants.

She leaned her back against a sturdy armoire made from indigenous conewood. Tree rings swirled along the edges and flat surfaces as fresh as its cut. She admired the sweet taste of the wood hitting her nose, a smell she had become accustomed to during her tenure in Silvetzen. Her tunics exposed her arms; a fresh gauze tightened around her bicep covering slathered ointments spread into her wound.

Cassica snoozed on Tijoa's bed underneath a torn woolen blanket scarcely enough to protect her from the biting cold creeping in from outside. The cold airs fought the warmth of the hearth shared between the rooms. Logs and coals lit the stone furnace splitting the walls reaching up the chimney stack. Ysalir dug the edge of her knife into her fingernails starting with her index finger and meticulously eyeing each one as she performed her cleaning in the pale light filtering from the single lamp in the living space. Cassica's breathing hastened, her body twitching from nervous impulses scratching the hay below her.

Ysalir slowed the cleaning on her right ring finger and studied the movements of the young woman as she twisted in her sleep. Ysalir turned her head towards the living space to study Kenat and Venna within sight. Cadeck slept on the chair at the edge of her view. Cassica stuttered inaudible speech in her dreams which Ysalir ignored tossing it off as nothing of importance.

Cassica's mind wandered towards visions untamed. Thrusts of carnal pleasure hammered betwixt her thighs. Her wrists and ankles bound with her legs spread eagle propped upon a velvet cushion with her back on a cold slab. Whimpers and cries went unnoticed with each thrust. Pains shot through every nerve fiber as a thousand knives sliced across her abdomen in sweeping motions simultaneously, cutting and twisting their way across her pelvis via her womb. Through her pains, the chiseled face of a man focused into her sight.

Raven hair graced upon her pale face mingling with her crimson strands like a symphony of oil and water. Cut and carved like a pristine statue, the chest and torso of the man above her scraped upon her supple bosom and toned abdomen in a harmony of perfect unison. Vermillion silk snaked along her backside and draped across her arms. Scant clothing exposed her frontal nudity in lascivious display.

Tears streamed down her cheeks; the sting unbearable with the perverse, yet godlike man pummeling her loins. Soft voices spoke to her amidst the pains of a crying child. Restrained in movement, she battled to glance around seeing only empty vacuum. Cassica tried to cry, words stopped short of leaving her breath. A soft hand wafted over her forehead attached to pale fingers leading to a bare arm.

Cassica craned her neck to look behind her position. Tattered rags covered the little girl's frame slinking towards her knees as the child stood at her head. A young girl, no older than sixteen. Curled and frazzled strands of brunette fleece draped across her shoulders and darted out from scraggly weaves atop her head. Sleeves were torn from the scarce tunics, holes formed across the neckline. The child laid both hands upon Cassica's forehead gracing her temples with soothing relaxations with the flush of warm water spilling through the digits.

Do not fear.
What is this? What is going on, I cannot speak. Where am I?
It is only a vision, Cassica. This is not happening to you, but to me.
What are you, who are you?
You do not know me, but you travel with my father.

Cadeck?

Yes. You must stay with Azthar Kherdmon, lest harm fall upon you.

How? What is going on?

He fulfills the prophecy. A prophecy which you share.

Me? I do not understand.

In time you will. I must go. They will be angry for what I have done.

Waves cascaded around Cassica as she laid spread upon the cold altar. As drowned by a waterfall, Cassica struggled to breathe through thick waters crashing onto her open body. Her breaths shortened, suffocating, gasping to clench for air yet she could not move. Water filled through her dreams as she burst awake with screaming pains like torrid torture coursing through her abdomen.

Ysalir dropped her blade at the cries of pain leaving her liege and rushed to sit beside her embracing the woman with her arms. Cassica huddled into Ysalir's bosom and collapsed into her shirt. Cassica's arms tucked against her face, curled digits constricted into a premature fist with her agonizing sobs. Puffy lips opened with teeth agape, strands of saliva strings ripped apart in her mouth. Cassica's legs stiffened into a rigorous state, her face turned pale as the sheets started to stain with blood seeping from between her legs.

"Wrem."

Cadeck shouted from the front room. Kenat's voice followed in a curdling scream as he shot up to full seat. Both Magi sat upright, motionless, and rigid in blank stare to their own deaths amongst oblivion. In the dimmed light dancing from the candles their erect bodies appeared as dead men resurrected by curse. Venna could only scream as loud as the piercing of shattered glass. The young Magi stiffened in agony to the magick filling over his body in the form of fire flames along his arms, hands, and spine.

She turned to see Cadeck engulfed in electrical arcs of light spanning the same extremities. Venna scampered backwards towards the bedroom screaming the names of the two Magi. Ysalir cried her sister's name as the younger girl stumbled to stand, her feet clamored upon the wooden floor haunted by a pair of revenant madmen looking to assault her. Matted and snarled, her blonde hairs clung against her face and chemise.

She breeched the threshold to the single bedroom, pawing her hands against the frame and walls. She flung around, reaching for the door frame stepping further away from the horror spectacle only to find no door to which to close her from the fright. No sooner than she stumbled into the back room, she turned to see the bloody sheets wrapped around Cassica's legs.

Venna's mouth took in the horror before her eyes could fully awaken and released a startled scream jolting her eyes to full attention as the copper stench of bloodied sheets fully engulfed her senses. Her innocence destroyed, she could only cower against the frame, falling with her head between her knees as she drowned the cries out with her own screams.

"Cadeck come quick," Ysalir commanded unaware of his condition.

Cassica coddled into her embrace. Her sobs slowed to pained whispers as she clutched her left hand against her abdomen, her right hand entwined against her face with Ysalir's hug. Venna ceased her screams, her mind hypnotized into a silent panic as her body turned rigid from the horrors before her. Her breaths turned to hyperventilation.

"Venna, calm down," Ysalir worked to silence her sister, "Don't be alarmed, you've bled before."

"But not like that."

Venna slowed her reaction in voiced sobs, pointing to the flowing blood soaking the blankets.

Ysalir studied her gaze near Cassica's legs, what began as a steady trickle flushed into a raging torrent of flow. She called for Cadeck's name once more to hear no answer.

"Eris," she issued in command.

"The Magi," the younger girl stammered her voice from the other room, "What's happening?"

"Your Princess, she's in trouble, come to her side," Ysalir ordered.

Cassica pawed her fingers into Ysalir's chest, pulling at her as the pains continued through her abdomen, "We need Cadeck, Venna. Get him."

"But he's," Venna turned her eyes widened towards the small door frame separating the rooms to see the Magi eased into relaxation.

Cadeck's palm rested against his head as his breaths returned. Kenat slumped over onto the mattress unaffected by the searing flames which had spilled over his hands a few moments before.

"My head," Cadeck moaned.

Cadeck surveyed the tattered tunics covering his body and the peasant rot trousers over his legs. He spotted a touch of blood into the fabric over his thigh. He reached to his nostril, dabbing his index finger to the top of his lip, feeling a spot of blood trickle evacuating his nose. Swift to cover his face, he stood to see Venna pouting in the back room and the noise of Ysalir calming those around. He turned to see Eris clamoring for anything to fend off whatever affected the Magi which in his own thoughts knew would be a feeble attempt.

Cadeck sauntered into the breezeway, struggling in pain to the physical torture and the spiritual beating he had endured. His left arm aided his limping leg as Ysalir's face flushed with fear.

354

"This is foul magick, Magi." Ysalir grunted through clenched teeth, "Killing the Si'rai wizard cursed her."

"Do not spout tongue you cannot recant, Ysalir," He struck her a scolding stare, wiping his hand over his nostrils, "His death was a necessary means to an end."

"Venna," Cadeck glanced downward to the young blonde, "you and Eris grab some clean sheets and padding; we need to stop the hemorrhaging."

Venna stood agape, her body rigid with fear.

"Go now," he shouted.

Go now.

Father. Please come help me.

Cassica strained her neck to see Cadeck's worry as he approached her bedside. Cadeck reached his hands upon her palms, sliding his calloused fingers over her own roughened hands, his fatherly approach turned her eyes from fear to an exasperated calm. Her legs cramped as pounded by hammers, the sounds of child-like voices echoing as pulsating pain. Venna darted away. Ysalir's hands entwined within Cassica's sanguine locks like twigs caught in a river.

Father.

Cassica heard the closed voice scream once more through her mind. No. *What is this? Who is this? Why are you here?*

Please, you must let me speak to father.

I do not want this. Leave me.

No please. I must tell him.

The girl's voice cut off to silence before the feminine laughter of insanity rolled through Cassica's soul like the voice of one thousand whores.

I AM risen.

"She's not going to die, is she?" Ysalir's eyes started to tear, "She is our future Queen, our leader. What if what the foul wizard says was true?"

Ysalir's mind formed doubts of her own confidence.

"We do not know, Ysalir. Concern should be for her returning to health."

Venna and Eris returned with matted sheets and torn pillows taken from the resting spots the occupants used. Cadeck motioned the pair to remove the soiled rags and replace them with the cleaner coverings. Venna worked to seal the blood flow by applying a clean white sheet between Cassica's legs.

"Venna, what are you doing? You are still an orange, you must not be near Her Highness' chastity," Ysalir barked.

Cadeck returned to scorn. Anger roiled in his face as Ysalir reverted to protocol for the maidens, "You're going to compromise her life over trivial procedure?"

"She is the Commandant of the Order of the Rose and future Queen of Sarat, only her maidens of yellow rank are permitted to tend to her."

"Right now, Venna and Eris act as her maidens. A few moments ago, you were concerned over her death. You cannot risk her life over trite drama."

Cadeck stood to his feet, "Ysalir, incline her abdomen above her chest. Use the pillows and other padding. This will help the blood flow return to her heart."

Ysalir steadied her hands and set Cassica calmly to lie onto the bed with her back. She worked with the younger ladies to raise Cassica. Cassica quietly groaned as the ladies comforted her with the pillows. Ysalir instructed the ladies to be careful. With Cassica's bent knees upon a propped pillow, Ysalir buttressed Cassica's back to be more comfortable with a wadded fur blanket. Cassica's breathing returned to a standard pace, convulsions in her chest and loins ceased as Venna cooled her head with a wet cloth.

Cadeck removed himself from the triage towards the single door and through the cramped quarters of Tijoa's hut, skirted past Kenat who huddled in his own arms. He yanked the satchel resting on the chair he called his bed and hurried towards the door. Cold winds bit into the cabin as Cadeck exited with a slam.

Ysalir rose from her crouched position and informed the pair to remain at their stations. Her trouser legs flowed to gravity, flitting in the calm breezes entering the back room. Kenat rested his head against the cold wall, his arms hugged his chest in the best way he could to enter the fetal position. She fitted a fur covering over her shoulders and cracked the wooden door to exit.

Cadeck stood outside, a few meters in front of the chopping block with his head cocked towards the sky as a strike of ruban stench filled the air. His mouth muttered vile curses towards a woman's name he only spoke of in the tongue of magick before taking a puff of his pipe. The prevalent band of darkness stretched through the night like a border on a map. The shadow of the moon's mask positioned in precise alignment with the empty void. Stars avoided the band of the Abyss like men to lepers. Crunches of snow and slush rang through Cadeck's ears, his head unwavering from his studious gaze.

"You addressed my true name in front of Cassica, Cadeck," her voice lowered in apprehensions towards the fact.

"Trivial formality, Ysalir. There is something far greater at hand. This is what I feared."

"What?"

"Above us, look at how the stars avoid it if death awaits them there, like they too know the harbinger around them. The moon is empty, crossing the dark Abyss above."

"Stories tell change comes with the Abyss. When man sees the Abyss, the Abyss changes him."

"Partially true Ysalir. But what makes tonight special is the moon is vacant in the sky. It has gone dark in time for its new birth. The stars speak the voice of the gods."

"I do not follow. The moon always goes dark around the twenty-eighth day."

Cadeck lowered his face to match hers as she stood to his right side. A waft of ruban smoke spilled from his pipe end to the lit ambers filtered from the holding basin. Ysalir's brunette hairs sauntered in the cold winds lit by a solitary lamp burning by the front door.

"Tonight, would have been my daughter's fifteenth cycle of the low sun. She was born on a night with no moon, not much different than tonight, when the dark band across the sky appeared just over the eastern horizon. Now it appears at its peak, a night the Aztmi refer as Astunox Graa, a night of absolute darkness, the Death Moon. Prophecies say when the Abyss has reached its apex, the gods go to war. As do the gods above, so does man below. May the gods watch over my children on this accursed night."

Ysalir brushed a cold whip of her bangs from her face. Cadeck's concern for his daughter touched at her heart with a spark of sorrow, "The Si'rai have looked forward to this night. The soldiers would speak of it as it were to be a religious fervor."

Ysalir's eyes trailed towards the horizon ahead touched by the kiss of starlight upon the snow, "This is a night of high libations known as the Drahak Abra'in in their tongue. They believe it is when their magick returns to the world when the moon is dark, and the Abyss rises high. They will mark this night with the coronation of a new queen," she turned back towards Cadeck, his face dropped towards the ground below. Her words fell like an empty sack upon the snow.

"Strong magick falls upon Roth this evening. Let it not curse us anymore than it already has."

"Tell me, in seclusion of solitude, could Si'rai magick have laid foul curse upon Cassica?"

"The hunter we killed was weak amongst his own, easy to remove and to have detected, but what befell Cassica eludes me. Did you not learn of their magick amongst their company?"

"I never saw Tivius perform any magick. Their soldiers spoke of it, only in the style of a myth."

"It's said their magick relies on the cold death of good hearts," a harsh wind shot across Cadeck's whiskery cheeks; "My children are alone without me. The longer they suffer, the more I fear."

Cadeck turned towards the hut to trudge through the slushy snow leaving Ysalir to the coldness of the north.

"Cadeck please, do not let my words bring sorrow to your ears."

Cadeck turned over his shoulder towards the brunette woman where ice accumulated over her eyebrows, "It is unwise to underestimate the gift of magick, more so theirs. The sacrifice you made to Sarat brings you honor, your words do not fall upon sorrow but only motivation."

#

Fur coverings bundled around Venna's head masking her face against the chilled winds blowing from the northwest. Strands of her golden blonde hair escaped in front of her forehead as though fleeing from entrapments. Lined with warm fleece covering her frail body to her feet, she stood next to the south wall of Tijoa's hut. The Si'rai war horse towered over her like a giant beast prepared to consume her. Sturdy reins tied the animal to a steady post rigged into the ground with makeshift skill. The reins wrapped around a sturdy crossbeam bolted to a pair of stakes hefted deep into the ground. With each strain of the horse's weight, the poles softened the slushy mud.

"My words the other day, Venna, I meant no harm."

Venna shook her head as she turned to a pile of hay beside the animal, "I didn't plan on spending Founder's Day in the middle of nowhere."

Venna ignored Ysalir and reached into the pile of hay beside her and wrapped her arms around a bundle of loose straw, offering it to the animal.

"Venna, did you hear me?"

Venna ignored Ysalir.

"What is it Cadeck is making again? Stew. Last year I had a full feast at the Academy. Stew is for the commoners."

"Venna," Ysalir grunted her voice to scorn, "I made apologies."

Venna continued her spite and moved in closer to the beast. Black as night with searing teeth sharpened and whittled for defense, the animal scoffed at her with flared nostril breaths. Whiffing the offering, the beast lunged for the food with a beastly grunt and nipped at the sleeves of Venna's gloved hand pinching at the finger as she pulled it away. Strands of hay filtered onto the ground like a steady loft of sifted dirt drifting into the muddy slush at her feet. The beast hoofed into the muddy snow snarling with hungry delight as it dropped its head to consume the treats.

"I don't think it likes me," she snarled at the beast, sharing mutual disdain.

Ysalir attempted to laugh but felt it better not to lighten the mood. She could sense Venna's ire with the world collapsing around her. She feared her distrust. Of anyone, Venna should be wise to trust her yet in this world she grew into, trust seemed scarce and Ysalir sensed this. Embraced in copious coverings of fur warmth she stood below the horse's shoulder at her height. Ysalir stroked the right side of the animal's neck in soothing manner ruffling her fur-gloved hands across the beast's hide. Thin hairs covered the beast's neck in ritual shaved decoration.

"Perhaps, it doesn't care too much for us white skins. Besides, these horses were not meant to be gifts for a young woman, but as a warrior's steed."

"I once wanted a horse for my Maiden's Day," Venna responded, "Instead, I received my Orange Petal. Had I a horse such as this, my, my," her voice trailed into whisper, admiring the beast's musculature for its form as bred and trained.

Ysalir smiled and continued the soft massage along the beast's muscular hides, stretching her arms across the girth of the abdominal muscles. The bulk of the animal struck through her nerves, her mind recalled the nightly pleasantries she eloped with her lover in Silvetzen. The muscles of the beast flashed to her the chiseled chest of training which she laid upon on that forlorn night. Soaked with emotional drain, she removed herself from the chore and stepped around the front of the animal's head and behind the hitching rack.

"Venna, we should leave the horse be. I will have to get him ready to hitch to the cart when Tesh returns," her head gazed into the open horizon to the south, "If he returns."

"How do you mean, if he returns?"

"I do not trust Tijoa. He strikes me odd. You saw how he acted towards us who were not Magi? Yet you were so quick to trust Cadeck when you met him? Mother and Father raised you never to trust Magi and likewise you learned within the Academy."

Ysalir led Venna with her hand upon her sister's shoulder before she shrugged her off.

"Cadeck caught me spying on them back in Telmen. He questioned me and I," Venna swallowed her next thought, "told him everything."

Ysalir could see Venna's embarrassment blush. Venna's uncovered eyes lowered within the fur shroud covering her face. Ysalir laughed at her sister's admittance, "I see why Cadeck joked about your shortcomings."

"No, it is not funny. It was my first job since I received color. I am just an embarrassment. I do not deserve my color, nor the Order."

"Do you think you failed the Order?"

Venna paused at her sister's question. They approached the wood frame door leading into Tijoa's hut. Crisp winds blew as wicked gales from the northwest. Ysalir and Venna cuddled close to one another as they stood in stance to fight the violent gusts.

"Please do not tell Cassica, Ysalir. She will deny me any advancement."

"Venna, I would not worry about it. We are this far and Cassica has learned quite a bit about the Silvetzenian treaty with the Si'rai. You served your role."

Ysalir gripped the curved iron handle and twisted it to enter Tijoa's hut. Ysalir and Venna slid within and quickly closed the portal behind them. Flecks of snow flurries followed with a rush of cold chill encasing the pair. Fiery warmth greeted them as Cadeck huddled over the twin stove in the far side of the entry room. A stew bubbled in a pot aerating the room with salty smells of seasoned poultry and the sweet tender broil of meat broth.

Kenat sat upright on the bed to the right side of the room. He propped his bare, left leg on a burlap pillow stuffed with hay as he fidgeted with the orange stone scarred with streaks of blackened sear within his fingers. White undergarments rolled up close to his groin on his left leg while his right covered with the full length of his protective vestments. A white shirt clothed all but his arms.

These were the protective garments fitting his body before his sacred robes. To the Magi, they symbolized the purity of his soul to accept the craft of which he was to undertake. The sacred robe of his order set the Magi to others to denote their connection. Each Magi wore a distinct color corresponding to the ancient spectrum of their followed deity. As the Magi took his sacramental robe over his body, the purity of his soul symbolized by the white underwear prepared him spiritually to master the requirements of the vestments. Robe and underwear completed his ensemble, offering covenant to wield the powers of his god.

Ysalir removed the fur hood from her head and untied the wrap covering her mouth and nose. Brunette hair clung to the static trappings, crinkling, and sparking as the fur pulled away. Falling loose and disheveled, her unwashed hair slid over her face and down onto her shoulders.

"How is Her Highness?"

Venna followed suit and removed her hood as Ysalir commanded her question to Cadeck. Cadeck lifted the spoon from the pot to inhale a slow sip to test the warmth and spices of the food. He tapped the wooden receptacle against the iron pot and rested it onto a counter space to his right. Cadeck turned his head to glance over his left shoulder.

"She is fine. Eris has tended to her this morning, and she is talking again. How is the war horse doing?"

Cadeck reached for a rag hanging from a wooden loop above the stove and used it to wipe his hands and the spoon. He placed it onto the counter and rested the spoon on top of the towel.

"It took a while, but I was able to break him this morning. He was hesitant, vicious, and nearly bit Venna's hand as we fed him."

"I'm alright though," Venna chimed in as she made her way to sit next to Kenat.

She removed her fur gloves and the overcoat covering her frail shoulders. Plain tunics covered her torso leading over a pair of loose legged pants stretching to her ankles. A light-hearted smile shorn from puffed lips towards the Magi, accentuated by doe-eyes of a crisp blue like the waters of a summer lake. Her blonde hair frazzled and frayed from the earlier release of static pulling from her fur coverings.

She muffled her hands into her hair in a vain attempt to make it presentable. Venna's graceful hands stroked the healed scars sealed upon Kenat's cheek and forehead. Kenat's pearly irises closed with a grin welcoming her soft touch as he clutched the stone within his palm.

"Venna," Ysalir shot a disparaging stare as her sister made affection towards Kenat, "What did I tell you about Kenat? What did I tell you about the Magi?"

Cadeck craned his neck over his right shoulder to watch as Venna jerked her body away from Kenat and pouted at her sister's reprimand.

"We should leave soon," Cadeck urged, "Ysalir, can you make sure Cassica can walk?"

"What about Tesh?"

Ysalir burst as she felt Cadeck's tone did not imply concern.

Cadeck dropped his head towards the bubbling stew. Pops and gurgles released seasoned steam towards his aging face as solemnity gripped his heart.

"They've been gone nearly a week," Cadeck dropped his voice, concern rolled through him as a limp dog begging for its mercy, "If he's failed the Trials, then we must be able to rely on Trebut for aide."

"But what the bad wizard said," Venna opened her mouth.

Cadeck extended his right arm upward with an outstretched index finger. He turned back over his shoulder and twisted his body to look towards the young woman. Empty and torn, the pits and crevices ripped across his face appeared more solemn and forlorn. A full-face beard covered the scars and marks of age around his chin and cheeks. His hazel eyes emptied of hope and turned into a vacant stare of collapsed worth.

"We do not express what he said within earshot of Her Highness," Cadeck whispered with lecturing undertones through gritted teeth.

Kenat reached his left arm to wrap around Venna's shoulders as she took a double shot of stark commands within a few moments of each other.

"Kenat. You are a Magi. Remember your vows."

Ysalir turned face towards Cadeck whose raised voice escalated into contempt. For the time, the pair acted as protective parents. He towards Kenat, she towards Venna.

"Vows?"

Kenat's voice rose in heightened intonation. He removed his arm from the young lady and scooted towards the edge of the bed. His face winced as pain tore through his left thigh with the applied pressure from the edge of the mattress. He struggled to lift onto his legs as he limped onto his right leg to balance pressure.

"What can you tell me about vows, Cadeck?"

Kenat stood on his feet shifting his weight onto his right side.

"Wasn't it you who betrayed the vows of the Magi? Wasn't it you who caused us to be in this mess? Because of your acts, Philos is dead," Kenat's palm tightened around the stone in his hand, "This was the Heart of Heseph, the fire from his power, scarred by the death of its holder, now nothing but a worthless stone."

His palms opened as he moved towards Cadeck's space, revealing the relic resting within a pair of skin lines upon his hand.

"Kenat, sit back down. Keep your leg rested. We will need you at full strength if we are to meet other Si'rai," Cadeck urged him with commanding tone.

"Cadeck, was it not you who betrayed the Council, made union with another Magi, and raised children; a clear violation of the vows with which you took? And you are going to tell me about the vows of chastity I promised?"

Kenat gripped the stone tight once more.

"Kenat."

Cadeck turned to face the stew pot, hunkered over the stove. Warm steam curled into his face. The younger man's words weighed onto his heart with stressful pains which his age took no welcome to bear. He calmed himself to speak slow and rational, taking heed to keep his pain held within.

"Do not remind me of burden which we all bear. Honor this day for Founders and keep tongue still."

"Cadeck, do not accuse me of what you yourself are guilty of."

"I demanded you to calm your tongue."

Amidst the commotion, Eris' slender frame darted from the back room. Ragged brunette locks flaked down the sides of her cheeks and draped along her shoulders to mid-back. She propped herself against the edge of the breezeway with her left palm. Ysalir leaned against the edge of the single table while Venna had sat upon the edge of the mattress in the living quarters. Venna's lips puffed with bubbling tears boiling in her clear blue eyes.

Eris interrupted the interaction between the pair of Magi, "Her Highness demands to know the circumstances of the commotion."

Cadeck resigned his thoughts, releasing his breath as a sigh through his salty beard, "Inform Cassica there is nothing more Kenat and I must discuss. Let her ready for Founder's Dinner, it is a day for praise and thanks; a day to honor her ancestors."

Cadeck returned his gaze towards the younger Magi and with a grimaced sneer forced his way towards the door, "The stew is ready, if you care to eat."

Cadeck approached the single-entry door and with a heft of his might, the iron latches crackled in disarray as he exited the room and slammed the door with a loud smash behind him. Kenat watched him as he trotted away, disbelief washed across his face as he turned to each of the women in the room. Ysalir and Venna shared the same dismayed reaction towards Kenat as they scooted behind him to grab a pair of bowls and dipped them into the stew pot.

Before Venna could dip her bowl, a hurling shriek rolled across the valley sending drifts of snow slamming against the north wall of Tijoa's hut. An explosion of white powder shook the small home knocking Venna and Ysalir into a quick clutch as they braced against the counter surface near the stove. Kenat tumbled onto the floor, his hands gripped his wounded leg as the vibrations flustered his nerves along his left thigh. Eris straddled the left brace of the breezeway frame before falling onto her knees, her right facial cheek taut with her tightened grip against the edge of the border.

Outside, Cadeck collapsed onto his knees with the violent flow of winds slamming into the yard. Snow flecked into his ragged tunics as the hurricane winds carried gusts of snow drifts rolling across the valley. Cadeck slammed his palms against his ears as another roar rippled across the open dell. Saliva stretched across his gaped teeth as the shrieks from above drowned out his own screams. The Si'rai horse bucked and kicked to release its reins from the post but resigned with frightened failure, stomping into the slush with its heavy feet.

Cassica rolled herself from the bed. Her hands covered her abdomen over a single shirt ending mid-thigh. She paused as her feet touched the cool floor and winced as she lifted to walk. Another shriek covered the sounds of the home, rocking Cassica to collapse onto her knees and fall to her left side. Pain ripped through her torso exploding as a loud scream only to be unheard as the occupants ignored her, covering their ears from loud screeches like a thousand trumpets blaring through the two-room house.

Æiutherion's wings flapped with the force of gales as he slowed his descent into the valley. Each burst of his crystalline appendages blazed snow-filled winds against Tijoa's hut as the dragon lowered his altitude onto the ground many meters north of the abode. As his momentum slowed to land, three of his crystal skinned legs propped his massive weight onto the slushed ground, digging into the soft mush with the imprints of reptilian feet. Sharp claws measured several feet in length clutched into the deep ground carving trenches into the muddy slush.

The dragon's right claw clutched tight, bent against his extended chest above the limbs attached to his wings. He craned his elongated neck towards the ground, watching as the Magi of Light shuddered to lift to his feet. Æiutherion blinked his reptilian eyes with curious stare while he observed Cadeck brush the snowflakes from his hands and beard. The door to Tijoa's hut sprung wide with Ysalir leading the exit charge.

Cold winds filtered through her brunette hair as she sheltered her hands upon her shoulders to warm them from the biting gusts. She rushed to Cadeck's side to aid the man to his knees. He clutched his right shoulder and through squinted eyes brushed by chilly winds marveled at the beast returning glare.

Ysalir followed his stare only to step over herself backwards in her surprise. Venna ran to the pair followed by Kenat who limped towards the freezing cold. Venna's blue eyes widened like the pristine waters of a river as she stared in shock at the crystalline dragon towering above the home. Skin shimmered in sunlight as a jeweled tower with spread wings. Æiutherion lowered his neck and with steady gait, he moved on three legs towards the fleshy creatures. Each step shook the ground as he treaded lightly, limiting his weighty stature to prevent the humans from falling.

Æiutherion stopped several hundred meters from the house and lowered his right claw. With the brush of powdered ice, his sheer blue claws opened with a tornado of snow-filled wind. As the whirlwind lowered to calm, Tesh lied in the fetal position within the palm of the dragon's reptilian claws. With staggered repose, the young man steadied to his feet, his right knee buckling in the chilled air. Tesh caught his weakness, rising with strained momentum.

Tesh's face wore twisted with pain and emotion. He shifted his weight to walk along the middle index claw resting into a crevice carved into the snowy mud. He dropped the few feet onto the ground, bracing his hands against the frigid blue appendage. His knees slid along the crystalline hide in near catatonic repose, his legs limp and body light of breeze. As he landed on his feet, Tesh's sword slinked along his back as his gravity shifted with the short fall. He lifted himself in the cold winds and staggered away from the mighty beast with a confident walk. When he cleared Æiutherion's claw with safe distance, the dragon rotated his palm to rest comfortably on his quadruped stance.

Tesh marched towards Tijoa's hut, regaining his tall gait. Gales skated across his hair blowing his bangs against his forehead. Heavy furs covered his shoulders and torso giving him the appearance of a large predator. He strode with proud gait, his arms hung at his sides with minimal swing. He curled and wiggled his fingers with each stride, his breaths syncopated with stout trudge. Icy breaths rolled from his nostrils carving circles into the air as he ignored the fierce winds roaring through the valley. He approached Cadeck, stepping into the icy mud shifting below his fur boots and as Kenat before him, stood to gaze at the older Magi.

"We have much to discuss, Cadeck," Tesh's voice was short and terse, reaching to his point of discussion without hesitation, "There is not much time. We should hurry to the next Temple."

Tesh turned his attention from Cadeck as his confidence harried past Ysalir and the younger adults who made clearance for him as he entered the warm confines of Tijoa's hut. Cadeck turned towards the dragon, his thoughts of concern for what Tesh may have experienced at the Wind Temple.

"What happened to him dragon?"

Cadeck spoke in common speech. His beard ruffled in breezes slowing to calm.

Æiutherion paused. Matters of the Primordials were above the concern of men and for a mortal to question his authority shuddered the beast. The dragon craned his neck towards the older Magi meeting his elongated snout to approach the front of the Wind Magi's home. His horny outgrowths lowered into passive stance to rest against the parallel of his beak.

"The Azthar Kherdmon has observed events of which there is no explanation," his voice rippled through Cadeck's soul in ancient tongue, paced slow as though time was an afterthought to him, "All doubt as to his legacy is no longer of concern. The Winds as they always do to other Initiates have changed him.

"However, I do have concern without a suitable Water Magi, by your own admitted transgressions Cadeck, his Trials may fail. To fulfill his lineage, one must administer the Trial of Water. Only with all seven Trials completed can we know if he is the Azthar Kherdmon. Failing his Trials, he will be of no use in this Aeon."

"Is this a… dragon?" Venna inquired, interrupting Cadeck's thoughts of speech as he communicated to the beast.

"Ysalir, take your sister inside. Allow Kenat and myself to talk to the dragon."

"Sorry Cadeck. This one is all yours."

Kenat shook his head, lifting his hands and entered the home with the women to permit Cadeck and Æiutherion to be alone.

Cadeck pulled to his thoughts. His mind raced towards his children and their uncertainty. His own actions caused the demise of his ways, his imprisonment and his offspring's pain. The dragon's speech spited him in tone. Kenat's outburst became a reaction of his own coercion and the need to carry the Magi lineages. By obsolete traditions, Kenat suffered too.

"I can find a way to have him train dragon and finish his trials. I have heard Jess call for me to the Temple of Water; I sense her presence when I pray. He will succeed, dragon, and my children must restore the Council."

Æiutherion lowered his head to meet the magic user. Bony outgrowths flared to full erection along the lining of his beak, "Your children will not restore the Council. The Council is dead, a curse by your Ascended's own greed. There is a future for your children, but it does not involve your Council. Guide them to Truth as the gods ordained. Your blood is the key, Cadeck. It was the Aztmi who hoarded their powers and their gifts, your children will see the truth.

"Your undying love for Jess is a testament to your species. I have felt, through the ripples of my own aztmudin, her love and pain, her loss and gain. She is strong. She will guide you and the Azthar Kherdmon for the truth, for the beginning of this Aeon. Do not believe your sin has caused pain to Roth, consider them the pangs of birth for Roth to be reborn as the gods intended."

Æiutherion's claw pawed next to Cadeck as he shifted balance soft into the snow, "If her aztmudin is as strong as I have felt, then even in death, she can provide this incarnation of the Azthar Kherdmon his Trials. I give your species credit, Magi. You are resilient and your confidence belies your failures. I must return to my Temple, Tijoa begins prayer to prepare himself for his servitude."

"Is he returning here?"

"No."

The dragon squat on his four knees and lifted himself into the air with a heave. As he gained height many meters above the hut, his wings flapped and lifted him into the sky. He circled the valley with an aerodynamic glide before thrusting his wings to gain speed and with an ear-shattering shriek, broke sonic speed towards the northern glaciers.

Chapter 33

Cold screams of horrid trepidation ripped through still, moonless air. Violent throes of torture echoed amidst the steaming embers of smoldered buildings and darkened alleyways. Tivius A'zum surveyed his destruction from a grand balcony jutting from a towering precipice of the Saratian royal estate. His left forearm leaned against the stone rail. Naked frail frame remained in the shadows of soft torch light glistening behind him casting ethereal glow upon his pale skin.

Tivius studied the city fallen before him. The final throes of his assault catapulted Sarat into a celebration of chaos. Like a flittering ghost, Tivius' feet skirted across an elaborate design set into the terrazzo. Pieced by small tiles, a gold-tinted herald of the Saratian two-headed eagle centered into the picture laid over a white background of tiles tickling his feet with a coarse texture. Tivius stood proud of the violence, his crimson spackled phallus reflective of the sinister grin on his face.

More yelps pierced into the nighttime air jerking Tivius' head into the direction, recalling icy cruelties imprinted upon his mind from youth. He gazed upon his opus of chaos, tracing his fingers across the balustrade. Static, circular columns stood at attention to support the carved rampart, the center column in even number etched with the Saratian herald facing Tivius at his thigh level. The dark stillness of quiet clouds raised above, creeping along the sky to cover the span of the Abyss splitting the symmetry of the stars. Fabric ruffled below him. A Si'rai banner clung to the bottom of the balcony stirring in calm breeze, its herald emblazoned in dark blood hue against a raven backdrop. Its very sight invoked thoughts of fear as evidence by those whom he dominated.

Tivius traced his spindly fingers across the scarred crevices painted across his body in broad strokes like a maniacal canvas. The largest scar cut below his ribcage, a testament to a brutal slash endured in a violent encounter decades ago. Lanterns emptied their shadowy light upon the balcony over his pale and slinky naked form.

Moans of youth interrupted his thoughts pouring through the bedroom behind him. He jerked his head with snarled sneer in response to the noise. He stood silent. A fondness tore into his emotions as he recalled the touch of a former lover. A lover who fell in the arena, a lover presented by him to his father as a prized acolyte. A lover who failed their emperor.

Each action, each conquest, and each order he undertook for his father he meant to erase his father's displeasure. With each action, he found embarrassment and disappointment. His conquest of Sarat was proof of his worth. Through his vizier, the Revered Magister, his father commissioned fifty-thousand soldiers to support him and weeks after his arrival, during a quiet seizure of the royal palace and its grounds, Sarat was his as well was the teenage boy shuffling in Trebut's bed.

The boy stirred with slurred groans as Tivius' lithe, naked form returned into the torch lit room. Lantern light illuminated the tightened, sculpted muscles on Tivius' frame. Arcane and sinister within his new quarters, the visage of Tivius' pale, scarred body stirred the shadows into unease. Thick curtains flapped cautiously as the mirror discriminated its reflections almost sentient of Tivius' own appearance.

Tivius approached the canopy bed whose posts rose as tall as he. Fitted, white sheets tucked firmly under the mattress with a thick, woolen blanket dyed with fine lavender scattered above the cushions. Heavy pillows positioned at the headrest, rotund as a firm pig. Sprawled crosswise across the width of the mattress, a young man lay spread-eagle upon his stomach. Blood thickened with semen trickled between the young gluteus of the boy, staining the sanctity of the white sheets below him.

"Where am I," a slow, disillusioned grunt evacuated his tongue.

Tivius reached towards his scabbard leaning against a decorative stand. Curled posts rested upon the marble floor leading towards a lavish swirl supporting a rounded surface carved from a mahogany wood. Tivius' outstretched digits gripped the onyx sheath reaching close to his height. A cord cobbled close to the guard which bound the weapon into the casing.

A curved hilt of bone wrapped in braided strands of hair, moistened, and sealed long ago, preserving the bone from rotted decay. The quillion was of an unknown make, metal dipped and carved prior to the casting, the material underneath lost to time. Etched upon the quillion shielding his open hands in combat were scripted characters written with precision cut by the maker, carved to the original material beneath the cast. Tivius unbound his weapon and with an ear-piercing shriek, ethereal steel exited the deep housing of the raven case.

He removed the sword in a swift motion, pointing the tip against the back of the young boy's nape. Ghostly glows burned from amber torches mounted on opposite ends of the room, burning their hues upon ancient steel tinted as ice. The flickers of the candlelight in the room tickled the markings seared into the sides of the blade written with an ancient script as carved by magick into steel.

Tivius knew not of its craftsmanship, nor was he fully educated upon its legends except to have found it in a cave commissioned to head an archaeological dig by command of his father, a dig envisioned by dreams since his youth. The words on the sword carried the legend through thousands of years. They spoke to him as from centuries past; the weapon smith who designed this blade foresaw great deeds when wielded properly to the name of their god and with each draw of the blade to strike a foe, Tivius felt its power. Raven hairs settled down Tivius' shoulders, caressing along his pale chest. An icy stare seared bright with displeasure as the extremities of the boy began to twitch.

"By this blade, I forge my destiny," Tivius began in his tongue.

"What do you want from me?"

Cries left the boy's mouth, dry like a desert, as he struggled to lift his neck.

"Your life will be spared should your body remain motionless, and your lips no longer speak," Tivius hissed and continued his prayer, switching to his speech, "By this blade, I honor Hadithem."

Whimpers exited the boy's puffed lips. Tears remained vacant as numb tingles shot through his body. Tivius' foreign speech incited fear into his mind. Were Tivius' words an insult, or were his words a sacred ritual meant to fulfill his desires? The boy felt his extremities twitch under reflex. His torso collapsed and expanded under heated breaths.

"Please, I beg you. Do what you will to me, I am your servant."

Tivius's demeanor remained calm, tickling the hairs on the young man's neck with the icy steel tip of his blade and continued his prayer in Imperium speech, "By this blade, I sacrifice my enemy."

In Common Tongue, Tivius addressed himself to the boy in mocking, boastful tone, "I am Magister Tivius A'zum of the Si'rai Imperium," Tivius' elongated sword flowed as an extension to his buffed arm stretching to meet his shoulder.

"Supernus Commandant of the Fifth Arm of Chaos, Son to the Exalted Supernus Magister, Lucivus A'zum. By the Supreme Lord of the Abyss, Hadithem, I have conquered Sarat and your pitiful sadakem."

Conquest: the word rolled from Tivius' tongue like a collapsing mountain to the boy's ears.

"I have already taken *my* desires boy; your death will be Hadithem's."

Tivius returned to the prayer, "By this blade, all are beneath Him."

Tivius lifted the point of his sword from the boy's neck and with ethereal strength in one swift action he pulled the blade's length away from the boy and penetrated the blade clean like a hot shiv inside the teenage boy's anus. The tip tore through the mouth splitting his tongue in symmetry. With a torrential thrust of quick, painless death, the boy's corpse sauntered and shook to the climax of nerve throes rippling over the flesh.

A wisp of purple mist swirled around the tip point of the blade, twinkling with the luminescence of a preternatural origin. Likewise, another exposure of deep, lavender spray encircled the blade around the entry point of the young man's ass, whirling in small, circular motions to central position around the steel of the blade. Tivius reveled in the slow removal of his weapon from the young boy's impalement. The corpse's neck relaxed into a slouch upon the bed. Crimson spewed from the gaping mouth in a steady drip like water pouring from a cruse.

Swirled marble tainted with liquid death below the boy's head. White sheets folded beneath the lavenders, stained with the flowing river of life exiting from the boy's naked ass. Tivius reached for the stained sheets splattered with fresh spray, held his sword with dull edge facing his chest and swiped it clean with one stroke. With a sloppy lump, the lavender sheet cleaned the blade of any residue as though the metal of the weapon repelled the stain.

He studied the quiet bedroom, eyeing the torn vanity of Trebut's portrait hanging above the fireplace across the room of which he had desecrated many days ago. Trebut's surname, Bovariàr, etched into a gold-plated marker below his portrait. Tivius cursed the image and declared the boy a symbol for Trebut's shame.

He moved towards the head of the cadaver, carrying his extended sword to his side, his left hand gripped the scabbard. As he approached the boy, he dropped into a squat resembling a pair of pale twigs sprouting from a single stump from the ground and sheathed his weapon to rest it at his side. His hair fell in front of his face like raven sackcloth covering a condemned man. Blood oozed from the willowy boy's mouth in steady stream, drip, dripping down the sheets and into a pool upon the marble floor.

Finding pleasure in the victim's pain, Tivius defiled the corpse with his own self-gratification, "By shedding your blood for the Abyss, I present to you my seed so your soul may live in eternal bliss. And with your aztunai, *mine* becomes stronger."

Tivius entered his phallus into the boy's blood-gurgled mouth and relieved himself into the cavity. Reciting ancient prayers borne from ritual, Tivius felt a rush flow through his brain as climactic expulsions released into his victim. Tivius opened an emotional memory to the stinging flows of salty liquid forced into his own throat.

Tivius unleashed a vile scream upon the lavish room. Echoes of horror spilled into the open balcony as his connection to aztunai released his pent-up pain. His spindly fingers intertwined into the boy's hair and with an unsurpassed strength, the cracking and breaking of skull bone shattered into a mushy, fragmented glop around his penis in a symphony of crimson and gray. Pulling away from the damage, he yanked at the head only to detach it from the base of the neckline with a powerful tug. Reaching his anger from the deepest recesses of his soul, he lifted his hands to have the bone-laden goo slip between his fingers as bone shards lingered in his palms.

Tivius clamped his fingers with a gnarled snare, crushing the skull pieces that remained. His fingers discolored from gooey brain matter soaked with crimson blood. He dropped his hands to his sides, streaks of organ matter splattered onto the cold marble. Drips of streaming gore trickled down his fingers as morning dew would leave a leaflet.

He smeared the slimy blood upon his torso and stomach, licking his hands of the matter in a macabre ceremony of crimson. Tivius leaned his neck back, his raven locks flowed behind him as he widened his jaw in a gasp of adrenal orgasm. The culmination of conquest escalated to this point as his mind blurred into comatose memory...

Sarat's pristine walls rose high in the distance as the hijacked wagon carried along the rolling meadows of farmlands flanking the Saratian Road. To Tivius, a ride completed weeks ago turned to distant recollection blurred by ecstasy. Giant towers loomed with their battlements as the azure cart with Saratian livery strolled into the main gates. As the cart lumbered into the city, Tivius recalled the shops bustling with the monotony of labor. Women and men cavorted to beneficiary production while citizens toiled in their open windowed homes above the shop districts below, and oblivious to the activities of the castle looming upon a western steppe.

The people took no notice of the vessel as the rickety wheels turned through the streets leading along the avenue beyond the market districts. Lavish homes erected around the wagon. Ornate columns supported the garish balconies of the upper class in contrast to the sodden poor plowing the outlying fields only for every bit of wealth and opulence to burn in damning blazes. Rows of elite chicanery mocked Tivius' resolve as the cart ventured deeper into the city, rounding streets of brick and garish accoutrements of the high wealth of Sarat's noble-borns.

The cart approached a pair of gates opening inward toward the city flanked by several guards. Massive gates led away from the city towards an intersection running north and south in parallel with the wide river ahead. On either flank of the Saratian Road, another pair of gates closed to seal from the north and southern ends. A secondary pair of gates opened as the first in unison, to lead onto a bridge spanning a river. Soft trickles of pleasant water tickled against rough rocks in the bed as the horse hooves paraded in rhythmic unison to the gentle ruckus.

A majestic bridge spanned the river leading from the city gates towards the castle built upon a steppe. The grade of the bridge lifted it at an angle towards the entrance of the castle at the summit. White rock erected as steps supporting the castle into an elevation rivaling the massive walls. Eons of geological formation built the peak into a soft, stepped pyramid lined with vines and grass in sporadic patches. A gatekeeper greeted the wagon as it left the bridge crossing into the portcullis of the grand courtyard.

A blur of memories washed over the swordsman. Pains of cuts mixed with his soul memories stinging through Tivius' brain with a pulsing power unleashed through the haunting halls as a dangerous beast ravishing its victims. Tivius dropped to his knees amidst Trebut's bedroom, flashes of death loomed before him as his thoughts washed over with a foreign spirit crushing through his skull.

Soldiers protecting the castle fell in swift strokes of his blade cleaved with single cuts as he shorn his blade into flesh and ribs. Several others fought his hardened men in vain attempts ending with their demise. Like a blinding shadow, Tivius' sword guided his actions towards exquisitely decorated halls where his enemy fell swiftly. Onslaughts of armored men felled quickly from his blade, painting the finely lavished walls with blood. He moved like a black wraith, unstoppable, an exterminating angel.

In his attacks, his attention turned towards several of the guard dressed in blue armor, a signifying feature of the assigned protectorate of the royal family as a conglomeration concentrated on shuffling towards the rear of the castle. Following them, he mowed down lesser ranks along the way, undeterred from his convictions before reaching a pair of iron doors sealed tight and guarded by four of the same armored guards. Each one wore the breastplate adorned by Sarat's double-eagle and covered in blue armor like the unfortunate lads who gave up their carriage along the way to Sarat. One strike. One unseen strike cleaved all of them in half within their armor before Tivius sliced into the split doors.

The iron entry pushed open with ease where Tivius' sword cut clean into the steel barricade which had sealed it from outside attack. In the elaborate receiving chambers, Tivius' blade cut into the thick armor of stronger men whose dark blue armor encased their bodies like tight jars. A supernatural glow burned upon his icy eyes extending along his arm across his ancient blade.

Before him stood the gray-bearded king, his adult sons flanked beside him as the two younger boys huddled around their father. Tresin and Desin, the oldest boys, red-haired twins with freckled faces, stood firm in their guard to protect their father and brothers. Right and left hands gripped swords respectively each in mirror reflection. Armor forged of blue steel encased their bodies; a mirror of the eagle crest adorned their right and left sides, as though the herald split with a single head facing in opposition to the mirror symmetry. Charging Tivius to outnumber him, the twins carried their swords in opposing dominant hands to reflect a symmetry of instinctive training.

Grinning as to mock their attempt, Tivius called upon murmured prayers in his arcane speech supplying him supernatural speed and strength as a burst of sprint carried him to leap over the synchronized swing of the blades. Tips of his toes touched where the tips of the blades met and using the tiny surface of the edges, propelled Tivius to leap forward into a somersault, landing perfectly on his feet. Mesmerized at their failed swing, the twins turned to see Tivius sneering at them, his icy eyes aglow. Desin swung at the enemy, Tivius countered, striking steel on ethereal steel sending a spark of lavender magick energies to wisp silently away from the impact point. Tresin repeated the attempt to catch Tivius off-guard only for Tivius to counter in rapid succession of defense. Both men carried forward in momentum, now with backs turned to Tivius. Tivius held his weapon to his side, arcing the blade in parallel to the stone floor.

Glancing at one another, the twins nodded and quickly synchronized a lunge towards Tivius. Turning around in quick succession, Tivius countered their lunges, facing a pair of expert swordsmen. Their lunges and swipes hustled Tivius' ability while he toyed with them in their struggles. His steps countered their steps, as neither twin succeeded to obtain a strike against Tivius' body. Tivius twirled over them, dodged their swipes, bending his back in unnatural arcs, whirled his body to parry against their swings, playing against their fears with a grin at their weaknesses.

"You delay the inevitable," Tivius jeered.

"You will never take this kingdom," one of the boys proclaimed.

From the distance separating the adversaries, Tivius had his back to the swordsmen, grinning and mocking at the cowering king huddled behind his throne. His weapon shaded to an eerie, blue glow lit aflame upon the hieroglyphs charging the magick within the blade. Both twins charged at him from the steps in front of the entry door, and along the cerulean carpet leading to the throne. Reaching a distance from Tivius, one twin leapt into the air, lunging his sword downward towards Tivius' neck.

The second twin slid along the floor, extending his sword to cut at Tivius' knees. Closing his eyes, Tivius held his weapon against his chest, meeting the bottom twin's momentum sliding into Tivius' blade as it cleaved him diagonally left to right slicing flesh and steel in splintered sparks severing him clean. In continued momentum, glistened by the sinister flames coursing along the blade, Tivius' weapon arced skyward controlled by double grip into the bottom torso of the flying twin starting at his groin and arcing across his chest from right to upper left. As Tivius' momentum continued, his body twirled into a full three-hundred-and-sixty-degree circle. In the swift strike, his weapon turned from his right hand during the cut and after completing his revolution rested in his left hand. His blade glowed bright blue, extending behind him.

The twin boys collapsed upon one another between Tivius and the throne. Faces immortalized in soulless pain. Blood congealed within their wounds leaving a pair of drained corpses flanking the Saratian herald upon the floor. Without hesitation, Tivius called upon his aztunai, focusing his power to his weapon, and in a single leap, hoisted his blade over his chest lunging it through the cushions of the throne into Trebut's heart. With his strike, Trebut's younger son, Tirerian scooped up his younger brother, Geraud and with sobs of suffering harried past their father's body as Tivius looked on. The boy with the child encased against his chest fled towards the entry door to Tivius' amusement. Entering the death doors, Xanos and Jagoth joined their master in the fleeting minute to meet the children's deaths in glorious conquest by their weapons.

Trebut's voice echoed in Tivius' memories as it gasped for final breaths, frantically clinging to remove the blade from his chest. Trebut's soulless eyes cried out in silent tears to see his younger children gutted by viscous cruelty, turning only briefly to look upon the glowing tattoo of the Abyss in Tivius' open hand.

"Si'rai magick… but it's only a legend."

"Legends cannot kill you, sadakem."

Trebut's body fell backward off the blade, slumping upon the stone floor drenching the grout with his blood.

*

"I could not consume your soul, boy. The sword denied me once again."

Tivius rested upon his knees; blood covered his pale skin, washing over his thighs and torso as a single tear streaked upon his face. An unnatural glow burned through his icy eyes as he gripped clenched palms closed tight. Lengthy nails scarred into his hands and mixing his own blood with the liquid life of his victim. Black like spade, his tongue split his lips licking them with savor. He stood to his feet. What blood had not dried, trickled down his thighs onto his knees like a river slowed by time.

"It drives me," he whispered in gasping breaths mixed of pain and pleasure, "consumes me," he swallowed his own spit, "Yet, denies me. Its power magnifies. With every life I take, Daihekda becomes…stronger. I crave its offerings."

His sword rested at his feet, the blood pool reaching towards the scabbard. The sheath glowed with a bright purple illumination as the crimson spill touched it, beginning to pool against the static barrier rested on the ground. Just as he tasted blood, he felt the importance of his blade to share in his delicacies. He picked up the weapon, lifting it palms upward. He pulled the weapon from its sheath, revealing a few words in the engraving shining with mauve radiation.

Muffled voices through the plated iron doors to the room diverted Tivius' attention away from his ritual. Listening to the inhuman voices of his ethereal guards mingled with those of a familiar man brought him to pause. Whispers left his lips to command his protectors. The arguments ceased. As a portal into reality masking his illusions, the sealed iron doors leading into the bedroom tore open with weighted might.

Standing outside was a silver-armored man, his head vacant of protection and flanked by a pair of inferior troops protected by the raven common mold. The crest of the Si'rai carved onto his breastplate in golden hue dulled by wear and scratches. Like others of his race, his face was dark-skinned with an olive hue with a slight red complexion. He wore his hair in a ponytail sprouting from a single stalk on the back of a shaved head.

"Why do you interrupt me, General Cisian?"

Tivius' face seethed his spoken language taut through clenched teeth.

"I have information which may be imperative to your rule here, my Lord." Cisian answered in their common dialogue.

Tivius closed his sword into the sheath and placed it onto the bed next to the corpse, "My guards could have torn you asunder. This could not wait until the morning?"

Tivius removed his feet from the blood-stained floor and tracked the crimson footprints as he crossed in front of the footboard.

"I am afraid not, my Lord. I can prepare men to act on this information with your blessing of course."

"Go on."

Tivius stopped at the foot of the bed, a wrinkled, velvet robe draped over the mahogany wood in a haphazard manner. He lifted the silk coverings and covered them over his naked body to soak the liquid remnants of his victim into the fabric as it stained brown. Stitched above his heart was the monogram of "TB" over the double-headed eagle herald of Sarat.

"My Lord," the general bowed with his right fist closed against his heart, "Our armies have yet arrived but for the last week, and already I have received word there are pockets of rebellion scattered throughout the kingdom. We have discovered crude propaganda pamphlets. These rebels captured some wervostri and tortured them. Those returned to us have had limbs broken, faces slashed or bodies stuffed with written messages coercing an uprising."

Tivius paused and turned his head towards the general, "Petty rebellions do not concern me, Cisian. Saratian citizens see us as occupiers, not liberators; liberators of their fallible gods, liberators of their vanity, liberators of those who keep them poor. They do not understand we will expose their gods for the truth they are. Do they not understand we are here to free them of their selfish nobles? We offer them a unified system under one rule, under one god. They need to understand the Council of Magi betrayed them, who turns nation against nation, brother against brother. It is the Council who killed their legendary Knights, we offer up an alternative. Unlike prisoners, make them understand those we enslave are workers redistributed for the betterment of the Imperium, for the betterment of all.

"What is the progress of the work camps?"

Tivius approached the open window. Chilled winds blew across his perked pores.

"The first one has been prepared south of Telmen. Its crude, but it can house the workers. Two battalions are building another between here and Racoren to support our invasion."

"Sarat and Silvetzen need to understand the Si'rai caste system. As a conquered people, they are nothing more than indentured labor. Those who can serve will, those who cannot, die. Through work, they are free."

Tivius turned his gaze over his shoulder towards the general, "Should the princess or her abra'ir be aware of these pockets of insurgency, the citizens could unite under a common leadership. Any you may find within these resistance movements; deal with them using any accordance. And should any Saratian citizen know the location of the princess or her abra'ir," Tivius turned and opened a smile towards the general, he raised his index finger towards his chin, "offer a reward."

Tivius waved his right hand, palm upward in a sweeping motion.

"Freedom. Freedom and land. Lands which did not belong to them before," his words trailed in his smiling lie, "Their choosing of course. Land, resources and of course, auduin, and the security the Imperium shall leave them to their means, should they obey our laws.

"These peasants will clamor at the opportunity. Those of lower class will certainly rise to gain their wealth if they had information leading to the arrest of the princess. Of course, we cannot offer reward."

Tivius tilted his head, his raven mane draped in a single swoop, "But our ruse is to remain secret from exposure. Their time in conscripted labor will be less… cruel."

Tivius smiled with spiteful grin. His eyes shone a ghastly azure as he motioned the general to dismiss. With a striking precision, the general saluted the Magister with his fist clenched upon his chest. The general, turned, exiting the massive portals. Behind him, the ethereal guards heaved the swinging doors with a whining creak, sealed with a low boom.

Tivius turned towards the corpse lying in his bed. Silence fell upon the room, undisturbed by spiritual agitations or violent outbursts of torture. Instead, Tivius gathered the serenity surrounding him. The low muffled screams continued from the open window as the rustling of a breeze beckoned him to close his robe tighter. He marched around the bed to the nightstand where his sword once rested. The boy's bloody anus faced him, carved in two as the open crevice ripped muscle and sinew between the buttocks. He made careful not to let it arouse him, calming his loins with closed eyes.

He turned his thoughts towards his future and the future of an Imperium without his father.

"There is but one chosen ruler of the Si'rai, one who holds this weapon. The Imperium will soon realize this, this secret I have kept in my custody all these years. In my father's place, a more powerful leader should arise. Once the Azthar Kherdmon has purified his aztunai at the final temple."

Tivius lifted his sword from the bed and unsheathed it. Tightening his grip against the curved hilt, his luminescent eyes glazed over the craftwork, "Daihekda will consume him and Cadeck as it has allowed me others."

Chapter 34

Nothing of value remained among Tijoa's possessions. Blankets and mattresses stripped bare like the cupboards holding his poultices. His words weighed heavy on my heart like the cold knife that nearly cut through it. Arctic winds seared through the open door, but I took solace with the brown and white furs draped across my shoulders. Sparse but warm, I tucked pelts into my boots as I rose to a standing position, lifting the Silvetzenian sword across my shoulder to rest against my back. Luck carried the guard to the afterlife to escape the fear of what may come. I can feel the surges tickling through my left hand as my golden veins turned to ice blue streaks of frozen rivers cutting into the canyons of my knuckles.

I watch carefully as my eyes stray through the open door. Like tedious bugs toiling in their chores, Cadeck, Kenat and the other women ready the wagon for travel. Cadeck coordinated the efforts, standing in the bed as Kenat rested next to him. Cadeck has much to answer for. Like his history wrapped in delicate lies, the fragile box he hoisted crinkled with the gentle touching of glass vials. Rensel minded the horse, taking caution so the massive Si'rai beast did not wildly buck taking the cart into a furious gallop. She is a strong woman, but spite burns into her soul. Venna and Eris readied the satchels holding their small weapons taking subtle care as to their handling. They are so innocent; they do not deserve this world.

Then there's Cassica, the heir-apparent to the kingdom of Sarat, that is, if the princes should ever fall. She is steadfast in her ways and quick to remind us of them. Delicate beauty defies her aggression. She handles the ways of the blade as a skilled master, as though the sword were an extension of her will. But her judgment of those not of position undermines her personality. I admire her, for she cares of those she governs despite her arrogance.

I see their turmoil as I walk outside this small hut for the last time. Cassica smiles as she watches me leave the door. I cannot decide whether she is being honest or not. Her words speak her mind, although I can detect her heart condescends her tone. I walk up to Venna and lift a heavy pouch of food into the cart from the sloshy ground. She is frail and lifting this package would surely topple her over. Eris giggles as grunts leave my gut to lift it into the cart. I return smile, as stark and simple as I need to.

Cassica struggles with her chores. I have tried to consult with her on her noticeable ailments, but both she and Rensel have brushed it off as little concern in their brash tones. She has welcomed mine and Cadeck's help, but insists once we return to friendly lands, she and her ladies return to Sarat despite Cadeck's warnings. I overheard him telling Cassica if we return to Sarat and nothing has changed, she is more than welcome to return, allowing us to continue our own.

But I do not believe those words and sensed in Cadeck's voice he too knows Sarat is in dire danger. Cadeck calls to board the cart and though my thoughts linger on my trials biting into my hand with every magical pulse of conscious, I cannot help but think there is something different about the people with us. I help Venna and Eris step into the cart, gripping them by their hands as they work their legs to step into the bed. Rensel and Cadeck ride on the driving board while I join the younger Magi, Venna, Eris and Cassica in the bed.

We huddle for warmth amongst our heavy furs and line them with thick hay. The cart ride southward turned ragged and rutted. I lean my head against the sideboard to ease my mind from the pains of the ride and cope with the meditations of my trials. My mind wanders as I focus on the past. I feel burning in my left hand within my veins, but as I dart awake, I do not see it showing on my skin. I breathe a sigh as these thoughts trouble me and should those I travel with see my hand, they will surely ask questions.

I hear the words of my mother, Senas Verdui. My conscience focuses on the vision I saw inside my old home. A memory locked away under my subconscious stream opened during my trials in the Wind Temple. Why was it held back, or did I choose to hide it? Cadeck called my mother, *cousin*. I needed answers. His chance meeting with me many weeks ago was not coincidence. Cadeck and I met under deadly circumstances and since then the past few weeks, death and blood fell upon my hands all in the name of a prophecy dictated by men who huddle in yearly meetings feigning over secret texts.

I never asked for this, and mother even drew concern from when I heard her in my vision. Mother knew something. What really was her role in all of this? Did she know better, or did she also hide something? If so, then my life has been full of lies. I travel with those who hide lies from me.

Cadeck has warned me about being loose to interact with Cassica's entourage that we ride with their aide and vice versa but once we are able to be safe, they may return home. I choose not to get too involved with them out of his respect. But I am not too sure I can respect him anymore.

But I draw empathy to him. He has been a soul tortured and lost for two years. I know not the warmth of a woman or the love of children, but deep down something inside me sympathizes with him as though his destiny is intwined with my own soul, or as the Magi refer to it as Aztmudin. They speak of words and phrases I know not and that I carry *Dra Nar Azt*, the spirit of the gods, a sacred bloodline. None of them have informed me what it means even in their old speech. I do not think they may know, a prophecy lost to time and books long since turned to ash from age. But each vision I have, I feel the power of a spirit within. I hear the Magi speaking in my unconscious thoughts with each Trial passed.

I hear Godwen's fear, Philos' anticipations and Tijoa's doubts. The ancient dragon called me the Azthar Kherdmon, but somewhere I know this language. He spoke to me in his own speech, a speech I have not heard ever but closely resembles the speech when Cadeck or Kenat recite spells. And I understood it.

And with my ancient past, I heard a small child. She spoke to me and told me to tell her father to hurry. I know it was Wrem. I felt her pain and heard her cries of suffering. I could not tell Cadeck as his thoughts raced into pleasantness I have not seen in some time. Once the dragon left Tijoa's hut, he placed a calm hand on my shoulder and told me we will talk when it is safe.

I understand his concern. He does not feel the others need to know the affairs of the Magi nor their secrets. Neither did Tijoa, but these women travelling with us deserved to know what the Council did to Roth. Tijoa did not believe mankind was worth saving and man has toiled for thousands of years under the guidance of the Council. They create wars and treaties made by their dictation and enforced by the Temple Knights.

My father was one of them. But as I learned, he was a vagrant, a thief, and a scoundrel. Cassica's father sentenced him to repay his debts by serving with the Knights. Godwen needed Knights and looked to the criminals for them. Many thousands came and many thousands died. A handful, my father included, passed the Trials successfully. As the Si'rai came to threaten Roth, service to the Temples called my father into war. He died doing his service as did the other Knights serving with him. The Council betrayed Roth to ally with the Si'rai. This was mankind's curse; this was the Council's curse upon the land. The dragon called the Si'rai the cursed ones and damned Tijoa and his Council for their actions.

All predicted, as they tell me. Since my introduction to Cadeck, this life, this myth all thrust upon me and somehow, I am the center of it all. I refused it and vowed to return home only to find my home destroyed. I had only one choice; to continue to travel with Cadeck.

Venna and her spry naiveté joined us first. Cassica and Eris continued along and when we entered Silvetzen we found Rensel. Kenat was the latest acquisition. He was quick to damn Cassica when she addressed his last name. Why? I do not know. Cassica claims he hails from House Denwich of Kora and addressed him formally. A family of debutantes, miscreants and libertines acting above the law as I have heard through passing bards in Telmen. Or, like my name, he is just as common.

Funny. Verdui was such a common name as Venna was quick to judge. Through my trials, from the giant dragon and from Cadeck's own knowledge, I was destined to save Roth. My father's name was legend within Sarat and Cadeck and the other Magi tell me I am destined to surpass him to become this fabled savior, Azthar Kherdmon. But for what? Each vision I see there is an ancient battlefield and thousands lay dead by the call of the sword. It is always the same. What did the Council do to mankind to call for this and how long has it been going on?

My mind stopped as we unloaded for camp. I joined the huddle as Rensel took first watch as she always does. By her estimates we were another three days from the Saratian border. We decided to leave Silvetzen and travel to Racoren, the closest friendly port. From there, Cassica can return home and Cadeck, Kenat and I could make it to the Water Temple. I drew the next watch.

As the chilled winds whined across my furled brow, I had time to watch them sleep. I huddled deep embedded into my fur coverings. The light warmth did little to comfort my chilled bones. The fields across the horizon were still with the occasional call from a wild animal or domesticated dog. The warm crackles of the fire soothed me to relaxation.

Whispers called to me in the still of the night. I did not hear them from the winds, but I heard them inside me. She called me to her thoughts like a graceful beauty beckoning her lover. Her voice soothed like a purring kitten. I turned to glance in the direction of the voice to see Cassica sleeping quietly huddled against Venna and Rensel, but the voice I heard was not Cassica's. It was sultry, like the lurid tavern girls that called for me in Telmen. Ethereal in tone, as it called a faint echo followed as though from the ancient world.

Azthar Kherdmon, I heard. The voice called the name thrice.

Together, we save Roth. You and I are destined. The Apophadi has no power over our joining.

"Who are you?"

I decided to answer the voice, knowing such an action would invite spite if Cadeck ever found out.

The Si'rai have a name for me, Visraair Abra. In the common tongue I am Babalon, the Sacred Mother.

"Babalon? Sacred Mother? I do not understand."

There is truth you must seek, Azthar Kherdmon; your Trials will show you truth.

"I heard you once. With Cadeck's daughter, Wrem."

Babalon laughed and I heard her voice no more this night.

#

We loaded the cart the following morning. Pink hues of dim sunlight crept across the eastern horizon painting the sparse clouds like a thin brush masterfully crafted across the sky. I left my thoughts to drift in mindless reflection while I aided Kenat. Kenat attempted to pry to my emotions, but I reminded him that visions returned to me, and I needed time to reflect upon them. He was more comfortable moving his leg this morning and walking with minimal aid as he lifted into the cart. The rest of the group seated themselves as I sat next to Cassica with our backs against the front board.

Rensel harried the horse to stride. The trained beast roared to life with a stubborn whinny as we carried through winding roads of snow-melted fields. Distant cries bellowed to the west with the hint of smoldering ruin rising from sinister flame. We heard guttural orders in the Si'rai tongue followed by faint voices speaking our speech before screams erupted again. Venna called to Cadeck we should stop and help only for him to enforce the notion there is nothing more we can do. Doing anything would only expose our cover and lead to an unfortunate conclusion. Rensel pressed on.

We continued to make progress. As day turned to dusk, we set up a new camp once again. A low fog rolled into the fields as we approached the edges of the forestry bordering the two lands. Rensel estimated a day trip through the sparse western woods would lead us to the border of our nations. Snows had disappeared in the warmer climate and any residue remained upon the shadows of the trees and rocky alcoves. But would not remain like such for long as the months of low sun drew closer upon Sarat. Fog lingered upon camp like a mist of frozen spackle.

My watch approached on third rotation. I entertained myself by forming breaths into shapes in front of me. The rigid wood of our cart caused a numbing pain in my thighs as I studied the shapes I made. The circles danced in the firelight before disappearing into the faint darkness ahead.

Nocturnal predators called around hunting the smaller prey in their midst. Most animals avoided us but the occasional curious wolf or verdasnik would approach camp within eyesight hiding in the tree lines. The lone verdasnik rubbed its nose upon the ground searching for the nocturnal insects composing its prey. Stray scents emanated from the animal which hinted as sour mash served in taverns. I could not tell if the animal was defecating, or it was their natural smell of breath from the carcasses of their food. Moments later another verdasnik approached the original and mounted it for reproduction. The animal's scent must have been estrus.

I listened as animals engaged in mating ritual. The ground below them shuffled in their exaltations. I turned to the firelight bouncing from the erected wood placed carefully in a small triangle shape. A reflection flickered in the orange flame of a sultry face, shaped with proportionate features with emerald eyes set in symmetry upon a soft pale. A river of scarlet hair draped upon opaque shoulders flowing further upon vermillion vestments made of a sheer fabric. The light robes covering her body accentuated her pale flesh and supple figure. My eyes wandered upon the image standing behind the flame as the most beauteous of beauty drifted upon the vacant foliage.

"Why do you haunt me woman?"

When the moon hides the sun, I will be ready for you.

"What do you mean? Who will be ready?"

The scarlet woman laughed once again as she did last night.

She will need you. The Apophadi did not take her. You must take her instead.

"I do not understand. Why do you come to me?"

I am the future of Roth. I am your future, Azthar Kherdmon. Together, we will change this Aeon.

With those final words, the vision disappeared as quickly and silently as she arrived. I continued to watch as the fire burned hotter after my vision. I kept thoughts to myself, the apparition called for me to lie with her, to lie with Cassica. I turned my gaze towards her as she slept. I watched her breathe softly through covered furs. Her body formed in shape as seductively as the ghost, her crimson locks buckled in furrowed matting against her scalp from days of maltreatment and dirt. Cadeck did not divulge to me why she was bedridden when I returned, nor did Rensel or the other two girls. As we prepared for return to Sarat, she moved as a cripple yet shunned any help from her entourage.

I steadied myself as I dropped from the bed of the wagon onto the mossy ground below me. With careful steps, I approached Kenat who snoozed softly, Venna's arms wrapped around him to keep her body warm. The lithe pair together coupled was about the thickness of a healthy wolf. I leaned down, squatting with my knees to nudge Kenat to wake and remind him to take his watch into the morning. Startled, he rubbed his eyes to embrace the dancing fires flickering into vision.

"Tesh my turn already?"

"Yes."

Kenat eased into a sitting position, the soft furs draped down his body exposing the gaudy lavender shirt snaking along his pale figure. Venna had a horrible sense of dress when it came to men. I account that to inexperience with them. Kenat rose to his feet, steadying his posture to prevent him from tumbling over Venna to his right, while Eris snoozed to his left. Kenat wrapped himself in tight furs warming him with deep solitude. We had been about a week's ride west of the Tanakian Ring as the crows would fly and on steady pace to Sarat.

I had learned the hunter who pillaged the Temple of Fire attacked Tijoa's hut during my absence and murdered by Cadeck. His limbs cut into a five piece and buried separately around Tijoa's property in perfect symmetry. Using the ashes of the torso along with an incantation to protect the homestead, Cadeck proposed that adverse magick using the Si'rai wizard would ward off any Si'rai encroachers allowing them a few days to hide till I returned. Surprisingly, his theory worked.

As Kenat took his position within the cart, I did not linger to sleep, but instead focused upon the fire burning to keep us warm and the fires within my heart. I rubbed my left hand that by now had begun to glow a light red to reflect the flame nearby. With each Trial, I grew more observant with magick. Each element presented a new danger and new surprises and each time I passed, I heard the Magi speak of the *Dra Nar Azt*. I noticed as Kenat observed my meditations and heard his quiet whisper from behind me.

"Are you not going to sleep, Tesh?"

"No. Something bothers me."

Not much younger than I, Kenat drew upon the biological politic of our generation.

"Is it Cassica? Or is it Venna?"

I laughed quietly at his jest.

"No, Kenat, it's neither," I rise to my feet, "You remember what Tijoa said, about the people of Roth and about saving them?"

"Yes. As a Magi, I abide by the Council's rules and respect his decision as being next to absolute."

"But you can't honestly believe those words?"

"I know no better, Tesh. It was how Philos raised me. I do not recall much of life before he took me into Temple. Philos tells me that I was an orphan wandering the streets of Racoren when he found me. I later discovered on my own whom I was, who my family was and what happened to me."

"Go on, I have ear."

Kenat stared into the open woods. Through his pearly eyes I could understand the pain he was feeling inside that he hesitated to divulge.

"Father orphaned me because I was different. My parents were of aristocratic lineage in Kora. I was once like them, but as I grew older my blue eyes turned the unnatural white they are now. Being of self-serving nobility, they could not have a child different than they. They left me an orphan. I later learned they continued to have children and continued to live the lifestyle of kings. Even our own Cassica has met them on many occasions, wined and dined by my father to garner favor by her father. They live a life I could have had, but instead of love, I faced exile. Shunned for being different and taken in to become a Magi, forced to serve a cause at the whim of the few. And to disagree with them, can bring me punishment.

"But I cannot righteously back them anymore. I have seen what it did, what it is doing, as a man, as a person, I cannot agree with the Council with everything. Why we are here? Why you are here. Without the Magi there can be no Quorum. Without a Quorum, the citizens of Roth know nothing of decisions by the Council deciding their fates, and that is a good thing, Tesh.

"You are different, Tesh. More different than you know. I have read the prophecies and the legends ingrained upon me since I could read. However, I have heard of deeper magick. Magick untold in the books Philos taught. Books the Council considered dangerous outside of our various temple archives and which I laid eyes upon in brief only for Philos to scold me when I had cracked them open.

"We are living in this new Aeon, the Aeon prophesied millennia ago. The books I mention tell of another Aeon after this one. This one ruled in harmony, an Aeon of the Aztun so the scrolls say."

"What about the next one?"

"You don't want to know about the next one."

"Neither of us will be alive, what does it matter?"

Kenat heaved a long sigh. In his words I have learned more than Cadeck's cryptic tongue has spoken, "That is the Aeon of Chaos, the final Aeon. You get one more shot then *he* gets one more shot. That is how it always is; the bickering and dick-rattling between the two entities. These are just words from dried up books written by men long turned soil."

"Do any of the books you've read talk about a *Babalon*?"

Kenat leered a slow turn into my direction. His beady eyes morphed into an eerie, predatory gaze and looked as though a hawk homed in on my weak, rat-like question.

"You should turn in for the night. Cadeck is better suited to answer the words you pose."

#

As our journey stretched into the midday, our rickety cart led by the single Si'rai horse approached the demarcated border between Sarat and Silvetzen. Along the dusty, lest travelled roads, the dense forestry to our east spread into sparse woods of rolling hills of colorful leaves shading orange and falling into the detritus. A hint of smoldering wood tickled our noses alerting us civilization may be close. Cassica's lips smiled with the hint of welcome arrival as the southern horizon opened. Low clouds lingered along the edges of the horizon blotting out the sun yet to burn off the early morning dew.

Rensel muttered inaudibly as the border approached us. I could tell in the tone of her voice a disgruntled disgust lured about her thoughts. Rensel warned us to steady down as she drove the muscular beast into a swift gallop. As quickly as the horse sprinted, within moments she reined in the animal to halt with a loud shout of commands in the only tongue it knew. I was thankful of her time spent amongst the Si'rai but wondered how she learned it.

Burning ash stung our noses like a violent onslaught of torture. Splinters remained of charred wood with the watch box of a tower crushed nearby. Flies buzzed around the ruins as the overpowering rot of death soiled the ashen stench. Venna heaved in frail hiccups before leaning over the edge of the cart to expel her stomach. The others covered their mouths as Rensel and Cadeck dropped to the rocky ground and examined the singed ruins.

I peeked up from the bed of the cart, holding my arm back to prevent Cassica from seeing the horrific scene. She insisted I remove my hand rising to stand beside me. Burnt remnants of a skeletal corpse sprawled within the crushed watch tower box, the tell-tale azure armor of Sarat scarred and scorched black as it fused to skeletal remains.

I heard Cassica's sobs. I felt the sideboard tremble as her hands rocked the wood. Rensel returned to the cart as tears flooded her face slashing through emotions stinging deep. Cadeck crossed his arms and remained in repose at the base of the collapsed structure. Rensel scanned the surrounding landscape and informed us we were alone in the area.

But we were not. A voice cried from the distance amidst a deep grove of trees to the west. It was a man's voice, straining in weakness and inaudible. Rensel commanded me to stay with Cassica as she led Cadeck to the voice. As the pair approached the clearing, I could see from my vantage a man dressed in a half-shirt emblazoned with the Saratian eagle in dark ink. He steadied himself to his feet before collapsing in front of Rensel. I could hear fear in his throat as Cadeck and Rensel worked to lift him.

I heard Cadeck speaking to him, and the man replied quietly. Rensel called us over, announcing he was safe and needed water and rations. I gathered the flasks as Venna grabbed a few pieces of stale bread. One by one, we lifted ourselves out of the cart and onto the ground, taking pace towards the humbled man. Venna and Eris walked ahead of Cassica as I trailed behind, covering the rear.

Venna produced a piece of bread for the man as I followed behind, uncorking the horned flask from my side marked with the Saratian crest. The man consumed the nutrition. Water drenched down his fuzzy cheeks as Cadeck tapped on his shoulders. He had the appearance of a man younger than I. Blonde hair matted across his head botched with blood from cuts on his scalp. Welted bruises swelled on his disheveled cheeks. Crusted blood speckled on his left hand clutching a deep cut below his right ribs. He struggled to eat as blood drained through the finger webbings of his left hand. I watched as Rensel carefully prepared a bandage using some torn fabric from her tunics to expose a tapered and muscled midriff below her ribcage.

"Tell us your name," Rensel requested as she hastened to place her fabrics around the soldier's wound. Stray blood pools stained the surrounding brush.

"My name is Vizin Tur," He opened in Low Accent and random breaths, "I am a soldier in the Sixth Regiment of Racoren."

"What happened to you?" Rensel continued. The soldier's eyes drew into a weary state.

"I do not remember much. Only the armies of black came swiftly," he breathed deep. I could tell his weakened state did not mark him to live too much longer, "Masked by the darkness of night, they came upon our outpost from the South. We fought for the Crown, but their numbers overwhelmed us."

Vizin coughed deeply, blood spittle came from his mouth.

"The enemies seemed to glow, like the whispering ghost lights in the skies over Silvetzen. They appeared as consumed, thriving for bloodlust. They lost few and fought like men whose souls were absent. They knew nothing but death and welcomed those opposing them into its embrace. I saw men like us, Silvetzenian men fighting against us. Then there were others," his voice trailed to stave off any panic inflections, "Those others, their war cries rang out like the bells of a funeral procession, sending even our bravest men into a panic. They did not speak our tongue, but what they yelled were fierce words of death and blood like billows of ash clouds. We lost our resolve and those who could fled into the surrounding forest. They moved from us and with thousands of others like them, and marched westward towards Racoren. We knew there was little we could do, Racoren would suffer the same fate as we."

As his story escalated into outright fear, Cassica clenched her left hand around my right. By this time, her face had turned into a blushed red, tears

390

flowing like a flood basin down her cheeks while her lips quivered from any syllabic response.

"These wounds, when did you receive them?"

I could feel Rensel questioning the man's bravery.

"The next evening. Wolfsblood. Tired and hungry, more of my fellow soldiers died. They stabbed me and left me for dead. Though, I had wished they had. I heard cries coming from the West as I lay overnight and thought to myself Racoren was no more. I do not know whether they were my screams or those carrying many miles towards me. But I heard and felt pain."

"No. Those are lies. You abandoned your post and fabricated a lie to cover your actions."

Cassica produced a knife from the hemp cord tied around her waist and raised it in a position to attack the young soldier. Cadeck motioned for me to restrain her with a cock of his head. Venna and Eris clutched one another either for fear of Cassica's actions or Vizin's words. I could not tell.

"I should have you murdered here, by my hands, for treason to the Crown."

"I'm sorry Your Highness," Vizin cowered towards the angered princess, "we did not repel the invasion. If you must, kill me for my lack of bravery in the height of battle."

"No soldier," Cadeck comforted him, "We will not bring you to fate. Are you able to walk? Are you able to help?"

"I do not think so. These wounds are deep; I can barely feel my legs."

I watched my travelers closely. Cadeck helped the young soldier, tending to his gaping wound as he consumed more of our rations. He beckoned Kenat over to help, spouting words to the effect it is the duty of the Magi to tend to the needy. Venna and Eris were still distraught over the news as Cassica came to a steady grip with the fact her kingdom lay conquered as she dropped her knife and coddled in her own arms shunning my protection. Rensel continued her enraged fury, panting and pacing alone away from the gathering. I studied their sadness but felt none of my own for the loss; for I lost long ago.

My mother died before my eighteenth harvest season. My father, I barely knew him, but we have all heard his fate. I lost someone I loved by a band of robbers looking to make a quick ransom. Now I see the loss before me. What these companions really mean to me is they are all I have left. Cadeck has treated me as a father in the absence of his own children whose pangs he bears daily. I have heard Rensel's concerns over a lost lover. Kenat has lost his heritage by the hands of intolerable parents. Venna and Eris have lost their own innocence in this land of war and destruction. Cassica has lost her meaning; her lifestyle and everything she had come to know during her childhood, the inheritance she swore to protect, and quite possibly, her entire family.

I understand loss and pain as each of my Trials reminds me. As I grow stronger with my aztmudin, I have learned to feel theirs; each of them and know their concerns. Tijoa's words echo to me. His harsh criticism of non-magick man, the 'profane' as the Magi refer, burns into my soul like the clouds of lingering doubt. He has written off man and by his opinion, so too seemingly has the Elders in the Council of Magi. But I see true suffering, true loss. I know what I fight for. These are my friends, and they are worth saving.

Chapter 35

Cassica's hands fidgeted her fingers, pricking her nails. Her hands tucked against her torso. Her lips pouted with fury at the soldier's betrayal. Cadeck maintained a vigil of comfort over Vizin Tur. His breaths heaved in and out of consciousness. Venna and Eris did their best to hold him down from the intense agony as Kenat positioned to cauterize the deep wound below his ribs.

Tesh stood nearby attentive and somber. Flicked, sooty hair drifted over stoic eyes as he crossed his arms. Ysalir calmed her erratic pacing, soothing her anger through clenched teeth as the clumps of grass and mud eased with each slowed kick. Cassica struggled to fight tears dripping down her cheeks and chilling her face. A rolling, cold fog hastened the frost forming upon her skin.

"We will need to move off the main road if we are going to set camp. We do not want any stray Si'rai patrols to meet us again."

"What about him?" Eris chimed in, pointing to Vizin.

"Kenat, can you use your fire to seal his wound?"

"I do not know Elder Cadeck. I think I can see his stomach in here," Kenat held a choke in his throat to the scent of untreated fester.

Vizin's eyes burned with terror as he clenched his left fist deep within Cadeck's ragged coverings. Kenat waved his hands over the wound sending sparks of burning heat searing against Vizin's inner flesh taking precautions to seal tissue and sinew damaged by a deep sword cut before working his way with precision to seal the outer layers of skin. Reaching for a twig with his free hand, Cadeck jammed the stick parallel to Vizin's jawline as Kenat made one more binding sear into the middle layers of his muscle to burn any infection beginning to form. Vizin hummed his agony into the rudimentary muzzle. Mucus evacuated from his nose mingling with the tears of pain coursing over his cheeks.

Vizin emptied the pain from his thoughts focusing instead on the comforting embrace of his mother as a youth. He numbed the stench of the acrid rot of his searing flesh and replaced it with the pleasant smells of the cadium flowers he gave his mother the day before he left for training. As she dipped them in a small vase, their petals blossomed filling the room with the warm hints of the summer sun and the tearful hug as he left the next day to join others of his age to live the life of a soldier. He reminded her he would stay for the required minimum; two harvest-seasons and return to continue their family's business. That was the last recollection he remembered of his mother.

He yearned to return home; to see the delight of his mother's face once more and see the pride in his father's heart. The sights of the approaching army delighted his heart as he knew they came with new recruits to relieve him of his duties so he may receive his leave papers, return to Kora, and begin a new existence for his father's enterprise. Instead of the double-headed eagle herald, the armies that came to him bore the eight-spoke sunwheel of the Si'rai.

The ensuing battle lasted for most of the day and in the end, dozens of Saratian soldiers at their border outpost lay dying and survivors scattered into the forests. The Si'rai wasted no time moving on. Those wounded they captured on the spot and taken to where? Vizin did not know. Of those who died, Vizin watched from a hidden distance as they fed them to the vicious beasts carrying their wagons standing as the size of houses. Minimal traces remained amidst scraps of clothing for the lesser predators to consume with the hints of sundered meat clinging to them.

As Kenat sealed the final strings of muscle tissue, Vizin heaved a sigh as he drifted into sleep, collapsing out of Cadeck's arms onto the soft grass beneath. Kenat stood from the wounded soldier's side, his face flush from any life. His bright, pearl irises dimmed to a pair of dull cataracts. Every fiber of nerves in his body twitched his muscles into minor spasms racing along his biceps and thighs, tingling onward onto his feet and hands as blackened scorch marks formed on his fingertips.

Cadeck draped his arms around the younger Magi as he dropped back onto his knees with the uncontrolled reverberations of his magick drain. Venna stood to her feet to step at his side. Cadeck moved his arm to block her attempt, scraping his extended forearm against her torso.

"He will be fine, Venna. He has gone into shock."

"What do you mean?"

Kenat closed his eyes as Cadeck cradled him with both arms.

"Kenat, when were you last exposed to your element?"

Kenat's mouth strained to form words as his eye lids squinted open with Cadeck's voice.

"Before we left my home. I see darkness…death… Abyss."

Kenat's dry words came with stuttered response as his lips deteriorated to a pale red and his body fell limp to shock. Cadeck turned to Ysalir, a shivering eye felling a single tear.

"We have no choice but to camp tonight. Tesh, you and Cassica get Vizin into the cart. Rensel, help me with Kenat."

"But Vizin said there are Wolfsblood in the forest," Ysalir protested, her concern drifting through her face like breaking waves crashing on cliffs, "I won't expose Her Highness to vile criminals."

"We can handle a few dregs; it's the Si'rai which should draw our concern."

Kenat relaxed into a sudden slumber, slumping in Cadeck's arms. Ysalir gripped Kenat's legs, wrapping her arms around his calves as Cadeck hoisted him by his shoulders. Tesh and Cassica struggled with Vizin's medium frame with the glint in her eye to take his life. Tesh took the heavier center of gravity around his shoulders while Cassica hoisted his feet, careful to be mindful of his injury. Strains emptied from his face followed by grunts and whines as Tesh lifted the injured soldier into the back of the cart.

Eris and Venna returned to the cart, straddling the side boards, while Cassica and Tesh sat inside resting next to the injured bodies. Ysalir drove the cart westward into the woods to avoid the main road through patches of rough grass and through the dense underbrush of the spotty deciduous trees lining the border crossing. Ysalir guided the horse through the thicket, turning into a clearing contained within the trees. A few moments later, she pulled the reins to stop the horse and stood upon the driver board.

Sounds of croaks permeated across her trained ears. Birds rustled upon the canopy while gentle corduks roiled along the underbrush consuming leaves and stems with the suckling sound emanating from their snouts. The echoes of the forest reminded her of the stillness and serenity of nature. Ysalir dropped down from the board and urged Cadeck to remain with the motion of her hand. She tread carefully amongst the brush with dainty steps of a dancer to prevent the disruption of spying bandits. She knelt to the ground as she brushed her right hand over a set of tracks.

"There's no human tracks," she whispered to Cadeck standing nearby, "We should be fine. If the Si'rai have made it to Racoren, any refugees will avoid the woods due to the gangs. We can set up camp in this clearing."

Cadeck stepped down the short incline and approached Ysalir, standing a few yards away from the cart. She positioned her hands on her hips in continued protest, "If we must fight here, how is Kenat to be of any help? He muttered something about death. Will he survive?"

The words of fear followed from her breaths as she straddled her legs to climb the slight rise of detritus and soil.

"Do not bring worry to your heart, Rensel. His health is my concern."

Cadeck's warm voice softened her tone.

"I'll be more comforted if we can find safety for Her Highness."

Cadeck beckoned the others to file out of the cart. He motioned for Tesh to find the wood for fire while Cassica demanded Venna, and Eris prepare the sleeping furs.

"If Vizin's words ring any truth, the Si'rai have overrun Sarat and the kingdom. We can hope Tarlakana is safe and free of Si'rai influence. We have at least a month's travel by sea. Our best chances lie with finding safe passage in Racoren. We must continue to provide Tesh his trials."

"Out of the pan and into the fire. That is your plan, Magi? Venture straight into Racoren where even before the Si'rai became a threat, the city was not much better. Every thief and murderer find haven in Racoren."

"I do not believe the gods have entirely forsaken us. Aeus will guide our way, Rensel."

Echoes of cooing birds rang across the forest while the dim dances of sunlight burned orange through creeping clouds along the horizon. Beams of glinted sparkles struck through the trunks of the large trees. As the early evening sun dropped into the horizon, fingers of lingering fog tickled billowing tentacles through the linings of the brush. The starting flickers of fire crackled in the early evening sunset warming the soft tissues of the small game roasting over them.

Tesh and Cassica rested Kenat next to the fire hissing before them. Cadeck shuffled to place himself on the other side of Kenat while the younger ladies consumed the small game legs across from his position. Ysalir positioned herself upon a small log, toned thighs bent to sit as her trim leggings cuddled her knees exposing bare shins. Leathery boots covered her ankles dusted by a fresh layer of grass and mud to amplify the pangs of her heartbeat with each trod of dirt and soil from her enraged pacing.

Cadeck lengthened his weary bones listening to every crack tearing from his thighs, knees, and ankles before popping his knuckles. His mind lingered on pressing thoughts and the fear of an imposing ambush in the night. Tesh had not spoken to him since he returned from the Wind Temple, only drifting into a threatening request for the pair to discuss urgent matters. Tesh had been quiet, obedient but kept to himself since they left Tijoa's hut. The Magi understood to keep his distance and his repose to allow the younger man to approach him. Tesh relegated to himself keeping conversations to a minimum. Venna lingered on Tesh's torn eyes sensing pain within them.

"Tesh, you have not spoken a word since you came back to Tijoa's home. What troubles you?"

Tesh brushed her notion away with a swivel of his body. Clouded mist lingered through the cavernous canopy shrouding their cover in the light forest region. A few days ride through hills and into marsh would bring them into

Racoren and with eventual passage towards Tesh's next goal. Mystery surrounded the Water Temple as his Trials have told him and the phantom creature haunting his thoughts calling herself *Babalon* provided little reassurance to his depression. Silence lingered on his dry lips.

Venna's demeanor turned to impatience as she sighed with defeat. Positioned between her and Eris laid Vizin Tur. His quiet breathing lulled an unsettled peace as he lay rested on his left side to prevent pressure applied to the sealed wound. Echoes of unease motivated the speech of the Mistress of the Rose, whose name he only knew as Rensel, and Princess Cassica while the two conscious men remained silent in their vigils. Vizin recognized two of the men were Magi and one of them lay unconscious after sealing his wound.

Vizin listened to the words of the meeting. Venna and Eris kept to themselves, their eyes focused on the conversations of the older women. The older Magi poked at the fire, removing a stick drawn from the embers of the camp and raised it to his face. Soft murmurs emptied from his lips in a speech Vizin could not decipher. The accent befell on his ears as Cadeck's Low Accent, but the words whispered did not reflect Common Tongue.

As he finished his prayer, he stood to his withered legs as bones creaked in obeisance and with the whispering fire at his side, he moved towards the ailing Magi. Cadeck's knees cracked into position as he placed the fire stick above Kenat's head in preparation to ignite Kenat's flesh. Venna pierced a bolting scream into the forest awakening the resting fauna.

"What are you doing?"

Her voice burst through the trees.

"Still her. I must perform this ritual."

Vizin continued his audience as Ysalir shot ahead of her sister grappling her frail body and pressed the blonde girl's backside into her chest. With sobbing response, Venna struggled to free herself with fists pumped and collapsing into restricted into subservience by Ysalir's grapple. Cadeck placed the fire-drawn poke against Kenat's forehead igniting fire onto his scalp before moving onto his chest, each hand, foot and leg, torso, and groin. Kenat's body erupted in flame engulfing the young lad in imposed immolation.

"You're going to kill him."

"Calm down Venna," Ysalir urged, "Cadeck appears to know what he's doing."

Tesh reacted to the flame, scooting away from Kenat's torching body. Cassica and Tesh remained in stunning pose. Eris' eyes reflected the burning pyre Cadeck created of orange flame overshadowing the camp's warmth.

Ysalir carried her sister to the ground, keeping her from the dangers presented by the wrathful fires.

397

"Feiaztmi Kenat, awake," Cadeck spoke in the ancient speech.

Cadeck called him in title, Fire Magi. Kenat's name rung like the tones of exploding magma.

Upon Cadeck's command, Kenat reached upright as his body lifted itself to seating position. Violent screams exploded from his mouth as the fires turned from a carbon orange into an ethereal crimson separating in form apart from his silhouette. Visible from the outline, Kenat's breathing resumed to normalcy. Pearl-white eyes brightened as the orbiting moon during cycle. Clenching his muscles into rigor, the boy's jaw line shrunk with the gritted gnashing of his teeth. As instant as the flames burst from his body to consume him, the fires sealed as a vacuum against his skin disappearing as immediate as the flames started.

Kenat's body hunched over, steam percolated from the starter points where Cadeck placed the stick. The tip still burned in his clenched hand as he stood over the young Magi in observation. The embers flickered against his sooty, ragged skin highlighting the folds within his tattered tunics.

"What did you do to him?"

Tears fell from Venna's eyes onto her quivering lips.

"I'll be fine, Venna."

Kenat comforted her relaxing sobs.

"You asked how I would get Kenat back to help us. This is what I had to do."

Cadeck tossed the stick back into the fire with the gush of crackles erupting with the welcome fuel. He reached into his satchel draped around his hips and removed the small smoke pipe and a pouch. He lifted a small starter twig from the flames and removed himself from the camp.

Ysalir released the grip around her sister's svelte body as Venna turned to Kenat and darted to sit beside him. Fires glowed in the older woman's emerald sea eyes; her breaths outraced her heart to keep pace with her anxiety. Cadeck turned his back to the troupe to empty his sorrows into the awaiting darkness of the forestry. Ysalir watched him while her sister approached Kenat to embrace his cooling body with lovelorn infatuation. Eris remained beside Vizin's body while Ysalir regained her thoughts towards Cadeck's actions.

Cassica rose to pace towards her older peer and sat next to Ysalir on the overturned log stump. She rustled her leggings loose to aid comfort in her seat. The soft flick of igniting embers rolled from the distance followed by sparkling crunches leading the sweet, titillating smell of ruban smoke to linger with the winds carrying over the camp. Cadeck's puffs followed in rhythm.

"Rensel, do you believe Vizin's words are true?"

Cassica's firm question came from her soft, puffed lips, addressing Ysalir with her Crown name so not to allow the ailing soldier to hear her birth name. Her skin glowed from the warm fires burning the wood before them as Ysalir pondered the weight of the Princess' question. Cassica's words carried the weight of their fate. She refrained to answer, but after releasing a short breath, returned her thoughts.

"No, Your Highness. We should allow him rest. I will learn more in the morning. If bribery or coercion allowed him to speak of such failures, he will tell me."

"Then we should return to Sarat, send him to the keep and have him interrogated."

"I cannot ask you to consider this choice, Your Highness. For now, I suggest we listen to the Magi. We do not have many choices."

"But he proposes travelling to Racoren. Surely, Cadeck cannot be serious?"

"He is your friend. Don't you trust his actions?"

"Of course. But my kingdom comes first. I must know if mother and father are still alive."

"I deplore you, Your Highness, we stay with Cadeck, and we find out the truth from Vizin. I have seen the Magi's reactions towards you, and he has no intention of putting you into harm's way. Neither do I."

Cassica furrowed her lips towards Ysalir, "But you take orders from me. Accompany me to Sarat so we can find the truth to this soldier's story."

"Then you return to Sarat at your own peril, Highness. As a loyal servant to the Crown, I am anxious to know as well, but we find out together. You, me, Venna and Eris. I do not intend to disobey, but for your protection I request to deny your orders."

Ysalir tightened her lip into a stern poise. Her eyes erupted into full bloom meeting emerald seas to clash against one another in their stares.

"So, you propose we continue to Racoren?"

Cassica retreated her stance to listen to Ysalir.

"Aye. Either there or Blorak and Blorak is in Silvetzen. We do not have many options given our current circumstances."

Cassica lowered her shorn eyes into the soft hints of the illuminated embers then returned towards Ysalir.

"We will need disguises if we enter Racoren, Your Highness. The citizens there already despise royalty. We barely hold the criminals there with our standing forces. If the Si'rai control Racoren, the criminal gangs will need to fend on their own and danger will be insurmountable. We will need everyone alert and ready."

Cassica returned gaze towards the glowing fire. Wood crackled and splintered under internal chemical reactions as the flames glistened against her pale face. Venna cuddled next to Kenat as he embraced her with slender, noodly arms. Tesh pecked at the ground impatiently with a stick as his breaths lulled towards internal thought. Eris stood vigil over Vizin; her soothing voice comforted him into relaxed attention.

Cassica's future existed with this band of adventurers. Each one of them taking part, entwined by fate, and all depended upon her decisions as the potential future queen of Sarat. What started between a wizened Magi and a young man entailed a conflict spanning the entirety of their world. The fates of her realm and subjects hung in the balance.

Cassica struggled to grasp her revelations she learned in the past few weeks. Her life hung by threads with each passing day, yet she continued to survive with the aid of those in her company. Vizin's words reminding her Sarat was gone, her kingdom in the grips of an empire that would have murdered her too had she remained in Silvetzen. Her denials overcame her emotions distorting her mind from interpreting the truth.

Cadeck intervened and Tesh took his own vows to protect her and her company. Yet something stirred within her of which she knew little of. She had felt it since birth and only with puberty had the spirit inside grown stronger. She kept her knowledge within her own mind and chose not to reveal it to Ysalir for fear should she worry further for her safety. Cadeck realized the apparition upon first introduction. Cassica heard the spirit awakening, calling in the night since her bleeding several days ago. The Spirit of Babalon was alive.

As the night waned onward, Cassica caught Eris awake as she ended her watch. Eris sat alone with her back against a tree as she whittled a small twig with her blade. Cassica followed the younger girl's actions to the painstaking efforts to carve a perfect tip, muttering words inaudible to Cassica's ears, while catching her attention. Cassica's light steps crunched the ground beneath her approach to the younger maiden whose hair ran down her back in disheveled flair. Eris wrapped herself in tight woolen blankets clutched against her hair in static disarray, a tunic covered down to her midriff, and leggings reached her shins revealing bumpy legs with weeks-old fuzz scraping across them. Covering her feet, a pair of damp leather boots with slight tears in the fabric peeled away from the mud-covered soles.

"Another restless night, Eris? Another bad dream?"

Cassica seated beside her.

"If I may, Your Highness, I request permission to refrain from discussion."

"If it jeopardizes our mission, I must request to know and in audience with Cadeck. For now, I will support your request. You will rotate watch when needed, but please, do try to catch sleep."

"As you wish," Eris whispered, coddling her blankets closer.

Cassica moved to the others in camp, taking a spot near Cadeck. Ysalir rested beside Eris with Vizin to her right. She studied the grounds, following the trail of Venna's silky hair along her backside coiled up over her shoulders. Arms resting against her chest as Kenat's head positioned to her feet.

Eris started her vigil with calm unease. Animals rustled and called in the distances and with each screech, holler or yelp Eris ran the sounds through her head whispering the names of the beasts as she heard their screams. Survival as a Rose depended on her ability to memorize the native species thriving in her land. Snickering snorts rummaged in the distance as coming across muted ground mixed with foliage and mud.

"Destersnout," she muttered to herself in high-pitched High Accent, "It feeds on the worms in the soft mud around the forest floor."

"No, verdasnik," a masculine voice whispered beside her.

Vizin's voice strained to breath. Speech stammered through his throat like a piercing knife cutting through flesh. Vizin lifted his eyes to wake, shaking his head from the pounding pain throbbing across his temples.

"No, I swear it's a destersnout," Eris condemned his correction.

"The shrieking yelp of the mating call should have clued you in, Maiden."

"I heard the sound, far, far away in the woods."

Vizin winced as he lifted himself to raise, his right hand clutching the bloodied gauze seeping the fester on his side.

"It was closer than you perceive. The verdasnik can throw their vocal calls to distract predators away from their prowl."

"My time in Academy did not teach me of such abilities."

Vizin laughed as the pain in his ribs made him grunt, "The Academy cannot teach you everything. My experience in the forest guided me to knowledge."

"You're an expert on matters of the field?"

Eris puffed her frame, turning her neck to gaze at the man lying beside her.

"Of course not," Vizin coughed, careful not to wake the others, "But I have worked in the woods for almost two years since my enlistment. When did you leave Sarat to be in the field?"

"My orders deny my right to comment on such matters. As you are also a man, I should not continue this discussion."

"Holding onto your orders, Maiden?"

Vizin gazed around. His view dimmed by the waning embers and rolling fog lingering over the camp.

"As a White Rose, I should permit my superiors to speak to you in the morning."

"Come now. You need the company, and I am an open ear."

Eris turned to him, sighed, and huffed a few flocks of hair away from her mouth.

"I suppose you may be right."

Vizin struggled to continue his inclined ascent, propping himself onto his hands while straining pain grappled over his right hips and ribs. His wound sealed, but two days without medical attention brought him to fate.

"I thought so. Tell me, Maiden, again, what brings you into the field? Why do you travel with Her Highness?"

"Her Highness sent as an envoy to Silvetzen. I chose to travel with her when I heard my sister had died in service to the Crown," Eris withdrew into her stringy hair as she uttered her last sentence.

"Murdered? By whom?"

"Those we fight against."

Vizin strained to reach his left hand onto her leg and soothed his voice into a tone to equal her pain, "I'm sorry."

"Do not be. She served His Majesty as we all do. I do not seek revenge for her but fulfilling my duties to Crown and King will honor her more than taking the lives of another."

"What of your friend, there, you're not jealous of her affection to the Magi?"

"No," she turned to Vizin, "I appall it."

"And your thoughts on Tesh?"

"Clumsy and aloof. His father was Teru Verdui. But he does not portray his qualities."

"Teru Verdui? The Temple Knight who commanded the Blue Guard?"

"Aye, the same. I heard a story from another Magi he was a common vagabond, a rogue and a criminal."

"Impossible. Teru Verdui was a brave man. He exuded qualities every soldier aspires to be. When I began service, our instructors and commanders praised him as refreshing the waters of the Saratian River flowing from the Tanakian Mountains outward into the sea. His death watered the grounds and gave rise to the Eternal Rose sprung from the gardens of His Majesty's castle. Please, do not tarnish my emotions with talks he was a commoner. If Tesh truly

402

came from his loins, then his mother must have been a common whore to taint mighty blood."

Eris derided his comments in her thoughts, puffing cool air through her lips, "Cadeck believes he is to become a Temple Knight, as his father."

"A Temple Knight? So, he is going to restore the order? I have heard stories, legends mostly where only a Temple Knight can conquer the Si'rai. But it would take an army. If rumor is true and they conquered Silvetzen and Sarat, who remains to support the Temple Knights?"

"I would not know of legends. I am just a common girl. You speak of fantasies and war tales in a manner to believe you strive to live them. I only choose to read and study and learn the ancient mysteries of the land. I am more appealed to books and scrolls than clanging a sword."

Vizin coughed to clear his throat, "Forgive me, Maiden. I did not mean to impose with my flights of grandeur. You never told me your name, love."

"Eris, Eris Fevyn. How is your wound?"

"Infected."

Through dim light dancing from the fire, Vizin looked onto the bandage covering the seal Kenat sewn into his side with his fire magic, "I don't think your friend's magick worked before the blood poisoning set in."

Eris withdrew to shock. She slipped to her side. Her hands crawled over Vizin's exposed torso taking care not to sneak her touch into a state of arousal for either of them, "But Kenat healed your wound."

She slipped her fingers over the wrappings torn from Ysalir's shirt. Brown stains of leaking blood seeped into the sooty clothing dampening the fabric in a gory wound of ever-expanding circumference.

"The cut severed a couple of organs. All Kenat did was close the wound to stop the bleeding, I was already dying before you showed up."

Vizin raised his right hand to grip Eris' sleeveless arm below her fur covering. His voice strained to exit his tongue.

"Permit me, fair Maiden, to enjoy the warmth of a woman once more before I slip to face my fate. I can hear Sokut calling to me."

Eris released herself from the soldier's grasp, her face lowered to scorn, "I am a Maiden of the Rose. I cannot allow myself to pleasure a man until I have earned my color. You disrespect the Order and the Queen by requesting such a service."

"Please, Eris, I mean no disrespect. Permit me the comfort of dying peacefully in the tender care of a lady."

"I shan't. And we will end this discussion and further talk. You may hold my hand upon your final breaths, but do not ask of me to warm your loins."

Eris reached her right hand to grip Vizin's left. Their fingers intertwined like spider webbing collapsing upon its prey within the soft soils of the forests. Mud and soot clung to her fingers as his hands tightened around them. Vizin relaxed his position onto his back, the pain pulsating across his abdomen and shooting across his legs and chest. He began chanting a Soldier's Prayer under his breaths.

Vizin begged to Sokut to grant him restful peace in the afterlife so he may once again his mother and father flowing into the oceans. As his breathing slowed, so did his grip upon Eris loosen before his body exhaled his final strain. Eris studied his death, watching patiently, allowing the surveillance to guide her insight into her duties.

To see a human die and to live his final breaths through their own eyes became the teachings of the assassin. To hear the final breaths, to feel their pain and listen to their desires and memories in death were the eruditions of the scholar and to prevent their death or make it as painless as necessary was the job of the spagyrist. Each of the qualities exuded by her profession, and either of which she could one day achieve.

Eris reached into her waistband and removed the soft cloth of her herald. Pure as white foam, the petals of the rose emblem symbolized her rank. Soot and sweat spotted on the burlap stitching which she clutched into her palms before she leaned over to kiss Vizin on blue lips. Eris' face lit up with the clutch of cold embrace as she jerked her body away from the corpse, watching Vizin's fading moments before she moved his hands to his sides.

For one moment, he no longer felt pain. Pain of which caused by his conqueror and the physical pain of vile men who feed on the sufferings of those they exploit. To Eris, the Si'rai were conquerors designed by nature to leave scorched earth in their wake disturbing their conquests to chaos. All she has seen, concluded to her the Si'rai were cleaners; cleansing old ways to create chaos for new. Their vicious attacks roared like a death wind howling through her ears and the shrieks of their war calls summoned demons through their bodies.

Her sister died by their will, but not by their hand or so Venna had informed her. She released herself from her vigil of Vizin's body and slumped to his side as the embers of the fire burned with a low hum signaling the termination of warmth. Likewise, with Vizin, Eris experienced his life though briefly snuffed out as the fire before her. She could only guess the suffering her sister endured, the horrendous defilement at the hands of her tormentors not dissimilar by the light of a fire as the one warming her.

Eris remained calm through the bristling sun rising against her back to the east as it pierced across the shadowy fogs snaking through the tree lines.

The light kissed frosty dew upon the crisp foliage settled on the floor. Shimmers of reflection twinkled along the leaves and detritus as daytime rodents scurried from their nests between logs and the underbrush to obtain their morning morsels. Eris cuddled close to herself amongst the fur wrappings lining across her shoulders while doves cooed their songs along the trees. Thoughts of death emotions drew her into serenity.

Chapter 36

Morning mists sprinkled across the sun streaks rippling through the forest grove. Chitlebugs floated through the slicing rays, their reflective carapaces bounced the light like slivers of dust floating through a dirty room as they swarmed for the tree sap. As he stood beside the cart, Cadeck puffed on his elongated pipe, savoring the spicy tingle floating through his nostrils as he exhaled his smoke.

"We do not have time to bury Vizin. We need to hurry to Racoren."

Ysalir sighed as she patted the Si'rai war beast against the lengthy mane flanking across its neck. Natural oils sheened a reflective sable coat as the animal stood in the sunlight piercing into the grove. Ysalir stroked her own mottled hair strewn with sweat and soot away from her face, her oceanic eyes dimmed into a lull with the emotions weighing on her heart.

"You won't give him the honor of a Saratian burial?"

"Cassica was quick to wish end to his life before I intervened. Why would you honor him with proper rite?

Ysalir arced her toned back as she ducked under the neck of the animal to face Cadeck who stood on the opposite side. Her eyes shot towards Cadeck's weighted face against his own emotions he struggled to suppress.

Ysalir continued, "He was still someone's child and you and I both know what happened here. He deserves it at least."

"Did you not inform Cassica last night?"

Ysalir lowered her chin and peaked over her shoulder to see Cassica aiding to dismantle camp.

"I could not. I could not so I could protect her. She believes he lied."

"Then why did you lie to her?"

"I could not speak truth. Knowing I told her, what would she do to me? She would see me killed. She nearly killed me while you were at the Fire Temple because of my broken heart."

Cadeck lifted his eyes in concern, "And if she discovers something far worse, on her own accord? How would you help her?"

"I… I do not know, Magi."

Cadeck peaked over Ysalir's shoulder continuing to watch the camp dismantle, "Her pains back at Tijoa's hut. I have pondered on horrid night in recent days. Your suspicion may be correct."

Cadeck paced to advance behind Ysalir, placing a hardened hand upon the muddied tunics covering her shoulder.

"How do you mean, Cadeck?"

"Consider such research an affair of the Magi. I should not tell you so I can protect you."

"But...."

Cadeck shrugged her thoughts off, interrupting her in mid-speech with a snide grin through stubble face. Cadeck's words followed from his tongue with the spicy tingle of ruban breath.

"Make it a shallow grave. Be quick about ritual and prayer. I will have Tesh and Kenat double effort to ready the cart."

#

Coniferous trees flanked along faint trails carved into the underbrush. Fog lifted from the assault of the mid-morning sun as the single, raven horse carried the rugged cart through the clearing at blinding pace. Ysalir bucked the reins to hammer the horse to speed with the confidence of a commanding driver over the fierce beast. A hooded cowl covered her face and head as another figure dressed in same seated beside her. Cadeck's graying beard covering his pitted face jutted from below the tattered coverings. Behind them in the cargo bed, hay mounds spread along the wooden planks hiding the other occupants.

Cadeck strained his neck to peak behind them, eyeing the hidden compatriots and to take account if pursuers followed. His breaths eased into relaxation as he released a heavy sigh before returning posture to face forward.

"The citizens of Racoren will not take kind to Her Highness making an appearance. Are you sure our disguises will not fail us as they had against the Si'rai patrol on our way to Tijoa's?"

"I have no doubts."

"And did you take into account what Vizin said about the Si'rai?"

"Yes."

Ysalir focused on her task, keeping vigil at the Si'rai beast's pace and careful to keep the cart from jerking or listing too far to any side to keep center of gravity level.

"I sense uneasiness in you, Rensel. Your confirmation did not sound too confident."

"Don't you think you've questioned my judgment enough today?"

"I apologize if you took harm from my statements, but your thoughts trouble you."

Ysalir sighed. Hair toiled across her face through the shifting winds tucked beneath a sullen cowl.

"I don't wish for her to know the truth, please honor me Magi."

Ysalir's words fell under her breath fading into the air as their sounds reached the back of the cart. Cadeck took her whispers in serious tone. For a trained killer with many scores under her belt, a knowledgeable spy with fluency in the Si'rai tongue, Ysalir's words billowed fear. Cadeck sensed this and withdrew inside. His face furrowed slightly below his cloaks as he contemplated her statements silently. His emotionless breaths danced in the airs flowing in concentric circles from his nostrils.

Ysalir shifted a quick glance over her shoulders and returned to face forward.

"We will need to ditch this horse before we reach Racoren. We will need to make it on foot starting at nightfall."

Cadeck's eyes stunned in stare at her words, "But wouldn't holding this animal, this beast of war, guarantee us safe passage if the Si'rai hold Racoren?"

Ysalir paused, releasing a slow sigh, "A safe passage to the axe. This animal is strong, the mane well kept. This animal belongs to nobility. If the Si'rai catch us with this animal, they will no doubt believe we stole it. Si'rai disdain those not of their race, not of their lineage. They have a word for us, sadakem. It means 'cursed people.' Even should one of their own, not of the noble families were to have this animal would mean instant death, excruciating beyond imagination. Imagine the outrage should one not of their race own an object of the nobility."

Cadeck grinned, "'Sadakem'? Words spoken in the ancient tongue as the name for man, amusing they twist it to be a cursed word."

Ysalir nodded off his comment focusing instead on her plan to ditch the animal, "The main road skirts the northern edge of Er'tahar. We will need to be careful on foot. Dangerous roads full of thieves and criminals. Its' rugged and ill-kept roads are unfit for heavy movement. A wervostrakgar should have difficulty in the sloshy terrain."

Cadeck shook his head, "I am aware of Racoren and its dangers. Many times have I ventured there but forgive me if I must ask you to repeat statement. I refuse my tongue to speak their vile language."

Ysalir spoke under her breath with the winds curling between her lips and Cadeck's ears, "War procession. The loosest interpretation of it in Rykanian Common Tongue. What Vizin described fits the details. There could be

409

hundreds or thousands of troops, supplies and cavalry. Our troops in Racoren would not stand much of a chance.

"Please, Cadeck. Do not let my words leave our ears."

Ysalir looked back into the cargo hold. Sun streaks peaked across the sky marking the early afternoon sun. The mounds of hay where the occupants hid remained still amidst the slow heaving marking their locations. Cassica's mound lay still, resting on the right sideboard covered well with straw. Dried strands of hay tightened inside her dirtied locks of hair. Scarlet weaves mottled together in front of sooty face. She lay on her side listening to Ysalir's words.

Her thoughts raced to her kingdom as Ysalir spoke to Cadeck; the decimation from Vizin's description reflected a brutal battle. She dared not to consider the capitol city laid plundered, burned, and destroyed should his words be true. Cassica calmed herself, focusing her thoughts on a hidden motivation of strength. Cadeck kept her safe, at least another day. The armored carriage carrying her to Silvetzen became a distraction to the Si'rai luring them into her kingdom. Her emerald eyes turned into a source of tears.

A fathomed death would have given little to no hope for her people, for her kingdom. Alive, Cassica could use her status to convince her people to support her efforts, support the Magi and support the reinvented Knights. She closed her eyes, harkening to a deeper meaning to her struggles whispering a small prayer to gods she never trusted.

#

Nighttime crept in lingering shuffle upon the travelers. Haunting odors wafted through the air like a dense fog. Silent croaks from amphibious creatures rang through the still air in a symphony of unnerving calm. Tesh lay on his back. Smoke billowed from the campfire, into the clear skies, and disrupted his count of the stars. He continued his silent vigil, refraining conversation towards Cadeck and remained isolated from the others resorting to his inner thoughts.

In the distance, Cassica led the ladies to dismantle the horse carriage. Venna and Eris removed weapons and garments from the cargo bed. They gathered what they could carry and hurried towards the center of camp. Ysalir took care to remove the tack from the muscular animal. She escorted the beast away from the riggings of the carriage and beckoned it to scurry. Rising into a whinny, the animal shifted back to all fours and sprinted in a northerly direction.

Cassica ceased her duties as Venna and Eris skittered towards the campfire. She watched as the younger women hefted the supplies within their

410

arms, tucked upon their chests as their shadows covered the campfire. She stood within the cargo bed as Ysalir's darkened silhouette returning to the cart.

"Why did you lie to me, Ysalir?"

Cassica spoke her real name with scorn, denying the woman the safety of her own anonymity.

Ysalir stopped in her actions, "Your Highness, you use my true name?"

Ysalir darted her eyes, sensing the unease in Cassica's voice knowing the reveal of her name was perilous to her own standing.

"I meant no lies, Your Highness."

Cassica's face withdrew to anger.

"I use your true name out of spite. Matters of my father's lands are my concern. Any knowledge you have kept from me is in violation of your oaths and subject to punishment. What do you know, Ysalir?"

The princess jumped over the side of the cart, landing on the soft ground with firm stance. Ysalir took defense to her princess, returning to the front of the carriage and meeting her superior to eye. Cassica furthered her advance as she paced a few feet to the front of the cart to meet the agent. Soft ground mushed below their feet creating slight tracks from thin shoes in Cassica's wake.

"Please, Your Highness, I do not choose to argue my reasons. Do not put me into this position."

Cassica ignored her plea. Anger rolled through emerald eyes glaring with empty soul through muddied crimson locks.

"My kingdom is gone. My cousin, murdered. And you refuse to inform me everything you knew. You knew about this. You hid your knowledge, and you divulged your legs and your thoughts to a Si'rai lover. You slept with Si'rai and Silvetzenian men alike and for what? I do not believe you gathered your information, but you exposed my father's weaknesses. You are a traitor and scores of my subjects suffer by words from your tongue and the pleasures of your loins."

Cassica reached to her right side and produced a small dagger from her belt and in swift motion raised it to bear against Ysalir's neck. Ysalir covered her face by crossing her arms from Cassica's thrust that brought the princess' wrist between Ysalir's. Twisting in reaction, Ysalir removed the knife from her assailant and hoisted Cassica across her back and dropped her onto the ground.

The violent outburst from Cassica's voice turned Venna's head towards the pair as her eyes witnessed Cassica drop to her back. Cadeck turned his head away from the campfire towards the commotion. Kenat followed suit. Tesh repositioned, gripping the hilt of the blade resting by his side. Cadeck brushed them both to still as he lifted himself to stand.

"I'll handle this."

Cadeck rushed pace towards the argument.

Ysalir positioned her knee into Cassica's back, the princess' face steadied into peat soil on her right cheek.

"Do not make me do this, Your Highness. I mean you no harm. I serve you, your father, and his lands. I have protected you. I have protected the Crown."

Hinted with a jade ferocity, Cassica's eyes shimmered with an increased brightness.

"Get off me whore. You are no Rose; you betrayed my father and worse of all my trust, Ysalir Rutin."

"I did no such thing."

"Enough."

Cadeck's order barked with emotional tone. He gripped Ysalir by her shoulders and heaved her away from the ailing royal. Ignoring the trappings of decency and respect of her position, Cadeck reached down and brought Cassica to stand by lifting her under her shoulders and reaching across her breast. She turned to react to his admonishment and met him to eye with stiff, muscular rigidity.

Cassica's eyes brightened into shimmered green wash glistening under their own accord, reflecting fiery disdain towards Cadeck. Her emerald gaze flared brightly along the pits and crevices scarring his aging face. He muttered ancient words with calm manner towards the girl inaudible to those around him. As his soliloquy left his spoken tongue, Cassica's body returned soft and flexible; her eyes returned to natural color as she slumped into his arms.

Ysalir stepped foot to approach. Cadeck turned and shook his head as Cassica breathed softly held by his arms. She steadied a push away from the Magi as her arms remained cuddled into his chest. He peaked down towards her face as her complexion emptied to return color. Ysalir retreated in her attempts to Cassica's aide and bent down to pick up the fallen weapon. Venna reached her sister and she rudely shrugged off the blonde girl.

"I think it's time we settled in."

Cadeck reassured the ladies, lifting Cassica away from his shoulders. Cadeck braced his arms around Cassica as Venna scurried beside him.

"Will she be alright?"

"She'll be fine Venna, return to camp."

Cadeck furthered his pace towards the campfire, draping Cassica across his arms to carry her to the fireside. Venna crossed her arms, shrugging with curled lips at the Magi. Ysalir slid the knife into her belt, tightened it against her hip and leaned against the cart, propping a foot against the wagon. Venna turned towards her, brushing disheveled bangs from her cheeks.

"What did you do, Ysalir?"

"Nothing. Return to camp and follow your orders. I will take first watch."

"It is everything isn't it? Everything going on now. The Si'rai, the war, the Magi, everything?"

"It is of no concern of your rank. Now return to camp as instructed."

"There's more you're not telling me."

Ysalir sighed, releasing angered breath, "I tell you not as a sister out of your concern but as your superior. Return to camp now or I will see your disobedience as insubordination and see your punishment accordingly. See to Cassica's rest. You and Eris must flank her and watch over her. Do not go near Kenat. This is an order."

"But…"

"I said go. For the last time, leave me."

Venna sunk her head and turned her svelte frame toward the small camp with audible groan. Ysalir sighed, her breaths roiled from her mouth in chilled halos. Amphibious animals croaked their nighttime songs along the distance. She gazed at the open sky. Clouds spread thin along stretched canvas covering sections of star-filled brightness. The dark patch of the Abyss hovered overhead along a north-south span splitting the sky like a wide chasm.

Figures wavered near the fire. Venna seated next to Cassica as Cadeck leaned over the royal and covered her with a blanket of fur. Ysalir carried stench of clinging sweat and blood-dried gauze. She unlatched the flask strapped to her hip, removed cork, and lifted to her mouth. Scant drops lingered on the rim as they collapsed onto her waiting tongue. She moaned, screwing the cork into the pit, and dropped it to the ground.

The camp settled to rest as Cadeck stood from his seat, proceeding towards Ysalir's position. The dim fires masked his silhouetted appearance as a ghost haunting the grounds. Scruffy and worn, Cadeck cleared his throat to speak as Ysalir interrupted his thoughts.

"I could have taken care of her myself; it was matter of royal concern. Let us remain of our own command while we help you on your journey."

"She would have torn you apart had I not intervened."

"You speak of disrespect towards her position. I do not believe she would have placed herself in danger at my hand. What did you tell her, Cadeck?"

"There is no translation in Common Tongue."

"You said there is something within her. What is it?"

413

"What it is, revealed itself in Tijoa's hut."

Cadeck crossed his arms, leaning beside Ysalir. Towering next to her close to a foot, he craned his neck to meet her face.

"I know little of this spirit but understand this being poses a threat to all of humanity should she fall into the hands of the Si'rai. I have felt this being since her birth, thus my interest to the Court against my Ascended's wishes. It is no coincidence such a being revealed itself on the night when magick was highest. As Magi, we do not believe in coincidences."

"Can you remove it from her? Is it dangerous? Was it Si'rai magick?"

"I cannot say for certain, Ysalir. I know too little of this creature. I would require more study and meditation. You are doing your best, and your service to Cassica shall not go unnoticed."

Ysalir lowered her head, "You and I both share many secrets Magi. She accused me of lying and exposing weaknesses of the Crown. She even called me by my true name, to a Rose, it is shame. I may as well oust myself from the Order. I want to know what I fight for. What I continue to protect Cassica and the Crown for. Tell me, Magi, is it all true?"

"Is what true?"

Cadeck turned towards her, shifting his body to face her.

"All of this. Do you believe Tesh is some great hero? What do you think happened to Sarat?"

Cadeck sighed, her questions weighed on his heart like rocks pressing on his chest on a torture slab.

"Do I believe in Tesh? It is hard to say. He shows great promise, but he has been silent with me since he returned from the Temple of Wind. His vision, his experience revealed something to him. Until he tells me and opens back up to me, I will not know. I will not pry. What he saw is between him, the gods and Tijoa. What do I think of Sarat?"

His words emptied into trailing breath as though the thought led his heart into cessation, "I choose not to."

Cadeck's words offered little comfort to Ysalir as her thoughts waned towards a fate she realized. Ysalir struggled to remove foul thoughts from mind, but the prospect Sarat and the royal family were no longer in control or worse, dead as Ragres tempted in his attack, brought little comfort into her body.

"The Council, is there nothing they can do? Surely not everyone voted with your Ascended."

"What remains of the Council is few and far. They are no match for the Si'rai if those we have met are of any sign of what waits for us. As it stands, Kenat and I are no match either. Our magick suffers with each day we idle under their grasp."

"Suffers?"

"Aye. I have felt it, as well as Kenat. Each use of magick gives away our position. We must make speed to leave this dark influence."

"Then we will lose, unless Tesh is able to defeat them alone, but how? He is one man."

"Once his training is complete, my dear, I have no doubt his ancient spirit will take care of your concern for us."

Ysalir reacted with open gape.

"I have heard the legends, the stories, and they are all myths. You cling to an ideal which cannot be true."

Cadeck reacted with a calm furrow of his brow, "Erase doubt from clouded mind. You must restore your faith in the gods."

Ysalir shook her head.

"I do not recall ever knowing faith. I once thought I lived and fought for something. Every life I took, every tongue I twisted and every cock which filled me was in service to the Crown. But knowing now what I know, what I have fought for has suffered in paralyzing agony. And for what? A prophecy? A legend? We fight for something unproven and all at the mercy of our king. What if he is dead? What if the Court is dead? Then what?"

Ysalir struggled upon final thought as tears welled from her eyes stifling the anger building within.

"Return to camp Ysalir," Cadeck patted her on her left shoulder to ease her dismay, "I'll continue watch."

His words reflected the tone she called for; somber, informative, and pleasant. She realized he thought the same but reiterated he wished not to divulge any further detail. Keeping Cassica in the dark as much as possible was key to keeping her sanity and preventing violent outbursts of anger and aggression manifesting from the spirit within. What it was, Cadeck never understood. He never carried weight to study the matter for his own teachings and those of his children were of importance.

In his mind, his thoughts lingered towards Tesh's future, reaching the Water Temple and furthering training. Distant stars twinkled against the chasm of the Abyss cutting across his field of view. What lingered there he dared not meditate upon for such answers might corrupt his soul. He reached into his soul, calling along his aztmudin struggling upon darkened taint.

Exhausted and spent of his magick, each call to meditation brought him face to face with a demon instead. Each call to magick weakened him with each passing moment. Cadeck reached hard to find inner peace against the still silence of impending uncertainty. Leaving Silvetzen offered little comfort only to feel the same darkness upon crossing realms. Cadeck and Kenat knew the truth before seeing Vizin's body but dare not reveal to Cassica. Her eyes soon discovered the outcome. Reaching into nothingness, he expanded his feelings. His aztmudin billowed through his soul. Feeling awash with regenerated energies, whispers lingered in his mind crescendoing into a loud roar finally silenced by the sincere clarity he once lost.

The night speaks still whispers, love. Foul stench waits in Racoren. Hurry to Temple, I have much to share with you.

Jess?

Chapter 37

Tivius A'zum followed the murmurs of the officers before him as their sounds echoed upon the vast war room chambers like haunting beacons of strategy. He seated himself in a high-backed chair topped by a pair of golden eagle ornaments on each side of the back. Leather entrapping wrapped around his chest and legs, covering him from neck to boot like a sadistic cocoon of constricted hides. His right hand stroked his chin, elbow leaned on the burnt colored oak rest. The accoutrements and association of the furniture deserved no respect from him as he carelessly positioned a foot onto a knee, slouching inattentively to the discussions around him.

Before him, a table positioned in the middle of the hall spanning a length of many meters. A rudimentary display of parchment drawn maps spread across the table as several officers discussed key strategy pointing their reddish olive fingers as their talking points converged. Their armor varied from the plating of Field Marshal Jabar, covered in reflective silver sheen from the neck plates down, to the generals covered in sable armor with silver etchings. The officers were devoid of helmets, faces were clean or marked with battle scars. Generals talked with a respected Imperium accent and slivers of gray splattered along some of their heads denoting their age.

"My Lord," a tall general before him began.

Etched lines of battle-hardened skin accentuated his nose and cheek bones as his chin ended like a carved point. A cropped ponytail perked from the rear of his bald scalp.

"I present an update on our progress. We have secured the major towns of Sarat; Kora, Racoren and the capitol. The bodies of the male nobility have traveled to the other towns as you ordered. We are nearing completion of the worker camp to our north with added space constructed on the camp to the south. Existing workers reassigned to the mines and worker camp there. We have forced into conscription those who resist, at the cost of life, or transferred them to Silvetzen for further sale as uristri. The transition of the 'material labor' has begun. Those of the durusta classes have had their wealth and possessions and other assets assessed, their lives evaluated for inclusion into the Imperium.

417

We have begun transition giving them proper documentation among Imperium durustristus so they may begin business as required by regulation.

"But the news is not all in good tone, my Lord. There is reason to believe pockets of resistance persist and are gathering at Yumphen, using the navy vessels in port. We have dispatched correspondence to Magister Malphas to supply ships to help in the fight."

Discouraged by the news, Tivius' icy eyes inflamed into a brighter hue. He shifted to lean forward; his hands firmly grasped as he settled both boots to the hard stone.

"We cannot hold this kingdom if we do not hold its major ports. Who commands our troops in Yumphen?"

"Commander Vuk'ian."

"Send another legion to aid him. General Isitar," Tivius pointed to a general to the addressor's right.

"Yes, My Lord."

"Command this legion to Yumphen, relieve Vuk'ian of command and punish him for his failures. Yumphen is your charge, do not fail me."

"Yes Magister," Isitar saluted with a closed fist against his chest and bowed in reverence. He excused himself from the counsel room with a lockstep of his metal boots clamoring along the chiseled stone floor.

Turning to Tivius, the general across the table from him held back the fuming thoughts bubbling in his head.

"Is this wise, my Lord? Our forces in Sarat and the outlying villages are thin numbering less than twenty thousand. We send any more troops to the other cities, and our hold in the capitol could falter. The complacent citizens still outnumber our own troops. If they realize we have weakened, we could face an uprising and lose control of the kingdom."

Tivius growled to the concerns expressed by his general.

"The people under our rule should be aware their attempt to resist shall not go without severe punishment. The display of their dead, ruling men should have subdued them enough and if we still hold the minds of the nobility, the lower classes will fall in line. Should they still resist, punish them that speak out. What is the progress of finding the former Princess and the Queen of this foul kingdom?"

"My Lord," the general swallowed a gulp considering his next words carefully, "there has been no current information as to their location. We are almost certain the Princess is still in Silvetzen. We have salvaged records placing the Queen in Kora on family business longer than an abranus ago."

"And yet, she stays elusive. Exposed in Kora on official business, reveling amongst her people and family? And we cannot find her?"

Tivius snarled through grated gums.

"No, my Lord," the general swallowed his words admitting failure.

Tivius erected his stretched leathery bindings into a form-fitted posture as he stood in front of the table. Towering over the table as a menacing monster set to devour its prey, his silk-screened eyes focused intention upon the general's thoughts. The thick-framed general gripped a silvery-metal glove against his bald forehead. His breaths strained with groaned, guttural pain emitting from his vocal cords. Veins bulged in his thick forehead and neck as he clamored backward in a struggle for equilibrium. Bulked armor jilted with his erratic movements as he swung his hips wildly with each jerked step.

"My Lord," his voice called, straining to form cohesive speech, "please, I…"

"Your thoughts," Tivius hissed, "discourage me. I have commanded them to be torn apart in the Abyss to join your soul."

"No Lord, no…not this."

The general dropped to his knees; his armor scraped the stone floor. The other generals and officers nearby circled around him, their mouths agape at the spectacle, staying silent as Tivius paced. As the general continued to exist in torture, Tivius' eyes brightened, his body posture ignored the general's pleas. Tivius' arms crossed behind his back, leathery confinements squeaking and gnawing against his skin.

"Let me continue to serve you, Lord," his words strained from his lips as the officer followed to the ground with his open palm before collapsing onto his side.

"You will serve me in the Abyss as a uristri when I return."

"No please…I…"

The general's voice trailed as he protested the curse. Before he could complete his sentence, a mushy crack expelled through his thoughts as his eyes blackened into darkness. Thick, vermillion blood spilled from his ears, nostrils and eyelids as his body collapsed onto the floor.

The officers around the dead general remained in awe. The commanding power of a Magister was well-known amongst them during their indoctrinations from youth, never to question. Never to anger. It was rare for a Magister to display his or her power to those in their command or presence below their equality. Thus, their secrets would remain hidden to their caste. Rumors persisted that magistri were madmen, insane receptacles of the Abyss, feared by all. Tivius' sneer proved their superstitions.

"This is why I do not trust the wervostri. You are weak, meddling individuals who clamor to your strength and rely less on your minds. Therefore, you shall always be an inferior caste.

"Commander," Tivius pointed to a sturdy man built as rugged as the fallen general. His existing armor shimmered as the generals with a raven crest of the Si'rai herald emblazoned on his chest.

"Assume General Cisian's armor and rank. You are in command of the forces in Sarat now. Send urgent message to our ally in Kora. He is to spend all efforts to find the Queen, the backing of the Imperium is at his command. Do not allow yourself to my wrath."

Tivius' words tore through the command staff like a violent storm pounding an eroded coastline.

"As you wish my Lord," the deep-voiced commander addressed in their tongue as he bowed reverently.

Tivius turned away from the newly appointed general towards a pair of iron doors stretching floor-to-ceiling. A pair of plain, raven-armored soldiers gripped a pair of bronze-carved handles flanking the seam of the doorway. With minimal strength, the doors tore open to reveal a foyer stretching before the lofty magician.

Tivius exited the strategy room as the iron doors clamored shut behind him. An outside pair of soldiers flanked the hingeworks of the chamber entry carrying pikes twice their height. In perfect unison, the outside troops crossed their spears with single hands in a symmetrical formation. Tivius heel-turned to his right as leathery bindings stretched against his skin like a suffocating cocoon. Ebony robes stretched across his shoulders pinned by hooks under armored epaulets and fell just above his heel line, drifting over the floor as a shadowy spirit. *Daihekda* strapped to his left hip, trimmed by bony hilt protruding from below his chest.

His eyes dimmed to a natural tone like a silver-icy lake simmering against a shoreline of pale, crusted skin. He felt his blood returning to normal boil as it warmed from icy cold. Raven hair billowed across his shoulders to flow with his gait. Tivius continued his journey along the hallway, his eyes focused on ancient portraits of rulers past as he paced beyond them.

Various names and tenure dates lined the walls emblazoned with a brass plate below their pictures. He admonished the notion to desecrate the portraits when approached for the command in earlier days, instead admiring the works of the artists that created them. Differing styles manifested with the series of depictions reflecting the styles of the creator with each progressive ruler. Tivius spotted consistencies with several rulers noting the same artist painted for the kingdom for several iterations of rule.

As he continued to the end of the hallway, a portrait of Trebut Geraud Bovariàr established the current ruling dynasty of the kingdom. Tivius paused at this portrait. Lamp lights danced in a chandelier above him contrasting the humble hues of Trebut's crimson beard full to his chest. His right hand tucked into a lavender robe with the crest of Sarat hung around his neck in a golden painted medallion whose brush strokes stood out to reflect his pompadour lifestyle. Golden rings highlighted upon his open knuckle. Tall boots rose to his knees covering white, seamless pants and topped his head with his elaborate crown. He stood against a table with a broad landscape of the city in the depths of the background.

Tivius craned his neck to meet the paintings' eyes. Dark hope appeared to empty from the subject's eyes as Tivius reflected on what would have been Trebut's thoughts as he ran his sacred blade through the man's heart. Tivius pondered on thoughts of hidden purpose. As interim ruler of Sarat, Tivius encountered willing subjects and unwilling slaves. Trebut's sons faced his blade or those of his assassins. The kingdom fell as tens of thousands of soldiers brutally marched their way into the capitol city with a supporting regiment of horses and artillery.

Other secrets lingered in Trebut's thoughts which Tivius raced to find. During his short term, Tivius exposed secrets of the kingdom the rulers kept from their subjects; Trebut's excessive gambling and drinking habits and his distrust for his Queen. Tivius smiled, relishing in the knowledge the Si'rai fabricated propaganda claiming the adult children were debaucherous and younger children were born of bastards who worked in service to the castle and even worse; the youngest child was born of incest by one of the twin boys and their princess in a bawdy orgy of libertinism involving the trio.

The weak-minded citizens believed it and those who betrayed the Si'rai met with harsh punishment. The nobility denied rumor, but in clamor to keep their properties followed the lies. Yet, something still escaped Tivius, something Trebut, with his devotion the Magi in study and piousness, may not have known.

Tuned to the Abyss, Tivius' soul reached for something existential. Each use of his magick burned a searing mark against his soul unlike which he had previously known. As he ripped General Cisian's soul from his mind, Tivius' blood burned cold with a feeling of greater power as to feel his magick itself heightened. The drain of life awakened something within him, undisturbed in his rites before as he had done in Sarat.

"What secrets do you hide from me, even in death, Trebut?"

Tivius growled with a low hiss through rotted teeth. Standing as a poised raven in demented solitude, Tivius sneered as he craned his neck skyward towards the face of the portrait. Crackled fingers of bulbous pus traced the darkened colors of the lower part of the portrait along the painted floor. Shuffled feet distracted his attention as he turned his face towards the disruption. A small child hurried towards the towering man; the boy's hair cut into a neat bowl.

Tivius sensed fear into the boy as the messenger approached closer. An olive-toned skin covered the boy's face and exposed arms as scant clothes kept the boy covered with minimal warmth. Bare feet scurried along the frigid stone in hastened pace to keep his warm blood flowing. He stopped a few feet in front of Tivius and removed a folded letter from the rope tied against his waist. Icy blue eyes focused upon the timid boy as Tivius requested of the purpose to his disruption.

"Lord Tivius?"

The young boy requested in timorous speech.

"What do you request, uristri?"

Tivius poked tongue through rotted gum, his raven mane flowing in front of his face.

The slave focused on Tivius' eyes with the dark-hazel hue of his own. He was a native of Iriq, a land known for its vast mineral wealth and one of the first lands held by the Imperium outside their homeland. As a slave, he held minimal privilege and feared for his life with each step of his day. Misplaced by thousands of miles and several months of journey, indoctrination of his service to the Imperium became the boy's guidance.

"A letter from Abaddon, addressed from Stritus A'zum."

Tivius yanked the folded parchment from the boy's intimidated stance, "Begone, uristri."

The boy bowed in respect and shuffled away. Tivius held the folded correspondence in his left-hand relishing in the coarseness of the parchment of the yusik tree. As he flipped it over, the sealed wax emblazoned with the sigil of the Abyss rested upon an unsheathed sword. Recognizing his house seal, he tucked the note within the leathery belt strapped around his waistband careful not to crunch the delicate parchment and distort the words respected as sacred.

Like a ghost, Tivius floated through the cavernous foyer, leaving the grand hall, and entered a primary chamber anchored by an elaborate staircase. A heavy carpet flowed down the steps like a crystal-blue river. Trimmed with gold etching flanked on the sides, the drapery spilled onto the baseline and ended in a half-circle pattern emblazoned with the double-head eagle herald. Spherical finials began on the banisters and led the balustrade as it split into two flanking runs at the fiftieth step. On the wall behind the first flight, the eagle herald was set in bronze above a pair of crossed, decorative swords. Tivius gripped the balustrade as he motioned his way towards the staircase. The rugged thickness of the polished bearwood steadied his stride as he appeared to float against the rails supporting the banister.

Above him, the sun burned through an elaborate crystalline rotunda where gold braces held the large sections in place. Each of the stones reflected the sacred sunlight onto the various décor in manner to highlight feigned significance of wealth. The braces arced high, leading to a sculpture adorning the apex of the rotunda, cast in gold, and bearing the twin-headed eagle likeness.

He carried beyond the first platform and split onto the right staircase leading to another story. As Tivius furthered the journey beyond minor chambers and windowed rooms, he approached a large wooden door nearly double his height, turned the latch, and pushed the door forward. Seas of shelves held vast volumes of books, scrolls and other bindings. Tickling scents of bearwood mingled with the aging dust of drying paper as Tivius walked to a table. Positioned behind the desk, he straightened his cloak and removed his weapon as his body lumbered into the chair on a leathery collision course. He lifted the sealed letter from his belt and rested it upon the table.

Sunlight burned through the high windows behind the desk illuminating the grand library before him. Ahead of his view, shelves of books positioned in neat rows against the walls, also running down the center of the room. Feet shuffled against musty stone as several men and women toiled amongst the books and scrolls, resting them upon risen desks for study. One man turned as Tivius entered the room, watching as the towering wizard relieved pain from thought as Tivius released a long sigh.

Each scholar wore the loose, raven shrouds of their position flung across their bodies like woolen blankets. A few slung medallions around their necks of golden chain and crimson sigil. The startled man strode towards Tivius. Diffident and spindly, the younger gentleman approached with consternation at the sudden arrival of the superior rank.

"Lord, you look troubled," his voice creaked with intimidation.

Tivius turned stare at the man whose height came to his chest. His face stretched along his z-axis into a pointed nose and extended chin as a man out of place amongst the most desirable traits of the Si'rai. His complexion was pale, in keeping with the lack of sunlight his work denied him.

"Do tell, magistri, you have better news than my generals?"

"Lord A'zum, we have combed these books and scrolls and have found only histories, stories, legends, and the occasional reference to magick. However, nothing leads us to a conclusion of the power that you feel in your aztunai here and the supposition that it is more far-reaching than that of Supernus Magister."

Erecting to full stand, Tivius' arm span reached across the wide desk onto the neckline of the frightened man's cloak. In one swing of his strength, Tivius cleared the weaker man over the desk and flung him into the massive window behind him. With a crackle of shattered glass emptying into a wide-rimmed hole, the man cleared the windowsill and plummeted to the courtyard below with his dying screams. The remaining scholars ceased their study and stared at Tivius as his eyes shorn with furious azure.

"There shall be no food or rest until you find the information I seek. I shall station a wervostri within these walls to insure my Volen. Do not let me render unto another as I did to him."

Tivius outstretched his hand towards the window behind him reminding his understudies of failure. Sunlight spilled into the gap trickling onto crusted fingernails enhancing their brittle, blackened spots marred with embellished amber decay. Tivius' mane stretched across his shoulders flanking the pale visage staring with malicious intent towards the scholars. Their faces fell to fear.

As Tivius returned calm, he lifted the sealed letter to his side and carried his slender tower towards the massive doors. Tivius slid across the floor with shuffling leather. The scholars' faces followed his exit with heightened unease. Tivius sealed the door behind him with a clamorous shudder as the workers resumed their research.

Outside the chambers, Tivius followed the hallway and came upon the first soldier in his walk. With pointed finger and anger in his breath, Tivius commanded the young trooper to assign towards the library room. Tivius continued pace, sighing deep with feelings of exasperation and planned failures. Had his father orchestrated the incompetent underlings towards his command? Was this his punishment for such short-sightedness fulfilling his orders and charge?

Doubt filled his mind as he continued along decorative pathways towards the northern wing along the highest story of the grand palisade. Here, he moved beyond the hall with the paintings and towards a pair of immaculately, carved doors which led onto a grand terrace overlooking the rear of the castle. He slid his hand along decorative railings lined by ivy and manicured plants where a large garden spanned far west toward the infinite edge of the steppe.

Spaced archways upon the terrace cast sunlit shadows on the white-marble walkway. Below Tivius, soldiers sparred and trained in an expansive courtyard which stretched outward along the steppe to an artificial pool flanked on all sides by a voluminous garden. War cries called from the training men in syncopated response to their commanding officers. Tivius advanced towards an iron door frame, flanked by the pair of silent, unwavering figures of a male and female, and released his concerns into Trebut's chambers.

Like gears of machinery, the metal doors craned open to reveal Tivius into the chambers of which he made bed. Clean, lavender sheets sprawled upon the mattress wide enough to accommodate several people. The canopy redecorated with sheen; black frill bound with ropes upon the four posts. A host of young boys and girls addressed the room, washing windows, and wiping the cold stone floors. The servants clothed in traditional uristri vestments; a simple tunic covering their bodies and ended at their knees, their scant and frail arms exposed through open sleeves.

Upon entry, the servants ceased their functions, turned to Tivius and with Saratian fear, bowed in reluctant reverence. Tivius pointed towards a small girl towards his right and addressed her in Common Tongue. He commanded the child to release his cloak from his shoulders and with obeisance; the child reached for a step stool and placed it at Tivius' right.

Jittery fingers tangled against lanky shoulders as she reached for the small hooks binding the cloak against his clothes. She untied the metallic epaulet and lifted it aside to reveal the upward hooks bound into metal loops. She released the first flank as another child came upon Tivius' left and repeated the process.

Released by restricted flocks, Tivius proceeded towards the desk positioned next to the fireplace. Scents of native bearwood danced upon his nostrils with bitter hints as he moved himself into the plush chair behind the surface. He ordered the children back to chore as one of the boys impatiently met eye contact with the imposing being.

"Your eyes are not worthy to look upon me, slave. Do it again, and I shall rip your heart asunder while you watch."

The boy obeyed, retreating to dip his cloth into the metal bucket next to him. He wrung out the fabric and furiously scrubbed the aging floor. Each movement by Tivius heightened the fear of the boys and girls. The recent uristri soon learned fear and oppression.

One of the girls, her eyes gleaned a light hazel in the spilling sunlight, pouted with puffed lips while fresh, quieted tears sullied her face. She continued to clean the bearwood surfaces, hiding her depression from her oppressor. The two girls that removed Tivius' cloak carefully folded it to specification and placed the delicate drapery within the armoire. They returned to task, washing the windows with soiled cloth.

Tivius guided a small knife against the seal of his estate, releasing the folds of the delicate parchment. Dried ziut ink hinted at the mastery of the script of the letter's author. The blackened ledger showed to Tivius the stationary of his rank and the correspondence had been genuine from its source. He unfolded the paper with eight, perfectly symmetrical folds; another indicator the author had been his entrusted eunuch. He gleamed with a rare smile as the words of his caretaker spilled from page with the educated eloquence befitting of his domain.

The author placed his address in far-left margin spanning to center of page. He began his body in Si'rai standard; top to bottom formed with the obscure calligraphy of the language. Characters held no pattern to script. Lifted angles emphasized power words, while soft words were arches and loops. Paragraphs began by double-space separation as the opening words pronounced by bold indentation drop caps. Tivius mouthed the words in his speech, careful not to utter aloud should his foreign labor dare memorize his sacred tongue.

Lord Tivius A'zum, Magnificum Magistrata, Lord Commander of the Fifth Arm of Chaos, and Son of Exalted Supernus Magister, Lucivus A'zum,

I would hope this letter receives you upon good news and your endeavors in the lands of the Sadakem return with glorious bounty. The affairs of the Stritus continue within your most entrusted hands at my command.

To matters of the Stritus: Durustratus Eikenor has requested one hundred auduin on loan to expand his shops outside his district. We agreed to terms at equal interest to the amount of the loan. Failure to repay within six abrani shall result in the requisition of two of his uristri with each missed payment. Durustratus Golgat passed quietly in his sleep on the morning of 14E.5.24. We dispatched a memoriam gift of two auduin, several bundles of food and the joyous revelry of his life by the sacrifice of a uristri in his honor. No further news concerning your allies follows.

To matters of the estate: On the morning of 14E.6.4, I discovered a uristri became with child and had carried close to full gestation. I accept full responsibility for not predicting this oversight, but you should be pleased the affair came with severe punishment. I learned the raka'ir to be another uristri in your Stritus; both recently taken from Silvetzen upon your glorious representation to the kingdom five abrani ago. The uristri were ne'er thirteen.

After the discovery, I ordered the raka'ir paraded in front of the other raka and the offending abra'ir and ritualistically castrated without sedative. The raka did not survive. The abina faced her own punishment when your ravactistri eviscerated the fetus from her womb as she watched. Likewise, she too did not survive the experience. As punishment, we sold the abin to durustrita of varying notoriety for cruelty towards the treatment of their uristri.

We invited the durustrita to partake in sampling their future wares to preview their purchases. We served the eviscerated fetus as an appetizer and proclaimed the feast in honor of Hadithem for punishment for violating the rules of one of His most noble servants. The raka have doubled their work until we can acquire more uristri. I have decreed, in keeping with your own preferences, that abina shall no longer provide services within your walls.

Your absence has worried some of the more loyal uristri, and me. When last you wrote, you described the ruggedness of the Silvetzenian people and tales of their blasphemous ways. I do hope your tenure with them has not displeasured your desires, Magistrata, and their devolved minds have supplied you with generous stock of satisfaction.

Has the Aztmi succumbed to his torture? Do his tuistrina still remain in Shaoltar? Tongues are loose in Abaddon concerning the Aztmi and his offspring as you have asked. The Durustratum has raised concern over your Raka'ir's continued infatuations. Although questioning Supernus Magister is tantamount to death, I trust I can raise my opinion that he may not be worthy of his title nor his name. Should a more worthy successor to his lineage come forward, such as you Magistrata A'zum, my loyalties would duly continue.

Euristri Stritus A'zum, Jeoph Renkarin

Tivius withdrew the letter from his reading view and placed it upon the desk. He shed a slow sigh as reflections of home boiled through his thoughts. The letter itself, dated almost a year prior, indicated his brief time in position in Silvetzen. There was motive to his madness as he sat thousands of miles from his lavish estate. Tivius had conquered a kingdom and sowed the seeds of doubt in his home capitol concerning his own father. Tivius would not allow denial of his rightful place upon his father's throne, but something else eluded him. A power grew below these castle walls tearing into his aztunai and burning like a hungering flame. As he sought to focus; the fire cooled, evading his attempts. Tivius felt taunted by the sentient magick billowing through the castle walls like a haunting ghost fading into the wall as he got closer.

He followed his eyes across the room, seeing the youth tending to his chambers. The oldest, a girl with Saratian blonde hair close to the age of twelve tended to the window draping by cleansing them with a dry cloth to remove dust and soot from the elaborate stitch work. He moved his eyes to the boys tending to the floor then the other girls who continued their menial chores. The slaves hid their suffering, learning quickly emotions led to anger on behalf of their new master. Tivius stood to full height and with a lingering stride, shifted position around the desk and approached the boy closest to him scrubbing the floor with unbridled fervor.

The boy ceased his duty as Tivius paused in front of him. Knee-high leathery boots stretched from the sole of the older man's feet tightened with strapped buckles as they spilled towards a strictly bound greave highlighting the thin musculature of the owner. Tivius reached towards the boy, wrapping crusted, spindly fingers around his chin as he coaxed the boy to lift. Loose-fitting tunics fluttered along the boy's shoulders, dripping on his left side as they clung with failing attempt on his right. Tivius seethed in soft tones as his eyes cooled to mellow ice. Rotted breaths evacuated through his crackled lips as he met the boy face-to-face.

427

The young boy startled with the putrid air leaving his master's mouth and nostrils. His face shriveled and winced to Tivius' breaths. Tivius held his chin firm, careful not to exude his preternatural strength onto the boy's skull.

"Do not be afraid, child," Tivius began in Common Tongue, "You serve your new masters well. A trait not shared among those who are citizens of the Imperium. In time, you will all learn obedience to the Imperium."

Tivius reacted, glaring his face around the room as the children turned attention towards his speech. The magister continued, "Your mothers and fathers were weak; permitting the grand army of the Imperium to conquer this land."

Tivius released the boy's chin and continued his chiding demeanor, "But amongst you are the futures of the Imperium."

Tivius outstretched his hands in calm motion to angle them short upon his hips. He moved in slow pace, approaching each of the children in paced rhythm.

"The boys, when they turn thirteen will become soldiers. The girls, when you first bleed, shall present yourselves to our warriors to bear their children and further our armies. Denial of this future shall result in certain death. As would any escape from your fate. You can forget about your mothers and fathers; your mothers are fulfilling their purposes to fill our ranks with noble soldiers filling their wombs while your fathers are either conscripted to the camps or trained into our armies. Those who are too weak to serve, serve Hadithem in the Abyss. This kingdom, your homes, and your future, belong to the Imperium."

The towering, iron doors lifted open flanked by the pair of ethereal guards positioned outside as they pushed the portals inwards. Silver armor glinted in the faint sunlight entering the chambers revealing a man whose right face succumbed in fiery confrontation. Bubbles of seared skin scarred pitted wounds below his eyes and across the lower half of his chin. His lip tore to reveal sinewy muscle of his jawline. As grievous as the wounds had left him, his speech did not falter, and he proved to his inferiors the superior might of his rigorous training. He addressed Tivius in Sheebal, the name of their tongue, revealing a hint of appeasing news to the Magister.

"My Lord, I have received information that is of dire request to be presented to you."

Tivius sneered at the interruption, pausing in his pace to revolve to the officer standing before him.

"If you displease me, Commander, this will be your last interruption."

"Understood, my Lord. We have received word from conscripted spies in the field of a small cart entering the northern borders from Silvetzen."

"I am not interested in trader traffic, Commander. What is the purpose of this news?"

"This cart matches the description of a wagon that left Silvetzen several weeks ago as we took the kingdom by force. As it escaped, many of our guards died in process."

"Why was this cargo vessel not followed?"

Tivius' anger incensed at the officer.

"My Lord, there were orders from the Iostana Magistrata not to pursue at the time. A secret proclamation took place preventing chase."

"The Seer."

Tivius whispered under his breath, inaudible to the inferior.

"When it was spotted," the commander proceeded, "it was led by a single horse; a Si'rai horse that matches that of Stritus Shabririn."

Tivius grinned with welcoming glee and the commander's statement confirmed his suspicions as to Ragres' fate.

"Where was this vessel headed?"

"Racoren, sir."

"Send word to Magister Nybas. No one is to leave the city and detain those who dare enter for questioning. Princess Cassica, the Aztmi and the Azthar Kherdmon are alive. They are my duty, and I will take the glory of seeing to their capture. Bring them forward to me. Kill any who travel with them."

"As you command, my Lord."

"One more request; return these uristri to their hold."

"Yes, My Lord."

The silver commander motioned for the pair of lesser ranks outside. The trio rounded up the children with unbridled disregard as to the might of their grips. Stuttering whimpers carried across their lips and mouths but as one of the soldiers reached for the young boy standing beside the magister, Tivius quickly reached across the boy's chest denying the soldier his command.

"This one," Tivius sneered with perverted tone, "remains here with me."

The soldier nodded the request and as he lifted a second child over his shoulder, the officer gripped the split handles and sealed the iron gateway into a shuddered slam, drowning the impending cries of fear that followed.

Chapter 38

Soothing whispers of a lumbering creek trickled against muddy banks. Clouds thickened into light gray puffs. The hint of an imposing rain sprinkled light mist across the vibark trees clumped in clusters hugging the nutrient-rich soil by the creek path. Leaves flocked in open array to shadow the ground below as wisps of a flittering moss clung upon their branches like hangman's nooses without a body.

Sloshed mud spackled upon tattered leggings as Venna squatted to ring out the soot clumped in her hair. Her eyes lowered with scorn; lips pouted with dismay as splatters of mud met her frocks. Venna looked up to see the source of her anger and watched as Kenat worked his limber hands into the swampy soil to ready another splatter.

"What are you doing?"

She whispered in anger. Her eyes lowered to an annoyed gaze.

"Enough," Cadeck ordered, his stoic pose approached from behind Kenat and ordered him to cleanse his hands, "We don't have time for antics."

"Cadeck, we have travelled on foot nearing two days. Can't we at least relax for a few hours?"

Kenat moaned as he turned towards his superior.

"We can relax once the Si'rai Imperium suffers defeat. Until then, we must remain on guard."

Cadeck towered the younger Magi by over a foot. Wrinkled crevices lined his face as a full beard seeded its way along the marked paths.

"Fine," Kenat sighed.

A splatter of mud slammed into his face and as he turned to the direction of the distraction. Venna waned off towards the older women with a cackling giggle. Cadeck placed a calloused grip upon Kenat's shoulder.

"Understand your training is still in my observation, remember this, for your Ascended's own memory. I have watched how you act with the young woman but be mindful of your oath. You may care for the girl, but do not see your skills restricted by feelings of your nature lingering upon your heart. Do not allow Ego between yourself and Gift. Be mindful of your powers in coming days. You must remain focused on those seeking our demise."

Kenat nodded his head as he followed Venna movement towards Tesh and Cassica as they seated upon a small rock.

"Our rest should be ending soon. We must travel the swamps and be in Racoren come morning."

"Elder, I need to tell you something."

"Now? Can it not wait?"

Cadeck shifted his body to face the young man.

"It has troubled me since I learned of it. I request to tell you."

Cadeck turned the pair to face their backs to the women to assure their exchange remained secretive, "Very well then."

"A few nights ago, Tesh mentioned troubling words to my ears."

"Go on," Cadeck lowered his emotions to listen intently.

"He spoke to me about a spirit lingering with us. He mentioned it by name. I asked him to speak word with you but as he has not spilled tongue in a week, you need to know."

"Babalon?"

Cadeck whispered as mind raced to thoughts of vile premonitions.

"Aye. How did you know?"

Cadeck lowered his chin to look towards Kenat and gave order for the boy, "Go; inform the girls we must get moving again."

"Cadeck, what about…"

Cadeck cut him off, commanding the duty once more. Upon his order, Kenat lifted himself from the sloshy banks and gathered a series of seven, full, canteen horns strung along a rope. He jogged across the creek and marshy soils to the small enclave where Tesh, Cassica and the younger ladies rested. In distance, Cadeck raised his vision to watch as Kenat approached the foursome and readied his creaking bones to cross the narrow waterway.

Cadeck's mind focused on future thought and Tesh's reactions since his arrival from the Wind Temple. He continued to remain quiet, ignoring Cassica's requests until she gave up and tended to Eris' sour emotions lingering from Vizin's death. Cassica's recent appearance belittled her status, soiled by sweat, mud, and disarray.

A fresh change of clothes denied her presence to keep their travel minimal at best. Simple cloaks with scant hoods covered their faces while the girls remained garbed with vague tunics of bland discoloration. Leggings covered down to their ankles protecting their legs from the elements and unwarranted predation should they come across a band of smugglers or other undesirables. Venna scratched at her legs just below her knees, groaning at the onslaught of unkempt hair growing upon her.

"I need a fresh bath," Venna grumbled.

"Acquaint to this, Venna. In the field, they will be hard to come by. Consider this part of your training."

"I wish not to be a Justiciar."

A hush fell upon Cassica's ears at Venna's retort.

"I'd rather be a Benedicer so I can help people."

"I shall place my Roses as I see fit, Venna. Do not argue with Command."

"What is the use? We are all that remains of the Order of the Rose."

Cassica turned in disgust at Venna's statement. Her eyes diminished to a scolding glance; her mouth puffed with anger as an outburst welled inside her stomach. Cassica shifted weight, lifting herself from the rock on which she perched to stand to Venna who remained seated beside her position. Her thoughts collapsed to fear and the uncertainty of her family's fates. And the words leaving the tongue of her inferior deserved reprimand.

"Dare speak disparaging remarks again, and I should see to it you're stripped of your color and removed from the Order."

Venna met her eyes with doe-faced impression. Tears welted upon her irises as she chose her next words to speak from risen lips.

"What good is the Order if there is no Crown to serve?"

With swift hand, Cassica affirmed her disdain for Venna's words across her face.

"How dare you mock me. So long as I may live, there is still a Crown to serve."

Venna craned her neck to look upon Cassica's emerald eyes through mottled blonde hair as she rubbed her left cheek. Cassica's eyes pierced into Venna's soul with a burning passion of an ethereal persuasion. Mind focused on dreaded thoughts as she dropped from the rock and shifted her stride away from Cassica to the running brook. Cadeck shook his head and set hand to Cassica's shoulder as he approached and urged not to pursue but to remain behind and allow the younger girl to remove emotions.

"Eris," Cadeck began, "Assist her with cleaning. When Ysalir returns from her scout, I will explain what happened."

"Cadeck, she is in my charge. She spoke against the Order and the Crown; she deserves punishment for her actions."

Cassica protested the hand placed on her shoulder.

"I am afraid this journey is putting toll on your younger ranks, and menses is complicating matter. There is doubt and uncertainty fomenting on impressionable minds. Even Ysalir is not immune I have noticed. The quicker we make Racoren, the better chance we have of finding voyage to sea. When Ysalir returns, we should know how best our journey is going forward. Even *my* patience is beginning to wear thin."

"How did you conclude her emotions were caused by bleeding?"

Cassica furrowed a dismayed look at Cadeck's assumed insult towards the limitations of gender.

"I've been around women long enough," Cadeck grinned.

He motioned past Cassica's stance, arms wavering to his sides as he trudged through the sodden soil. Cassica followed his actions with stern eyes as the Magi raised question to her own command. For once, Cassica felt alone as Tesh remained seated on the rock, watching the proceedings with wavered interest.

Cassica returned to seat, her bottom hitting the rock with furious dismay as she lifted her left knee to her chest in solemn concern. Mottled hair flowed against muddied tunic; her leggings flowed loose against her thighs and shins. Cadeck continued beyond the resting stop towards a figure lingering in the distance returning towards the group.

"What did you find?"

Ysalir's approached Cadeck midway through her walk. She brushed her bangs aside, emerald-teal eyes peaked through. Towering vibark trees anchored tight into the soil around them. Sodden paths lay along their route lined with pillowed grasses cleaned like a spring rain. Ysalir craned her neck over Cadeck's shoulder and whispered in low tone to prevent Cassica to hear.

"A large war procession followed to the south along the main roads. If we stick to the north flank, we could sneak into Racoren."

"How many do you assume?"

"About five thousand. Their wagon ruts cut deep, which means they used their heavy weapons with iron barrels that weighed down their procession. I have seen these weapons, Cadeck," Ysalir's eyes turned sullen, "one shot brought a large house to the ground. The iron barrels shoot fire from their ends, the metal sphere that ejects burns bright and obliterates anything it touches. I dare not consider what happened to Sarat if they used these weapons there."

"Ysalir," Cadeck lifted hand to comfort shoulder, "we have the gods on our side. Whatever the Si'rai may raise against us, we can smite down with our magick. I only ask you regain faith, dear."

She returned his locked stare and met his gaze. Furrowed bangs slipped along her forehead to grace her right cheek dirtied with sweat and muck.

"I cannot. Not yet at least," Ysalir returned forward stare towards the resting position, "Where's Venna?"

"Go easy on her. The journey is taking toll on young mind. Starting menses is not helping her cause."

Ysalir nodded in confirmation, "I'll be mindful of her emotions, Magi."

"We should move soon. The daylight turns to noon, and we should be close to Racoren before nightfall."

"Aye."

Ysalir jogged towards the camp, meeting Venna and Eris as they lifted themselves from rudimentary cleansing. Cadeck stood poised, watching the interactions of the ladies but kept vigil of concern over Tesh's behaviors. The man sheathed his weapon and gathered supplies to string across his back. Ysalir met her sister, looking upon her as handprint bruise began to form. She grew concerned as Venna shrugged her thoughts and attention away to join Eris into making the marching formation Cassica beckoned.

Cranes swooped overhead, gliding from vibark tree to vibark tree; their necks jerking with stimuli at the sights of prey or the humans beneath them. Flittered whispers of buzzing insects circled around the trees and marshy grasses as Ysalir took point in the formation. She trudged her muscular legs along muddy paths burying her feet in procession. Kenat followed her as Venna, Cassica and Eris marched in succession separated by several meters. Tesh and Cadeck took the rear allowing the older Magi to watch over the party.

The journey led them across creek banks whose waters remained still as folded bed sheets. Heavy rut lines embraced the group running parallel to them as Ysalir led them through the median cut into the wet grass blades sprinkled by cascading mists. Tall grasses lined the water ways while their feet trudged through thick stalks of grass and soil. Rows of vibark trees mingled in various states of decay and vitality to mark the edge of the swampland as gray clouds billowed overhead coinciding with a chilled breeze whispering from the northern edge. Cold-blooded animals scurried into their hovels against mud shelters and holes to hide from the winds. Bubbles from breathing fish stilled in the waters as small gusts frothed along the creeks with rippling waves.

Muddied waters lingered on Venna's nose as she lifted her grubby hands to hide from stench. An olfactory onslaught of chlorophyllous mixture, swamp water, and grass assaulted Venna's senses inducing a gag reflex.

"You'll be fine, Venna."

Ysalir urged her sister to hold her gut as she trudged along the single mound of dirt and grass. Ysalir led the group around the various puddles to avoid the old ruts scarring the path.

Yet, she did not heed Ysalir's request. Venna stopped to the side of the path and released an upheaval of empty bile with a gag reaction to the tingling odors. Ysalir reacted to the sounds and turned to see her sister dropped to her

435

knees, leaning over in successive evacuations. Eris hurried to her friend's side and aided her to stand. She wiped her face with the tattered long sleeve upon her wrist. Strips of mucus and bile clung to the fabric as she sneezed in reaction to the tickling in her nose. Her face flushed red as tears welled into her eyes with histamines. Venna returned to her position behind Kenat. Disfavor clearly set upon her eyes, Ysalir turned to continue the march along the northern edge of the Bogs of Er'tahar.

"We should clear the bogs before nighttime, Ysalir, or do you prefer Rensel? We would not want Er'tahar's ghost to snatch Eris and Venna in the middle of the night."

Ysalir continued pace with a slow sigh ignoring Kenat's superstition.

"You may address me with my true name, Kenat. Venna and Cadeck already do, and where would you hear such tales? Your Ascended told you?"

"Neigh, I heard it a long time ago by a woman I care not to remember."

Kenat continued his march.

"There is no such thing as ghosts, Kenat. The Si'rai and wild predators are more dangerous."

"Wasn't Er'tahar one of your own?"

"As my mother told it, and her mother before her and many other mothers and fathers in Sarat before them. It serves as a warning to all girls and boys growing up in the kingdom, that the old king's ghost haunts the swamps, preying on those of ill repute and bad little boys and girls who have yet to atone for their misdeeds. Legends say that the old king was a gambler, a womanizer, and a tyrant whose actions spread ill comment about his person and title upon the lands. Seeing his disregard for the kingdom, a few, well-intentioned nobles led by a Bovariàr ancestor, long before they assumed the throne, had kidnapped him under the guise of a hosted meal and brought him out to these swamps where they murdered him and left his body here. That is why his ghost is rumored to haunt here, why legends speak of fainting whispers and muddled screams in the swamps. You just would not want to spend many a night out here."

"Fascinating. If I were a king, I would rule the land with forgiveness and care for my people. I would show them mercy and give them liberty. I would abolish all crimes and let my people do as they please. I would remove taxes and allow the people to keep their monies to further their own gains. The people would love me."

Ysalir smirked, hinting at a condescending giggle, "The people yes, your nobles no. They would draw and quarter you before you watched over your first harvest season. Nobility hates free peasants. That is how it has always been and how it should always be."

"Why does your tongue carry hateful words?"

Kenat's eyes glistened with white fire at his intuitive tone.

"The ruling classes can be cruel, Kenat. With a just king, like Trebut, there are a few exceptions. Rathmana, however, reminded me of those legends."

"He was a fair king, I would say, from what I saw. I never interacted often with Silvetzen. Philos did not allow me to leave much."

"Rathmana was a loathsome person. Even to this day, I can still smell his stench."

Kenat swallowed for his next words, "I would only know what I have seen. I had only ventured into Silvetzen briefly. Ran errands for Ascended Philos as needed and stayed low. I had heard rumors from the heralds about Saratian advancements to the south and the propaganda about Trebut. The taverns told me what I needed about Rathmana."

"Taverns? But aren't you denied libations?"

Kenat coughed with a slight pause then a giggle, "Cadeck puffs on ruban, Ysalir. Besides, I had to know. If I were not wearing my vestments, no one would know I was a Magi. They would see me as some inquisitive little page, or a nuisance. I would venture into the taverns, hear rumors, and see the Si'rai."

"What you saw in the taverns were not Si'rai, Kenat. They were conscripted men, torn from their native lands in service to the Imperium. True Si'rai do not revel in drink on the battlefield."

"I suppose you know a bit about them."

"A subject matter I dare not reveal in full, if you please."

"Then you know what we're up against?"

Kenat's words trailed into stale fear as the trainings of his Ascended failed his mind to lend his voice to cowardice. Ysalir only nodded her head to his question.

#

Like a lavish menagerie of marching innocence, the party continued along the path Ysalir led. Tight furs clung to Ysalir's shoulders covering the loose tunics leading to her hips bound by a pouched belt fastened along her waist. Behind her, Kenat followed a few paces like a garish harlequin. A frilly lavender overshirt billowed from his shoulders and dropped to long sleeves tight against his wrists. Mud caked from his discolored shoes up to his ankles marring the teal leggings hiding his under clothes. Venna strode behind him, loose tunics exposed arms under fur shoulder-coverings. Dressed as a peasant, unbecoming of the stature she accustomed, the tunics flowed below her hips and led to a pair of trousers ending just above her ankles. Eris dressed similarly; furs covered the younger ladies offering scant warmth while their outfits presented them as a pair of nuisances.

Tesh carried the weight of the equipment. Stacks of gear carried across his shoulders strapped with leathered buckles around his hips and waist. Cleverly wrapped burlap fittings disguised the heavier weapons slung across his back. Cassica carried herself with a wavering gait as the pouch-laden belt swayed with her hips. Tesh caught glimpses of her curves as he over-reached Eris' height by several inches. Thoughts of the sultry spirit that visited him lingered on his mind as she had spoken words to him on his watches coaxing him with perverted enticement.

Tesh shook those thoughts with the wriggling of his neck side-to-side, focusing on the walk ahead. Tesh had never known a woman, yet cavorted with a local girl, a fellow farmer's daughter from near Telmen named Jaena, but they never came to consummating. That was the closest he learned how to be with a woman before this spirit, this sultry succubus visited him along this journey. How did it start, why did it start now and not sooner?

He had met Cassica just several weeks ago. Her attitude reflected her position in life and had taken surprise at his sudden gesture to kiss her. Tesh remained distanced from her since then; continuing his own journey of self-discovery and aiding as Cadeck recommended. Not once did *she* make an advance.

Self-discovery - a phrase Tesh learned all too well in his quest. An order existing as legend became reality when he spoke to Godwen in the Temple of Light. He lifted his left hand to his chest, stretching the golden tendrils seared into his flesh ripped asunder by foul magick along his vein lines. With each passing Trial, the hand conducted powers unknown to his former existence which he had only learned from stories told by his mother or those he heard amongst roaming bards. Since his encounter with Cadeck, he had learned his father was a felon, only granted pardon should he survive the Trials presented by the Knights; not the legend the citizens of Telmen revered and praised.

What lies fed his ears in his youth. His mother kept dark secrets from him only discovered in the torn soul exposing itself in his Trials; unruly men, indebted servitude to pay off the land issued to his father left to Tesh's mother upon her widowhood. The lie haunting him the most when Cadeck called his mother *cousin*.

Tesh peaked over his shoulder at Cadeck behind him. The older man's face weathered with age and pain from an experience of distant horrors in a prison whose tenure he dared not to allow leave his tongue. Cadeck revealed

438

small pieces of his past, but Tesh understood the thoughts lingering within him. Through his subconscious recognition, Cadeck's appearance at the Wind Temple seemed a happier moment of a man in opposite position, a man from another time and place non-existent on Roth. He smiled as he told Tesh's mother he was to welcome his bonded with their first child, the daughter known as Wrem. Tesh could not fathom the suffering he currently felt tearing through Cadeck with weakened thoughts of self-pity.

Tesh's thoughts turned to the small girl's voice he had scantly heard. The girl called to him and through intellectual processing deduced the child was the daughter Cadeck lost to the Si'rai. She screamed of pain ripping through her mind like a scythe slicing wheat sheaf. Wrem's cries wailed across Tesh's thoughts and at once he knew Cadeck's suffering. And for this, he spoke nothing.

Tesh needed to process his vision as Tiasu's winds shredded his existence into tainted cloth clinging like torn curtains in an abandoned home. Tijoa warned him this vision may be the most difficult, the hardest to grasp which rendered many Initiates into psychotic vegetables. As his stark visions returned to conscious thought, his left hand shivered into a sudden cold as icy crystals grew along his golden veins. He clenched his fist with gathered strength and rested it to grip his left shoulder strap as Ysalir positioned ahead, motioning the party to come to halt with a tightly clenched fist raised with an elbow bend.

Ysalir knelt to the ground as the trodden path came to join a wide road trampled with fresh muddy rain. Knees bent, crouched with statuesque position she ran a bare finger in front of her body, pointing towards sets of tracks in the road and murmuring to herself. Kenat caught her first as the following procession hurried to her position.

"What is it?"

Cassica's eyes opened with fear.

"Your Highness, Vizin was right. Your doubts about him were wrong. The Si'rai used two flanks. The main road had a smaller battalion, the tracks are fresher," Ysalir pointed and traced the tracks with extended arm, rising to full stand, "The tracks we just followed were first to go probably about two weeks old."

Ysalir turned to face the scarlet-headed woman. Tears dirtied Cassica's cheeks as soiled hair strung like tattered dress against her freckles.

"I'm sorry Your Highness."

"They used the surveys," Cassica swallowed her emotions, "That's the only way they knew how to navigate the northern bogs."

"Surveys?" Kenat postured.

"Aye," Ysalir followed, "every passable nook and rut in our kingdom has been mapped to the degree; every rise, every plateau, every hill and valley."

"Then our entrance into Racoren must be met with caution."

Cadeck moved from behind Tesh and placed comforting hand upon Cassica's shoulder, "You must contain your emotions if we are to remain in disguise."

"My family is resourceful, Cadeck, I am certain they are safe."

Cadeck smiled to respond sending positive intuition towards Cassica while hiding the thought they were all wrong.

Chapter 39

Rows of vibark trees stretched the expanse of the winding road carved in the risen soils. Tall grasses scattered across the flanks of the road barely wide enough for two-way traffic as marshes sprawled muddy waters in the distances beyond the visible horizon. The travelers huddled close in formation with Ysalir leading the pack. Cadeck and Tesh covered the rear as the rest travelled in tight formation between them.

They passed along the main road leading into Racoren. Stinging insects hovered around them in the murky climate, lingering their lives with the late autumn airs, attracted to the human perspirations. Venna swatted at one landing on her wrist and flicked the carcass from her flesh. Eris gazed around, soaking in the sounds of the swamps as various native fauna croaked and yelped in the midday sun, singing their encores before the snows settled in.

She studied the various states of vegetative care nature had performed on the flora. Some of the vibark trees had grown to decay while others had been lush with their vibrant leaves sprawling along the canopy enclosing the bogs. Planted footsteps spread dirt and mud clumps to collapse in the deep wagon ruts they followed causing Kenat to slip a few times to catch his footing.

Ysalir turned her attention to the ambient sounds of the region. She focused on her training, recalling the isolation lessons while in the tutelage of the Magi named Mornika. Relying on other instincts besides her tangible focus, she paid close consideration to the details of silence haunting the marsh. Native birds perched upon branches overhead. The songs and cries billowed over the swamp canopy.

She carried the group through the dense marshes along the carved path laden several decades before her time. Through trodden highways surrounded by sticky swamps, Ysalir toiled her princess and their friends while persevering blistered heels. As the sun lowered westward into early evening hours the aromatic sting of ash and smoke carried the sickening hint of burning flesh. The caustic odors drifted through Cassica's nostrils with the stagnant waters surrounding their pathway. With a disparaging emotion upon building tears, Cassica realized the gravitas of the situation she was about to face.

Rounding a designed curve in the road, faint echoes of dim lights bounced in the distance like a pair of wisps lingering in the swamp gas. Wooden planks lined the lane signaling the edges of the path for wayward travelers preventing stray carts to abandon the road into the dark swamps surrounding them. A stone bridge lay across a stagnant waterway, sturdy in stature for heavy traffic. Lingering odors of singed wood and the dust of crumpled rock and mortar floated along the still nighttime airs while the evening calls of insects seeking winter's hibernation produced haunting symphonies.

Beside the road, stretches of marsh expanded through the horizon. Vibark trees clung to sparse patches of wetland muds in the nutrient-rich soil. Daytime creatures slithered or crawled towards their nighttime homes as though they readied themselves to guard from the nocturnal predators waiting to wake for their nightly devour.

Cadeck hastened to Ysalir's side, whispering reminders of their cover. Cassica slipped clammy grasp into Venna's right palm. Venna craned to meet her eyes and in a silent moment, Cassica had forgiven her for her outburst amidst the outcome Cassica had dared not consider.

Inside a makeshift shack, Cadeck recognized a pair of men in Si'rai armor built of slight frame and olive-toned complexions. Despite their physical disadvantage, the pair displayed familiar markings and rugged bone structure, a hallmark to their race. A third man had seated at a desk carved from the front panel of the structure. Dim lamps shone upon his form matching him with the white-skin paleness of the neighbors to the north.

Strings of ruby hair reached along his scalp entangled with sideburns stretching towards the beard and goatee marked by weeks or months of filth-laden disorder. Behind the shanty post marked the remnants of a battered pike fortification separating the outskirts from the wilds. A mangled sign clung above them with a solitary nail noting the town's name as Racoren in both the Common Tongue and the script of the Si'rai language.

Approaching cautiously, Cadeck took the lead with Ysalir following at a distance behind. He approached the brawny soldier along the path from the north. Fatigue settled into his bones and muscles. His knees ached and his breaths wavered with each step. The Silvetzenian soldier remained in his seat and released a blackened blob of spittle onto the ground next to the soldier upon his right. He moaned through decayed gums as his rusty beard parted to highlight disfigured teeth clinging to the rotted flesh lining his jaws. The man's face released sweat like a happy hog wallowing in mud in contrast to the cold mists birthing from the swamplands around him. As Cadeck stood firm to the man, a message posted on the wall behind them on a thin, portrait-styled parchment.

442

Cadeck caught notice of the details of the message and in no pleasantries did he acknowledge the contents of the medium. A message scrawled onto the parchment in Common Tongue shared with the glyphs of the Sheebal dialect underneath. The poster called out his name, Cassica's by full title and Tesh's commoner rankings. Cadeck noticed a peculiarity; the parchment did not include a likeness of their appearances. Stationary had strewn along the desk as stacks of papers with prefabricated notices. A small burning chalice released the smell of bubbling wax sealants, and a small quill with ink bottle rested beside.

"Halt, traveler," the Silvetzenian guard erupted through strained words as his husky form caught breath, "What is the purpose of your visit to Racoren?"

"Forgive me," Cadeck answered, "but we are but a travelling troupe of entertainers seeking coin in this port."

"Coin," the Silvetzenian man stood, leaning his left hand on the table, "you are in the wrong town if you want coin. I would advise to turn back now."

His accent stung to Cadeck's ears like the rough bark of bearwood slammed upon his skull.

"Please, syr. We have scant resources of which to feed ourselves and we have come a long distance to reach Racoren. My youngest daughter needs medicine for her wounds, a band of brigands confronted us recently. We have no money for her concerns and have been starving these last few days."

The Silvetzenian soldier rose to full attention. Links of chain mail stretched over his chest and torso like splintered fragments of steel straining from his bulbous belly. Stringy hairs clung to his arms exiting a torn shirt below his armor. He waddled away from his position in such a pace as though Cadeck held a fresh roast. The Si'rai guards behind him unsheathed swords from hip-mounted scabbards to defend the man. Thick legs positioned the man into position; gluttony folds betrayed the man's stature as a soldier. He met Cadeck to height and through sweaty breaths carrying scent of ale-soaked pig fat, interrogated Cadeck where he stood.

"And what is it that you do?"

"I am the master of ceremonies, the narrator of our stories. My oldest daughter here," pointing to Ysalir, "and her younger sister," moving to Cassica, "perform a knife throwing routine. Dangerous, if you ask me."

Cadeck moved finger to point to Eris and Venna, "These two, the dark-haired one, and the blonde perform juggling and mimicry while the slender boy here performs as our jester and prankster. You would best watch your wits about him. While our mute, he is a strange one," pointing to Tesh, "He is the

443

steward of our equipment. He plays the lute and what an outstanding job he does while our jester carries out the antics of the songs we sing."

The guard took notice to each of the members of the party Cadeck pointed out. His mouth watered at Ysalir's toned build. Her brunette locks draped across ragged tunics hiding her rank to the likeness of a peasant girl. Cassica's silk-red hair folded into a thick hood like stringy twine over her scalp betraying her nobility. As he continued to survey the travelers, the nubile figures of Eris and Venna lulled the dirty man into slithering tongue of grotesque perversion relishing the chance to defile their innocence. Kenat's laughable outfit sent the man into a roaring chuckle as he patted the young Magi with hearty palms on his frail shoulder. Kenat winced, followed with a breathy *ow*.

"If he plays the lute, old man," the Silvetzenian soldier caught eye to Tesh's hand wrapped in sackcloth as he made his stop towards the young man, "how does he do it with one 'and?"

"Quite simple really," Cadeck replied, "he is a strange one indeed. I have never seen such a dumb bastard before I ran into him in Telmen. If you ask me, it is like Desed Themself gifted him."

"Your gods bear no meaning anymore. You would be wise t' relinquish your religion if you want to make a living in Racoren. The Si'rai rule here and their one god, and they detest the Androgyne most of all. But before I let you enter, have you 'ad any dealins with any of the persons on my poster 'ere?"

The guard pointed towards the paper bearing the names of three in their retinue.

"Cannot say that we have. Her Highness is a fickle bitch, lemme tell you, and I had never entertained a worse hostess than on her Maiden's Day. I can tell you stories if you want to hear them?"

With a jolly chuckle, the Silvetzenian soldier motioned them through his post, "That's alright, old man. Find you an inn and rest your weary bodies. I look forward to your entertainment tomorrow after the grand announcements. Before you go, you will need a writ of passage to enter town."

He returned to his outpost and removed a small paper from a stack on his right. The man scribbled his rudimentary signature on the canned response and marked it with the hot wax sealant on the footer of the note. He provided Cadeck with the statement and motioned Cadeck and the others to shuffle past the outpost. Ysalir followed close to Cadeck, hovering to his side.

As they cleared the tattered poles, splintered, and fractured by recent battle, the outskirts opened to reveal a life no longer. Scattered homes lay in burning ruin still smoldering from planned extermination. Mud clamped onto the brick-paved road continuing beyond their pace towards the north. Sprawled along both sides of their travel the stench of waste mingled with the decay of uncleansed hygiene.

Boats sat in shallow harbor on their left flank, some left burning in the bay freed from the moorings entrapping them to the splintered harbor decks. Dogs milled about the tattered decay of corpses and rotted fish that had once been the livelihood of the shanty village outside the main city. Chaos of putrid leftovers stretched around as the path carried them towards Racoren's gates. Vagrants and homeless gathered scant resources, fleeing the berating tongues of the foreign oppressors.

Cassica's eyes darted around her, enveloped in the scenery of the supporting village. Silence befell her soul as the decimation wrought by the ancient antagonists had taken hold in the empty gazes of her former subjects. A solitary man stood by the shoreline. His frail frame balanced upon a walking cane matching his height. He met Cassica's stare through his shallowed soul reflected in his weathered eyes as though contemptible not for her and her family, but his very existence. He stooped down to fetch something in the ground and wiggled his left hand in the mud for a few moments before clutching a mudfish from the deep slush and raised it to his mouth. He bit into the spine of the animal, severing its central nervous system as it writhed in final agony from the appetite of the solemn man. Blood gorged along his muddied face as he sloughed through shallow waters to a small tent with the grime of stolen pride.

As the group continued to trail the central road gradually turning to a steep grade, fresh construction began by the shoreline. Several Si'rai soldiers and conscripted Saratian citizens had begun construction on a new facility. A pair of Si'rai soldiers hoisted a large sign on a pulley. Sheebal script written upon the sign turned Ysalir's curiosity. She pressed on, turning back to the road ahead, not allowing her eyes to linger too long for her to translate.

Approaching the main gates at the height of the slight grade, a pair of bulked Si'rai soldiers had taken guard. The primary entrance stood to former glory; the gates violently dismembered from the wall and exposed the town. Mounted archers positioned atop collapsed ramparts and stretched armed bows at the oncoming party. Cadeck eyed the small parchment in his hands written with the designs of Si'rai calligraphy. Sinister to his own body, he thought curses upon himself to even touch the script but knew better than to call his aztmudin. He politely released the note into one of the guard's hands who alerted the snipers to stand down. Behind the guards positioned a foreign weapon bearing no resemblance to anything Sarat possessed.

The guards motioned them past handing the note back to Cadeck as he led them into the town proper. Buildings lay in destructed ruin as crowds dressed in higher-scale fashions lingered around their former houses or businesses, toiling for what scraps they could muster while groups of Si'rai guards gathered to round up those of any class who disobeyed approaching curfew. A barrel made of nightmarish obsidian posed in front of Cadeck mounted upon a heavy cart supported by thick-ply wheels made of an iron cast. The primary cylinder stretched to length as Cadeck was tall while a pair of soldiers stood behind in idle chatter. Steel orbs stacked in a foot-high pyramid beside them while one man leaned on a pole fitted with a sooty brush on the tip upon the ground. Ysalir's eyes widened at the recognition of this weapon.

Kenat coddled the younger girls in close arms. Venna welled tears upon her cheeks as she huddled into Kenat's shoulder. Tesh stood behind them gathering the sights of the destruction. He covered his left hand wrapped as best he could. Stings ripped through his left arm with the ferocity of a lightning storm. Cadeck pressed them further beyond blocks of ragged decimation and crying victims beaten by the lash of whips and curse speech.

The town pulpit stood center within a ring lined of buildings and shops. Citizens toiled against their will at the barking orders of Si'rai soldiers; preparing a tall object draped in a black cloak where folds bent the red markings of the Imperium sigil. Sunlight waned towards the early evening hours as several soldiers mounted lamps on tall posts. When the preparations of the tall, covered object had completed, the Si'rai guards yelled obscenities in their guttural language. One of the guards slammed his fist upon the jaw of one of the four men refusing to cooperate.

Cassica restrained herself. Her eyes saw torture and pain. Ysalir placed a firm arm against her chest and solemnly shook her head. One of the Si'rai guards perked attentive eyes towards the fluffed woman and disregarded the troupe as nothing more than a band of curious entertainers before he lifted the fallen slave to his feet and punched him once more.

Around the edge of the ring, Cadeck caught notice of an advertisement hanging along the edge of a building. Bound by chain strung along a slender pole jutting from the brick, a sign swayed in solemn breezes. A doldrum energy of the befallen city creaked in the slight shifting of the iron which held the sign aloft. Surrounded in an alley with buildings stretching for several blocks, *Undine's Hole* presented itself to welcome the weary. Lively banter of a loud-voiced woman eschewed from the tavern's open door frame lending credence to truth to the sign promoting a seaman's tavern where ales flowed, and women loosened.

"Not much different than last I was here."

Cadeck muttered to Ysalir as he surveyed the room full of drunken sods passing out on their tables and in the floors. Cadeck made passage towards an open table to accommodate the full arrangement and motioned the travelers to follow. Ysalir entered behind him as a flurry of catcalls spilled from the back of the room. Faces lingered perversely upon Venna and Eris' bodies from men not pleasured by a woman's loins for days. As Kenat entered the door frame, a few burly men glanced from frothy mugs to chuckle at the effeminate clothing the younger Magi wore and paid no attention to the covered redhead or the common steward carrying packs of gear upon his back. Others murmured and whispered displeasured remarks towards the newcomers lacking the smell of sea.

A husky tavern owner yelled at the single lady who served a pair of drunkards with a fresh pour of stout. She cursed at her boss with the language of a seasoned sailor as a few of the men nearby heard her retort and moaned a long *ohhh* followed by drunken chuckles. Bare feet shuffled towards Cadeck in a gait that had borne several children from her loins. Her constant, unrested labor created a disheveled appearance to her hair and a solitary mole positioned below her lip. She turned to Cadeck. Sweaty breasts bulged out of her low-cut shirt; the buttons stressed tight.

"What'll you 'ave?"

Her Low Accent fell upon their ears with fresh phlegm seeping through her speech.

"Do you have any rooms?"

"Y' gots a ship?"

"Pardon?"

"I ax'ed, y' gots a ship? We only pour fer sailors in 'ere."

"No," Cadeck replied.

He looked around the confines of the tavern and stole a quick glance at a man on the corner of the bar taking a long drag from a smoking stick.

"But I suppose you take coin. We ask for rooms, drinks, and no questions."

"Yu's are't one of them Si'ry men," her rotted breath pushed ahead of her face as she leaned towards the strangers.

"Y's look like 'uve seen bettuh days. I tell you wha, if yu's gots coin, I will f'giv yu's for b'en land scrubs."

Cadeck nodded, placing the hefty coin purse from his satchel with the whispered clink of metal from within. She yelled back across the tavern, wide mouth filtered through scarce teeth.

"Whaddaya know? We got us 'ome High Ones 'ere."

"You ign'r'ant quim," her boss exploded, "take thar orders and muve on."

His balding head scrunched around his eyes to form a grimacing stare.

"Suck my tit ol' troll."

The woman smiled at the man and loosely revealed a sagging breast exposing an areola with warts orbiting the radius. Ysalir sighed, surmising this to be a common occurrence as the remaining patrons erupted in perceived laughter. At the corner of the bar, a brown-skinned man perked up from his drink and a stick of smoke rose from between his fingers with a reddened sear of fresh smolder on the tip. He watched as the antics of the hefty waitress mingled with the new strangers.

"Well, whaddaya wan'?"

She returned attention to Cadeck, forgetting her civility, and leaving diseased breast exposed. The patrons continued their distractions, slobbering fermented ales and sharing stories. A nearby table filled with bearded sailors reeking of sea water and cheap liquors recited ill tongue against the Court with lecherous abandon.

Cassica overheard the men sharing sour gossips mocking her that she shared cock with her twin brothers. Another chimed in that she had conceived the youngest prince, Geraud, in a secret liaison with the same twins. The third commented that if he would ever see her, he would plough her like a cheap whore to which the fourth replied in common taste that with his pecker, it would be like throwing a candle across a banquet hall. All four men erupted in cheerful laughter baring scant teeth, crusted faces, and straggled beards.

"For the older ladies, a pair of ales. The younger girls will have rugeberry with light ferment, the rest of us boys will have swamp stout."

"Well, I's got a secret to tell ya," she leaned down to whisper to Cadeck, inaudibly to the rest of the tavern, "Y' see, Sarashun Crowns won' be good 'ere much longa.' You gotsta have what the Si'ry call owdooin."

She turned eyes around the table glancing over her shoulder to assure no Si'rai soldiers were present, "But m' sheets mate 'ere will still take any Sarashun coin y' 'ave. We don' rightly care for the redskins, but you cannot let 'em 'ear you say that."

"Much obliged, and caution is heard."

"Ten 'naves," she whispered.

Cadeck produced ten pieces of Saratian minted copper and one piece of golden coin.

"Here," Cadeck returned quiet speech, "one Crown for your bond mate. Provide us with two rooms next to one another, one for the ladies and one for the men. Again, no questions and no trouble."

"Aye," she gripped the coins into tight hands and shuffled back towards the bar.

She lifted her fist over the bartender's hand as the pair sought eyes for any of the dark-complexioned oppressors. As the bar was clear, she placed hairy knuckles into her bonded's hand and released the coins. He scurried into the side room with the illegal currency, then returned to his position. Her vocal recollection of Cadeck's order recited towards her bonded mate in slurred and broken dialect.

Setting cup to table, the brown man continued to watch the newcomers. With low, hazel eyes he scanned the group assessing their purpose as he lifted his right hand to inhale a taste of his rolled paper smoldering with the light hints of ruban sweetness. Slathered with a sip to follow his smoke, he wiped dark-purple ferment from his chin. Dirt clung upon his nails as though a pig had wallowed within his fingertips.

Cadeck followed the room with his eyes before catching another quick glimpse of the man in the corner. Ysalir scanned across the room in full rotation. Drunks and unsavory filled the shadowed tavern. They reeked like the perversion in their minds and the sea waters they sailed upon. Their jests and angered tones disfavored royalty, and should they discover one attended their midst, Ysalir had no reason to doubt they would react accordingly. A full house consumed ales and kept to themselves amidst occasional burps or spilled vomit. Drunkenness eased pain and suffering and soon curfew would fall as the sun began to settle upon the western horizon.

The waitress returned with order, recalled correctly. The non-alcoholic drinks she poured in clay cups and placed first in front of Venna and Eris while clear, thick glasses held the pale ales in front of Ysalir and Cassica poured a foot high. The stouts filled clay steins, allowing the flavors to mingle with the ocean scents of mud and soot, giving the name credence to swamp stout. Venna stared at the liquid in the clay cup, discouraged she was not to consume ferment. Kenat peaked into his cup, held his nose, and produced a gag at scents of fermented kelp and clay spilling from the glass like a sloshy brew.

"Where do you propose that we'll find a ship to get us out of here?"

Ysalir motioned Cadeck to conversation as he sipped on his concoction. Tesh turned to the Magi to await Cadeck's response and consumed a sip before twisting his mouth in contorted disgust.

"We will need to find a captain in the morning. I doubt it will be easy. These men in here seem tired and weakened as though a void enters their hearts and souls stealing them of life and they drink to forget. Probably not much different before the Si'rai but keep an eye out. I am going to talk to the owner and obtain our room keys."

Cadeck lifted from the bench and straddled his right leg across the seat. He hoisted his left to follow suit before struggling through creaking bones to hasten towards the bar in the center of the room. A single, vacant stool among the full house invited him beside the brown-skinned man seated at the apex of the corner. Ysalir followed his movements, downing a large gulp from her glass before turning to the rest of the table. Cassica stared at her drink as she raised it with clammy hands which shuddered to her lips. A sip of the ale danced upon her tongue. The bitterness fell down her throat to drown the bitterness ringing in her ears.

"I thought I'd seen a spirit," the brown man slurred to Cadeck.

He sipped slowly on the fruity rugeberry cider swirling in his cup. Notes of citrus and lavender hung upon his tongue. The taste of burned ruban leaves followed with a puff of his rolled paper.

"Then I realized I may as well be looking at one."

"Good to see you too, Cruxien," Cadeck muttered to the brown man.

"Aye."

He sloshed the drink in swirling motion in his cup a few inches from his mouth. Cruxien took a sip of the drink as streaks of purple stain cascaded down the sides of his roughened lips.

"What brings you here old friend, and why the company you keep?"

Cruxien lifted his ruban stick to point towards Ysalir who at this time had focused radiating eyes on the pair. Cruxien returned her gaze as the drift of smoke trailed from his pleasure to linger high with the collection hovering over the room.

"Interesting story, really. But we should not discuss it in the open."

Disfigured hands dropped a pair of bronze keys on the bar in front of Cadeck. He perked upward to greet the balding owner's face with a simple nod of accommodation.

"Would you care to join us in our rooms upstairs?"

"I suppose it's better than this stool that's bruised my ass the last few days."

Cruxien consumed the lingering drops in his cup before slamming the vessel onto the bar.

"Care to cover me again?"

Cruxien took a final inhale of his ruban before dropping it into his used cup. A pillar of exhausted cinder rose calmly from the chalice in extinguished linger.

"Like old times," Cadeck grinned.

Cruxien slipped off the wooden stool in a manner befitting an intoxicated slob. Cadeck reached for Cruxien's muscled, bare arm protruding from an open-sleeved tunic and lifted the appendage around his neck. He motioned Ysalir with a nod and steadied the brawny drunkard upon his shoulders. His knees shuddered with the added weight. Ysalir approached the right side of Cruxien and hoisted his other arm around her neck as she called for her sister to bring the others to follow.

Inebriated patrons ignored the activity as many had lulled themselves into a drunken coma to pay any relevant attention. Scant candlelight blanketed the tavern as the outside light slipped into evening. Cadeck and Ysalir carried Cruxien towards a short staircase on the far side of the room and with steady grip, planted heavy foot onto creaking wood. The incline moaned with weight as the pair shuffled Cruxien to the top of the staircase and made a right turn into the room hall.

Cadeck flicked the keys into his hand. Soft candles shined in the hall offering his withered eyes scant reprieve to read tarnished numbers. He handed one of the keys to Ysalir and took the room to his right. Ysalir's key matched the number on the room to the left side.

Ysalir aided Cadeck with his friend into the room where Cadeck scurried and propped Cruxien onto a musky bed which the sheets had not changed in months. Cassica and the others spilled into the cramp quarters behind them, a solitary bed the only comfort to rest Cruxien's weary body. They stood tight to shoulders in the confined room. Ysalir squeezed behind Kenat and Cadeck and met the single window. Verifying the integrity of the design, she locked the window in place with the latch. She knelt to the table in front of the window, lifted a flint and lit the lamp sitting on the surface.

"Kenat, go downstairs and fetch some water," Cadeck made slight turn towards the younger Magi on his left.

Leaving tight space behind, Kenat pressed his way past Tesh and Cassica and closed the door behind him.

"I suppose you're going to tell us who this man is?" Ysalir demanded.

Cruxien breathed in relaxed stupor. Each breath heaved his tightened pectorals beneath tattered shirt cut just above his navel. Light-brown skin covered his complexion. Various scars cut valleys into his symmetrical face along his cheek bones and chin as his head topped in a faded buzz of flat hair.

"Cruxien Balax. We have shared drink on occasion."

"Cruxien Balax? Cadeck how can you put trust with him?"

Ysalir turned her face in angered twist towards the Magi as Cruxien looked on her with concern.

"He's got a ship," Cadeck looked upon Ysalir in discerning scorn.

"Had a ship my friend," Cruxien slurred, rubbing his beaded eyes with dirt-trodden fingers.

His speech carried the tone of High Accent with a foreign dialect. Kenat barged into the door carrying a small flask of water in his right hand. He slipped his way past Cassica and Tesh beside Venna and towards Cadeck where Cruxien set himself up on his own strength and removed the vial from Kenat's hands. After ingesting a small swig, he forced the rest of the contents upon his face then called for more water. Cadeck motioned Kenat to obey with a nod of his head and Kenat repeated his procedure. Water dripped along Cruxien's cheeks onto his clothes as he leaned forward supported by tree trunk thighs covered in bulging trousers.

"What do you mean *had a ship?*"

Cadeck leered towards Cruxien.

"The Imperium confiscated it four days ago," Cruxien peeked up from the slosh dripping from his face to open eyes toward Cadeck.

"Can you get it back?" Ysalir urged swaying to Cadeck's quick persuasion, "We have priority to travel as emissaries of the Crown of Sarat."

Cruxien smiled. His eyes wandered towards Cassica, then Cadeck.

"I suppose you do carry burden. Your names are everywhere. Cassica, I recognize, but which one of you is this Tesh Verdui?"

Tesh slipped his left hand from sackcloth to raise it in response prompting Cruxien to comment about his injury.

"That's a horrid wound you have there, friend."

"And one of the reasons we need your ship," Cadeck followed.

Cruxien nodded his head as Kenat returned. As he made his way towards Cruxien, the sailor took the cup and gulped the contents in one try. With a relieving sigh, Cruxien continued, "I suppose you can just use your magick and take it back then?"

Cadeck shrugged, "You know that is not possible. What happened to your ship?"

"I came into Racoren about a week ago, full crew, empty vessel ready for our next charter. The port was in ruins, barely an open dock to port to. Upon landing and finding a safe dock, the Si'rai welcomed me. They required title to my ship, or they would remove it from my bloodied corpse. They promised they would allow it to sail under new charter, as with the other ships able to find port. They said something about needing supply vessels to run between their coastal behemoths and the port and all ships able to dock here would be repurposed for their use.

"You see, this port's too shallow for their ships. My caravel is light enough to sail into harbor and past your father's ships, Red. But your ships lie in hulks in the middle of the bay, half sinking, or others no longer seaworthy. The Si'rai require the smaller ships to transfer supplies to their heavies. My ship will not stand a chance past the blockade without their charter."

"Then we go when you have new charter."

Cruxien shook his head, "I go beyond blockade, and I get bombarded, or so they tell me per the charter they drafted. Getting the princess away from Sarat... well, I do not want to risk my neck for task old friend."

Cruxien rubbed the fresh stubble around his neck and rose next to Cadeck's side. He muscled through the tight quarters towards the door.

"I need favor of you Cruxien and its fortune of the gods we met today."

Cruxien stopped as his heavy hand put grip onto the wooden knob of the thin-ply door. With a heavy sigh, he responded to Cadeck's request, "If Sokut favored my prayers these past few days then that whore could spill her waters unto me and allow me to fuck her dry. Otherwise, you would best find another captain."

Cruxien twisted the knob.

"Then, you can tell Sokut when you take us to the Water Temple."

Cruxien paused, giving thought to Cadeck's words as his statement floated on his mind like wisp ghosts in the swamp. He put trust into the goddess, praying to her regularly. However, recent prayers weighed heavy on his heart as they fell unanswered. He no longer felt purpose to his goddess, but Cadeck's words ripped into the void within his soul.

"I'll return here in the morning, I'll come up with a plan tonight."

Cruxien returned his hand to twist the knob and with a creak of iron and wood, the door swung tight in the musky quarters as he exited the small room. Eris sealed the door behind him in the cramped space. Ysalir erupted into a ferocious stare as anger boiled within her thoughts. She curled velvety lips with the sneering temper of a rabid wolf assaulting prey.

"I do not trust Cassica with a wanted pirate. How can you just volunteer our passage to this man?"

Cadeck turned back to meet her gaze.

"I have known him for more time than Cassica has been alive. He may be a scoundrel on the outside, but he is a man of good heart. You would rather us leave onboard a ship belonging to the Imperium?"

Ysalir fell silent. Locks of straggled brunette hair mangled over her shoulders as she lowered her pose to a solemn defeat. The Magi's words carried a heavier weight than the burden on her heart to Cassica's safety and to trust him meant security.

"Now, leave us and take to your room. We must be thankful we have comfort below our bodies and roof over our heads. Tomorrow, I hope to eat a hot meal, and we can work with Cruxien to leave this place."

Ysalir led the women out of the room with disgruntled moans. As Eris became the last to exit, Kenat breathed an open sigh as the aeration of the confines opened from the cramped environment. Tesh moved to the bed, setting his sword and various other utilities of equipment onto the head position. Cold tingles covered his veins as his index finger slid along the rough patches of crystalline ice formed upon the golden traces on his left hand. He counted twenty marks of gold traced in a tree pattern along the back of his wrist as his eyes slumbered.

Cadeck settled onto the small stool beside the table and positioned his rucksack to open the latch. Aromatic leathery bindings unbuckled with the clanks of bronze as he lifted his pipe from the bag. He relaxed a small fabric pouch from the satchel and a wicker stick and placed the stick on the table. He loosened the small tie around the pouch and squeezed a pinch of his fingers into the container. He reached to remove a small nip of crinkling grass with a pungent tinge and filtered the narcotic into the receptacle of his pipe in a method he memorized to rote. With the wicker stick, he lit the end of the lighter into the lamp, snuffed out the light and settled the burning torch to light his pleasure.

Cadeck took a slow whiff of the ruban. Ruban's tingling sensation lingered along the back of his throat; an imprisonment of addiction he enjoyed. He held the smoke deep into his mouth before exhuming his breath into a relaxing release. Coils of puffed smoke rolled out in a dance macabre of symphonic exasperation. His artistry of breath reflected in the dim light specks creeping in from nearby buildings across the alley. Tesh lifted his legs and extended them along the hay-stuffed mattress. Kenat seated himself on a firm piece of flooring, checking the creaks to find the load-bearing beams below him and propped himself against the wall in a solemn manner in attempt to find sleep. A low hum in rhythmic verse emptied from Cadeck's throat as he whispered words in a syncopated nursery rhyme.

Words fluttered from tongue as his mind drifted to old thoughts. He closed his eyes, recalling the soft words he once sung to his boy resting in a bed. The song reflected the legend of an ancient Magi who once loved a common woman. In the second verse he left his position to raise their family only for his Ascended to discover him in the third. In the bridge, the song reflected love for family, and another knows no bounds, where neither dogma nor position could separate the pair. By the fourth verse, the Ascended understood and by this time sought position for a replacement allowing the subject to live happily with his bride.

Ysalir led the entrance to the ladies' room, followed by Cassica and the younger women. Impatiently, she reached the lone window in the room and set iron hook latch to the loop securing the opening from any outside notice. She continued her survey, verifying neither holes nor other leaks of flooring or wall could allow others to hear or see their existence in the room. Through soft whispers, she gave instruction to Venna and Eris to pay attention to her methods for their purposes in future rank. Cassica positioned herself on the lone bed, sinking her sultry build into the soft hay mattress. A comfort she sought in many days of travel from Tijoa's hut.

Her eyes followed Ysalir as the woman lectured Venna and Eris in her repetition. Strands of bright vermillion hair streaked down her cheeks highlighting sorrowed tears spilled over jade. Cassica brought her knees to her chest. The loose side of her tunics slipped down her exposed right shoulder releasing pale cleavage into the still darkness of the room.

"Permission to speak informally?"

Ysalir turned to Cassica with a whisper who nodded in response.

"Begging pardon, but are you going to permit Cadeck to hire this scoundrel?"

"What choice do we have?"

Cassica shot a glare at the confrontation through puffed lips hiding tear in lowered whispers, "Silvetzen, fallen. My lands, fallen. We have been lucky thus far and evaded capture. How much longer can our luck last? For generations, my family has trusted the judgment of the Magi and Cadeck is a loyal friend."

"And trust in the Magi is what puts us in this position."

Ysalir seated firm onto the hard stool. Her conflict resounded through Cassica's heart as though the weight of her kingdom pressed upon her chest.

"I've supported you," Ysalir continued, "but I cannot support this decision. I have made promise to protect you and cannot perform task among criminals. We should find Saratian passage and make way to Tarlakana without Cruxien's aide."

"Cadeck has kept us safe this long. As much as I personally distrust his kind, I can trust him. As a Mistress of the Rose, you must obey my orders, and I order you and the others to respect *my* trust. We did not have to remain after we escorted him to the Fire Temple, but he suspected danger. When Tijoa told me how the Council views us humans and human governments, it confirmed my suspicions all this time and my father placed undue trust in an archaic body.

"I may never agree with his decisions in my capacity in Court and the strained dealings Sarat has with the Magi, but as a friend, I trust Cadeck's choices. We must rest. We follow Cadeck to Cruxien, charter ship as best we can and," Cassica swallowed her next thought as though the words haunted her from her past, "continue to Jorin."

"Aye, milady."

Ysalir bowed her head in acknowledgement. Ysalir reserved to defeat yet her loyalty to Cassica persisted. In recent days, she sensed Venna's distrust, the slap mark on her sister's face matched Cassica's hand, but it was not Ysalir's position to question. She was the last to fall to rest instead making sure Venna and Eris found comfort huddled amongst themselves on firm seating upon warm furs.

As a pair of ladies, they matched perfect symmetry cuddled amongst one another with arms entwined and faces buried in each other's shoulders. Cassica turned her back towards Ysalir, huddled in the fetal position facing the wall. A fragment of her tunic rose above the grimy trousers covering her hips, exposing a segment of her pale skin. Columns of vertebrae outlined upon Cassica's skin shuttered among whimpers.

Ysalir turned attention to the soft muffles coming from Cassica's sleep. Glancing over, Venna and Eris did not move and remained in breathing solace in their dreams. She kept to herself, piercing her eyes through darkened window and observed the stillness of the town below.

Lights flickered along building walls and the crashing sounds of ocean waves littered her auditory senses into enchanting thoughts distracting her from duty. Entranced by the soft waves, she drifted to a subtle time as she lifted her head to arc her neck against the wall and closed her eyes to meditate on dreams once welcomed.

Her mind flowed to recall the sharp features of her former lover's solid frame as carved from quarry. Sensuous pulses rushed through her abdomen and down her loins as the vibrating tickle from his thrust pulverized her insides in endorphin ecstasy. Ysalir hiked her right foot upon the windowsill and caressed the prickling nerves along her inner thigh. Moistening her fingers and with hushed silence she slid her longest down her pants reviving cries of pleasures she had once favored in attempt to calm herself from their dreaded surroundings.

Chapter 40

Chilled fog rolled atop Racoren's buildings like a rampaging ghost consuming lights and sustenance as the low morning sun broke through from the eastern horizons. Crows cackled in flight as startled foot stomps clamored along the cobblestone streets in lockstep unison. Armor-clad clanks broke through the morning stillness pounding on doors to homes and surrounding buildings shouting obscenities in Si'rai language followed by a censored translation from a scruffy-voiced Silvetzenian repeating the words in Common Tongue. Startled, Venna yawned amidst the calamity outside and moaned in exasperation.

Stringy hairs clung to fabric as she pried herself from Eris' embrace with the static sparks of their hairs separating in violent storms. She frazzled her blonde locks into a semblance of order as she skirted eyes around the quiet stillness of the sleeping inhabitants of the room. Goose skin reached across exposed shins by the loose leggings she had worn. She propped her knees to her chest and with graceful ease of a lithe dancer, lifted herself to stand barefoot upon mold-stained wood. Venna hobbled with bleary eyes scratched and crusted by sleep scraps as she fingered them loose into her hands to ease herself into consciousness. Doe-like eyes that propelled her child-like looks blinked as she darted towards the window.

In the alley below, pairs of Si'rai black troops commissioned their way towards the building proclaiming with Common translation for the louts in the tavern below to make their way towards the town center in one hour. Yelling continued as the trio of men met staircase and with lockstep steel preceded the incline towards the rooms. Wood clamored with foreign metal, heavy with burden creaking with wear as the formidable gear weighted aged and sea-brittle lumber. Venna's ears perked to the creeping sounds of iron as the men's progress continued closer. The Silvetzenian man pounded on the doors down the hall screaming the same command to meet in the town center within one hour. He repeated his command as he hammered on each door with heavy fist.

Patrons' doors swung open prompting ad-libbed replies as to the person's state of undress or disgruntled remark requiring their response. A plea came from below in uneducated accent of the owner announcing his rights to hold business without intrusion of soldiers who will not pay for tabs left open. As he made the top of the flight of the steps, a loud welp threw from his voice as a calamitous slam met him to the side of the wall. The Silvetzenian guard cursed him violently before threatening his life should he ever to make threats again. The door beatings continued as Venna stood next to Ysalir to shake her to wake.

Forceful tugs caused Ysalir to moan and with violent response, threw blanket off her body sending Venna onto the floor beside them. Exposed from the waist down, translucent skin glistened with pale white. Sunlight spackled into the musty window glass upon Ysalir's flesh. Like a nest of strewn fabric, Ysalir's pubic regions shaped into form between curvaceous thighs with defined musculature. Ysalir bent knee to her side as her face shook to ponder the startling calls coming from outside.

"Sister, there're guards outside."

Ysalir jerked her head towards Venna, "Do they disturb us yet?"

Venna shook her head. The clamoring beatings stopped as a more violent knock slammed into their closed door.

"'Ey, what was that noise in 'ere?"

Ysalir answered with a blurting response to wake the others, "'Tis just a lady fumbling to put her clothes on."

A slow giggle billowed through thin door, "Jou don' mind if'in I peek do ya?"

"If you don't mind the stench of the blue rot, you can look at my cunt all you want." Ysalir unveiled her lie with buoyancy. She smiled to Venna and covered herself with the blanket.

"You dirty whore. Get dressed and get into the town center in one 'our."

Ysalir did not respond, instead reached for her trousers resting on the floor in front of her and pulled each leg to her hip. Quickly, she fastened the muddied and sweat-drenched pants around her waist. She reached over to Cassica's shoulder and with a nudge alerted her to wake.

"We must go, Highness." Ysalir's hair draped down her shoulders in front of her face, "We do not have much time. We must get the men."

"No mother, just one more hour," Cassica murmured.

"Your Highness," Ysalir jolted her shoulder again.

Cassica's eyes fluttered open to see Ysalir standing above her.

"What's the matter?"

Cassica's body slowly adjusted to the morning arousal as she stretched her legs and arms to full length. Crimson hair tangled over her shoulders as emerald eyes caught glance of Ysalir peering outside the window.

"The Si'rai have requested us to move to meeting. We must hurry and find Cadeck's friend. Cadeck must know where he hides out here."

A low rattle beckoned at the door to the ladies' room.

"Is everyone decent?" Kenat's voice whispered from outside.

Ysalir took a quick glance to see all the ladies were in proper attire and remained clothed.

"Aye, Kenat. Enter."

Iron bolt latched open as the doorknob twisted. Kenat swung the hollow door to full wide as he, Cadeck and Tesh entered. Tesh arranged the weaponry upon his back to hide his sword amongst thick sackcloth. Cadeck squeezed into the space leaving Tesh with the heavy bulk of equipment at the front of the room and closed the door behind them.

"We must find Cruxien, Cadeck. I hope you would know where he hides out. We must hurry."

Cadeck paused, lifting his right hand to stop Ysalir's advance of further inquiry.

"I am afraid I do not. I've only shared drink with him on a few occasions in Racoren and only to pass through. However, if we were in Yumphen, I would be more than obliged."

"Then how do we find him?" Cassica demanded.

She sat upright onto the bed, untangled her hair as best she could with the absence of brush and sought response from the Magi.

"He said he would come to us. But this presents a challenge. The Si'rai are going building to building and if we linger in this tavern for too long upon the called time, we will be at risk of revealing our motives. I recommend we adhere to their commands and migrate to the town center."

"Let me get to Cruxien," Ysalir turned towards Cadeck.

Her eyes flared with anger as the thoughts of safety came to challenge.

"Just like we did in Silvetzen. I can sneak away."

"No, Ysalir. This is unlike Silvetzen. They caught us by surprise after we had a well thought out agenda. There is an old saying amongst Magi that to deviate from Natural Will is ill-fated for the distracted. If we value the protection of Cassica and ourselves, we do as they command then return to plan."

Ysalir resigned in defeat once again. She turned stare towards Cassica who reminded her through facial expression of their conversation a few hours ago. Ysalir harried Eris and Venna to organize belongings and ready the armaments for travel. Eris and Venna laid out the small knives into the pocket satchels for the older women to wrap around their waists. Working meticulously for time allotted amidst whispered clanks and leather slips the weapons had laid out in two sets of elongated belts each woman gathered and wrapped around their waists discreetly.

Cadeck exited first, followed by Cassica and the remaining entourage. Through dim halls reeking of molded wood seared by aging smoke and fish gut, the group carried single file down the rickety staircase in desire to collapse at any moment. The cramped space tavern had been devoid of occupancy save for a slender waitress clothed in ragged dress covering a dingy white undershirt bound at her wrists. She tended to the wiping of the counters in diligent fashion as Cadeck approached the girl.

"Are you able to serve us morning meal?"

"Sorry syr," she opened with mousy tone in Low Accent, "Kitchin's closed by order of the Imperium."

She pointed towards the bald-head tavern owner resting on the edge of a crusted table of rotted wood. He winced as his foul-tongued waitress for a bond mate placed wet cloth on his fresh wounds. Disgruntled and dreary, Cadeck rubbed his stubble whiskers with crackled hands as a slow moan evacuated his lips.

"We've only had scraps and what we can hunt the last few days, is there anything you can offer?"

The girl glanced around behind her and shuffled through sturdy wood shelves in between the wine casks stacked against them. She reached for a sprig of velvet bulbs set in a bowl and a length of bread resting beside them. Next to them a bowl held skinned filets of stale fish meat.

"You look like 'onest folk. Here is some rugeberries, a couple of fish cuts and some day-old bread. I doubt my father would mind."

She swatted flies away from the food and placed the nourishment on the bar in front of Cadeck. She looked towards the injured owner who shrugged off Cadeck with a wave of scraped hand and painful grimace.

Cadeck followed her finger to the man.

"The gods smile upon you this day. We will not forget this deed."

Cadeck distributed the morsels into rations amongst the group as he shuffled them further to leave the tavern. He made sure each member received a pinch of fish and a couple of rugeberries before giving them a piece of bread enough to clench between two fingers. It would work for now, he thought, meat and bread for whatever may await them.

As they left, Venna considered what would become of her as their eyes met upon Venna's hastened exit. Would the Imperium leave her and her family alone, tending to her own devices in her duties or would there be a harsher fate, one much like Bri's met many weeks ago at the hands of cruel punishers. Such a lithe and carefree girl close to Eris' age was ripe for abuse and Venna had only wished to take her with them. She knew better than to ask Cadeck or even Cassica to free the girl in the moment their eyes locked. Their new world was harsh and unforgiving, a fear Venna understood in the young girl's eyes.

Multitudes of citizens pushed their way through thin alleys furrowing into widened streets, streaming at the pointed end of pike men following with the rhythmic calamity of steel jointed armor. Seas of population spilled towards the central ring crowding the small group amidst raucous banter of pain. Honest men with buckled and defeated faces stammered with their families. Pain gripped on the children as Cassica sensed the fears of those around her.

A little boy walked beside her, barefoot and with muddied face. Shiny blue eyes peeked through hair dipped in grime fluttering in all directions. He gripped the hand of his mother whose tender face looked aged by several decades in the matter of a couple of short weeks. Echoes of similar sentiment carried around her as innocent boys and girls turned to her in still life appearing to gaze to her with hope; the innocence of childhood ripped asunder from a war she could have avoided.

Guilt weighed on her mind as the children seemed to mouth their distrust. As though their own parents did not exist in this split moment of time, but the haunted cries of the offspring who were either orphans or taken to one parent, cursed her very name in their sorrow. She wanted to cry. Yell and scream to the citizens that she is there for them, she will take care of their needs and they will fight back. She knew better. Doing so would mean her capture and the end of all hope these children and their few parents had to hold onto.

The multitude stopped at the town's central podium. Cadeck seated himself upon a small, overturned crate. Hay spilled around his seat next to a two handled cart parked against a wall belonging to a building. Kenat stood beside him, gazing his pearly eyes towards the white-wood stage where several troops armored in black shells stood to attention. The mark of the Imperium had meshed into the breastplates in crimson ire. Behind the group, olive-skinned men in similar fashion stood at full attention armed by swords resting at hip. Ysalir followed her eyes to the rooftops where positioned snipers armed with crossbows trained onto the podium as to guard a dignitary from assassination.

A row of seated men gathered on the podium flanked by a pair of raven banners marking the Si'rai sigil in full bloom. A couple of the men wore silvery shined armor capped by crimson feather plumes on their helmets and fleeced gold formed to the shape of their herald on their breastplates. A third man stood out from the rest of the known Si'rai ranks.

461

Sunlight caught the crimson robe into full flair as the star rose to mid-morning. Spiked epaulets rested upon his shoulders stretching out a few inches off his robes dyed to match his outfit. Wrapped around his neck like a gaudy accessory, a gold medallion hung just above his torso suspended by a striking gold chain.

Behind the men positioned a scaffold draped by a large black sheet. Folds of fabric stretched through the sheet in strain from the weight of the coverings bending the fashioned herald of the Imperium within the pleats. The man with the garish robe sat in perfect center to the curtain in a manner befitting a ritual. His face hid behind a crimson veil flowing from an elaborate skull cap with eight spokes emanating from his crown. He covered from head to toe, gloves to boots capped off by a red silk neck piece ensuring no skin exposed from his clothes.

A Silvetzenian man took to the front of the podium covered in standard chain mail assembly. Bare-arms protruded from tattered tunics like a hairy mangle of peach-tone skin. Thick thighs covered by dirt and soot-stained trousers reached down to a pair of hefty, untied boots. His battle-hardiness wavered through the air amidst the worn armor and the scraps of scars struck upon his face.

Cassica's mind raced to impossible tangents. A once proud kingdom of her dynasty now betrodden to this hellish nightmare before her. She stood to Cadeck's left flank, her eyes wandered to his stubble then over to Ysalir standing opposite. Venna and Eris propped themselves onto the back board of the cart while Tesh and Kenat positioned beside the younger girls.

"Cadeck, what do you suppose this is about?"

Kenat leaned to whisper.

"The puppeteers will show us once the veil has been lifted," Cadeck's cryptic tone pointed his eyes towards the ominous sheet draped over the tall backdrop.

Cassica reached inward to adjust her emotions. Calm rested over her subjects. Necks craned over taller bodies as children sat upon their parents' shoulders to get unobstructed view. Tensions built around the nervous silence before the Silvetzenian man took to tongue.

"Citizens of Racoren," the Silvetzenian growled in Low Accent through thick and protruding beard, "The Si'rai Imperium welcomes you into their lands as they did with your neighbors to the north, Silvetzen."

His voice vibrated with hidden discomfort and hesitation as he continued, "It is with great honor that I present to you Magister Secuminius Nybas."

The Silvetzenian man turned around on injured leg as the covered man stood to full height. He moved like a bloodied ghost fresh from the grave, floating above the podium and towered over the brawny white-skinned Silvetzenian to his left. Whispers muttered upon the crowd in shocked response to the ethereal figure erected before them. Patiently he waited for the murmurs to settle, unwavering in motion. Fingers crossed in formation to an upside-down triangle rested firmly above his loins as in meditative prayer. So still in contemplative pose, not even his chest heaved.

Secuminius did not move nor flinch nor waver in stoic position. His head remained still, resolute; should any crane of his neck, any jerk of his body would topple his heavy headdress and expose his true form. As a demon hidden by veil, he preferred anonymity to recognition. Inferior men and women need not know him; he cared not for their volitions only those demanded from his vicar. As the silence carried, he waited still longer. Restlessness lingered upon his audience in anticipation of a drastic gesture. Every cough or whimper delayed him.

"Citizens of Racoren," he opened in Common Tongue, the inflections in his voice steadied into confident monotone.

He paused after his introduction like a programmed automaton, "Blessed by Almighty Hadithem and His Holy Vicar, Supernus Magister Lucivus A'zum, Exalted God-King of the Imperium and on behalf of Tivius A'zum, Supernus Commandant of the Fifth Arm of Chaos, Lord Magister and interim ruler of Sarat, I proclaim it is with great pleasure you are welcomed into our empire."

The introduction met a cacophony of boos and cat calls as he steadied his posture in response. Secuminius did not choose to exude the chicanery of his superior, the Revered Magister, Torkas Philatané, nor did he own the might of his immediate report, but what he did master was uncomfortable calm amid adversity. His mind sowed undesirable madness upon his subjects, reaching out through his aztunai, he could detect the slightest vibrations of his audience through the physical contact with the ground and connected to them like roots of a tree. His pose remained as a blood-drenched statue as the citizens eased on their displeasure with frightened agitation. The man standing before them remained in his pose sowing their minds to his madness.

"It is understood resistance will come," the priest continued, "and resistance will meet with hostility. You work now, not for yourselves, not for your own improvement, but to the improvement of the Imperium. The Imperium assumes control over your business, over your roads, your farms, your docks, and your pleasures. What you do not contribute to better the

Imperium is a vice. Vice is a sin, and with impunity, we cleanse such sins from our Imperium.

"We are your saviors. We bring you a new beginning. There is no individual, there is only the Imperium. You will apply for status in the Imperium. We shall assess criteria for you to keep your positions and those who do not meet them we shall reassign as the Imperium sees fit. Your abilities to the needs of the Imperium, and those needs distributed as necessary.

"Citizens of Racoren, hope is a dream. Change is inevitable. Your rulers did not see this and abandoned you in desperation to save their wealth, wealth they do not dare share with you. To this day, the Queen and her daughter flee like cowards. They deny you freedom for the sake of their own vanity."

Cassica shuddered to calm herself. Thoughts raced to pain; the faces of the children stared like empty death into her soul. Cold numbness ripped across Tesh's wrist slicing through the embedded golden veins as vibrations in his aztmudin commanded the gods' strengths from his Trials. He ruffled a piece of fabric around his hand to disguise it from curious onlookers. Cadeck stood to height. Surges rippled through his soul unlike those he had felt since his enslavement.

Cadeck. Jess' voice called to him.

Jess. He whispered.

His eyes shot across the blue skies as distant thunders boiled to the west. Only it was he who heard them. Venna heard his whisper, shooting a stare at the spoken softness spilled from his mouth as though inside she felt what he knew. Kenat closed his eyes, fiery pains burned inside of them. A raging lava spilled through his veins like a devouring liquid ready to ignite.

"It is this vanity," Magister Nybas continued, "denying them their fate. The inevitable outcome of the suffering they have caused you while you toiled your lives for a vain king who spent your coin on games of chance and females of loose resolve.

"Vice is a weakness upon the Will of the people. A vain king cannot understand the labor of his subjects if he indulges in self-pleasures. A vain king does not improve those he rules, nor does he see to their needs. A vain king does not reward work. The Imperium will reward you. To understand this, you must work. Work will set you free.

"Freedom to improve your life. To improve the Imperium is to improve life for all. At the hands of a vain ruler, a kingdom cannot thrive. At the hands of your old king, you have suffered in punishment. With your vain king, your Queen, and their whore of a daughter, they have brought this upon you. They have brought you fear. Fear of this Imperium. Instead of choosing alliance, they chose to run. And to that end, the Imperium offers you justice."

On command, the thick sheet of raven lifted with pulley and dropped to the ground. Magister Nybas broke position, lifting his hands in welcome gesture. Palms faced skyward with arms in full extension. Commanding the gesture and orchestrating the audience through his own theater, Nybas anticipated the crowd's reaction, feeding on their gall and fear.

Behind him, impaled upon a thick pole, rested the corpse of a young boy around the age of nine. Tattered vestments of royalty covered the lad in bright lavender tones draped in silk wrap around his frame. Sever marks carved across the boy's naked chest as the drape unfurled in fluttering winds. His neck split apart beneath the jaw, eviscerated from the pressure of the pike. Preserved by ritualistic medicines, the skin of the boy sheened in the sun like a glimmer of glass crust faded green.

Time ceased. Streaks of sobbing saliva eviscerated from Cassica's reddened lips as she widened her jaw in silent, unbreathing sobs. Blush tinge filled her cheeks as her left hand stopped in mid reach to cover her mouth. Instant tears streamed like torrential rains washing over her face at the sight of her brother. Tirerian's nubile flesh had torn along the pike like a skewer. Cassica's existence paused with static disarray. Around her, the subjects yelled, screamed, some began to riot, stricken down by flailing arrows from the rooftops.

Cassica lunged into Cadeck's chest. His face boiled with searing anger as thunder rolled upon the sky in ever widening symphony. Flames erupted from Kenat's fingertips like candle wicks while flowing fires spilled along his wrists and forearms as though he dipped into accelerant. Cadeck twined hands within scarlet mottle as he made quick to bring hood upon Cassica's head.

He turned to Kenat and ordered him in whisper to calm his aztmudin to not alert the Si'rai priest to their presence. Venna yelled a deafening scream unnoticed upon the culminating roar of the crowd reacting fervently to the reveal of the royal son. Ysalir rushed to Cassica's front, gripping a sidearm knife tucked beneath her hip cord in preparation should any strike against her. Sea-spackled eyes ripped a striking stare at the red-robed master as lips puffed in fiery fury.

"Do something Cadeck, or I will."

Ysalir motioned, inaudible to those around her as the riot erupted to full bore. Si'rai soldiers began to enter the fray in attempt to calm the mayhem.

"No."

Cadeck warned, placing tranquil hand upon Ysalir's shoulder. With a rush of his magick, a cooling surge filled his arms and rolled upon his hands as he summoned the effect upon Ysalir's own form.

"We run. We find shelter. It is too dangerous to work here, in this now, in this moment."

Cadeck's teeth gritted to find his own serenity.

Although hidden from view by his audience, Nybas grinned condescendingly upon the chaos he had wrought. In meditation, he projected into his audience the deafening madness he had desired. The visual effect culminated his implantations, and the reaction was as expected. The citizenry feared their fate, feared his command, and feared the army at his disposal. Criminals and commoners hustled to escape in common goal only for those who resisted the most to find an arrow through their chest or a sword swiping their thighs. His magick had completed as commanded by ritual. In resounding boom, his monotone voice projected final words to his audience.

"You will learn to accept us. You will learn to obey. Learn what your nobles did not. In your major cities, the remaining male nobility is on display, punished for their sinful vices. The Will of the Imperium is absolute. The Will of Supernus Magister is Eternal."

Cadeck huddled Cassica within his chest, clenched tight in his arms, he encased her tangled crimson hair. Tears drenched the ribcage of his tunic with weeping outrage. He set pace to turn them into a nearby alley next to the building they rested and motioned for Kenat, Ysalir and the young girls to move with him. With pouted lips, Ysalir shot her neck towards the ambushing crowds, the nonchalant scarlet robe, and the snipers positioned on the roof striking those who advanced towards the podium. Her mind raced with calculations taking factors and variables into her procedures she reached for a stiletto tucked within the leather belt. Kenat passed her with Venna and Eris tow in hand.

Venna disappeared into the alley, her voice calling her sister's name amidst the commotions in faint whispers at her distance. Sea shorn eyes flowed as violent rapids hidden by brunette locks against her face, Ysalir turned around into the alley to see Venna's tear-stricken blonde hair screaming for her. Dying now would strike Venna's heart like a poison dart. Cassica would be void of a protector and easy to prey upon. Her eyes darted back to the man on the podium as though through his thick veil she could pierce his soul in a projected image of a blade striking at his neck. Resigning to defeat, she left Tesh to stand at the chaos as she made swift run into the backstreet.

Tingles of ice fire static surged along Tesh's left hand wrapping his swollen veins in a menagerie of flowing aztmudin. Unravelling the sackcloth around his hand, he tossed the fabric onto the cobble street as his left hand ignited with a fiery tinge sharpened with crystalline ice wrapped around electrical arcs. Si'rai soldiers occupied themselves to control the riot around him. They ignored the single man in nondescript rags who had unsheathed the hidden blade rested against his back. Boiling with a fire beyond Ysalir's own revenge, Tesh faced stare down towards the red-colored man many yards in the distance.

All is in motion; life is in motion. Go. Spoken through his aztmudin through ancient eons, the crystalline ice ceased to circuit along his veins.

Life begets death. Death renews life. Those may die so others may live. Go. A second voice lingered on his mind, stopping the fiery orange flow encapsulating through his bloodstream.

You are the first, the last, and the only. We are your Mind, Matter, and Soul. Go. As the third voice spoke to him, the final arcs of violet electricity seized eruption calming his hand into the bruised color of golden leaf splintered along the traces. Tesh dropped his sword to the brick stone as he released control to his destiny and made haste to catch up to the advanced members.

Cadeck led the group through blighted alleys, skipping over piles of trash and slipping past sludge waste spilling from dripping buckets. He made careful attention to avoid the main streets. Cadeck turned one corner leading into a main road and without hesitation, motioned the group to circle back as a cadre of Si'rai troops marched towards the screams of riot. He continued the advancements through dimly lit paths following the strong odor of sea and fish as best he could amidst the lingering sting of ash hanging upon the town like death manifest.

Cadeck snaked down inclined slopes following into the wharf district leading Cassica who stumbled and continued to sob by his hand. Cheers for aide struck the air in the Si'rai speech with the grumbling shakes of heavy wagons splintering cobblestone streets nearby. Ysalir caught to Cadeck and urged him to stop to catch breath as the younger members had paced a few yards behind them. On request, Cadeck ceased running, permitting Cassica to slam her back against a wall wailing in distress before she plunked her body in slow tears to grab her knees in seated position. She buried her face into her thighs, pain tore from her chest amid thoughts of uncontrollable pity.

"What do we do now?"

Ysalir raged silently towards Cadeck.

Cassica quieted her following wail as Venna, and Eris rushed to her side.

"I must meditate. Father Aeus must have a plan."

"We have no time, Magi. Tirerian is dead and if that robed sack of shit bares any truth, the rest of her brothers and father are too. You do not have a plan. You did not have a plan once we got here."

"I had a plan, Ysalir," Cadeck turned to meet her face, towering over her forehead by mere inches. Fishy breaths rolled down his chin upon her face, his moustache snarled through gray grizzled flair.

"Yeah? Well, your drunken friend blew it," Ysalir's voice erupted in seething anger quiet under her breath to avoid detection.

"Hey sweets," a gravelly voice echoed behind their position in the alley.

Tesh turned over his shoulder to see Cruxien standing next to two white-skinned men on each flank.

"I'm right here, you don't have to call me names."

"Cruxien, how'd you find us?"

Cadeck pushed his way towards the sailor, stepping over Venna's huddle with Eris next to her. Cadeck approached Cruxien with a startled relief at the sailor's surprised approach.

"I heard the commotion, came out to see what it was all about. We do not have much time. I have shelter nearby; you'll be safer there than in the open."

Cadeck slapped Cruxien's exposed shoulder with a comforting grin then turned over his shoulder to lecture Ysalir.

"What did I remind you about faith?"

Ysalir gathered herself, brushing her hair away from her face with flared anger. She looked onto Cassica who remained slumped with knees against chest trailing whispered sobs within her thighs. She called Venna to help her lifting Cassica to her feet and followed as Cruxien navigated the slim alleys amidst furthering decay and the wafting smells of sea sludge and fish waste. Cassica's tears lessened to a low whimper as she huddled against Ysalir's chest, wrapping arms tight along her hips in a motion to remain sane.

Tirerian's laughter frolicked in her mind as reflections of his ghost pattered their way through the ancient castle walls, a distant memory now. The young boy had only learned to wield a sword when she returned from Mornika, never knowing of his oldest sibling. She had told him a few weeks ago how she had an important assignment to carry for father and she would return to him with reassurance in her tone of voice she would complete his training. The last smile she shared was the innocent lamentations of a child begging to assure promise.

Cruxien led the group towards an alley as common as others filled with filth and grime. He set eyes upon a small doorknob and with curious glances, shifted his neck in either direction down the path to ensure none followed. The portal swung open leading Cadeck and his travelers into a dingy, ill-lit quarter chamber cramped smaller than their last confinement. Before Cadeck could speak as to his disagreement with the restricted room, Cruxien turned his back to his friend and advised Ysalir to shut the door behind her as she entered.

Packed into the room barely fit for one stood ten grown adults in manner imprisoned in a shelter awaiting torture. Cruxien had pressed against an internal door and with a rhythmic knock a slit revealed a pair of bejeweled eyes set in clear blue irises.

"Sokut's tears bear the sweetest fruit," Cruxien spoke towards the other figure.

"That fruit shall bear the bitterest nectar." She replied, lifting the inside latch.

A fresh flow of perfumy air filtered into the musty space. Cruxien led the group into a lavish chamber decorated in crimson sheets draped along the walls and ceiling like soft whispers accentuated from a luscious lover's lips. Beside him, the maiden who allowed entry stood close to his height, her raven hair bundled into a tail reaching towards her back with glistening jewelry embedded along her eye sockets. Her dress made of Tarnian silk, a sheer piece covered across her ample chest splitting at her navel and continued to her ankles. Cosmetic spackles of golden lines traced along her fingers and bare feet as she greeted Cruxien with a peck on his cheek. A tight palm soft as a newborn babe fluttered along his chin.

The group filtered into the antechambers. Venna scrunched her nose at the sweet perfumes flowing through the air sensing the aromas were common occurrence to the room. The smells reminded her of the distasteful brothel in Silvetzen as Eris and Kenat brushed her aside. Candlelight dripped upon the room from a chandelier clanking in the ceiling, suspended from cheap trinkets straining to keep the set piece from crashing to floor. The lithe maiden shifted her position towards a nearby wall and readied herself for Cruxien's next words as the two men beside him closed the internal door behind them.

"Cadeck, welcome to my home."

Cruxien opened his arms to full width with a grimy smile punctuated through week old stubble.

Cadeck furrowed his brow, shifting aged eyes along the ceiling and walls. Perfume lightened the smell of seawater. The room devoid of meaningful furniture, a lack of a bed, lamps, and tables. An empty floor remained, covered in mildew stains betraying the glamor of the delicate linens.

Dismayed at the treatment of Cruxien's guests, Cadeck mocked him.

"My imprisonment with the Imperium had far superior accommodations."

"But this is only the first room, my friend. Ophelia, if you may."

Cruxien pointed to the lanky maiden as Ophelia reached behind a small shelf bolted to the wall. With a twist of her wrist and push of her strength, the wall slid open to unveil a spacious room filled with laughter, friendly banter and a host of men cavorting with ale and food.

"Iosta, serve my friends fresh food and drink."

A blonde-haired woman behind a counter nodded at his command.

"Ophelia, summon the other maidens and when the ladies have finished, bathe them, clothe them, and arm the oldest ones. Men, open table for my friends and I."

On command, five of his men lifted themselves and emptied the table. Cadeck widened his grin with a whiskery smile. He opened his mind to a lull he had not relished in over two years. Steaming food piled onto his senses as Eris and Venna rushed beyond him towards the opened table. Cruxien's men paid the fair maidens no attention, returning to the sultry mistresses serving them drink and sustenance. Tesh positioned seat next to Eris. Kenat followed suit, seating himself next to Venna. Kenat crackled his stretched knuckles.

"Cadeck, friend, it will be a long journey. Break bread with me, you are my guest."

"So, this is how you squander the money you owe me?"

Cadeck patted Cruxien on his shoulder as the pair shared a sympathetic smile towards one another. Ysalir followed Cadeck and Cruxien to the table, keeping her eyes on the pirate as she permitted Cassica to sit first.

Ophelia slid the false wall behind her as she latched the room shut from the inside of the dark chambers. Small sconces shone candlelight upon the floors and walls, hiding the interior amidst haunting orange glows devoid of sunlight. One of Cruxien's maidens stood next to him, placing a bowl of bread loaves before him. Dangling earrings looped below her lobes, while beaded jewelry of fashionable gold weaved along her hair strands tightened against her scalp. A lavender ensemble covered her breasts exposing tan-skinned cleavage with a piercing of a golden dolphin accentuating her navel. A jeweled waist cord wrapped around her hips holding leggings together with beads exposing her thighs just below her toned waistline.

Cruxien reached into the breadbasket and split a loaf to hand one half to Cadeck. Ophelia lowered a vase and emptied a serving of juyo wine into a clay chalice to his left. She followed suit to the other adults and began to serve Eris and Venna. Cadeck turned to Ophelia and without hesitation, welcomed her to pour to them. Iosta approached the table bearing seven bowls of steaming stew, placing each upon the table beginning with Cassica and working her way around the table before she left to gather her master's meal.

"Cruxien, your hospitality is unwavering. To what is the purpose of this treatment?"

"Cadeck, friend, I have known you for over twenty harvests. It is time we cut ourselves even cloth. I take you and your party to the legendary Temple of Sokut and points further, if necessary," Cruxien then turned to Cassica with a leer of coercion in his eye, "The princess here waivers our warrants till our lives have fallen to grave."

Ysalir's suspicions boiled in her gut. She lowered shallow eyes as though to curse his request. Cassica toiled her spoon into the stew. She rested her left temple upon open palm, slighted hair sifting against weathered skin like crimson rags torn against sharpened stone. Through saddened eyes dried of tears, she observed Venna and Kenat hastily taking their accommodations.

"You mock and cheer and revel in drunkenness while all around you, the Imperium has taken over Racoren? You spoke tongue yourself the Imperium has stolen your ship and you dare insult Her Highness by requesting her to pardon your crimes? All for repaying any coin you may owe to Cadeck? What do you take the Crown for, pirate? Fools?"

Ysalir stood and removed a sinister blade from her left hip. She stabbed the curved, Si'rai blade taken from the blind magister into the cracked table. Cruxien leaned in his seat, resting his right arm with drink into an angled position. Soft accent spilled from his tongue as the rest of the room fell silent; his tone implied a seriousness betraying his introductions.

"No, assassin, I take them for dead. And to good riddance."

Cruxien sneered at Ysalir, his mouth widened with sinister grin at his seething words of disgust, "Seeing as Cassica is the only royal capable of meeting my demands, I do not think it is an unfair request. I can transport Cadeck, Tesh and the boy Magi to the Water Temple and points onward. You ladies are fair game in this new world."

Cruxien leaned forward and slammed his cup to the table shattering it in a splash of purple soaked clay. He curled his fingers to rest on the table in calm manner.

"You are more than welcome to return to Sarat if you so desire, I have no time for your plight."

"Ys," Venna paused realizing the gaffe in pronouncing Ysalir's true name in front of strangers, "Rensel please," she begged.

"I offer my gratitude as a token of my wealth, Rensel. If that is your true name, assassin," Cruxien sneered at her in snide grin, "My shelter as a means of appeasement. The rest of this town would see her turned over to the Imperium of which I am not too fond of, but their reward is quite exquisite.

However, any friend of Cadeck's is a friend of mine, but assassin, your attitude is straining my outreach."

"Rensel, ease."

Cassica raised her voice to a low whine. She moved her palm away from her face turning strangled mats of hair away from her ear. With dying emerald flare wavering in her eyes, she turned towards the criminal in a plea of desperation.

"As the last known living member of the House of Bovariàr, heir to Sarat, I welcome your request in exchange of our passage. But only when the kingdom is free from the tyranny of the Imperium shall I grant pardon. You have my word as Trebut's oldest and as the word of Crown Law."

Cruxien wafted his thoughts with a whiskery grin. The glimmer in his hazel eyes lifted lip to smile. He stood to height, the scraping of his vibark chair brushed against stone. Sweaty grime traced his muscle tone along his neck and biceps. Fit thighs covered in burlap leggings as he looked around his room to see all eyes turned to his attention; men, women and a couple of spotted curs resting in a distant corner. Men focused on him through beards, clean shaves, or disfigured scars. A few were bald or smiled with diseased or missing teeth. The women stopped their chores and waited on his breath.

"To Roth, to Sarat, to Cassica and the Crown. Today, my friends, we will be part to bring down the Imperium."

Cruxien reached for Cadeck's cup still full of pour. He raised drink for his followers as they erupted in revelry. The pair of dogs yelled in howls. Cadeck opened with wide smile as Cruxien returned to seat.

Ysalir did not follow the celebratory stance, instead refrained to the negativity of guilt as she resumed her seat. Cassica's safety troubled her and resigning to the demands of a criminal were beneath the promises of the Crown for generations. Her oath was to the Crown, its laws, and its rulers. In one swift stroke, all she had known, fought for and risked her life for became evidence of a changing tide. Cadeck's anecdote about the loss of two kingdoms for the sake of all man tore through her skull as an arrow would shatter frail glass. All she had promised to protect ripped apart by an unwavering enemy, an enemy to the Crown, an enemy to the Council, an enemy to Roth and an enemy to the gods. Worst of all, she had welcomed this enemy unto her sheets in fleeting instances of unadulterated emotions.

Chapter 41

Light wavered within burned lamp glass as the lamp wick danced its image upon an old dresser. Crusted wood splintered at the joints, while faded panels crisscrossed the edges and surfaces of the wooden vanity desk. Light filtered upon a mirror in Cassica's hand, bouncing Cassica's image against shadow. Fickle hands danced within crimson locks behind her as she focused attention to her left eye. Blush powder flakes suffocated the hairs of a brush she set against the soft skin of her left cheek. Flickers of powder dust swept over her skin to settle as flakes in the dying shadows of the low light. She stretched her eye again, opened and closed but the fine line below her eye lid would not leave. Defeated, she settled the mirror back to the surface with a low sigh.

Fear trembled through her heart abetting stress reflected on once graceful skin. Behind her, floating hands turned curled vermillion strands into a braided flow wrapped around her scalp. Delicate hands toiled behind her head and gracefully settled her sanguine hair upon freckled shoulders like a waterfall over white foam. Curled bangs flanked Cassica's cheeks extended just above her dimples. Shimmered loop lay on each shoulder binding a sleek piece of, crimson, Tarnian silk split upon each breast exposing her sternum down the center towards her waist.

She sat with crossed legs clothed in fire-red legwear, loose fitting against her thighs ended below her knees. Bound to her hips with her top, a slim chain graced her waist accentuating her fit figure. Cassica turned attention towards the falling sunlight in the western distance. Racoren stung her eyes with soot and ash filtered by the natural cling of fish rot. Screams permeated in the background, echoing sentiment weighed upon her chest like the stone torture as her emotions caused burden about the fate of her brothers. Tirerian's laughter died in her thoughts as a waning chill shivered down her spine. Secuminius' monotone shot through her heart at the words of his announcement concerning the male lineage. Father Trebut, twin brothers Tresin and Desin, and her youngest brother, Geraud; all murdered in cold blood by an enemy who snuck into the kingdom as part of a revenge ousting.

Had she signed the treaty, would it have spared them? Cadeck's words lingered on her emotions; is she doing the right thing by fleeing with him? Could he guarantee safety? Cassica moved her left hand towards a rolled scroll, bound tight by leather ribbon strapped around the center. She held the starched parchment in tight grip wrapped by slender fingers and recently manicured nails.

"Eris," she muttered, "Summon Rensel to my chambers. Assure Tesh and the Magi settled for the evening. Upon completing this task, you and Venna may retire for rest."

Eris removed her hands from Cassica's silk hair, settling a comb next to the mirror on the table, "Aye, milady."

In private, Eris returned to needed purpose in capacity as a White Rose. In service as a maiden, she wore a plain white tunic covering her body up to her neck with full sleeves. Fashioned for plainness, a similar virgin white skirt covered her from hip to ankle as she bowed in reverence and turned her back to Cassica before exiting the door.

Alone, as she was in Court, Cassica had a moment to fill her heart with thoughts of pain and sorrow. Rumors of alleged libidinous debauchery stabbed into her chest with the claims of Geraud's false parentage produced of her and her twin brothers by incestuous orgy. This was Racoren, a town disloyal to the Crown. She waived the rumors as mere suspicion by the populace to foster ill-tongue against her family. A patter of light foot interrupted her thoughts as a thick wooden door swung open with welcome request.

Ysalir entered the chambers with the eloquence of a composed servant. She brought herself to curtsy and address at the majestic presence of her leader. Cleaned hair sprinkled against her face enticing the scents to her nose. Washed face refreshed her emotions as she lifted herself to full stand. Cassica craned neck over shoulder, shifting her eyes to stare behind her. Vermillion locks escaped from pale shoulders, collapsing behind her back.

"Rensel," Cassica held tongue to gather her thoughts and reached for the letter resting beside her, "I task you with a new assignment."

Cassica rose from the stool. Scarlet wrappings filtered loose against her skin. In flittering light, the sheer fabric accented the outline of her naked form underneath. Blessed by curved, yet slender measurements, her figure resembled a goddess statue erected in a town center. She let her hands drape to the front of her waist, her note held firm within her grip.

"Your Highness," Ysalir addressed with concern.

"I require you to leave Racoren at once. Seek out my mother and inform her of my safety."

"Your Highness," Ysalir's eyes widened to exasperated response, "Please. I ask to remain with you to be your steward and guardian."

"No. You have new purpose. Locate my mother and protect her instead. Tesh and the Magi can comfort my security."

"And what of Cruxien? I will not leave you alone with his criminals."

Ysalir stepped to approach Cassica as the princess stopped her with a wave of her hand in command.

"He will not bring harm to me if he wishes pardon. I will honor his request once Sarat is under my House again. Take this warrant," Cassica approached Ysalir and tangled their fingers to place the note within, "I have no instrument to seal it, but I have contained instructions for delivery by a Rose and such transfer makes this document bound to the Crown should you encounter any able-bodied Saratian men along the way. They are to form a militia and encourage others to do the same with stipends paid upon my restoration of Crown. And if any of those men are of the criminal society, I shall pardon their vices."

Tears welted within Ysalir's eyes as she lifted the rolled paper to her chest. She lowered her face. Her hair draped along her open shoulders. Pain boiled in her stomach lifting to her throat within the nightdress dyed with raven silk. She reached an open hand towards exposed navel as she thought only of her sister and how empty Venna must have felt while duty made absent correspondence from her.

Defying formality, "Cassica, please. Do not make me abandon Venna. I do not trust Kenat with her nor Cruxien's men. And should our mother and father be dead or imprisoned, I do not wish for her to learn of fate or suffer the same."

"Your concerns are noted."

Ysalir met Cassica to the eye, "For all the blood I gave and the dignity I sacrificed, promise me, she won't become one of my ranks."

Cassica touched Ysalir's chin with slender fingers. With a glaze in her eye forming tears, the pair shared emotion as one entity. Cassica pulled Ysalir to embrace, her arms stretched around Ysalir's shoulders and entangled their despair united. Ysalir reacted in kind, wrapping arms along Cassica's shoulders at same height. Tears drenched hair and silk as Cassica craned her mouth to reach Ysalir's ear.

"Venna is strong. Perform task and we will meet again."

"Your Highness, promise me," pulling away, Ysalir attempted one more plea.

Cassica surveyed the tears swelling in her guardian's eyes.

"If she is alive, beg of my mother. You know my position cannot honor request."

The pair relaxed embrace. Ysalir looked to her princess in leaving thought. Training intuition gathered her emotions inside her chest, savored like the last pieces of a forgotten meal never to render again. She curtsied and reached for the heavy door and with a creak of iron hinge, snaked through the open slit and sealed it shut behind her.

Blathering screams tore through the slim pane window from the outside town followed by barked commands in the Imperium tongue. Cassica was alone, helpless. Her protector reassigned to find her mother, Selen. Was Ysalir on a suicide mission? She could only rely on the thought of Ysalir's perfected training to remove her from danger and allow the skilled woman to succeed in the return of Cassica's family to the throne.

#

Guttural ruckus lifted high spirit through tiny, darkened hallways lasting for what seemed like complete city blocks. Eris skirted her way past various chambers of scant space and vast expanse. She passed a couple in ravishing romances on a rickety table. The man's pants wrapped around his ankles, sweaty gut hefting away as he fornicated with a tan-skinned woman bent over and dress lifted over her hips. The pair kept to their appeasement ignoring the virgin white dress flying past them on errand. She motioned her way through snaking halls towards the open meeting hall she had dined within.

Cruxien and Cadeck shared laughter and tales at the extended table, having returned to seat since evening meal. Ophelia poured darkened cider from a clay pitcher into a stein beside Cruxien, then followed to Cadeck's. Ghostly smoke rose from Cadeck's mouth as he puffed on pipe filtering the room with the titillating sweetness of ruban burn lightening the reek of sea rot outside the thick walls.

"Cadeck, do you remember when I found your boy rummaging through port? I had all my cargo ready to load through mismarked crates and in his carelessness; he toppled over one of the shipments of Koran brandy I was to transport, knocking the whole load all over the pier."

Cadeck nodded his head in stifled laughter.

Cruxien continued, "And what did you tell the port guards who nearly caught it?"

"I gave them an illusion that it was bushels of wheat intended for export to Cratia. Legal and taxed and procured an illusion of documents to the same," Cadeck huffed on his pipe, "One whiff of the spill and a couple of bottles bought from you to ease the pain."

476

Cruxien ruffled his fingers on Cadeck's exposed shoulders, freshly washed of muck and grime. Ripped from strained fitness, Cadeck bulged in open arm shirt from a regiment of his own doing requiring shape and health to focus on his aztmudin. A perfect figure, for perfect thought.

Cruxien smiled, "I thought as a Magi, you couldn't do those things?"

"There's a lot we shouldn't do," Cadeck reached for a clay chalice beside him and took a gulp of rugeberry cider.

The stench of the ruban smokes lifted to coil along the wood-beam ceiling. Eris approached Cadeck, interrupting their conversation briefly. Brunette mane draped over pure white tunic woven from thin, Tarlaki cotton allowing her skin to breathe in the humid, port airs. A perkiness shone through the wrappings of her slight frame.

"Excuse me, Cadeck, but Her Highness wishes you comfortable rest and bids goodnight."

"Thank you, Eris."

Cadeck nodded, keeping his right hand positioned in manner to hold his pipe. The young girl turned away from the pair and carried herself in calm manner away from the meeting hall.

"She almost looks like Wrem. I almost thought she was. How is she? Did she survive the fire as you did?"

Cruxien's mood lowered to grim state for the welfare of his friend's family. Cadeck took a long huff on his pipe to erase pain and swigged the rest of his inebriation to soothing burn down his chest.

"What fire?"

Cadeck's eyes curled to inquire keeping focus to the scratched and splintered surface. Nail heads poked through the table planks in front of him like hazardous steps on a delicate road.

"Your farm. When I was last in Yumphen a season ago, I had heard rumor Wenfier farm burned a year before. I hired ride to see for myself and there was nothing left. The townsfolk said it was sudden, that a burst of lightning angered by Aeus struck the house, trapping all inside."

"This is why I travel with Tesh."

Cadeck turned aging wrinkled eye towards his friend. Clean face exposed scarred pits and craggy age drooped in folded pain along puffed eyes and weathered cheeks as he clutched his tunics to grip the locket hanging around his chest.

"Two years ago, my Ascended turned tongue to my disfavor. In the silence of night, a group of Si'rai men accompanied Tivius A'zum who came to take them. Three of those men died to my magick as I ushered Wrem and Dal to hide. Then, I saw that sword he held. A magick enveloped that weapon as none I had ever seen, bound in death unlike any blade. As I spoke my spells, the sword absorbed them, only to feel my power returned to me, flinging me unconscious upon my back.

"Tivius saw no use for Madelynn. I lie on the floor, bleeding from wounds of impact, begging for Aeus' magick to flow. I could only witness as Tivius eviscerated her from sternum to womb. The last I saw, her body turned gray, lifeless, and cold. Like her soul removed. I awoke later in a cold prison, absent the comfort of my children.

"I did all I could to keep my children from becoming bound to a Temple," Cadeck moved his thoughts to stare into the wooden table. Ruts and protruded nails scarred its surface.

"I made promise to Jess as she lay suffering from birthing Dal. Her words, her visions guided my thoughts. We met all those years ago in Tarn and fell in love not over our own desires, but out of reciprocated trust. In her visions, she saw Wrem and Dal. In mine, I saw Tesh."

Cadeck reached for the locket hidden beneath his tunic, "Godwen translated prophecy as he considered necessary and as I learned, turned the Council against all of mankind over his readings - a prophecy written Aeons ago; The Sun, The Moon, and The Falling of Stars. It is why I travel with Tesh; I take him to become a Knight. Just like his father and many others before him."

"But the Knights are long dead. And the Magi? Did the others know of Godwen's treachery?"

"Aye. They voted on it only by fear if to defy him would mean punishment," Cadeck lowered his eyes for grave tongue, "You dare not wish to know how punishment would occur. The Knights demise came at the hands of Godwen as well."

"I remember hearing of news. My homeland fell not long afterward. Tongues spread the Knights were gone, no more. You, Jess, and another Magi, what was his name," Cruxien turned to his drink trying to recall, "Rechold, I believe. You three tried to prevent that war. And the propaganda that spread soon afterward; the Knights were corrupt and met their demise by their own greed, harboring bargains for favored kings and lords, selling their services to the highest bidder, and amassing a wealth far exceeding any kingdom jeopardizing the people in the process. Gossips I heard insisted the Council issued decree seeing their properties seized, their lives punished, and their weapons smelted down. Rumors spilled from tongues that the Magi themselves took them out, by their own magick, thus ending a centuries-old quarrel."

"And thus, the lies worked."

"Lies, Cadeck. I could not fight them. What I saw in those younger days in Tarn, my first experiences with a Magi in yourself and Jess, you were honest and decent. Yet every port I went to, the people believed the Council's news. I took to sail and fled Tarn after the carnage the Imperium wrought, and I believed nothing I saw afterward."

"The lies spread by the Magi continue to this day. Even those I travel with have believed them. Cruxien, I travel to bring Tesh to train as a Knight. He is our last remaining vestige to bring down the Imperium; to remove Roth from its threat, and to rescue my children from them. If they die, magick dies in Roth. Would you allow Tarn to fall in vain? And then to what purpose do your people have if the magick of the gods does not exist? Without magick, without what we call, aztmudin, the gods die too."

Cadeck's story soured Cruxien's heart. His face grimaced with a long sigh. Cruxien gritted his teeth. He had constantly remained neutral, running illegal market trade for those who could pay his hefty prices, excising contraband in risky raids and delivering it to his clientele.

He had come under the ire of most kingdoms, including the Imperium and its generals. He had no family; just his crew and the harem of ladies he kept in various port cities for front operations. Yet Cadeck never judged his activities, finding him in Yumphen on occasion to share drink and story, keeping his connection quiet should future favor require. But Cruxien knew how to ply his trade and how safe markets, safe ports and wealthy clients would keep him alive so long as he had money to bail and skills to match and lungs to breathe. Under the Imperium, his trade lessened. The Imperium's war restrictions kept his ship away from the extended hemisphere only to risk high-yield rewards if times came tough and he dare not fathom the results if the Imperium continued their warmongering.

"I am not a righteous man, friend. I have done things I am not too proud of, but I am a pious man. Until lately, Sokut has blessed me with guided sail, skilled crews, and consistent pay, but as your friend, I shall not let your sorrows be burden in Her eyes or upon Her ears. Your bonded was a good woman," Cruxien patted Cadeck on his shoulder, meeting face to continue, "and as she was vicar to my goddess, I shall honor my goddess with commitment to your goals.

"Yet, Cadeck, defeating the Imperium requires a large army. They have thousands upon thousands of soldiers; conscripted, conquered, and natural born. We cannot win with diplomacy. How can one man, two Magi, an assassin, a princess and two girls take out their entire regime?"

Cadeck accepted his question, "If the legends are true, there was once a man, the Azthar Kherdmon, the savior who vanquished the ancient Si'rai. He led thousands into battle, thousands of believers, enough to consume a landmass of continents upon a battlefield. Tesh too, must lead that army if his bloodline is pure as the legends say."

"But Sarat is now gone," Cruxien uttered in muttered growl. His foreign dialect faded in and out with his High Accent, "He would need an army larger than Sarat or Silvetzen could ever field, including the three kingdoms of the Tarlaki."

"And what of the Tarlaki? Are they still free?"

"Aye, but rumors persist in Jorin of civil war which may well erupt over disputed lands they all share. It has all the earmarks of what happened at home. A divided people are a conquerable people. If the Imperium ever learns of this feud, they could easily distract through war or diplomacy."

"Agreed and we must be cautious. But the Tarlaki are loyal to their soil and their warrior creed. Rechold has Ascended to be Gedesh's vicar, and another of my contemporaries, Ascended Mornika, keeps his position at a Temple there, and where Tesh shall need to advance his training. Cassica and her bodyguard should remember where his Temple is. We have a good bargaining posture on our side. The kings may very well see what happened to Cassica, side with their vicar and take sympathy.

"We go to the Water Temple, permit Tesh his Trials, then make way for Tarlakana."

"Then it's agreed," Cruxien extended his right hand, removing himself from the chair. The pair embraced their forearms in mutual accord, "It will take a few days to ready my ship. Make yourselves homely, but I would not leave these grounds given the situation outside."

Cadeck nodded, "Agreed. Now, if you will excuse me, Cruxien, I will make towards my bedchambers. It will be nice to rest without affliction for one night."

Cadeck removed himself from the rickety chair, sliding it away from his body over distressed flooring. He stood to full height. The feel of fresh clothes and the scents of bathing salts refreshed his mind of the pains bothering him if only for one evening. Cadeck's gait rocked as stiffened joints stifled his motion while he cleared the open doorway leading into shadow. Cadeck stumbled his way through poorly lit walkways narrowing to mere feet, snaking along twisting paths opening into various chambers towards noticeable gaps where walls tore away to join buildings in the block together.

Strips of cobblestone interrupted wooden floor path as he entered the false room of another building next to the one serving the dining hall. He motioned his way towards a crusted staircase. Wood whined as he planted steady foot and escalated the structure in recollection to the chambers assigned.

Ocean stench soiled the walls as he moved further down hallways and past hollow rooms where rats expressed their sentiments. Drunken burps filtered his advance beyond other rooms isolated for Cruxien's men.

Cadeck split his walk towards a wing of the floor. A wooden planked bridge beckoned his advance into an adjacent building over an alley where a pair of thin walls and rudimentary thatch ceiling had erected to enclose the path from the elements. He counted the number of doors on his left before coming upon the sixth entrance. The door whined open to full reveal.

Soft lamplight flooded the room, washing the sackcloth blanket with an orange glare. A paned window positioned in front of his nightstand. He paused briefly before closing the door behind him. His body suspended in shadow behind the flickering light. A pulse shuttered across his chest; a reverberation of his soul rippled like a skipped rock on a lake as he continued course towards the glass. Rolling thunder crackled in the thin air outside amidst a cloudless night. An empty moon night darkened the outside as his reflection from the lamp faded into view upon his window.

"If I wasn't a Magi, Rensel, I'm certain my life would be taken before I addressed you."

"If you were my target, Cadeck, your assessment would be accurate."

Ysalir removed herself from the corner provided by the door's arc. Cadeck revolved to see the young woman standing in lighted shadow. Her features hid in darkness sheltered from the soft ambers.

"Something troubles you."

"I'm leaving Racoren, tonight."

She moved to seat herself upon the stuffed mattress resting on the floor space. Her voice shifted towards unrevealed emotions as inflections tightened puffy lips. Fitted to her torso as a noblewoman's corset, she wore a formed leather cuirass which creaked as she raised her left thigh to chest. She buried slender cheek into her leg continuing to watch Cadeck as he remained standing before her. A clean, leather boot heel hung onto the mattress.

"And your heart wants you to remain?"

"Aye. I cannot let Venna know about new purpose Cassica assigned."

"But she'll know you're gone in the morning."

Ysalir buried her full face into her leg disguising softened emotions and preventing tears from staining her fitted raven leather.

"Take care of them, for me. Won't you Cadeck?"

"It is my vow and my honor as a Magi to protect those who do not bare magick. That has always been our promise," Cadeck's voice trailed as he shifted thought to betrayal, "Although promise has been forsaken in recent years."

"Cassica trusts you with her heart, this much she's told me," Ysalir raised her head, turning to the Magi. She rose to her feet meeting Cadeck's stare towering over her.

Tears melted inside her crystal teal eyes resonating against sparse light casting an eerie glow upon Ysalir's face.

"You have a warm heart with meaning and clear purpose to find your children, and complete Tesh's training. You are different than the others, Cadeck. The Council and the gods turned their backs on us humans, but you… you remained true. You defied your ruling body and you have proven even laws can be wrong.

"I know I've done the same, violated oath, and I know those actions jeopardized Sarat and people I hold dear," a tear shifted down her cheek, "I just want to make it better. I do not want Venna to grow up in a savage world where men take her as property, and she has no meaning anymore. I do not want her to be like me," Ysalir followed into open sob.

"I do not want men to fool her as I. If we are not successful with Tesh, if we are not successful rescuing your children and if I cannot secure Selen and the survivors of Court, then our lives no longer share meaning and Venna and Eris risk becoming Si'rai property. But I cannot ensure Venna's safety while on new assignment.

"I want to know they will be safe, both. Should I die, I wish to know my sister will not live in a vile world full of suffering."

Ysalir buried herself into Cadeck's chest as he wrapped muscled arms around exposed pale shoulders. Calloused hands wriggled within brunette locks draped down her bare back.

"You did what you did. Your actions did not bring Sarat's downfall. Do not place blame upon your heart. If anything, your actions will offer us a vital ally in this battle if he is still alive. Calm your tears. Serve renewed purpose and we will reunite in this journey. You have my promise; no harm shall come to the ladies you leave in my care."

Ysalir lifted herself from Cadeck's embrace as he stroked aside a misplaced strand of raven locks behind her ear. She leaned lips towards his cheek and with a strain of her neck, planted a firm peck upon his lower jaw. She removed herself from his space and sauntered towards the window.

Open-gloved hands unlatched the bolt lock and flung the window to swivel outside. Slinking her way within the window frame, she lifted a leathery leg outside and left herself in crouched position with sealed leggings firmly encapsulating her fitted figure. She shot a parting glance at Cadeck, before leaping into a hay cart below and landed on her buttocks with closed arms.

Cadeck rushed towards the window, his eyes catching her lithe sprint between the alleys as the shadows swallowed her.

Cadeck rested his hand against the open sill while he reached to close the glass portal. A burst of lightning shot from the sky striking the ocean surface miles away. Tremors punctuated his soul as the calm surface of the distant ocean exploded from a tsunami wave as struck by a colliding meteor. He gazed into the distant, northward ocean as the frantic wave barreled into the shore shelf yet the dock workers in the northern piers continued their nightly shift, bells and horns remained quiet and flecked lights of the Si'rai blockade kept motionless.

"Father."

A girlish voice whispered behind him. Cadeck cocked his head towards his left shoulder, settling halfway in motion to listen again. He heard the voice repeat as the ethereal waves made landfall, colliding with the port town. Foam tides cascaded through the alleys and streets of an otherworldly origin. Cadeck turned to full rotation, keeping his body facing perpendicular to the window. Before his closed door, shadows danced in a tempo with the light against an image of a young girl of the age of fifteen. Washed hair like salty resin clung to the girl's face and tunics. Sea salt brine punctuated scent into the room as a fresh tide were to roll to shore.

"Wrem, is that you?"

Wrem stood in his room like a half-ghost; existing to touch the wood flooring while faded into the room like a phantom's vision. Azure eyes of a gentle stare perked to meet her father's pitted face like weathered leather. Cadeck kneeled to one knee stretching exposed arms to embrace his daughter where her ragged clothes stretched upon her malnourished body. Graying hair fluttered upon his scalp as tears emptied into his bare face.

"Where's Dal? Let me hold you."

Wrem distanced herself as though his time would be torment should they embrace.

"My time is short, father. Mother calls for you."

"I know," Cadeck opened tears to leave his cheeks as he reached to brush brined hair upon his daughter's ear, "I have shared words with her spirit too."

Like a distant memory, his calloused hands reached towards ragged locks, only for his hand to slip through an illusion.

"Then you must hurry. Mother will show Azthar Kherdmon the truth in her trials."

"But your mother, she is spirit. She communicates as a ghost."

Wrem reached to her father's lip to silence him with her index finger. A salty wash flowed along his mouth as she met his touch. A solid finger pecked upon his mouth as endorphins rushed within his head to the memories of his daughter's touch.

"The doubts of the Council cloud your mind, father. Can you continue to trust them with your heart? Deny the Ego of their teachings. What I have seen in pain has given me patience to know you will come for me with the Azthar Kherdmon and this pain is temporary."

"Pain? Are you hurt?"

"Do not concern father. The Apophadi draws close. I can hear them coming now. They are taking me away, far from here where they do not want you to find me. Know that Mother protects Dal and I from him. We will be safe once we reach the oceans."

Tidal floes washed over Wrem's hair as they spilled onto her body like a full tub. Cadeck reached to hold her as a wall of water covered her shape. A liquid wall emptied her visage as his clasp collapsed the water to crash into the floor at his knees. With an ethereal surge, his room remained dry returning to the stench of carbonized wick sprinkling against the sea rot oceans behind him.

"Wrem, no. Do not go. Wrem."

His cries fell upon empty chambers as though he screamed in a dead wood. Silence answered his cries as they remained internal, exploding from his soul in cacophony. Pains seared through his heart, pumping through his arms and legs, vibrating within his head a sheer pulse of resounding torture. Thunder crackled outside his window, an echo only his soul understood.

Hairs stood upon his head and arms, sparkling static shocks bounced and danced between his follicles like an awkward storm, sending minute tings of ionized sparks over his flesh. Cadeck lifted his right arm as the electrical tempest on his wrist magnified outside his bedroom chambers into the open airs with calamitous thunderclaps. The same occurred upon his left hand as he held his digits split apart, separating palms a few feet from one another.

A jolt of shock erupted from his left index finger to streak open space onto his right palm followed by a rushing whiff of electrical burn crackling through the oxygen air. The flux of energy swayed the previous sparks dancing across his hairs to cease towards an infrequent state discharging his hair to rest on surface skin. Cadeck clenched his fists, stiffening muscles and joints into bulges rippling his flexed biceps. He lifted to stand, wiping his left hand over his right arm as the remnants of static sparkled with stroking motion. Cadeck reached sight to glance towards open ceiling. Rotted coverings enclosed him from the elements, desecrated linens clung like heavy limbs draping downward in tattered rags. *Father Aeus, you have returned gift. You truly have not forsaken us.*

Chapter 42

Venna darted through hallways as quickly as her body would allow and turned down a narrow corridor opening into a wide room stacked high with crates and supplies. An aura of fermented wine danced into her nostrils as she continued beyond the leaking casks and bolted into an antechamber shifting into a narrow passage. Spry frame squeezed through the room as she continued her way through another occupied by half-naked women in changing preparations.

Women giggled as Venna crossed through, exiting through the opposing door. Clearly lost, she came across a closed chamber where a false door painted upon a wall lined by planks for door frames. She remembered the rooms contained false walls and poked her hand around the suspect wall for a catch lever. Click. She felt into a small bookcase mounted onto the panel and with the release of the lock, the door inched open as a metallic conveyor slid the door to her right. She came across a staircase piled with years of collected dust and continued her way to climb to the apex.

As she came to the platform, she angled her sprint to the left. Still lost, she listened for any signs that may point her to the rest of her party. Ophelia had shown the girls their rooms, but did not present to them where Tesh, Kenat and Cadeck stayed. Amidst the unfamiliar maze, Venna was as disoriented as she had feared when she came across a planked bridge straddling a pair of crude walls below her feet. A split between buildings, she continued past the bridge and into another building below a thatch work covering.

A door swung open amidst the dim sconces lighting the halls. A single person left the room and as Venna slammed on her tracks, she feared she may have stumbled upon a segment of Cruxien's hideout where she was unwelcomed. Dim candlelight shadowed the hall as blonde bangs fell over her face, spilling over a soft peasant's shirt and exposed a few inches of her left shoulder through the neckline. The hem of her skirt flowed to a halt. Through the dimly lit corridor, she watched as the stranger stepped towards her. She shifted her right hand to grab at a hilt of a small blade tucked within her bodice.

"Venna," the calming voice recognized her face through the shadow.

"Kenat?"

Venna watched as the sconce above her bounced his pearly eyes into her view. Heaving a sigh, she relaxed her right hand and approached the young man slightly older than she.

"What are you doing over here?"

"Have you seen my sister? I went to her quarters when called to wake, and she was gone."

"No, I have not. You look worried. Have you asked Cassica?"

"It would be improper to ask Her Highness of the whereabouts of one of her ranks, unless I too was a Red," Venna's eyes drooped in defeat.

Kenat stepped towards Venna. The light bounced off his pale white hair and continued along a new set of leather features to cover his torso. A set of black trousers covered his legs as they spilled over to a pair of ankle boots.

"Tesh and Cadeck have made their way towards morning meal. I was finishing our gear for the trip as requested by Cadeck to perform. Surely Cadeck may know where she is. But we do not have to leave just yet."

Kenat lifted his fingers to soft blonde hair as he twirled her locks against the side of her ears. Nerves coiled tickling sensations down Venna's neck and back, tingling her navel and extending into her thighs before she batted his hand away.

"No. I am serious. I need to find her."

Venna mocked his advances with a glare in her eyes as they widened fierce, "C'mon."

Venna reached for his offending hand and gripped it tight as she turned to make sprint. Kenat stumbled to follow, relinquishing her grip as she outpaced him. He managed to keep stride as the pair followed in single file through the various catacombs and archways splitting the block of buildings Cruxien had renovated. The pair weaved through narrow paths leading to large rooms before engaging gravel trails between hollowed buildings. They turned down a planked path built as a porch covered on both sides by fabricated walls and the original awning.

"Do we have to run, Venna? Cadeck would not leave us behind."

Venna stopped in her sprint and turned to the Magi, "And what if Rensel has left us all behind? Her Highness must know so there might still be time to catch her."

Venna resumed her run leaving Kenat trailing. She turned a corner into dark shadow away from Kenat's view as he hastened to catch her pace. A bustle of activity filtered, voices talking in harmonious unison to one another as Venna approached the mess hall. As she carried down the hallway, the wide arch leading to the dining hall emptied to her.

486

Orange lamp lights mounted on the left of the arch while sparse candles supplied hidden light within the remaining chamber. Seated at the table in the center of the room, she observed Cadeck seated next to Cruxien as Tesh sat across from him. Cassica's vibrant crimson hair braided down her backside cascading over an azure bodice covering a white tucked shirt. Venna moved in to sit next to Cassica who crossed her legs beneath an emerald cotton dress. Iosta stood behind the counter orchestrating smells of back fat and boiled fish.

Positioned beside the princess, Venna set herself onto the bench and waited patiently for Cruxien to finish addressing Cadeck. A large map of the Oradan Sea laid out to cover the table reaching towards Cassica's position in its length.

"Where have you been?"

Cassica turned to Venna and as she lessened the distance between their faces, she whispered to Venna in a lecturing tone.

Venna lowered her eyes, "I got lost."

Regaining her composure, she lifted her head to inquire motive, "Your Highness, may I speak freely?"

"Not now. Cruxien is completing his escape plan to get us to sea."

Kenat positioned across from Venna listening as Cruxien continued his speech. Cruxien proceeded to announce his crew had stayed in the harbor overnight, readying the ship as best as possible under the cover of darkness and remained in hiding in their bunks while the Si'rai enforced curfews. He advised Cassica and Cadeck about the dangers of moving during the day, but Cadeck accepted that would allow them to be the least suspicious. Running during the night would lead cause to the Si'rai there may be contraband onboard. Cruxien concluded by removing a rolled parchment from a satchel resting on the table and with the flick of his wrist, the ribbon pulled the crisp yusik parchment to unravel open.

He passed the document to Cadeck. Common Tongue script written on the front of the paper and when he flipped it over, the elaborate glyphs of the Sheebal dialect adorned with flashy curls, edged straight lines in perfect symmetry and emboldened markings to denote important words. On both sides, Cruxien had assertively placed signature in a manner extolling his dissatisfaction. Cadeck flipped it back towards the legible side and perused the contract.

"I can understand your displeasure, friend," he addressed to Cruxien admiring the anger exemplified by the furious handwriting, "And if you break this charter by sailing past the blockade, it says that lethal force may be used."

"Aye, I signed contract with a pair of swords readied at my back. I was not the only captain in that room either. It also came with a flag to raise; signaling I have agreed to charter."

"Your faith in Sokut will guide us past the Si'rai, Cruxien. Of this I have no doubt."

Cruxien placed his hand upon the document to return it to his satchel, "Sokut herself couldn't lift my ship past that blockade."

"I have faith Sokut will guide us as She sees, Cruxien. A visit last night reaffirmed me."

Cruxien smiled at Cadeck and leaned back into his seat, "Did one of my whores visit you, Cadeck?"

"I'm afraid not, Cruxien."

Cadeck smiled in return and turned to Venna appearing as he were prepared to share information. Cadeck inhaled a long sigh before returning his gaze towards his friend.

"If we leave during daylight," Cadeck proceeded, "We must surely hide ourselves from any prying eyes. We are in a town inhabited by those who would just as soon turn in their mothers if it meant they remain free from Si'rai encounter, much less a trio of individuals whose names placed upon posters for the town to see with a reward far exceeding what any of these folks would earn in a lifetime."

Cruxien smiled, rubbing his week grown chin stubble, "I have a supply cart in the stables. You can lie in the cart with a rag thrown over. We can complete the illusion with coverings soaked in pig slop."

Venna grimaced at the thought of pig rot covering her skin and clothes. This adventure has led her to lie in hay, wade through slushed snow and swampy rivers and nearly got her killed by a man with scabs for eyes. How she longed in thought for simple life in Sarat, which as she had learned in recent days is a memory long erased to time.

"Crude but seems effective. No one will question a corpse cart."

"Once on board, we will have to smuggle you three in special panels I have built for smuggling goods. They are false boards within the decks to hide contraband and those whom I do not want port authorities to see apart from the legitimate cargo. At least until we have cleared port."

"How far out is the blockade?"

"I estimate they have anchored a mile from port. The coastal shelf turns shallow further inland which would scrape against their keel lines."

Cruxien pointed to a position on the map to scale off the coast of Racoren. His fingers roughened to his experience upon the map stenciled with carbon tints to outline the shorelines. Wide lettering noted the notable features such as names of the ocean, coastal features, and shore towns. The map stretched to plot the coastal waterways of Western Sarat and Silvetzen and ended as the northern expanses of ice floes drawn to the northern edge. Shipping lanes had crisscrossed in dotted line patterns between various ports in Sarat, Silvetzen and Tarlakana to the East. A compass rose positioned to the far corner of the map pointing the northern edge towards the map where Tesh seated across from Cassica. A crude index grid had outlined the border of the paper.

Cadeck observed the instrument, reading to himself the various locations he recognized such as Racoren and further to the south, the Saratian River which spilled into an inlet at the edge of the ocean. Further south along the coastal shores, the city of Kora marked with a series of channels and waterways noted with crude scale roads spanning the various islands on its coast. The town itself plotted along a series of islands and swamps carrying a watery network between the charted land and buildings.

His eyes caught the peculiarity of a spot of the ocean south and east of the continent of Tarlakana. On Cruxien's map the ocean cartography had a curious lettering in scripted writ whose handwriting Cadeck did not recognize.

"What is this," Cadeck pointed out to the illegible scribble. He moved his eyes to gaze towards Cruxien to meet his scowling face.

Cruxien followed Cadeck's finger to the part of the map noted south of the scale line.

"Just scribble, friend," Cruxien's eyes drew low towards Cadeck's inquiry, "nothing important. This is just a map of the Oradan Sea, shipping lanes and points of interest along the shore."

Cadeck reached to his instincts calling to him. As though Cruxien began to lie to him, Cadeck opened to pry.

"But this scribble, Cruxien. My eyesight is crude, but it looks like it reads..."

Before Cadeck could continue his sentence, Cruxien drew anger at his friend, rolled up the map in haste and with a flair for the dramatic muttered through gritted teeth.

"My pay as promised is to deliver the princess safely from Sarat, is it not?"

Cruxien smiled with a sneer and removed himself from the mess hall. Cruxien stammered with leather boot upon wooden plank and exited through the opening archway. Cassica shot an alerted stare towards the Magi as Cadeck looked towards those in his company in equal resonance to Cassica's emotions.

"Did you have to upset him?" Kenat lowered his eyes toward Cadeck and rose to his feet.

Cadeck resumed his composure and rose to meet Kenat followed by the other members of the group. He requested to Tesh to string the ladies from the room and follow Cruxien's lead out of the refectory. Venna moved towards Cadeck and began to address him before Cadeck brushed her off to follow Tesh's lead. As Kenat proceeded towards him, he rested his hand against the young man's shoulder. Kenat turned his neck towards Cadeck who felt a cold scolding coming upon him.

"There was something about his map requiring inquiry."

"A scribble as he told you. Nothing more."

"It is an older map, Kenat; sixty, or seventy years, judging by the age of the ink. His scribble was fresh; smears were still visible on the aging paper. He is a pious man, Kenat. In all my years of his company, I have known him to pray to Sokut regularly. He was uneasy about going to the Temple of Water.

"He has never sailed empty, always carrying charter. An empty vessel's wasted money, he would say. Coercion prompted him to come to Racoren at quickened pace. The writing mentioned he lost his faith."

"Lost faith?"

"Aye," Cadeck carried himself towards the opening, his full-length cloak loaded heavy on his shoulders draping towards his ankles. Dilapidated, torn and tattered the robe became a pleasant change from the soiled rags he had worn for several weeks since leaving Telmen, "Ysalir was wise to question his trust."

Kenat paused on his statement as he continued behind Cadeck, "Where is she? Venna came charging to my room to find her, asking if her whereabouts were known to me."

"Cassica sent her on assignment," Cadeck turned to Kenat as the younger man met his proceedings down the darkened hallway.

"We should tell Venna," Kenat raised an eyebrow, his pearly eyes softened by scarce lighting.

"No. It is a matter of the Order of the Rose. As I should remind you, their affairs are not our own."

"But she trusts us."

"As she should," Cadeck motioned his right index finger to gesture in lecture, "But if we become privy to disclosure of their secrets, we become biased towards them. As a Magi, we are to remain without opinion on matters of kingdoms. Ysalir trusts our protection for Venna and as such, you should be mindful of your feelings. While we are on assignment, your dealings with Venna should remain professional."

"But Cadeck, you…" Cadeck placed a finger on Kenat's mouth before he could finish speech.

490

"I know what I did, and I do not regret it. My actions have created this mess, but in turn could have implications to the future of the Council. A future you will be inheriting along with my children. Cruxien allowed us to stay a few days, please be mindful of your emotions, Kenat. You shall Ascend soon; I am certain of this. One day, yourself and Wrem might lead the Council."

#

Venna stood against the buckboard cart with arms crossed and pouted lips of discouraged mood. The sun shone down upon Racoren beaming with a vivacious light against the buildings and alleys, shadowing her underneath a stable erected into Cruxien's complex. Wooden beams shaped like a bent cross supported the structure as a pair of horses lingered in stable pens behind the wagon. A small boy, no older than ten tended to the animals as he fed them handfuls of hay. An older man, dressed in tattered tunics, limped upon his right leg towards one of the horses with a pulling harness.

With a scruffy voice, the man coaxed the horse to wear the device. Lowering its neck, the animal penetrated its head into the gear as the man slipped it over the horse. The stable master motioned the boy away in condescending command. His stark eyes lowered into a furrowed brow whose scrapes and scars exemplified his scowl.

Venna observed attentively as the man unlatched the iron bolt keeping the horse penned into its chamber and swung the gate to full width. She caught whiff of manure trailing the horse as he led the horse out of its pen. The young boy sighed and reached to grab a small pitchfork hanging from the wall to scoot the soiled hay into a corner of the vacant stable. Through delicate locks, she turned her eyes to her right to watch as Cruxien discussed the plan with Tesh and Cassica. Tesh listened closely to the plan as he hefted a smaller sword upon his shoulder, the sheath wrapped down towards his thigh.

As the stable master finished binding the horse to the carriage with iron bolts and leathery reins, he removed himself from the stable gantry. Eris stood to Venna's left, her curious eyes inquired of her friend.

"I have not seen Rensel for days, Venna. What do you suppose happened?"

"I don't know," Venna turned towards the younger girl, their eyes meeting in naïve stare. Her voice lowered into a whisper, "Her Highness has diverted my questions."

"You know it's not proper to ask concern regarding the affairs of higher ranks of the Order."

"I know, Eris. But she is my sister. Did Cassica mention anything when she requested you to summon her?"

"No, she did not. I saw a letter on her table, folded with a ribbon, nothing more. Did you ask the Magi?"

"Do not be silly, Eris. Kenat is just a simple doof," Venna giggled, "Besides, he did not know when I asked that first morning. And Cadeck, he would not know either. He makes sure he and Kenat know as little of our affairs as possible. Remember, he wants Tesh trained and to find his children. I doubt concerns of the Rose are any of his business."

"But I thought you like Kenat?"

Eris moved into whisper on Venna's shoulder. The small page boy shuffled hay in front of the pair as they stood next to the back rail of the buckboard.

"I do," she blushed, "but he can still be a doof."

"What about Tesh, did you ask him?"

Venna shrugged, shaking her head, "Tesh? The man has not said nary a word since we left that old man's hut. He was cute at first, but he has become agitated about something. I think all this magick is getting to him with the way his hand sparkles and glows sometimes. Although it has saved our butts a few times, he is becoming loony."

Kenat and Cadeck entered the open-air stable from a split iron door behind Cassica and Tesh. Cruxien returned to cheerful boast as Cadeck filtered into the fresh airs filtering of sea rot and horse manure. Gulls cawed along the distant piers in search of morning prey as the slaps of ocean waves rolled into Cruxien's ears. Cruxien carried to the edge of his open stable, stretching his muscled arms to full width through a sleeveless tunic.

"The smell of the ocean, friend; smells like… money."

He turned his eyes towards Cadeck as the pair made their way towards the buckboard cart. The stable master returned inside the overhang with a large burlap tarp rolled up and rested on his left shoulder. The small page boy shoveled hay and manure from the open stable into a bucket to prepare for disposal. With the plops of solid goo, the messes spilled into the metal bucket to the dismay of Venna's nose.

Cassica hurried next to Venna and Eris, her two maidens who remained behind to carry with her. Her face carried a mystique of solemn joy as she lifted a cowl over braided crimson strands. With subtle voice, she informed Venna and Eris they would ride in the cart sitting upon the blanket resting upon her. Cadeck and Tesh hurried to position within the vessel. Climbing reluctantly, the pair followed order and lifted into the cart to set their backs against the driver board.

492

The bed line was short framed, barely a few inches high, enough to cover the sides and any cargo onboard. Cadeck and Tesh aided Cassica into the buckboard as Cruxien met his stable master with the rolled blanket.

"I hope you don't mind smelling of pig shit, my friend," Cruxien smiled towards Cadeck.

"I tended a farm, remember?"

The pair exchanged smiles as Cadeck and Tesh positioned to their stomachs and flanked Cassica. Cruxien and his stable master unraveled the tarp and threw it over the trio. The rush of air whiffed up Venna's face, sending her hair into a flurry of pig rot and manure stench as she coughed and wheezed the smell away from her mouth. Cruxien handed the brunette maiden a trio of small, hollow chutes of wood.

"Pass these to your friends, this will allow them to breathe."

Eris poked the chutes under the blanket and whispered to Cadeck who lay before her to extrude them from their sides. Kenat lifted himself to the passenger side of the driver board. He covered his head with a loose cowl to detract attention from his silvery hair and pearly eyes. With toned arms, Cruxien gripped the side posts and lifted onto the driver side. His stable master hoisted him a small canteen with fingers of gnawed scars covered in half-hand gloves.

"Will yu be back sewn, Mastair," the scruff tone of mucus-lined language erupted from the stable master's tongue. He heaved a cough emptying green fluid in spit.

"Maybe," Cruxien looked into the alley ahead, sun filled the streets amidst sparse clouds wavering to conceal it, "But I'm about to sail for an adventure that pays dividends more than I've ever seen."

"Safe sail tu ya' Mastair," the stable master nodded his head and Cruxien returned same.

Cruxien whistled the horse to stride through clenched teeth as the high, iron wheels turned into motion. The carriage removed from the overhang into the bright sun-lit sky, Cruxien's height slid just below the low clearance as he ducked to avoid the support beam. Venna shielded her fair complexion from the light, raising her hand to parallel with her eyes to hide them from sudden blindness. The sunlight highlighted her milk white flesh absent the brightness of the star for the days cramped up in Cruxien's hideout.

Concerns for her sister faded as Cruxien eased the carriage into the mid-morning bustle. He turned into a street as resigning pitch smoke simmered into a quiet burn of a building downwind. Citizens remained in tormented disarray, their homes and livelihood questioned on their faces reflected the horrors unfolding with the invading forces. A young woman held her small baby suckling against bare breast approached Cruxien's side, begging for just a sliver of coin to which Cruxien shook his head to offer none. Her Low Accent spoke in broken dialect as she continued to beg while he hastened the cart to quick pace. As the cart passed her, Eris studied the woman with shock and dismay, her eyes lowered in morose queasiness through strands of brunette locks draped over her face.

"You couldn't offer her coin?"

"We must keep illusion, Kenat. I am a sailor offering three of his men to sea, nothing more."

Cruxien continued his ride down the incline road to port. Rows of storage houses and shattered dreams crumbled around him as the streets narrowed into steep trails leading into the harbor. Hammered nail and lifted stone began to replace destruction to bridge the gap between conquered and assimilated. Hundreds of workers, fair-skin complexioned of the Saratian heritage began conscripted labor on new buildings along the harbor to hollow out the decayed remnants of those damaged. Si'rai soldiers berated beggars and peddlers in the harsh cruelty of their boisterous and staccato speech at times to the brunt of pommels or heavy fists. Silvetzenian translators barked commands towards the unwilling servants who toiled in the rebuilding of their ruined city in the images of their new conquerors.

Cruxien turned his cart into a lane next to the harbor as rows of seaworthy vessels lined against the piers. Like silent monuments, the empty sail ships swayed in the calm rocking of the shore waters. Each ship tended by overseers from the Si'rai and the various crew who argued in Common Tongue which the Si'rai did not understand, as the oppressors ended arguments with a reveal of steel unsheathed. Towers had erected upon viewpoints of the harbor housing a solitary soldier armed with a sniper's crossbow in sheltered perch above the docks.

"Maybe she's already boarded the ship," Eris whispered to Venna with confidence.

Venna returned her glance, "Maybe. I doubt it though. Why would she already be there?"

"Perhaps working ahead of us and getting our quarters ready. She is the toughest out of all of us, you know. It makes sense to me."

Eris peered over the storage docks lining her side of the path. Si'rai soldiers patrolled in two abreast, escorting a Silvetzenian man dressed in the clothes of a duty clerk. The Silvetzenian man approached Saratian citizens amidst arguments between them over documents. The tone of the Saratian worker showed his displeasure of the new bureaucracy and by the speech that Eris could surmise, the rules were ever more rigid. Beside Eris' feet, Tesh's body stirred slightly.

494

"The Si'rai seem as bureaucratic as we are," Eris pointed to the observed scene.

Venna pursed her lips to watch where her friend directed her to, "But you see what they have done. Doesn't it bother you what happened to Sarat?"

"No," Eris' tone turned somber, "This was only a matter of time. When I looked upon Vizin in the swamp, his words echoed truth. We were not ready for this, Venna, and my sister's death affirmed it to me."

Venna observed the activities around her as Eris pointed out the similarities one by one; the constructed rigidity of tyrannical order, the marches of troops who extolled justice where they moved and questioned those who may be slightly disobedient, the formalities of ranking officers addressing their subordinates and the citizens beneath them. How the time managed to filter since the initial invasion. A span of mere weeks if their calculations were true. Venna surmised the installation of the Si'rai was swift since their departure from Silvetzen and in the entirety of their time within the northern realm, did not allow a full-scale force of many thousands. To what resources did they channel, she wondered, to invoke a massive operation in such brief time?

"Look around us, Venna, they defeated us in quick pace. Our soldiers were no match for this enemy. These, these monsters," Eris scanned the rooftops and streets as she whispered her thoughts aloud and noted the reddish features hidden beneath raven armor of their oppressors.

"Their cruelties are primitive, but ordinal and precise. No army on Roth could equal what they have, and we are going to trust those with us to their defeat? Look at us, Venna, we are refugees. A once grand kingdom, fallen, over an ideal even Her Highness believes is archaic."

Eris' similarities became true to Venna's mind as she parlayed them to her friend.

"Every night I can only perceive what torturous sufferings my sister endured, and how it haunts me. I see them as clearly as I see you, Venna. Then, a whisper. A word, I cannot pronounce, in their tongue. A man, eyes like icy lakes and a sword at his hip. I hear something each night, from his sword and in his hands, my sister's face. Then, I hear her screams filtered out in echo and surrounded by iron walls. All because of this, these monsters before us. And I have come to accept it.

"Be honest with yourself, Venna," Eris turned to her, their eyes locked upon one another, "You see it. We all see it. Her Highness may try to hide it, but even she cannot."

"Why did you say nothing before departing Sarat?"

"And given unto the sanitarium? Should I not make attempt to learn why my sister died over an oath? I have lost my twin sister to that oath and your sister is gone for days, because of oath. The soldier we met days ago, the one who died in my sight, he had a family. A family upended by chaos, but a chaos wrought upon him by the very people we travel with. The chaos that killed my sister, it gives me my dreams. The old Magi claimed a curse, and I do not doubt him. This curse is destined. Who brought it upon Sarat? The Si'rai? The Magi? The King? Or Tesh?"

"Eris, please, not now. Your words speak of treason."

Venna glanced towards Cassica. In her mind, she knew Cassica heard their words but could do nothing to act. Cassica fell from the prestige of royalty to lying in a cheap buckboard covered by pig-slop laden blanket.

"No Venna. Search your heart. Look at what has become," tears welled in Eris' eyes, "We are both too young for this, Venna, too innocent. Can your heart change how you feel towards the Order? You and I should be bearing children, not fighting. The Order would not exist if the Knights were still in service, and you know this. Innocence ripped from both of us, my sister, your sister, and Her Highness. Do you respect the oath you made? For what you fight? Would you still honor the Crown if you were not in the Order?

"Neither of us had a choice. Your parents signed you into the Seed; it was an honor and privilege for yourself and Rensel to serve the same Crown you and your family coddle. As orphans, the Crown forced my sister and me. How does your heart guide you in knowing this?"

Eris retreated towards her side of the carriage. She stared towards the bustling activity looking away from her friend. Her own emotions drifted into a teary sob. Eris lowered her face into her knees as she raised them to her chest, burying her feelings with her hair.

Despite her own loyal thoughts, Venna surmised Eris was right. She watched her friend bury within her emotions, closing herself from any further discussion. Bound by oath, Venna became an orange rose of the Order. Her next assignment dependent upon Cassica's own will despite her wishes. Would she be a spagyrist, a Benedicer, working in the infirmary and healing those wounded soldiers or caring for a Justiciar in support of her goal? Would she be a scholar, a Scrivener, issuing the information gathered by the Aspirants and Maidens below her and assigning it to the Justiciars in the field? Or would she be a Justiciar, acting for the Crown much as her sister, killing targets by task or sneaking her way into bedrooms for better intelligence?

Like all nobles, as a youth, Venna studied at the Academy by her parents' direction. By this time, Ysalir served among the ranks of the Order of the Rose having completed her training under the tutelage of the Magi Mornika. When she turned thirteen, her studies opened for her entry into the Seed, the training required to become a Petal of the Rose. Like Eris beside her and her deceased sister, she excelled in her studies advancing into the Order of the Rose when she was only fifteen. She remembered the look of glee on her mother's face when her acceptance letter returned, but at the same time, sorrow. Once committed to the Order; there was no return.

As Cruxien carried the cart towards his ship, Venna followed sight of Si'rai soldiers marching in lockstep patrol. Her thoughts faded towards her mother and father and what their fate may have become since the invasion. Ysalir saw them briefly before leaving for Silvetzen. Venna too attended reunion, but returned once more since, to inform her parents of promotion to color. She told her mother how the visits would be sparse, life committed to a cause and travel to unknown lands. Warm sun trickled onto her face as her mother and father's final hugs turned into a distant memory.

Cruxien ceased the cart as he approached the dock his ship had moored. A pair of Si'rai soldiers stationed at each pier where a ship had landed and like other sailors who had approached their ships, performed as expected towards Cruxien. The sun beat down on their raven-pitch armor, cooking their skins. Brisk puffs of air curled along their tanned-red faces producing chill sweat to slide their brows. Cruxien reached into his satchel and produced the rolled orders he had shown to Cadeck and presented the papers to one of the soldiers.

The one soldier flipped the document towards the side in his speech and with grunted nods of acceptance, he returned the document to Cruxien and ushered him forward. Reining the horse cart along the mortar pier, Cruxien's ship came into sight, docked parallel to the lengthy berth. Venna gathered her sights upon Cruxien's vessel. *I have seen bigger.*

"Wha d' ya 'ave 'ere?" A brisk voice echoed from the deck of the boat. Cruxien gazed towards the ship to see a pudgy man dressed in fluffed, blue shirt and puffy pants he held to his waist with one of his hands. He stopped the cart close to a wide ramp leaving his boat's top deck to settle upon the mortar pier.

"Three dead sailors, nothing more. I planned to bury them at sea this afternoon. Just stopped breathing on me last night."

Cruxien's accent dug out from his faked despair.

"Cruxien Balax, yer cargo manifest sed nothin' bout no dead men."

"I know what it said, dock master. I am to carry supplies for the blockade," Cruxien reached into his satchel to produce a manifest sheet, "I am to go to the... What the fuck is this shit?"

He cursed upon a word on his orders scribbled in the Si'rai language, undecipherable in Cruxien's native language. In hesitated gurgle, the obese dock master waddled his way along the ramp to meet Cruxien's side of the cart. Walking behind the cart, he covered his rotund nose at the stench of pig-rot death. The man stopped at Cruxien's side as the captain stepped down from the transport wagon.

"Lemme see yer orders," the dock master reached towards Cruxien with a hand of chubby digits, the loose pants slid a bit to expose rounded gut. His middle finger siphoned through a pair of rings as the dock master snatched the orders from Cruxien's hand with impatient demeanor. Cruxien furrowed an angered brow at the disrespect.

"Yes, yes," the dock master muttered thought as he looked at a rolled-up scroll in his hand. "Here, hold this."

The feisty little man returned the orders back to Cruxien and unraveled the long scroll in his hands. Venna sighed at the gentleman who judging by his accent and features became a turncoat of the Crown. The chubby man perused the scroll he had laid out to the length as he was tall reaching close to Cruxien's neck in height. He reached onto his tattered waist band to lift his pants back up.

"Okay…Mmmhmm…letssee…"

The dock master continued to read the scribbles of the Si'rai written word. Each ornate word had corresponded to a phrase or word connection to the right side of the page in Common Tongue as to appear written by a club-handed blind man.

"Oh my. They've assigned you to supply the flagship of their fleet, *Tiamat*. The ship will sail a green flag on top o' the crow's nest. Admiral Focalore is the cap'n… well, I woul'n just call im cap'n if you favor your head upon your sholda."

"Focalore? Goborah Focalore?"

Cruxien's eyes drew low, his voice muttered in growling whisper.

Hesitating in stutter, the short man answered, "I don' know. I only have a last name."

"Very well," Cruxien sighed to admitted defeat, "May I board my ship now?"

Cruxien raised an eyebrow in threatening demeanor towards the dock master of his impatience.

"I… I cannot let you, Cruxien. I must documen' their names," the dock master pointed to the three bodies in the cargo bed, "Make it official. I must know I have seen the bodies and turn over any new manifests to the Si'rai. I must weigh and measure. I cannot let you board the ship until then."

"What about the cargo? Won't it spoil?"

The dock master shook his head, "C'mon now, it'll onlee be a few hours to process the new manifest."

The tiny eyes leered towards the nubile ladies in the back of the buckboard.

"I don't recall you sailin' wit cunts before."

Cruxien stifled a chuckle, "They did not make good whores, so I'm setting them to sail. They will earn their keep some way."

The dock master nodded, "I guess so Cruxien. Shame really, I would rather have liked to savor their sweet flowers."

The dock master licked his scabbed lips at Venna and Eris as they recoiled with disgust at his features. The pudgy man waddled towards the back. Cruxien's eyes followed, discerning the man's every move as he lifted his left hand to grip hilt on his right thigh. If the man knew any Sheebal, even a simple command to alert the guards at the foot of the pier, Cruxien would have a tough fight on his hands.

He had not seen a Magi in action, much less two and knew nothing about Tesh's skill with a sword other than practice swings at the armory. And the girls, the Rose's reputation preceded them, having met a few in his day, but of Eris and Venna they appeared too young to match skill with steel. He too wondered in thought of Ysalir and why she did not join. Cruxien had seen her tattoo as it snaked its way past her waistband at the dinner table in fleeting glimpse and could use her ability should the harbormaster waiver in his tasks.

With stifled lift, the dock master set his foot upon the running board in the back of the carriage and as though every movement ceased his breath, inched his way into the bed. His loose pants slipped below his belly, spilling his exposed gut to the young girls. Timidly, Venna lifted herself from her seat and positioned to stand. She motioned Eris to join as she propped herself to a sitting position on the edge of the sideboard. The buckboard buckled with shifted weight as the harbormaster fidgeted both feet into the cargo bed. His eyes squinted to perceive his sight as three wooden tubes exited from the forward part of the bed and the light lift of breathing heaved the rotten blanket beneath his feet.

"Do not touch that blanket," Cruxien warned, his hand full grip onto his dagger.

Several men of Cruxien's order prepared stand-by readiness with weapons drawn at the deck of Cruxien's boat.

"Your blood may spill today if you do."

"Cruxien, I only have to yell one word, and every Si'rai soldier on the dock will come to my position."

The harbormaster leaned his burly stomach over to reach the tip of the blanket and with a swift sweep, revealed the likenesses of Cassica, Cadeck and Tesh. The furled crimson hair laid over Cassica's head and neck and as the shock of his observation settled onto the fat man, Cruxien and everyone paused at his next breaths. Cadeck gripped his hand over Cassica and Tesh as he swung his head to watch the rotund man's next thoughts and actions.

The harbormaster clutched at his chest as he waddled to sit at the edge of the buckboard's bed. Gasping for breaths, he made quick focus onto the Si'rai guards at the foot of the pier as they paid attention to his moves. He reached his neck around, looking to see if the sniper nests caught sight of his scene. Catching his heart within his chest, he dropped his feet onto the ground as he motioned for Cruxien to help him down.

"Understan' I have only done this to stay alive, Cruxien. Go and keep her safe."

He turned towards the cart and with an inaudible whisper heard under the calling of the seagulls and cresting waves, he spoke to Cassica, "I hope you can forgive me, Your Highness. By the grace of Sokut, leave your kingdom for safe sail."

The harbormaster gathered his thoughts and glanced towards Cruxien as his fears overpowered him. He scuttled away as his pudgy frame could carry him towards the beginning of the pier where the Si'rai soldiers stood watch. Cruxien studied the man as he waddled the distance to the pier. The harbormaster met the pair of Si'rai guards and harried past them in the haste of his job.

Cruxien turned his gaze towards the western curvature of the horizon. Faint outlines of ships settled in the distance spanning the breadth of his view. Cruxien studied his caravel and the folded sails gripped tight against the pair of masts. Confident feelings swirled through his veins as the cold sweats of early winter chill brushed against tanned skin. *We have outrun these ships before, old girl, we can do it again.*

Sweat glistened from his cheeks and muscled arms. He shaded his eyes from the sun and turned to his men standing on the top deck, "Get down here and load the cart into the ship, I don't pay you to stand around."

A pair of Cruxien's men billowed down the ramp to latch the waiting reins of the drawn cart. With simple calls, the sturdy-built men turned the horse to walk the grade of the rickety wood. Venna, Eris and Kenat dropped out of the cart to stand by Cruxien's side. Kenat's simple cloak covered his visage; rustling winds twisted the fabric around his ankles swaying the sleeves into the current. The horse obliged to the men's lead as though routine procedures garnered instinct from the animal.

The men commanded the horse to its own pull, shifting the animal's weight with the heavy cart onto the top deck of the ship. Cruxien motioned the ladies first with courtesy and proceeded behind Kenat as they strode single file towards the ship. The same pair of men who led his horse scurried behind the cart after Cruxien joined them and with swift muscle, lifted the ramp and hoisted it onboard with the fulcrum of several men behind them. In rhythmic march, ten men sprinted towards the aft staircase leading towards the middeck. As the group shuffled below decks, the five men on the main deck secured small chains around the wagon wheels, positioning the cart amidships then moved the animal to the foremast to secure him.

The five men scurried to the anchor wheel and in strained rotation, began the chain to lift the anchor from the bottom of the harbor. Slotted windows slid open along the topsides upon the port and starboard, setting flat oars into the water. Leaned upon the bulwark, Cruxien studied the anchor chain as water dripped from the iron during ascent. Cruxien barked commands into a middeck grate as the anchor cleared the keel line

Oars set to water line, men moved in unison to propel the vessel forward as the anchor completed its journey to its home. The five men running anchor watch secured the chain with a brake and scuttled to follow order to position upon the masts like nimble animals climbing trees. Kenat lifted his cowl, observing the finite details of which Cruxien's men followed procedure as the captain continued aft towards the helm. As the oarsmen cleared the harbor, Cruxien motioned Kenat to remove Cadeck, Tesh and Cassica from the cart.

Kenat removed the grimy blanket as Cadeck coughed his displeasure at the scent. Cassica scooted along the buckboard as she dropped to her feet upon the sturdy deck. Sea smell air flowed along the curvature of her visage in the cool winds. With assistance from Kenat, Tesh settled foot upon the wooden planks steadying against the sway of sea. Venna and Eris remained close to the port ladder at stern.

Cassica positioned herself against the portside bulwark. Wind brushed her eyelids catching her tears to frost. As the oars below her skimmed the ocean, various artifacts of wrecked ships dotted the landscape of sea, creating a hazardous wasteland of sunken vessels once belonged to her father's navy. From the few meters away from the shore, the totality of destruction befallen upon Racoren took hold upon her heart as tears began to well.

Cassica turned her eyes towards their forward direction. An outline of several massive ships loomed upon the close horizon appearing much larger than the small caravel Cruxien employed. Her thoughts trembled at the trust she had bestowed. Her heart raced inside her chest at the sight of the enemy blockade closing in the distance. Cadeck moved beside her, lifting himself to the helm by Cruxien's side.

"We will not be safe until we've cleared the blockade. Then, I will lower sail and set us to full speed."

"And you can outrun them?"

Cadeck did not share Cruxien's optimism.

"The *Willow* has legs, friend. She has outpaced those ships many times before. At full weight, we are still five times less than they are empty. If we aim for the smaller ships, we should be able to bypass the blockade."

"I sure hope you know what you're doing," Cadeck's pessimism spilled from fresh stubble.

Venna remained in position below the helm on the aft deck, crossing her arms with an air of disgust towards Cassica. She released a sigh as Kenat approached her, leaning against the aft ladder on starboard. He brushed a strand of silvery hair as to rake a field of silk rustling in wind swept sunlight. Eris observed his advances towards her peer in abject disdain. Tesh joined Cadeck beside the helm.

"Did you ever find out about Rensel?" Kenat's voice sprinkled with the waves of the ocean.

"No." Venna's raised voice intoned a disparaging remark.

"Don't get mad at me," Kenat raised his arms in defeat.

Venna retreated to lowered face as she turned her back towards her peer, "I didn't mean to."

She lifted her face, watching the afternoon sun bounce along the flowing streams of waves in the harbor. Venna looked westward setting her palms against the rigid planks of the bulwark to steady her sorrows upon the ship.

"Someone must know, and we just left her. How will she find us?"

"She very resourceful Venna. I am sure we will see her again. There is purpose for her absence, and I am sure Heseph will guide her on journey."

"Heseph? In Sarat, we pray to Sokut."

Venna scowled at his god.

"Of course, Venna, my apologies," Kenat bowed, "I only offer guidance from my deity as his representative."

"I understand. I want to be alone, please."

Kenat slid away from behind the girl, moving to the aft deck to stand next to Cadeck. Cadeck smiled at the exchange, warming to Kenat in his sly sarcasm. He patted Kenat on the shoulder and turned him towards the bulwark laden upon the stern.

Behind the vessel, Racoren's dock skyline lowered in view. Docked ships cradled into their moorings, harbor warehouses turned tiny in view as the momentum of Cruxien's ship carried forward. Cadeck turned to Kenat to lowered voice, inaudible to Cruxien and others nearby.

"Be mindful, Kenat. Remember what I told you of emotions. You are to hide them."

"I know, Cadeck. But Venna she is…"

"You are young Kenat. Do not make the same mistake I did. Do not allow Ego to deter you from Gift. You need to stay close. There is something misplaced about this vessel I cannot quite figure out as well why Cruxien has not permitted us to hide within his secret panels. I suspect something."

Kenat nodded to Cadeck's instruction. A whip of wind caught Cadeck's eye skyward to gaze at the crewman hoisting the green flag upon the crow's nest as Cruxien admitted being his indication towards the Imperium.

Venna released a sigh, her doe-eyes returned to look out upon the harbor and upon the junked Saratian ships resting in the grave of a shallow port. Somewhere, in the maze of buildings behind them, her sister remained. Ysalir either took to hiding in the city or left town for some greater purpose none cared to divulge to Venna. For once, Ysalir remained true to herself and her sister.

She heard Ysalir cry the night they settled into Racoren but said nothing. Heavy heart weighed upon Venna, and she saw the same on Cassica's face as the kingdom her father once ruled no longer existed in original form. Her mind raced to young prince Tirerian, the body impaled on the large spike in the center of the town square and the lost hope of Sarat gone with his brothers. Now, the hope of Sarat lay with the man she saw as common, Tesh Verdui.

Cruxien's yell silenced her thoughts as he burst forth a command to the oarsmen below decks shouting at the top of his lungs for them to row expediently. The outline of several ships grew larger upon the distance as Cadeck began to make details from the offending blockade. Cruxien's ship rocked against the shallow waves opening into the continental shelf. The oarsmen in syncopated rhythm shouted a timed cadence below the decks.

"What are they doing, Cruxien?"

Cadeck's eyes scrutinized the behavior of two of the ships in their view. Their distance margins increased slowly as the ships opened all sails to catch wind. The heavy ship on the right supported a quadruple mast configuration, several sails draped open from its rigging, each of the main sails adorned with the herald of the Imperium. The ship on the left, a much smaller vessel loosened the three masts and allowed the sails' full envelopment of current. Both ships angled in directional configuration with the bow of the right ship directly behind the stern of the other.

"They are aligning us between them. The ship on the right is turning its portside inward while the other one is turning its starboard side to face the other. They must have predicted our breach of the blockade."

Cruxien's scowl gave hints of fear, "We can't open sail, they tower over *Misty Willow* by many meters, and we won't be able to catch enough draft to escape them."

"Can't we just go around one of them?"

Cadeck's eyes widened. His weathered face hoping good news.

"My oar configuration sets us in a straight line, with minimal grade to turn. By the time we can angle to turn, taking consideration of ocean currents and the tide level, we will be ramming them. We will not survive a head on collision."

"Your wheel, can't you…"

Cruxien interrupted Cadeck with a shake of his head. Fear noticeable in Cruxien's eyes, "This controls the rudder, which can jerk the oarsmen if I shift it too swiftly. I could lose several oars; the force of momentum could break arms. I only steer with it once I am open sail. I do not lose equipment or injure men by doing so."

Icicles formed within the golden veins on Tesh's left hand. Tesh glanced to the tingling appendage, lifting it to his chest as his injured vessels tinted into icy crystalline. Tesh surveyed the blockade ever approaching their position with the momentum of the oarsmen below. The pair of ships impeding their progress turned to full line permitting a swath of ocean for Cruxien's ship to pass. Tesh closed his eyes, permitting his thoughts to reach into the moment listening through his meditations for guidance.

Tesh closed his eyes. Cassica hurried herself to approach the aft deck, Eris beside her on the portside bulwark. Cadeck's gaze turning to his friend, then to watch as Cassica lifted herself to join him and Tesh upon the helm. The Magi's eyes drifted towards Tesh's hand, now sparkling with the cerulean glaze of his power.

"Continue course, raise your oars and drop your sails, I have an idea," Tesh eased his statement with an air of confidence breaking his silent vow.

"What do you mean, farmer boy? I am captain of this vessel, who am I to listen to a land scrub?"

"Cruxien, I believe I may know his plan," Cadeck assured his friend, "If you wish to live today, we'll do as he asks."

He turned a lecturing gaze towards Cruxien.

Belittled upon his own ship, Cruxien's eyes widened to full setting, "You better be right, friend."

He shifted focus towards the bow as the outline of his figurehead loomed ever closer to the width span separating the two larger vessels. He commanded order to his oarsmen to lift and retract and on unison; all ten oars rose from the current, set parallel to one another and retracted into the hull of the ship. Portholes closed as the last of the oars spilled into the vessel. Cruxien commanded his other crew to unbind the riggings keeping sails tight against his masts and with the full gust of available wind, the linens billowed forth blossoming the vessel towards the ocean breezes.

"Cassica, get your ladies below decks."

Cassica nodded at Tesh's suggestion, her thoughts racing towards escape gave her little time to question his command. In a fleet of grace, she grasped the rails providing safe incline to the aft deck and with two hops down the ladder, set foot upon the main deck of the boat and harried the two maidens towards the bow where a ladder positioned in front of Cruxien's horse. The last of the five men lowered from the mast as the sailors steadied themselves against the bulwarks.

Comforted with knowledge the women secured below decks, Tesh lifted his left hand towards the main sail on the aft mast. Slow swirls culminated around his fingertips in the ether, whirling around and in-between his digits as though a cyclone of minuscule scale boiled within his palm. Ahead of his position, the figurehead of Sokut loomed against the edge of the plane separating the two Imperium ships. Portholes raised on each of the ships' side as sets of iron barrels poked through the hulls on either side of the *Misty Willow*'s approach.

"Tesh, whatever you're doing, you better do it now."

Cruxien muttered through bit lip.

"Patience," Cadeck's lips widened to grin. Kenat steadied himself against the starboard bulwark as Tesh's hand circulated with a glowing burst of ice. His face widened to full grin; his pearl-white eyes glinted as his own aztmudin reflected the growing magick in Tesh's arm.

The All is Vibration. Nothing rests. Everything moves.

Tesh repeated the phrase within his mind, guided by the ancient dragon's speech pounding through the very fabric of his skin, muscle, and bones. Deep-rooted into his own blood, Æiutherion's words called his name, addressing him in ancient tongue, echoing the mantra he repeated now made into breath upon his tongue. As the beast's prayers rose to crescendo, tremors rippled upon Tesh's body fabric. Sweat boiled down his face as his cheeks swelled to full blush. His veins completed transmutation into a crusted patch of crystalline lattice. Tesh envisioned the ancient call of the dragon. The mythical beast raised his neck to full extension and widened his wings to full span. Ancient echoes from Æiutherion's beak broke the calm, unleashing a torrent of hurricane winds exploding from Tesh's outstretched palm.

With the momentum of shifted gales, the *Misty Willow* lurched forward as her sails opened to full receipt of Tesh's magick. Tesh's face clenched tight muscle, his reddened expression exhibited the strain of his power. Coasting between the enemy vessels, Cruxien's ship created a rocking wake behind her rippling towards the larger ships on her flanks. The unsecured sailors, dropped to the decks towards the stern as the direction of magical wind forced the *Misty Willow* to a sudden increase in unprecedented speed. The crimson-painted keel line lifted above the deck of the water in hydroplane.

The two opposing ships readied their attack. Aiming the precise location between the pair, the Si'rai ships opened cannon fire towards an invisible target surpassing the calculated position. The wake wave collided with their keels, pushing the two ships in sideways momentum. Their keels listing appropriately, jerking a shift in their projectiles sending several rounds of cannon fire to cascade towards their own friendly vessel instead of the ocean deck where the smaller ship skimmed the water between them.

Simultaneous eruptions exploded upon each of the Si'rai vessels as a barrage of iron balls rained upon the unsuspecting pair. Trailing behind Cruxien's ship, a chain reaction of fire and death split upon the port and starboard sides of the vessels in the carpet of cannonade. The shift in weight brought upon by the sudden destruction of each of their opposing sides created a deprecated morale upon their crew as the attacking ships suddenly listed towards their damaged sides.

Expended, exhausted, the remnants of Tesh's call upon his aztmudin weakened his left hand to return to normal. The ice covering it receded as in a spring thaw; the veins retreated to golden hue. With the weight lifted, Tesh dropped to collapse, first shifted to his knees then finally to his left side. Cadeck dropped to ease the man to his descent. As the *Misty Willow* cruised with the scattered gusts lingering in her sails, Cruxien turned around to watch the shifting events in their favor.

A pair of Si'rai ships crackled under fire, their weight sinking them. Tesh cleared the *Misty Willow* from Cruxien's port several thousand yards beyond the blockade and slowed to a steady drift as the sails caught the offshore winds. Cruxien's sailors raised themselves to the main deck, followed by Cassica, Venna and Eris. As the scruffy sailors caught sight of the blockade behind them, several erupted in cheers and shouts signaling their joy of the feat.

Cassica shoved her way beyond the revelry. Her peasant's dress shifting with her motions while the wind caught the opening of her cowl forcing it back upon her shoulders. Kenat and Cadeck sat stooped upon the aft deck while Venna and Eris pushed ahead of the princess. She raised herself to the helm and stood next to Cruxien as the flaming wreckage began to shift smaller in the horizon.

Tesh's body lay prone on his side. Exposed arms turned clammy with pale face as Cadeck shifted him to his back. Blood loosened from his face, exposing his lips to purple hue.

Cassica turned to Cadeck, dropping next to him, "Is Tesh going to make it?"

"We will need to cover him, get him away from the open air. Cruxien, request your men help me get him below decks."

Cruxien commanded the order and several of his sailors took to the aft. Various throes of dress covered them from bare chests to covered shirts. A couple of the sailors built and stocky, sported tattoos on their arms or faces. As they lifted the younger man into a steady support, they took care to ease him down the ladder and onto the main deck before continuing towards the bow of the ship to move Tesh into the lower decks. Cadeck followed them, dropping his aging body with a slow ease onto the main deck before proceeding to pursue the men below leaving Cassica to stand next to Cruxien.

Cruxien sighed, the ire of the Si'rai fleet behind him in his wake, "We owe him our lives, Red."

Cruxien's eyes drifted to the flaming horrors behind them. Fainted screams seared his ears from within billowing, blackened smoke. In his experience, nothing could have amazed him more.

"But at what cost? The Imperium will certainly follow us. And Cadeck worries about them finding their Temples."

"I know nothing of their goals, but if my itinerary was of any truth, we have outwitted their most skilled naval commander."

Cruxien retreated from the helm, handing command to a man beside him with an eye patch over his right eye. He dropped to the main deck in motion to follow Cadeck's stride. With a weighted sigh, he craned his neck to the sails above him filled with light winds drifting his ship in a southwesterly direction. With sturdy oak arms, he shifted weight to shake the steadfast masts with full strength. Without budging, his face grinned to confidence as the masts held as tight as their construction day. He turned over his shoulder towards the stern and the open ocean separating his crew from Racoren.

***

Calamitous commands roared around as fair skinned and red-toned sailors sprinted across the large deck swelling with wild cacophony. Officers barked orders in Si'rai and Common Tongue; their features adorned in sleek raven coats and pressed trousers. They bellowed to their inferiors to take the davits and lower lifeboats to the surface. As smoky ashen sparks sprinkled fiery death across Racoren's harbor, a similar scene played out upon several ships clouded by the chaotic soot. Fidgeted screams faintly billowed from below decks, gnashing and wailing from a void of the air sending the morale of the men into a tizzy while they scrambled to listen to spoken orders.

Upon the forward deck of his ship, *Tiamat*, tall and statuesque, a salty blonde-haired man fitted to the open air as a puzzle piece suitable to the perfect slot. His right hand bent to elbow behind his back, ending with an iron-made fist tucked against his gentleman's sleeve. A starched white coat adhered to his frame as a popped collar stiffened around his neck as rank required. Epaulets adorned his shoulders wrapped with rank cords below his armpits and turned back upon themselves. Brass cufflinks tightened against his wrist; brass buttons cut like small pins down his torso.

Like his stiff coat, a pair of white pants stretched to formation as calf-high, leather boots swallowed the hemlines. Sooty ash carried with the westerly winds covering the escape Cruxien made. Fiery sparkles drifted with carried breezes aloft like orange snow carelessly collapsing where nature intended. The ranking man outstretched the gloved left hand while ashen glow slivers cascaded to his index finger. He lifted his finger to flared nostril and closed his azure eyes to relish the tinge of the odors, his pale skin in stark contrast to the red-tinted man standing beside him.

"It's amazing, Azal," the man began in Common Tongue, "The Imperium builds its ships from the sidgen trees, the strongest of woods available in your lands. Such marvel that when this wood is cut, the bark emits a foul taste upon the nose making one wince with disgust as though drinking a sour beer. But as it burns, it eludes the nostrils with its scent of a pleasant wine. What do you make of that?"

The admiral turned to his left. He scrunched his index finger against his thumb to dissolve the ash. His first mate, Azal dressed in sharp raven uniform, crisp to meet his superior officer's credentials. Vermillion highlights lined his sleeves and the over-lapped lapel buttoning brass on his right torso.

"Admiral Focalore," Azal nodded, returning tongue with gruff dialect, "I don't have an opinion."

"It really is a shame; never able to admire the work of your own people, leaving it up to the… durustrita, as your people call them. Your caste system is fascinating."

"I understand sir. The final lifeboat from this ship has been set to sea to search for survivors and take them to shore," Azal hid his infuriation with his superior officer's distraction.

Admiral Focalore returned his gaze towards the faint ship drifting distant in the horizon, "What is our remaining crew capacity?"

508

"Three-hundred seventy, sir."

"Have the men prepare to sail. We pursue as planned. Cruxien Balax uses his itinerary wisely, although death was not part of the scheme. Supernus Magister shall get his temples."

Sailors behind them railed against the bulwarks with grimaces of concern flowing onto their faces. Lower officers walked the deck, taking count of the emptied davits. Screams gnashed and wailed below decks while loud murmurs whispered upon the crew with unsettled concern.

"And what of *her*," Azal tilted his head and jostled his right thumb towards the aft, "Should we tell her an Aztmi was involved?"

Azal requested of his admiral with timid tongue. Slicked black hair settled upon his scalp, ending in a trimmed square just above his shoulder line. Thick lips were set upon a rigid face of experience below a shortened nose with nostrils curling upward.

Admiral Focalore turned over his left shoulder, reaching his left hand behind his back to grip the cold iron of his amputation.

"Judging from her screams frightening my men along with the destruction before them," Focalore sighed, turning back to Azal, "I don't believe that will be necessary."

Chapter 43

Asoothing fire crackled upon murky aromas of swamp mud and sour grass. A stick entered the warming flame, poking the fires in a concealed pit sending crisp embers to escape to the sky before settling like incidental debris upon the nearby soil. Darkness fell upon the great swamp; echoes of nocturnal predators poisoned the landscape with their calls and gurgles. Unperturbed, Ysalir continued her vigil over her small camp, her back arced against the rugged trunk of a vibark tree. Putrid stench flared into her nostrils from the embers of the detritus fuel keeping her warm.

Ysalir permitted herself a moment of solitary relaxation. Her feet struggled with pain as pulses from the sluggish sprint which consumed her evening cascaded along her calves and ankles. She rested her head against the tree trunk, her thoughts wavered to secluded emotions. She crossed her arms against bent knees as cold chills scrapped against her bare biceps. She relied on her teachings, permitting her body to react by heating her blood with intense concentration so as her warmth would deny nature's claims to frostbite.

Ysalir remained calm, her meditations sent her blood into a warm trance as she worked to control her feelings. She slowed her breathing to an inaudible lull, her lungs opening and closing in rhythmic release like permutations of smoke from an incense burner. As she propelled her body into relaxation, her thoughts wandered towards intense memories permitted in her solitude.

That chest, so rippled upon his untied tunic. His hair, covered in sweat as black oils upon water. His confidence echoed in his commands to those who obeyed his orders. They were simple commands to move heavy crates and items into a shop with the aid of carts, but his stone-chiseled face glowed in that high-sun day with each clamor of his jaw. Something about his demeanor rippled tingling surges through my stomach while embarrassing scrapes tightened upon the front of my shirt, unwelcome and uncommon in the high-sun months of Silvetzen. This man, this shop was new to Silvetzen. I had to focus on my function, my purpose. Find a lead.

Setting the washed laundry at my feet, I asked his name.

"Barest," he told me.
"Rensel," I replied, a welcome grin exchanged.

Barest. The name he had told Ysalir like a distant memory lost to time. Before he exposed his own lie and before she told him hers in the later months, the last moment she saw him. Ysalir closed her eyes within the darkness of her curled-up thighs. Tingles pulsated across her chest as her heart palpated into a rhythm shivering her mid torso and upper thighs.

"Why did I fall for him?"

She whispered to herself. Ysalir continued to let her mind wander, lulling her amidst the solitude permitted to her this evening. No longer under the concern of Cassica and the prying questions from Venna, she was truly alone within an expansive swamp adorned with predators of its own natural environs, the probability of Si'rai patrols or scavenging refugees left to the wilderness.

But for this brief instant, she could reflect upon a lifetime long gone. In a standard living, she would have become the matriarch to a family as permitted by her father. Another noble man who seemed fit to sire his grandchildren and merge their businesses together for profit. Under the current rule of House Bovariàr, vast reforms were made to allow private property and wealth. For five hundred years, the ancestors of the dynasty had accosted millions of Crowns to promoting lifestyles benefitting those of close association with ruthless contracts of resource affiliation or other unfair deals. Those who fell short of the favors of the ruling house, turned disgruntled, yet their level of wealth resided them to the lesser Houses of the Court, muting their retaliations with small rebellions easily quashed in a few months, forcing them back into appeasement and gravelling to the ruling king.

The Rutins had become one of those benefactors in the early times, savoring in the rise of military might of the Saratian kings since the onset of the civil war separating the old Rykanian Empire to split into Sarat and Silvetzen. In recent decades, Ysalir's ancestors reconsidered, turning their fortunes back to those of which they presided over, repurposing the taxes they accumulated to share upon the less fortunate, opening orphanages, tending to hospitals, or establishing soup kitchens. The demise of the Knights brought a new requirement of close nobility, bringing together both mighty and weakened Houses to repurpose their strengths to a new directive.

As a young girl, she had no choice. Her father told her she was to be part of something special, by commission of the Crown. Her parents told her Queen Selen required special maidens to help the king. Using only women, her directive had requested upon all the noble families with daughters to request their service to the Crown. To those who agreed, tremendous compensation would follow for the loss of valuable resources which would otherwise unite them with other noble houses. Ysalir was one of the first in a list of women accepted to the program and at the behest of the directive, should Selen bear a daughter, likewise her assignment led by example into the new Order of the Rose to show Selen was committed to the order as much as she had asked of her own.

Fourteen years passed since the call. When she turned ten, Ysalir travelled overseas to train with the Magi known only as Mornika. She learned instruction limited towards her training, and spent eight years among the Magi among others, learning the methods of deception, stealth, and subterfuge. Mornika instilled the methods of the warrior into all those Selen sent him, without the guidance of the Council and without the Trials permitted of the Knights.

Ysalir graced the hilt of the blade resting into a sheath against her ankle. It was of Si'rai craft, acquired from the dead magister Cadeck killed at Tijoa's hut. Her fingers recalled the exquisite details of the Imperium herald encrusted upon the pommel, the intricate curves of the blade and the hilt made of bone. A dagger of a purpose she cared not to know, only to meet blade to flesh of her enemy in poetic justice.

Her mind drifted to thoughts of her mother and father back home. She did not know if they survived the attack. She knew her mission, to return to Sarat, locate those who could aide in any manner of resistance and then find Selen who may be in Doningsen. Should she discover the whereabouts of her mother and father, she could escort them to Doningsen if warranted. Mind wandered to sleep as she meditated on her course of action, resting her head against the thick trunk of the vibark tree at her back.

On her third day of travel, violent whispers of distant explosions startled Ysalir to waken. Her eyes darted to full width as faint, pinging echoes of pulsating shockwaves filtered through her inner ear canal. She shook her head, bearing mental grip upon the source location of the resonating sounds channeled across the swamp. She readied her hand against the hilt of the Si'rai blade resting against her hip as she forced herself to full stand and focused her thoughts on the distant sounds.

Sunlight crested through the swamp canopy, falling in faint beams of narrow light like a rigid march formation upon the murky waters and muddy soils. Ysalir listened intently, watching the distant westerly direction from whence she heard the echoes pulsating into her ear. The sounds jarred in her mind as a memory she had heard before.

Wervos'kiga, as the Si'rai called them. Up close, their booms shatter ears as large iron balls spill from their metal snouts with intense velocity. Ysalir recalled the one she saw in Racoren and the damage even one of those weapons could do.

She readied her open hand against the tree bark, stepping off with her left foot as to carry sprint back into Racoren. But her mission came first. She heaved a sigh, whispered a silent prayer to herself for the safety of the ladies entrusted to Cadeck's security. She trusted her instincts to believe Tesh and the Magi would ensure their well-being for she had every reason to put faith upon Cadeck.

Faith; a concept fallen out of touch with her. She had witnessed firsthand the dangers of the Imperium and the betrayal the Council of Magi took to man and in recent weeks, she found herself into the heat of the conflict; the very core of the Imperium's hatred for the kingdoms of what they dubbed, the "sadakem." The Magi, as legends told, had waged wars against the Si'rai once before. Myths, mostly, of ancient battles which time forgot.

Raised among the nobility of Sarat, she had every reason to believe them as nothing more than lost lore, tales of a more primordial time lost to history. But, as she would learn from Cadeck, to the Magi, those stories were fact. He reminded her of faith; faith that he was true to the heart, to the inspiration of the original Magi before they had become corrupt with power and presence before their methods condescended to those who looked up to them.

Ysalir scouted her campsite. The fire died to a slow rising smoke surrounded by a boundary of crude rocks she scavenged nearby. She had managed to make her campfire rudimentary and concealable, digging a pit to hide her fire and permitting a side pit to promulgate the air to fuel the blaze. It was simple enough for a solitary person to keep warm, not adequate for several others. She leveled out the soil, pushing the mound of mud and detritus back into the pit to disguise her camp and filled both holes in a matter of a few minutes.

Taking mental inventory of her belongings, she wiped her hands upon the tree trunk, gathered her small knives wrapped around her hips and continued a path to set her southeasterly. Ysalir managed to tread along the swampy outcroppings, taking care to avoid the main road leading through the Bogs of Er'tahar and continued along the deeper recesses of the dangerous marsh. Using her survival training, she recognized the plant growth noting the edges of the deep waters and avoided the hazards as she came to them, seeking alternate routes around them.   Vicious reptiles would stop at nothing to count her amongst their prey, and she stepped lightly in the swamps to avoid setting off their audible organs to hint to her location. She knew the larger ones would prepare for their low-sun hibernation time, but the smaller predators continued to roam the landscape. What did not hunt at night hunted during the day and at any time the Bogs were a dangerous place. She recognized edible berries and those to avoid, taking random stops in her trek to pick a few of the ripened cydia fruits growing as small bulbs along their bushes. Ysalir picked off small mammals consuming the berries nearby to sustain her proteins and tied their carcasses against her right hip to cook later.

By mid-morning, she encountered a trail which did not resemble a travel route. Footprints lined single file in the trail as she stopped to crouched position and examined the steps. Fresh mud had crept over the soft prints as Ysalir calculated the age. She gazed to her left and right, following the many footprints. Some ran abreast, many stepped upon others creating a pair of mismatched shoes impressed upon the soil. They flowed in a direction leading to the south, away from Racoren.

"This might be a trail of refugees. If I can follow it, I may be able to locate help for Her Highness' message."

She continued her study of the trail, taking care not to step into any of the pressed soil so her tracking would not grow cold. The path weaved and wavered along the soils, crossing shallow swamps Ysalir waded through and picked up again on the opposite shore. As she continued the path, a rotten corpse of a man had lay still in the mud.

Clothes tattered against the corpse while limbs had turned up missing, its head partially detached from torso and ragged skin torn from remains. Maggots had begun to feast around the festered wounds and the exposed eye sockets. Scant hairs covered the scalp, still gray from weathered age and minimal decay.

"Poor soul. Likely died en route and left here to the swamp. The tears are postmortem, the wound at the neck," Ysalir dipped a finger into the open gash and examined the saliva residue surrounding the circumference, "scavenger bites, well after other animals had their feast."

She moved beyond the corpse, picking up the trail once again and setting light foot towards the midday sun. Ysalir set her hand firm against the left side of her cuirass, Cassica's letter tucked neatly between the shoulder strap and covered breast. Tied in the back, the leather clothing split upon her cleavage and fitted to cover her midriff below her navel. Ysalir quickened her pace, remaining light-footed as she strode along the trail in effort to find refugees.

As the afternoon sunlight stretched low over the western horizon, the canopy of vibark trees dimmed with an eerie green glow settling upon the swamp floor. Low croaking echoes created an early evening symphony. Cool winds of the early, low-sun months sprinkled Ysalir's breath with rolling frost.

She crept along the edge of the path, the tracks becoming bunched up as though unsettled footsteps paused in step only to slowly pick up like siphoned liquid into a small opening.

Amber lights flickered in the distance as her journey carried her into dusk. Faint hints of cooked laundry mingled into her nose with others of sour meats roasting over a large pit. Echoes of whispered laughs penetrated from the direction of the smell. Ysalir crept to a crouched position, dropping herself into a low profile to straddle the ground with quiet creep.

Ysalir ducked behind a brush of low growing weeds sprouting from the rich soils they rooted upon. Bitter scents of the plant stalks filled her nose as she stifled a low sneeze to avoid breaking cover. Footsteps pushed mud near her position, sloshing thick hide boots into the soil. She calculated the gait and surmised a set of two men. The weight of their splattering gait permitted Ysalir to estimate one of the men was heavyset, the other man was a lanky person and malnourished. She had heard a third man walking behind them, his voice higher pitched than the others as his breaths set him to be in a position struggling to catch up. He was the more vulnerable target, a young man, younger than Venna. The voices spoke in Common Tongue informing Ysalir that the men were of common company, a patrol group guarding the camp of whose aromas trickled through the swamps.

The patrol of three continued their march towards her position. She resisted making presence known and steadied herself into the brush. Despite years of training, survival programming and steady hand, the slip of her foot alerted one of the men to the sound of a break of stems in the swamp bush. Breaths of rot tongue broke her nose with the putrefaction of swamp water as the burly man steadied his footing to approach her position amongst the thick brush. Steel blade advanced from his hand to set grasses aside for clearer vision.

"I heard sumthin' move 'ere."

"C'mon. It's prolly just a frog. Y' skered of a frog, Teaumar?" The skinnier man addressed his compatriot.

Teaumar turned over his left shoulder, his right arm extending blade. His gluttonous neck sloshing with thick pronunciations of his jowls.

"I'm tellin' ya. I heard and saw sumthin' move 'ere. Imma gonna kill it an' cook it damn you."

"A frog," the lanky man laughed, "those refugees are cookin' hogs back at camp. Hurry up, let's go, I'm starvin' 'ere."

"You call that cookin' Harold. Those privileged cunts could burn boiled water if they did not already have servants. There's sumthin' 'ere."

Full weight of a lunged thrust split Teaumar's blade through the weeds in a threatening attack. Ysalir jerked her body away of the throttling blade in anticipated reflex. With a quick burst, she shot to full stand and gripped her right hand against the leather vanguard supporting the husky man's right wrist then shoved his sword thrust away from her. Startled to react, Teaumar's mouth opened with a questioning grunt. With leveraged position, Ysalir jabbed her right knee into his rib cage several times, shattering his ribs with her defense.

Teaumar dropped his heavy sword, screaming through pain of the cracked bone that stammered his breathing. Teaumar fell to his knees, coughing, hacking, and wheezing to catch breath. Harold released his dagger from the side sheath upon his hip and admired the brutal beauty before him. Sweat drenched along Ysalir's skin. Raven hair draped over her face hiding the sea foam eyes seething beneath them. In her right hand, she had removed the dagger at her side as her first victim dropped to the ground. Ysalir positioned herself into a closed fighting stance; her torso facing to the right of her body, ready to force her right-handed dagger with the full power of her training.

"Well, I don't know if I should thrust my sword or my cock into you. But you don't really give me a choice, now do ya' luv?"

Lying on the ground, Teaumar whimpered loud cries reddening his face with salty tears. The muddy swamp soiled his bare-armed shirt strained over the stomach girth and tight-fitting pants.

"The only thrusting you'll be doing is the convulsions of your dying breaths, Harold."

Ysalir addressed the guard in a condescending tone, dropping her voice to threat. Harold attempted to rush Ysalir, only for her to parry his dagger plunge aimed for her pale-skinned bosom. Blocking his blade with hers, the pair of blades glided to an angle away from her body as she revolved her back facing the exposed man permitting her right elbow to thrust into his face. Splintering nose bone into skin, Harold dropped his dagger to the mud, blood expelled from the open wound between his eyes where his septum forced upward into his bridge.

Teaumar's hacking screams mixed with Harold's as the pair lay prone onto the ground. Harold gripped his face; blood seeped between his fingers as throbbing breaths stung his lungs with copper taste trying to breath and not hyperventilate. Unawares of the smaller man, she miscalculated the threat he presented. Ysalir felt the nudge at the nape of her neck, followed by a sharp pain rippling into her head before fainting blackness collapsed her body to the ground.

#

Primdils. Reds and purples, how they adorn the white petal bases. Oh Barest, how my knees weaken at your generosity. They smell lovely, like the tender warmth of cider. You remembered my colors. You take me in your arm as we leave the market square, the high-sun smashing upon our faces with the calm breezes rolling off the shore.

We talk for hours. I told you of the little lords and ladies I delivered the past week while you educate me on life in the Imperium and how your shop master wishes to expand trade into Silvetzen and on towards Sarat. You trust me with words and language, educating me on the dialect. While foreign to your Rykanian complexion, you speak fluently. The Si'rai are but a race of the land known as Sheebal.

Your voice is like rugged cliffs as you pronounce each of your words with meticulous detail. I enamor your position. We move into the King's Square, harried by those of Silvetzenian high class. You take me to dine.

Of my outward appearance and profession, this is all foreign, but to the secrets you do not know this was my life as a youth in Sarat. You regale me with legends of battles and bore me with the laborious details of commerce and trade. The servant pours glasses of Seuveratian wine which you reveal you had imported specifically for this night. You show me how to savor the glass, swirling the aromas in my nose before I drink; a task of knowledge I hide from you yet listen to your lesson assiduously. For to you, I am but a peasant girl serving as a nurse maid, your boasts of claim of high civility tickle my loins with giddiness.

We dine on a meal of spiced meats and salads glazed by light oil, a meal chosen for the complimentary flavors. You planned this evening with everything arranged prior to our arrival. You offer the coin for meal and take my hand to return to the Square, proceeding towards the amphitheater as the sun settles to evening purples.

We enjoy a play; a tale of two lovers of rival clans, their love ending in sorrowful death. I weep, you comfort me. You walk me home, sheltering me from the cool air by the warmth of your chest. We stop at my small room on the edge of the peasant's district. I reach to kiss you, but you shy me away. You doff your wide-brimmed hat to me and offer to see me again. I yearn to accept only for heart to mourn till our next meeting.

Ysalir's fond memories did not recall the drenching chills dripping upon her hair and face. She suffocated to breathe, jarring her consciousness into awakening. She coughed the icy water from her mouth splashing once more upon her face. Cascading water trickled down her neck as she tilted her head against the back of a chair. Her breasts turned cold, exposed to the watery air. Ysalir's wrists felt tight; reddened to purple from the bindings stretching her arms behind her to the seat.

A heavy fist pounded into her lower jaw, cracking her neck to jerk her right. Drenched water blurred her vision of a husky man standing to her left as she spit sparse saliva to miss his face. A swift backhand against her right cheek shifted her face to the left.

"Wakey, wakey, eggs and bakey, bitch," the burly man grumbled.

His bald face contorted with whiskery folds of skin and flabby jowls. He set the wooden bucket onto the floor next to the chair where Ysalir was bound.

"Now. That's no way to talk to the lovely lady," a smooth-talking voice called from behind her attacker.

Ysalir's eyes took in the scene as she lifted her head. Strands of sable hair fell across her face hiding the men from her vision. She huffed through clenched lips to clear the locks away from her face only to fail in her efforts. Swelling grew upon her lower lip as she realigned her jaw with angered twitches to correct the disjointed mandible.

The smooth man approached from the open door in front of her. His blonde hair fell to his jaw line. Dark stubble covered his face as though shaved by thick blade of recent attempt. The untied neckline of his tunic caked of sweat drenching over his covered pectorals and muscled abdomen. The point of a blade twisted into his left index finger to clean his fingers of the acquired soot. Blue eyes concentrated on his task as the heavy man set aside to permit him to approach Ysalir's bound body.

He knelt in front of Ysalir as the water continued to drench onto bare thighs onto the hard chair below her. Blonde hair leaned over, setting his blade against her naked shoulder, snaking the dull side down her left breast running with the ample curve below her perked nipple.

"Well, sweet cheeks, this is where you tell me what you were doing in my swamp," his Low Accent swaggered from his tongue with the breath of cooked swamp weed.

"You tell me first where my clothes are," Ysalir's sea-teal eyes churned to revulsion.

The man turned his head over his left shoulder towards a table at the edge of the room. A leather cuirass lay atop a pair of sable leggings. A soft cloth fitted to match her hips set on top of the pants in a gentle pile respectful of their fabrication. A gleaning blue eye squinted into her direction.

"They're right there if you can get out of them ropes. But you won't," he shook the pointed edge of the knife in front of her face, "Y'see, I had to make sure you couldn't escape."

The blonde man stepped away, pacing towards the table with Ysalir's attire sprawled upon it. Bitter chills coiled across her naked body. Tight wrappings bound her ankles to the chair legs with her thighs tied together with thick cords. Hints of mildewed wood tickled Ysalir's nose with the putrid taste of swamp water.

She craned around to spot features in the room, aiding to her escape. Beams spanned the ceiling supporting the roof structure, an open door ahead of her. A small candle lamp rested on the table by her clothes and another chair in front of it. A whispering patch of burlap behind her indicated a window was open to her back. The chair below her bottom sweat with its own moisture acquired by exposure in the deep recesses of the outlying marsh. She assessed her surroundings, calculating the chair could distract while she climbed along the beams and out the window. Ysalir had to plan her actions and with the two men in the room, she would have to wait till one of them left.

"You disabled two of my men before Patryck knocked you out. That right there is accountable for two of your limbs. But I like the color of your skin. See, you weren' one of them, Imperium types."

The criminal leader turned back around to face her, his head cocked slyly to his right side, "So you had to be one of two things; either working for them as a spy, well trained I might add, or a remnant of the Order of the Rose. Seeing all your knives, well, we Wolfsblood don't take chances and had to be 'thorough'."

"You wretched…"

Ysalir sprayed disgusted spittle towards the man in a vain attempt to attack him with saliva.

"Now," he waved his knife as if to shake a finger before continuing. "We don't need none of that. We hadn't touched ya yet."

He paced towards her seated position. The damp air trickled down her forehead into a cold sweat dripping down her cheeks and onto bare breasts. She studied his every stride; his every intricacy taking notice of the crimson wolfs head tattooed on his right arm above his wrist. The candle lamp on her clothes table lit the room with shadowy folds.

"See, 'bout coupla weeks ago me and my boys was, well we was mindin' our own business when suddenly about three hundred of your people came a knockin' on my door. Now, we don't take kind to your kind, but they were accompanied by close to two dozen of Sarat's finest. These people, well these people were trodden, weakened, beaten, and sickened. They'd seen something that I can only describe as a…horror."

The gang leader crept close to her face, eyes shifting to peer into hers.

"I wasn't gonna fight them," putrid breath fell upon her nose, "there were about twenty-five well-trained Saratian soldiers and about fifty more men capable of picking up their slack and besides, it was as though they'd seen enough fightin.' I had recognized some of them. Some of them we'd stolen from before and harassed up there in Racoren. But this… this was worse than any damage we'd ever inflicted.

"We'd already known of the invaders coming into Sarat but didn't expect to have any of your people come to visit us here in the Bogs. We've kept a close eye out, but we figure we're deep enough in the swamps, the Imperium won't bother us. The way I see it, these folks just rightly fit in. We take in some of the women, convince the soldiers to join my cause and it's all for good. The Imperium wouldn't mind a few mercenaries I'd imagine; puts the pressure off their regular members."

"What makes you think they won't do to you what they did to the refugees?" Ysalir sighed, her emotions damaged and torn.

"All I gotta do is tell them what you're about to tell me, and they'll leave me well enough alone. In fact, they may commend my work."

The gang leader set his knife edge against her neck and cocked her head back with his free hand, "Says in your letter that Ol' Red is offering reward and freedom to any who you may cross paths with. What I wanna know is," his eyes widened with a demented fervor and sly grin, "where she at?"

Ysalir stammered internally, her face sweating as the knife blade set to taut skin on her neckline. Her lips pursed with fear.

"She is not even in this kingdom anymore. She set sail last night. She found passage with a pirate to exchange her body for his cock and sail."

Her words expelled with intimidated honesty.

"A whore in charge of whores. That's what your Order is. You ladies taste good, but you sure don't act so lady-like. Reckin' from what I know of your Order, what if I said I didn't believe you?"

The man set the edge of his knife against her left cheek and with a sharp prick, created a quick cut against her cheek bone promoting Ysalir to wince in pain as a slow stream of blood trickled along her face. Ysalir strained to kick the man, but her ankles were bound tight creating a thick rash where the rope twisted on her skin. He moved himself away from Ysalir's naked body, set himself a few feet away and sheathed his dagger.

"Now, I'm gonna come back in 'ere come mornin.' If you like lookin' that purty an' I suspect you do, then you'll give me the answer I want."

He turned his back from Ysalir and with a swift strike, turned and swung a hard punch against her lower jaw, cocking her neck in reaction before she slouched to pass out. The man then turned around and proceeded to exit the room. Tattered trousers covered his legs, tied by hemp cord around his waist. Caked mud started at his shins and worked their way to crudely stitched boots covering his feet. He approached the husky man at the door entrance, whispered a few words taking off-glances towards Ysalir before exiting the room leaving the man to guard her.

#

Barest, how your serenade fills my heart with emotions I dare not expose. Your fingers pluck the lute as for you to make love to it, your voice ripples through the mid-spring airs to entrance the beasts around us. That beast is my heart, my emotions, and my loins.

How I have clamored for you these past couple of months, you never permitting me to lock my lips to yours. I have ne'er heard this tune, but you educate me it is a story of passionate betrayal sung in a major key to belie the insidious undertones of a lover scorned. As you complete the last verse, you reach into the small wicker basket we carried to these meadows and shared picnic. A wind flushes over me as I sprawl upon the soft blanket.

You remove a small box to fit in the palm of your hand. You release a latch and swing it open removing a gold chain necklace. Attached upon the end is a magenta stone shaped as a tear drop.

You motion me to rise to seat. You are too close. The loose ties around the neck of your raven shirt reveal to me a fraction of your rigid muscles. I could puncture the bone in the middle of your chest with a swift lunge of my fist. You reach around my neck, placing the dangling jewel to set loose on my tunic between my breasts. Our breaths sync, my chest heaving in anticipation of your movements. I spot at least three points of your body of which I can disable you.

I yearn to sneak you closer as you pull away. Upon my question, you tell me the jewel is a sample of trinkets you sell. It is an Erabian luck charm. You explain the origins from the distant land of Erabu and the belief behind the amulet. The words roll from your lips to exasperate me to smile. We stare into each other's eyes. I want you.

You do not deny me. I reach over to you, the blanket falls to my hip as I place soft hand upon high cheek and settle my lips upon yours. You welcome me. We share tongues if only briefly before you pull away. In my nineteen harvests, I have never felt like this to another man. You tell Rensel that you will be leaving shortly, to settle some business in Sarat. I am close Barest if that is your real name.

Moaning sounds of distant romance lulled Ysalir to awaken as guttural snores startled her nearby. She stretched her eyes to open in pain through swollen eyelids, bruised by the last punch. In blurred vision, she could see the husky man leaning against a chair near the table with her clothes, his weighty snores rippling in the now darkened room. Faint lamp light on the table had lulled to a soft sputter. Her lips had crusted with dried goo filtering onto her chin. She moved her tongue across her chin and recognized the sour taste. She winced in disgust surmising the grotesque man on the chair had given her an evening treat before he slouched to sleep.

His weapon, a long dagger, rested on the table beside her clothes. Ysalir moved to grab it, the ropes binding her to the chair reminded her of her confinement. Her chair rustled wooden legs against the aging planks, startling the man into sputtered snore before his wide neck slouched to sleep.

Distant moans faded into a joint release of groans male and female. Ysalir turned her head in gradual pace to the left and right, looking for anything she could use to free herself from her constraints only to meet with disfavor. The only sharp object was the dagger and trying to grab it while the husky man slept meant scooting her chair towards the table, alerting her guard and others in the house.

Ysalir had to move. She relied on finding Saratian aid and this highwayman's stronghold was impeding her on her assignment. Her ears tuned to faded snores coming down the hallway. *Typical man*, she thought to herself, *gets his and passes out.*

Footsteps proceeded in the far room. Ysalir paused. Her swollen eyes turned to the door; her hair drenched over her face in cold sweat. Her breaths formed into frosty rolls of air as increasing cold chilled her skin into bumps. The tingling frosts of air danced upon her exposed skin, tickling her chest and her loins with the damp chills of the early months of the low sun.

A door opened before shifting to close with minimal noise. Ysalir froze, watching the darkened hallway exposing her room. The shadow of a lithe figure shuffled the hall into her direction. She could make out the build to be a woman. Dim light shone from the girl's back, clouding her face from view. The shadow danced over the crusted wood with the grace of a floating apparition before she entered Ysalir's prison room. The woman's flowing gown whispered against the open air as she moved into an elegant stance and ended behind the slouching man.

She removed a bracelet from around her wrist, extending it like it were a fine cord and proceeded to set it against the man's throat. With tensile strength, the cord fit around the man's neck girth as she yanked it tight around him. The snug cord embedded into his skin, piercing it to bleed as he struggled to catch breaths. He futilely reached to the restricting weapon. With a swift yank, the woman snapped the cord tauter into the man's throat as the snap of his neck ended his life. With death gurgles, his body slouched over in the chair.

Waiting, she attuned herself for any noise alerted from the man's stammering. Hearing none, she moved towards Ysalir and hustled to unbind her wrists.

"Can you move, Sister," the assassin asked of Ysalir with low whisper.

"Get me out of these ropes. I need to continue my journey to Sarat."

The mousy voice answered, "You are in no shape to advance your purpose, Sister. Visit camp, there are a pair of Yellows who can provide you salves and poultices."

Ysalir considered her options as the throbbing pain in her left eye settled over her face, "I can manage."

The rescuer released Ysalir's hands from the ropes as she followed to question, "How do I get out of here?"

"There is a patch of burlap behind you, covering the window. It is a simple bolt latch and should not cause too much noise."

The rescuer moved swiftly towards the table and readied Ysalir's clothes. Ysalir continued to watch the hallway, making sure no others startled and heard their soft voices. She freed her legs and ankles and tried to lift herself before her knees buckled from serrating pain inside her ribs. The other woman sprinted to her, catching her before she could fall to the rickety floor. She settled Ysalir slowly onto the ground allowing her to rest on her knees as she regained circulation to her extremities.

"What's your name?"

"Jasa Tyrell. And yours?"

"Rensel Fiasti."

Both ladies looked at one another knowing the given names were not those their mothers called them. Ysalir kneeled to an upright position. Her face swelled with throbbing bruises as she motioned for Jasa to lift her to her feet. Ysalir hurried to dress into her clothes as Jasa handed them over, taking care to keep from startling any others who may be in the shanty house.

Fitting her loinpiece first, she followed to squeeze the tight leather pants upon her curves. As she squeezed into her clothing, pains pierced in the side of her ribs. Jasa stood behind her, her hair strewn in carnal disarray and assisted Ysalir to tighten her cuirass. As the binding ties knotted together, Ysalir grimaced with the sensation of short breath pain.

They worked quietly, taking care to watch their steps so their light feet did not disturb the distressed planks holding the floor together with rusted nails. Ysalir finished her dressing, taking visual account of all pieces of her assembly including the count of her knives. The articulate Si'rai blade missing amongst her possessions. One meticulous detail remained vacant. She pursed her lips and turned frazzled hair towards the smaller girl.

Jasa stood a few inches shorter than Ysalir. Her body frame poised like an upright twig. Her smaller features discarded her underlying threat to those who would harm her. She kept her confidence in her walk as she turned towards the open doorway to assure their actions remained silent. The simple gown covered her svelte features, masking them in the shadows of the dim light.

"The letter, where is it?"

"Erian ordered it burned after I read it to him."

524

Ysalir's face hung in despair, Sarat's freedom rested upon the words of her letter and its contents forever lost to flame, "You memorized the writing?"

"As required, Rensel."

"Let us move. I need to reach Sarat."

Jasa studied the hallway once more and spied none approaching upon their chambers, "You must leave quickly. I am told, Erian is a light sleeper and if we have startled him at all, he will be quick on us."

"We can both take him."

"While true, he'll be accompanied by several men."

"His men do not concern me."

"No," Jasa urged, her face drawn to concern over her and Ysalir's safety, "he is like a rat. Timid and fearful. He poses no threat to you or the cause of the Crown."

Jasa shuffled Ysalir by her shoulders as the pair strode towards the burlap draping hanging over the window. Jasa lifted the curtain and moved an iron bolt to unlatch the window on the side of the pane. The opening built to allow enough height for Ysalir to slide through.

She set one leg through the opening and examined the roof with her foot taking into consideration the estimated age of the structure and determined the weight she could press onto it. Straddling the windowsill, she clutched one edge with her right hand and turned her face towards Jasa.

"What of yourself? You must return to Sarat with me. I will need other Justiciars to coordinate any insurgency."

"No. Erian will expect service in the morning; I must make him believe I have not left his side."

"Does he not suspect you are as I? He has seen my mark."

"He has only taken me once. Tonight, happened to be my lucky night, I guess. But it was a position preventing him from seeing it."

Jasa lowered her head and turned over her shoulder to watch down the hallway assuring none heard the commotion and stumbles.

"Then return to Sarat when you can," Ysalir assured, "Do not let your shame deny you comfort for purpose to the Crown. We are Justiciars. Our bodies, our hearts, our minds serve the Crown in all roles."

Jasa nodded her head for the comforting words.

"I have three others in my command. With your wounds, you should consider the offer for medicines. There is a triage in the southern camp. Likewise, I must see to it that nothing changes here so the small groups of soldiers along with Erian's men, hold no suspicions."

"Thanks again, for your consideration, Jasa, but these wounds are modest. I will be fine."

Ysalir surveyed the outlay of camp from her point on the windowsill. Insects chirped nocturnal songs. Small fires had lit in camp as the lull of sleep induced the surrounding shanty tents and shacks into a calm ease betraying the inner emotions of those who occupied it.

"I will send you word once I return. Await my commands; take them to be issued by Commandant. The population need not know her whereabouts other than she lives. Any words you receive from Sarat by my signature are as official writ from the Crown."

Jasa nodded her head in agreement with Ysalir's ploy, "For the Crown, Rensel."

"For the Crown, Jasa."

Ysalir's fit figure lurched from the windowsill, took a step off the awning of the roof, and caught a jump towards a nearby vibark tree. Her arms wrapped around the robust trunk as she grappled tight with her hips and thighs. Her nimble limbs eased her towards the ground before setting light foot onto the trodden peat grass. Jasa closed the narrow window behind her and loosened the burlap tarp to hide it once again.

Ysalir crossed through the campgrounds, running with the throbbing pains permeating her swollen left eye and bruised ribs. Her breaths lightened into repeated pattern, signaling pain flowing across her torso. The restricting cuirass hampered efforts to regain breaths.

She cautiously hid behind trees to prevent the armed patrols from catching her. As she caught sight of a patrol, she fit her back against a vibark tree and watched over her shoulders as the ragtag patrol moved across her field of vision from behind the thick wood. Clearing one patrol, she leaped over a fallen, rotted trunk. The throbs in her right side caused her to slouch onto the ground to a cascading tumble.

Mud splattered on her face and caked into her hair. She feared the cackling of her steel blades would alert the passing men to her position, only for her to regain purpose and ignore her bruises. She lifted to her knees and with a rush of adrenaline, continued her sprint through the ramshackle camp.

She passed by tattered tents covered by sparse roofs made of the vibark leaves and various stalks of thick grasses growing in the Bogs of Er'tahar. She took care not to startle any who may have slept and continued into a southerly direction to lead out of the swamps. Ysalir approached the position of another pair of guards, seated and drinking crude mash stouts. Their banter signaled they were men of Wolfsblood. No fire light highlighted their features as Ysalir inched behind them. Hurting them would alert others, fighting them would bring an onslaught of which Ysalir was in no shape to fend off nor would she see herself back in Erian's torture room.

Ysalir's dash cut through the high grasses behind the pair, stirring the winds to bend the stalks and crackle the lower plants below them. She discerned her movements would startle the men but relied on their drunken stupors to deny their attentions. She waited behind a nearby tree on the other side of their position and listened for their actions. A burp, a scratch and a raunchy joke paraded the pair's antics to have ignored the rustle of the flora.

Her stifled pains dropped her to knee on various occasion as she exited the refugee encampment. Having cleared the outskirts and the prying eyes of Wolfsblood criminals, she turned over her shoulder to watch the embers of dying flames and quiet still of downfallen citizens. Her thoughts lingered on Jasa and the hope her motivation could incite the local men to Cassica's cause. Spreading leg for Erian, he could be sentimental to her words if Ysalir could get them to her. Ysalir could only hope Jasa returned to his chambers in time to not arouse suspicion, leaving the empty room with the dead guard to suspect only Ysalir herself escaped her confines.

Ysalir turned her gaze towards the south. Rows of vibark groves and marsh impeded her advance. Tightened pains pressed against her ribcage and pulsated against her eye socket to a purple blob settling over her left eye. She stood and pressed her right hand against her ribcage. A limp carried her further towards another grove of trees before collapsing once more. She cursed under her breaths as she slowed her wheezing to soft whispers.

Your training prepared you for this, Ysalir.

Her thoughts remarked back to her days under the Magi named Mornika. The pounding of her pains felt like the padded staves she had difficulty blocking as Mornika pummeled her sides until she could keep his pace.

Move, she told herself. *You are unable to fail. You do not understand failure. Sarat does not accept failure.*

Mornika's speeches motivated her in youth as she recounted his harsh commands in her subconscious. Ysalir needed more distance in case any outwardly patrols came upon her position in the morning. She picked herself from her seat on the soggy ground. Her ribs burst pain, crackling as she rose. Ysalir inhaled a large breath, pushing her ribs as tight as she could to train her mind into a threshold. With crying sobs, lowering her face into whimper, she exhaled the suffering from her mental focus.

One breath inhaled naturally, followed by a second then a third as her lungs relaxed to normal capacity expelling the surging ferocity with each lament. Refocusing her mind on her task, her legs carried her deeper south from the camp as daybreak began to rise in the eastern skies. Ysalir pushed to continue moving well into daylight, her journey lasting several hours on foot as the sunlight beams tangled into the groves.

Beaten, tired, drained, and hungry, Ysalir rested to pause a few moments and regain her bearings. Resting in daylight would be dangerous if a Si'rai patrol came from the south and into the swamps. Her body fought rest. Her battered frame coerced her to sleep, but her mind fought the weakened state focusing her composure that sleep would come the next evening when she could safely rest under the cover of darkness. But darkness would need to wait. Ysalir rose again, agonizing pressures hinged against her ribs. She struggled to breathe, her legs stammering to hold her upright. She pushed forward, relying on vibark trees for support. After moving several yards, she collapsed again. Pain intensified.

She lowered herself to her knees, dropping over to her side as her movements intensified into a sobbing cry. Every breath ached; every spasm of her ribs to expand brought her to stutter to shortened gasps. A final breath inhaled. Ysalir rolled her right eye into the pain, welcoming the warm embrace of unconsciousness.

#

Barest, what secrets do you hold from me? This arcane shop holds trinkets and artifacts of an exquisite gaudiness. I take a browse through your books, each one written with an elaborate etching, a glyph of which I know nothing of its tongue. Each of them an exorbitant wage, far exceeding any income of the common man. Others, written in an old dialect of Rykanian, rumored lost to dust, now sitting on your shelves. I recognize titles, and in awe of your collection, were I not to pursue a purpose.

You have buyers; endowments of which equal those of lords or dukes. Noblemen who have ordered exotic words in a tongue so foreign that none in all Rykana could dare pronounce it. An order placed for a large statue standing taller than you by King Rathmana of his own personal accounts.

As I browse through your closed shop, the lush ornamentations of the woodwork fall upon my eyes with a lure of exotic decor. The desk, the chair, etched against the wall to the back of the long aisles. You deal with the esoteric artifacts of a civilization on the other side of the ocean as to make me believe you yourself invoke magick. As I peruse the dressers of your desk; a pair of documents strikes my fancy.

Amidst your orders, lying around your official brochures of business, a letter written in Common Tongue addressed to Rensel Fiasti. Your words lift her heart, titillating her loins with the flutter of a maiden on her union night. I stuff the letter back to its spot and remove another document.

This one written in the script of your language, Sheebal, with the sigil of your kingdom sealed to the foot of the message underneath a scribbled signature. The signature stands out with its elaborate loops and hieroglyph as stamped by block print. This notice addressed in a way to make it official, as to be from your craft master. But the block does not look like a common stamp; instead, its etchings give it purpose to your business. I stuff the note into my dress, my intuition serves me well; you are more than just a shop owner. But to what your true intent in Silvetzen is, I must let my heart turn closer.

A scent of bitter salve tickled at Ysalir's nostrils. The warming paste settled over her bruised eyelid sealing it shut. Prickles danced across her left eye with soothing sensations. She moaned softly, calling her sister's name. A reply came back in a voice spoken in familiar accent. It strained in wheezing tones as the voice described Venna as a precocious little girl. The sounds of wood stirred against clay summoned Ysalir's head to turn into the direction of her left. Dark shadows encompassed her limited field of view.

She lay on her back; a soft hay mattress comforted her ribs. Croaking chirps of distant frogs bickered outside. She could feel herself within the confines of a room, a mattress to her back and a ceiling above despite lingering darkness clouding her normal senses. A blanket and pillow propped her left torso. A wool blanket covered her naked body as her breath rolled off her tongue in crisp wisps of frosty chills.

Tight bandages constricted around her ribcage below her breasts, binding her still painful cage in relaxed tortures. Her mind fizzled from the application of an oral anesthetic administered to her. Its bitter, numbing taste lingered on her lips and tongue permitting her body into a soothing calm.

Ysalir paced in and out of consciousness, stuttering the name of Cadeck in her visions. The other voice called back, telling Ysalir the taint of Ego carries him, but his Soul struggles to fight. Unnerved by the voice who replied, Ysalir's body fell to dream again and in moments called Cassica's name. She heard shuffling as a foot on dirty wood.

The strained voice remarked, speaking a phrase in a dialect similar she heard from Cadeck or Kenat invoking magick, then followed in tone which Cassica would become a wise queen one day. Her tests for such are still undetermined, the voice later extolled Ysalir for leaving her in the hands of the Magi. Following Cassica's name, Ysalir spoke of Tesh to which the voice commended the Azthar Kherdmon shall fulfill destiny and a new Aeon will arise.

A creak of a chair settled next to Ysalir's head. A soft rag dripped soothing water onto her face as she strained her neck to catch droplets into her tongue. Ysalir felt a clay cup lift to her lips. Her tongue spilled through her lips as the warming porridge seeped into her mouth. She coughed up the foul food, hacking the viscous liquid away from her lips.

"Drink this, child," the whining voice beckoned once again into her ear, "Your body needs to replenish for your journey."

Too weak to fight, Ysalir obeyed, opening her lips once again as the cup spilled the warm goo into her mouth. The darkness covered the goo spilling from the clay chalice to fill her throat like caramelized paste. The heated mixture traveled her throat with a numbing lubrication as the rest of the morsels glided towards her stomach. Ysalir's stomach growled to digest the gruel, pushing against the insides of her ribs now soothed by the delayed reaction of the intoxicants streaming into her body. Ysalir licked her tongue against her lips, fragments of the meal clung to the bottom of her busted lip.

"Where am I," Ysalir's voice whined.

"You're still in the Bogs of Er'tahar, child."

The voice distinctly feminine; aged and strained with the confines of wheezing lungs.

"Wolfsblood?"

"Those scallywags? They are timid men, fearful of legends and myth."

"Sarat?"

"Dangerous now with the Imperium there. I fear for their children. The lord of Sarat is a cruel creature, preying on the little ones."

"Sadar, where are you?"

"Your lover, child," the voice lowered to a soft whisper, "A man you should never trusted."

"I can hear you, but I can't see you."

Ysalir turned her head towards the voice.

"It is better this way. For yours and my protection. With light, the Imperium can find us."

"Imperium?"

Amnesia settled into Ysalir's mind.

"Their God-King seeks to draw the powers of the Aztun to become immortal. He is a Creator of Chaos."

"I need to move. I need to go to Sarat."

"Patience, Ysalir. Your wounds are not yet healed well to leave this place."

"Jasa?"

"A spry woman. Capable of her duties, yet timid in the face of adversary. She will be an asset to your cause if you can motivate her in time."

Ysalir questioned the omnipotence of the woman's words as she brainstormed the conversation in her head. She fought the dulling intoxicants selling her body to calm ease. With her remaining strength, she lifted her head against the pillow and propped her left side with her elbow.

Under the strains of shifted weight, her ribs settled with gravity against the bind causing the trained woman to whimper the pains vocally. No hands helped her as her elbow collapsed her side back onto the bed. She rolled onto her back, gripping her left hand upon her ribs. Her arm and fingers numb to touch, unable to feel any effort to her attempts.

Desperate and fearing impending death, Ysalir grunted her next statement, "Who are you? What am I doing here?"

"To answer your second question; I rescued you from the swamp ahead of an Imperium patrol. Your body was weak and in need of resuscitation. Had you remained laying in the bog, the Imperium army would have stabbed you to verify death. There were no witnesses to return to their camp. But to answer your first, would require you to reacquaint yourself with faith.

"I know why you run, Ysalir. You do not run for your creed. You run from yourself."

"I run to Sarat, woman. I must gain sympathy towards Cassica, the ruler of Sarat, for her people, so she can motivate them to rebel against the Imperium."

Ysalir moaned on every word. Her ribs settling with the soothing drugs administered with the goo she absorbed.

"That is what you run for, on the outside. You have let your mother break your faith. You have let Sadar break your faith. You let the Imperium break your faith and worse of all; you let the Magi break your faith and why my name should forever remain a mystery, well after you return to health and leave here."

"But the gods have forsaken us. Tijoa said as much, Cadeck said as much, and I believed them."

"And you rely on what a Magi says to a woman? Remember, Cadeck's words once softened the heart of a woman which puts us into our current situation. The gods did not leave us. The Magi left the gods. Their power over Man influenced them to turn their backs on Man all for the sake of holding that power, a power which curses them. You run from your faith, Ysalir, stripped from you by the codices of Magi."

"But Sokut tore Sadar from my heart. His words - his purpose in Silvetzen was all a lie. Then, I learned of the Magi Godwen's role in all of it and it all made sense. The demise of the Council and of man was at the fault of the trusting of the Magi."

"The tears in your faith are far deeper than anything a man has done to you. If Sokut herself came to you and told you there was nothing to fear; to tell you she still loved you as one of Her own, a child of the Aztun?"

"Then I would turn to her," Ysalir craned her neck towards the direction of the mysterious woman, "and after tearing off the Blessed Robes, spitting on her naked body for throwing me into this wretched torment, I would kiss her cheeks and lips, and drop to my knees for sacred forgiveness and to guide my heart with courage and wisdom to unite Sarat against this oppression."

A glimmering light erupted from the darkness in front of Ysalir's eyes. The soft glow emanated from the ether floating above a gnarled hand and with a faded shimmer danced corporeal shadows onto the graying and withered palm. Amidst the flame, Ysalir distinguished a woolen robe ceasing above the woman's wrist. Whispers of gray hair trailed over her shoulders and chest like wisps of moss clung to vibark trees hiding her face in pitch.

"I have lived this world since Great Mother put me here. I have loved as you love, and I have also seen death. I am of many names, yet I carry none. The ruffians in Racoren call me the Swamp Maiden," the hand inched towards her face. "The sailors and merchants in Yumphen call me the Sea Crone. The scholars and teachers in Kora call me the Wise Woman."

The flame sauntered closer, lifting to her chin as the holding hand rose the light. Ysalir could make out the features of an aging woman, defying mortality with creases and wrinkles tearing across her cheeks and chin. Her eyes were set back, awash in dark pools of ashen water waves as though forever removed by a curse. The woman's nose faded from face leaving a hollowed triangle of a mummified corpse.

As she spoke her next words, skin tore from decay along her jaw line, splitting apart like fractured paper where her teeth once rested, "Saratian mothers warn their little girls to stay from the Forest. Whispers forbade them not to call my name that I may snatch them up for their youth. You know my name, Ysalir."

"Fersyn?"

Chapter 44

*M*isty *Willow* lumbered alone amidst darkened oceans. Sea swells lifted and lowered the vessel in calm crests against the backdrop of a cool, starry night. High along the apex of the sky, the dark band split the star field separating the expanse like a chasm ripping across a meadow in the middle of a catastrophic quake. The silhouette of the new moon appeared as a ghostly orb over the lower horizon of the western sky. Around the pirate vessel, dark oceans cast in the pall light of lantern shimmer from Cruxien's boat like ghostly spirits dancing upon the waters.

Atop the main mast hung a pair of lanterns shining dim glazes upon the surface deck of the vessel. A red lantern mounted upon the stern, casting its crimson hue with each rock of the boat upon the waves, while on the forward deck, behind the figurehead, shone a green-tinted lantern swaying to alert for approaching vessels. In isolation beneath the starry night, Cadeck hefted himself over the starboard bulwark and leaned his hands to counter the shifting oceans unsettling his nerves. Vomit expelled from his mouth.

Cadeck expelled a fresh heave as the ship rocked in the calm seas. His knees buckled. He settled his hands upon them and tapped his head in depressed agony against the posts supporting the bulwark. Cadeck moaned as his stomach gurgled once more signaling an impending eruption of bile with his dizzy equilibrium.

A creak of iron hinge from the hatch in the forward ship paused his laments. He turned his gaze, gripping white knuckle fists upon the rounded posts. Spittle ran down his chin and onto the shirt he had worn for the several days since departing Racoren.

The stalwart frame of a tall woman moved towards him. Dancing lights of oil lamps flickered against the vibrant, crimson hair settling upon Cassica's shoulders. The dress she wore covered her shoulders and wound tight around her neck to enclose her body from prying eyes, ending in wrist-long sleeves and ankle-length hemline. She cuddled within a thick woolen cloak rolled around her. Her breaths rose in the cool airs, disappearing as quickly in the swaying lantern lights.

Cadeck hastened to lift himself as Cassica approached. He counted the stress lines caressing her face beneath her dazzling emerald eyes. Cadeck's stomach churned by guilt and the sea sickened nausea. Deep down, he suspected he was fault to cause. He had heard the blame before from others. His sin against his Council, against his order and against his oath allowed the bearing of children. The same children became the cause for the devastation mounted upon Sarat and Cassica's people, the murder of her siblings and father and the disappearance of her mother for which she had no further right to trust his words or actions.

"I heard you leave your bunk, Cadeck. Are you well?"

"Gratitude for your concern, Cassica, but I am never accustomed to ship travel."

Cadeck leaned on his elbows and lowered his head to face the crashing waves against the keel.

"If only my magick could carry me over oceans."

"Why don't you?"

"Water interferes with the method. Over land, my magick is uninhibited, between cities or towns is draining, but trying to go over oceans can result in risks I dare not mention. Magick is a gift one must practice studiously and in seriousness."

Cassica nodded. Cadeck's lecture reminded her how powerful and how trusting a Magi could or could not potentially become.

"Have you come across a Magi who tried?"

Cassica motioned Cadeck to a history lesson, her mind inquisitive to the intricacies of his trade.

Cadeck grinned, scanning his eyes across the darkness of vacant ocean.

"No, Your Highness. Books written long ago; long before the last Aeon tells of these legends. I wish I could understand why it happens, why some of our abilities contaminate upon others, why some of our magick counters another, never the two shall meet you can say. Magi have dared not try for fear of death and lack of an inheritor, and such words became warnings, not lessons.

"The Si'rai sure wish I had learned of such abilities. You should have seen my confines onboard that infernal ship. The sailors were none too pleased at the mess they had to clean."

Cadeck sequestered laughter before turning to a more solemn question, "How is Tesh?"

"He is still asleep. It has been three days. Neither has he awoken or stirred to speech. I am beginning to draw concern for him."

"I've never seen one produce magick of that strength before, with as little learning as he has acquired," he turned to her, leaning his back against the bulwark. His stomach growled and churned, "Give him time, according to Cruxien, we still have a few weeks before we come close to the location he suspects is the Water Temple."

"Are you sure of Cruxien's findings?"

"Not in the slightest. I would like to observe his map in deeper detail and learn what he knows."

"Cadeck, you trust him, don't you?"

Cadeck grinned, "As far as I can throw him, yes."

He sensed trouble in her voice as her words trembled from her lips.

"And what of his men?"

"I know them not. They are a band of vagrants and miscreants. I have never known him to associate with respectable company."

"I fear them, Cadeck. I have seen the way they leer at the girls and myself. They outnumber us."

Cadeck sighed. Cruxien agreed to keep his men in line with ladies onboard, ladies of the Crown. Cadeck had Cruxien's word; his men would leave Cassica and her ladies alone.

"I promised to Ysalir, I would allow no harm upon yourself, or your maidens."

Cassica listened to his words as Ysalir's name came into thought. She never found difficulty trusting Cadeck despite the ultimate cause of her stresses.

"I wish to ask you something, friend. What did she tell you when she left?"

Cassica leaned her elbows upon the railing. A cool wind fluttered her bangs as she stared into the empty nothingness of the darkened seas.

Cadeck swallowed his saliva. It was no surprise she knew. She trusted him and relied on his advice. Confidently, he turned back to her gaze. Deep eyes focused onto hers. The crevices in his face tore upon the whiskers with aging wisdom.

"She was worried for yourself and Venna in present company. I assured her Kenat, and I will protect you."

"Does Venna know of her new assignment?"

"No. I have instructed Kenat to never divulge for it is the business of the Crown. Not ours. But if I may," Cadeck broke from his boundaries, "as your friend and not as a Magi, I advise you to tell her."

Cassica lowered her head, tears began to form in her eyes and cascaded upon her cheeks.

"I am afraid, Cadeck. My leadership, my dishonesty back in Silvetzen caused this pain. Eris and Venna question my guidance. How can I be their leader of the Order, much less a Queen if I lead death to my people? How are they to trust me again?"

Cadeck felt the urge to comfort her with an embrace, but instead allowed the woman to sob at his side. Cassica needed a release of her pain, a pain she had held for days to keep from exposing her identity in Racoren.

"None of this was your fault, Cassica. It is hard to know what the gods decide. My magick permits me to see all possibilities, but none would have been favorable to Sarat. Our choice to leave Silvetzen provided the better outcome. Remember what I told you; the loss of two kingdoms is greater than the whole of Roth. Your leverage with the Tarlaki could provide us the advantage we need to reclaim your kingdom."

Cassica ceased her cry, sniffled her nostrils and wiped a tear from eye and cheek. Her head remained lowered to watch as waves crested against the keel of Cruxien's vessel.

"What do you know of treaty?"

Cassica returned to a formal stance, rose from the lean and furrowed her lips to Cadeck's assumptions.

Cadeck smiled and patted her on her covered shoulder, "Father Aeus guides me in more ways than you can know, Cassica."

Cadeck hobbled towards the aft deck with an infused relief of regained equilibrium and disappeared into the door between the two ladders into the lower decks. Cassica watched as the older man removed himself from the main deck, leaving her to switch her attention towards the splattering waves clapping against the keel. The helmsman kept busy, whistling a sailor's tune as he coordinated activity with the navigator beside him. Cool winds rose Cassica's hair into frenzy as she returned to lean against bulwarks. With calm oceans below, her mind let go towards recent events. She trusted Ysalir to carry her message and sought guidance in her own intuition Ysalir's purpose would be fruitful.

Now her people suffered under the hands of a cruel enemy. An enemy which would never back down nor give to her rightful leadership. Leadership: an ability she felt she could not convey. Her leadership led Sarat to ruin. Her leadership wrought distrust amongst the pair in her command. She was a princess forced into a paramilitary role at the command of her own mother. What cruel fate was that? Like Venna and Eris and even Ysalir, she should be suckling children, watching them play or learn how to be kings and queens.

On this ship, she was no longer a princess, but a fugitive. Like Venna, Eris, the Magi and Tesh, she was on equal status to those she sailed with.

Cruxien risked his life to help her escape, Tesh aided to rescue her from the chaos in her home and on the open ocean, she was now contraband cargo. The events in Racoren left her stripped of title, worth and dignity. She owed thanks to Cruxien for the medium and to Tesh whom she had only known in recent weeks.

Tesh Verdui, a man of low status in Sarat. He had come from the blood of a known criminal who served his punishment by becoming a Temple Knight. Arcane and foul as the stories and rumors told, the Knights devolved into nothing but criminals, liars, cheats, and thieves. He was just a young man, a villager learned in several crafts. Paranoid and superstitious like most low-born men, she had seen his lack of trust towards her and lately towards Cadeck. Yet, there was something innate within him she admired. Was it his morality? His humility? His compassion? Or was it deeper, more instinctive?

When he reached to kiss her, she overcame with shock and scorned him of his place. Now, she was alone; a woman of nobility travelling with pirates. She had never had a tongue for prayer, doubting the gods her mother told her about. In her youth, she had felt the presence of another being haunting her dreams, guiding her, and tricking her into shy child-like giggles. The spirit played to her charms with broken vases, scratched paintings, or other malicious deeds she had only accused to the ghosts which regularly haunted the castle.

However, on this night, Cassica felt heart to call to other powers beyond her own reasoning. She prayed Tesh would wake soon, muttering a chant to Sokut taught to her as a child to promote fortune upon the ill for good health. Despite Tesh's lower class, she trusted in him. She sighed heavy after her chant and brushed her hair with her hand behind her ear.

The nighttime listened to her. The dark sky opened her thoughts. Whispers floated in her ears as though to answer prayer. Stars danced above her head as a twinkling show. The night listened and so did Babalon.

Azthar Kherdmon; a worthy blade for chalice. Likewise, is the Destroyer. Chalice shall receive none other.

Cassica looked around, hearing a distinctive feminine voice through the air. She jerked her head towards her side, peering towards the aft deck to see the two sailors working their business at steering ship. She twisted again, this time to gaze towards the figurehead and finding no persons there.

"I prayed to Sokut. Why did you answer?"

Cassica called to the spirit echoing within her heart. Thoughts feared delusional acquaintance by the men steering ship; she retreated her head to look upon the oceans below.

For the duration of your life, I have never known you to pray and when you have, I heard them.

"I've heard you before," Cassica muttered to herself, "In my dreams always before the moon lights again."

I am you. You are me. I am Sacred Mother. Contained, I am destructive. Unleashed, I redeem. So long as I remain within, Sarat, like other profane kingdoms, will suffer.

"I never asked for this. I do not understand."

The spirit laughed.

When the moon joins the sun along the Abyss, blade shall strike chalice.

Cassica's face drained. Emerald eyes glossed with hints of tears. Her head shot back and forth, trying to find the voice speaking to her only to see bewildered amusement from Cruxien's men sailing the vessel. Cassica stood alone. The haunting words of the spirit within her lingered on her tongue as it had muttered the prophecy. Could she consult Cadeck to its meaning? What could he know? He confided to her he has followed the apparition since her childhood, only to divert studies away as quickly as he made progress. She thought, even he feared the results of lesson.

#

Morning sun rose over the calm seas as *Misty Willow* continued a southerly trek. The boat drifted with open sail draped to fill with the pushing winds cutting her keel to slice through the waves. Sea crests rocked the boat against the waves as it sailed perpendicular to the current. Rigging line stretched and whined as the sails pulled taut. Crewmen hustled to perform chores, whistling tunes, or grumbling their tasks as they spoke to themselves.

Sea winds guided over Venna's gentle hair. Soft, blue eyes glazed over the oceans as she leaned against a bulwark on the forward deck below the foremast. A brown dress covered her fae frame in a drab brown cloth bound at her wrists and neck stretching down upon her ankles. She thought of her sister and the abandonment she felt as she awoke days ago to find Ysalir gone. She wrapped her arms around her chest, holding her body warm in the cool winds settling over her. Wispy clouds lingered overhead strung together like cotton strands stretched across the blue skies as pasted upon a canvas.

Footsteps rattled the wood behind her as they approached the ladder leading to the forward deck. Rope lines tensed as weight applied to the cracked planks, footsteps ascending to her position. She turned to the distraction to find Kenat's lanky body inching towards her. He wore his traditional garments with the crimson robe stretched to his ankles, the edges trimmed by golden etch and full sleeves stopping below his wrists.

Kenat's mix-color hair tousled in the winds as she found herself lost in his pearl-glazed eyes. Venna turned back to her watch over the gentle seas. A pod of dolphins arced over the surface in close distance to run parallel to the vessel.

"May I join you?"

"I suppose."

"I hope you understand I meant no insult the other day."

"Don't worry yourself over my thoughts, Kenat."

"You never heard about Ysalir?"

"No. I care not to ask Cassica. I know what she did. She dispatched her to another mission. It is not my concern, for I am only an Orange Petal of the Rose, the business of my superiors is not mine. Kenat, do you ever wonder if your life would be different were you not a Magi?"

Kenat stood at pause. Her question caught him off-guard as he slowed his approach to her side, "Why do you ask?"

Kenat leaned against the bulwark. He followed her gaze to the dolphins in the ocean.

"We both serve orders to a greater purpose. Neither of which was our choice," she turned towards Kenat, "How would your life be different?"

Kenat sighed, "I would be Koran nobility, flaunting my father's wealth with the libertine carelessness befitting of my peers. I would be either bond in union or fathered bastard children with wily debutantes. Bards would sing of my perverse scandals and woo more women my way."

Venna drew in a long breath and held her chest with her hand. Her heart pattered beneath her breast as her face flushed with embarrassment.

"Ribald tales of which I have only heard amongst the more flirtatious spirits at the Academy. I hear gossip of such vanity befitting of the Denwiches. They are well known in Sarat for swaying loose harlots towards their affections. Surely, Kenat, you do not revel them in your tongue? Certainly, you just spoke inane fantasies of which you have read in stories?"

Kenat lowered his head, grinning slightly to hide his secrets, "I was just short of my eleventh day of name when Philos found me, I could only dream of such debauchery in the tales I read and the bards I heard."

Venna's radiant skin glistened in the morning light easing over the decks. Her crisp blue eyes as clear as the oceans below. Delicate hands rested on the edge of the rail, clipping the wood as she tapped her fingers in repeated succession against the bulwark. Kenat felt to move in, grip her hand and sweep her away. His covenant denied him bawdy pleasures.

"So, if you were Koran nobility, what House do you reside, Kenat?"

"Denwich, madam."

Kenat lifted himself to face her, bowed, and with the elegance befitting of his birthright, slipped his hand to grip one of her palms and kissed the back of it. Her hands were like a bed of flowers in fresh bloom. Nails trimmed with spackled mud. He glanced towards her face to remain in bow as her face flowed with crimson blush.

"Kenat Denwich, at your service."

Venna's heart dropped within her chest at the name rolling from his tongue, a name belonging to the young man before her who defied the libations of the family she had heard in her days back home. Why him? Why now? Why on this ship away from home did he entrap her with a name which carried stories of carnal depravity and insidious glamor?

"Kenat."

Cadeck scowled from behind them. Startled, Kenat turned around to see the older Magi in visual dismay at the affection he saw. Kenat released Venna's gentle palm and allowed it to flop to her side. He straightened his robes and sleeves in amusing effect which caused Venna to giggle. Venna waved her hand to her face, fanning the blush from her cheeks. She fluttered like a giddy schoolgirl as he turned his back to her to scuttle down the ladder leading onto the main deck.

Venna followed a short distance and leaned over the railing overlooking the main deck behind her. Cadeck set his firm hand upon Kenat's shoulder as the pair glided towards the aft section. Eris caught her attention as her peer stood with the horse, dressed in a bland black dress fitted in the same manner as her own. Her dark hair draped over her covered shoulders blending with the fabrics of the clothes. She held a small clump of hay in her hand and approached the horse bound by a chain to secure the animal from leaving the vessel.

Kenat and Cadeck moved beyond the chained cart and towards the mizzenmast. He visibly scolded him with pointed finger and calm demeanor about his actions towards the women. Venna followed suit, leaving the forward deck and met with Eris to aid with chore.

"What happened?"

Eris asked as she patted the animal on its cheek while it consumed the straw in her hand.

"Nothing, Eris," Venna shook her head.

"Kenat said something to you, I saw you blush. He clearly likes you; don't you like him?"

Venna paused, aghast. Stuttering, she darted her eyes, "I do not know. I mean…"

"Well, if you like him, kiss him."

"I shan't. He is a Denwich. Father would never approve, even if he were not a Magi."

"A Denwich," Eris widened her eyes, dropping her jaw in response, "You know what that means?"

Eris turned a flirting eye and a smile at Venna.

"I am fully aware of what that means, Eris. He would conquer me, then you and however many others. He could never be faithful until his father arranged union pair to some other wealthy daughter to secure business. And even that is in name only."

Eris giggled, "He seems so polite for a Denwich."

"That's because he's a Magi."

Venna followed in giggle as the pair continued to gossip and treat the horse to meal.

#

"I should remind you to keep focus away from Ego."

"I understand Cadeck," Kenat turned back towards the pair of women, then back to Cadeck.

"There is something afoul aboard this ship, something I cannot quite place."

"What do you suspect?"

"I do not know. I sense unease amongst the crew. Whispers of dwindling supplies and rumors of mutiny. There may be danger afoot if we are not cautious."

"I can pry into their hearts. Listen to their inflections if their words match intuition."

"Be mindful. These men seem a superstitious lot and wouldn't hesitate to consider your presence a curse upon them."

"Without Tesh, it is only you and me. I've seen how Tesh's magick works. It is remarkable and unmatched. Philos never lectured on such innate skill. We could use him."

Cadeck nodded, "I agree. Yet, it is best we do not wake him until he is ready. Cassica maintains watch over him. Sometimes she's spoken of unintelligible murmurs. He speaks of an island shrouded in a fog.

"The night we left Racoren, I saw a vision of my children, alone. They seemed they were adrift."

Kenat turned to him in query, "I saw a fire in my dream the same night. Ships sinking."

Cadeck leered to him in concern, "It wasn't this one, was it?"

"No. Much larger. A warship I think."

"I hope it is nothing. The lingering rocking of the waves and my concern for their safety merging into my mind to one incohesive memory. On a lighter concern, have either of the girls expressed concern for Cassica?"

"Only their growing distrust. Nothing more. I fear for their safety, I have seen how Cruxein's men eye them."

"Keep to their protection. I promised Ysalir nothing would happen to them and Cassica."

"And what of Captain Cruxien, Cadeck?"

"I have requested an audience in his cabin more than once and denied each time. I wish to seek answers about this anomaly onboard, but I am unable to place it. He denies access to the cargo deck, only supplying food as needed."

Cadeck leaned against the portside bulwark, "I fear for the security of Cassica and her girls. If the crew folds into mutiny against their captain, they will no longer be safe."

"I'll keep to their side, Cadeck."

"I will be mindful of Cassica. She is still mourning for her family and stands to Tesh's vigil for the duration of his sleep. I dare not pry into her sudden passion, but the desperation in her voice lends me to believe she has placed newfound trust into him."

"How long will he remain asleep?"

"Hard to say, Kenat. I have never seen such an expense of magick like he displayed. I would like to review Cruxien's map to see our distance to the Water Temple to wake Tesh. Cruxien posited his faith to doubt, and the reverberations called to me in my aztmudin lends me to believe it is in the cargo decks."

"He's your friend, why does he deny your inquiry?"

"I suspect unease in his speech. Should I pry further, it is likely he would abandon us on a remote island out of spite."

"Should Heseph lend me guidance, I will surely follow through."

Cadeck pat Kenat on his shoulder and shared a smile, "The future of the Magi is safe with your faith, Kenat. With you and my children, the future of the Council is not in doubt. Do not allow Ego to wander from your convictions."

Kenat nodded his head before the pair left towards opposite ends of the vessel. Kenat moved through the cramped deck beside the chained cart and shuffled past a pair of burly sailors who eyed him with disparaging grunts as

they edged past him. He tousled his robes back into form and glanced at the
threatening man intimidating the young Magi with a leer. He stumbled over a
pile of wrapped rope and caught himself against the rickety buckboard. Venna
laughed at his efforts from the forward section of the deck. He turned to her
and blushed before setting foot in her direction.

"Did you listen to the whole conversation, Venna?"

"Pieces," Venna blushed, swaying her hips with hands clutched behind
her back.

"Where's Eris?"

"She has returned to quarters. Talk to me."

Venna flicked her eyes at Kenat to coax him to follow.

"About?"

"So, you're to protect us?"

"Well, to keep you and Eris safe should Cadeck's suspicions come to
head."

"Oh," Venna shifted towards the forward deck, lifting herself onto the
ladder to climb towards the figurehead.

Kenat followed and elevated to the deck. She rose to the deck with
swaggered gait and stopped short of the foremast.

"You said you were a Denwich. Is it true about your family?"

Kenat looked down to his sandals. He stood a few paces behind her.

"I only know of what limits there were to my discoveries. I learned my
mother and father continued to have children and live their ostentatious lifestyle
well after my absence. I had the displeasure of meeting my father once in
Silvetzen. He arrived on rumor of extravagant baubles at auction by an
Imperium importer. My mother did not attach to his hip, only a strange woman
who licked at his ears and pulled at his pants as he sat upon that balcony in
Rathmana's castle, eyeing the wares before the audience and the unsavory ladies
who accompanied the wealthy. He saw me, scoffed at me, and turned back to
his entertainer."

"How sad, Kenat. Are you sure it was him?"

She moved in closer. His heart raced.

"I had no reason to doubt. He looked as I do; taut face, protruding
nose, and furrows of faded blonde hair. I discovered a list of dignitaries invited
from around to make purchase of these artifacts," Kenat smiled, "I do believe I
first saw your sister that day."

"Please, Kenat," Venna sulked.

"Apologies, I thought it might uplift spirit."

"Finding her will uplift spirit. I would show my disagreements towards Cassica's decision if allowed. Yet, the contrivances of our oath deny me an outlet to pain."

"You shouldn't hold grudge."

"And why not?"

Venna raised her chin, her face angered by his suggestion.

"Did your father not tear you from his fortune, from your family? Do you not hold anger for him? Cassica lifted Ysalir from me again. Anger is all I hold towards her and the Roses."

Venna turned her back to Kenat, sauntering off towards the bulwark to overlook the figurehead of Sokut. The hair of the wooden statue adorned the edge of the bow, wrapping around the railings in twisted knots of carved finesse.

"I ponder daily how my life could be different. But what if it was? What if it was as I told you, full of drink and loose women? Am I angry? Only if I think about it. To never love, to never hold. It burns me."

"Why can't you love? Other than, well, bringing on the destruction of the world?"

Kenat approached to her side, "Affection distracts from my convictions."

"But it didn't stop Cadeck."

"I cannot answer for him or his lover. I was wrong to question him at Tijoa's hut. I know my place and that is to take over the covenant to Heseph upon my return. To uphold my covenant, I should remain faithful to my…"

His voice trailed as Venna reached up towards his neck and pecked a full lip kiss on his cheek. She tasted silk butter on her lips. She slinked away. Small flames erupted in his pearl eyes reflected onto hers.

"What was that for?"

He pondered her action, rubbing the cheek where her wet smooch lingered in thought.

"To change your mind."

Venna slid past him. He caught whiff of her salty hair brushing against his shoulder. She slid her hair away from her face exposing her milk white neck to his thoughts. A curious birthmark distracted him beneath her ear. Kenat felt a deep fire in his blood boiling through. He closed his pearl glazed eyes and released a sigh as her footsteps trailed her to reach below decks.

He hid thoughts betraying his commitments and envisioned him in the lifestyle of his family running with Venna. In his blasphemous feelings, he treated her with lavish gifts and whispered salacious words of vulgar poets upon her delicate ears he followed with a nibble. Kenat shook his head to erase such reflections and listened to the words of his own Ascended and Cadeck for his duty in life was to follow the teachings of Philos and to take stewardship of the Temple of Fire.

Kenat permitted the gentle winds of the open ocean to brush upon his skin. He opened his eyes as strands of silver clouds blew over the sunlight casting random shadows over the deck of *Misty Willow*. He focused on the rocking crests of the ocean as the ship broke through waves in its advance towards waters unknown. Bustling chores broke his concentration as the commands of men in broken accent ordered the inferior sailors to routine.

Kenat focused onto their slurred voices and the hints of dialect wavering from their tongues. Rampant syncopation of beating hearts chanted into his head. He allowed his heart into a lull rhythm, reaching with his aztmudin to touch upon their chests.

Intentions manifested in the pulses as Venna moved past a pair of men towards the aft section. Kenat craned his neck to watch as a man sneered in her direction with disfigured gums. His heart yearned to step in to turn the man's attention away from Venna with a terse rebuttal only to hear Cadeck's command to interfere in case of imminent danger. A whistle and a gander would have to suffice the unsavory man for now.

The young Magi watched as she progressed into the aft cabin, sealing the door behind her. Heartbeats slowed to a dull pace while he continued to listen to their words. He moved quietly, shuffling down the ladder and proceeded towards the main mast to close in on speech. A trio of sailors ceased their chores to meet up with a huskier man and flank him on the portside bulwark in seedy conspiracy.

They smelled of fish rot and slippery grease. Kenat scooted by them, their hearts pounded upon the Magi's skull in maddening orchestration. They need not to speak, Kenat heard their words before their tongues moved to form them. He knew them all by the intentions of their hearts within, his aztmudin crying louder than in recent days as though relieved of the darkened haunts in Silvetzen and Sarat. Reaching the aft cabin, he grasped the wrought iron bar handle and pulled the release to enter. Iron scraped on wood, distracting a skinnier sailor with tussled ginger hair. The leading man smashed his palm against the ginger kid to return his attention to plan.

Kenat slammed the door behind him and moved down the ladder leading to the officer decks. Like coiling strands of twisting ropes, he felt the heartbeats of the men speaking amongst themselves. His eyes shone a dull red hue as the four sailors formulated their plan to reach an agreed upon time. Hearts beat in rapid succession, each synchronized to the other while their words spoke of cunning plans. Kenat continued through cramped passageway.

He reached a small door on his right and with a slip of a slide; the door ran along a channel to open to his entry. Inside the narrow room, a pair of bunks fitted to the right side. A small plank had lifted upon the horizontal axis to latch in place opposite the bunk bed. Seated on the lower bunk, Cadeck's hulk squeezed into the constricting confines as his satchel slung over a hook on the bed post. Kenat's pearl irises burned to attention, alerting Cadeck to a hidden danger. Slivers of sunlight spilled into the porthole washing the younger Magi in daylight.

The hearts of the men continued to give their motives away. As their words grew into sinister ambition, the rapid pacing of the muscles echoed their rising stress. A strained voice called to him, reaching from beyond the men's words as though touching him personally. Tesh's voice called his name several times, begging for his ear. Kenat listened to his voice as the whispers hinted his calling. Kenat shuttered his eyes, shaking his head and with a sudden release from expended magick, collapsed towards Cadeck who reacted to catch the young man.

The fire burned out of Kenat's eyes revealing their pearl-white glow. His breathing increased to a rapid pace as Cadeck reached to the pulse in his wrist to feel the rapidly changing heart rate. Cadeck swung the young Magi onto the bottom bunk, patting his cheek to call his name. The boy grunted through gaped mouth; his tongue rested against the back of his throat. Cadeck called his name again beckoning him to wake.

Upon the last hit, Kenat blinked his eyes, closing the gap in his mouth and coughed several iterations. With tight clasp, his fingers wrapped around Cadeck's exposed forearm scratching at his flesh with trimmed fingernails. Kenat scrambled to regain traction in his prone state, as he hoisted himself towards Cadeck's chest with repurposed invigoration.

"Kenat, what's wrong?"

Kenat coughed again, releasing his breathing into a normal condition. Cadeck rested his thick arm around the man's chest as Kenat clutched to him.

"Elder, we are in grave danger."

Chapter 45

Cassica's cabin betrayed the pleasantries her upbringing allowed her throughout her youth. A small bunk rested upon the bulkhead, fitted as though it sprouted from the vessel. Beside it a small table had locked into place parallel to the opposing wall, fastened by brass latch with a tarnished mirror just wide enough for a face.

Tesh lied upon the bed on a thin hay mattress, his frazzled hair rested upon a stuffed, feather pillow. Silent murmurs spilled from his lips; his hands set at his sides above a scant blanket covering him to his chest. Arms spilled along the sheet exposing his naked shoulders and tapering chest frame. His left hand moved in short syncs as his lungs filled slowly with each breath.

Cassica set beside him at his head, her hips close to his ear. She crossed her legs within her drab woolen dress, unchanged in the weeks at sea. Her hair strewn around her neck and shoulders withered from the sea brine air and mangled by unwashed hygiene. Slender hands traced over Tesh's forehead, scraping a growing bang away from eyes which fluttered behind his eyelids. She had given her room over to the young man who had exerted himself to save her from Imperium hands. She relied on the scant comfort afforded to her body in her sleep upon the wooden deck.

Inside her heart she felt compassion from him. As noble of a deed as he had done, he had given up his breath to save those he had only met. Tesh pushed himself, or so it seemed, exerting powerful magick to command the winds to lead her away from Racoren. Was it simple self-preservation or the need to fulfill a worthy cause? He shared not a word to anyone prior to that act, muttering only for Cruxien to listen and follow heed.

Cassica arranged for Tesh to move from the common quarters, relinquishing her bunk for him to rest well. Placed upon her bed, words and whispers opened from his tongue. She could not read his lips that day, but understood his brazen act meant her escape from her war-torn nation implemented by his deed. In so doing, she sat by his side for three long weeks, coming up for a few moments at a time. The smell of sea winds caressed her body in those brief moments. Cassica kept to herself, meeting Cadeck for small talk or to gather her daily rations with the other ladies.

Her rations, like those of Cadeck and the girls relegated to a piece of fruit for breakfast shared amongst those of gender. On odd days, she would be provided a filet of fish, while most days, a staple of tack biscuit and a mixed grog to which she learned swiftly the grog softened the hardened bread to become edible. Each day she saved her rations of grog and tack to make a mash which she would offer to Tesh's lips, which he ignored to partake.

Venna and Eris disregarded her, condemning her with their body language and the spite of their tongues in silent whispers. Her command structure slipped away in gradual decay. The Order of the Rose a shell of itself with the defeat of Sarat and the need for such a regimental cabal. She prayed to Sokut for Ysalir's progress only to hear discouraging whispers from the spirit haunting her since her youth, filling her mind with doubts and furthering her separation from Venna's trust.

She urged seclusion onboard the ship, leaving her with Tesh so he would be in helpful hands should he ever wake. Cadeck argued against her request several times, hinting to her in grunted whispers of the jeopardy Kenat envisioned. He had spoken to her about the rations they receive are the only luxury provided to them while the crew subsisted on mildewed tack and souring grog.

As with any night, Tesh whispered with his sleep and uttered phrases unpronounceable in Common Tongue. Her cabin grew dark as the sunlight faded into the west, edging into her porthole within the starboard cabin. She looked upon him. Cold lips glazed with purple tint; his wounded hand etched by golden lace reacted to the setting sun like sparkles of dust rushing by a window in their fleeting moments of life.

Cassica reached her dainty fingers towards Tesh's scarred appendage. An urge came upon her mind as curiosity stole her heart to touch the wound. Arcane mumbles tore into her skull bouncing between her ears in hushed calls spoken in a tongue unaware to her.

Like the grace of a dancer, her index finger pushed upon his chest as the fingertips rose along the folds and creases of his sheet. Dirt and soot settled below her nails as her middle finger followed suit. Mere inches from his hand, Cassica let out a sigh.

The sun burned orange into the room. The sparkles in his left-hand danced vividly in her eyes with the reflection of the rays striking his wrist. She waited patiently, reminding herself to leave Tesh be and rose to her feet. She forced the creases from her dress starting at her hips towards the flow of the hemline.

A repeated knock startled her from thought as she called out to request name. Cadeck's rough voice responded as she urged him to enter the cabin. His aging husk skirted into the doorway carrying a small bowl in his right hand. He wore a ripped-sleeve shirt with dusty trousers tied together by a hemp cord. Her nose accustomed to the lingering ocean odors commonplace the better part of recent weeks. He held a pouch in one hand and quickly removed the wrappings to reveal a single piece of crumbling tack.

"No grog or fish?"

"No fish were caught today, and the grog is turning sourer," Cadeck turned to look to Tesh, "It's been three weeks, has he taken any meal?"

Cassica shook her head, "I have tried, only for his lips to remain pressed. When he mutters prayers, I place spoon to lips only for mouth to close again. What if he does not wake? You are a Magi, have you seen this before?"

"In my nearly forty harvests of being a Magi, no."

"Before we left Racoren, he was so," Cassica dropped her eyes, turning over her shoulder to Tesh, "quiet. He spoke nary a word only to offer glimpses into the distance. I heard him speak to Kenat one night during his watch and opened my eyes to listen."

Cassica crossed her arms, "He spoke to Kenat about someone, or something, named Babalon."

Cadeck paused, his shoulders sank below his chest as the words muttering from her mouth signaled the gravest revelations he could ever foretell. He closed his eyes to wait for her follow through. Within his heart and mind, he considered every possibility as he controlled his breathing to calm rhythms.

"What did he mean, Cadeck?"

The inevitable question, a spirit he had sensed within Cassica since Selen expelled her from bloody womb. He denied her a response; instead, he turned his back and set his firm hand upon the edge of the door to try to catch his breath. He summoned the will to relay to her stories of folk tales to stave off any chance of her making conversation of the matter.

"She is a demon, nothing more, sent to haunt the dreams of young men in their sleep, encouraging them with sinister beauty so they may wake up with soiled linens."

"Then what is it that haunts me? Is it the spirit you sense about me?"

Cadeck tightened his grip upon the side of the door like a noose bound upon a condemned man. He positioned his weight to the lean of his grip and sighed loudly, craning his neck towards the ceiling. He reminded himself of the day Wrem first turned to him of the growths in her chest upon her thirteenth year only for Cadeck to encourage her to discuss the matter with Madelynn. A conversation he had wished he had carried sooner only to have his life forever changed a few weeks later.

"A conversation for another time Cassica."

Cadeck set foot outside the cabin and with a rush of force, pulled the door behind him.

"Cadeck, wait," Cassica whispered behind the door.

He fluffed her notion out of his mind as he moved along the hall towards his cabin. He passed his door, continuing towards the ladder rising towards the main deck. Cassica's door opened behind him as she commanded for his attention once more. He ignored her request again, lifting himself towards the door leading onto the main deck and slammed her voice behind it.

Defeated, Cassica sighed and turned her attention back into her cabin. She posed questions he hesitated to answer, haunts and visions of a demonness of which she scarcely understood. She leaned upon the door to close it. Tears formed upon her eyes as she truly felt alone. Withdrawn and stressed, she moved towards Tesh whom supplied her the only comfort in his isolated coma.

Cassica lied parallel to him, sliding her hips against his and raised his right arm over her shoulder to drape around her. She placed her right hand upon his chest, her tears streaming down her blush cheeks as she whispered her sorrows towards his ear. Each word, each syllable forming out of her lips had preceded an ethereal echo tickling into his ear.

She wept for Venna and Eris; divulging the desperation of her isolation as they ignored her commands and disobeyed her intuitions. Tesh's ears heard her human speech followed by sinister whispers. Cassica permitted her hand to drift across Tesh's left hand resting on his chest and with uninhibited inclinations, set her finger upon his.

Upon touch, the golden veins reacted, rippling with a wave of violet tendrils coursing along his hand and wrist to trace the outline of his injury. She lifted her index finger to slip over his as his body reacted to her titillating touch. With the push of her sliding digit, the veins arced as a finger sliding across sand while she saw the mystic antiphons she promoted. Cassica moved her middle finger to touch, repeating the procedure, his hand responded likewise.

Each touch titillated her like gliding her hands across frozen rose petals shattering with each slide of her fingers. His veins formed as gold, sparkling flakes while her digits floated on his skin like silken sheets filled with restless spiders. Tesh groaned with reaction. Cassica turned her eyes towards his cheek and cuddled closer into him allowing their warmth to match in rhythmic heart rate. She placed her hand upon his heart, feeling his chest lift with each pulse. Every breath quieted her mind with each unspoken word she heard coming from his soul. Connected in spirit, the one she had heard inside her for the entirety of her life had quieted into somber calm.

#

Crested waves gently rocked *Misty Willow* into the painted morning strokes of purple sky. With struggled resistance, Tesh's eyelids ripped open with the crust built from weeks of closure. Like ripped fabric the residue crackled apart. He reached up with his left hand and scratched his eyes to wipe away the rheum. His eyes squinted as he strained to process the rush of faint light pouring into the room across the horizon.

Overhead, he heard the clamor of feet rushing across the wood. Cadeck's voice echoed from down the hall, clearly upset with Cruxien as the pair spoke in mumbled opposition. Tesh attuned his ears to Cadeck's words as he blinked to understand his own disposition.

Around him was a room painted of white wood panels, a mirror hung from across the room from where he lay, and a tattered sheet covered his bare chest and body. But the woman who rested beside him supplied a reprieve.

His right hand had entwined within the burnt orange hair like a tangled weave of ribbon. Cassica's flush cheeks felt like silk cream lavender as she rested upon his right nipple. A right thigh draped over his hip, clothed in a plain dress of earthen colors covering her from neck to ankle. The fabric slid upon fuzzed shin up to her knee bringing to his vision the sight of pale, freckled flesh.

"Cassica," he whispered. Her body reacted as she drew herself closer towards him, "Cassica, wake please."

Her eyelids fluttered in dreaming slumber, "Let me sleep till noon, mother."

"Cassica, it is me, Tesh. Where am I?"

Cassica groaned, "Tesh."

Her eyelids stuttered to open. She wiped her eyes with her right hand and expelled a loud yawn. She met his face and gazed upon his open eyes.

"Tesh."

She shot up to sit upright, her face widened as though fresh inspiration flushed over her.

"Where am I?"

"Tesh."

Cassica could not hold her voice as she screamed his name at the top of her breath. She jerked from the bed, landing her feet firm onto the deck as she stumbled backward against the opposing bulkhead. Feet clamored along the hallway approaching her door followed by a rapping of the wood.

"Are you decent, Your Highness," Kenat's timid voice billowed from the other side.

"You may enter."

Kenat turned the handle and slid into the frame. His crimson robes softened in the morning stir of light flowing into the cabin. Venna and Eris followed behind him crowding the cramped space.

"Where's Cadeck?"

"To that question is my purpose for seeing you, Cassica. He has been with Cruxien all morning."

Cassica's eyes widened to fear, "I heard raised voices. Do you know the matter?"

"Cadeck did not invite me, and thus it is not my business to pry."

Cassica pursed her lips, "He should know Tesh is awake."

"Agreed, yet as he is my elder, it would be untoward for me to approach him if he does not wish for me to assist. He has tasked me to assure your safety while he is dealing with Cruxien."

"I am more than capable of protecting myself and the girls."

"A feat I am more than familiar with, Your Grace."

"Then leave me, please. Find Cadeck."

"Your Grace, with all due respect to your position, you carry no authority over me. I will stay here and protect you, Venna and Eris. We will remain in the room as is best until Cadeck returns."

"You will go and find him."

Cassica's voice rose to anger as preternatural hints of emerald shine covered her eyes. Venna cowered behind Kenat, clutching against his left sleeve. Eris stood her guard behind her, ready to defend should Cassica's anger turn violent.

Cassica approached Kenat with a small stride. An ethereal aura haunted her eyes. To his ears, her tongue spilled the speech of invocation, cursing his name against his god. Her lips puffed to her words, mimicking the vocal intonations leaving her mouth.

As Tesh lay propped against the bed, tendrils of pulsating energies slithered along the wounded hand against the golden veins. Kenat stood his ground. His eyes darted upon Cassica's countenance never wavering from his duty to protect them as commanded. The demonic murmurs continued from Cassica's soul berating the young Magi with profanities and insults against he and his god while she stood silent grasping for the right phrases. Tesh slid his legs over the bed, clutching his forehead with his good hand while his left hand remained upon his lap. The energies shimmered upon his bare chest as he raised his hand to face in front of him.

He continued to watch the silent exchange. Kenat never faltered as the princess stood like a silent peasant in awe over the shaman before her. The tirade from Cassica's soul called from his hand as though filtered from the rest of the mortal women in the room. He rose to stand and with a stretch of his left arm, placed hand against her covered shoulder. Her mouth gaped open as the haunting glow lifted returning her eyes to hints of mortal green. Only Kenat and Tesh observed and heard her vile aberrations, the pair of younger ladies saw only a scorned ruler who faced challenge to her authority.

Cassica lifted her right hand and touched Tesh's wounded appendage. Tickling stings rubbed on his fingers as he pulled his hand to his chest to scratch the biting tingles away.

"Go, Kenat. Leave the ladies here."

"Are you certain, Tesh?"

"Please, find Cadeck. I have words to share."

Kenat bowed.

"You can listen to him, but you're unwilling to take orders from me?"

Kenat looked to Tesh, then back to Cassica, "In time, Your Grace, his words will carry more weight than the Council."

Kenat turned to both ladies and promised them to return. He pecked cheek kisses on Venna and Eris before leaving the confined space with a swift seal of the bulkhead door.

Ocean breezes sifted over Kenat's dusty, silver hair as he closed the bulkhead door behind him. Moving onto the main deck from the aft, Kenat observed several of Cruxien's men loitering around, toiling about their chores. Sea song whistles whispered to Kenat's ears like code. Neither Cadeck nor Cruxien appeared amongst the men. Kenat followed the deck towards the forward hatch leading into the lower decks.

Kenat's heart raced inside his chest as he tuned to the intentions of the men. Each man clued him in on the finalization of plans. Each heartbeat signaled to Kenat the dangers of his separation. Kenat declined to continue his walk, instead trailing away to return towards the quarterdeck cabins. A husky sailor watched as the Magi backtracked in his steps, following beside him as Kenat skirted past.

Kenat moved over coiled ropes aside lanyards holding the middle mast sails taut to the wind. Two other sailors continued in his chase as he heard the increased race of their hearts. His blood sizzled with fires coursing across his hands and inside his chest. Pearl glazed eyes fell to an orange tint as his thoughts predicted the movements of the pursuers. On the open ocean, he had nowhere to turn, no place to run and with the fragile construction of the ship, unleashing his fire would certainly turn his transportation into kindling.

Sudden darkness covered his face as a man rushed behind him to hide Kenat's head inside a burlap sack as another struck him hard with the blunt end of a sword hilt. With little effort, the younger Magi collapsed to the deck as the men rushed to bind his hands with rope. One of the sailors grunted to smile as a string-haired man stood over Kenat. He signaled towards others to make their way towards the lower decks.

Cadeck did not prepare his heart or his mind for the spectacle he saw this morning. As he stood silent in the lowest decks, holding only a small lamp in front of his face, his eyes filled with tears upon the visualization of the sealed bulkhead in front of him. An Imperium Sigil had cast upon the symmetry of the barrier in the whispering hints of wick flicker. A solid steel frame sealed the portal upon the outlying bulkhead consuming the remaining space in front of him, cutting off half of the cargo deck from access.

No visible lock closed the partition, but the presence of a darkness carried onto Cadeck's soul. His knees quivered as haunting memories of rusted chains, rotten stench, and the absence of his children flashed into his head. The energies of a sinister magick flowed over the alloy door like a tangled menagerie of violet pulses as he lifted his hand towards the barrier.

He turned around, setting the lamp upon an upright cask. Other casks lay littered upon the floor, their contents long ago removed. Emptied crates scattered around, stacked neatly upon the keel. Cadeck stared with disgust at the man standing before him.

"What is this, friend?"

Cadeck clenched his teeth.

"Assurance to safe sail, Cadeck."

"Your cargo is half filled and nearing empty, yet this abomination seals the rest? You would starve your men to strike a deal with demons."

Cadeck's anger echoed in the lower deck as he stood to toe with Cruxien. His hands short of gripping the split vest exposing the sailor's rippled chest.

"What is behind this door?"

"They never told me. They only paid me to take cargo to Jorin," Upon Cruxien's words, several of his sailors lowered themselves into the cargo hold. Cadeck's eyes shimmered with yellow hues.

"But the blockade?"

"It was part of the deal."

"What deal?"

An ear-piercing scream shot through the decks prompting Cadeck to look upward.

"You were the cargo, my friend."

Before Cadeck could lunge for Cruxien, a husky man with exposed belly swung a club at the Magi's face, sending him to the deck.

Cadeck felt a nudge against his face, sharpening the pain in his left jaw as it bruised into a tight puff. Forced to stand upon his feet, the sea airs filled through his lungs covered by a heavy rucksack. He heard sobbing to his right as Cruxien's voice lamented on as to the decision of his fate. Cadeck's blood soured into fury. Hands bound tight behind his back, his mouth stuffed with a dirty rag taut against his cheeks in a rope bind preventing him from chanting magick.

He could only muffle the sounds of voice through his gag trying to call for his fellow travelers only for them to not hear his lamentations. Instead, Venna's screams dragged across the deck as he followed the sounds of stammering feet with her voice. Eris followed her and within moments the sounds soon muffled by sobbing cries through bound jaws.

Anxious breathing warmed up the rag over his face, "I'm sorry friend, but unlike Red here, the Imperium pays up front for their transport fees."

Cadeck's gag silenced the choice words leaving his stunted tongue, likewise, preventing him from incantations.

"The deal is to take you to Jorin, with Red and Gold Hand. Your younger Magi is expendable and the girls… I am sorry friend, but their mouths look more like things go in than words come out. I did not count on running into you, you see," Cruxien's voice trailed away from Cadeck's face, "but the Imperium drives a hard bargain. They told me a Magi would enter Racoren within three moons, and with a redheaded woman and a man with an injured hand. They informed me while I was in Jorin. I doubted them, questioned their ability to foresee such specifics, but a hefty purse convinced me to sail empty. I didn't expect it to be you."

"You lied to us."

Cassica's tongue burst through the crisp airs. A soft yelp left her lips as a hard smack punched upon her cheek.

"I did not lie Red. I am a businessman and I make profit. I agreed to terms, so long as my ventures in Imperium lands stay untouched."

His breaths returned towards Cadeck, "They have found three of my hideouts and burned them. Hung my men and raped my whores before enslaving them. I could not bring fate upon the others. I make no profit when those under my coin die."

"You are a monster. Rensel was wise to distrust you."

"I am no more of a monster than your father, Red. How many men of prestige escaped charges of conspiratorial murder? How many families whose coffers enhanced your treasury soon elevated into Court? I merely run against your system because my ventures escape your taxes when your system runs anathema to my own, they cannot coexist. You could only dream to know how many friends of your father I have taken across the oceans to escape the courts when he signed charters for their warrants."

"If my father were alive, he would see your body hung from your mast as he orders the armada to sink your vessel."

"Your father is not alive, and neither is your armada. You would be wise to remain still, Red. Stuff her mouth so her ill tongue does not speak till she is handed over."

Tesh could only watch the exchanges from his prone position lying on his stomach upon the deck of *Misty Willow*. The sailors did not bother to tie him as his weakened state put him in no position to fight them off. His hands rested in front of him, the digits curled in pain from the beating he endured to bring him out to display.

He looked up to see Cadeck's head bound by a sack. Cassica kneeled beside him as she tried to bite at the surly man wrapping the gag around her jaw as he spoke profanities of her. Torn dress covered her body in her vain attempts to ward off the attackers. Venna and Eris cried likewise, their faces rosy and red from their strained sobs and eyes shot by dried tears. Their mouths bound in torment with their hands behind their backs forced to prone. Through beaten eyelid, he saw Kenat's bound body marched towards the forward deck, sack wrapped upon head tightened by a noose cord.

Cold, fast winds whipped the sails into frenzy towards the southerly direction keeping the helmsman busy to steer the vessel in proper vector. Winds caught him off guard periodically and forced him to turn the rudder wheel into marked course. The wooden build of the ship creaked with pain as the oceans churned beneath the cutting keel resisting the tides. The sounds of one thousand cries shot through Tesh's soul, rippling across his chest and ears before following towards his injured hand shimmering with a teal hue across the veins.

Cadeck's covered head turned to the ethereal current he sensed flowing into Tesh's hand. As to paused time, the uproarious winds ceased with sudden force, stilling the boat into a silent bob upon the surface of the ocean. Curious eyes looked around, sailors, Venna, Eris and Cruxien. All eyes focused on the quiet sails shifting position to rest. The helmsman released his hold on the wheel, startled at the precise position the wheel remained motionless.

"Cruxien," a man shouted from the forward deck pointing south, "Look."

Cruxien rushed to the bulwark to catch a better glimpse of the anomaly to his attention. A cresting wave rippled across the surface of the ocean like a silent rock had skipped in front of the ship. Cruxien climbed onto the forward deck, reaching the figurehead of Sokut to watch as the pushing tidal force lifted the vessel a few meters before calmly setting her to rest. He continued to watch as the crest moved under the vessel, following the anomaly as it headed towards the stern racing with it along the main deck. Wood creaked and shuttered amidst the quietness of the observers as a listing shift positioned *Misty Willow* back to a steady position, leading at the bow and continued till the stern resumed a level lull. As the crest pillowed under the ship, Tesh's hand brightened to glow, reacting in ripples with the action of the wave from his fingertip into his arm.

"We are in the Oceans of Wavering Tides. Cruxien, you have sent us to our doom."

One of his sailors clamored to keep his calm as the inflection of his voice echoed his own fears. Within moments, Cruxien's betrayal crumbled around him as he ordered men to scramble to turn sails into a direction to put them out of harm's way. A sailor behind Cadeck pushed him to his knees and turned to follow orders. Fistiros, Cruxien's first mate, ordered all but himself and the helmsman below decks to ready oars to reposition the *Willow* and remove the vessel from the region.

But his command would not be without confusion. Before the first man could lift the hatch leading into the lower decks, a loud thump slammed into the starboard side of the vessel rocking the boat with the momentum. A gust of wind blew in from the starboard, shifting the sails taut and sliding the mass to list in the forced direction. Kenat and Cadeck fell from their kneels to their sides with the push from below the water line. Venna and Eris screamed beneath their bound ropes as Kenat struggled to free his own wrists from the cords. Cassica fell backward onto her hips, landing her head against the edge of the bulwark besides Tesh.

Tesh's left hand froze into position, unable to move even to wriggle his fingers. Cased within stiffened ice, the tendrils upon his veins cooled to a frosty glaze. Another attack hit the port side followed likewise by another gust of wind shifting *Misty Willow* to slide westward across the surface of the ocean. A jolt of the keel caught the helmsman off guard as he slid over the bulwark railing, screaming into the ocean below. His death call rattled nerves of his colleagues as several men clamored to move below decks to heed command and ready oars.

A shadow loomed from the stern, blotting out the sun like a drifting cloud. Fistiros turned around to see a massive wave pushing towards the ship in forward direction. The force of the cascading crest slammed into the stern of the ship, rocking the vessel to raise its keel above the crest line allowing it to skim across the surface. The occupants of the vessel slid into the aft section across the main deck. The bound cart jolted and shifted loose from its moorings sliding forward into one of the sailors and pinned him at the ribcage against the starboard bulwark. He screamed until the heavy cart crushed him silent.

Chaos erupted from the junior sailors. Screams shred through their sanity as several louder thuds slammed into the sides of *Misty Willow*. Cruxien's horse clamored and trotted to free itself, only to collapse to its right side. Cruxien fell to his knees as his command buckled around him and humbled himself into a crying prayer.

"There's something under the ocean."

One of the sailors proclaimed. Cruxien ignored the call begging with sobs to Sokut to spare the ship. He reached for a blade held in a sheath against his hip and with service to the goddess, cut a slit into his left hand to spill blood into the salty waters slapping onto the decks. Cadeck and Cassica tumbled near him followed by Tesh. Venna and Eris managed to clamor towards the abutments leading into the quarterdeck cabins in apparent safety.

Cadeck's tumble spilled upon Cruxien's knee only to slice his cut deeper towards his small finger. He paused in fear, his heart nervously split into his chest rocking his ribcage. Destruction wrought upon his livelihood as Cadeck struggled to release himself from his binds. Tesh clawed towards him, his left hand aglow with mystical energies blinding Cruxien's eyes in the pain of humility. Cadeck removed the cloth from his head then the sooty rag; he spit out fibers of rope cord and dried saliva. Cruxien remained humble upon his knees, his face white like a ghost at the sight of his freed friend.

"I'm sorry, friend."

Cruxien turned to Cadeck with honest eyes welling tears of guilt.

"You can apologize when we make it to safety."

"No. She punishes me. I sold you out."

Cadeck furrowed his eyebrow as though Cruxien spoke cursed death.

"This is where my faith is tested," Cruxien continued.

Cadeck turned his back on Cruxien to move towards Cassica and remove the rag from her mouth. Impacts rocked the ship from underneath the keel. Scratches and claws clamored from below, jarring the ears of the seasoned sailors. Cruxien moved towards Kenat to aide him with freedom only to find

558

the younger Magi stood to his height, the sack removed and his hands glowing bright orange with flame. Kenat jumped from the forward deck, crouched when he landed and pushed his way past the screaming sailors who had taken up arms and stood on either side of the vessel aiming crossbows into the ocean.

Thwipping recoils of flailing arrows followed each of the ethereal poundings below the surface. Cadeck hoisted Tesh to stand and as Kenat approached the pair Tesh's hand glowed with a teal-green hue bright as the sun hitting the sea. Cruxien shuffled past the men and made towards Venna and Eris. Cadeck led the others towards Cruxien's position as he finished releasing Eris from her confines.

"Cruxien, are we where I think we are," Cadeck gritted his teeth.

"Yes. Where all sailors fear."

Cadeck crunched his lips into a scowled grimace, "Without a Magi, the undines will kill us. All of us, Tesh and myself included."

"I deserve death. I sold myself to those who bring it."

"Cruxien, humble me this moment and I shall see you spared."

Arrows continued to whip and plunge into the ocean depths, missing their targets. Several men infuriated over their poor aim as their targets below swiftly jolted from side to side. By now the sounds of thousands of oceanic inhabitants burned through Tesh's ears as he covered his head to ward off the screams.

"Those bitches have cursed us," another sailor proclaimed, pointing to Cassica and her ladies.

The ire of the men removed their efforts from the attackers below and turned their attention towards Cassica and the two girls. Several men ceased their defense and moved with substantial effort towards the hunkered guests to alleviate their balance with the attacks from below.

"Your men seem to have an idea, Cruxien," Cadeck followed.

"Give us those women. They have cursed us Cruxien," Fistiros screamed.

A crossbow rested on his shoulder as he lowered it to aim at Cruxien, "Or I'll kill you myself and take them from you."

Cruxien rose and intervened to meet the arrow tip, pressing it firmly against his heart.

"This is testament of my blasphemy against Sokut. This is Her doing. I will sacrifice myself for misdeed."

"No Cruxien, they brought a curse upon this ship," Fistiros uttered through foul breath, "They're the ones who deserve to be tossed overboard."

His boast riled the men to angered applause. Without warning, brutish sailors pushed towards the younger girls, grabbing Eris by her hair, pulling her away from Venna's embrace. Venna screamed Eris' name as they dragged the brunette girl away. Cruxien pulled the crossbow from Fistiros' slender hands and tossed it aside towards Cadeck before shoving the smaller man out of his way.

"Leave her alone."

Cadeck's eyes lit to fury as he pointed his left hand towards the offender. Screams from below continued from all around the ship like a wild orchestra out of tune and playing a lambasting reveille of supernatural song.

"No Cadeck, stop."

Tesh rose from his crouch. His breathing erratic like a man given welcome breath after long days depleted of air.

"I can hear them all, shouting and calling to be abated."

He caught himself as he collapsed to his right side against the bulkhead beside him. His words drew a silence from the panicked sailors.

"The goddess will kill us all, Cadeck. You know this," Tesh panted.

Cadeck lowered his head, all eyes turned to his next breath. The man who held Eris withdrew his grip, allowing her to collapse towards Venna. The young ladies embraced, tears rolling across their cheeks. The continued assault of the vessel below hammered into Cadeck's mind as his thoughts turned to Jess, his children and the future of Roth before him. Should Tesh fail in his trainings, destiny and fate both with his next breath.

"Then it is only fair to them for the ladies to draw sticks," Cadeck uttered. Cassica's eyes turned to tears through moist locks of clung hair.

"No Cadeck," Cassica teared, "You cannot leave this to fate."

"Faith guides me dear; I never rely on fate."

"Why now?"

Cassica rose to her feet shifting herself as the pounding continued below decks. Several men rushed towards the forward section to try to find small splinters of assorted sizes.

"It is only fair, Your Grace."

"No. My people need me."

She turned back to Tesh, "Tesh, do something, please. Stop him. I will not allow chance to permit you to take me."

Her tears swelled to volumes as she took Cadeck to task. Her eyes lit aglow with emerald flame as she rushed to his face.

"Cassica, I will not argue this. You *will* draw as Venna and Eris."

You are a fool, Cadeck. This body is not yours to command.

Cadeck caught the spirit inside her speaking to him through his aztmudin and with subtle speech under his breath, silenced the roars within her. With his might he caught her wrists and set her aside, ignoring her continued pleas spoken from her physical tongue. Venna begged for Cadeck's mercy asking not to meet fate. He turned his back towards the women, uttering a chanting prayer to his god and begged to hear Jess once more for guidance.

Without hesitation, a sailor approached Cadeck with a trio of sticks and rested them in Cadeck's open palm. He opened his hands, inspecting each one and concluding one was shorter than the other two. He clenched them tight, allowing only the tops visible above his index finger and turned to face the three ladies who had by now come towards him. Each of them sobbing; their fate rested in Cadeck's palm.

"You know how to do this," Cadeck extended his hand towards the women.

"No Cadeck, I beg you. You were to protect us. Did you know of this?"

Cadeck ignored Venna's request. Kenat could only watch as she turned to face him silently begging for his influence onto the elder's decision. Kenat could only hold his tears as he withdrew himself from her look. Hesitantly, each of the women handled a stick and removed it from Cadeck's hand crying their anticipation of fate. Tears welled as delicate fingers plucked at sticks gripped by Cadeck's hand.

Cassica gazed upon her choice and with panting reprieve saw she had the longest one. Her thoughts turned to Venna and Eris. Cassica would have to live with this guilt to the survivor of this ordeal, forever untrusting her with regards to her recent actions in lackluster leadership. What could Cassica glean from this? Death had no winners, but for Cassica, she would need to be exemplary to the younger woman who lived while the demon inside her reveled in the outcome.

Venna's knees quivered as she dropped to the deck and with a raging scream released the two-inch stick from her hand.

"I'm sorry, Venna," Cadeck uttered as he helped to raise her, "Sokut has spoken."

"Kenat, please," she begged.

Cadeck lifted her and dragged her over the deck towards a bulwark.

Eris could only watch as Cadeck and another man led her friend towards certain death. She glanced down towards the stick and extended her fingers to open her palm. It was slightly longer than Venna's much to Eris' dismay. Eris brushed her hair aside watching as Venna fought and kicked at Cadeck who surpassed her physicality. Venna had more value to life. A sister who cared for her and a man of whom Venna adored that could only watch as her futile screams ignored Cadeck's calm prayers to her.

Eris had nothing. Her sister died at the hands of Silvetzen led by the Imperium. She lived youth as an orphan and forced into Academy by the Crown. What type of fate was that she often wondered? Her life held at the whim of a Court forever bound to order and fulfill the commands of a Queen and her daughter serving a corrupt kingdom. She never knew love, only fleeting moments of passion filled with the tawdry gossip of Venna or other girls. The only man of whom she felt a match to, died in her arms on the battlefield a few weeks ago. Cadeck prepared to lift Venna over his shoulder as she kicked and begged pleading further for mercy.

The word lingered in her mind again, whispering louder, calling her name with the dialect of their enemy. She heard the whispers calling the vile pronoun and the shared dialogue as the visions returned, flashing in her head. Tivius' snarling grin formed below cold stare as hints of lavender mist spilled from the hilt of the blade resting at his hip. She looked up in the form of her sister, crying and releasing her breaths to fate. The voice whispered again, spoken not of Tivius' tongue, but feminine, darker, and sauntering in sinful lust. Breathy, haunting words spoken as two tongues in conflicting languages.

"Cadeck, No," Eris yelled, catching his attention, "She does not deserve this. Permit me to take her fate."

"I'm sorry Eris."

"No, Cadeck."

Eris moved towards the elder Magi; her tears now streamed like rivers carving paths in mountains.

"Eris, have you gone mad?" Cassica requested.

The sailors and Cruxien could only watch the exchange, acting on nothing.

"I take her place, Cadeck. Give me over to the undines and permit Tesh his training."

Cadeck set Venna to the deck, releasing her towards Eris. The pair of women sobbed as they embraced one another, each of them gripping the other's cheeks as they pushed matted hair aside.

"No, Eris. You do not have to do this," Venna's emotions jittered with her unease.

"No Venna," she whispered, "Move away."

Eris pushed her aside and with morbid grace approached the bulwark. She turned to Cassica, then to Venna standing beside her. She looked up at Cadeck and set herself to sit upon the bulwark. She glanced towards the ocean below her. Trails of large fins skimmed the under surface like swift arrows shooting through the sky in every direction.

She reached into the cord binding her dress and removed the small felt fabric noting her rank and turned it over to Cadeck.

"Promise me this, Cadeck, if you should ever see your daughter, give her this for me."

Cadeck clutched the fabric tight into his fist as she turned towards the others.

"I won't let *them* take me for *his* will."

Her words curdled from her tongue, speaking in foreign manner against her learned dialect. Cadeck listened to her words coming from her lips in the vile reverberations of perverted magick borne of bloodlust and pain.

Eris lowered her dress below her shoulders and down her small frame, revealing full nakedness.

"*He* has watched us both, Venna."

Cadeck could only watch as Venna burst towards the bulwark next to him, hearing the only distinguished word of Eris' unnatural speech, that of Venna's name. Her face turned full red as tears echoed her sadness at the loss. Eris splashed into the ocean, her body collapsing into the swells of her impact. Swirls of seas ceased their attack onto the boat as the slim, fish-like creatures honed onto the new body. With rabid response, the beasts transformed the ocean around Eris into a crimson feast of death.

Venna slammed her fist onto the bulwark, her face emptied of blood out of panicked fright covering her eyes. She sulked to sit onto the deck, hiding her sorrow with her hands. Cruxien stood alone, stunned at the events as Tesh struggled to lift himself onto his own feet. The sailors could only watch the horror unfold, dropping their weapons and muttering personal prayers to their goddess. Before Kenat stepped towards Venna, she buried herself in the folds of his robe. Cadeck motioned for Kenat to escort her below decks.

A scream of attention tore through the monotony of mourning when a sailor called to the starboard side. Cruxien turned to see the skies unfold as clouds shifted into a vortex several hundred meters from the ship. Below the opening of the heavens, a similar occurrence spilled like a circular drain into the ocean. Cresting waves cascaded across the keel of *Misty Willow* in pulsing shocks from the event. Men braced against bolted or fastened mounts, their legs giving way to the violent jolts slamming against the ship.

The rotating clouds intensified escalating the ocean into a whirlpool draining into a singularity catching the *Willow* in its riptides. Time paused in motion as Cruxien yelled a command to the occupants, his words stuttering to leave his gaping mouth by the utter shock of the spectacle. Men slid towards the starboard, yelling as their grips released them into the spiraling vortex of ocean below. Like waste down a drain, the whirlpool caught *Misty Willow* on its edge, cycling the vessel in a counterclockwise motion towards the bottom.

Cassica clung to mooring. Water spilling over her face bound her dress tight against her fit figure. Cadeck slid into Tesh as Kenat and Venna cascaded towards the starboard side. Kenat gripped the edge of a stair ladder, clasping the blonde girl tight with his open hand as she screamed in fear. Wind and water whipped around the crew and passengers as the ship spun in a downward spiral towards the epicenter of the singularity. Within moments, the water closed above them in a slow procession as the outskirts of the vortex cascaded downward to fill the void.

Cruxien beckoned for mercy, praying to the goddess he worshipped as the ship lowered itself towards the floor with filling waters. He closed his eyes, grasping against a lanyard with seawater flushing over him. He could only ponder on the disastrous events leading him to Cadeck as his life began to linger in front of his face harkening him to pay toll for his sins.

As his prayers turned to unanswered screams, he could only envision his afterlife in a manner of finding peace in a world which knew none. He heard a beckoning call to him, yelling his name. He raised his head and squint his eyes, glancing around and wondering if he fell into Sokut's welcome grace or his soul fell to torture in the Great Void. A voice called his name once again as he pressed his hands upon the firm, stone surface.

"Cruxien," Cadeck's familiar voice called and reached a hand into his direction.

"Where are we, Cadeck?"

Cruxien struggled to regain his sight as it blurred into focus. Seaweed strewn about, covering the ancient stone he stood upon. He heard the moans of Cassica, Tesh and others and quickly learned to assess the outcome of his own vessel.

"This is where Jess called home, Cruxien," Cadeck's furrowed face saddened.

"The Water Temple?"

Cadeck nodded to confirm, "Aye."

Cruxien's vision opened further to consume the sight around him. He looked up to see dancing lights of fading sun floating above them. He took a gasp of air to exhale a welcome release of carbon dioxide byproducts. Cruxien craned his neck to look around. Water spilled around them as they occupied a void of air in a massive bubble.

Around the confines, majestic creatures swam and glided through the oceans with fin-like tails and androgyne, humanoid torsos. In the center of the circular platform, a grandiose structure composed of gritty stone and coral rose above them. Stairs spilled into the center of the architecture leading from the platform and into the diameter of the stone circle.

This was the home of his goddess. For years, he had pondered the existence of this structure, praying daily for good blessings to the goddess inhabiting this ancient tomb, only to deny his faith with recent charter. Cruxien dropped his tongue in awe and fell to his knees to weep. He chanted open prayers in Common Tongue filtered with the accent of his people. Cadeck admired his professed piety as words of contract and self-guilt spilled from his tongue calling for the goddess to forgive him of misdeeds and gave thanks of his survival to see the Temple meant atonement.

Cadeck turned to the Temple building and surveyed the area to ensure Kenat and Tesh, Cassica and Venna were safe. He processed thoughts of Eris' sacrifice and the words she spoke as she fell to fate, words spoken not of the Common Tongue, but that of a blasphemy had befallen her with curse. He closed his eyes, pondering the dreams she spoke of with Venna as the group approached the dock in Racoren, thoughts of her sister and the voices she heard to feeling trapped in iron walls.

A speech she should never have known, much less studied without years in the lands of the Imperium or even longer in study as a Magi. Not even an Elder or Ascended dared to utter such vocabulary. Nonetheless and even then, the tongue spoke stylized and eloquent with the resonance of a foreboding voice of deep baritone.

Her words carried weight upon his heart, crushing his resolve if only met with brief comfort at the sight of the swarms of schools of undines swimming around and through the pillars of the Water Temple before him. He closed his eyes. Jess' voice called from within the Temple, echoing from behind the coral vibrations of the structure. Once more, he saw a cave, situated upon an island in the middle of the ocean. This time, a sword lingered behind him with raging anger followed by a vacuum of silence.

Chapter 46

"Cadeck," Cassica shouted.

He opened his eyes, filtering in the sights of the *Misty Willow* situated upon a wide platform made of coral, supporting the weight of the vessel as the men awoke around him; confused, and startled by the sudden appearance of the structure before them.

"Cruxien," Cadeck began, "round up your men and take them back to the ship."

"Why show kindness towards me after my admission? Take my life, Cadeck. It is only fair, in front of my goddess on Her sacred ground."

"Your goddess has spared it so you may atone," Cadeck lifted himself with creaking bones, "Honor your friendship with apology later. My only vengeance is for those who continue to hold my children captive."

Cadeck looked across the stone platform watching as several of Cruxien's men dropped to their knees and wept for forgiveness to the building in the center of the amphitheater. Their sobs and cries reflected penance. Grown men, husky and cutthroat men, all fell in humility towards the gracious representation before them of their goddess.

"Your men humble themselves. They only obeyed you but see the error of your folly. I present Tesh his trials. Then we shall discuss your bargain."

Cruxien nodded as he rose to his feet smiling at Cadeck's acceptance. Cruxien gathered his thoughts. Cruxien tightened grip upon Cadeck's hand into a muscular handshake and embraced by a one-arm hug. Cadeck removed himself, allowing the pirate captain to descend the stairs and move along the circular venue gradually descending towards the coral-structured temple. Cruxien followed the many walkways of coral to several of his men, gathering them as requested before marching them towards the raised structure where *Misty Willow* had rested upright. The ship floated upon a suspension of air, contained to set the ship level against the circular structure.

Cadeck turned his attention towards his party, seeing each member absorbing their responses to the outcomes. Venna wrung pockets of water from her once golden locks turned into dampened curls of soaked brown. The dresses of the girls soaked into their skin tightening to form, fitting along their curves and hips. Kenat did the same as he squeezed the sleeves of his crimson robe turned watery maroon. His gray-tinted hair turned into stringy locks spiked across his head as seawater dripped from his ears and face.

Venna approached him, aiding his task. She scowled at Cadeck as they began their approach, the loss of her friend upon his words and deed turned her heart and emotions into a blackened husk. The fear of this new world, magick and the Si'rai lifted her from comforting confines into an unpredictable and unsecure outcome. Dried tears burrowed against flush cheeks lending themselves to her pouting lips full of sobbing cries. She continued to dry herself and kept her misery of Eris' loss from moving beyond her facial expressions.

Now she had no reason to trust either of the authority figures. Cassica dismissed her sister and now her only friend in the Academy deceased by Cadeck's faith. To her, she wondered, what were the gods other than vile portents of sinful power? A power denied her. A power in constant play for the worship of mankind. A power of ego and greed. A power shunned and disgraced. A power, she now wondered, could be destroyed.

A cackle whispered in her mind – *Beleth*.

#

Cassica carried herself in a more dignified manner while sharing disdain for Cadeck's motives. The demoness boiled inside of her, only calmed when she aided Tesh to his feet and noticed as his left arm ebbed with violent tendrils arcing along his wrist and fingers. Her hands like wrinkled linens as she turned Tesh's fuzzy cheeks with her palm to face her. Cassica's eyes reflected the blissful seas above them like emerald, green stars jolted by mystic forces. Tesh could only meet her stare listening to the whispers burning from her soul.

"Why could you not save her?"

Tesh shook his head releasing himself from her clammy hands.

"My ears rung from the screams of those creatures calling for a girl. I cannot explain it, but the speech was not like ours. I cannot pronounce it, but I heard it and recognized the words. I am sorry Cassica."

He lowered his face as he stepped away. Helpless, Cassica folded her arms under her breasts and pursed her lips.

"Then what good is one of us, if you cannot save us all? You are supposed to be this legend that saves Sarat."

"Then maybe I'm not who you want me to be," Tesh continued to move away from her and approached Cadeck.

Tears filled her eyes as she truly remained alone listening to the voices inside her.

"Tesh please," she whispered to herself through pouted lips.

He ignored her quiet plea as he met with Cadeck.

Cadeck took to Tesh with an open arm as he patted the young man onto his shoulder.

"Cadeck," Tesh addressed him, "shall we proceed?"

Cadeck smiled welcoming Tesh's sudden change of attitude towards him. The pair carried down the stairs leading towards the center of the circle. Cadeck's knees creaked as he moved, hampering his progress one leg at a time down the expansive steps. He called to Kenat to move the women to the ship with Cruxien as the young Magi obeyed. Venna followed Kenat's lead as Cassica's pouted lips and shorn eyes displayed her hesitation to listen to the Magi. She brushed him off, choosing to position herself upon the steps and watch as Cadeck and Tesh advanced towards the bottom of the stairs towards the temple in the center.

Trapped by the ethereal forces around her, she knew of no other place to turn. Cassica wrapped her elbows around her knees, binding herself tight as she sat upon the coral steps. Kenat and Venna moved away from her as Cruxien continued to gather his men towards *Misty Willow* resting next to the platform unnerved in the ethereal waters around the structure. The stench of salted water settled on her tongue as she gnawed on a stray lock of hair attached to her lips.

Cassica confined herself to thoughts of her actions. They weighed on her with heavy heart as each day replayed over again in her mind. Before her stood a testament to the goddess her people worshipped. Here in this mystical realm, the portrayal of the wisdom of Sokut guided her father and his father before him tracing back many generations. Statues devoted to Sokut existed in her castle gardens within the town and along each port city of her kingdom. The mighty navy under her father's command had Sokut to praise for their skills.

And with each action she heeded herself to the secular authority guided by the egoism where no gods existed. She scorned the tithing her father gave for lip service and made it known to Cadeck. She trusted no Magi, save for him, but did not bear to bring self to piety. She had read legends of a Sun Warrior, a man with a gold hand to redeem Sarat and assumed it for Tesh. To her, magick was a chicanery of illusion brought on by the Council and true magick, she believed, came from within oneself, not forbidden or kept by the Magi and passed down to man after the gods died on Roth. All had the gift she thought but suppressed by the Magi over the years. Were these her own thoughts formed of self-sentience and superstition or that of another being, the spirit she had heard since she was a little girl?

#

Cadeck approached the side of the building with Tesh behind him. Cadeck's arms outstretched to feel for an entrance amongst the stiffened coral and stone formation. Coral cut into his fingertips, scraping them with tears of unbloodied skin. Perplexed, he ceased his procedure and stopped to arc his neck looking upward. He scanned the precipice of the rock structure and the three spires towering towards the tip of the air bubble.

"This would be easier with a Water Magi," he sighed, "Sokut if your grace is pure, permit me to find an entrance."

Cadeck's defeated tone weighed upon Tesh. Tesh leaned his back against the structure and placed his left foot to press against it. He eased his back onto the surface and placed his left hand onto the wall to support his body. As his digits made connection to the wall, his arm tingled with a spark of cerulean energy flowing along his hand and expanded with spidery tendrils embedded into the coral. The connection forced Tesh's hand to embed onto the structure as he twisted around to pry away only to find his fingers sinking into the hardened wall as one would sift through sand.

Tesh screamed for help as Cadeck reacted to aid his release from the ethereal bond. The tentacle sparks continued along the edge of the Temple, arcing higher towards the base of the spires in patterns of spiraling ladders reaching ever higher towards the twin steeples. The teal-green light marched onward, twisting around the left spire first like a winding snake around a branch before following through to the right spire in the same manner. At the tips of the flanking pinnacles, the energy shot towards the apex of the center steeple before collapsing in a surging burst of raw power along the central tower and into the base of the building.

As the force of the energy grounded into the base, the wall released Tesh's hand and knocked him and Cadeck several feet onto their backs. The observers of the spectacle stunned frozen in shock silence at the display of focused energies surging upon the building. Cassica collapsed to her side, covering her ears at the deafening shockwave rippling across the air. The others reaching *Misty Willow* all dropped to the surface from the bow shock of pressurized air ebbing in a radius around the Temple.

Cadeck rose first as the compressed energies subsided with Tesh under his chest protected from any fragments expelled from the building. As he focused his eyes onto the Temple, an arched opening had formed in front of him spilling pleasant green lights onto the walkway. He rose to his feet and grasped Tesh by both hands, urging him to stand. The quiet light laminated their faces into an awe of subtle calm.

Cadeck set his left foot forward, continuing towards the opening formed of the brittle coral. Tesh followed his lead as the pair walked into welcoming light. Kelp covered the sheen coral arc carved into a perfect form as cut by tools of otherworldly precision. As the others, glyphs scored the walls in the dialect of its ancient builders.

Cadeck limped slowly towards the epicenter of the building. As the men approached the end of the tunnel, Cadeck leaned with his left hand against the wall, glancing towards the center room of the Temple. A pool of ethereal energies waited for Tesh's trials. Cadeck coughed to regain his breath. Tesh leaned into him to help ease him to rest.

Cadeck investigated the main chamber to see it empty of an occupant. Testament to the absence of a Water Magi on the Council. The sacred table at the rear of the pool remained undisturbed, its artifacts and relics to its goddess as stable as the day of their last usage.

"We have come this far, Tesh. What are we to do?"

Cadeck shook his head, "I cannot administer this Trial. Jess never trained an Adept, instead counting on Wrem to take her place."

Cadeck pushed himself away from the wall, hobbling towards the steps leading to the central pool. Energies guided them into the primary chamber. There, he collapsed, energy spent. The realization to see the Temple where his bonded once called home.

"Jess," he whispered clutching his locket, "I have heard and followed you. You called me to bring him here. I have succeeded."

Cadeck's eyes rolled into his head as he could only embrace the fainted darkness from his exhaustion. Tesh rushed to his side, falling to him to beckon him to wake.

"Cadeck, no, we've made it this far."

Tesh jiggled Cadeck's shoulders. Cadeck's breathing quieted to slow exhalations followed by relaxed heart rates quieting to near stillness. Through all his pain and his journey, Cadeck realized calm serenity in the sacred grounds. He lingered on visions of passing here, embraced by the warmth of the calming oceans Jess once commanded under the guidance of her goddess. He watched as the spry brunette girl he sired and named Wrem ran through the wheat fields outside of his home, laughing and taunting her younger brother Dal to give chase. She crouched down into the crops to hide from the boy only to rise to scare him into disjointed laughter as the pair embraced one another in their child-like innocence.

Cadeck's spirit leaned against a supporting post holding the thatch roof of his small wood-framed home. The sun beamed upon his golden robes; a gelded crown wrapped his head in semi-circle. Wrem and Dal continued to play

571

in the fields as Cadeck watched them with glints of delight and serenity. Beyond the fields, gracing the edges of his property, approached a figure shielded in the glimmering light of a full moon. The hands outstretched to touch the tips of wheat stalks; the light shimmered upon a shadowy figure approaching the pair of children.

The hand revealed first. A pale hand extended by slender fingers and delicate nails cropped short against the fingertips. The features were perfect in their tone and absent wrinkles of age. The arms exposed in sequential fashion revealed the sleeves of a silvery dress flowing along the arms and ending before the base of the wrists. A lithe frame shed the moonlight energies around the shoulders, forming the torso of the dress glimmered within the light of a moon upon a backdrop of starry sky.

The hemline of the fitted garment flowed over the ankles of the figure. Sandals made of leather guided the feet along the grasses. Moonlight encompassed in a backdrop of darkness embraced the being as it approached Wrem and Dal. Wrem and Dal ceased to play in the fields watching as the being came closer to them. As the final strands of energy formed the figure, the backdrop of daylight met in center to that of moonlight. The gentle face of a blonde woman revealed itself to the pair of children.

"Mother."

Wrem shouted from her position and sprinted towards her parent. Jess leaned down and grasped Wrem by her waist, hugging her as tightly as she could. She called Dal's name as Wrem beckoned the boy to come towards them. Hesitant, Dal shared the gentle cuddle with his sister.

Jess' comforting touch eased the girl and her blonde-haired brother into a relaxing calm. She smiled and pecked each of her children on their cheeks. Her glistening blue eyes comforted Wrem without a word as she held the sides of her daughter's cheeks with soothing assurance.

Jess rose to her feet, leading the hands of her children to her right and left as Cadeck walked to join them. She allowed the children loose of her grip as she moved towards Cadeck's space to grace him with a soft kiss on his lips. The pair shared affection as they stared longingly; Cadeck in the sunlight backdrop with Jess surrounded by moonlight.

"You have brought the Azthar Kherdmon to his Trials, love, but your journey is yet completed. Our children need you. They will stand with the Azthar Kherdmon as he frees Roth of those wishing to lay harm to it. You have not given up; you will not give up. Rise, my love, and see me with your own eyes."

Cadeck growled in fury as his lungs rattled a strained breath. His eyelids cracked open to allow the bright green glow to spill into them. His body felt

572

warm through his blood pumping in soft syncopations along his extremities touching every vein and capillary through his system. He gazed skyward, prone on his back to see the familiar face of the one he once loved.

Jess' eyes glistened from a deep pool of sacred water beneath her. Her gentle features promoted a beauty exceeding her position as a Magi. Stark cheeks rose high on her face in proportion to her skeletal structure. Silk hands nestled into Cadeck's hair from the back of his neck, supporting his body soaking in the pool of water.

"My love, where is Tesh?"

"He is in the living quarters, Cadeck. I have asked him to rest."

"Where am I? I am still alive?"

"Yes Cadeck. You still breathe, blood still flows."

"Then how…"

Jess shushed him with a gentle whistle through her lips.

"Do not ponder on such wonders. Know in death, I have grown in power, an achievement not met by other Magi. I have only felt this power since the birth of Dal."

"I have heard you many times before. I do not believe I am with you."

"What does Aeus tell you, love? Is our love so sacrilege where in death I cannot embrace you? Is our love so vile the gods have deemed us to never kiss again? Or does your Ego still profess to the codices of archaism?"

Cadeck turned over in the shallow pool. Before him, seated Jess. Her body shimmered in the glow of emerald essence; her svelte frame barren of clothes covered by clear water below her shoulders. Likewise, was he, as strands of scars streaked in wild patterns along his back.

Sensations of pleasantries flowed through his veins as he met her blue eyes as crisp as icy plains. Cadeck looked around through the clear water to see the naked beauty of his beloved standing firmly on a stone surface. In the center of the surface at the bottom of the pool, carved a single glyph, an upside-down triangle where the solitary point aimed behind him towards the entrance. He reached his hand to caress her cheek. Her physical form as pure as the day he met her. She closed her eyes at his touch.

"But I can touch you as the day you left me," Cadeck sighed, tears welling upon irises.

"In these walls, I am whole. I can speak to you as we were together. I can embrace you as we were lovers."

"But I immolated you as you requested and scattered your ashes into the ocean."

Jess nodded, "And I returned here."

"Then you will provide Tesh his Trials?"

"Yes, Cadeck," she nodded, "here, truth shall reveal to him. A truth I have mastered in my death. Your Ascended feared this moment and feared him and is why you and the children suffer."

"Wrem, Dal," Cadeck cut her off.

"Do not fear for them, Cadeck. Their resolve will provide them strength."

"Will I see their faces once again? Please Jess I yearn to see the look on their eyes as I do in my dreams."

Jess glided her hands over his weathered face, creasing through every whisker. Her hands followed across his neck and onto the golden chain wrapped around his head leading to the small locket.

"You still carry this locket I once gave you."

Cadeck nodded, "It is the only connection I have to you. It keeps me whole; it affirms my belief in the gods when one day I would see you again."

Jess coddled her hand around his neck, "Your faith is strong Cadeck. You do not need this to remind you of your devotion."

Her soft touches continued down the back of his neck. Her delicate hands ran along his rugged shoulders traced by the marks of scars.

"I have made you whole once again, Cadeck. But these scars shall remain a reminder of why you travel with the Azthar Kherdmon and the tests you must face."

Her eyes dropped to follow her fingers as she moved her hands along his arms. She reached her mouth to press against his, pairing their tongues together as the night of their first consummation under the light of a silvery moon. Cadeck withheld his hesitation and with the passion of his emotions, wrapped his rugged arms around the complete body spirit of his beloved. Eyes maintained bond as the sacred pool filled with mystical waters reacting to the hoist of her legs around his hips and allowing him to love her as their first night of union.

Tesh stood before the sacred pool as the day he was born. His naked frame did not slouch, instead he remained poised for the test he was about to endure. Yet he was not a mold of human perfection with the slight bulge around his abdomen betraying the toned muscles around it. His arms and legs structured of a farmhand, but still unlike a trained and disciplined soldier.

The apparition of Jess remained inside the pool; her figure naked as she was once with Cadeck. Water covered her from the shoulders down, her blonde hair draped in watery bind to her neck and shoulders. Her eyes glistened as the pool they set in as water draped down her face and neckline. She lifted her right hand above the water, bending her elbow as she coaxed Tesh to join.

This trial would be as any other, submerging into the inner pool of energy to experience another vision of which his experiences with Cadeck, magick and those who he travelled with, prepared him. Cassica fluttered his heart secretly while the fears of Venna and Kenat's exuberance and boastful demeanor echoed into his mind. For once in many days, he saw a smile upon Cadeck as he remained in the company of his lover.

The water felt cool initially and the longer he lingered, his blood rippled with mystical energies warming his skin. He sunk into the energy vortex; his shoulders slightly risen above the water level. He closed his eyes, listening to inner voices calling from around him. Visions began to encapsulate the waters of the pool swirling like hasty fish in erratic directions.

The events formed around him. Many of them foreign, unknown to Tesh but in particular ways he heard the voices, saw the faces, and felt the experiences. Other images mingled as his own memories; thoughts of his mother, his childhood and other whispers calling to his present. The pool shimmered into reflections of Cassica with a soft kiss upon his lips. Venna appeared in following vision, her eyes stained in red tendril streaks of fear. Kenat loomed beside her, his hands formed of fire magick, twisting in fire spiral ladders. Jess approached him and with warm caress, graced the sides of his face with her tender fingers. He opened his eyes to see the Magi. Her lips sealed yet she spoke to his soul.

"Hear me, Azthar Kherdmon," her telepathic voice soothed, "By the Light, you opened your Mind to the All. By the Fire burning your past, you understood Correspondence; as within, so without. By the Winds enraging you, you saw Vibration; all is in motion. Here in the Water, you shall see Polarity; all opposites are but degrees of the All. Your life renews, Soul prepares to enter Matter, so the final truths lead you to Oneness."

With the force of her might, Jess lifted herself over the water level exposing her nakedness and forced Tesh's head to submerge into the viscous waters. She followed thereafter to join his submersion. The mystical waters swirled within the pool clouding the pair within a cerulean glaze pulsating from the center of the voided seas. A high wall of water rose from the edges of the circular bath and lifted to the height of the ceiling several meters above. The whirlpool charged with magical auras. Mystical sparks arced across the edges of the water wall spinning counterclockwise as though the sky itself opened to receive the hydrodynamic forces.

To Cadeck, the feat stayed the same. He seated himself beside the altar pool, his back turned to the dais leading into the vortex rising over his head. His legs crossed over one another as his palms remained closed, pressed together, and rested against his chest. He bowed his head reverently at the ceremony

575

behind him respecting the rituals of the Water. He listened to his own aztmudin whispering across the void, tuning himself into the Trials behind him and the soft voice of Jess administering the sacred words of chant and initiation.

To feel her face once more, to taste her lips and smell her fragrant scent. To embrace her honey silk skin white as breast milk and allow himself once more to fill her as he once did in her mortal life renewed him. For the fleeting moment, he reconnected and rejuvenated his mission. He listened to his soul as it branched across the void magnified by the pulsating energies behind him.

Cadeck heard Jess calling to Tesh as the boy swam in a dark water blinding him from seeing his own hands.

"Jess," Tesh called, "I hear you. Where are you?"

"Follow me. Hear my voice."

Within the murky waters, Tesh swam. Flashes of his past lingered before him swirling in the coldness of death. His mother washed in front of him wiping instantly away as her thought form dissipated in the darkness. She wore a commoner's dress with a bonnet covering her head. She lied on her death bed; boils covered across her exposed skin in darkened yellow bruises of pus. His mother called for him, chanting his name repeatedly begging to live only for her pleas to remain ignored as she wavered off into death's embrace. He could only watch helplessly as her memory faded within the waters as Jess beckoned his name.

Hammers hit anvils in the sweaty shop heated by steamed steel formed and shaped by master hands. Before him sat a bitter old man who barked orders berating his apprentices. Tesh obeyed numbingly as each call to his attention derided him in some way. Several men commanded Tesh in daily chores to make coin, each one of them yelling harder and louder than the last all for the meager earnings of various trades. Swordsmiths, tanners, armorers, cobblers – all trades Tesh learned, yet mastered none. Each shop owner taking a beating to the young man, cursing his name repeatedly.

Verdui. Verdui. Your mother should have cut you from her womb. You are worthless. Your father's name is a curse upon you boy.

He swam deeper, watching as visions of his life continued to replay around him. Thoughts of his blonde friend, Jaena began to appear. He wrapped her hand in a small ribbon, promising to bind together in his heart with her father's permission. For months, the bald man refused to allow it citing Tesh to be nothing more than a misguided boy working a toiled wage and never amounting to wealth. He too cursed Tesh's name as nothing more than sin. Each time before their liaisons, Tesh would hear screams and cries coming from her upstairs window as she begged to her father to let him have a chance. Tesh presented to her a small gift of saved fortune, a slightly tarnished ring he bought from a wandering tradesman, unbeknownst of origin nor quality of craft.

The day he was to present it, she had gone missing and found several days later along the road to Telmen having never made it to market. His heart paced into a sudden withdrawal, returning to his home with quieted despair begging to the gods for mercy. He felt no reply from the gods, only emptiness as though none could hear him nor wanted to. He cried to the gods that evening, disavowing their existence forever, chastising them till the end of his days.

As the visions of Jaena left his soul dissipating forever into the murky void, the water cleared before him into a war-torn valley awash by the ocean waters. It was the same vision he had seen of scarred landscape drowned out by tidal forces encasing him as he walked amongst the dismantled siege and dead bodies. He pushed further; leaving the embattled weapons, bodies, and cavalry to wither in the bloodied wash. Slain armies of varied heraldry rested before him as far as he could see as he followed towards a bright stillness in the far horizon.

As he approached the light, the luminescence enraged to encompass his full vision. He met the edge of the water formed in front of him like a wall; on the other side was the source of the light. He touched the edge with his hand as it rippled around him. He heard Jess' voice calling through the void.

Tesh stepped through the liquid wall and found himself as a dripping nude along a white vacancy. Jess stood at the far edge of his sight surrounded by a pure whiteness canvassing the entirety of the vision. Tesh moved towards her and struggled to calculate the stark outlines of the blonde woman who called his name.

"What did you see?"

"I have seen my past, Magi. As with the other Trials, but I burn inside, I can no longer feel them. A feeling as having erased them."

"A Past held by Ego. A past you must reconcile to complete Oneness. You have impressed me as you did Cadeck."

Jess now clothed in emerald robes of her covenant, covering her shoulders down to her ankles.

"Do you feel worthy to continue your Trials, Azthar Kherdmon?"

"I do, Magi," Tesh kneeled before her, "I have seen love and joy, sadness, and despair. I know what I must do to complete my journey."

"Do you?"

"The waters have cleansed my Soul, prepared me to fulfill destiny ahead."

"I have felt your aztmudin since you first met Cadeck."

Jess' spirit reached towards Tesh's wounded hand and lifted it to her waist. She traced the delicate veins with her fingers as each movement created an arc of azure energy escalating across his wrist.

"This wound; a testament to his intuition and where in your worst moments, you should always place trust upon the gods and yourself. You have *Dra Nar Azt* within your blood, Tesh, but only if you are willing to utilize its purpose."

"Purpose?"

"To cleanse Roth of the evil cursing it. The curse placed by the Si'rai as the Magi have forsaken True Will. Magi. Si'rai. All the same. Duality of opposites. Two degrees to the same conclusion. For what is darkness, without light?"

"I don't understand."

"Light and Dark, Polarity of the All. Roth needs cleansing of all evil, man and Magi alike. Evil: true evil, is the ego of man. Magi. Si'rai. Both have used magick to fulfill their egoist ways. Magick is to be a gift. A gift to Man. A Gift of Mind, Spirit, and Matter. If you fulfill purpose, you will be the vessel to spread the gift. Mother, our Primordial and Sacred Mother shall fulfill her deed to replenish this gift upon Man."

"Babalon?"

"She travels with you, and she has risen. You must keep her safe from the Apophadi. Death will follow if he consummates with her."

"Cassica?"

"She trusts you, Tesh. Protect her and those you travel with."

"I have seen her. Should I fear her?"

"Difficult to say. Sacred Mother burns within her like a volcano to erupt. Be mindful and do not let her sway you until prophecy fulfills. She can be fierce, deadly. But you can soothe her."

Surges of water collapsed the pale construct of Tesh's soul cascading along Jess' body and onto Tesh splashing the pair into a pool of sacred energies. Tesh's back jerked in an arc, shifting his body into a back float position with his hands spread out to width. His body lifted to the surface of the pool. Tesh's breaths slowed as his body lay unconscious face up.

Jess stood at the head of the pool in front of the altar table garbed within her sacred vestments. As Tesh lay on his back in her sacred waters, pockets of emerald sea energies formed upon his head and hands, feet and knees, neck, groin, and chest. The spots of magick rippled like small ponds on his skin.

Cadeck rose from his vigil, clothed in the lavender silk vestments of his commitment. He saw with Jess, liquid streams of rippling energies trickled upward into Tesh's forehead before disappearing entirely. Jess moved into the pool to catch Tesh at his feet as Cadeck squatted to his head and together, lifted Tesh out of the sacred waters and back upon the edge of the dais.

"It is true, then? *Dra Nar Azt.*"

"Yes Jess. What my Ascended feared."

"I felt it when he entered the pool."

"Then the prophecy is to be fulfilled."

"But which one?"

Cadeck turned to his beloved with a smile, "All of them."

Jess escorted Cadeck down the steps, permitting Tesh to regain consciousness behind them. Tesh's guttural coughs echoed through the coral room as water expelled from his lungs. Jess' slender fingers graced her lover's calloused hands as the pair intertwined their digits leading to the base of the platform.

She turned to Cadeck and graced her fingers along his rough whiskers.

"Now you must go. Lead Tesh to his next trial at the Temple of Terranroth."

Cadeck shook his head, "No. I wish to stay with you. Here. Cherish you till the end of my days."

He placed rough hands against her tender cheeks.

"No, Cadeck. I have fulfilled my role to free Roth and bore our children as the visions instructed me while my heart still beat. Your purpose is not yet complete. Lead Tesh to his trials."

"I will bring Wrem and Dal to see you. I promise you."

Tesh lifted himself from the platform and plopped his head onto his left hand.

Jess shook her head, "No my love. Once Wrem fulfills her role and completes her gift, my soul will leave this incarnation and return home. Neither could see me again. Rest assured, I have visited them, and they have heard me."

Cadeck swallowed his words as tears formed on eyes, "The witch in the forest gave me a vision. Tell me Jess with the honesty that bears my heart pain, has harm come upon them?"

Jess withdrew from his hold bringing herself to focus thoughts. Tesh ignored their conversation, moving swiftly to clothe himself in the ragged and soggy outfit he had worn several weeks. The leather shirt reeked of sea stench and kelp as he fitted each sleeve over his arms and lifted pants around his waist.

"Do not bring me to this, love."

Tears began to roll along her silky cheeks.

Cadeck interpreted her reaction to the truth he did not need to know.

"I will bring Tivius A'zum pain beyond which he considers pleasure. After he has fallen at my hands, I will focus on the Master of the Imperium. To his flesh, I will tear asunder from bone and to his mind will he forever to lament in vacancy."

"No, Cadeck."

Jess placed her hand on his shoulder with his back turned to her. His face fumed with the horrid thoughts of what suffering his children may have known.

"Do not give yourself to such emotion. It will bring you misery and failure."

"Should I reunite with Wrem, and she is no longer chaste…"

"Cadeck, love, do not think of thoughts."

"Cadeck, she is right. We must go."

Tesh glanced at the older Magi, his hands at his side as Cadeck glanced from the floor to meet Tesh to face.

"Do not let your anger cloud your purpose, love. Give Tesh to his trials so our children will be safe. You must go soon. Cruxien awaits you."

"He is pious towards the goddess, but writ deal with the Imperium. Give us another passage to the Tarlaki so he may go about his ways."

"Cadeck, it is neither your place nor mine to deny Natural Will. What he has done is worthy of finding penance. Fulfilling his task to take you to the Tarlaki will supply worth. Do not let your friendship wane over this misstep. His heart means well, but the sword and coin coerced him to deed."

Cadeck sighed, turning to face her again, "Your words only lift my heart from pain, Jess. To have seen you and touch your skin, filled your flesh, and tasted your lips provides me hope."

"Your faith in our love and in Tesh guides you. Through my love I have made you whole once again. I grant Tesh the blessings of my Aztmudin and from here, lead him to prophecy."

Jess reached her hand around Cadeck's neck, lifting herself to place a soft kiss upon his scarred lips. Cadeck cherished her embrace, leading his tongue to part her lips as they had always. As their arms wrapped upon one another, teal and lavender vestments entwined in a display of committed affection.

She moved towards Tesh and slipped her gracious hands upon his cheeks. Speaking in the tongue of magick, she closed her eyes and blessed the man with the vibrant glows webbing along her spread fingers. As she finished her prayer, Jess looked upon his hazel eyes and shared a warm grin. She leaned to whisper towards him. Nodding his head, he gathered his resolve, breathed deep, and stepped aside towards the tunnel opening to the outside.

As Tesh departed the primary chamber, Cadeck turned back to Jess. Tears flowed down his rutted cheeks sealing into scarred crevices and covering the fuzzy whiskers forming against his skin. She reached to the chain around his neck pulling out the tiny locket from his cloak.

"I will always be here Cadeck, by your heart where you wear this chain."

Cadeck snaked his fingers through her hands raising them to mutual chest, "I will find our children, Jess. I promise you this."

Jess closed her eyes as their foreheads touched.

Lifting her eyes to his, "Do not ignore your visions my love. Guide Tesh. Only in his company with Sacred Mother will our children be safe."

Cadeck nodded his head and with tears, placed his lips upon Jess' to share one final kiss. She walked with him to exit the Water Temple. Outside the entrance to the tunnel, Tesh waited with Cruxien. A blessed radiance befell upon Cruxien as his eyes widened to the sight of Jess in her vestments. Hypnotized by the aura, he dropped to one knee in reverence to the Magi.

Jess' elegance boasted the youth she emanated before her death. Cruxien recalled her loving nature towards Cadeck, how her welcome tone kept their home hearty and filled with cherished memories. The last time he had laid eyes on her, the bump of Dal had just grown noticeable. That evening, Cruxien lured Cadeck with warm ale and a night of libation and forgotten deeds that left the pair jaunting through Yumphen half-naked and screaming sailor songs past curfew.

He reached to touch her left hand, gracing his lips in piety towards her, "Blessed Magi, forgive me for I have sinned."

His tears covered his voice with emotional moans of penitent suffering.

"Cruxien, you have not sinned. You follow the path of Natural Will," Jess lifted an arm to aim at Tesh.

"Tesh is your path. Take him to Jorin. Your true path is yet to resolve. Take care of Cadeck for me," she leaned down to his ear and smiled, "and keep him away from hard drink."

Cruxien rose sharing her thoughts, "I will Jess."

They shared embrace as they pecked each cheek to one another. Cadeck, Cruxien and Jess parted their ways as they joined Tesh leading back towards *Misty Willow* docked behind the temple structure. The captain led the pair onto the main deck level with the circular platform. Venna and Kenat stood in front of them. Venna embraced the pair individually. Cassica stood behind them, her face shorn of pleasantries only embracing loneliness she never knew. She approached Tesh in effort to comfort him only for him to shrug her advance away with a pull of his left shoulder.

Cruxien called commands to his crew as he observed Jess' silhouette glowing with her enchanted words thundering within their ears. The Magi raised her hands while Cadeck and Cassica approached the starboard bulwark to watch his lover creating her magick. The mystical bubble holding the Water Temple split apart as it surrounded the rising ship. *Misty Willow* floated upon still oceans below it as the sphere of air lifted them away from the sacred structure.

Cassica observed Cadeck's fleeting tears as the words of his beloved had drowned in the surrounding oceans outside of the bubble barring him from hearing her ever again. He leaned onto the wooden rail, his tears soaking onto his lavender robes. Kenat and Venna joined to his side as the ocean surface began to appear above them. Cruxien continued to issue commands to his men now humbled before their goddess erasing thoughts of sinister treachery.

As the ethereal container surrounding *Misty Willow* cracked the surface of the ocean the taste of sunlight seared along the edge sending sparkling prisms of rainbows along the circumference. With the heat of the star shining upon their bubble, tears began to form along the topside of the effervescent shielding. The mystical ampule shattered whole and spilled the ship to splash in a rush of tidal displacement. The action jerked the men to falter before the current rocked the ship into a steady list.

Cruxien ordered the men to open sail allowing the wind to catch the ship westward. *Misty Willow* ran full speed to his command. Cruxien hurried towards the aft deck taking command of his helm. Cadeck set foot to join him as he permitted Tesh, Kenat and the ladies to make company. Setting himself to stand beside the captain, Cadeck felt the tight winds slapping his loose robes to match with the sails above him. The smell of fresh ocean breeze comforted him as he touched his calloused hands to the tarnished locket around his neck.

"Cruxien, I believe there is a matter of importance we need to discuss."

Chapter 47

Cold stinging air bit into the young girl's arms and legs like a steel pike once poked at her back. She curled tight into her chest to fend off the sharp cuts of air rustling against her skin. Her efforts dashed by the tight space upon the small boat she shared with her younger brother, Dal, who lay tight against her back. The gentle sway of the ocean beneath her covered her senses in the rocking movements of the winter-chilled waters as darkened clouds lingered overhead in puffed curls to signal an incoming front.

Hints of icicles glistened against the locks of brunette hair draped upon her face as they mingled like puzzle pieces with her eyebrows. She scraped a strand of raven hair away only for the wind to curl it back against her face. She shuddered once more as the bitter wind knocked against their boat sending her to hide in her tears. Her bare arms tightened against her knees; the small tunic supplied limited warmth to her discomfort as she lay on her side in fetal position.

In sleep she faded to memory of which seemed like distant nightmares forming together in strands of mangled chaos. Several women dressed in crimson robes hovered around her, a few displayed various stages of pregnancy as they tended to her in an ill-lit chamber. Several other moments flashed to her; large halls blackened in vacant darkness, the massive hulk of man dressed in foreboding robes extending to his ankles and the brief glints of the armor encased by his cloak.

His dark features towered over her; deep set eyes highlighted his face as his nose extended downward as to guide his eyes to the rest of humanity. In his beauty, she would admire his ruggedness had he not displayed the cruel totality of his reign upon herself and Dal. She heard names chanted by a chorus of women above her. Several times they repeated the name. *Ba'met. Ba'met. Ba'met.*

Wrem shot upright to seated position and leaned over the side of the dinghy clutching her hands against the keel. She dug her short nails into the sidgen wood as her stomach unleashed a bile flow into the ocean below her turning the sea water into a mix of green sludge. She repeated this action for two more times, moaning after each release. Her head collapsed to her left as she grimaced at the thought of another release.

Fragments of driftwood floated into her clouded vision. Other debris soon followed as the currents carried the small boat into a southeasterly direction with the churning winds behind their stern. To the east, sea-blue eyes caught glimpse of the orange glow reaching over the horizon painting the sky above into pastel shades of washed pinks and blue. Ruffled noises and scattering sounds alerted Wrem to Dal's unease as he shifted positions with a soft yawn of his mouth.

Dal scratched his blonde head and rubbed hazel eyes. His hair matted with icy glaze as he fluffed particles of the crystalline fragments off his head. He looked behind him to see Wrem leaning over the side, her breathing light and rhythmic. He leaned over to touch her back covered by a damp raven tunic.

"Wrem, why are you sick every morning?"

"The dreams I have. They bother me," she muttered under her breath. She did not react to his touch pressing the damp cloth deeper onto her back.

"You've been sick ever since we left that castle."

"I'm sorry, Dal."

Wrem lifted herself with slow strength she mustered from her arms.

"Grab yourself some food from that box if you're hungry," her inflection moved to change subject.

"Those green sticks? They are gross."

"It's all we have, Dal."

Dal slid towards the stern of the small boat to reach for a box underneath a beam holding the keel pieces together. He hoisted the box into his crossed legs and set it upon his knee-length pants. An elaborate calligraphy of an undecipherable language marked the box.. He fidgeted with the latch and lifted the top on hinge to tilt backwards from his sight. Inside the simple crate about the width of his knee-span, rested pouches of tightly wrapped parchment stacked in neat rows in small, individual cylinders which fit snugly within his small hand. He reached for two on the top row and carefully closed the box and set it back to its resting place.

He offered one of the cylinders to Wrem who snatched it from his hand before curling herself into her legs. She bound her knees within her elbows tight into her chest. Dal did not hesitate to open his portions and split the fragile parchment down the edge opening the wrappings to a sour, slimy colored rod of hardened nutrients. He grimaced at the sight of this simple meal and took a small nibble off the top to test for taste.

The morsel had the texture like epoxy on his teeth with the stale taste of week-old bread. He did not know if this was the proper taste or if in fact the pair had been eating rotted food. But each bite of these rations tasted the same and after consuming each cylinder, Dal felt stuffed. He ignored the taste as he munched down a quarter of his ration, his teeth discolored from the dye of the food he consumed. He watched his sister who continued to pay attention to their direction upon the bow of their small vessel.

Dal picked at the tasteless rations with his index finger looking at the bland composition of the visual textures. The paper sealing it wrapped in such a manner of preservation laden by a honey paste which supplied a sweet-scented pleasantry to the otherwise dull taste. Wrem did not touch the meal given to her, only to remain motionless staring forward towards the southerly direction.

"Do you remember what happened back there Wrem?"

More pieces of driftwood settled nearby washing with the current carrying their boat.

"Let's refrain, Dal."

"All those men started to glow as a light was coming out of them."

Wrem turned over her shoulder, "Dal, I said I don't want to talk about it."

"Then the ships began to be broken up by…"

"Enough."

Dal retreated to his side of the boat on Wrem's harsh command as he stared longingly at the half-eaten bar in front of him.

"You're mad at me, aren't you?"

Wrem huddled to her knees closer.

"No, I am not. I just cannot seem to grasp what happened yet."

Lonesome feelings tugged upon Wrem's heart as she gathered her senses to surmise their surroundings. Miles of ocean encompassed their tiny vessel as they drifted aimlessly in the freezing waters of the northern climate. Wrem did not see land upon any horizon only the tiny glints of sunlight cresting over the eastern ocean washing the sky with streaks of orange and pink pastels. She fondled the wrapping around the stick in her hand and ripped it along the edge. Using her left hand, she broke off a piece of the rations and set it upon her lips.

Her tongue hesitated to recoil the dry taste into her mouth as she chewed it slowly wincing with each pass of her taste buds upon the food. Whatever this packaged food was, the sailors onboard their prison vessels had consumed it on a regular basis while Dal and herself had enjoyed the finer pleasantries of prepared meals; juicy game birds as large as fists, bean and fruit salads, dark breads baked with a honey center and washed down by a thick honey milk. Even the superior officers had reduced their meals to these dry bars to supply their passengers with a veritable resource of needed energy. Alone in the unforgiving oceans, Wrem understood food became scarce and to exist on minimal sustenance would assure certain death.

With each morsel she swallowed, her stomach rumbled to digest the foreign cuisine as she had felt several times before. Each morning, the dream repeated; forcing her to wake to an unforgiving removal of her stomach contents however she surmised the involuntary reactions were not a result of the sparse meals. Wrem realized this before.

Her mind wavered to a time months before Dal was born, their mother would excuse herself from the farmhouse in the mornings for the same result. Wrem grasped at her stomach, closing her eyes to the quiet waves of the ocean and listened for murmurs within her spirit. Stillness. Relief. The expulsions of vomit were something else.

Wrem listened to Dal's quiet whispers as he delved into an imaginary world of his own, calming himself with song. She indulged herself with his words as a calm smile opened her cheeks, opening her eyes to the constant view of sea. Strands of ice-fused locks of hair whipped around her face with a new gust. Wrem crossed her arms and took another bite of the green stick allowing her mind to wander into the horizon and watched the sun as it broke the surface of the ocean with golden dawn.

As the distant sun lit her face with welcome warmth, she closed her eyes once again on the calm winds humming into her ears. The night recalled like a burning fire blazing upon her skin to see the faces of the captives lit as from a source within. The multitudes of olive red-skinned sailors and soldiers scattered about in the calamity dressed according to rank or duty.

A clean-cut man wearing a raven uniform denoting high rank, hurried to catch her. His reddish skin covered in grayed beard and sideburns. Wrem motioned Dal to a small boat resting on a davit displaying signs of fracture. As she turned her back, the man ran towards them with a vengeful laughter. Then, his flesh ripped asunder from a streak of lightning rippling from the sky and struck him upon his skull.

She hopped onto the small boat. The added weight shifted the stern side to collapse from the broken davit, sending them to buckle with the pull of gravity's embrace. She tugged the rope hastily as rain pelted her face and mingled with her tears blinding her vision from her actions. Wrem cried only to watch as several men took to the sides to escape certain death. A chance to swim away in the open waters yet struck down one at a time by instantaneous attacks of ethereal sparks bursting around them. The air they breathed consumed them with electrical energy without a source.

A cascade of ocean current cut a nearby ship of the small flotilla in half while men screamed for their own salvation amidst prayers unanswered by an invisible god. With weight of a collapsing mast, the forward section in the split had crashed into the ocean with an instant deluge to consume all onboard. Moments later the stern followed as it lifted upright to sink at a full tilted angle eased by the mass of the mast that carried the ship into a doomed vector.

Wrem teared up again as the night played out in her mind. The rope binding the lifeboat to the davit tore apart with the strain crashing into the ocean surface below. Their own demise a flitter upon her mind, Wrem held to her brother tightly only for the pair to pass out amidst the disaster. Her mind numbed in shock, setting her into a coma.

She awoke the next morning, sensing a drift southward and saw her brother passed out beneath her chest. Pieces of sidgen wood scattered around her location mingled with fabric sails and tattered bits of clothing. She surmised the swords and heavier materials had already descended. Afraid Dal would see remains, she hastily turned in every direction to find the ocean derelict of bodies or other organic decay.

The cataclysmic storm spared the pair of which her mind focused to calculate. Faint whispers from her mother called to her now. A tarnished locket clouded her thoughts glimmering with wavers of a hand as it passed through azure glow.

You still carry this locket I once gave you

"Mother?"

Wrem whispered into the open oceans as to reply to the voice she heard escaping them. She yearned to feel the gentle caress of her mother's touch, the loving speech from her lips and the warm feelings she remembered by her gaze. Nine years had gone by so long ago since she last hugged her mother and told her how much she loved her. Now in isolation amidst the expansive oceans, Wrem could only hear her mother's whispers; unaware of their origination or to whom they spoke.

For now, Wrem embraced the ocean scents which meant freedom. Time lost to her senses in the dark dungeon she had known in captivity. Amidst the vermin crawling across her, she would trade any minute of that hell for the loneliness of wayward drifting. For another hour of the moldy stench of hay, the fish stink gave her reprieve, and to remove herself from the dim wavering candle which would burn out for days unattended, the warmth of the sun gave her confidence.

Rickety creaks continued to penetrate her ears as the small boat swayed to each direction the current carried them. Dal turned his attention from his distraction to watch as Wrem kept her back to him.

"Why don't we go to Yumphen?"

Wrem did not hear him the first time, her mind focused on the trailing whispers Jess' voice imprinted upon her thoughts.

"Wrem," Dal inched towards her, "did you hear me?"

Dal shook his sister's shoulder. Startled, her shoulders arced as to shiver when she turned over to look upon the young boy behind her. His innocence shown on his face, their father's features clear with his hazel eyes and tiny lips. Like her, he shared their mother's high cheeks. Dal's blonde hair mingled with icy fragments upon his scalp. Her face settled to calm as she shed a small grin at his sight before returning to glance upon the oceans.

"It's dangerous Dal."

"Dangerous? But that's where father is. That is where the farm is. He will protect us."

"How do you know he's back there?"

"I don't."

"Then why would we go there?"

Her tone did not lecture but only to inquire as to his reasoning.

"That is where the Saratian ships are. Certainly, they could go after those bad men."

Wrem smiled at her brother's suggestion, "You'd have to convince King Trebut first."

"Well, if father is at home, then he would certainly go before the king."

"And how do you know father is home?" Wrem grinned as she released her legs to extend from her chest.

"I saw him, Wrem."

Wrem giggled to lighten the mood, "In a vision several weeks ago, Dal, and you told me he was in Silvetzen."

Dal retreated to look down upon his hands as he fidgeted with the rest of the small stick of food.

"I guess you're right."

He looked back up towards her, "Do you know where we are?"

Dal's question worried Wrem. She would be unable to supply an answer. The expanse of the sea supplied her only clue as no visible sight of land gave her indications of their bearings. They floated with the current shared by several pieces of driftwood from the destruction they had escaped. Within her heart, Dal trusted her to protect him in his most dire situations. But Wrem felt no safety within herself. Wrem was as scared as her brother but mustered just enough strength to hide it. Cold shivers crossed her thin, wet shirt chilling her nubile chest. She covered herself tight with open arms bare from tattered sleeves.

The sun beat down minimal warmth to hide the damp, chilled air. Within her soul, Wrem closed her fears to the outside so to keep Dal from noticing. Wrem pulled strength from within to force her resolve, releasing a sigh heard by the winds.

"I don't know, Dal."

She had no confidence in her answer, nor did she consider a lie.

"Are we going to die here?"

Dal's cheeks turned to rosy red. Wrem turned her head to see a small tear forming within his left eye. Wrem leaned over to embrace him within her cold, dimpled arms and squeezed his head close to her chest. She rested her chin upon his frazzled, blonde hair matted by the grungy confines of their former dungeon.

"Don't let those thoughts enter your mind."

Dal coddled into her chest, "But Wrem, I want to go home."

She quietly shushed at him as she rocked him gently.

"I know you do. As do I."

Icy tears flowed down Wrem's cheeks and onto puffed lips. She wiped her right cheek as her nose filled with mucus. Tightness churned below her stomach into the deep recesses of her abdomen like a slow grinding wheel pressing grains to flour. Wrem fought her own fears turning them into a confident song chiding Dal into quiet relaxation. She soothed him with calm words, lifting her voice with otherworldly angels as she whispered under her breath a child's rhyme she had heard their father's nurse maid sing to quiet him.

As Dal rested in her caring embrace, Wrem had a moment to reflect upon her own feelings. Her mind lingered on thoughts of pain and the thrusting tortures penetrating her thighs. Foreboding chants pierced into her ears amidst the bitter smells of sweat and burning oils. Her naked skin pressed against the icy stone slab; the long locks of silk raven hair clouded by her tears. The pain endured for an eternity only lessened by the vision of her mother. As her mother promised her salvation, the perpetrator to her penetrating pain propelled from her loins against the wall.

Wrem knew it was magick, untamed and fierce with an unyielding nature. Within her own soul she searched for a method to control it. She had no formal guidance in the aftermath of her actions, only the company of several cloaked women tending to her in the ensuing days. Each of them covered in crimson robes, their faces covered likewise by vermillion veils. Their linen robes led to hints of thin fabric covering the bulbous bellies in various states of incubation. The only words she heard them speak were ancient chants. When she tried to ask a question, they would raise their voices with their songs.

Each of the women would tend to her body, soaking her nude, nubile features in scented oils lit by slow candle flames. Wrem concluded their accents were like the others of her captivity. As the feminine voices scarred her ears with their shrilled, heavy accents, Wrem could only calm herself with her tears. She cried aloud then silenced by their incantations chanting the name in their tongue; *Visraair Abra*. She could not understand the purpose of the ceremonies she endured each day. In her isolation, she felt her brother calling for her. Alone and scared, she called to him only met by closed doors holding her in privacy.

The cold prick of icy steel graced against her pale cheeks and curled frocks of raven bangs. Like an obsidian tower of massive bulk shadowing a subservient valley below him, the cloaked figurehead of the Imperium gave her simple words in Common Tongue admiring her resolve and gracious splendor before he commanded the women servants in their native language. Soldiers returned with chains to bind to her, masking her face with a dark hood before lifting her from her feet.

Wrem heard her brother beside her mumbling through a muzzle as they rode upon a transport. She sensed the decline of a hill before taking scent of the oceans within a few moments. Strained sounds of wood planks groaned beneath her feet as soldiers escorted her into a cramped space.

She heard the cries of others as they collapsed to the floor around them. Their curses in heavy accents frightened Dal as others carried the absence and escorted them to their cabins. She felt her hood remove to show them the candle-lit space of a ship's cabin complete with a pair of beds. The glinted armor's red highlights reflected in the soft candles as the olive-red man removed himself with a slam of the rigid door.

Her day of redemption came as a blur. Icy cold tingles tore across her arms and legs, reaching over her chest and neck. Her conscious mind closed her thoughts to external stimuli as her vision walk closed into a darkened void speaking only to her from an ethereal distance. Echoes of suffering reflected in her mind as she followed the calm voices of ancient chants only she heard. Beside her stood Dal, his eyes covered by bright orbs paving their way amidst complete darkness.

Screams of terrified horror and guttural growls stabbed at their ears, yet their shared vision kept them focused on a blinded void, an ancient voice beckoned them towards the outline of a small boat. She set her foot upon the edge of the keel of the vessel and turned to gaze over her shoulder. The voluminous emptiness of the Abyss faded to reality. The vision of suffering men and a shattered fleet of ships tore her emotions to express stressed tears as she hurried to free the boat from the davits.

Wrem opened her eyes from her memories. She chose not to explain them to Dal for fear he would react unfavorably. He lay asleep in her arms, silenced by her rocking and quiet lullabies. She chose to hide her memories from him as she once was isolated, hidden by her own conscious and to harness them to amplify her magick should she ever use it again. The sun reached to full height of the noon beating upon her and warming her damp clothes.

As she came around to her senses, her ears opened to the sounds of quiet hums burrowing like a worm into her mind. The absence of fish stench startled her nostrils to detect an anomaly. Her neck twitched slowly to each side, gathering the outlying periphery of a clouded fog behind her expanding the horizon around. Wrem licked her lips to the startled taste of blood.

She reached up to her lips and pressed her index finger to her mouth. Smooth traces of crimson liquid settled within the canvas of her fingerprints. She touched her thumb to her finger and wriggled them together, smearing the crimson to stain the crevices of her flesh.

Wrem paused as she studied a drop of liquid falling onto her arm when her stunned face concluded the source of the bleeding. She set two of her fingers to her nose. In desperation, she reached down towards Dal and tilted his head against her left arm, painting her own blood to his cheeks. His pale face alerted Wrem to his condition as blood oozed like crimson rivers along his lips and chin.

"No."

Her heart paced to her terror. Her breaths turned erratic; her eyes rolled backward as her head fogged over into blurred vision before her body fell backward.

Rocky beaches adorned a distant shoreline as the current carried Wrem and Dal's lifeboat towards the isolated landmass. A towering mountain cut into the sky on the eastern edge of the continental island sloping towards a valley of vegetation of various heights. The current sloughed with the waves kissing the shelf of a beachfront. As the small boat rose with the high tidal waves, it settled as quickly into the low currents as the ocean carried it towards a craggy shore.

Ocean water splashed upon smooth, blackened rocks chiseled by eons of water erosion. A shoreline composed of finite stones arranged in a menagerie of various minerals and soot. A hard collision scratched the tough keel against the pebble beach as the waves pushed the boat with the high tide. The waves retreated, then shoved the craft further with the next action. Gravel shifted with the pace of footsteps crunching into the deep soot in gentle rhythm.

A figure dressed in black approached the small boat. A wide-brim hat protected his pale face from the afternoon sun beating upon the beach. A shirt flittered around him in the light winds; the strings dangled at his sternum. Dark, cotton pants shifted loosely upon his legs and bound at his hips with a leather belt. The man's shadow cast in even length behind him as he stood above the pair of children resting inside the vessel. A squared, white-flesh jawline poked from the shadow of his hat as he leaned, bending his elbows to rest at his knees.

He graced a gloved hand over the steel plate bearing the Sigil of the Imperium bolted to the bow. Beneath the blood-red symbol engraved the name of the mother vessel, *Abzu*. The dark-metal plating contrasted to the bright-red paint of the sigil.

If catastrophe struck this ship, I do not imagine Supernus Magister will be all too delighted of the news.

The man removed the raven, leathery glove from his right hand and revealed light-skinned flesh like Wrem's. A Rykanian such as she. He reached to her nostril and swiped the blood caked in the crease beneath her nose. He shifted his index finger against his thumb allowing the blood to embed into his fingerprints. As he lifted the blood to his nose, a tiny blood bubble popped from Wrem's nostril with the slow heave of her chest.

"You're breathing," he spoke in Common Tongue, "and," he sniffed the blood trickled on his finger, "you're in moon cycle."

He stood and turned his attention towards the dark fog encompassing his horizon which swirled in snake-like maneuvers, twisting and turning for miles in the far distance. Sunlight contrasted to the blackness of the mist which separated blue sky and blue ocean in an opaque barrier that rolled in a counterclockwise direction from his viewpoint, before turning at an angle to either end of his view on the horizon.

He looked back towards Wrem and Dal resting peacefully in the bottom of the craft.

"Yet, there is something more to your blood."

He reached towards Dal's nose and repeated the procedure to sniff. The stranger closed his eyes, then once more with Wrem.

"Your blood is that of a Magi and you survived the fog."

He smiled, "You must be Cadeck's children; the Moon Child and, by all appearances her brother, the Sun Child."

.... To be continued....

Appendix A: Glossary

Language of the Si'rai Imperium (Sheebal)

Abin – ab-inn; daughter

Abina – ab-ee-nah; girl

Abra'in – ab-rah-in; moon

Abra'ir – ab-rah-eer; mother

Abra'ni – ab-rah-nigh; sister

Abranus / abrani – ab-rah-noos/ab-rah-nee; Month (plural)

Acta'unas Vohm Volen – ak-tah ew-nahs vōm vōlynn; "My blood for your Will"

Antexum Cruci – antex-oohm croo-chi

Apophadi – uh-poff-uh-die

Asta – ahz-tah; health

Asti – ahz-tie; bad health

Astu – ahz-too; womb, can also mean female genitalia as a system.

Astini – ahz-tuh-nigh; bloodline

Astutni – ahz-tuht-nigh; life taker, assassin

Aztmi – ahzt-my; Ancient name given to the Magi.

Aztunai – ahz-tew-nigh; Life force, essence, aura.

Boshani – bo-sha-nigh; female hound, derogatory.

Daihekda – die-heck-duh; Wrath blade, blade of Wrath.

Durustrate – duur-ooh-straate; singular of noble

Durustratum – duur-ooh-straht-oom; Parliamentary nobles, ruling council.

Durustrista/u – duur-ooh-strist-ah/oo; King, Queen

Durustri/u – duur-ooh-stry/stru; nobility m/f

Durustristus – duur-ooh-stris-tuhs; plural of noble.

Duruwervos – duur-ooh-wahr-vuhs; high rank officer or clans leader with title and claim.

Drahak Abra'in – draah-hauk Abra-een; Celebrated rite, translation as "Death Moon."

Eeristri/u – eer-uhs-try; commoner.

Gertoum – gehr-tomb; massive beast of burden, can reach the height of a house. Used to haul heavy industrial carts or war machines.

Hadithem – Haahd-ee-them; the masculine, high god of the Si'rai Imperium, the source of Will and their Magick. Symbolized by the empty circle within their sunwheel.

Hekda - blade

Iostana Magistrita – eye-ohs-ta-nah mahj-is-try-tah; Revered Magister

Magistri/u – mahj-is-try/troo; Si'rai priest m/f

Magister – Si'rai High Priest, one versed in the more occulted spells and ritual.
Raka – rahk-ah; boy
Raka'ir – rahk-ah-eer; father
Raka'ni – rahk-ah-nigh; brother
Raki – rahk-ee; son
Rak'in – rahk-in; Sun
Rakin/i – ra-kuh-nigh; day(s)
Ravactistri – rah-vahk-tis-try; loosely translated as "doctor."
Sadakem – sadé-uh-khem; humans that are not of the Si'rai religion, race, or culture. Used as a racial epithet.
Saruf – sahr-oof; master, used by the slave caste.
Sheebal – she-ba'al; native nomenclature of the language spoken by the Si'rai, also the name of the continent the Imperium resides.
Si'rai – sheh-rye; name of the people, race, and culture on the continent of Sheebal.
Strita – stry-tah; house
Stritus – stry-toos; specifically a noble's house or preceding a noble's surname.
Templarus – older dialect referring to the Temples of the Aztun pantheon.

Uristri/u – yew-rist-try/u; slave m/f
       Euristri/u – favored slave, sometimes overseer of other slaves on an estate.
Visraa – viz-raah; sacred, the addition of "ir" or "in" denotes female or male conjugation of the verb.
Wervos – wear-vohs; war
Wervostri – wear-vohs-try; warrior
Wervos'kiga – wear-vohs-kee-gah; cannon, war gun
Wervostrakgar – wear-vohs-strek-gar; war procession
Xiat – hand
Xiatutni – shia-tewt-nigh Assassins of the Hand, used to denote Tivius is the Hand of his emperor and thus his specialized assassins use this title.

Language of the Magi (Tereswa)

Aztun – az-tuhn; pantheon of gods worshipped by the Magi from whom they derive their magick.

Azthar Kherdmon – az-tar caird-mahn

Aztmudin – ahzt-mew-den

Graa – grah; moon

Graa'vael – grah-vae-el

Telaac Graa – tehl-eck grah

Pantheon (Aztun)

Aeus – aa-ewus; rune is a triangle sitting atop a cross.

Heseph – hesh-eff; rune is an upright triangle.

Tiasu – tee-ah-soo; rune is an upright triangle with a line through the bilateral.

Sokut – soh-koot; rune is upside down triangle.

Gedesh – gehd-esh; rune is an upside-down triangle with a line through the bilateral.

Vebest – vehb-est; rune is a circle with a line across.

Desed / udesedu – deh-sehd/oo-deh-sehd-oo; circle with crescent moon above, cross below.

Places

Rykana – rye-ka-nah; Continent where Silvetzen and Sarat reside. People are referred as Rykanian.

Rykanian – rye-ka-nee-an; language of the people of Rykana. Common tongue, spoken of three accents; Low, High, and Proper along with their dialects and verbiage associated to each.

Sarat – saihr-at

Saratian – saihr-a-shun

Pronunciations associated with characters.

Cruxien Balax: crew-shi-en bahl-ahx.
Ysalir: ees-ah-leer
Lucivus A'zum: luch-uh-vuhs ah-zoom
Verdui: ver-dwy
Trebut: treh-buht
Fersyn: fair-sin
Sadar: say-daar

RYKANA

TEMPLE OF WIND

N

TIJOA'S HOME

SILVETZEN

BLORAK

VOSTOK

	IMPERIAL ROAD
	CAPITAL ROAD
	PROVINCIAL ROAD
	LOCAL ROAD
	SERVICING ROAD
	EXISTING BORDER
	CAPITAL CITY
	PROVINCIAL SEAT
	MAJOR TOWN
	TEMPLE

MAP NOT TO SCALE

TEMPLE OF FIRE

BOGS OF ER'TAHAK

RACOREN

BOVARIAR ESTATE

SARATIAN ROUTE · RYKANIAN IMPERIAL HIGHWAY

YUMPIEN

WENFIER FARM

SARATIAN CASTLE

SARAT

KINGDOM OF SARAT

TESH'S HOME

SARATIAN RIVER

HIGHHORN

TELMEN

WOODSAN

TEMPLE OF LIGHT

KORA

GERMBEATO

DONINGSEN

ORADAN SEA

TEMPLE OF WATER

About the Author

Native Texan, born and raised in DFW. Currently an IT /network technician for the past 20+ years with industry certifications. An avid fan of sci fi and fantasy, began my journey to be inspired after watching the Star Wars Trilogy as a child in the 80s. Continued my love for fantasy when I discovered the Wizard of Earthsea stories in seventh grade. Raised with Stephen King novels easily accessible and soon explored a love for horror which broadened to Clive Barker, HP Lovecraft and others. In my free time, I hobby build computers (built the one I write from) and enjoy the occasional meetup for Dungeons and Dragons or any other Tabletop RPG. I found inspiration from many authors aside from already described and musical genres from classical to more eclectic, metal tastes.

When not writing, I find myself reading or researching or the occasional video game. Inspiration can be found in anything if you look for it.

Legacy of the Knight

Hand of the Sun

Sword of the Moon

Fall of the Stars

Made in United States
Troutdale, OR
11/25/2024

25268811R00369